(continued)

THE
CHOSEN

kusheqárós-shu cháguda uthe
knákusheós tsur kókátha tsurán
ksárathas tyeyehue umyártahe shesheles
sháh mánya sháh mumuya
chiyáqeyeke-shu yáresh keru
yáreshira chiyaqeyensha-shu qányaye
knátiyeinsha-hue tungóqerónsha
shánguós-shu osráhrata lyeyecha huágata
kuyushimuntheónsha-shu lyeyeshi
churutniryinsha-shu chuyiruth niryike-shu
lyeyehash ksirushhua keru
knáksyekshákeamha ksósheáthase
ruyuchádayetnirónsha-shu shile
ruyuchádayetnirónsha-kshu tyeyehue
ksuyiruyitha-shu charata thumya
juyireithata tyeyerea
qayakáyas-kye tyeyere cháguda
knarenál tyeyehue dájaqea
kshiruis-che shayaguyas-che

kureóke-shu káreónsha-shu
tyeyeshile tuya kshiransha
knátsáyansha miruthe susheóke-shu
sásheónsha-shu kshán shile
knápóyánsha káradahua
huáyechádeqeransha-hue jirishán
tyeyenán nunyána nangáqerán-sha-hue
uthe chyeqetheleqeransha-hue uthe
lyeyehuea qányátla kise

Flesh, knit bone to bone
Your withered earth
Ancient Mother
Scorched tearless You await
The Sky Lord come to thunder
Rumbling His stormy belly
Withholding His urgent seed
Till He shall pierce You with His shafts
Quench the burning air
Rill and pool Your dusts
Fill Your wombs with spiraling jades
Till Your flesh swells up
In the midst of breaking waters
Clenching for release

Thrust forth the Green Child
Ten thousand times reborn
Squeeze Him into the air
Enjeweled by the morning
To take sweet nurture
At Your breasts
That He might dance again
And once more blow His scents
Beneath the skies.

*Part of the "Song to the Earth" from
the* Book of the Sorcerers, *shown in the
original Quya and accompanied by its
translation into English.*

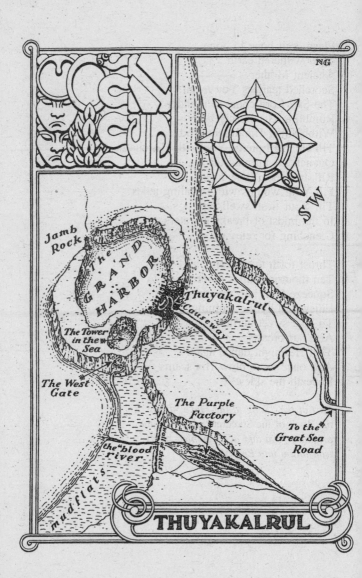

THUYAKALRUL

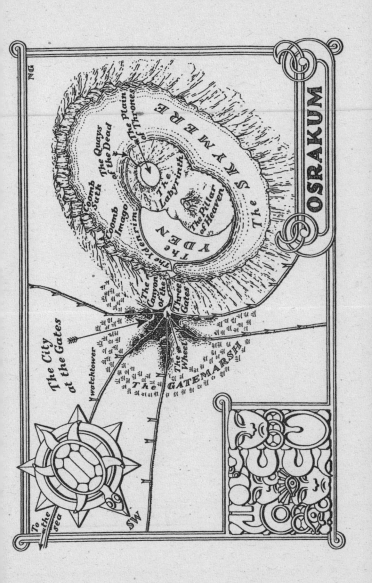

VISITORS

Ice winds strike a flint-edged sea

Splintering flakes that scatter like birds.

There, trees turn to gold then die

As does all that is born of the sun.

—ORIGIN UNKNOWN

All that day the wind had rattled the shutters and slanted the sky with snow, but in the warm heart of the Hold Carnelian sat with some of his people around a fire, listening to their talk. They were telling stories, the stories that those who could still remember told of their lives before the child-gatherers came for them. The words bleached his mind with the light of summers far away. He settled back into the chair dreaming, his eyes narrowed against the leaping dazzle of the flames. The tale rumbled on amid the whisper of women weaving, the remote clink and clatter of the kitchens, someone humming a song. Behind all this was the keening wind which made him shiver, then sink deeper into the comfort of the chair.

A child's voice cried out, muffled, outside somewhere. The spell broke. Reddened faces turned from the fire. They looked down the hall, between the pillars. The great door opened and a girl slipped in. A gust of snow-spotted air lifted some of the tapestries. Carnelian rose with the others and drew his blanket round him.

The girl ran toward them, all eyes, breathless. "A boat." Her lips shaped the word with exaggerated care. She made sure she saw the disbelief on every face. She grinned, delighted to be the center of all their staring.

Carnelian frowned. "A ship?"

The girl looked up at him and gave a hard nod. "A ship, Carnie, I swear, a ship. It's there, on the sea. I saw it."

Carnelian gave his blanket to someone, strode away to pick up his cloak, threw it on, came back to the girl and offered his hand. "Come, show me."

The girl reached up for it, sinking her chin into her chest, blushing. Her own fingers were very small and dark in Carnelian's milk-white hand. Together, they led a procession out from the hall. The cold hit them. Carnelian sent the old people back into the warmth. "There's no need for you to come. I'll send word back if it's true."

Then he was letting the girl pull him off across the slushy courtyard. Some youngsters followed. They all huddled together against the wind but it slipped between them, ballooning up their blankets, ruffling the feathers on Carnelian's cloak.

They had to cross two courtyards to reach the halls that looked east across the sea. Pavilions, slender-columned, in summer cooled with tiles and water. Now they were abandoned to the frost, but then they caught the breezes and were filled with sun and laughter.

Their ear tips were burning when they reached the door to the tower. A stairway lay beyond down which the wind came screaming. They fought their way against it up steps treacherous with ice. Slits let in spear-thrusts from the storm. They reached the top, girded themselves and staggered out into a raging roar.

Turmoiled grays and blacks. Flurrying snow spitting at them, furring their eyes. Faces began aching. Carnelian went with the pull of the girl's hand, leaning into the gale. They reached the parapet and clung to it with numbing fingers. The girl gripped Carnelian for support. They both squinted. The sea was rolling its glass toward them all scratched with white. They felt the thunder as each wave detonated on the shore. Carnelian had to wipe his eyes. The girl was grimacing up at him, shouting something. Her hand shook as she pointed. Carnelian shielded his face with a cross of his arms and stared out. The disappointment was crushing. There was nothing but the mounding terror of the sea. He was about to turn away, but then his heart quickened. He saw it, a sliver, a ship with sails stretched open like fingered wings, a ship flying toward them on the wrath of the storm.

Leaving the others to make their way back to the Great Hall at their own speed, he leapt down the steps, almost soaring on the wind. He slipped a few times and fell once, scraping his elbow against stone. Then he was up again and running. He splattered his way back along the trail they had made. He reached the hall door, paused a moment breathing like a dragon, indecisive, heard the chatter and turned aside. Too many questions lay in that direction. Let the others spread the news.

He used another smaller door, wound through some storerooms, passed along a corridor flickering with doorways. He could smell the spiced stew. Through clouds of steam he glimpsed people working in the kitchens. Nobody saw him. He reached the covered alleyway that snaked off northward toward the Holdgate. A vague brightening down there showed where the alleyway opened into the Long Court. He went the other way, jogging along the ridged floor. He came to some steps and took them two at a time. The guardsmen of the tyadra were up there muffled in blankets, playing dice around a brazier. Their faces came up, each identically marked with his House tattoo: the chameleon, its goggle-eyes at the center of their foreheads, its back swelling down their noses, the tail curling on their chins. A leg splayed out over each brow, each cheek. Glad to see him, they smiled, making the chameleons dance on their faces. They began to make a space for him, thinking he had come to share their watch.

"It's not you lot I've come to see. Naith, there's news for the Master. Please announce me."

The man grinned crookedly. "The Master said—"

"I know, Naith. I'll take the responsibility."

Naith shrugged. He walked off to the end of the passage where a pair of sea-ivory doors caught his shadow. Standing before them the man seemed as small as a child. He hid his eyes in the crook of his arm and thumped the sea-ivory three times with the palm of his hand. His shadow shifted as it opened a crack. A mutter of voices. The door closed. Naith came back stiff-faced. "I hope you know what you're doing."

Carnelian squeezed the man's arm, jerked a nod, then walked past him. The door jambs were painted with the warding eye: a warning to all that none must enter save at the express invitation of the Master. The paint had faded many times and as many times had been repainted. Waiting before the door, Carnelian ran his finger around the lip of a face that grimaced out of the sea-ivory. Only a year back he had been unable to reach so high. He felt the surface move away as the door opened. Through the gap he could see the fire that was the center of the hall and off, beyond, in the half-light, loomed the shape of the Master of the Hold, the Ruling Lord Suth, his father.

His father's beautiful face hung above Carnelian like the moon. "Why do you disturb my meditations?"

"I have seen a ship coming here," replied Carnelian in the same tongue, court Quya.

His father's eyes narrowed. "A dream?"

"No, Father, I have come here straight from the East Tower. From its brow I saw the ship."

Suth noticed the water that beaded the feathers of his son's cloak. "A ship, you say?" He did not allow himself to smile, not wanting to hurt the boy's feelings.

"It looked black and was in size and shape like my finger and had many sails spread to catch the gale."

His father frowned. "A long black ship, with sails set, in this storm?"

"Upon my blood, Lord."

"A baran," his father muttered.

The word was unknown to Carnelian and he did not like the pale expression that washed across his father's face as he spoke it.

His father turned away. Opals woven into his robe blinked like the eyes of birds. He turned back looking severe. "If your eyes have seen true, then we must make preparations to receive our visitors with proper state. Please go you to your chamber and make ready. You will not leave it until I send you summons and then only to come directly here. There shall be no deviation from that path."

His father's hand clamped his shoulder but it was more the gray eyes that held Carnelian fast. "You do understand me?"

"I do, my Lord," said Carnelian and wondered at his father's manner.

"Then go, and do as you are bid."

Carnelian set off back to the sea-ivory doors. He was halfway round the fire when his father spoke again.

"It is Naith who commands without, is it not?"

"It is so, my Lord."

"Please send him in."

Carnelian strode down the alleyway with the memory of his father's face nagging him. He dismissed it by turning his thoughts to the visitors. What kind of people would be brave enough or, he corrected himself, foolhardy enough to be upon the sea in winter?

He reached the arcade bordering the Long Court. Through its wooden colonnade he could see the air thickly feathered with snow. It drifted down into the rectangle of the court, dulling all familiar detail. In the wall opposite, orange light chinked out through closed doors and shutters. He squinted up to the eaves. The sky had an angry look. Night was nearing.

He went to the back of the arcade and fumbled for the ring that opened another door into the Great Hall. He slipped into the warmth with its smell of spice and bodies and burning wood. Between the pillars people huddled gossiping.

"Carnie," cried many voices as people rushed up, "what news? Can it really be true? A ship?"

"I have seen it with my own eyes." They clamored round him. He lifted his hands and they quieted. "Look, I've no time to talk. The Master will be sending his commands to you soon enough. We must make ready for the visitors." He pulled up the edge of his cloak. "Even I'm to be made ready."

There was much grinning.

"I'll be off then. Someone please find Tain and ask him to come to my room."

Carnelian went back out into the cold and continued off down the alleyway into a tunnel. At its end an arch gave into the Sword Court, but before he reached it he turned left onto a stairway. It took him up into the noisy warren of the barracks. He had slept here since he was five and had long ceased to notice the musky smell of men, though it made him feel safe.

When he reached his room, he lifted the catch on the shutters, yanked them back, opened the parchment pane and craned out. Churning roaring sea and wind. Snow flocking in the air. His hair whipped his face. He saw the shoreline fading off to the western tip of the island. The road curved down from the Holdgate out onto the quay. Its long rectangle was a stillness amidst the undulating sea. He looked out along the rocky edge of the Hold. The cliff rose up to the bone-smooth masonry of his father's hall on its southern promontory. The blizzard blurred the view. Out there, beyond the shelter of the cliff, the sea lifted in a mountain that avalanched, foaming, into the bay. There was no sign of the ship.

He closed the window and the shutters. It was a relief to shut out the storm. He unfastened his cloak, hung it up, went over to the fireplace, stooped down, raked away the mantle of ash and began to pile sticks over the embers.

When his half-brother Tain arrived, flames were shaking shadows up and down the walls.

Carnelian jumped up. "Gods' blood! I thought you'd never come."

"I didn't realize you were in such a hurry, Carnie, it's just—"

"Never mind the justs. Come on, Tain, I need to get dressed."

Tain peeled the sodden layers off until Carnelian's body was revealed dull white, lean, shivering. Tain touched his skin. "You should have stripped, Carnie, you're corpse-cold." He coaxed Carnelian closer to the fire. "Do you know what's going on?" he asked as he faded off into a corner of the room.

"You mean you don't know about the ship?" said Carnelian after him.

His brother came back with a stone flask, a bowl and a handful of pads. He made a face. "Of course I do. I meant with the tyadra."

"The tyadra?"

Tain was pouring smoking liquid from the flask into the bowl. He looked up. His face was still too young to have the House tattoo. "They're arming themselves and I just saw the Master sweeping past. He not only had Grane with him, but also Keal and several of the other commanders."

Carnelian felt uneasy. Their father rarely came out of his hall. In the past, he had been known to go to the Sword Court to supervise the training of the tyadra. When the spring came, he took them all hunting outside the Hold. On those occasions the tyadra bore weapons but at other times only those guarding his father were armed and even that was ceremonial. What threat could there be on their remote island?

Carnelian had a hunch. "Hold on a moment." He went to the door and opened it. Sure enough, there were guardsmen in the corridor outside. "What're you doing here?"

"The Master sent us to protect you, Carnie," one of them said.

"From what, Krib?"

The man shrugged. "The visitors?"

"What's up with the tyadra?"

"I think we're being readied for a fight, Carnie." Krib glanced at the other guardsmen for support.

Seeing their long faces, Carnelian frowned. "And you're stuck here having to look after me, is that it?"

They looked down at their feet.

Carnelian went back to his fire. He stopped in front of Tain, and did not see the question on his face. The bowl lay on the floor between them. Carnelian was remembering his father's look. Clearly, the Master thought the ship was bringing danger to the Hold.

As Tain stooped to the bowl and dipped a pad in it, Carnelian's head fell automatically. Tain stretched up to swab his forehead. The dullness came away to reveal the white gleam of skin beneath.

Carnelian was only faintly aware of the cold then burn, and of the smell of camphor. He stood stone-still as Tain wiped off his bodypaint. He grunted when the pad stung his grazed elbow.

"It's your own fault, Carnie," said Tain. "I don't know why you felt you needed your paint today. There's not enough of the sun to make a shadow, never mind taint your skin."

When Tain had finished the cleaning, he insisted on combing the tangle of Carnelian's black hair. Carnelian bore each yank in silence. His brother brought his best robes and put them on him one after the other. They were cut so that each layer beneath was partially revealed.

"Do you want to wear jewels, Carnie?"

Carnelian looked down and saw that his brother was offering him an open casket. He stirred the contents with a finger and fished out a brooch of apple-jade and ivory. He gave it to Tain. "Do I look presentable?"

Tain had heard the guardsmen discuss Carnie's beauty. Towering there he looked as if he might be fashioned from snow. "The brooch matches the color of your eyes and shows off the whiteness of your skin."

Thinking that he was being teased, Carnelian threw a punch. Tain ducked away, chuckling.

"What now?"

"Now I get to sit and wait," said Carnelian, affecting cheerfulness.

"You mean, we get to sit and wait." Tain did not even try to hide his gloom. He had hoped to run off and find out what was happening, but he would not desert Carnelian. He brightened. "We'll be able to see the ship coming in from here."

Carnelian leapt up. "You're right."

They ran over to the shutters. Tain caught Carnelian's hand as it reached up to the catch. "I'd better do this, Carnie. You might dirty your robes."

Carnelian scowled but gave in. As the parchment window flew back, snow gusted in. Everything in the room flapped. They both peered out into the twilight. The blizzard had thinned. "Can you see anything?"

Tain shook his head, then reached back to tug on his brother's robe. "Look!" he cried, pointing with the other hand.

Carnelian leaned over him and saw the huge shape creeping toward the quay. She rocked slow and heavy. Lights flickered here and there across her deck. Her sails had been furled, leaving the trunks of her masts bare.

"She's going to smash herself to pieces," cried Tain. And sure enough there was a terrible grinding that they could hear even over the wind. The ship grated along the quay but she did not founder. Carnelian watched, chewing his hand. He was not sure whether he wanted her safe. Flames flared as torches moved across the deck to collect on the ship's landward side. Their pulsing line defined the curve of her hull. Suddenly, the torches were sparking from the ship to the quay. Most snuffed out as they hit but others splashed spluttering light. Soon after, figures began flinging themselves over the side, trailing ropes. Some landed on the stone, others fell short and dropped into the sea. Carnelian watched with horror as the ship lunged away. Ropes tautened. Some of the men were pulled off the quay to disappear into the narrow channel of sea lying between the hull and the wall. When the ship came crashing back more men jumped off regardless. Those still on the quay were leaning back on their heels, straining against the ropes, struggling to tame her.

Carnelian left Tain at the window and rushed to look into the corridor. The guardsmen were still there. "No message come for me, no news?"

"None, Carnie." They were shaking their heads, looking worried.

Carnelian tried to send one off to get news but he was refused with, "The Master must be obeyed." Whenever one of his people said that, he knew it would take all his power of command to press further. He let it go. Why make trouble for the man?

He ran back to join Tain. Dozens of lines were stitching the ship to the quay. She was being pulled in. More lines were thrown over and secured. Men slid down them like oil drops on a string. There was a constant milling on the deck. Then it stopped. Suddenly. Two or three huge figures had appeared and were moving to the bow. Everything else was still, save for the ship's rise and fall. Even the wind had dropped.

"Masters," said Tain, flickering uneasy eyes at Carnelian.

"They can't be," Carnelian said, though he had been thinking the same thing.

"But look, Carnie, all those around them," Tain pointed, "they're making the prostration. And look at them, look how huge they are. Only Masters are so big."

Even in the twilight, at that distance, the shapes had some quality of grace that suggested they were indeed of the Masters.

"What can they be doing coming here?" Carnelian muttered, but his words were snatched away by the wind.

Carnelian and Tain had watched the tall figures leave the ship and move along the quay towering amidst the smaller men who carried torches. The procession had climbed the road round to the Holdgate and out of sight. Then, nothing. The brothers were left to sit waiting by the fire, each wrapped in his own thoughts.

The sound of the door opening made them both jump up. Two guardsmen appeared carrying a white chest between them. Carnelian pointed to where they could put it down.

Another man had come in behind them. His eyes were stitched closed. "The Master bade me say to the Lord his son that he should be attired as if he were in Osrakum." The blindman spoke in accented Quya. Tain looked round. The words were just sounds to him. Only a few in the household understood the mysterious tongue of the Masters.

"He said that . . . you're certain he said that?" Carnelian asked, shifting the conversation into Vulgate.

"I'm sure, Master."

Carnelian mused, now certain beyond any doubt that the visitors were Masters. He went over to the chest. With customary unease he noted how the eyeless man followed his movement. The creature came toward him, held out his hand and opened it to reveal two packets. "These the Master bade me put into his son's own hand. I'm to say that, once he's properly dressed, his son should attend the Master in his hall."

Carnelian took the windings of soft leather and unwound one. Inside was a long narrow piece of exquisitely worked jade pierced by three finger holes.

He gaped at it. "A Great-Ring."

He turned the ring until its carving held the light. It had been his mother's. He unwound the other package to find that it contained a second ring. Worn together, they were a sign of his blood-rank. His mother's blood had been so pure, she had been entitled to wear a third. He slipped the rings on. His hand had not grown into them yet.

He hooked his fingers to make sure that the rings would not fall off and lifted them. They made his hand look gashed.

Tain was kneeling before the chest, running his hands over the smooth ivory. It was worked all over with a writhing of chameleons whose eyes were the rivets of copper that held the chest together.

For a moment the brothers looked at each other, brimming over with excitement.

"Come on, Tain, we must hurry," said Carnelian.

They pushed back the lid, then gasped. Inside the chest wondrous garments were dulled like butterflies in chrysalises of waxed parchment. As they drew them out the room filled with the scent of lilies. They marveled at them. Tain stripped Carnelian and then one by one he put the garments on him. The first few were tissues so fine they floated on the air. The ones further down in the chest were heavier and interwoven with precious stones. The garments fitted over each other like the pieces of a puzzle. The final robe was of gray samite: stiff silk brocaded with coral pins. It hung as heavily as chains and was a little too long.

At the bottom of the chest Tain found a box holding a circlet of black-grained silver wreathed with turquoises and jades. Carnelian had to put this on his head himself because Tain could not reach.

Tain stepped back, wide-eyed. "You're transformed into a Master, Carnie."

"I've always been a Master, Tain," snapped Carnelian. He felt vaguely silly, weighed down, overdressed. "I suppose I should go."

"But you must see yourself," his brother cried. He ran over to a copper mirror. As he struggled to set it up against the wall, it shot glimmers through the rafters.

Scowling, Carnelian allowed his head to droop under the weight of the circlet. When he lifted his head again he drew back. "By the Two . . ." A strange being was lurking in the copper. Carnelian had to move from side to side to convince himself it was his own watery reflection.

He thought of the tall men drifting along the quay. Masters. The Chosen, he corrected himself, using the Quya name they called themselves. His stomach churned. In all the world there were only three kinds of men: the Chosen, the half-caste marumaga and the rest, the barbarians. He realized Tain was looking at him, and could see that his own unease was spreading to that marumaga face. Remembering who he was and the duty he had to the boy, Carnelian dragged up some confidence and put it into his voice. "It's time for me to go, Tain. Please fetch my mask."

His brother went off to find it. When he came back, he offered the mask to Carnelian in both hands, with reverence. Carnelian took the hollow face and held it up so that it looked back at him. Flame light poured over the gold and put hidden life into its eyeslits. Its straps hung like thick tresses. It had a cold, unhuman beauty. Carnelian fitted it over his face. It chilled his cheeks and forehead. He held it there while Tain went round behind him and reached to do up the straps. He breathed slow and deep through the nostrils of the mask as his father had taught him and fought down the feeling of being trapped. He had never liked wearing it. Many times his father had insisted that he must, so that he might get used to it, even though Masking Law required only that a Ruling Lord conceal his face from his household.

The mask slits shielded Carnelian's eyes from the fire glare and he found that he could see into the dark corners of the room. He distracted himself with this until Tain was finished with the straps.

"I will go now." His voice sounded very close to him, flat, dead. "You may as well go off and join the rest of the household, Tain."

His brother's face was half turned away, looking at him obliquely with a strange expression Carnelian had never seen before. Tain bowed. "As you say . . . Master."

*　　*　　*

Tain's look was also there on the faces of the guardsmen. Carnelian disliked this new reverence, and the way they kept calling him "Master." It made him feel as if they were setting him up in his father's place. This was not his only unease as they walked through the barracks. He could see his escorts were sensing something too. He tried to locate its source. Silence. It was the silence. The barracks were never silent. It was unnatural. He became aware the air was dank and shivered. When they passed along the arcade it was all he could do to stop himself escaping through the door into the familiar warmth of the Great Hall.

He noticed his men tensing and then he straightened too as he saw the strangers. They were ranged in groups up the steps, men whose faces bore the marks of other Houses. He stared. Until that moment, every adult face he had seen, other than his father's, had had its chameleon. The strangers' faces were different. Some were bisected from hairline to chin by a horned-ring staff. Others were marked with the cross of dragonfly wings. A third group had the disc and crescent of the evening star tattooed like manic smiles. It was not only the tattoos that made the faces strange to him. The bisected ones were round and yellow. The dragonflied ones were oval, with almond eyes that peeped out from between the wings of their tattoos. Those who wore painted smiles were swarthier than any people Carnelian had seen before. All the strangers were swathed in stained brown traveling cloaks. While some had two-pronged spears, others had their hands on sheathed sickles or four-bladed cross-swords. All this Carnelian saw in the instant before the strangers fell with a clatter before him into the prostration.

He froze and his escort halted round him. The only men still standing had chameleoned faces. Two of these were his brothers: Grane, grim commander of the tyadra, and handsome Keal. Carnelian saw the uncertainty in the guardsmen's faces as they looked at him. He watched them glance at Grane, anxious, looking for an order. The commander ignored them. Instead, he gave Carnelian an almost imperceptible nod. Carnelian watched his own hand rise up before him. It shaped the sign, *Kneel*. In twos and threes they went down. Proud Grane, the eldest of his brothers, was last of all to obey. He pressed his brown hands together and pushed them out, as the others had done, as if offering himself to be tied up like a slave. Carnelian went cold, disliking their abasement. His hand was there before him, the sign still locked into it. It looked like his father's hand, for only he used such a command gesture. Carnelian forced himself to ascend the stairway. The doors of sea-ivory opened before him and he passed between them into his father's hall.

Four masks turned toward him. Carnelian faltered under their gaze, awed by the serene, unearthly beauty of those faces of gold. Four giants stood there beside the circular hearth. One he knew: his father in his jeweled robe. The other three, though much like him, were enveloped in great black hooded cloaks grayed with brine. In all his life Carnelian had seen no other Master save for his father. He realized that in spite of all he had been told, until that moment he had believed him a being without peer.

Behind Carnelian the doors closed and the giants dropped their masks into the cradles of their hands, revealing white faces, long, finely boned, with eyes the colors of winter. Carnelian remembered that the Law commanded he must unmask when those higher than him did so. Fumbling his mask off left him feeling exposed. He clutched it as he approached. Their skin was like light passing through ice. It took strength to keep his eyes up looking back at them. He found it. He would not bring shame on his father or himself.

"Great Lords, behold my son, Suth Carnelian," his father said, looking at him. Emotions were shifting in his eyes.

"So, Lord Suth, this is the son whom you have been hiding from us all these many, long years." The voice seemed to be coming from a bronze throat. Its owner was even larger than his father. He was also older, much older, though unlike any old man Carnelian had ever seen. His skin had not wrinkled, rather it had thinned to alabaster. His eyes' intense blue searched Carnelian's face. The voice sounded again. "He has the jade-eyed beauty, this son of yours."

Suth frowned. "You flatter him, Lord Aurum." Their eyes locked together. Though their lips did not move, nor their hands, Carnelian was convinced they were communicating with each other. He saw the other two Masters were also watching them.

Flames spluttered, hissed. Sparks seeded the air.

"Perhaps I do," the old Master said finally, breaking off from the contest. He smiled but only with his lips. Suth turned back to his son. Carnelian could see he was controlling anger.

"My son, let me make known to you our blood-pure visitors." His father opened a fist and lifted the hand to indicate the old Master. "Aurum, the Ruling Lord of that House and your uncle." The old Master gave a slow nod but his eyes never left Carnelian's face.

Carnelian stared back. He came back to the sound of his father's voice. ". . . Ruling Lord of House Vennel." The Master who bowed was more slender than the others, younger, paler-eyed. His hand unsheathed from a sleeve and melted into the sign, *Charmed*.

Suth turned to the last Master, who wore the serene smile of an idol. "This is your second cousin, Jaspar of House Imago, who one day, if the Two will it, shall be its Ruling Lord."

"As you say, cousin, if They will it," said the smiling Master and inclined his head elegantly.

Carnelian tried to return the smile.

"Now that the introductions have been made, my Lords, I might suggest that we retire," said Vennel. He had a woman's voice and his Quya was like singing. "One must confess to a certain weariness."

"What resources we have here are at your disposal, my Lords," Suth said. "Apartments have been made ready. I hope my Lords will forgive the little comfort we can provide. If we had been advised that you were coming . . ."

"We have come in haste, my Lord," said Aurum. "There

was neither the time nor the opportunity to herald our arrival."

Jaspar smiled again. "A little comfort will be rendered great by comparison with our recent accommodation."

"Shall we then tomorrow meet in formal conclave?" asked Vennel with his woman's voice.

The others lifted their hands in assent.

"Until the morrow then."

When Vennel and Jaspar began to move toward the door, Aurum remained behind. Vennel turned. "You are not accompanying us, my Lord?"

"Not immediately. I shall remain here and reminisce with the Lord Suth. Nostalgic nothings can resurrect the past."

Jaspar raised an eyebrow then dropped it again. Vennel's expression froze for a moment.

Seeing the sag in his father's face, Carnelian went up to him. "You are weary, my Lord."

His father smiled a bleak smile. "Perhaps I will find refreshment in reliving the past with the Lord Aurum. Go now, my Lord, and see that our guests are well looked after."

Carnelian bowed. Aurum was looking at him with gleaming eyes. Carnelian blushed. As he led Jaspar and Vennel to the sea-ivory doors, blinded slaves appeared. Carnelian stared at their puckered eyelids, then, copying the others, he held his mask up before his face and a blindman bound it on. As the doors opened, he looked back. His new uncle, Lord Aurum, had stretched a long arm across his father's shoulders and was moving him off into the shadows.

THE
CONCLAVE

A child can oft more fates decide

Than can a meeting of kings.

—PROVERB,

ORIGIN UNKNOWN

He surfaced from a murky dream, the mist of memory thinning into vague uneasy recollection then fading to nothing. It was cold and dark. Carnelian sensed it was not long until sunrise. The shutters rattled under a volley of sleet. Perhaps he had dreamed the visitors with their long black ship. His heart beat hard. He did not know which was worse: that they had come or that they might not have come at all. He put his feet onto the floor, fumbled a blanket round him and walked over to the shutters. When he swung them back, the wind and snow set him trembling. In the morning twilight the waves swayed their sickening surge. The ship was there in the anchorage, black as a hole.

*　　*　　*

Tain's breathing was fitful. The night before, Carnelian had returned to find him sleeping there on a makeshift bed and had not had the heart to send him back to his own room. In truth, he drew some comfort from having him there. He decided not to wake him. He would just have to do without paint.

He hunted around in the half-light until he found an under-robe. He slipped into its icy grip then hurriedly threw on more layers until he began to feel warm. His gull-feather cloak went over everything. He walked towards the outer door and stopped. "Gods' blood," he hissed. He returned for his mask. He had no intention of running into the visitors but it was safer to be cautious. He hitched the cold thing by its straps to his belt and returned to the door.

He should have expected the guardsmen outside. They eyed his cloak. One of them stepped forward. "You know you're not supposed to leave your room, Carnie, not until the Master sends for you."

"If there's anything you want we'll go and fetch it," piped up another.

"Who told you this?"

"Grane," said the first.

Carnelian glared at the man, who flinched. For a moment he considered putting on his mask and commanding them to let him pass. Grane's granite face appeared in his mind. It was one thing to play the Master in front of the visitors, quite another to do so in front of his own people. He nodded and bit his lip. One of the guardsmen sighed the general relief as Carnelian retreated back through the door.

His hand kneaded the door handle. With the arrival of the visitors his life had changed, and not for the better. His father had warned him of the restrictions of life in Osrakum but Carnelian had never expected these to come to the island. All his life he had heard his father say that life in the Hold was very lax. Still, he burned with questions and would have them answered before the conclave.

He considered his options and made up his mind. He strode back to the window and let in the gray sky.

"What are you doing?" said a voice from behind him.

Carnelian turned to look at Tain. He was propped up on one elbow squinting past a hand. "I'm going to find out what's happening. If you could bear it, Tain, I'd appreciate it if you'd hold the fort until I come back. You know, pretend I'm still here."

"What . . . ?"

Carnelian was not in the mood for long explanations. He climbed into the window space, braced himself against the wind and looked down at the swelling anger of the sea as it foamed and mouthed the rock below. He mastered his fear and peered just below the sill. The ledge was there, slushy, slick with spume.

There was a tugging at his cloak. "By the horns," he heard Tain spluttering, "are you trying to get yourself killed?"

Carnelian craned round. "There are guardsmen at the door and this is the only other way."

"But you'll kill yourself!"

"Rubbish. We've both done this a hundred times."

"When we were little, Carnie, and even then, never in winter."

"Let go, Tain," Carnelian cried and pulled away.

Tain let go, afraid Carnelian might pull so hard he would lose his balance. Tain knew well enough how obstinate his brother could be. "Yesterday, when he wasn't going out, he needed to be painted," Tain grumbled. "Today, he's prepared to go out on ledges with naked skin."

Carnelian ignored his brother, stooped down to remove his shoes and tied them to his belt beside the mask. It was better to feel the ledge. He lowered a foot down to it, ground his heel into the slush and bore the stab of cold that went up his leg. The other foot joined the first as he turned to face into the room. He walked his fingers over the stone of the wall outside searching for the once familiar handholds. The last time he had done this he had needed to stretch for them, now he actually had to bend his arms. Below him the sea was ravening at the cliff. He edged along. His foot slipped, thumping his heart up through his throat. He made a shuffle to the side, another, one more and he had reached the next window. It would not open. Shoving it, he almost pushed himself out into space. He did it again, with more care. The catch gave way and the shutters snapped into the room. He looked back to his own window. Tain's face was there, sick with fear. Carnelian winked at him, then disappeared.

Carnelian slipped into the barracks. He was anxious not to run into the Masters or any of their guardsmen. He found a balcony that looked down into the Sword Court and saw that a path had been cleared across it through the snow. The training posts with their wooden arms and heads were buried up to their waists in drifts. Carnelian smiled. There was nobody about.

He skirted the court, avoiding the main corridors. When he reached the final stairway he heard voices. He listened for a while. When he was sure they were men of his own tyadra, he went down to the alleyway. Its cobbles had recently been scraped clear but were already smearing with new snow. Two of his men were there. One had a brush and a cake of paint that was oozing its indigo over his palm and trickling it down his arm. The men looked up and saw him.

"What're you doing?" asked Carnelian.

"Making wards, Master."

"Don't you 'Master' me, Poal."

The man showed gaps in his teeth as he grinned.

Carnelian looked north toward the Holdgate, then south into the Sword Court. The eaves' icicle jaws clamped a leaden sky. There was no sound, no movement save for fluttering snow flecks. He turned to inspect their work. An eye was already painted on the archway. The run of the paint was making it cry. Below this they were daubing a crude chameleon. The first sign warned against any uninvited intrusion: the second removed the restriction for those belonging to the House Suth.

"Where's this being done, Poal?"

"Everywhere, Carnie."

"Are the strangers wandering around?"

The man shook his head. "I've not seen any today."

"Where's Grane?"

They both shrugged.

"Keal?"

"In the kitchens, I think," said the other man.

Carnelian thanked them, crossed to a door, opened it and slipped into the warm gloom beyond. He felt his way down narrow corridors, met no one and managed to reach the kitchens unseen.

Pungent smells. A steam of air. Enough smoke to sting his eyes. Fires hissed and danced their gleam across walls paneled with platters of precious brass. Endless clatter, clanging and the scolding of the cooks. Stone slab tables stood on either side of the firepit, the center of each jammed with condiment boxes and bottles of sauces. Round them people were chopping with flint cleavers, slicing with obsidian knives. Along one wall were the cisterns with their chipped-lipped spouts where dishes were being scrubbed. Cracked flagged floor, tiled walls, the whole huge room funneled up blackening into a chimney.

Carnelian wandered into this world with his customary delight. He almost forgot his reason for being there when he saw they were cooking feast dishes. The storerooms had yielded up their treasures. Dried fish wallowed in pools of marinade. Air-mummified birds were being soaked in red, honeyed oil. A boy was binding their feathers into fans for garnish. There were flint-gray shrimp just drawn from their tanks, still trembling their combs of legs. Fruits like wizened jewels were being sorted into their kinds. The seeds and bark of rare spices were being pounded into pastes with garlic and rounds sliced from the segmented giriju roots, whose gnarled golden fingers had to be handled with leather gloves because their juice burned skin. Carnelian insisted on sniffing everything and the cooks indulged him. One of the older women slapped his hand away when he stole an apple. He made a face at her and she waggled her cleaver threateningly. Everyone laughed. He bit into the fruit and grimaced at its bitterness, and she called out that it served him right.

He came to the firepit and peered into the pots. Some had green sauces, others yellow. In one a pair of carp swam round in the warming water. He stirred another, fishing for morsels with a ladle, curious to see what might be wandering in the depths.

He reached the pool into which the Hold's spring was pouring its liquid ice. Girls were ranged around its edge, drawing water out with pitchers. He asked for Keal and one of them pointed. He did not see her shy adoration or the way the other girls exchanged meaningful looks. He made for his brother's broad back and slapped it.

Keal spun round cursing, but the anger quickly slipped from his face. "What're you doing here? Grane will be furious—"

"Grane's always furious. Besides, his bird will be back in the cage before ever he finds that it's flown."

"The order to keep you there came from the Master himself. You do know that, don't you?"

Keal's eyes were storm-gray. His skin was a pale honey-brown. He was tall enough to reach Carnelian's chest. Of all the children his father had sired upon the household women, Keal was the one who looked most like him. Those eyes, that severe look, were the Master's. Carnelian felt a familiar pang because Keal would never see this for himself. In the household only the eldest had seen his father's face.

"Come on, you'd better get back there anyway," said Keal.

"Before I do I'd like to know a few things," said Carnelian. "First, tell me what happened last night. The warlike preparations—"

"Hush!" Keal grabbed his arm and dragged him off into the intoxicating stink of one of the storerooms, whose walls rustled with dried squid.

Keal looked so serious Carnelian almost laughed.

"I'll tell you what I know but you must keep it to yourself."

Carnelian nodded.

"I don't know why I'm doing this."

"Because we're brothers, of course."

"Actually, I'm just hoping that you'll make less trouble if your damned curiosity's satisfied."

"And because you know you're no good at hiding things from me." Carnelian grinned.

"Do you want to know or not?"

Carnelian made his face serious, then nodded.

"Well listen then. The Master armed us and made us man the Holdgate. I was with him as we watched the Masters coming up the road. I think he was as shocked as the rest of us that they were here."

"How do you know that?"

Keal shrugged. "I just do."

Carnelian let it pass.

"He put me in charge of the Holdgate. He told me that when the Masters demanded entry I was to delay them, tell them that we were waiting for word to come back from him in his hall before we could let them in. He told me that I mustn't on any account open the Holdgate until he sent word. Then he left with Grane and—"

"They left you there to face the Masters by yourself . . . to openly disobey them?"

"Well, it wasn't quite like that. It was their tyadra that actually demanded entry. Mind you, even then it wasn't easy."

"Go on."

Keal's eyes blanked. "Though the Masters said nothing I could feel their anger rising. They just loomed in the background. It was terrifying."

Carnelian shuddered. "I can imagine."

"At last, a blindman came from the Master. I can't remember all he said, you know how weirdly they speak when they're carrying one of his commands, but the gist of it was . . ." He stopped and walked to the doorway to make sure there was no one nearby, then came back. "The gist of it was that we were to let them in with all proper respect and to escort them to him, leaving none at the Holdgate. They were to be treated as the Masters they were but . . . we should think of them as being pirates come to plunder the Hold."

Carnelian stared at his brother. "He said that?"

Keal nodded, his eyes big and round. "Or something very close."

"Was that it?"

Keal chewed his lip. "Not quite." He had lowered his voice. "The blindman also said that, at the Master's word, I was to be ready to destroy them."

"What?" Carnelian was stunned. Even the suggestion of harming a Master was blasphemy.

"That's what the man said, and he brought the Master's ring to prove it."

Their eyes locked.

"Is there more?" Carnelian said at last.

"I was to stay at the Holdgate and expect an attack from the ship. If any of them came back through the Hold without their escort they were to be destroyed."

"And later?"

"Things changed. When you came out of his hall with the two Masters, you remember, I took them to the west rooms. That's where they are now . . . I hope. When I came back Grane was there and the other Master was still inside. The Master came out—"

"Which Master?"

"Our father." Keal blushed from the use of the word. "He came out and told us that we could relax our alert a little. He made most of us stand down. He said he wanted us rested and fresh for this morning."

"And today?"

"Today he's told us to paint wards everywhere. Grane was told to protect you and stop you wandering about." He gave Carnelian the severe look again.

Carnelian patted his shoulder. "It'll be all right. Tell me about our people. How are they feeling about all this?"

"What do you think, Carnie? They're all dancing for joy."

"What're they afraid of?"

"The Masters, of course, and do you blame them? They're a scary bunch. People know something's up but they don't know what."

Carnelian nodded grimly. "I suppose I feel a bit like that myself." He saw his brother tauten and reached out to touch him. "We'll be fine. My . . . our father won't let them harm us."

"But, Carnie, they're taking so much, so much of everything."

Carnelian remembered the kitchen. "You mean food?"

"That and other things. Their demands just don't stop. We've already started digging into our reserves. If they stay even a few days they'll eat into our stores, and you know as well as I do that there's nowhere to get more before the ships come."

Carnelian nodded. He knew how carefully they had always had to husband their resources, especially in winter. He was still brooding as they walked back into the kitchen.

"There you are," a voice cried.

Carnelian's heart sank. His aunt Brin was sweeping toward them across the kitchen.

"You do know it was the Master himself who ordered you to stay in your room?" said Brin as she reached him. The kitchen clatter faded away as people turned to stare. She turned on Keal. "And I would have thought you at least would show more sense."

Keal flushed. Brin was not only the Master's sister but she also had control of all the household except for the men of the tyadra, though that did not stop them fearing her tongue.

Carnelian grew angry. "Don't you dare take this out on him, Brin. I was the one who forced him to talk to me. He was all for getting me back to my room."

Brin grunted. The legs of her chameleon tattoo disappeared into the creases in her cheeks as she showed her distaste. "Look at the way you're dressed, Carnelian. Do you have any idea at all what might happen if any of the strangers were to see your face?"

Carnelian drew his cloak back to reveal the mask hanging at his hip.

"It's a lot of use there under your cloak. Besides, the Master's command is the Master's command. Go back to your room." She turned to Keal. "And you, since you're so easily *forced* away from your tasks, maybe you'd better give up what you're doing and escort him. Make sure he gets where he's going, then go and tell Grane that I don't want to see you or any of his other boneheads in my kitchen for the rest of the day."

Keal hung his head. "Yes, Brin."

Carnelian let his anger go. He knew Brin was right and that she already had enough to do without having to run around looking out for him.

"What are you lot gawking at?" bellowed Keal, glowering.

Brin made just enough room to let them pass. The clatter resumed as they fled her disapproval.

For most of the morning Carnelian fretted in his room. Tain went out several times but each time came back with nothing new about the visitors. They both became sullen, infected with the general foreboding.

When the summons came at last, Tain dressed him in the gray robe, circlet and Great-Rings. When Carnelian was ready an escort came for him from Grane, gleaming in their polished leather cuirasses, their hair freshly oiled, their blades honed and waxed. Carnelian said he was proud of them and they all beamed. He marched between them through the Hold. Every door, every arch Carnelian saw was warded with a freshly painted eye and the Suth chameleon. Only the three doors that stood on the final stretch of the alleyway were any different. They had the warding eye but below it the cipher of the Master who had taken possession of the halls that lay beyond: Vennel's disc and crescent evening star, Jaspar's dragonfly, the horned-ring staff of the Lord Aurum.

In the past, Carnelian and the other children had sneaked

into those dismal halls with their views of the anchorage and the bay. All his life they had been a haunted, musty hinterland of the Hold. He tried to imagine them transformed into mysterious luxury by the households the visitors had brought with them, and failed. It was far easier to imagine the Masters lying in dusty state like kings in their tombs.

Carnelian was relieved to find his father alone. He formed a pillar of shadow against a rectangle of glowering sky. Carnelian crossed the hall toward the window. A carpet of embers glowed in the circular hearth. The nearer he drew to his father, the louder spoke the wind and sea.

"I am come, my Lord, at your command."

The apparition turned. The face looking down at him was like a lamp. The eyes seemed of a piece with the sky. "I wished to speak to you before the conclave." His father turned back to view the sea, a vast slate-green plain stretching off into the south. "It is likely that we shall be returning to Osrakum."

That name reverberated through Carnelian. Visions flashed through his mind with the quickening of his heart. He saw a memory from childhood of his father cupping his small hands in one of his. The little bowl of fingers was Osrakum: a crater hidden within a mountain wall. Circling the inner edge, his father's finger had let him see and feel the coombs cutting into the rim which were where the Masters lived. Tender pressure for their own coomb. A swirl showed where the sky lake filled the bowl. A touch at the center where the edges of his palms met allowed him to feel the Isle with its Forbidden Garden within which lay the Pillar of Heaven and the Labyrinth.

Carnelian realized that his father's bright face had turned to him, its stormy eyes deeper than the sky.

"Long have we lived here remote from the turning of events across the sea. But now they reach out to us and we can no longer remain untouched." His father became granite. "A time of peril comes for me . . . and for you, my son. In the days to come we will have need of every resource."

"What danger have our guests brought here?"

"Amongst many, themselves."

"Lord Aurum?"

"He most of all."

"Even though he is aligned to us by blood."

"Blood trade insures neither amity nor alliance. My father gave my sister to be Aurum's second wife because he sought a son to replace the one who died in infancy. She has borne his House three daughters, a vast wealth should they live. But still, he has no son."

"I did not know the children of the Chosen were so frail?"

"It is a curse of our race that so few come of age. Though the ichor of the Gods is watered down with mortal blood its fire cannot easily be contained by human veins."

"I suppose it is that fire that kills their mothers too."

"Your mother would have died a thousand times to give you life," said Suth, misreading the look in his son's face.

Father and son examined each other's eyes. This was a subject they never spoke of.

Carnelian broke the silence first. "And if Aurum were to die without a son?"

"The second lineage of his House would inherit its ruling and House Aurum would be diminished among the Great."

"Then he should get himself another wife."

"Do you forget that high blood-rank brides are the rarest commodity?"

"He has daughters that he can trade."

"They are too young."

"Iron then?"

His father's eyes pierced him. "If he could have used such wealth, he would have."

"And what of Imago Jaspar?"

"His House once ranked among the highest of the Great. More than two hundred years ago it sold the Emperor Nuhquanya a wife from whom today all those of the House of the Masks descend. Yet in the crisis over the succession of Qusata they lost their ruling lineage."

"Slaughtered at his Apotheosis?"

His father nodded. "Many Houses suffered."

"So we are linked to House Imago's second lineage?"

"For more than a century it has been their first."

"What is the nature of the linkage?"

"My grandmother was sister to his grandfather."

"But our blood is purer than his?"

"Not so, in spite of your mother's blood having gifted you a blood-taint almost half of mine."

Carnelian nodded. Notwithstanding her august blood, he valued the father that he knew more than the mother he had never known.

"As you know, like all Chosen of blood-rank two, your taint has zeros in the first two positions. The largest fraction of your blood that is tainted is the eight-thousandth. In this third position you, Aurum and Jaspar have a one in contrast to my three. It is only in the fourth position, or the sixteen-thousandth fraction, that your blood differs from theirs. Whereas you have a nineteen in this position, Jaspar has a sixteen and Aurum has a fifteen."

"So their blood is purer than mine."

"Marginally, though neither of them can claim as you can to be the nephew of the God Emperor."

Carnelian nodded at that familiar evocation of blood pride. "And Lord Vennel?"

His father looked as if he had bitten into a lemon.

"He is of inferior blood. His father and his uncles, all of blood-rank one, conspired to buy for themselves a bride of blood-rank two. Their House had no blood to barter and little iron coinage and so her bride-price had to be paid with vulgar wealth."

"Nevertheless, Vennel is of blood-rank two?"

Just, Suth's hand signed with a flick of contempt. "He has the two zeros but a nineteen in the third. His blood is more than five times less pure than mine; ten times less pure than yours."

"I like him as little as Aurum, but cousin Jaspar seems amiable enough."

Suth clamped Carnelian's shoulders with his hands. "If you think that, then he is to you a greater danger than the others. All who are Chosen are dangerous. In the Three Lands there are no beings so terrible as are we. Few of us know mercy, fewer still compassion. Inevitably, the greatest among us are the most rapacious. This is a necessity forced on some by the contest of the blood trade, on others by their nature. Constantly we hunt each other. Our appetite for power cannot be sated. We would eat the world though the gluttony destroy us."

Suth stopped. He could see that he had frightened the boy already more than he had intended.

"Of course, you will think you know this," he said more gently. "After all, have we not spoken of it many times before? But accept it when I say that you cannot truly understand, for you have never walked in the crater of Osrakum. This is something that you feel with the fibers of your flesh or not at all. You have heard my words?"

Carnelian swallowed, nodded.

"Then believe them." His father's hands dropped away, his shoulders slumped.

Compassion made Carnelian bold. "What burden are you carrying, Father?"

"The greatest burden. Choice."

The word was like a gate slamming shut.

They stood in silence. The green glass of the sea swelled up and from several points began to shatter white from side to side. Carnelian watched it, brooding over his father's words. Thoughts of the visitors worked their barbs into his mind. The salt wind blew hard upon his face but was not strong enough to lift the brocade of his robe.

"Why have they come, my Lord?" he said at last.

"You will know that soon enough. Suffice to say that we will return with them to Osrakum."

Images, hopes, dreams spated through Carnelian's mind. Osrakum, the heart and wonder of the Three Lands. More a yearning than a word. A bleak thought squeezed the vision still.

"Is their ship large enough to take us all?"

His father's eyes were fathomless.

As they looked out, both their faces turned to stone. The ominous movement of the sea seemed a mirror to their thoughts. Neither saw the storm brewing its violence along the southern margin of the sky.

A clanging on the doors called them back.

"Your mask," his father said in a low voice and Carnelian remembered it and held it up before his face. His father's hand was a heavy comfort on his shoulder. The doors opened remotely and the beings came in, glimmering like dark water, their masks like flames.

Carnelian went with his father to greet them. With a clatter the day was choked out with shutters. They met the Masters by the fire in the crowding gloom.

"We trust you found sufficient comfort in your night's repose?" Suth said.

One of the apparitions lifted a jeweled hand. *Sufficient*, it signed.

Carnelian found the sign curious, made as it was by an unfamiliar hand. The Masters had discarded their traveling cloaks and were now clad in splendor. Their haughty faces of gold seemed a gilded part of the long marble swelling of their heads. Each was crowned with dull fire. Each wore many-layered robes, plumaged, crusted with gems and ivories.

"We shall needs be rid of uninvited eyes and ears." It was Aurum's deep swelling voice.

Suth lifted his hand and at its command shadows flitted along the hem of the hall. The movement passed away. "We are alone, my Lords."

As they unmasked, Carnelian felt something like surprise that the gold had managed to contain the radiance of their faces.

"Suth, your son is still here," sang Vennel's liquid voice.

Suth's response was cold. "Is he not at least as entitled to be here as are you, my Lord?"

Vennel's head inclined back and his eyes flashed. "He is a child."

Carnelian glared at Vennel's perfect face and was pleased to find his neck too long.

"In Osrakum, he would already have been given his blood-ring by the Wise," Suth said.

Carnelian looked at the Masters' hands. Each was knuckled with rings like stars but on the smallest finger of each right hand there was a dull, narrow band. A ring of skymetal that grew bloody when not oiled. Iron, most precious of substances save only the ichor of the Gods Themselves. It fell from the sky in stones. A gift from the Twins to Their Chosen. The sign of Their covenant.

Jaspar smiled at Carnelian. "Whether he wears a ring or not, I for one can see no reason to exclude him from our conclave."

"Nor I," said Aurum with over-bright eyes.

"Then let us begin," said Suth.

Carnelian saw that five chairs had been set in a half-circle round the hearth. There was a hissing of silk as they each sat down. Their faces hung in the gloom like moons. They closed their eyes. Gems in their robes trapped fire-flicker. Carnelian looked down at his hands and wondered what was happening.

"Even now the Heart of the Commonwealth is failing," Aurum rumbled, making Carnelian jump.

Understanding, Carnelian almost gasped. The God Emperor was dying. He watched his father's hand rise up to make the sign for grief. The other Masters followed him. Carnelian hesitated, then copied them. He stared at his hand, making sure the sign was well made. He was relieved when the others' hands flattened to palms. Alone, his father kept his hand raised, but then he too let it go.

"This crisis imperils the Commonwealth as it has always done," said Vennel. "Her subjects must not know of this ere a new candidate is made ready to receive the Dual Essence."

"And so we are come with great urgency, to offer the Ruling Lord of House Suth the ring of He-who-goes-before," said Aurum.

Jaspar fixed unblinking eyes on Suth's face. "Will you accept it, Lord?"

"Is this the will of the Great?"

"It is," said Aurum. "Their Clave, in formal session, elected you."

"Why?"

"We were in some disarray, my Lord," said Vennel.

"More accurately, at each others' throats," said Jaspar.

Suth smiled though his eyes were flint. "That at least has not changed."

Vennel's colorless eyes lingered on Jaspar, who ignored them, saying, "We need you, my Lord, to speak for the Great in the interregnum before the election of the next Gods."

"The Great must be much diminished if they need seek leadership from one so long away," said Suth.

"From being so long away, the Ruling Lord Suth might be assumed untainted by narrow factional considerations," said Aurum.

"From being so long away, the Ruling Lord Suth might be assumed dismissive of *all* considerations," said Suth.

"So it was said," said Vennel.

Suth looked across the fire at Aurum. "Was it indeed?"

"The Commonwealth must have another God and he who shall be They must be rightly chosen," said Aurum.

"There is, of course, a difference of opinion as to who should be chosen," said Jaspar. "There are two candidates, the Jade Lord twins, Nephron and Molochite."

"And three factions?" asked Carnelian.

The three visitor Masters looked at him and then inclined their heads.

"Of course, the matter had been decided," said Vennel.

"But not to the general satisfaction," said Aurum.

"Certainly not to your satisfaction, my Lord."

"I am merely one among many. Those whom I represent

THE
CHOSEN

Book One
of the
Stone Dance
of the
Chamelon

RICARDO
PINTO

A TOM DOHERTY ASSOCIATES BOOK
NEW YORK

This is a work of fiction. All the characters and events portrayed in this book
are either products of the author's imagination or are used fictitiously.

THE CHOSEN

This book was originally published in 1999 by Bantam Press, U.K.

Interior map © Neil Gower

By arrangement with Transworld Publishers, a Division of the Random
House Group Ltd.

A Tor Book.
Published by Tom Doherty Associates, LLC
175 Fifth Avenue
New York, NY 10010

www.tor.com

Tor® is a registered trademark of Tom Doherty Associates, LLC.

ISBN: 0-812-58435-X
Library of Congress Catalog Card Number: 99-088106

First Tor edition: March 2000
First mass market edition: February 2001

Printed in the United States of America

0 9 8 7 6 5 4 3 2 1

FOR MY MOTHER AND FATHER

ACKNOWLEDGMENTS

A number of experts have provided me with invaluable support in the writing of *The Chosen*. In many meetings, Ben Harte helped reshape the geology of Osrakum and the Three Lands. David Adger helped me invent the language Quya, and it is his translations that appear in the book and that have allowed me to form grammatically correct glyphs. Dominic Prior checked my math and produced much of his own. He was instrumental in devising the watchtower heliographs and gave me the equations to calculate the lengths and directions of shadows. Frank Neuman helped me devise a plausible monsoon. Nina Mandel delved in Hebrew scriptures to find, among other things, the orders of the angelic host. Billy, a tattoo artist in Leith, Edinburgh, bemusedly answered a question or two. Jane of the Edinburgh Zoo found out for me the color of a flamingo's tongue. Any errors are my own.

All my friends and family are to be pitied for the years that they have put up with me working on this book. However, it is my partner Robbie who has most patiently overseen this monstrous labor. He kept me from starving and has had besides to read the thing too many times. My brother David justly found early versions complete rubbish and told me so. A few friends read drafts and gave me valuable criticism and support: Jo Bateson, Bridget and Peter McCalister, Rosie and Tom Hall. For years, my T'ai Chi buddies Bob Gillies, Ian Thompson and Graham Gibson have had to endure ranting in the pub about this book. Exchanging madnesses with James "Moonie" Worrall helped keep me sane. Liz and Stanley Rosenthal brought me to the attention of my agents. Fred White, Philip and Simon Bolton, Mike Forrester, Steve Rizza, Mark Haillay, James Hutchby, Ali Pickard, Sue Macarthy and John Scofield, Richard Jordan, Grace Cheetham, Anoop Pareikh, feathers and Apple computers have all made significant contributions.

I wish to thank Broo Doherty for her incisive editing and unflagging support, Claire Ward and the other people at Transworld for all their enthusiasm and hard work, Neil Gower for his interpretation of my glyphs and maps, as well as Nancy Webber and Antonia Reeve.

For this edition additional thanks to Claire Eddy, Jenna Felice, M. Longbrake, Bryan Cholfin, Mark Harrison for his artwork and Martha E. Sedgwick for her lovely jacket design. I owe a special debt to my friend Stephen Rizza, whose post-editing has contributed immensely to this edition.

Finally, there is my agent, Victoria Hobbs (masterfully abetted by Alexandra Pringle), for whose belief in me, encouragement, patience and indefatigable championing of my cause I am deeply grateful.

would feel closer to being satisfied if the Lord Suth were to oversee the election."

"We must all bow to the will of the Clave," said Vennel sardonically.

Aurum's head angled in irritation.

"My Lords," said Suth.

All faces turned to him.

"No more words are needed. I will wear the Pomegranate Ring."

Jaspar hid his surprise quickly under an idol's smile. Though Vennel's face was as blank as a drift of snow, his eyes looked startled.

Aurum's eyes blazed with triumph. "Then we must make preparations to return."

Carnelian watched his father nod slowly, staring into the distance. His face seemed a piece of marble.

"Perhaps we should wait for the clemency of the storms," said Vennel quickly.

"My Lord knows our purpose can brook no delay, the weather notwithstanding," said Aurum.

"Still, the baran must be repaired and we require provisions," said Vennel.

Carnelian's guts wrenched. "Surely you have supplies upon your ship, my Lords. Here, we have barely enough to last the winter."

Aurum fixed him with his glassy gaze. "You will have enough, nephew, for our needs."

"For two months, my Lord, we have been upon the sea," said Jaspar. "The provisions that the sea did not spoil were all consumed. The baran's holds are as empty as the stomachs of her crew."

"Carnelian," his father said. "She must be filled up from our storerooms."

"But our people—"

"There is no other way, my son." His father's eyes dulled. "Whether we stay or go, there will be some who go hungry."

Jaspar smiled indulgently. "My Lord does of course realize

that the Commonwealth will compensate his House in full measure for any loss?"

"Of course, my Lord," Suth said quickly, glancing at his son. The boy was holding in his pain as he had taught him, but only just. "But let there be no talk of compensation until the full cost be known."

"Wood will be needed, rope, sail parchment, tar," said Aurum.

"I shall instruct my people to give you access to everything we have, my Lord," said Suth, and as he spoke his eyes returned to linger on his son's tight, resolute face.

When his father left the hall with the other Masters, Carnelian stayed behind. He stared into the fire and tried to work out what he would say to Tain, his other brothers, his people. No one must starve. He would not allow anyone to starve. Surely there was time enough to work something out.

He rose and left. Nothing would happen until the morning. He would sleep and rise early. He walked back through eerie quiet, the only sounds the scuffling of his escort and the whining wind.

Misery was crowding in. He tried to turn his back on it by preparing himself for bed. When Tain appeared complaining that some strange men had come up from the ship, Carnelian told him not to worry.

Tain looked unhappy. "But they're sticking their noses everywhere. The Master's given them leave to pass our wards."

"I said things will be fine," snapped Carnelian. "Now either go back to your own room or get to bed."

Tain's cheeks went as red as if he had been slapped.

Carnelian turned away to face the wall. For a long time sleep eluded him. He watched the shadows tremble up the wall. He could almost feel the ship out there, a cold fist pushing hard against his back.

PILLAGE

Ruins smoking on a hill

They stole my hands' work

My children

And in their place

With violence

This child of hatred planted

—EXTRACT FROM A

BARBARIAN LAMENT

Carnelian woke. Each breath clouded the air. Wrapped in a blanket he went to the window to look out at his enemy. There the ship lay like a mouth in the sea. That sight of her fixed his resolve. He woke Tain. His brother sat up tousled and confused. "It's the middle of the night."

"No, it's near daybreak and the household will be stirring. Today I must be painted as well as dressed."

Tain stood up grumbling. He stumbled off to get the jars and brushes while Carnelian played with the fire. When Tain came back he was still grumbling.

"I don't know what you're complaining about," said Carnelian. "I'm the one who has to stand here naked."

"Do you really need to be painted?"

"Would I ask you if I didn't?" Carnelian saw his brother flinch at his tone. "I want to be free to go out into the open," he said more softly.

Starting at his sooty fingers, Tain began to wash him. "How do you think you'll get past the guards this time?" he said humorlessly. "I'd like to see you manage the ledge in your Master's robes."

"For your information, dear brother, I intend to use my Master's mask. I'll order them to let me pass and they will."

"They might at that," muttered Tain.

When Carnelian was cleaned, Tain began the painting. He stirred the pigment in its jar with a brush and began to apply it to Carnelian's skin with long even strokes. The chill paint made him come up in goose-pimples. Though the pigment was duller than Carnelian's skin, there was so little light that Tain had to keep turning him to see which bits he had done already.

When it was finished Tain hurried the drying with a fan. Carnelian shivered with each gust. "You're enjoying this aren't you?" he said through rattling teeth.

"Of course," said Tain and they grinned at each other.

When he was ready they put on all the robes. They tied his mask on, then went out together and were surprised to find no guards outside the door. They made off through the barracks. Everywhere was the same; the Hold seemed abandoned. Neither voiced his dread. When they came down into the stretch of the alleyway that ran between the Sword Court and the Long Court they began to hear a rhythmic thudding.

In the Long Court the snow had been trampled gray. Doorways and windows gaped all round its edge. Carnelian and Tain were scandalized to see the snow blowing into the rooms beyond. The thudding rang round the court. It grew louder as they passed along the arcade. The door to the Great Hall was ajar. They approached it as if it were the opening to a monster's cave. The sounds grew sharper with each step they took. Suddenly, the chopping stopped. They peered round the jamb. Tain gasped. Carnelian froze, staring. There was a long stuttering eruption. One of the columns was falling, dragging down a piece of the ceiling. It butted another column with its carved head. Both boys shuddered as the falling one scraped down, trailing a smoke of plaster. It crashed into the floor. The impact shook up through their feet. They watched it bounce and rock still. The dust settled. Snow drove down through the ragged hole that had been ripped in the ceiling. Flurries danced among the columns still left standing.

Carnelian strode into the hall in fury, trailing Tain after him. Three columns had already been felled. He reached one of the stumps and touched its splinter teeth with tender disbelief. The chopping began again. He kicked his way toward it through the debris of the mosaics. Five strange creatures were hacking into the smooth skin of another column. The thin gray light filtering down with the snow revealed them to be as bony as old men's hands, their skin spotted with bruise-blue wave glyphs.

Carnelian planted himself before them, bellowing, "What in the names of the Gods do you think you're doing?"

He saw the sailors' narrow faces look up, sweat-glazed, taut with effort. Their eyes grew huge and then they collapsed to the ground. An axe clattered to the floor. The blue glyphs had been branded, not tattooed. Joints knobbed their limbs. They reeked of bitumen and fear. Carnelian could see their shaking. Their terror and frailty rebuked him. He saw Tain wandering lost amongst the devastation.

A voice cried out in anger, and a man burst into the light. He was taller than the sailors, but still much smaller than Carnelian. He scolded the bony creatures, jabbing at them with a stick. The man must have seen Carnelian looming there, for the next moment he fell to his knees, mumbling, "Master."

Carnelian came further into the light. "Has this been sanctioned by a Master?"

"Yes, Master," the man replied without looking up.

"Why is it necessary?"

"Long timbers are needed, Master, to repair the masts."

"And who are you?"

"Ship's captain, Master."

"Look up when I speak to you."

The man lifted his face but not his eyes.

"And my people who were here, where are they?"

"They've been moved elsewhere, Master."

"Show me."

"Instantly."

As the captain rose, Carnelian noticed the thick ring of brass circling his brown neck. Where it widened at his throat, it was inscribed with a wave glyph. To the right of the inscription the collar threaded a slider showing the number eight. To the left were other sliders. Carnelian knew this must be a legionary collar detailing the man's rank and recording his service to the Commonwealth. Only the Masters could make brass. Only they could put that collar about a man's neck, or take it off. Any man found wearing such a collar outside the bounds of his service faced crucifixion.

Carnelian called over to Tain. He came, sullen, cowed. Carnelian reached out and squeezed some reassurance into his arm. Together, they followed the captain out of the hall. Behind them the axes had already resumed their chopping.

As Carnelian accompanied the captain through his home, he found that it had become strange, unknown. Order had passed away. The passages were choked with people, with bundles, with rolled carpets. There was a clatter and echoes and the angry voices of his guardsmen as they herded the children and the women. These last were strangely silent. Thin chameleoned faces, fearful-eyed. When they saw him they looked up with hope. He tried to smile until he realized that all they could see was the disdainful fixed expression of his mask. They made way for him and, as he passed, hung their heads.

The captain brought him to the training hall of the tyadra. Carnelian's people filled it like a colony of birds: jabbering, marking little territories with the salvage of their belongings.

Weapon racks were ranged behind them on the walls. The target manikins had been shoved into a corner, with all their ropes and pulleys, their blunted swords and spears.

The captain was standing head bowed, eyes averted, waiting. Carnelian dismissed him. Tain's face expressed incomprehension as he looked around him at the refugees. Carnelian knew his own face must look much the same under his mask.

Silence fell. People stood still, their arms clutching their belongings, looking at Carnelian, expecting something, needing something. He felt a fraud. He had nothing to say to them, nothing that could make sense of what was happening. Outside more axes were chopping. There were other violent sounds of pillage. Carnelian could not bear their eyes. So many eyes. He could not resist the cowardice of lifting his hand, to command prostration. Then there were no more eyes, no chameleoned faces, just the backs of heads. Even then he felt they were accusing him. These people were in his keeping. It was not only his father that had taught him that, but his own instinct. He turned his back on them and walked out into the Sword Court. His steps were measured enough but Carnelian did not deceive himself, he knew he was fleeing.

Out in the cold he stared, not understanding what he saw. Something moved beside him. He glanced down to see Tain looking queasy. The snow that had been swept from the cobbles had been piled in dirty mounds. In one part of the court Carnelian saw some of his people laboring in the mist of their own breath, stacking shutters, pieces of flooring, tables. A queue was filing in from the Long Court alleyway carrying more. Nearby some of the branded men from the ship were splitting these things into planks. Across the court, parchment was being cut from windows. Sleds were being banged together. One already made was creaking as it was loaded. Some more of his people were standing at its head, dejected, hands wedged into their armpits, puffing, the ropes to pull the sled coiled at their feet. Carnelian saw here and there the leather jerkin of a guardsman of his tyadra. Over against a wall a handful of Aurum's guardsmen were leaning on their forked spears. Their yellow tattoo-bisected faces showed the uncaring arrogance of conquerors.

One of Carnelian's guardsmen came walking straight toward him. It was Grane, his nose and ears red, his hands rasping against each other. "It is unseemly that you should be here, my Master."

"Perhaps I can be of some help, Grane."

Breathing heavy clouds of vapor, his brother came closer. "This isn't the place for you," he said in a low voice.

Carnelian grew angry. "Do you really expect me just to sit back, watch this happen, do nothing?"

Grane looked up at him, frowning. "It's not only yourself you shame by coming here, it's all of us."

"Don't you talk to me of shame. I find enough shame in allowing this . . . this desecration. I'll go and see the Master and put a stop to it, now!"

Grane looked down at Tain and jerked his head. "You. Go and help load that sled." Tain looked up. Carnelian could see that his brother was hoping he would countermand the order, but pretended not to notice. As the boy stormed off, Grane leaned close. "Don't be a fool, Carnelian. From where do you think the orders came for this?"

Carnelian looked away, knowing Grane spoke truth.

"You can't do anything here." Grane took a step back, bowed and moved away.

Carnelian stood for a moment looking at nothing in particular. His mirror face made him a pale sun in the chaos of the court. Slowly he turned and walked off toward the barracks.

All that day Carnelian hid in his room. Several times he slept. He tried to distract himself. In flickering firelight he played with his Great-Rings. He tried to conjure up those visions of Osrakum that had always been brighter to him than summer sky. There was no brightness, only the lonely lightless room. All day he longed for Tain to come, but when finally he did, Carnelian had only pain to share and so pretended to be asleep.

His brother was there, sleeping in his makeshift bed. His breathing sounded as fitful as the gale outside. Despair lurked in every corner of the room. To escape, Carnelian tried to fill his mind with a vision of wide untainted blue sky.

Next morning, Tain uncovered the glow of the embers to make some light. Carnelian's brow was creased. His lips twitched as if he were speaking to someone far away in his dreams. The boy leaned forward and pulled the blanket up over him, then slipped away.

Carnelian woke to find Tain kneeling beside him looking agitated. "You must come, Carnie. I wanted to let you sleep but you must come and make him move."

"Eh? Make who move?" Carnelian sat up bleary-eyed. "Open the shutters, will you, Tain?"

The morning flooded in. Carnelian hid his eyes, smiled with pleasure as the light fell on his face, then, remembering, frowned.

"Crail. Crail's refusing to move," said Tain.

Carnelian looked at him, confused. "Move . . . ?"

"His room's to be pulled apart like the others and he refuses to move."

Carnelian stood up. "And Grane, Keal?"

"They're down at the ship and can't come up."

Carnelian saw the pleading in his brother's face. He chewed his lip. "You'll have to get me dressed first."

They hurried through it, and when Carnelian was ready Tain sprang toward the door. Carnelian ignored him, went to the window and stood for some moments looking out at the ship. People swarmed over her hull, spilling onto the quayside. One of her masts was down. She had a skirt of boats and rafts bobbing in the swell around her. A carcass awrithe with maggots, he thought. He turned his back on her and walked over to join Tain.

They had to cross the alleyway. It was loud with people.

Things were scraping along the wall, feet scuffing and kicking. From either side came workshop sounds. Carnelian looked neither left nor right. He kept his head up and only relaxed once they had passed through a door on the other side.

He faltered. His body had anticipated warmth. The floor was dusted white and chunked with plaster. Holes gaped on either side where doors had been ripped out. Even their frames had been torn away, leaving the walls ragged. He and Tain picked their way along the passage. In places where the ceiling had caved in, water had soaked into floor and walls which were giving off the derelict smell of wet plaster. Even a waft of cooking smells brought only resentment.

The noise had been growing louder. Tearing, ripping, thuds and cracking. They came into the Little Court and Tain gave a yell. The courtyard had been ploughed to mud. The buildings that had hugged it were crumbling shells. They had played their games here as children. The older people had lived here because it had been the most sheltered part of the Hold. Amongst the rubble, strange creatures turned to stare. Chalk-faced, hair powdered white. Seeing Carnelian they began to kneel. Carnelian jerked his hand up, *Rise*. "Continue your work," he said, his voice too shrill. They turned away and stooped to fish bits and pieces out of the wreckage, passing them back hand to hand until they were added to a pile in the center of the court.

One building was still intact though its face leaned out. A slate scraped down from above and shattered on the cobbles. Carnelian pulled Tain after him as he ducked in. It was hard to see anything in the corridor. They found Crail's room. Carnelian pushed into the small space. Two women were there, bent over an old man crumpled in a chair.

"Master," one of them said.

"Thank the Gods," said the other.

Carnelian whipped off his mask and knelt before the chair. "Crail, you must leave." He looked into the old man's rheumy eyes. This had been the commander of the tyadra. Now he was wasted to a bony sag, his mind so faded that sometimes he did not even know his own name. He was also the Master's brother and so Carnelian's uncle.

Crail shook his prune of a face. "Won't."

Carnelian looked round, saw the cracks that had spread like branches up the walls. "This is all falling down, Crail."

"And me with it. I'm too old for this." He reached up a trembling arm and touched Carnelian's face. "Just leave me be, child."

Carnelian was seeing him through tears. He snapped round. "Get out." The women fled. He turned back. "Come on, Crail, don't do this," he sobbed. He reached his arm out to gather the old man up.

Crail sank back. His soft face bunched itself into a well-used expression of stubbornness.

"You will move, you old fool," cried Carnelian, stepping back against someone. Tain. He had forgotten him. There he was, his hair dusted white in a mockery of the old man's. Two stripes had washed down from his eyes.

Carnelian raised himself to his full height and then put his mask before his face. "Crail, you will leave this place," he said in the level tone his father used. "For I command it."

The old man looked up, straining his eyes. "Master . . . ?"

"Tain, help him up."

For a moment, Tain was startled by Carnelian's tone, then he bowed. "As you command, my Master." Soon he had the old man propped up and was maneuvering him out of the room. Carnelian followed them out, helping as he could without being seen to do so.

People had gathered outside. Carnelian went out to meet them. He pointed here and there into the crowd, affecting brusqueness. "Help Tain take Crail away to some place of safety." He watched the old man being carried off. People started kneeling, in ones and twos. They surrounded him with their abasement so that he would only be able to walk out of their circle by treading on them.

"Make way," he said, controlling his voice, glad he had his mask to hide behind.

No one moved.

"Master," one said and then another, and then their voices rose all around him, breaking, almost wailing.

He wanted to be a child, to run away, but there was nowhere left to hide. At last he lifted his hands for silence. He bent down. "Mari, what's all this?"

The woman he spoke to lifted up her face. Her eyes were red, sunken. "Carnie . . . Master . . ."

Carnelian removed his mask. "Carnie will do fine," he said gently.

"They're taking our food, Carnie."

There were murmurs of assent. He looked at them. They all wore the same face of hope. He felt his lip quiver. "It's needed for the ship."

"But they're not leaving us enough," someone said.

Carnelian nodded. He was trying to hold in his tears but they could see by the way the paint was smeared around his eyes that he had been crying. "It's the Masters who have demanded it, and their needs are greater than ours." Even he could hear the hollow betrayal in his words. Their heads sank as the fight went out of them. He almost let his pain out in a wail.

"And you'll be leaving us too, Carnie?" asked Mari.

He could not bear to look at her. "Yes . . . yes, I must go with them," he looked up, said fiercely, "but before I go I promise I'll do all I can."

He stood up and hid his face behind the golden mask. They made way for him. It was all he could do to put one foot in front of the other.

Carnelian went to the storerooms and saw that it was as they had said. Fish were being sealed into jars. Dried fowl were being baled in woven seaweed. The walls were blank with naked hooks, the shelves bare. He opened one of the stone flour bins and had to lean over to see its level. Behind him on the floor, stacked and packaged, was by far the greater part of what the room had held. The faces that had gathered at the door told the story. Children frightened by their mother's looks. An old woman gnawing her hand. Even with rationing he knew she would not see another summer.

Carnelian pushed through them and stormed back through the kitchens, where lavish dishes were being prepared for their guests. The sight of all those riches patterning the plates made him rage. He stumbled into the shambles of the Great Hall. In among the columns there lay a clearing with its stumps. He walked into it. Most of the roof had come down. Capitals for so long hidden up in the ceiling dusk, showed their colors. It was already difficult to remember the way it had been.

Of the doors to the Long Court only the splintered wooden hinges remained. Beyond was another scene of devastation, like a view onto a battlefield where the camp women were despoiling the dead. He moved into the shadow of the archway to watch them shredding covers, blankets, clothing. The tattered ribbons they produced were being twisted into ropes. Others he saw with waxy faces, painting tar over the jeweled colors of the tapestries they themselves had woven. One woman paused to wipe her eyes with the back of the hand that held a brush. She scanned the pattern under her hand then with a jerk she turned it black.

Carnelian wanted to close his eyes, clap his hands over his ears. He passed through the arch and almost ran along the alleyway. The arcade had lost its roof and the row of columns down one side. He ignored the women. He refused to turn his head even though they cried out to him. Reaching the covered way he passed the Masters' three doors, and at each, guards fell to their knees. He ignored them, reached the steps, climbed them into sight of his father's door. His own men stood to one side of it but on the other there was a contingent of Aurum's yellow-faced guardsmen. All knelt. He bade one of his men announce him to the Master. The sea-ivory doors sounded as the man struck them. There was a mutter of voices. The man came back with a strange expression on his face. It took some moments for Carnelian to recognize it. Fear. The man was afraid of him. He fell before Carnelian and bowed his head. "The Master says he can't see you"—his head nodded—"my Master. When the time's right he'll send for you."

Carnelian looked up at his father's doors with hatred. He wished to throw them down. To erupt in among the gathered Masters. To drive them like vultures from the carcass of his home and send them winging back across the sea to the vaunted glory of their roosts in Osrakum. But he could not. His father's words lay across those doors like the seal on a tomb. His shoulders fell. The man was still there at his feet. He wanted to lift the fear from him. He put his hand out to touch him. Its shaking betrayed him. Carnelian snatched it back, turned and walked away.

THE
BLOOD-RING

Apotheosis transubstantiates the blood of the elected candidate into ichor. The fractions of this holy blood that run in the veins of the Chosen derive ultimately from consanguinity with a God Emperor. Blood-rings are worn as symbol and proof of this relation. Each ring is inscribed with a blood-taint that can be found tabulated in the Books of Blood. Entries will be found arranged according to the Houses. The blood-taint of an offspring is derived by averaging the blood-taints of its procreators.

—EXTRACT FROM A BEADCORD MANUAL USED IN THE TRAINING OF THE WISE

Carnelian went to seek solitude among the summer pavilions. The courtyards he crossed were empty, unmarred, familiar. He entered one of the pavilions where a bloom of frost dulled the tiles. He wandered maskless, blowing his cloudy breath. He warmed a tile with a puff. Rubbed away the cold traceries to reveal the poppies beneath. He broke the pane of ice that filled the fountain bowl. He sat on a stone bench and recalled summers there but refused to indulge himself with tears.

At last he put on his mask and slipped back through the ruins, a shadow with a gleaming face. He passed scenes of torchlit industry that showed his world being destroyed. When he reached his room he closed the door and slumped back against it. The ache around his eyes had spread to make his face as stiff as the gold of his mask.

He waited, blinded by the flames. Tain came at last. They saw each other's pain. Before Tain had a chance to say anything, Carnelian sent him off to find Keal, and they came back together.

Carnelian looked at Keal. "You look drained."

Keal was sure Carnelian looked worse than he did, but he just nodded. "I've been overseeing our work on the ship." He hung his head. "It's a nasty business."

"Our stores?"

He looked up. "That as well, but I was thinking of the ship. It's strange to wander in the warrens beneath her decks. You can feel the floor moving under your feet and hear her creaking all round you. It's brought back memories of coming here as a child." His frown creased the head of his chameleon tattoo. "Locked away in her sunless depths there are men, or something like men." He shook his head, as if he were trying to dislodge the image from his mind. "There was only enough light to make out the merest outlines, but they were there all right. I could smell them."

"Sartlar," said Carnelian.

Tain's eyes opened wide. "They brought those monsters here?"

"Not monsters, Tain, half-men. Don't judge them too harshly. If it wasn't for them the Commonwealth would starve. They work all her fields. Their labor is used everywhere by the Masters. They're not monsters but beasts of burden."

"Monsters or not, I pity them there in that ship," said Keal.

Carnelian looked at him. He imagined living out his life in the belly of the black ship, and he grimaced. "You've been to see the Master?"

Keal nodded. "He and the visiting Master, the gigantic one, check on everything we do. Grane reports back to them about the work in the Hold and I tell them about the ship."

"Work?" snorted Tain.

They both looked round at him.

"When will she be ready, Keal?" said Carnelian.

"Three days, maybe four."

"Who's to go?"

Keal glanced at Tain. He began to list the names of guardsmen. Carnelian nodded at each name, considering the choices, asking questions. He stopped his brother when he began to list those not of the tyadra. "You've not spoken your name, Keal."

"I'm to go, and as commander. Grane's to remain here in the Master's place."

"You don't seem overjoyed by your promotion."

"I feel the honor, Carnie, really I do. It's just . . ."

"I know."

"We're leaving them to die," said Keal, close to tears. Tain's eyes were already wet. Carnelian would not allow himself to share their despair.

"Come, let's not give up yet. I've brought you here, Keal, to ask you if you'd do something for me."

"Anything."

"You've access to the Master."

Keal paled.

"Are the other Masters always with him?"

"Not all of them, just the terrible giant."

"He frightens me too, Keal, but if I'm to do anything I

must speak with the Master. Will you ask him if he'll give me a private audience?"

"You ask when you could command."

"There will be no commanding between us."

"Of course I'll do it, but don't count on it, Carnie. The Master's not been alone since they came."

While they waited, Carnelian had Tain clean off his body-paint. He was ready when Keal came back to say that the Master would see him. Keal had brought an escort with him.

As Carnelian walked through the Hold with Keal, he prepared in his mind what he would say. He must stay calm. He knew his father did not appreciate fevered argument.

When they reached the sea-ivory door, Carnelian was relieved that only men of their tyadra stood outside. He squeezed Keal's arm. The doors opened before him and he went in.

"Carnelian, perhaps you could help me choose which of these to take," said Suth. He held up a folding-screen book whose binding was twisted with jewels. Many more books glimmered on the table beside him.

Reluctantly, Carnelian picked one up, smoother than skin, eyed with leather-lidded watery tourmalines. With care, he opened the first panel. Tracing his finger down the parchment, he began unraveling the pictures into words.

"Books are doors," his father muttered.

Carnelian looked up. "And the glyphs are the keys that open them."

His father smiled. "You remember that . . . ?" His eyes fell briefly on the book in his hand. "Do you remember the lessons we had here?"

In this hall, his father had taught him the art of reading, and had guided his hand as he scribbled his first thoughts on parchment with wavering lines.

"Thoughts are like butterflies," he said.

"Take care when capturing them lest you crush their wings," his father responded. "You know, it was necessity that drove me." He shook his head in disbelief. "A Ruling Lord . . . teaching a child his glyphs . . ."

"And the crabbed, lifeless merchants' script . . ."

". . . with which they trap wealth in their ledgers." His father's lips always curled when he spoke of the merchants. Like all Masters he found commerce distasteful.

"But wealth is power. . . ." said Carnelian.

"It is a fool who covets wealth, but he also is a fool who discards the way to power," his father said. He saw Carnelian's expression. "Have I said that many times?"

"I have it by heart. You showed me that my hands could"— *speak*. The last word was a sign. *Fingers are the lips and tongue of the silent speech. Their poetry of movement betrays the emotion behind the words. The words themselves are spoken without breath or sound by forming signs.*

"You have a strong, clear hand."

His father lifted up a book paler than his skin though not as radiant. "As we have traveled together through these, so shall we travel through the greater world of which they are only impressions."

"But what shall we be leaving behind, my Lord?" asked Carnelian.

"Famine," his father replied. His lips compressed to a line.

"Is there no way, my Lord, we might ameliorate its harshness by reducing the amount that is taken by the baran?"

"Everything that can be done, my Lord, has been done." Suth watched his son's face harden with pain. "You will have to face the situation as it is. The sharper blade leaves cleaner wounds."

"Will the baran not accommodate more of our people? It is so large."

His father shook his head. "For all her bulk she really has very little space."

"But the children, the elderly."

"The voyage would be as dangerous for them as staying here."

"Father, are you not desolated by such loss?"

The marble of his father's skin was stained around the eyes. "When we came here this place was a perfect mirror to my mood. That first winter was terrible. Many died. When they did not think I heard them, our people whispered that I had brought them across the black water to the Isle of the Dead. I think I almost shared their belief. As bleak and colorless as the Underworld is said to be, this island was worse. Perhaps if you had not been there swaddled in Ebeny's arms I might have let it remain always so. For your sake I let the household work upon the Hold. So far from Osrakum my hopes were ailing and wont to die. And yet, in the years that have passed, this desolation has become my home. It sits deep in my affection, perhaps more even than our palaces in Osrakum, of which all this"——he curved his arms out and round as if he were embracing the Hold——"is not even a reflection in dull brass." His father shook his head again. "If my memory gives me true recollection." He frowned and muttered, "Sometimes that other life I had seems an impossible dream. Strange transformations have come upon me in this shrinking compass of my world. You know, my son, I have played roles that not even a Lord of the Lesser Chosen would stoop to. I have been brought closer to our barbarian children than I would have thought possible. So, in spite of all I am, all I know and all that I have been taught to feel, I must say, yes, I am desolated by this loss."

They looked at each other, drawing a pale comfort from sharing their misery.

"Will Crail go with us?" asked Carnelian.

His father nodded.

"Tain?"

Another nod.

"And Ebeny?"

"She has asked not to go and I will not command her."

Carnelian considered this. She was more mother to him than nurse and, besides, his father's favored concubine. He knew his father had feelings for her. "I shall speak to her myself."

"As you wish," his father said and there was something like hope in his eyes. "Now let us return to the problem of selecting which of these worlds we shall take as an accompaniment to our journey."

Carnelian turned to the books. He looked sidelong at his father. The beautiful, tired face was intent upon the jeweled oblongs. A wave of dread washed its ice over Carnelian. His father was powerless. The Master, powerless. The Hold seemed suddenly precarious, as if a single wave might wash it into the sea.

That night, Carnelian slept hardly at all. Tain was having difficulty too. They played dice so as not to have to talk. Both played badly. Neither dared confess his dreams.

With first light Carnelian woke. He had left the shutters open just a chink and set a table against them to keep them from flying open. A thin light slipped into the room. Tain had turned away from it. In the corner, his blankets held him in their tight knot. Carnelian lay for a moment thinking. Noise carried up from the ship. Hammering. Voices. He rose and woke Tain to help him dress in his Master's robes.

From the alleyway, the Long Court looked like the carcass of one of the sea monsters that sometimes washed up in the bay that the gulls soon turned into a basket of bones. The remains of his home stood as stark against the colorless sky.

There was a sickening smell. Cauldrons had been set up from which palls of steam were spiraling into the air. Beyond, the cobbles were red with slaughter. Dread drew Carnelian to look closer. One cauldron was filled with birdlike heads and three-fingered hands jiggling in the boil. The long narrow saurian heads quivered white-eyed on pillows of pink-brown scum. He looked across to where they were skinning them, hacking the flesh free from the bones. Red hunks were being wrapped in leaves, pushed into jars, and the spaces between, packed with icicles. Carnelian was horrified. He surveyed everything with pain-ringed eyes. All around him the mottled bodies lay, their gashed necks bleeding puddles over the stone, their arms and legs and tails curled stiff. This flock had been one of their chief treasures, the only source of eggs. He had loved to feed them from his hand. He recalled their bustle and their chatter.

He snatched at someone walking past. "This was done for the meat?"

The man was all fear. He tried to fall to his knees but Carnelian held him up by one shoulder. "And for glue, Master." The man pointed crookedly at another of the cauldrons.

Carnelian let him go and went to look. Bones and skin, the few feathers, all boiling up in a thick translucent broth. He recoiled from the stench. Through the steam he could see parchment laid out on the ground being glued up into sails.

He turned away, disgusted. Once more he plunged past the visitors' doors and onward, but before he reached his father's steps he turned right. A small door gave onto a passage lit by a slit in the end wall. Once this had been his way to and from the Hold. It led to his old room overlooking the sea. Ebeny would be there. She had always been there.

He rapped on the door in the special way so that she would know it was him then opened it gently. The room was large, frescoed with squid-headed ammonites and saurians with paddle limbs. The floor was scented graywood. This had been his room. Her room was off to the left. Unmasking allowed him to drink in the smell of the place. He took off his shoes to feel the whorls of the graywood with his toes and walked across to the window. Through its panes of cuttlefish cartilage he could see the sea and the familiar curve of the bay. He frowned when he saw the ship lying against the quay.

"Carnie, it is you?" Ebeny called out. He went through the doorway. Her brown, chameleoned face was lit by her bright smiling eyes. She stood up. She was less than half his height and had been beautiful. With a pang he remembered something his father had said about a barbarian's beauty being but a spring flower and quick to wither. He went forward and knelt before her.

"Come, come. You mustn't kneel to me, and certainly not in your Master's robes."

He stood up and moved to sit on a low stool beside her.

Ebeny looked at him, her eyes large and round. She reached out and touched the samite of his robe. "You carry it well, Carnie."

He blushed.

"You're upset."

"They've slaughtered the laying flock."

Her lips pressed together, then she forced them into a smile. "There's been much destroyed. But you can't make mosaic without breaking stone."

"If it were only the stones of the Hold."

She nodded. "I know."

"And yet you won't come with us?"

"The Master told you?"

"Why won't you come?"

"Because, little one, I'm too old to travel on that sea." She waved her tiny hand vaguely. It was the color of sun-dried leaves and marked with the green of a childgatherer's tattoos. Those tattoos had been among the first glyphs he had ever read. Eight Nuhuron. The God Emperor's name and the reign year when she had been compelled to come to Osrakum as part of that year's flesh tithe. He reached out, took it, covered the tattoos. Her hands were always warm.

"You are not so very old."

She gave him a quizzical look. "But I am so very afraid of the sea."

He laughed, too loudly. "You? When have you ever feared anything? You don't even fear the Master."

"But still I'll not go. Your father came here before you and I gave him the same answer."

He almost asked her what encouragements Suth had offered, what threats, but he did not. She had never broken his father's confidences.

"What's the real reason you won't come with us?"

She lifted up his chin and looked into his eyes. "What I've become here, I cannot be in the Mountain. There, I'll be nothing but a faded concubine to be thrown away like a worn shoe. Would you hasten me to that?"

"My father will protect you."

"Even he must bow to the customs of your House. No. The journey will be hard and your father's been long away. There might be problems and I don't want to be a burden to him."

He drew her hand to his lips. "But I might never see you again."

"Nonsense," she cried. "It'll take a lot more than a little famine to rid you of me."

He laughed though his eyes were filling with tears. He leaned forward again. The coral pins of his robe rasped along the floor. He nestled his head into her lap. "I can't leave you behind," he mumbled into her thigh.

She ran her hand through his hair. "Sush, sush, little one. You must do your duty to your father and your blood. You're a Master and can't allow yourself to get upset over an old barbarian woman." She lifted his face up with both her hands. "Do you remember when your father took you and Tain from me to live with the tyadra?"

He nodded his head in her hands.

"Then you were leaving me to become a man. Now you're leaving me to go off and become a Master, one of the Sky-born. Would you choose instead to waste your life out here so far from the center of the world?"

He stood up. While she adjusted the stiff folds of his robe, he looked around her room, a room of treasures. He counted the plain waxed chests where she kept her robes and the ochre blankets that she made herself with their blue embroidery. He still slept with the blankets she had made for him though he had far finer. Even in the depths of winter something of the summer seemed to linger in their folds.

He turned round to look down at her. "Will you give me one of your blankets to take with me?"

"You've several already."

"But they've lost their smell of this room . . . of you."

She smiled and kissed him and together they chose one. She pressed it into his hands. The blanket was dull and crude against the beauty of his Master's robe. He pushed his nose into it and breathed in. It gave him a chance to wipe away the tears. "This will do, old woman." Once she would have boxed his ears. He realized now that even if she had wanted to she could not reach. He lifted her in his arms and kissed her neck. He left it wet with more tears. She was crying too. He put her down.

He made to leave but then her hand clasped his. "Will you do something for me, Carnie?"

"Anything."

"Take care of my Tain."

Tain was her youngest child. Carnelian nodded. "I swear on my blood, Ebeny, that I'll keep him by me and look out for him as best I can. Have you forgotten Keal?"

"He's a man now. He can take care of himself. One last thing." She reached her hands behind her neck, undid a thong and drew an amulet out from her robe.

"Your Little Mother?" Carnelian looked at her uncertainly.

She held it out for him. "Wear her for me."

"But she's all you've left of your mother."

"As she gave her to me, now I give her to you."

"Why do you not give her to Tain, Keal, one of your sons?"

"Pah! You're as much my son as they are. Besides, if she protects you, you'll be able to care for my boys. Take her. She has power over water."

"My father will disapprove of her."

"Well then, wear her where he won't see her."

Ebeny kissed the Little Mother and put it in his hand. The carved stone was all belly and breasts with stump limbs and head. Carnelian closed his fingers over her.

The next day he went off into the pavilions but found no solace. He climbed up into the East Tower to survey the leaden sea. There, where he had first seen the ship, he spat curses into the wind that she had ever come. He longed for the old comforts, the old certainties. Yet, although he tried to deny it, Osrakum was drawing him with her siren call.

Masked, he returned to the pillage to see it all: the fallen halls, the gaping windows, the blood-rusted cobbles. He went out from the Holdgate and stood against the parapet. Handcarts creaked down to the ship, his people strained under barrels and boxes. He wanted to rail at them that they were collaborating with their own rape. The compulsion froze him to that spot for fear of what he might do. The ship became the entire focus of his vision, wallowing down there, gorging herself on the general misery.

At some point he became aware of an ache in his knees. He looked down. Brackish water had soaked up from the hem of his samite robe. The silk was discolored, spoilt. He remembered what Grane had said. His people had had shame enough. As he turned away the robe swung against his legs like an apron of lead.

He went back to his room. He lit neither fire nor lamp but chose to brood in the blackness, his robes and mask discarded, staring sightless, letting the misery take him over.

When Tain crept into the room, he raked the ashes but there was no glow left to find. He fumbled for a lantern that they kept in a corner. It fluttered into life. He jumped back startled. Carnelian was sitting cross-legged, black eyes narrowed against the glare.

"I'll not go," Tain cried at his ghostly brother. "I'll not leave my mother here, nor all the others. I'd rather die with them."

Through the glare Carnelian could vaguely see that Tain's eyes were red and swollen. "If I go, you'll go," he said. He had neither love nor energy left to put any caring into his voice.

Tain stared at him blankly for a while and then ran away. Carnelian felt nothing. It was as if the winter had numbed him to the heart.

* * *

Later, a blindman brought him a casket of leather, ribbed and water-stained, which he put into Carnelian's hands. "The Master bade me tell his son that he should attend him in his hall attired in the robe that has now been given to him."

Carnelian asked him to leave one of his escort behind and then sent the man off to find Tain. When he looked round, the blindman had gone. Carnelian took the casket near the window to look at it. Outside, the twilight appeared to be sucking its darkening up from the sea. Carnelian pulled the cloth out from the casket. It was the color of spring leaves, but did not seem a robe at all, even though it had the hollow tubes for arms. The central band was plainly woven silk. The edges were brocaded in panels and fringed with eyes and hooks of copper. Carnelian ran his fingers over one of the panels. He peered close, feeling the beads. Rows of them. Jade, minutely carved.

Carnelian heard the door closing. He looked up and saw Tain's sullen face. His brother stared back at him. Neither spoke during the cleaning. At first they tried to put the robe on so that the panels were to the front. With much cursing they found that only when they put them to his back could Carnelian put his arms into the sleeves. Tain hooked the robe closed from top to bottom. It fitted well enough, though it was not sufficiently thick to keep out the cold. Carnelian did not allow his body to shiver. He took his mask from Tain's hands and put it on. "I'll see you later."

"As the Master commands," Tain said, a cold fire in his eyes.

Carnelian had finally made up his mind. The destruction he saw everywhere strengthened his resolution. He reminded himself of the empty storerooms and the gluttony of the ship. He catalogued all the desperate looks he had seen on the faces of his people. But when he neared his father's hall all he felt was the shivering cold.

Through the doors he saw a huge shape standing before the fire. It lifted up a hand in a sign of welcome. Carnelian crossed the floor to it. Its face was a shadow.

"The Ruling Lord Aurum has brought you this," said his father's voice.

The mass of his body swung round and Carnelian could see the hand held out in the firelight. He approached it. On the palm there was something like a hole. He reached out and took it. It was hard and warm. A ring of iron. A blood-ring that entitled him to cast votes in the elections of the Masters. He turned it in the firelight. Along the edge of the band were the raised glyphs of his names and the spots and bars of numbers.

"He was given it by the Wise who had it set aside for you." He gave his son a tender look that Carnelian did not see. The ring had him wholly in its spell. Its symbols were in mirrored form so that it could be used as a seal with both ink and wax. The eleven numbers confirmed the fractional tainting of his blood. He knew that it should be put on the smallest finger of the right hand. As the right hand signified the world of light so its smallest finger signified purity. It was too big.

"There is no time for proper ritual. Even the preliminaries take many days. But there is much that is not essential. It is the Examination and the Rite of Blood that are the very nub and core of it."

Carnelian looked up warmly at his father, then froze when he saw Aurum's face floating beyond his father's shoulder. Turning round he saw that Vennel was there too, his pupils the merest spots, and Jaspar with his idolic smile. Carnelian felt that his father had led him into an ambush.

Suth saw the change come across his son's face and said quickly, "Witnesses are essential."

The Masters circled Carnelian like sleek predators.

"Shall we begin?" said Aurum, his voice reverberating round the chamber. "Lord Jaspar, it might please you to read the rings."

Jaspar gave a little bow and accepted something from Aurum's hand.

"The blood-rings of the Lord Suth and of his Lady wife, now long expired," said Aurum. He turned to Vennel. "Perhaps, my Lord, you would care to read the scars."

"My hands do not have the seeing of the Wise."

"Nevertheless, my Lord, we wish to be certain of impartiality, is that not so?"

"Oh, very well!"

Vennel began to move round behind Carnelian who, alarmed, turned to keep the Master in sight.

"Keep still, my son," his father said.

Carnelian stopped turning and felt Vennel come up behind him.

"The robe must be opened for your taint scars to be read as proof of your parentage."

Carnelian fought a grimace as Vennel undid the hooks down his back. He felt the robe begin to slip off and hunched his shoulders so that it would not fall to the floor.

"Exquisite," he heard Jaspar say.

He closed his eyes. His perception was all in the skin of his back. He could not suppress a shudder when he felt Vennel's hands on him. Fingers sliding down the right of his spine, feeling the bumps and ridges that had been put there by the Wise at his birth, with a scarring comb.

"Zero, zero . . . three, ah . . ." Vennel was reading out his father's blood-taint, "fifteen, ah . . . nineteen, another fifteen . . . ten . . . two, no, three, now two, a final ten."

"Is that what is inscribed on Lord Suth's ring?" asked Aurum.

"Exactly," said Jaspar.

Carnelian felt the fingers lift away. He waited, grimacing. Vennel's hand was there again, to the left of his spine.

"Zero, zero, zero, two, one . . . three . . . nineteen, ah . . . nine, sixteen, ah . . . seventeen and a final . . . ten."

The eleven fractions of his mother's taint.

"Confirmed," said Jaspar.

"You can do the boy up, Vennel."

"I certainly shall not. Am I now to become a body slave?"

"I will do it, my Lords," said Suth.

Carnelian's shoulder was squeezed and the robe quickly hooked up. He turned and glared at the other Masters. Vennel was rubbing his hands as if he had touched something unclean. Jaspar was smiling. Aurum was as impassive as marble.

"The Rite of Blood," he said.

As the Master came toward him, Carnelian became enveloped in his odor of lilies. Aurum held out a vast hand. An oval bowl lay along the palm, of jade so thin it might have been water.

"This is the edge of the night," intoned his father and Carnelian saw that his left hand held a razor of obsidian like a mussel shell. It sliced into the palm of his other hand. The cut beaded blood all along its length. The bowl in Aurum's hand was there to catch each drop.

"Thou art my son, dewed from my flesh, Chosen. The ichor of the Two will burn thy veins; the same that once gushed from the Turtle's rending." His father dipped his finger in the bowl. "With this fire I anoint thee. In the names of He-whose-face-is-spiraling-jade." He daubed a vertical stroke upon Carnelian's forehead. "In the unspoken names of He-whose-face-is-the-mirror-in-the-night." Dipping his finger once more, his father applied a second stroke beside the first.

Then Aurum's hand offered Carnelian the bowl. He stared at it, not knowing what it was he was supposed to do.

"Drink now thy father's blood that its fire might ignite thine to its own . . . fierce . . . burning," said Aurum.

When Carnelian took the bowl he could not avoid touching the Master's stone skin. He looked up at his face. It seemed fashioned from dead bone with only two points of living light. Carnelian resisted its menace and drained the bowl with a single gulp, grimacing at the metal taste.

"On this day thou art come of age," his father said.

"Truly thou art chosen a Lord of the Hidden Land," the others chanted, then they glimmered away like a tide on a moonless night leaving Carnelian angry, amazed, uneasy that he was now fully one of them.

"Soon the fire will begin its burning in your veins," sang Vennel.

"Some days it will course like naphtha in a flame-pipe," Aurum growled.

"It is one of the myriad burdens that we bear," said Jaspar.

"The price that must be paid for near-divinity," said Aurum.

"Nothing is without cost," said Vennel.

Suth allowed his hand to brush Carnelian's. "Yet, for many years, I have felt no burning."

"How so?" said Vennel, his eyes frost.

Suth shrugged. "Perhaps so far from its source its vigor fades."

"Perhaps," said Aurum. "Perhaps."

"Tell me, my Lord Suth . . ." said Vennel.

Suth raised his eyebrows.

"Why did you have us perform this ritual here and now?"

"My son was past his time, and we had the ring here . . ."

"Ah, the ring. My Lord Aurum was so thoughtful to remember to bring the ring. But still, are you sure that the Wise will consider it valid?"

"The ritual had my Lords as witness," said Suth.

"Are we qualified?"

"Our journey will be perilous. The awakening of his blood might afford my son some protection."

Vennel nodded sagely. "I see. And I suppose this coming of age could have nothing to do with the fact that the Lord Carnelian is now entitled to cast his twenty votes."

"I do not entirely comprehend your meaning, my Lord."

"My meaning, Great Lord, is that with your son and one other of us," he glanced at Aurum, "you can henceforth determine every decision that we make in formal conclave."

"That presupposes that my son will always choose to vote with me."

"My Lord," Carnelian said. His stomach knotted when his father turned toward him. "My Lord, this conflict is unnecessary since I have decided that I shall stay with our household and follow after. It is for the best. I could be nothing but an encumbrance to you."

His father's face hardened. He turned to the others. "Great Lords, it would seem that I have need to talk with my son. It would be unforgivable that we should presume so much upon your patience, my Lords, as to expect you to stand by while we resolve a matter internal to our House. The baran is ready now. If the wind be not against us we shall depart on the morrow. I am sure my Lords must have numerous arrangements to make."

Vennel looked amused. Jaspar looked uncharacteristically serious. He stepped forward. "Lord Suth, your rings." Carnelian watched his father take them.

"Perhaps, Sardian, I should stay," said Aurum, his eyes like evening sky.

Carnelian stared, startled by the use of his father's personal name.

"I would rather you did not, my Lord." He was twisting his blood-ring back onto his finger.

Aurum stood for a moment, then turned away. He and the other Masters drifted off toward the door. Carnelian watched them to put off facing his father's anger which he could feel beating upon his back. The last of the Masters disappeared through the door. It closed.

Round the circuit of the chamber the shutters rattled. Twigs snapped in the fire and jiggled up a spray of sparks. Carnelian's forehead itched. He was determined to brave the heat of his father's fury. He turned. His father's face seemed cut from polished stone.

"Why did you feel it necessary, my Lord, to defy me before our guests?" his father asked in a quiet voice.

"I had made my decision and would inform you of it."

"And no doubt you thought that if you spoke it in the presence of the other Lords you would ensure that my response should be constrained?"

Carnelian looked at his feet. "Though there were several

reasons, my Lord, I am ashamed to say that was one of them."

"Tell me, my son, of this decision you have made."

Carnelian looked up and saw his father's face had softened. "Our people and the famine that will come here once the baran is gone—it is a betrayal, my Lord, that we should leave them here to face it all, alone."

"But, Carnelian, they live to serve us. Besides, I have put into motion certain policies that might somewhat reduce the severity of their need."

"Nevertheless, I would stay. I cannot find it in my heart to abandon Ebeny, but to mention one of them. Our people will miss your rule, my Lord, and though I would not presume to suggest I could replace you, I might provide some measure of compensation. The sight of a Master sharing their privations will give them hope, and hope is the mother of strength."

"Ebeny is a stubborn woman. I will command her to come with us. I am leaving Grane to rule here in my stead and, without too much offending you, my Lord, I would suggest that it is evident that he would do it better than you. As for this notion of yours to share their privations, have you completely taken leave of your senses? You would choose to sink yourself down to their level? Do you forget who and what you are, my Lord? Where is your pride?"

"I have pride, my Lord, and because of it the feelings of duty that you taught—"

"It seems I have taught you badly. I blame myself. Too long have I made myself blind to your familiarity with our slaves. Perhaps indeed I have shared in it. Being so far from Osrakum we have sunk into a mire of barbarism. It should come as no surprise to me. But that you should dare to speak to *me* of your feelings of duty to *my* slaves. Do I hear you speak of your feelings of duty to your father and your blood? Is my blood to be so traduced in you? Does that ring you newly wear mean so little to you, my Lord?"

Suth had become a tower of wrath but Carnelian squared up to him. "Your blood I cannot give back to you, but this . . ."

He pulled off the blood-ring. "This trinket you can take back to Osrakum or hurl in the sea for all I care, for I see that in the receiving of it I have acquired nothing."

In the vibrating silence that followed, his father seemed to narrow to a blade. "You will put that ring back on." The tone was level, dangerous. Suth lifted up his hand. Upon it were several rings, but above his blood-ring was another, the Ruling Ring of House Suth. Its black adamant was forced into the center of Carnelian's vision. "While I still wear this," the level voice continued, "I will be obeyed within the borders of my House. Tomorrow you will leave with me, my Lord. The only choice you have is whether you shall walk down to the baran or be carried. Reconcile yourself, my Lord, for you *will* cross the sea with me."

THE
BLACK
SHIP

They'll sew the black sail

Then we'll leave our dear land

For we've heard the call of the sea.

—SEA-SHANTY:

AMBER TRADE ROUTE

Frosty cobbles sparked with moonlight. Carnelian stood where the arcade had once been. Ghostly edges defined the column stumps in the blackness of the Great Hall. He turned round to survey the Long Court where the cauldrons lay abandoned. One had rolled over and spilt its lumps and liquids as an inky puddle. The walls behind were pocked with the dead eyes of window holes. Such were the ruins of his home.

Breath-clouds blossoming on either side of him made him remember his escort. It was bitterly cold.

* * *

Lamps stood in opposite corners of the room. Tain was hunched over a chest. Carnelian watched him for a while. His brother was sorting through his robes. He held one up and turned it into the light. He grunted, rolled it up and threw it onto a pile.

"Packing?" asked Carnelian, trying to sound matter-of-fact.

Tain whisked round. "By the horns! Are you trying to kill me creeping up on me like that?" But then he saw Carnelian standing there like a tree, with his cold metal face and bit his lip.

Swiftly, Carnelian reached up, unfastened his mask and dropped it into his hand. He did it before Tain had a chance to "Master" him. He lurched forward. "Here, let me help." He tried to bend down but the tightness of his robe resisted him.

Tain stood up. "Come on. Let's get you out of that thing. Is it as uncomfortable as it looks?"

"Worse," said Carnelian, and grinned.

Tain quickly undid the hooks and released him from the ritual robe. Naked, shivering, Carnelian threw on some of his old clothes. He sighed with pleasure. They were so comfortable, so familiar. "I feel more like myself."

"And you look more like yourself."

"About earlier. I didn't mean to—"

"Don't worry, Carnie, I understand."

"I wanted to stay too, but the Master has forbidden it. You'll come with me though, won't you?"

"Do I have any choice?"

Carnelian gave him a ragged smile.

"I see. I'm going whether I want to or not. If it makes you feel better, I'd go with you anyway."

Carnelian reached out and pulled him into a hug.

Tain looked sheepish. "My mother would never forgive me if I didn't. Someone has to look after you." He turned away. "Come on, let's get this packing done. Or were those just words?"

"They weren't," said Carnelian cheerily.

They talked well into the night about the long summers of their childhood, about the autumns when the trees turned gold, flamed red then were left black and naked. They recounted often-told anecdotes about the people they loved and found them freshly funny. Each gave the other reassurances: that the food would last, that it would really not be all that long before the household was together again in the Mountain. Wherever their talk went it always came back to the Mountain, Osrakum. Her dark alluring wonder lay heavy in the center of their thoughts. Thus, journeying far away, they found that they could leave their grief behind. Off into their dreams they soared, like gulls tumbling from a cliff into the wind. For Tain it was dragons. All his life he had longed to see dragons. Some people in the Hold swore they had seen them, had felt them shake the earth. His mother Ebeny had stood beneath one but was reluctant to talk about it. For Carnelian it was the home his father had spoken of, that lay in the crater of Osrakum beside the waters of the Skymere. As he spoke in a kind of rapture, he became aware that Tain no longer answered him. He sat up and saw that his brother lay with the faintest of smiles on his sleeping mouth.

Carnelian felt alone. As he lay back, the vision darkened, contracting down to the black ship outside with her distending belly. Most of what brought warmth and comfort to his people she had consumed. Tomorrow he and his father would go down too and she would have eaten everything. He ached for his old life. He begged for sleep, but the night was merciless.

They were woken by the rapping on the door. A voice cried something on the other side. Carnelian sat up, confused. The voice cried out again.

"It's time to leave," said Tain from somewhere nearby. He sounded surprised. He coaxed a light into being. Carnelian squinted through his fingers at him bustling round the room. "Yesterday, the Master sent this and that for this morning." His brother was holding a jar and pointing at a bundle on the floor.

Carnelian rose and braved the cold. Tain pulled something on, then came back and started cleaning him. "It'll not be long now," he said as he felt Carnelian's body shudder. He broke open the wax seal on the new jar and stirred the stuff inside. "It's thicker than the usual paint and apparently proof against the sea air." He began to apply it in wet strokes of chalky white.

"It smells disgusting," said Carnelian who was still only half awake.

After he was finished, Tain produced some old clothes.

"I'm really to wear these?" said Carnelian.

Tain shrugged. "The Master sent nothing other than the jar and the cloak."

When they had finished dressing him, Tain shook out the cloak. It was like a billow of tar smoke. He threw it over Carnelian, then did up its belts, managing to hoist it up so that only a little of it would drag upon the ground. He nodded sagely. "You could be wearing anything under it and nobody would be any the wiser."

"At least it's warm," said Carnelian, and pulled the hood over his head. Tain's clothing was flimsy by comparison. Carnelian went into a corner and came back with his gull-feather cloak. "Wear this, Tain, it'll be better than that rag." His brother put it on, protested that it was far too big but was clearly delighted.

There was another rap at the door and Tain went to see who it was. He came back. "Well, this is it, Carnie." He looked very young, very grave. "They've come for our things and I'm to go with them . . . onto the ship."

"We'll go together." Carnelian put on his mask and stood by the wall, out of the light, as Tain let in the bearers. When he saw they were his people he came out of the shadows.

"Master," they cried and fell flat on the floor.

"Oh, for the Gods' sake, get up." Carnelian took his mask off and scowled at them. They gave him watery smiles and then started picking up the bundles.

Carnelian and Tain followed them out. Every door they passed was closed. There were no sounds other than the scuffling of their feet. Carnelian was glad. He was feeling numb enough already and could not bear any tearful farewells. "Better to just get it over with," he muttered. The face Tain turned to him was wooden.

They came down into the alleyway. Carts lay angled among a scatter of debris in the Sword Court. Brown snow was carved by wheel-ruts, littered with straw. The place already looked as if it had been a hundred years abandoned.

The bearers were staggering down the alleyway to the Holdgate. They came into the court before the gate towers. The sky beyond them was paling gray. The wall all around the court was black. Carnelian could see the gate was open. When he and Tain reached it they stopped. The cobbled road curving down to the quay was lined with a long line of their tyadra. Each man held a torch aloft. Behind them were all their people. The ship was down at the end amongst a dense fluttering of torches.

"They've been gathered to see us off," said Tain, his voice breaking.

Carnelian reached out to steady him, then together they lurched forward toward the wall of gray faces. At first the people bowed, but soon they just nodded so that they could follow the two of them with their eyes. Carnelian's mask felt to him like cowardice and so he took it off. That act cost him dear. Their eyes were like wounds. He forced himself to look from face to tattooed face. Swollen-eyed, stressed tight, lips just holding the narrowest of smiles, all but the youngest bearing the winding tattoo, the mark of the chameleon, his mark, his servants, his people.

He moved down that avenue of faces sideways, a step at a time. He nodded at each face. He knew most of them. Children stared from between the guardsmen. They could feel the tension but did not really understand it. He smiled at them, and some smiled back but others had already begun to cry. Pain ran up and down the line and was wafting on the morning air. At first he thought a wind was coming up from the far distance, but then it swelled into human keening. The women had begun wailing. The guardsmen looked back over their shoulders, embarrassed, telling them to hush. But the noise was catching the throats of the men in the crowd and soon they were adding their feelings to the dirge. The guardsmen could not resist for long. Their torches wavered as they too began to groan.

The sound cut Carnelian to the bone. His tears distorted the hands they held out to him. He could not deny their grief and went to touch them. Their moaning enfolded him. He stretched into the crowd as far as he could reach. The guardsmen who had not kissed him since he was a child did so and were left white-lipped by his paint.

He noticed that their cries were fading all around him. Everybody was drawing away until he was left behind like a rock by the tide. A clink of armor made him shove his mask up before his face. The people were falling down into the prostration. The act of abasement ran down the road and out along the quay. Carnelian turned and saw with consternation the Masters sweeping down from the Holdgate. He felt Tain brush against his leg as the boy knelt. A glance showed that he was pressing himself down against the cobbles.

The Masters were upon him. Chinks in their hoods showed slivers of gold. Carnelian knew his hand must look obvious against the rim of his mask. He expected reproach but they ignored him.

". . . so many aged," he heard Aurum say.

"And where does my Lord think I could obtain replacements?" Suth replied with a tightness in his voice.

"Famine will winnow the aged from the young," said Vennel's woman-voice.

Jaspar had thrown back his hood to reveal the long, painted volume of his head. He was looking out into the bay where clouds hung like smoke above the mounding sea. "It seems we shall indeed depart today." His mask lent him an air of divine indifference.

The Masters avoided Tain's body as if he might soil their feet. Carnelian saw Grane and Brin walking behind them with more of the tyadra. Brin's eyes were red. They paused to gaze at him. His free hand rose, hesitating between several gestures of farewell. Brin clamped her hand over her nose and mouth. Carnelian's hand gave up, fell to indicate Tain. He waited for Grane's nod, then reached behind his head to tie his mask and followed after the other Masters.

In the spluttering torchlight the ship's wall of tarred wood slid up and down. She was huge. Carnelian had not imagined just how large she was. He looked down her curving flank. Hawsers strained to hold her and with each gentle lunge she pulled the stone rings up and, after, let them fall with a clatter. The sea gargled in the murky squeeze between her and the quay.

Grane and Brin were kneeling before his father receiving some last instructions. Beyond, his people formed a mat of flesh that clothed half the quay. Carnelian followed its swathe up to the Holdgate. So many people. He looked at the Hold to stop seeing them. He surveyed those dear gray walls. He knew which of the tiny holes was his own window, which Ebeny's. There, on the southern promontory, was the finer masonry of his father's hall. Only a single scratch of smoke slanted up where there had once been so many.

"We must embark," a voice said near him. It was Jaspar. His mask turned to look up at the Hold. "My Lord surveys his old dominions?"

Carnelian wondered if mockery was intended. "It has been the only home I have known."

"My Lord should not worry himself with that. The glory of Osrakum will soon dim all this deprivation into gray memory."

"And what of my people, Lord Jaspar, shall they also be

dimmed into gray memory?" Carnelian said bitterly.

Jaspar's gold face inclined to one side. Its aloof expression made the gesture seem almost comical. "Your people, my Lord? This is no cause for great concern. Your palaces in Osrakum will have many and better slaves. Perhaps my Lord is unaware of how much those here have been degenerated by the . . . climate.".

"And has my Lord detected perhaps such degeneration in myself?"

"Tut, cousin, the Chosen are made of finer clay."

Carnelian thought that if he spoke any longer to the Lord Jaspar he would say something he might regret. He turned toward the ship. "I think my Lord was suggesting that we should embark."

Through seeing her so close, Carnelian had almost forgotten how much he hated her. Jaspar showed him where staples of bone made a ladder up her side. The Master leaned out to one and jumped across. He rose and fell with her as he climbed. Carnelian wondered how his people could possibly have reached over to the staples. He looked down. He watched the water rush up and then suck down again. There was no point in thinking about it. He waited until the ship moved toward him, snatched at a staple and pulled himself across. He hit the hull with a thud. His foot struck something and he managed to stand on it. He adjusted his mask. The ship's black hide was before his face, reeking of tar. The hull lifted him as easily as if he were a wasp on a bobbing apple. He looked up and grasped the next staple. Its bone had weathered yellow and showed its grain. He went up one at a time. Before he reached the deck, the hull cut away to show a wide deep space under it, with supporting uprights like the trunks in a thicket, shapes under tarpaulins, more solid massings of shadow sprinkled with faces. The whole space was roofed with the grating of the deck.

He climbed higher, was looking down to place his foot when hands took hold of him and he was pulled up to be greeted by Keal's grave face. "Welcome aboard, Master," he said and tried a wink. Other guardsmen knelt around Car-

nelian. Over their heads, he could see the whole length of
the ship stretching off to the rise of her prow. Here and there
were capstans, openings in the deck and peculiar bronze engines clustered in threes on platforms extending beyond her
bows. Before him, from a collar of brass and a ring of posts
topped with pulleys, a mast rose higher than a tree and was
taut with rigging to which tiny figures clung. The deck
shifted under his feet like something alive. He saw his men's
faces still turned up to him and gave them the sign to rise.
Before he left them he asked that they be sure that Tain made
it safely aboard.

The Masters stood a short way off by the prow, wrapped in
the flutterings of their cloaks and speaking with their hands.
Carnelian was glad they had not invited him to join them. He
walked toward one of the engines. It had a huge bow, a
greased track, release hooks, and beside it a stock of barbed
harpoons each as long as he was tall. One was ready, threaded
like a needle with a coil of oily rope. He leaned against the
bow rail and gazed down forlornly at his people who stood
there looking back.

A rasping caused him to peer over the edge and see the
mushroom-headed poles pushing out toward the quay. One
after the other they clunked against its stone. The ship's rocking lessened as she was pushed away. Sailors on the quay
untied the hawsers and, in twos and threes, they strained
against them. The poles continued to push. The ship moved
further from the quay and dragged the hawsers and their
sailors closer to its edge. Carnelian watched with disbelief
as they plunged into the sea like stones. On board more of
their fellows drew the hawsers in. The heads of the sailors
bobbed up and soon they were being dragged out of the
water. Their feet had barely touched the deck when there
was a sudden rattling on either side, rude cries, scraping. The
ship sprouted wings of wood as oars were pushed out from
the hull into the water. Under his feet a heart began beating.
Driven by its rhythm the oars ploughed the sea. The banks

rose and fell, churning the slate sea white, and the ship began edging backward into the bay.

The quay was receding. Standing in uneven ranks, his people neither waved nor cried out. Their swarthy faces grew more indistinct with each thump of the drum. When they had become a single gray mass he turned away, his face stiff with pain under his mask.

The shuddering of the deck changed its rhythm. The sea was threshed to spume as the ship's prow was brought about. He watched the cliff and the Hold slip off slowly to the left, until, past the prow stem, he saw the hills of the sea sliding toward them. The drumming changed again, quickening with his heart. They moved forward. He looked with horror as a smooth glassy slope came rushing on. The world lifted until it seemed the ship was going to fall back upon herself. Then the deck lunged forward and down taking his stomach with it. Up, up, up, then rushing down so that the next wave rose high enough to wash away the sky.

There was a snapping and a rustling above his head like giant birds taking to the air. He looked up to see the fansails stretching open their hands. He watched them punch forward as they caught the wind. Though they seemed as fragile as autumn leaves, they held. He looked up the deck again as his grip tightened on the rail. The prow was knifing into another wall of water. It cut a widening white gash that sent a wind of foam hissing back. He felt the cold splatter on his robe and smelt the salty terror of the open sea.

Alternately he was climbing and then descending the deck. He bent his knees to keep his balance. Every so often spume would lash his back. There was a constant roaring; everything clattered and shook around him.

He saw Keal ahead hanging onto some rigging. He looked as if he were coming to help him. Carnelian put up his hand and commanded him to stay where he was.

"Down there, Master," Keal cried above the wind. He was pointing into the mouth of a large funnel that opened behind the mast. Carnelian thanked him but his words were lost in the roar. He staggered up to Keal, nodded his thanks, and then passed him. Behind the mast there was some respite from the wind. He lunged toward the funnel, swayed at its lip and peered in. A narrow stairway led down into blackness. He had to duck his head to enter. He fumbled for the balustrade and went down.

With each step the sea noise lessened and the creaking of the ship's timbers grew. He reached a dim corridor that had small doors all the way down on both sides. As his eyes adjusted he saw that the bulkhead on the left had been daubed with crude representations of House Aurum's horned-ring staff. The right bulkhead bore Carnelian's own chameleons. He almost felt like kissing them. As he walked along the corridor he had to bend his head down because the ceiling was so low. He knocked on one of the doors. It opened to reveal a familiar face.

"Naith," he cried in delight.

The man knelt. Past him, Carnelian could see the cabin with its inset bunks. It had a faint smell of home that almost caused him to release his pain in tears. "Get up, man," he said, remembering Naith. "Just get up."

The guardsman looked at him with concern.

"Where's my cabin?" asked Carnelian.

Naith leaned out, grasping the threshold lip, and pointed down the corridor.

"The door beside the stairway?"

He nodded.

Carnelian stepped back and let Naith shut the door. The corridor angled up then down. He edged along it to the door that had been pointed out. He tried to listen at it, opened it, lifted his foot over the threshold and then stepped into the tiny cabin beyond. Tain was there. "Thank the Gods, Carnie. I thought you washed into the sea."

"Apparently I'm made of finer clay."

Tain looked puzzled.

Carnelian looked around the cabin. The floor curved up to form the bulkheads and then further round to form the ceil-

ing. A single bunk was set into the bulkhead opposite the
door. A tiny lantern swinging from a hook in the ceiling
easily lit the place.

"There's not much of it, I'm afraid," said Tain.

"I've worn bigger robes," said Carnelian.

"Can I stay here with you, Carnie?"

"Where are you going to sleep?"

The corners of Tain's mouth turned down.

"Of course you can, but you're having the floor."

Tain managed a grin as he moved aside to reveal a bed
already made on the floor. Carnelian saw that some of their
clothes had been unpacked. He took two steps across the
cabin, turned and wedged himself back into the bunk.

"I'd like to watch the other Masters getting into one of
these."

Tain was staring into space. In his eyes, Carnelian could
almost see a reflection of his people on the quay. He busied
himself tracing the graffiti carved into the bulkhead. Obscene
pictures. Strokes in rows as if someone had been counting
days. All the way up his back, he could feel the sway and
shudder of the ship.

Carnelian was curled up in the dark, rocking as his stomach turned inside him. He was exhausted. The ship was
pressing in. She was whispering. He forced himself fully
awake to listen. It was just her body creaking all around him.
The bunk was too short for him to straighten his legs. He
swung them out and hunched on the edge. He imagined her
decks above his head, her tree masts, her bronze machines.
Up there against the leaden sky, her fan sails. He made their
shape with his hands, stretching his fingers until the skin
between them hurt. He slid his feet out until they found the
warmth of Tain's body. Below them the baran's belly swelled
into limitless sea. Carnelian recalled what Keal had told him
about the sartlar oarsmen. A vision of them writhing in her
bowels like worms made him snatch his feet up from the floor.

DREAMING

Sweet lady let me taste

Your bitter kiss,

Mother my forgetting,

Bind me with dreams.

—EXTRACT FROM

"SLAVE DREAMING"

It was too much bother to have himself cleaned. Besides, Tain was all clammy misery and found it hard to stand up. Carnelian asked only that his brother touch up his bodypaint where it had rubbed off in the night. When Tain was done he sank back to the floor. Carnelian wriggled into his robes, put on his mask and, shrouded in his traveling cloak, opened the cabin door.

The corridor smelled of men, urine and brine. The swilling sounds of the sea coming down the stairway almost made him retch into his mask. He stepped out of the cabin, closed the door so that Tain would not be disturbed, then padded along the corridor. The faint scent of lilies suggested that one of the Masters had walked there not so long ago. He knocked on Naith's door, and when the man showed himself Carnelian asked if he could take him to Keal. Naith said that he had been forbidden to leave the cabin but that Keal was quartered further down the passage, beside the Master's cabin.

Carnelian followed the directions. The corridor grew gloomier with each step, but his eyes adjusted well enough. He reached a round space with a central column. A yoke of bronze as thick as a man's waist gripped its base. It could only be the shaft of the central mast. Peering round it he saw that the corridor continued on to another stairway down which some daylight was filtering. Four doors led off the mast-columned hall. Each had been painted with the warding eye and one of the ciphers of the Masters' Houses.

Carnelian retraced his steps, found the door he thought Naith must have meant and knocked on it. It was opened by a guardsman he knew. The man began to kneel but Carnelian stopped him with a command sign. "Rale, is Keal here?"

"Yes, Carnie," the man said and stepped aside to let him in.

Carnelian squeezed into the cabin. It was perhaps twice the size of his own. Men were sitting on the floor playing dice. The six bunks hedged them in. One man lying on his bunk looked green. The others looked sickly, uncomfortable. They smiled, but avoided looking at his mask.

"Get on with your game," Carnelian said more gruffly than he intended. "I'd speak with you, Keal."

His brother stood up from among them. "I'm sorry, Carnie, but I'm not allowed to leave this room unless the Master sends for me."

"You can leave with me and tell him if he asks that it was· I who commanded you."

Carnelian squeezed back out into the corridor. Though he still had to stoop, it was less constricting than the cabin. His head scraped against the ceiling as he turned to look at Keal. He wondered that his brother could stand unbent. "Let's go up there," he said, pointing.

He walked up the steps and coming out of the funnel raised himself up to his full height and stretched, groaning. "The luxury of a straight back," he said into the freezing wind that was lifting his cloak up around him. The deck grating gleamed with water up to the rails. The foremast blocked his view of the prow. Beyond the narrow solid limits of the ship, a vast blinding sky melded into a silver sea.

He turned to his brother. "How are things?"

Keal was gazing blank-faced at the world. He focused on Carnelian and gave a nod toward the stairway. "The lads are well enough down there, but those that are here under our feet . . ." He tapped the deck grating with his foot, then pursed his lips as he shook his head.

Carnelian peered into the space beneath the grating and thought he could make out murky movement. "What protection do they have down there?"

Keal looked grim. "Some blankets and tarred tapestries to keep out the spray."

"The other Masters' people?"

"They're just as badly off, worse even. One of them was so ill that his Master sent word and he was chucked into the sea."

"Into the sea?" said Carnelian with horror.

They both looked over the rail at the swirling water.

"Apparently, this was to stop what he had spreading to the others. If you ask me he was just underfed."

Carnelian peered down through the grating again. "I should go down there, talk to them."

"Don't even think about it, Carnie," Keal said. His voice was tinged with anger. "It would be unseemly. Down there, even I'm forced to stoop."

"My Lord!" A cry in Quya.

They both turned to see a huge shrouded apparition bearing down on them. Carnelian cursed under his breath as Keal collapsed onto the deck.

"Lord Carnelian, have you no fear of coming up here on deck?" It was Jaspar speaking in Quya.

"Fear, my Lord?"

"Sea air burns the skin. Your hands, my Lord, your poor hands."

Carnelian looked at them. They looked fine.

"You should wear gloves," said Jaspar and lifted up his hands. Each was sheathed in silvery leather streaked like serpentine, so thin his hands seemed merely painted.

"Is that your only protection, my Lord?"

"Not so, my Lord, not so. But to reveal the other we must needs first clear the deck."

Carnelian remembered Keal. His brother's hands were numbing yellow on the grating. Carnelian almost spluttered out an apology but remembered who else was there. "Return to your cabin, Keal," he commanded, biting his lip once the words were said.

"Yes, Master," muttered Keal. He stood up, head bowed, and moved off.

Jaspar's mask was scanning the rigging. He looked off across the deck, spotted the captain and raised his hand to summon him. The man came jogging and flung himself at their feet.

"Clear the decks," said Jaspar.

Carnelian wanted to escape. "That is not really necessary. We—"

"Nonsense, my Lord. I for one would breathe the air unmasked."

The captain crept away and began shouting commands. Soon, sailors were scrabbling down the rigging, tying up ropes. Their branded bony bodies jerked across the deck and fell out of sight through a large, horn-rimmed hole.

Jaspar dropped his mask into his hand. "It will be more pleasant to converse without these."

Carnelian took a step back, staring at Jaspar's face. It was blue. His entire skin was lapis-blue. Jaspar pulled off one of his gloves. His hand was the same vibrant color. He regarded it as he turned it this way and that. His blue lips gave a little horizontal smile. "It is an interesting cosmetic, neh? Of course, it is exceedingly outlandish. One would not dare use it in Osrakum. But out here . . . so far from civilization, well . . . Besides, cousin, I intend to show it to none but you." He leaned toward Carnelian. "It can remain our little secret, neh?"

Carnelian stared at the gleaming idol's face. "W-where did you find it?"

"One of my slaves brought it to me in Thuyakalrul. Apparently it is rather in vogue among the marumaga there. My Lord might not know that the more neutral pigments have been forbidden them by a recent statute of the Wise."

"They copy us?"

Jaspar flourished his hand in the air. "Does not all the world? The pretensions of the marumaga are legion. They are like children aping the ways of their elders. But we were talking of the pigment. The creature . . . my body slave, has sworn upon his skin that the paint is proof against the sea-air burn."

"His skin?"

"His skin against mine. It is an unequal wager, but he has nothing else to hazard."

"Is it necessary to resort to such terror?"

"Say whim rather than necessity. But after all, is terror not the birthright of the inferior?"

Carnelian turned away to hide his frown. He pretended to survey the rolling surface of the sea. Spray flickered chill across his face. He wondered if it was burning through his paint.

"Would my Lord be amused to try the pigment for himself? I have a jar spare."

"I thank you, no. It would be wasted. I do not intend to venture much abroad."

"Indeed, I too do not intend that the day should often look upon my face."

"The other Lords?"

"The Ruling Lord your father I cannot speak for, cousin, but as for the others, if the voyage out was any indication, we will see nothing of our dear Vennel."

"Perhaps he does not mind stale air."

"Rather he does not thrive in the company of his . . . peers. Even when we were blown off to the east and daily threatened with foundering, he affected a disdain to meet with us. He sent up word that he should not be disturbed. At the time, I ventured to suggest to Aurum that our Lord might well find shipwreck most disturbing."

"He is brave, then?"

"On the contrary, he is craven. His blood lacks the true passion of the Great. His thinking bears comparison with the cold calculating of the Wise. The most I would say of him would be that he is, shall we say, capable of serving?"

"And Aurum?"

Jaspar regarded him with a blue smile. "Whenever I came up he was always here surveying the sky as if he were marshaling the winds."

"He is powerful?"

Jaspar chuckled. "Not that powerful."

Carnelian put on a smile.

"Once he was mighty. Intimacy with Nuhuron, the last God Emperor, gave him much influence. Naturally, this ceased with the accession of the present God. In spite of this, Aurum is still one of those who channel the currents of power in the Clave. Recently, many of us had hoped that his channeling days were finally coming to an end."

"He supports one of the candidates and you support the other?"

"Not so, cousin, not so. My father's faction supports neither of the Jade Lords, as yet."

"Then it is Lord Vennel's faction that supports the other candidate."

"No, no, no. It is Ykoriana, sister and wife of the God Emperor and mother of the contending twins who supports one of them, Molochite. Vennel is merely a puppet. It is her hands that move him."

"I am confused, my Lord," said Carnelian.

Jaspar examined his hands as if looking for some chink in their blueness. "It seems that my Lord requires clarification," he said at last. "When we left Osrakum, Aurum could command the support of three-quarters of the Great of blood-rank two. With Nephron's ring, that of the God Emperor's mother, and the Pomegranate Ring, Aurum could count on about twenty thousand votes. The Empress Ykoriana could rely on only a quarter of the Great of blood-rank two, but almost all the blood-rank one Houses whose cause she espouses. Additionally, she also had in her hand the rings of your maternal grandmother, the Lady Tiye, and of her own mother, the Lady Nayakarade, both of blood-rank three. Throwing in their rings, that of her son Molochite and her own she had something over twenty-one thousand votes. My father's party had the support of those of the Great whose blood pride keeps them from siding with the lesser Houses. With a few others this gave us nearly thirteen hundred votes."

"Your faction then controls the balance of power?"

"It did, but as each day passed the Emperor grew weaker and the aura of his endorsement dimmed about Aurum's faction. When we left, Osrakum was murmuring with rumor of the desertions he might expect to Ykoriana's party. After all, as the Gods' power wanes hers is in the ascendant."

"So you all came to our island?"

"Aurum used his power in the Clave to elect your father, He-who-goes-before."

"How could he carry the vote there when he could not win the sacred election?"

Jaspar raised an eyebrow and sighed. "Because, cousin, since they form part of the Imperial Power, the members of the House of the Masks cannot cast their votes in the Clave. Will you allow me to continue?"

Carnelian lifted his hand in assent, annoyed with himself. He had known perfectly well that the Imperial Power was excluded from the Clave.

"When Aurum announced that he would go and put the offer to your father, the other factions insisted that each would send its own representative."

"But why did Aurum come himself? Will his faction not crumble in his absence?"

"Almost certainly. As for why he felt the need to come himself," *who knows*, he signed. "At the Clave it was not considered likely the Lord Suth would return. Aurum must have hoped to persuade him."

"But what does he expect that my father can do for him?"

"For too long Aurum has forced his rancor on the Clave. He caws and caws, seeming to forget that, for all its wisdom, none will give ear to a raven. Your father has a reputation for a certain old-fashioned, patrician virtue. He can remind the Clave of its ancient and glorious opposition to the Imperial Power. He can make all the traditional speeches about blood pride, responsibility, honor." Jaspar shrugged. "Besides, his voice has not been heard in Osrakum for many years. The novelty of such a voice might be listened to, perhaps by enough of the Great to shore up the breach in Aurum's faction. Nevertheless, it was a desperate gamble."

"Not so desperate, my Lord. After all, we are here with all our old-fashioned virtue."

Jaspar regarded him with his wintry eyes. "That may be so, my Lord, but there was little reason to suppose the Ruling Lord Suth would wish to terminate his absence from Osrakum merely because we dangled the bauble of the Pomegranate Ring before his eyes. After all, the Ring has been offered him before and he turned it down."

Carnelian stared. "Offered before? But . . . our exile . . . ?"

"Exiles are as varied in their kinds as precious stones. It seems in keeping with Lord Suth's fabled eccentricity that he should choose to retire so far and to such a forbidding shore."

"Choose . . . ?" said Carnelian feeling that lightning had flashed before his eyes.

Jaspar drew back, his head leaning to one side. "Surely you knew, Carnelian, that your father's exile has always been self-imposed?"

Carnelian was not even sure where he was. He jerked a nod, fumbled on his mask. "Lord . . . Lord, excuse me."

Jaspar's blue face was frowning as he watched Carnelian disappear into the funnel.

The sea folded into hills and valleys and the ship slid heavily up and down the slopes. Carnelian lay in the cabin, falling in and out of sleep, brooding. Soon the vomit was burning up into his mouth and he forgot everything else as his stomach turned itself out onto the floor. Tain was suffering as much, and Carnelian ordered him to stop trying to clean up the mess. They shared the misery, wanting to die. They were not alone. Above the ship's timber-groan they could hear the retching coming from the cabins round about.

Carnelian heard the knock, then Tain talking to someone and he sat up to see who it was. When he saw his father squeezing into the cabin he was appalled. He was wound into his sheets. Both he and they were streaked with body-paint and soaked with sweat. Filth puddled the floor. He knew the cabin stank. He tried to smooth his hair and rubbed at his face with a corner of the sheet. He swung his feet out, winced as the stuff oozed between his toes, then began to stand up, an apology on his lips.

Stay, his father signed, his huge frame crammed into the other half of the cabin. "This is not the time for ceremony, Carnelian. I am just a father come to see his son." Suth looked around the cabin, then reached behind his head to release his mask. His face was haggard, his eyes bruise-rimmed red. "You look ill, my son."

Carnelian stared. His father looked terrible. He covered his dismay with a wan smile. "It is mostly the waves. Does the wave-sickness also ail my Lord?" For a moment he forgot the resentment he had been feeling toward him.

"No . . . No . . . well, yes, as you say, the waves." Braced against the ceiling and a bulkhead, his father seemed a part of the swaying cabin. "It occurred to me I might bring you some relief." He handed Carnelian a small silver box. Its lid was wrought with a crying eye: the moon's cipher. Opening it, Carnelian saw it was filled with a red-brown powder whose acridity stung his nose.

"It is made from the juice of young poppies. Get Tain to hide its bitterness in honey. Give him some. Its dreams will deaden you both to the storms."

Carnelian searched his father's weary face.

"Take care you do not consume too much. Poppy has a power over men's minds." His father looked as if he were seeing something far away. "And dreams can be as enslaving as the legions."

"You should not have incommoded yourself, my Lord. A servant could have brought me this."

His father almost smiled. "You see behind the mask, my son. You force me to own that I come to make a peace between us. This is no time for us to be at war. There are dangers coming that we should better meet with our shields locked together."

Carnelian felt his heart melting. He wanted to open up, to lean on his father's strength, to trust him. But he wore the discomfort of Jaspar's words like wet clothes. "May I ask my Lord a question?"

His father's brows lifted.

Carnelian clamped his teeth together. The taste of vomit was still in his mouth but his question lay more bitter on his tongue. He spat it out. "Was our exile freely chosen?"

His father's face darkened. "Who told you this?"

"It is true then!"

Father and son glared at each other. Then Suth's head fell as if it had grown suddenly heavy. Cold fear flushed up Carnelian's chest. The Master, hanging his head in shame? He had never expected to see that. He withdrew back into the bunk in a hunch. His father looked up with dull eyes. "Long ago, I swore before the Wise the blood oath that brought us here. All you need to know is that I have been released from it."

The sadness in his father's face punished Carnelian. The massive shoulders seemed to be curving under the weight of the decks above. Carnelian felt how unworthy had been his doubts.

His father made an elegant gesture to take in the cabin. "Shall I send one of my servants to clean this?"

"No, Father, Tain will manage well enough."

"I can see how well he is managing, but it is up to you."

He turned to leave. "There is one task that Tain should be capable of. You are no longer a boy. Have him shave your head. Wait until it is calm. It is not becoming to a Lord to have his head a mass of scars."

Tain was mopping up the last of the vomit. His face crumpled as he wiped it off his hands. He looked up at Carnelian hunched on his bunk. "You know, Crail's worse off than either of us." He busied himself rubbing the cloth between his fingers.

Carnelian dropped his hands from his head and glanced down. He felt a pang of guilt. He had altogether forgotten the old man. "Surely he's being looked after?"

Tain looked uncertain. "You know the tyadra. How likely do you think it is that they make good nursemaids?"

"Well then, he must come here where we can look after him."

Tain's eyes grew huge. "In here?"

"Why not?"

"Well, it might have escaped my Master's attention but there's very little space."

"If you don't think that you can squeeze in here with us then you could always take Crail's place in the other cabin."

Tain frowned.

"Go on, Tain, I'm sure you don't like the idea of him suffering uncared for any better than I do."

"I suppose," said Tain.

He went out and returned soon after with a sly grin. "He's refused."

"I bet you didn't try very hard."

"I did! You know what he's like."

"Well, go back and don't bother saying anything more to him. Tell the others in his cabin that I want him carried in here and that it's a command, not a request."

A little later Carnelian could hear grumbling and scuffing in the hall. He had risen, made himself presentable and knocked together another makeshift bed on the floor. He stood shakily on the tilting floor and had to look away from the swing of the lantern. Everything was lurching. Tain came in and held the door open and a guardsman backed into the cabin. Carnelian could see another over his shoulder. The first man had to trample on one of the floor beds. When they were both in they turned to reveal Crail hanging between them. Though sallow and feverish, the old man still managed a scowl. The guardsmen began to lower him to the floor.

"Not there," said Carnelian. "Put him on the bunk."

"But, Carnie, *you* can't sleep on the floor," said Tain. All the faces round him were aghast.

"Look at the bunk," Carnelian said. "Go on, look at it! Now look at me. I'm sure you can all see there's a difference in our lengths. I haven't slept comfortably since coming aboard this accursed scow. Now, if none of you object," he gave them all a bow, "I'd like to sleep stretched out on the floor."

Some of them blushed. It was making Carnelian queasy to see them swaying and so he turned away. When he looked back, Crail had already been put in the bunk. The old man's face puckered into a grimace that folded his chameleon tattoo into the wrinkles. "I knew I shouldn't have come," he grated. "I told the Master I didn't want to be a burden."

Tain's eyes rolled up to the ceiling. The other men slipped out. Carnelian and Tain arranged the beds that now took up almost all the floor. They settled down with groans of relief. The old man was still grumbling. Carnelian offered them each a morsel of poppied honey. Crail turned his face away. Carnelian forced it on him. "Take it. If it's good enough for a Master it's good enough for you." The old man gave in but put it into his mouth as if he were being poisoned.

"Tell me, Crail, of the time you saw the dragon," said Tain and winked at Carnelian.

The old man looked over, still scowling, suspecting mockery, but when he saw their expectant faces, his own began uncreasing. He chewed absentmindedly on the honey. "Yes, it was a wonder, and I saw it sure enough." The grooves in his skin bunched as he spoke. "By the God in his Mountain and his four horns, I saw it sure enough."

Carnelian and Tain had heard it all so many times before. They settled back into the comfort of his drone. ". . . a tower on its back that touched the sky." The old hands struggled to make a pyramid of fingers. "Its hide was bronze. It was larger than a hill." His arms trembled out a volume in the air. "Its horns were four men long." He spotted the corner of Carnelian's smile. "I swear it, boy, by all the hidden names of the God in his Mountain: four men long and curving like the moon." And four of his thick knob-knuckled fingers were hooked out around the head he'd made by pressing his callused thumbs together.

The lantern cast out a deeper gold. Its gilding warmed the cabin like sunlight. The swaying of the cabin had become the summer wave surge upon the beach at home. Everything was just fine. They all felt it. Carnelian could see the truth of it in the blissful sleepy smiles that Tain let slip across the smooth distances that lay between them. The smile he sent back was a dove loosed into a blue sky. He tried to speak but his words came as a surprise to him. They had acquired a breathing of their own. He lay back and listened to the drums. How deep they were and purple-voiced. That other strain, flutes, many flutes close-tuned and narrow-throated, singing. Voices crying like gulls. He sat up to listen. Not gulls but men, shouting. Panic in the wind. Thunder so bass it made his head, bell and thrum. He tried hard to listen. That was it, voices shrieking over shrilling wind and thunder. A storm, he smiled, lying back again, a storm so musical and lithe.

For eternities he was a needle darning in and out of sleep. The difference between the two, merely an attitude of mind. Sometimes he tried to work out how long it was now since the old man had come. It was no good. There was nothing to go on. Everything was always the same: Tain lying like a sandbank on the floor, Crail up there on the bed, wearing his mask of wrinkles. The cabin slipped and turned and spun and looped and the three of them went along for the ride. It really was a marvel that he felt so well. He had never felt so well. He knew he glowed. Only a single piece of grit spoiled his oyster bliss. He made it smooth with pearly dreams and forgetting. He knew it was there. Let it work its own way out; he was not about to bother delving for it.

His people. The thought popped into his dream and woke him up. There was a tempest and his people were up there, exposed between the decks. That single lucid thought was a stone falling into a well. He was eyeless at the bottom of that well. The lantern must have run out of oil. He climbed up until he found that he was standing. He searched. He became nothing but the feelings in his fingers. Squid at the bottom of the sea. He chuckled at the idea of it. His fingers found his cloak. Finding the door was a greater quest.

The corridor was filled with the swinging suns of lanterns. Their blaze blinded him. The door at the stairway top was rattling. Something was on the other side trying to come in. Crashing thunder, felt as much as heard. He turned to face the first step. He put one foot in front of the other. His body was a puppet he hardly remembered how to control. He took it up the stairway. The door clattered and shook. He lifted his wooden hand and watched it turn the handle. Nothing happened. He leaned against the door; it struggled to push him back but then gave way and he tumbled out.

He was kneeling in the throat of the roaring night. Its tongue sloped up wet under his hands. The pressure of its breath squeezed his eyes shut. It roared on and on and on. He felt a terror that, should it pause for breath, he would be swallowed up. The world shattered with a crash that left him deaf. Sudden white. Painful afterburn. He strained against the wind to open his eyes. When he did he squinted round him but could see nothing. He was reaching his fingers up to test that his eyes were really open when a livid crack appeared across the inky black. For a moment he saw the deck sloping up before him. The mast jutting out above his head was an axe waiting to fall. Beyond that the lurid gleaming foredeck funneled up to the prow behind which the whole sky was strangely streaked and mottled, like a writhing wall of snakes. His eye could just see up to its flint-sharp top and he realized that the ship was climbing an immensity of water. High above, where the wave edge touched the sky, Carnelian detected the faintest curling white. His heart stopped. The wave was breaking above them.

The light snuffed out. Ghostly scratches printed themselves wherever he looked. He tried to listen for the roar of the breaking wave as it raced down to get them. He waited for the unbearable touch of its cold thunder. Then the deck began toppling forward. For a moment it hung, horizontal, floating suspended in the night. Then it started angling down. His nails dug their anchors into the deck but he slid forward all the same. On and on as the deck fell away ever more steeply. He hit something hard. One of the brass posts around the mast. He hugged it with trembling desperation. The world shook again. The post rattled in his embrace. It was a kind of ecstasy waiting for the lightning. When it came it revealed far below the abyss into which they sped. That well was the starkest terror. Down into the deep it screwed its wall of circling iron.

"Carnie."

Impossible.

"Carnie." The word was the merest rustling in his ear. He had only eyes and they saw only the well.

A vise gripped his jaw and swiveled his head round. Something bleared in his sight. His eyes took time to adjust back to the dimensions of a human face. His father's face. "Carnie," it mouthed. "Are you all right? What's wrong with you?"

The circle of his arms was torn open. His body was being dragged. He squeezed his eyes closed. He could not bear to look down into the well again. His heels bobbed across the deck grating, catching like ratchets. They tugged free. The storm muffled, and he realized he was inside.

"Are you all right?" a human voice asked.

He dared to look. His father's face wearing the chameleon. No. It was Keal, wild-eyed Keal.

"My p-people . . ."

At first Keal stared at him as if he were mad, but then he grimaced, understanding. "They're lashed down," he shouted, "and safer than you or me out there." He looked back toward the shuddering door with terror pulling the skin taut over his skull.

"The well," cried Carnelian, seeing it in his mind where his eyelids could not hide the sight.

"Let's get you back to your cabin, Carnie."

Keal took his weight and helped him stagger. Carnelian patted the bulkheads. "It's better not to see what's outside."

Keal opened the door into the cabin. The corridor lanterns swung their shadows inside to where a figure was lumbering around like something in a trap. It was Crail, staring blind, mumbling over and over, "Must get out, must get out." Tain had fitted his spine up a corner and had a blanket clasped to his chest which he was peeping over with clearly no understanding of what he saw.

Carnelian settled them down with talk. He had to sit against the bunk because Crail would not let go of his hand.

"What's it like out there?" asked Tain.

Carnelian had watched his brother shudder with every thunderclap and all the time, the image of the well was turning in his mind. "It's just a storm," he said. "Now get some sleep." He was sure it was the poppy that had put this stain of dread in their minds.

Tain began a muttering whose rhythm was enough to insinuate familiar words onto Carnelian's lips: ". . . our Lord in the Mountain, who is two Gods but also One, whose angels are our Masters that must be obeyed, I plead my prayer . . ."

It was part of what his father called the "slavish superstition." Carnelian slid his hand out of Crail's grip, doused the lantern and lay down. He felt that he made a poor angel. A juddering came up into him through his back. His feet were higher than his head. His mind walked him along the corridor, up the stairway, through the door, into the raging night, the deck frozen in lightning glare, the prow cleaving a way into . . .

With a jerk he snatched his thoughts back into the cabin. His body was shaking. His body was leveling. The floor was bringing his head up. He pressed back against it. He ground his teeth, then gave a gasp as the ship began to fall. Down, the angle so steep he had to brace his feet against the bulkhead. Down. Down into the well until he was almost standing on the bulkhead. He tried to smother his fear with memories. The Hold. He thought of the Hold. Of Ebeny. Her gift. The Little Mother was there against his chest. He clutched her for warmth but the stone stayed cold. We are the lucky ones, he told himself. At least we have food. He squeezed the Little Mother. In truth, he envied those left behind their solid ground far from the abyss. The abyss. He crunched up his ears in his hands to shut out the baying of the wind. Then before he could use his fingers as a muzzle, the scream came up from his stomach and he vomited it out.

Endless night. Swimming in a coruscating sea of dreams. When he came up for breath, he surfaced in the cabin, each time with surprise. The silver box was the tearful eye of the moon. He would smother its light in his hand, dip his fingers in, let the others drink, then dive back. There was no where, there was no passing time, he ceased to be, his unblinking eyes saw only an endless undulating vision of now.

STORMS
AT SEA

Down the dark roads of the sea

We fled

Before a driving squall

—EXTRACT FROM "THE

VOYAGE OF THE SUNCUTTER"

Sharp gull cries superimposing over each other like their angles in the sky. Not gulls, men jabbering. A shout. Answers spaced by distance. Carnelian felt heavy, muffled by the dark. Stillness. No, his body was nudging up and down. It was as if he lay on someone's breathing chest. He did not open his eyes. He knew that he would see nothing. His limbs had been replaced by new ones cast in lead. His head was a stone. Something was different. It was the voices alone that defined space. He searched for the difference. The tempest. His hearing went out past the voices. The tempest was not there. Under him the ship seemed almost still. Unbelievably, she had survived his dreams.

*   *   *

When he decided to rise he found that every joint in his body had seized up. He propped himself onto his legs and drew them together like a pair of compasses. He tottered on his feet. No amount of fumbling would find the lantern. His fingers tried to locate the door, the shape of the cabin forgotten. When they found the door he opened it the merest crack and revealed a diamond thread of light. He opened the door wider and sprayed the dazzle across half the cabin. The sheer beauty of it left him gasping for breath.

He found the lantern and lit it. It ignited into a sun. He smiled through his squint and looked around. Tain was there like a bone carving abandoned in a wrapping of blankets. He stooped and carefully woke him. He gave him time. He watched the life seep back into the little face. There was something unfamiliar about his brother, but what? He turned to Crail. His skin looked empty, as if the old man had squeezed out of it and left it behind.

A while later Tain was sitting up and Carnelian was staring at him. Carnelian's first attempts at speech sighed away to nothing. He swallowed several times and waited for his tongue to be wet enough to move. "You're . . . so thin," he managed to rasp. Tain looked up at him. Carnelian saw that his brother had aged. His face had narrowed. His eyes were huge. They grew larger. He tried to speak but managed only a croak. His thin arm rose and pointed shakily at Carnelian. He nodded several times. Carnelian took his meaning and reached up. He stopped when he saw a stranger's bony hands. He put them to his face. It felt like someone else's.

"You'd better get me cleaned up," he croaked. "I want to go . . ." He jerked his finger up at the ceiling.

They went through the cleansing like old men. The pads were so cold. The smell of the unguent pricked their noses.

Tain's hand brushed the stone dangling at his chest. He peered at it, looked up. "My mother?"

Carnelian blinked down. "She . . . for us . . . protection for all of us."

As they continued with the cleaning Carnelian felt some strength returning. "Like butterfly birth . . . uncrumpling its wings." He chuckled. He almost asked Tain to shave his head but thought better of it. Tain's hand looked none too steady as he unpacked some clean clothes. Putting them on was a long, exhausting process. At last Carnelian edged into his cloak. He adjusted his face into his mask. It felt very loose. He turned to Tain. "Do you want to come with me?"

Tain shook his head. "Maybe . . . later." He slumped to the floor.

Carnelian stepped out into the corridor as if his feet were raw with blisters. With each step his body felt as if it might shake apart. He climbed to the deck with his eyes almost closed against the glare. When he reached it, he stood for a few moments getting used to the rolling and the light. He looked round. His neck was as stiff as an old door. Sea and sky were calm and gray. A breeze threatened to blow him over. He closed his eyes and sucked its saltiness through the nostrils of his mask. He almost swooned, as much from delight as from the burn in his lungs.

He took some steps away from the funnel, round one of the brass posts, and leaned against the mast. He looked at his unfamiliar bony hand and recognized the colors under it. It was sad to see them there. A fragment of his old life: a column from the Hold's Great Hall. He caressed it.

"Carnelian."

The voice carried across the deck. Carnelian looked for its source. He saw a pitchy mass against the sky. It was Aurum unmasked, his face outshining everything else.

The Master lifted his hand. *Greetings*.

Carnelian responded, struggling with his fingers to make the sign.

Lord Aurum's black form swept toward him. His face was glazed with white paint. Suddenly he tensed, shooting his eyes' misty stare past Carnelian's shoulder. The menace was so palpable that Carnelian backed away. Something grabbed him round the waist. He folded forward, almost falling. Looking down, he saw that it was Crail, haggard, confused, blinking, his arm up to ward off the bright sky.

Carnelian turned back in time to see Aurum's whitened

lips bending into an unpleasant smile. Bone fingers were drawing his mask out from his robe. With one smooth languid movement he put it on. The cruel gold face drifted toward them. Aurum's shadow falling across Crail allowed the old man to drop his arm. His eyes cleared. Then he saw the Master and jumped.

Aurum's mask looked down at the old man, who crumpled to his knees.

"Unfortunate creature," said the Master in Vulgate. "It's too late for that." He looked at Carnelian. "The creature saw my face unmasked," he said in Quya.

Carnelian stared with horror at the Master's mask. In its exquisite polished surface he saw his own mask, the ship and all the world trapped in reflection. "The slave could not have seen your face, my Lord, he was dazzled."

"It was looking straight at me."

"But you must have seen, my Lord, that he was shielding his eyes. It was only your shadow that allowed him to see."

"Sophistry. Is the slave blind?"

"No . . ."

"Then he has broken the Law of Concealment."

"But it was not his intention . . ."

"Do you really think the creature's intentions form any part of the Law?"

"But the slave is weak, delirious. He suffers still from the aftereffects of the poppy."

"Who gave the slave poppy?"

"Well, I did . . ."

"You see the result?"

"The fault is mine, my Lord."

"Assuredly that is so, but of course it is the slave that shall be punished."

"Be merciful, my Lord. He is weak. The blinding would surely kill him."

"Do you deliberately belittle me?"

"What? I am sorry . . . I do not understand."

"Even you must know that as a Ruling Lord of the Great my prerogative is the second Order of Concealment. The

Category of Punishment is thus also the second and not the first."

Carnelian closed his eyes, then opened them quickly when he started to feel dizzy.

"Not only blinding but mutilation shall be this creature's fate."

Carnelian looked down at Crail, feeling nausea. He coughed. "He is old . . . witless. Lord Aurum, please show mercy."

"Neither its age nor its wits are pertinent, but only its sin. Even if I wished to do so, it is not for me to show clemency. The Law is precise. It does not concern itself with mercy. You have been careless, Carnelian. Suth Sardian has shown too much license and this is the result. You should take this as a salutary lesson. Thank the Twins that your life in Osrakum will not be what it has been." The mask looked down at Crail. "Let us forgo the formalities of the proper punishment. I shall summon my guards and they shall dispose of the creature here and now."

Carnelian was close to vomiting. He used his anger to control the nausea. "If you insist on pursuing this matter of the Law to the full, then I must insist that the forms be adhered to. This slave is mine and thus his punishment is my affair not yours."

Aurum straightened. He loomed over Carnelian. "So be it. At least for now." A strange dry sound coming from his mask caused Carnelian to draw back. Aurum was laughing. It seemed the most dreadful thing of all. The Master lifted one of his huge hands and locked it round Carnelian's arm. "Truly you are your father's son." He laughed again. Then the golden mirror of his face came down close to Carnelian's. "However, it would irk me if I were to find it necessary to remind my Lord of the creature's sin. My Lord will not forget, will he?"

Carnelian saw his own serene reflection looking back.

"Punish the creature, Carnelian. If you do not have the stomach for the blinding and the amputation, then give it to the sea. What loss will it be to you? Replace it in whatever function it performs with a younger creature." Aurum nudged Crail with his foot. "It is long past its best use. Aaagh! It fouls the deck." He wiped his foot on Crail's back, released Carnelian's arm, then walked off.

Carnelian stood with Crail at his feet until his anger shook away and nothing was left but a paralyzing chill.

Carnelian took Crail back to the cabin. Tain and he cleaned him up. Then he made the old man lie on the bunk and sat with him stroking his forehead until he fell asleep. He told Tain that in no circumstances should Crail be allowed to leave the cabin. Tain nodded and Carnelian went off to find his father. When he knocked on his father's door a blinded slave opened it and told him that the Master had gone up on deck. Carnelian went to search for him there.

Sailors were calling to each other from mast to mast as they opened the sails to catch the wind. The enormous hooded figure of a Master was off near the stern with smaller men beside him. Carnelian saw it was Keal and some others of the tyadra. As he walked up to them the Master turned and he recognized his father's mask inside the hood.

"Carnelian?"

"I have urgent need to speak to you, my Lord."

"What about?"

"A matter concerning one of your servants and the Law."

"Very well." His father looked round the deck and then up at one of the masts. "I would speak to you face-to-face but it would not be advisable to send the crew below." He looked toward the prow. "We shall speak there." He gave some commands with his hands to Keal, then turned back to Carnelian. "Come."

Together they walked up the deck. "I see that you have found your sea legs, Carnelian."

"It is calm, Father."

They both looked out over the undulating flint-green sea. "It will not remain so for long," his father said.

"I had hoped we were through the tempest."

"We merely pass through its eye." His father pointed ahead to where the prow stem was forming a cross with the bar of stormy sky that ran behind it across the horizon.

As they approached it, the prow stem curved above them. Tracing its trunk down, Carnelian saw the green face surfacing through the wood as if up through water. Below it was set a trough of stone.

"A representation of our divine Emperor," said his father. His lips curled. "Primitive superstition."

"Why are They here, my Lord?"

"Not only the Commonwealth but also the legions worship the God Emperor as the living Twins and this is a legionary vessel." He pointed at the number eight carved high on the prow stem.

"An altar, then?"

His father lifted his hand in the affirmative.

"Where is the other Twin?"

"He is on the other side, looking out from the prow. Even now he and the tempest glare at each other."

Carnelian realized that the bronze hooks curving on either side of the stem were not, as he had thought, cleats for fixing lines, but rather the four horns of the Black God. "So the Green Face oversees the baran while the Black looks out over the sea."

"Quite so."

At that moment Keal appeared with the others carrying tall screens. They formed these into a wall around Carnelian and his father.

"Now we can take these off." His father removed his mask. His eyes were red-edged holes in his painted face.

Carnelian unmasked.

"By the Essences, what ails you?" his father cried. His hand came up to touch Carnelian's face.

"My Lord?" Carnelian said, alarmed.

"Your are so thin. Your eyes . . ." His father's eyes narrowed. "You have been taking the poppy that I gave you?"

Carnelian nodded.

"Have you also been taking regular sustenance?"

Carnelian thought back. He had vague memories of dreams, vaguer ones of waking. He realized that he could hardly remember eating at all.

"And Tain let this happen," said Suth, his voice cold with anger.

"Do not blame him, Father. He was as drugged as I."

"But—"

"You yourself told me that he should have some."

"Some, a little, and not through all these many days. Did I not tell you that you would feel no hunger?"

"I do not think you did, my Lord."

"Then it is I who am at fault. Come. Put on your mask. You must go and eat immediately."

Carnelian put his hand up to stay him. "Before I do there is the matter I need to bring before my Lord."

His father looked hard at him.

"It is Crail."

One of his father's brows arched.

"Lord Aurum is insisting that he looked upon his face."

His father frowned.

"I gave him poppy too. I am sure that is why it happened. He followed me up on deck in a delirium. The Ruling Lord was unmasked. He is insisting on the punishment the Law demands. But Crail could not have seen his face. He was blinded by the glare of the sky."

"What exactly did Aurum demand?"

"Blinding and amputation."

His father closed his eyes as if he had been struck. He opened them. "How did you leave this matter?"

"I told him that Crail was ours and that if he insisted on it we would carry out the punishment. But you can speak to him, Father, you can do something . . ."

His father looked ashen. "You put me in a difficult position, more difficult than you can know."

"You will save him?"

"I will do what I can." His father slid his mask back over his face. "Go now, eat, and for the sake of your blood, henceforth, be sparing with the poppy."

* * *

Before he ate, Carnelian made the round of all their cabins to see that his guardsmen were bearing up. He asked Keal how their people were coping between the decks. Nothing to worry about, Keal said. Carnelian knew he was lying and made him tell him the truth. One had been washed into the sea. Several were burning with fever. Carnelian had expected worse.

Back in his cabin he made sure that Crail ate something first. The old man was confused. He was recounting a nightmare he had had of a Master and a deck. Carnelian showed him a smile. When he ate with Tain, it surprised him how hungry he was. He gulped the food down though his stomach ached. He joked with Tain. They talked about dragons and the Three Lands, but all the time he was listening. Steadily the wind moan had become a keening. He eyed the silver box with its promise of dreams. There was a crack so loud he thought a mast had snapped. Snatches of voices screeched over the gale. Then the storm front hit them. The ship spun round to one side, and then was walloped round the other way. She leaned over. The lantern smashed against the ceiling. Crail was tipped onto the floor. Cries erupted on every side. The ship juddered once, twice; each time it seemed she had struck a rock. Tain's eyes were as round as his mouth. She righted herself, rocking heavily.

For an age they clung to her as she rode the tempest. Each time her hull broke a wave, there was a thud that shook them to their bones. This would be followed by a hiss rushing over their heads to the stern. In the lulls they could hear the running in the corridor, the cries, the lamentations, the slam of doors. Once Carnelian looked out to see the corridor awash with foam.

Tain's eyes kept straying to the silver box. Carnelian only knew this because his eyes were there too. He relented and nipped pellets from the honey.

He was despairing that it had lost its potency until he felt the flames of comfort licking up his body. Fear burned away. The rocking seemed gentle.

The three of them sagged back into poppy dreams. Carnelian took care when he woke to send Tain out to bring them food. They forced it down. Stale water lubricated tedious chewing. Their bodies mimicked every shudder of the ship. Even before the bowls were clean their eyes turned greedily to the silver box.

On a day when there was a lull in the storm, Tain and Carnelian were sitting eating though they felt no hunger. Both had noticed that the cabin floor had acquired a permanent slope down toward the door. Neither had said anything. There was a knocking that they ignored. They had grown used to ignoring every sound. The door opened and a Master's mask came into the cabin. They both recoiled. The poppy still lingered in the folds of their minds and so it seemed to them that this was some terrible being arisen from the sea.

"Carnelian, why do you stare so?" It was his father.

"You . . . you startled me, my Lord."

The Master crowded into the cabin and hunched forward. Tain found a space in which to perform the prostration. The door slammed open in a draught that caused Suth's cloak to billow up and fill the cabin. His gold face turned to look at the bunk where Crail was a crumple among the sheets. It lingered, then turned its eyeslits back to Carnelian. "We are to have a conclave," it said. Carnelian could hear a nuance of emotion in his father's voice. "When you are called you must attend. You are required to do nothing, save that, should it be required, you will vote with me."

Carnelian said that he understood and his father backed out of the cabin. For a few moments, Carnelian remained slumped where he sat and then found the will to stand. Tain cleansed him. They stood there, Carnelian bowed by the ceiling, Tain bracing himself by holding onto his arm. An eternity later they were finished. Carnelian was like some dead thing that had been wedged between the ceiling and the floor.

It was Keal who came to get him. Carnelian was alarmed when he saw how much life had gone out of his brother. Keal rasped some words that Carnelian could not make out, then pointed down the corridor. Around the mast column were several immense shapes. As he came toward them Carnelian saw that all three Masters were there with his father: each masked, each shrouded in his traveling cloak, each a being of a power that the wooden bulkheads looked too flimsy to contain. In their midst the mast shuddered and the bronze shoe that held it squealed.

"Now that we are all gathered, my Lords, I would beg your patience to hear first the evidence of the baran's captain," said Vennel. His voice played above the ship's creaking like an oboe. "Captain, make your report," it said in Vulgate.

"The Twins Themselves are against us, my Masters." The voice spoke from the ground. Carnelian searched among their feet and saw the captain groveling there.

"You were asked for a report, not a theological conjecture."

"Apologies, Master." The sliders on his collar chinked as the captain thumped his forehead against the floor.

"The ship, my Masters, has been blown far off course. For nigh on twenty days we've struggled south against the westerlies."

Twenty days. Carnelian was startled. Twenty days already.

"We've lost several sails and one of the steering oars is close to breaking. The ship's been taking on water. Because of the storm we couldn't go down there. I must regretfully report that two starboard bulkheads have been breached and that sixteen oars of sartlar have been drowned."

"Have the affected bulkheads been sealed off?" asked Suth.

"Yes, Master."

"And they can be bailed out?" asked Aurum.

"We attempt it even now, Master."

"So there's no immediate danger?" said Jaspar.

"If we're hit by another storm we could sink, my Master."

"You appreciate the risk, my Lords?" Vennel said in Quya and then, in Vulgate, "What's our current position, captain?"

"According to the lodestone and what reckonings I can make, Master, we should be somewhere near the Woadshore's southern reaches."

"And how far from Thuyakalrul?"

"Under the right conditions, depending on our real position, taking into account—"

"How many days?"

"Perhaps three or four, Master. But against the wind?" He peered up with a twitch in one eye. "I just can't say."

Vennel turned his mask on them. "My Lords, it seems to me the height of folly to keep to our present course."

"And what then is your proposal, Vennel?" asked Jaspar.

"It seems, my Lord, that our captain knows of some anchorage that should not be too far from here."

"And this anchorage, I presume, is in the swamps?" said Aurum.

"And what will we do if we should miss it?" said Suth.

"The winds will take us there," said Vennel. "We would be sailing before the tempest rather than against it. We would hug the shore. If there is some error in the captain's calculations, no matter. There are countless trading posts all the way up this coast."

"And what does my Lord suggest that we should do once we find this salubrious spot?" asked Jaspar.

"We should carry out what repairs we can and wait until the tempest has blown itself out. From there we would need only a few days of clear weather to make a crossing to Thuyakalrul across the open sea."

"I can see that you have given this matter much thought, Vennel," said Aurum. "But you seem to have neglected one factor."

"And what, pray, is that, Great Lord?"

"Time."

"What matter time if we should end up among the fish?"

"You well know, my Lord, that time in this matter is

everything," said Aurum with an edge to his voice.

"You heard the captain's words. He said that we will founder if we pursue our present course."

"He said that we *might* founder."

"You also forget, Vennel," said Suth, "that it was not one of the Chosen who spoke those words. So, the creature fears. What of it? It is a condition of its state."

"Valor will not make this vessel move against the wind," said Vennel.

"But oars will, my Lord."

"Even a full complement of oarsmen could not maintain such an effort. How much less can we depend on the animals we have below?"

"That is true, and that is why we must needs bend our own servants to the task."

"My votes and my slaves are yours, my Lord," said Aurum.

"I too will throw my ring in with Lord Suth's," said Jaspar.

"In that case it is decided," said Aurum. "We shall continue on to Thuyakalrul."

The drum beat its dirge in the rotting belly of the ship. In his cabin, Carnelian clapped his hands over his ears. It was a long time since it had started and its insistent pounding was driving him mad. He stroked the eye on the silver box. It was a door he was reluctant to pass through even though it promised escape. Twenty days. The captain had said that they had been at sea for twenty days. Truly it had been an eternity. He could hardly remember when his life had not consisted of dreaming in this cabin. Tain was snoring. Crail seemed less alive than something carved into the bulkhead. Those twenty days were all lost time. A single unending night. The wooden bulkheads pressed in on him. Carnelian wanted to stretch, to stand tall. He rose and curved up against the ceiling. He shuffled on his cloak, put on his mask and left the cabin.

The drumbeat pulsed louder in the corridor. He climbed

the stairway and passed through the door onto the deck. The sky was striped with cloud. The moon hid its silver eye behind some tatters. A voice cried from the deck. Others answered from above. He looked up the mast. Only a few sails were unfurled, great hands running their fingers through the sky. The ship's heart beat on and on. The deck leaned off to starboard. He walked down it to the rail, leaned over and saw the oar heads flying out into the air. The drum thumped and they plunged back in. His people were down there on the end of those oars, in the stinking dark, pickling in brine with the sartlar half-men. He slid his hand along the rail. Where the harpoon engine had been there was nothing, a gap and the deck torn where the bolts had pulled through. The moonlight suddenly brightened and sketched an eddying silver inlay over the sea.

The melodies of Master voices fluttered his heart. He turned and saw the two apparitions come up out of the ship and drift off toward the prow. Carnelian was sure that they would see him but they kept right on until they stood under the stem. He could hear the lilt of their Quya but could understand nothing of what they said. The moonlight dimmed. Carnelian looked up and saw that the moon now passed mysterious behind a veil of cloud. He looked to the prow and saw that one of the Masters was looking up at the moon. His mask caught a rill of its light. He stooped and ignited the Gods' fire on Their altar. Carnelian was uneasy under the Green Face's lurid stare. The Masters turned so that the firelight fell on their hands and then began to make signs.

Carnelian looked up again. He estimated the length of the cloud behind which the moon was sliding and decided to take the risk. He lifted his bright hands up into the sleeves of his cloak, then crept toward the prow trusting to the darkness. He came close enough to see the signing hands.

. . . *her eyes are not only here.* The signs were shot through with a jewel glimmer that spoke of Aurum's hands.

. . . *even she would not dare.* Those signs had his father's familiar framing.

Do you forget what she has already dared? made with strong, bold gesture. Aurum.

If she should even for a moment suspect. His father with a certain nervous slurring between the signs.

Aurum made a sign of reassurance.

His father's hands began signing again. *Her arm has grown long indeed if she can stretch it even to the sea.*

Her arm has grown long, the signs precise with emphasis.

Carnelian sensed more than saw the moon waxing. It was as if he felt its color on his back. He turned, hoping that the Masters were focused on their conversation. When he reached the mast, he moved behind it and from there went down the steps two at a time.

When he had closed the door of his cabin Carnelian stood for some moments listening. Wind. Timbers creaking. He removed his mask, threw off his cloak, and shrugged off the various robes. He lay down and slowed his breathing to match Tain's. His heart quietened until it seemed to Carnelian that the ship's pulse was his own. His feet managed to find their way to Tain's warm back. Tain moaned a protest but did not move away.

Of whom else but the Empress Ykoriana could they speak with such dread?

TRAPPED
IN
AMBER

The Categories of Concealment are: first, the offspring and the consorts of the God Emperor; second, the Ruling Lords of the Great and the Grand Sapients of the Wise; third, other Lords of the Great and the Ruling Lords of the Lesser Chosen; fourth, the remainder of the Chosen and the Wise; fifth, the ammonites of the Wise.

The Protocol of Concealment states that those in a lower category must unmask whenever those in a higher category do so unless this contravenes the second Law of Concealment.

The Categories of Seeing are: first, Lords of the Great and Ruling Lords of the Lesser Chosen; second, the remainder of the Chosen; third, a Lord's own household or the ammonites of the Wise; fourth, the household of another Lord; fifth, marumaga; sixth, all other creatures.

The Categories of punishment are: first, blinding; second, the addition of mutilation; third, the addition of flaying; fourth, the addition of capital crucifixion. At Chosen discretion, the third and fourth categories may be commuted to immediate destruction.

The Laws of Concealment are: first, that the God Emperor must always remain concealed; second, that the number of a Category of Seeing determines the Category of Concealment in which concealment may be waived; third, that, for the Unchosen, a Category of Punishment is referenced according to how much the Category of Concealment exceeds the Category of Seeing.

—EXTRACT FROM THE LAW-
THAT-MUST-BE-OBEYED

The word dropped like a stone into the water and rippled its black mirror. The sky was up there, far, far away, its bright disc like the moon in the night. Another word dropped into the well, cleaving deep into the water, trailing a churn and froth.

"Land." A muffled word. Carnelian came vaguely awake. "Land." He could hear the word clearly above the creaking of the ship, distinct from the dull thudding drum.

He sat up in the blackness.

"The land, the land."

The words caused him to breathe again. Land. He fumbled blindly for clothes. He fought his way into something. His hands wandered until they touched feathers. He grabbed them, pulled them to his nose, smiling at the smell and feel of his feather cloak. It fell around him, comfortable, familiar. He opened the door. Land. They had reached land at last. He stumbled up the stairway, throwing his arm up to shade his eyes from the high sun. He reached the deck, saw faces, walked round the mast. There, beyond the prow, was a blue horizon. His heart pounded against his ribs.

His ears came alive as if he were coming up out of water. There were fearful cries and shouting. There was a man kneeling off to one side, staring at him, his mouth hanging open, his eyes unblinking. It was the captain. Carnelian could not understand that horrified stare. He looked round and saw sailors flattening on the deck. Aurum was there like a pillar of tar smoke, his face impassive gold. Guardsmen stood around him holding forked spears, their eyes hidden in the crooks of their arms.

"Carnelian," his father's voice called out.

Carnelian was turning to find him when he heard Aurum say, "Cover the Master." He looked back and for an instant saw the face glowing white. Eyes like the heads of nails. Mouth a razor edge. Then it was gone as Aurum's slaves hid him with screens. The Master shifted behind their membranes, a god in a shadow play. A guardsman who knelt watching this, turned round with horror staring from his eyes. He held Aurum's mask out with stiff arms as if it were slaked with poison. Carnelian reached up to his face. His fingers found his cheeks, his nose, uncovered, naked. He masked himself with his hands and stared through the bars of his fingers as the guardsman crept toward him with the mask. Carnelian took its weight and put it quickly over his face. It was still warm and smelled of stale perfume. It was too long for him. He slid it down to peer through the eyeslits and held it still.

"Carnelian," said his father behind him. But Carnelian did not turn. Trapped behind the screens Aurum's shadow was scanning the deck. He lifted his arms.

"Attend me," he said over the sounds of fear. His guardsmen were reluctant to pull their heads from their hiding places. "Attend me, I say." A hint of impatience was in his voice. His men looked up, timid, hesitating. Through the screens their Master's hands were making chopping motions. The guardsmen turned where they pointed, lowering their spears. They looked as frightened as everyone else. Carnelian was surrounded by shaking bodies sobbing like children.

"Spare only the captain," said Aurum.

A shriek became a gurgle as one of the sailors was suddenly impaled. Carnelian twitched as each body was skewered. Blood ran along the deck grating and trickled into the space below. Bleating broke out under their feet. The sweet smell of blood clotted the air. The guardsmen unstuck the sailors from the deck with kicks and threats. They forced them to drag the bleeding bodies to the gaps in the rail and throw them into the sea. Then they were ordered to kneel. Red to the elbows, with tears coursing down their faces, they urinated down their legs. Forked spears shoved into them, making a sound of slicing cabbages. The guardsmen yanked the blades out, then kicked their victims over the edge. They came back grim, the redness running down their spears to stain their hands. One slipped on the deck and fell. They clustered round the man who was still on his knees before Carnelian.

"Stand back, my son," his father said quietly beside him.

Carnelian backed away. The man looked round at his companions as they closed on him. He looked up into the face of one of them: a youth, eyes bleary with tears. Carnelian could see the familial similarity in their faces. The man gave the youth a nod then bowed his head. The youth unsheathed a sword, his eyes huge and white, then he brought it down through the neck. It caught. He had to jerk the blade out. He seemed to be choking, but he managed to chop again. The head came loose and rolled drunkenly toward Carnelian's feet. The trunk sagged over onto one side, showing its meaty neck, spraying blood everywhere. The youth edged toward Carnelian with the dripping sword hanging from his hand. Carnelian prepared himself for the blow, almost welcoming it. He flinched as the youth looked up at him. Grief had cut stripes in the spatter of gore that was his face. It was a boy's face but hatred gave him the eyes of a man. He stooped, laid the sword on the deck, then lifted the head and cradled it as he moved away.

Carnelian looked down at his cloak. He remembered he had given it to Tain. Its feathers were darkly matted with blood. His father walked past him toward the captain who was a huddle on the deck. He nudged the man with his foot. "Clear the deck." The huddle flinched. "Now!"

The man rose mumbling as he stared at the blood-coated grating.

"You can have that cleaned later," said Suth.

The man stumbled off with horror printed on his face. Carnelian watched him mouthing orders. There was a taste of acid in his mouth. The stink of the blood mixed with the mask's perfume. He gagged. All he could hear was the wind, the relentless beat of the drum, the hiss of the oars.

Carnelian watched Aurum come out from behind the screens. He had expected anger but there was only contempt on the Master's face. "You stupid boy." Aurum reached out and snatched his mask from Carnelian's grip. It had been like a shell. Carnelian blinked, exposed. The smell of death and Aurum's sneer were all the world. "Look at this mess."

"Do not be too hard on the boy, my Lord," said Suth.

Carnelian could hear something like pleading in his father's voice.

"I have lost one of my tyadra, Sardian," said Aurum.

"I shall give you his worth or a replacement."

"And can you also replace the sailors upon which this vessel so much depends?"

Carnelian watched his father's head drop a little. Then Aurum turned on him. "How do you explain this, boy?"

Carnelian shook his head.

"I knew you were provincial, callow, but I did not think to add stupid."

"You will leave him be," Suth said.

"And what will you do, Sardian, if I do not?"

Carnelian waited for his father to confront the old Master in his defense, but once more his father dropped his head and said nothing.

Aurum stood with his legs planted wide. "I shall go now to ready what people I have left. See if you can find a way to keep your son under some measure of control." He put his mask up and strode away.

Carnelian turned to his father, red with shame. "My Lord—"

"It is my fault, Carnelian. I had thought you better trained. I blame myself."

"But—"

"You will stay here, my Lord, until Tain shall come with your mask. After that you will return to your cabin and remain there until I give you leave to come out."

Carnelian hung his head. "Yes, my Lord."

He heard his father move away. Feathers were sticking to his chin. Their smell was sweetened by the crusting blood. Carnelian lurched to the rail from where his stomach pumped vomit out over the threshing oars.

Tain came up with the mask. Carnelian watched his brother eye the bloody deck. "We heard the noises . . . below." His face was pale. "Why did it happen?" he whispered.

Carnelian looked down at his hands. "It was my fault, Tain. I forgot to wear my mask." He could feel his brother's eyes. He looked up but could not read their expression. Was it pity? He took the mask from him and put it on. He was glad to have it to hide behind. Through the eyeslits, he watched Tain regard the deck as if it were something dangerous.

"Look, there's the land," Carnelian said, to wrench his brother's eyes from the blood. He took some steps toward the prow. His foot slipped. "You'll see it better from here," he called back. He felt that Tain had not moved. He turned. Tain was still there, looking very small.

"I can see it well enough from here, Carnie."

Carnelian nodded and returned to Tain's side, defeated.

In the cabin they stripped him to the skin. Carnelian bundled everything into the feathered cloak, thrust it into his brother's hands and told him to go and throw it in the sea.

Tain packed quietly. They had said nothing to each other since he had returned without the bloody bundle. Carnelian woke Crail and told him that he would have to start thinking of getting ready. Then he tried to help Tain. Each time their hands touched Tain flinched as if he were being burned.

There was a knock on the door. It was Keal, grim, haggard. "The Master's sent me to escort you up on deck. He wants to talk to you."

Carnelian's stomach churned. "I'll be ready in a moment." He asked Tain to touch up the paint on his face and hands. He shook out his black cloak and put it on. He took the mask from Tain's hands, thanking him, and grimaced. The smell of blood was still on his fingers.

He followed Keal up the stairway. When he reached the top, he closed his eyes, sucked some deep breaths through the mouth of his mask, then stepped out onto the deck.

Slaves were scrubbing the grating. A path through the blood had already been cleaned from the stairway to the prow. There Carnelian saw the huge rectangle of his father's back among the smaller shapes of their guardsmen. Carnelian followed Keal along the path. His father turned as they approached. His mask lent him a cruel look. He moved to one side and the guardsmen cleared a way. "Come, stand beside me, my Lord."

Carnelian moved into the space and immediately their men formed a wall of screens to separate them from the rest of the ship. His father reached up to unfasten his mask. Carnelian's hand shook as he was forced by protocol to do the same.

His father's gray eyes fell on him. "How are you feeling, my son?"

Carnelian forced back the tears. He was no longer a child.

Suth reached out and touched Carnelian's cheek. "You will have to get used to death. Perhaps I have erred to keep you so shielded from it these long years. The Chosen are great dealers in death. You would have found this out in Osrakum had you been raised there. I fear you have acquired an unnatural sensitivity to it."

As his father looked out across the sea, Carnelian followed his gaze. He let the strain out and it saddened his face. A blue wall of cliffs had risen before them that edged the whole horizon. The wind washed him. It squeezed some tears out of the corners of his eyes and ran them back along his head to his ears.

"Behold," said Suth. He was careful not to look at his son lest he should weaken the boy's self-control. "Behold the shore of the province of Naralan, the edge of the Three Lands." He shook his head slowly as if he did not believe what he saw. "Once you set foot upon her brim, Carnelian, your life will be for ever changed. You cannot know, my son, who and what you are. It is not your fault. It will come slowly at first. You will see such beauty, and such terror, but the wonders." He sighed the last word. "Such wonders as not even your mind's eye has beheld."

Sensing that his words were soothing the boy, he dared to look at him. "But though you shall acquire the freedom and the thrill of power you shall always be restricted by the Law-that-must-be-obeyed. Today's bloody lesson you will not soon forget." He waited for a reaction but his son merely nodded. He continued, "Duality is the essence of creation. As certainly as night follows day, all gain is balanced with loss.

"Now, listen. There is a perilous game. The Law forms the matrix in which it is played. The Emperor, the Great and the Wise are its players. We must all play. I have almost forgotten how to. My moves are unsure, but it is coming back to me. You too must learn to play. There are such forces ranged against us . . ."

Carnelian had at first been glad of the distraction of politics but now he felt as if a shadow was being cast over them.

His father made a sign of dismissal. "Still, by the grace of the Two we shall yet prevail. Remember the warnings I have given you. All is not always as it seems. A knife is often concealed behind a smile."

He looked back towards the cliffs. Suddenly he lunged forward, bracing himself on one of the curving horns of the prow figurehead. He was searching the sea before them. "Look," he cried and pointed.

Carnelian leaned out and saw the shadow in the sea moving ahead of them. "A turtle," he said. The creature must have been as large as the ship. Its vast oval wavered just under the water, its paddles rowing like huge oars. The Wise taught that the world had been made from the dismembering of the Lord Turtle. His eyes had become the sun and moon. His carapace formed into the firmament of the sky. His flesh was the earth that floated on the sea. All life had sprung from his blood. Now, that ran pure only in the veins of the God Emperor, and in Carnelian's own veins, as in those of the other Chosen, tainted by mortality.

They watched the turtle veer away. "For a moment it was guiding us home. Creation through sacrifice," his father said. "The best of omens."

Creation through blood sacrifice. Behind him, Carnelian could hear the slaves' brushes rasping at the deck. Was it not also an omen that his first sight of the Three Lands should be an occasion of massacre?

"See there," his father said. He pointed off across the starboard bow to where a narrow feather of smoke seemed pinned to the cliff wall. "That is the Jamb Rock where a fire burns night and day to guide ships into the Grand Harbor of Thuyakalrul. Do you see that lower, darker band of cliff that spreads on either side of the beacon? Well, that is the outer wall of the harbor. Thuyakalrul is well named; she is indeed a ring of blue stone lying in the sea. Within her circle lies the harbor. It has but a single door: a breach in the northern curve of the ring. The town itself is set into a depression in the southern wall. From there a causeway crosses a lagoon to the mainland and the road climbs a valley up to join the Great Sea Road."

"And that road leads eventually to Osrakum," said Carnelian.

Suth almost sighed with relief as he saw the color come back into his son's face.

"But if all this is so, my Lord, why then do we not sail directly toward the beacon?"

Suth smiled. "Because, my son, Thuyakalrul is ringed about by another yet greater wall and even now we seek one of its gates."

"My Lord speaks in riddles."

The captain was barking commands.

"You shall see soon enough, but first we should remask."

They did so, and then his father dissolved the wall of screens. Keal was there with the others. He shot Carnelian a look of sympathy. In the rigging, slaves were closing up the fan-sails. Under the curving fishtail of the stern, the captain stood between the two steersmen with their oars. He said something to the man standing behind him. The man operated one of the levers set into the sternpost, and in response the pounding of the drum slowed to breathing pace. The threshing of the oars slowed. The wind fell and with it their cloaks which had been surfing on it. The captain spoke to another man and pointed up the ship. There was an argument as the other man refused to do what he was told. The captain shoved him out of his way and then came forward himself.

"Now you shall see," said Suth.

As the captain came closer, Carnelian could see the twitch in his eyes, his mouth pinching into a quivering smile. The man fell to his knees and did not move.

"Up, man, up. Get on with your business."

The captain's face came up gaunt. He rubbed his mouth with his hand. Muttering something he crept past them, nodded unconsciously to the altar of the Gods and then went to the starboard bow. He scanned the water ahead. Carnelian leaned on the rail to see what it was he sought. He noticed a darkening in the sea in front of them. The captain looked back anxiously and shouted something. The steersmen leaned on their oars. The ship turned her head slowly in response. The bruising in the water rushed toward them.

"A wall under the sea," gasped Carnelian.

"Even when it is submerged, few channels lead through it and only one is deep enough to allow the passage of a baran," his father said.

The captain kept whisking round to shout frantic commands. Then the black water was upon them. The ship jolted as if she had struck something and then the blackness was pouring past them.

"How do they find it?" Carnelian asked, amazed.

His father pointed to a tiny spine jutting up from the cliff. Then he pointed back the way they had come to where a crooked bronze post rose out of the sea. "The post and the cliff tower in a line will bring a baran safely through the reef."

Other posts went past. In some places the reef came up almost into the air. Sinuous filaments of light quivered over it. At the captain's cries the steersmen nudged the ship first one way then the other. At last she was through into the green water beyond. The captain passed them and jerked a bow before rushing back to the stern.

Carnelian chewed his lip. "He is terrified of us."

"With good reason," his father said grimly. "But come, let us resume our places at the prow. I would share this homecoming with you, my son."

Keal and the others remade the wall of screens, allowing Carnelian and his father once more to unmask. Carnelian rubbed at the side of his face where his mask had pressed into his skin. "I will never get used to this thing."

His father took the mask from Carnelian's hand and looked at its edge. "This is poorly made. In Osrakum we shall have our craftsmen fashion you better ones." He handed back the mask. "A well-crafted mask should fit its wearer as comfortably as an eyelid does its eye."

The drum beat faster and with it Carnelian's heart. The banks of oars made a hiss in the sea. The cliff loomed up. From far away, it had seemed mottled white. Closer, Carnelian could see that its corrugated face was peppered with birds. They wove the air with their flight and pierced it with cries. High above, sky-saurians drew wide arcs in the sky. Carnelian took a step back as one plunged toward them. Its dive veered and it seemed that it would crumple into the sea, but at the last moment it pulled up and its huge gray-feathered anvil-headed shape flashed past as it skimmed the surface on its fingered wings.

Behind Carnelian there was a consternation of mechanical sounds and voices. He turned reluctantly from the dance of birds and looked over the screen. He let out a cry, "The mast falls."

"Calm yourself, my Lord," snapped his father. "One should observe before giving voice. Look how slowly it comes down. We simply strike the masts for which we no longer have any use."

Putting his mask before his face, Carnelian parted the screens to look through. The forward mast swung upon a cradle of ropes that hung between the brass posts that had ringed its base when it was upright. The nearest rigging sagged. The rigging on the other side was straining and a gang of sailors was squealing it out through pulleys. The mast settled slowly to the deck. Other sailors began swarming the central mast. They wove a cradle of rope between its brass posts. They fitted new ropes that came over the pulleys on the posts. They pulled on these and the mast began to rise. Up it went while others kept its rigging in tension so that it would not topple. Once its base had cleared the deck they let it fall to one side and the rope cradle caught its weight and lowered it toward the deck.

Carnelian pulled the screens closed. "I cannot see, my Lord, why it should be necessary."

"Where we are going there will not be the height clearance for masts."

Carnelian turned his gaze back to the cliff. At its foot, rocks were ripping white tears in the green hem of the sea. The rock piled crag upon crag up into the sky, the whole mass veiled behind a mist of birds. They wheeled and dived and circled round and it seemed a miracle to Carnelian that they did not collide.

For a while there was a view down the lagoon to a bluish valley cutting up into the cliff. Then the harbor swept its basalt wall across the scene.

"In all the lands this wall is surpassed in towering majesty only by the cliff of the Guarded Land and by the Sacred Wall of Osrakum itself," his father said.

The ship moved near enough to allow Carnelian to see the cracked, jointed surface. Craning he could just see the sky. The rock mass slid past the ship's port rail. As it came closer it washed its cold shadow over the ship, spilling ink into the water round about. Carnelian shivered. In the shadow the waves frothed their lips up the rock but could find no grip.

Further along, the wall ended in a headland. Beyond that the sea was apple-green and gleaming as though some vast door had been left open in the cliff. They came round the headland. Light swelled and burned on every side. Carnelian could hear the captain shouting. The ship was swinging round on the coruscating mirror of the sea. He had to squint.

"Behold, Thuyakalrul, the Blue Ring of Stone," his father intoned, "greatest of the Cities of the Sea, gateway to the Three Lands."

The colors in Carnelian's vision oozed slowly back from white. He gasped. The sea was so green it might have been liquid jade. Two long arms of cliffs embraced the bay, the eastern a curving sweep of stone made turquoise by the sun, the western dark in its own shadow. Sunk between them he saw a many-towered citadel. Above that, a misty blue valley faded up into the sky.

The deck rolled up and down as the ship passed through the doorway in the cliff. Its starboard jamb, a stone column, rose shadowy-vast from a collar of rafts floating chained around its foot. Ropes dangled down from above and ladders formed a dizzying scarring up its flank. Shadowing his eyes, Carnelian looked up and narrowed his gaze in disbelief. Cranes and other machines formed a crown of spikes around the head of the column, which was plumed with a billowing of smoke that made Carnelian sway with vertigo.

"The beacon seemed so slight from out at sea, did it not?" his father said.

Carnelian gripped the rail, closed his eyes and nodded. He felt the ship's bucking, calm. He opened his eyes and saw that they were through into the bay. The cliffs on either side were banded with gray houses. A filigree of walkways traced across the stone. Here and there a palace formed a silver crust mossed with the heads of tiny trees. His eyes darted everywhere.

"Here people nest like gulls," he cried in delight.

"They flee the stench of the town," his father said.

There it lay, crowding the depression in the cliff and tumbling down to fill the further side of the bay with brown confusion.

"It is warmer here," sighed Carnelian in a trance. The drumbeats shook up from the deck and pulsed the air. From across the bay there came a distant murmur. Everything appeared to stand still, trapped motionless in the sun's amber.

"The ring traps the sun's rays," his father said remotely, making a circular motion with his hand to take in the cliffs. His fingers fell to stroking his mask as if he were thinking of hiding his face from the sun. He turned to check that all of his son's skin was painted. Carnelian was smiling closed-eyed, basking in the sun's warmth.

"You should take care, my Lord," Suth said. "The sun can taint even painted skin."

Carnelian opened his eyes. His father appeared to be an ivory carving of a god seeing the future. The more Carnelian looked the more he could see the man. With a pang he saw that the face had lost some of its beauty. The paint could not hide the faded youth. It made him melancholy.

His father came back to life with a sigh. "See the ships."

With each thump of the baran's heart her oars sliced into the syrup of green water. She was making for the wharves of the town. Carnelian could just make out the moorings, the masts like a stand of reeds, the clusters of white tenements that rose up behind. "So many ships," he said.

"They sleep now, but soon they will slip out from this harbor and sail up the coasts, navigate rivers, cross to islands and fetch back for us all that is curious and wonderful."

And our people, Carnelian thought. He said nothing. He did not want to take the brightness from his father's eyes. He watched his white hand point here and there among the nesting ships. Some were large, some small, some as brightly painted as kites.

"In less than a month this whole bay will be filled with a waft of sails." His father's hands made airy gestures that were almost words. "As a boy I came here and passed disguised through the markets. The smells . . . ah, the smells and the shimmer and the play of color. So many people." He looked down with his cloud-gray eyes. "Sometimes, however mean and squalid, however poor, sometimes I have almost envied our subjects their earthy lives."

Closer and closer came the mess of boats. The baran swung slowly round to starboard. All the time his father recited a litany of names, of places, of the rare and costly goods that were bartered all along the edges of the sea. Strange scents of spice, rotting fish and wood and tar mixed with the underlying stink of the town. Though Carnelian curled up his nose, delight was in his eyes. Looking above the forest of masts and rigging, up at the mud tenements of the town, he saw the purpling haze of the valley beyond. He was sure that he could see the thread that was the road winding up into the interior. Everything was gleaming in the sun, making the town seem a trinket fashioned for a Master. Carnelian turned and saw that the sun was already melting its yoke down behind the cliff ahead where the rock swelled into a buttress. The town thinned toward it so that only a few buildings and some roads clung to its black flank. The rest of its body was naked rock.

The marble of his father's face had dulled a little. He was looking up the valley as if his eyes could see all the way into the far south, to Osrakum. His thoughts had retired somewhere deep inside him.

"Do we not go to the town, my Lord?" Carnelian said, trying to reach in.

His father did not respond for some time. He seemed not to have heard, but then his head began moving from side to side as if he were trying to rid himself of a dream. "No. We shall disembark in the Tower in the Sea."

Carnelian looked at the swollen cliff ahead. "If that is a tower, then it was not one made by mortal hand."

"Men often use what the Gods have made for them," his father said.

The cliff and its tower were daubed with birds. Specks wheeled in the sky making screams like tearing copper.

His father tore his gaze at last away from the valley. "I must take counsel with the other Lords." He put his mask up over his face. "Remember what I have said about the game, my Lord."

Carnelian tensed at the return of formality. He masked. The metal face made it hard for him to breathe. The wall of screens came apart and his father walked away trailing guardsmen after him. Carnelian sent off one of the two men who had been left with him to fetch Tain. He wanted to please his brother with the view but, more than that, he needed a friend.

Tain looked uneasy when he came up. The deck was clean but he picked his way across it as if it had just been painted, skirting the masts that now ran the length of the ship. He knelt before Carnelian.

"Come on, get up. I thought you'd like to see all this," Carnelian said, opening his arms wide, desperate to make everything as normal as possible between them.

Tain stood up, fished inside his tunic and came out with something that he offered furtively. "I thought you might want this."

Carnelian took the silver box. Its tearful eye looked up at him. He could taste its bitter-sweet memory of dreams, the dreams that had led him to slaughter. His hand closed. He was glad of the mask that concealed his desire. He drew back his arm and hurled the box in a glinting arc into the sea. He clenched his fingers into a fist, trying to squeeze out the feel of the solid shape.

Nothing more was said. Tain found a place beside his brother and together they watched the tower rising from the sea bulge out to meet them. Its head was lost in the deepening blue sky. It made a somber sight.

The drum beat dolefully under their feet. The two wings of obedient oars plunged into the sea and then flew out sowing curves of foam. The ship carried them into the cold shadow of the tower. At its base gaped a blacker mouth. Only the curving of its high arch bore witness to men's work. Above them flickered a screeching shroud of birds. The sky began to disappear as the ship passed under the pot-bellied rocky swelling. They could smell wet rock. Gray-blue stone rose around them from the sea and made the ship seem as fragile as a poppy.

"If she touches the sides she'll shatter to driftwood," whispered Tain.

The tunnel arched above them. Bird excrement streaked its walls. A pair of sky-saurians flapped screaming out from the blackness. Dank shadow swallowed the ship and made the boys stand closer.

The drum fell suddenly silent. Its last beat echoed away to nothing. There was a terrible scraping. Carnelian felt the pull of Tain's hand on his cloak. He dared to look over the rail. He watched the bend then splinter of a shadowy oar that had not been drawn into the hull quickly enough. Behind them the captain was shuttling from side to side, shouting orders, guiding them through. Slaves thrust bronze-shod poles against the rock. Straining, leaning against them, striking sparks, cursing, they coaxed her down the narrow channel.

Ahead, surprising daylight glowed. A shock of impact forced a gasp from Tain. The ship scraped herself along the rock. Panic-edged cries echoed as, laboriously, she moved out of the tunnel. Carnelian and Tain, their eyes already accustomed to the dark, were dazzled by the light. Squinting past his hand, Carnelian saw that the Tower in the Sea was hollow. They were drifting in yet another wide, almost circular harbor enclosed by stone. Its wall was pierced all around the water's edge with archways in which he could see other ships lurking half drawn out of the waves.

Like rattling spears, the oars thrust out, then hung limp in the water. The drum sounded a dull thud that vibrated through the deck and then rose up echoing round the walls. The ship came alive again. The rhythm was dismally slow as she swam across the inner harbor. The further wall drew nearer. The captain gave a cry and she swung toward the cavern of a shiphouse where some faint lanterns burned. Carnelian felt her ail, her heartbeat slow. At least half her oars rasped back into her hull. She slid ponderously toward the shiphouse. As she passed the gateposts many of the crew flung themselves over her edge onto the netting that covered the inner walls. There was a sudden lurch. She juddered still. Carnelian and Tain held each other up. The crew swarmed along the netting into the darkness further in. They returned struggling with two enormous hooks of bronze. Behind them hawsers snaked out from the dark. The hooks bit somewhere into the ship's hull and then a grinding started somewhere in the shiphouse depths. The hawsers tautened and then, with a shudder, the ship was dragged screaming into the blackness.

Her deck began to slope upward. Carnelian held onto a rail. She bellowed as her hull scraped against a ramp. The captain struck the right-hand hawser with a billhook and made it sing. He scrabbled across the leaning deck and did the same to the other. Its voice was slightly higher. "Starboard!" he shouted into the darkness. The ship was coming up out of the water one tug at a time. The captain lumbered back and forth. Each time he sounded the hawser like a bell. Each time he flung a command into the darkness.

When the dragging stopped at last, Carnelian was able to hear the mutter of voices. Torches came alive all along the walls. The crew flung ropes from the ship's sides that others on the netting caught and looped round the mooring knobs studding the wall. She settled, gave one last stuttering groan and then fell silent. With an ache, Carnelian remembered her flying wild and free across the waves. Now she was tethered like a slave, deprived of the water that gave her life.

THE
TOWER IN
THE SEA

Characteristics required of a legionary tower are:

Firstly, that its personnel shall be segregated according to their kind: the marumaga shall not be quartered with the Chosen; the barbarian shall not be quartered with the marumaga; the barbarian shall be maintained in isolation from the huimur.

Secondly, the manner of this segregation shall be, if possible, in descending strata, otherwise in wall-separated courts.

Thirdly, the spatial elements of this segregation shall have no communication with each other, save by means of linking stairs or corri-

dors. Access to these must be controlled by suitable military gates that are lockable from the
stair or corridor.

—FROM A MILITARY

CODICIL COMPILED

IN BEADCORD BY

THE WISE OF THE

DOMAIN OF LEGIONS

"One always likes to make a grand entrance," said Jaspar as
he walked toward Carnelian, leaning forward against the
slope of the deck.

Carnelian gave Tain a little shove. His brother moved off
down the deck, ducking an obeisance as he passed Jaspar.
The Master watched him go. "My Lord seems quite attached
to that waif."

Carnelian disliked the tone in Jaspar's voice. "He is my
brother."

Jaspar glanced back at Tain. "Your brother?"

"This mode of entry seems rather unsuitable for the Chosen," Carnelian said, to change the subject.

"This is a vessel of war and not intended for the use of
the Chosen. She hunts pirates." Jaspar vaulted up onto a
ledge. He tucked his cloak up between his legs. His mask
looked down at Carnelian. "Would you like my hand,
cousin?" He offered one.

"There is no need." Carnelian emulated the other's vault.

"My Lord now stands upon the Three Lands." Jaspar
turned away. "Presumably, one is supposed to hold on to the
ropes."

Carnelian looked down at his feet, considering Jaspar's
words. Below him people were moving up the deck. Towering among them were the other Masters, silhouettes against
the bright undulating water of the harbor.

Carnelian drew his cloak tight against the clinging damp. The tarry air caught his throat. Jaspar was already some way along the ledge. Carnelian followed him, using the net as a support. The oily rope stuck to his hand. As he passed the baran's curving prow he averted his eyes from her leering horned figurehead. Ahead, pale light sketched an archway in the wall. A dull clang made him peer deeper into the ship-house. He was sure that he could make out shapes like hunched men. He hurried forward to tug at Jaspar's cloak. "What are those, there?" he whispered.

Jaspar's mask looked back at him. "Most likely they are sartlar. Be thankful the blackness conceals their fearful ugliness."

As the Master passed through the archway, Carnelian stole another look into the dark where he fancied he saw a glimmer of eyes. With a shudder, he followed him.

"Where are the guides?" snapped Aurum. Each word quaked the sailors who had come with them to light the way. Their torches made the escorting shadows shake with fear.

"This is intolerable," said Vennel.

"Perhaps, my Lords, we should wait for our tyadra to disembark," said Suth.

Here and there cavern stone showed between the sail parchment shrouds, the stacks of capstans, cleats in clusters, blocks, coil upon coil of rope. Hawsers swagged down from the darkness. Above their heads, a single mast bellied off in both directions. Far away the passage narrowed to a dim lozenge of light.

"I will not wait for my guardsmen," said Aurum. "You there!" He strode toward one of the sailors, pointing an enormous finger. The creatures dropped to their knees in bunches, their torches spurting the Masters' shadows up the walls.

Aurum spoke over their sounds of terror. "Take us to your Master's halls."

They cowered away with their unblinking eyes fixed on him. Carnelian saw a dark hand regrip its torch more tightly.

He remembered similar hands scrubbing blood from the grating of the deck.

Aurum strode among the sailors, scattering them like pigeons. "Do you not hear my command? Lead us up, I say, lead us up to your Master's hall."

"He pushes them beyond terror into panic," said Jaspar in a loud whisper.

Relentless, Aurum herded the sailors and their light before him, threatening to leave the other Masters in blackness. Suth and Vennel strode after him. Carnelian was reliving the horror of the massacre when Jaspar put a hand on his arm. "A lute string already taut should not be tightened further lest it snap. Better to pluck it until it slacks and needs retuning."

"My Lord has such exquisite sensitivity," hissed Carnelian.

It was only when he reached the others that he became aware that he was grinding his teeth.

The slaves found them a stairway winding up into the blackness. Carnelian had to feel for each step. The Masters filled the stairwell with their bodies, squeezing what little light there was into a random flicker. Worse, the stairway narrowed and rock rasped his cowl, eventually forcing him to bow. After the cabin, Carnelian had acquired a loathing of confinement. He was relieved to reach the top.

Although the sailors held their torches aloft, the flames were at his eye level. He wished they would hold them steady and not cower every time he raised his hand to shield his eyes from the glare. The air was stale with the odor of oil and sweat and fear. Roughly hewn pillars bulged under a ceiling low enough to stoop Aurum. Columns faded off like trees in a moonless forest.

"This is probably not the Legate's hall," said Jaspar.

Vennel turned on him. "I find your levity distasteful, my Lord."

"One shall refrain from telling my Lord what one finds distasteful," said Jaspar.

Carnelian noticed movements out of the corner of his eye. The darkness rustled with whispers.

"Evidently, this is not the upper stratum," said Aurum. "We have not climbed nearly high enough. But I swear by the Twins, my Lords, that if these slaves do not quickly find the proper stairway I will have their blood emptied upon the floor." His mask turned upon the sailors, sweeping their line with its serene malice.

A torch sparked thudding to the floor and Carnelian saw the man who had held it melt away. The dark mounded with many heads. Other sailors had come to look at the Masters, many others, ringing them with their splintered mirror eyes.

More torches hit the ground. Carnelian became convinced that he and his companions were being surrounded, that they had been led into an ambush. He glanced quickly round with a warning on his lips but the impassive golden masks muted him.

Suth stooped, scooped up a torch, then another. He thrust their glare into the faces coming into the light. The sailors fell back moaning, bowing, tucking their heads away into the shadows.

Following his father's lead, Carnelian plucked up a torch.

His father continued to swing fire to awe the sailors.

"We terrify them," said Carnelian.

"Overmuch," said Jaspar.

"We will have to find the way ourselves," said Vennel.

"Come, my Lords," Aurum said, "perhaps that light yonder is what we seek." He launched himself at the sailors blocking the way in that direction and they shuffled from his path. The Masters followed him toward the pale rectangle. Carnelian was nervous. The sailors were close enough for him to smell them. He held his torch aloft and scrutinized their faces. He could see their blinking terror of him but also a stubborn resistance.

Aurum brought them to a gateway closed with a grille. He slapped its wood. It shook but held. "How dare they lock this against us?"

Carnelian turned back. He scanned the mob, feeling them closing in.

Jaspar drew near him. "They are so much like animals."

"And dangerous," said Carnelian, distrusting every movement.

"What an outlandish suggestion."

"We shall have to wait until this portcullis is lifted for us," Suth said to Aurum.

"Wait? Wait for what, my Lord?" Aurum struck the grille with the flat of his hand, striking his rings against the wood.

Carnelian edged his way to the portcullis, always keeping his eyes on the mob. Through the bars he could see a landing stippled with red light that filtered down from above. A flight of shallow steps that came up to the landing continued climbing on its other side. He turned to see his father standing with both torches raised, his mask looking out blindly into the gloom. He was a pillar at the center of a region of light along the edge of which there was vague movement.

The rapid striking sound of Aurum's rings broke out again as he rattled the gate with his blows. Light welled up on the other side of the grille, accompanied by footfalls. Carnelian peered through and saw some small dark men lit by the lanterns they were carrying. One came up, cautiously, holding his lantern before him. Its light rayed through the grille and played around the Masters in shafts.

The small man must have seen their masks. "Masters!" he cried, and crumpled to the floor. Most of his companions joined him though one ran off down the stairway crying out, "The Masters. The Masters."

"Open this gate!" boomed Aurum.

"These creatures are so craven," said Jaspar.

Carnelian's unease ignited to anger. "Who makes them so?"

There was some commotion on the landing, a rattle of machinery. One of the men came up toward the portcullis, touched it as if it might be hot, then pushed against it and it slid up smoothly.

Aurum ducked under it before it was fully open. Carnelian

followed with the others onto the landing. Abandoning their lanterns the men scurried down the steps. Carnelian moved to the edge of the landing and saw that the stairway below was filling from wall to wall with men and a dazzle of lanterns. Amidst the dull eddying of leather jerkins several glinting apparitions floated up much taller than the rest.

Carnelian drew back and took his place beside the other Masters. With a clatter and the odor of men, the mass of soldiery spilled onto the landing. While the soldiers clunked into the prostration the apparitions kept coming at them. Their bronze carapaces had an insect mottle. Ridged plates of samite were underneath. Each wore an elaborate horned helm into which was wedged a Master's mask. Carnelian was amazed when they all sank down upon one knee.

"Great Ones, I do not know how came about this affront to your blood," protested their leader. His helm turned its four-horned mass and Carnelian had the feeling that he and the others were being counted. Their obeisance, the mode of address, suggested that these Masters were of the Lesser Chosen. The leader spoke again. "When your vessel was sighted I commanded this tower be made ready to welcome your return. Imagine my dismay when we reached her berth to find you already gone. This is—"

"An outrage?" suggested Jaspar.

Aurum stepped in front of the kneeling Masters. "The injury is forgotten, Lord Legate. We desire to take counsel with you that we might leave as swiftly as we have come."

"You are kind to condescend, Great Lord, but still—"

"Believe me, there is no ill feeling. Dispense with this speech that we might repair to the privacy of your halls." Aurum swept round and billowed up the stairway like a cloud of smoke.

Halfway up the stairs to the window that lit the cave of his hall, the Legate turned off onto a platform. Carnelian stopped where he was and looked back down the avalanche of steps. The door they had entered through was remote. All around him giants in the walls pushed out through veiling rock. Their vague faces frowned into the airy spaces above his head. He was beneath their notice.

He had to squint to look up the steps to where his father and the other Masters were still climbing toward the window. Against that slab of burning sky they were drawn as quivering charcoal strokes. Bronze urns taller than men squatted up the edges of the stairway. Platforms recessed here and there into the steps. The Legate stood on the nearest one of these. Smaller creatures perched around him were taking his helm apart one gleaming piece at a time. Carnelian watched as each was laid carefully on its stand. When the Legate's head was naked save for his mask, he dismissed his servants. Watching them fan out across the steps as they went down, Carnelian saw a figure coming slowly up through them. Though it wore a mask, it did not have the appearance of a Master. The silver mask snared a curve of light so that it appeared to be smiling.

A swelling of attar of lilies warned Carnelian that the Legate was there beside him.

"Great One, shall we join the others?"

Carnelian stared at the Legate's tiny head. He was wondering if this was an affliction peculiar to the Lesser Chosen when he realized it was an illusion caused by the contrast with the massive armor. He remembered to jerk a nod and side by side they began to climb, ahead of the silver mask.

The window widened until Carnelian could not see its edges and he felt that he was climbing into the heavens. He stumbled when his foot tried to find a final step. Shapes crowding the platform moved and Carnelian assumed from their size that they were the other Masters. He moved to one side of them and turned his back on the window, hoping to lose his near-blindness.

He watched the Legate move aside to reveal the creature standing behind him on the last step. Its mask was reflecting a fragment of the ochre sky. It made the prostration and when it rose Carnelian saw that it had unmasked to reveal a yellow marumaga face, spotted and striped all over with the dots and bars of numbers. The man's eyes were like glass. He lifted a hand with fingers splayed. Four fingers, the center one removed so that the hand naturally formed the sign of the horns.

"Seraphim," he said in Quya.

There was a swish of cloth. The Masters around Carnelian were making the sign. Self-consciously, he followed them.

The Legate came to stand beside the throne that piled up from the center of the platform. "Great Ones, I had begun to fear your blood mingled with the winter sea."

"Burning blood is not so easily quenched," Vennel said severely.

The Legate made a sign of apology. "I meant no offense, Great One."

The Legate watched as Vennel's mask turned away. His hand flattened and he looked round at the Masters. "There are more of the Great Ones than there were."

Carnelian saw his father step forward. "I am Suth, returning to the Three Lands."

The Legate made an uncertain bow. "They have yearned for your return, Great Lord."

"Before we conclave, Lord Legate, I should tell you that it became necessary to destroy some of the crew of your baran."

The Legate shrugged.

"The captain too was slain."

Carnelian looked at his father, thinking that he had made an error. Then he recalled the captain's looks of horror and that the man had seen his naked face, and his hands glued together as if they were still covered with blood.

The Legate lifted his hand, *So be it.* "Captains are more difficult to replace . . . the training, you see, Great Lord? But perhaps the Great Ones might allow me to turn to more important matters. I have here a communication come from Osrakum that has been in my hand for nigh on twenty days."

"I had expected this," said Aurum.

The Legate held out a long folded parchment bearing a square seal larger than his fist.

Aurum began to move forward, his hand outstretched but Suth lifted his own hand on which something blinked red. Aurum nodded as he retreated and Suth took the letter from the Legate's hand. He angled it to examine the seal in the light, then snapped it open. He unfolded the first panel, read it, then moved on to the second. Carnelian could see there were many panels and he caught glimpses of the glyphs that were pressed like butterflies between the pages. He wearied of waiting. The other Masters were statues. The only movement came from the yellow man who had still not come fully up onto the platform. Carnelian peered at his costume. He realized that it was not black as he had imagined, but a thick purple whirling brocade eyed here and there with bone buttons. There were spirals in the precious purple samite, the spirals of ammonite shells. From his belt hung several strings of many-colored beads. Carnelian regarded the yellow man with renewed interest, wondering if this could be one of the Wise.

"Quaestor?" said Suth.

"Seraph," answered the yellow man.

Carnelian turned. His father was holding up his hand. A bloody eye wounded his palm: a ruby thrusting down from a ring he wore on his middle finger.

"I who am He-who-goes-before make declaration that this letter concerns a private proceeding of the Clave."

The quaestor's eyes fixed birdlike on the ruby. "Does the Seraph invoke the Privilege of the Three Powers?"

"I do."

The quaestor frowned but resumed his silver mask and, bowing almost to the floor, turned and disappeared down the stairway.

The Masters began to unmask and Carnelian followed their example. He was surprised that the Legate's face had the same luminous beauty as the other Masters. He could easily have passed for one of the Great.

Suth held up the letter. "This contains matter pertinent to our mission, my Lords." He turned to the Legate. "Lord Legate, the Great require your assistance. The God Emperor lies dying, and—"

Vennel gaped at Suth. "Have you taken leave of your senses, my Lord?"

Suth turned toward him and his brow wrinkled.

"Have you forgotten, Lord Suth, that it is utterly forbidden by Law to speak of this to any outside Osrakum?"

Suth looked almost amused for a moment. "It is you, my Lord, who forget. Am I not become He-who-goes-before? When I speak, the voice may be mine but my words are the Clave's. Hear them now when I say that it would be foolish to underestimate the Legate. Did he not himself witness you coming down to the sea? What I have revealed, the Legate already knew."

Carnelian watched his father lock eyes with the Legate. His father waited for the startled man to give a slight nod before returning his gaze to Vennel.

"Is it not more prudent, my Lord, that we should take him into our confidence than that we should make vain denial? My presence alone would serve to confirm his conjectures." Suth looked at the Legate, who now hid behind a hand shaping the sign for grief. "My Lord, you have the confidence of the Clave, and it shall owe you blood debt for your discretion and for any aid that you might be called upon to give us. Rest assured that this in no way compromises your service to the House of the Masks."

"Even He-who-goes-before must obey the Law," said Vennel.

Suth did not turn. "Lord Vennel, the Law's intention was to avoid disturbance in the Commonwealth."

"And to avoid the legates being tempted to use their legions against the Three Powers."

Carnelian, who had always feared the look his father's face now wore, watched it wither Vennel.

"Does my Lord fear that my Lord Legate would sail his barans against Osrakum?"

Vennel's face deadened as he retired somewhere behind its icy surface. Carnelian fought his desire to smile.

His father lifted the letter again. "The Wise have made the Clave send this to warn us that a rumor is abroad."

Aurum stepped forward. "A rumor?"

"It has been noted that several Lords of the Great have gone down to the sea. It is said that they seek the return of the Ruling Lord of House Suth. Further, it is said that this Lord is being recalled to oversee a sacred election. The Wise command that we do all we can to avoid giving credence to this dangerous rumor."

Vennel gave a snort to which Carnelian could see only the Legate pay any attention.

"This should come as no surprise," said Jaspar. "Even though we came here with no banners the faces of our slaves proclaimed who we were. Even the mind of a barbarian would surmise that three Lords of the Great would not come out of Osrakum and down to the sea on trivial errand. Many of the Lesser Chosen know that the Ruling Lord Suth had gone beyond the sea. For some time it has been common knowledge that the God Emperor was ailing. Taken together, these would form a singular coincidence."

"Then we cannot return upon the leftway," said Aurum.

Carnelian watched the Legate's pale eyes linger on Jaspar before passing raven-sharp to his father's face.

Vennel looked incredulous. "Surely you do not suggest, my Lord, that we forgo the leftway to travel on the *road*?"

Jaspar pretended to be intent on adjusting his blood-ring. "Without banners to open up a way through the throng there certainly will be no making haste."

"Besides, how could we hope to hide ourselves?" said Vennel.

Aurum threw up his hands. "What else would you have us do, my Lords? Should we instead defy the Wise and imperil the Commonwealth?"

Carnelian watched the Legate turn his ivory head to look out through the window. The ochre sky looked painted. The sun's brass still crowned the towers of the town and ran a burning band round the edge of the further cliff.

The Legate turned back. "Perhaps the Great Ones might allow me to lend them my banners."

"You presume too much, Legate," said Vennel. "You dare suggest that a Ruling Lord of the Great should so demean his blood as to use the banners of one of the Lesser Chosen?"

Aurum fixed Vennel with a baleful eye. "This is no time for blood pride, my Lord. Have I to remind you once more of what is at stake? Pomp will be fatal to our mission: the lack of it, to our speed. If we take the leftway as ourselves all the world will soon know what transpires in Osrakum. Only under the banners of another might we hope to pass unnoticed."

"If the Great Ones might allow me to interject . . . ?" said the Legate, making vague gestures of apology.

Suth asked for his words with his hand.

"I intended to lend the Great Ones the banners of my *state*."

"And your ciphers?" asked Suth.

"Indeed, Great Lord, those would be essential. The Great Ones would maintain their anonymity if they were carried in palanquins. Then they could use the leftway. My duties oftentimes take me inland into the heart of the Naralan, as far as the city of Maga-Naralante, so such a party would excite little notice or question. Beyond Maga-Naralante"— he lowered his head—"matters might be more difficult."

Suth nodded and looked at the other Masters. "I find this idea to have merit."

Vennel's face was blank. "Will My-Lord-who-goes-before accept the responsibility for such an action before the Wise?"

"He will," said Suth.

"Very well. I shall bow to your will expressed. Now I shall retire. My Lords." He gave a curt bow, slipped his mask elegantly over his face, then turned to go down the steps. Carnelian watched him sink into the edge of the platform.

The Legate moved quickly to the top of the stairs and called after Vennel, "Any slave you find beyond the door, Great One, will be able to guide you to your chambers."

"You should go too, Carnelian," said Suth, "to make sure

the household is set in order for my coming."

Carnelian stood looking at him, resenting the dismissal, but he could think of no way to avoid complying.

"As my Lord commands," he said and put on his mask.

From the brink of the platform the steps looked perilously steep. He gazed out across the cavernous space. He could see the raised walkways that led to the door, and the audience pits on either side. He began descending.

When he reached the foot of the stairway he looked back up but he could see nothing of the Masters; only the glow from the window. The murmur of their talk was like the rumble of a distant storm.

Up ahead, Vennel was passing under a tower lantern. Carnelian began to follow him along the walkway on the journey to the door.

In token of his deafening, the slave's ears had been shorn off. The Legate's cipher, a sheaf of reeds, had been cut into the man's face and traditional tattoo-blue had been used to fill the scar channels. He had been loitering with others beyond the door. Carnelian had to show him the chameleon glyphs on the lining of his sleeve to indicate where he wanted to go. The slave's eyes flickered in the swathe of blue stain as they followed Carnelian's hand-speech. He must have understood for he lit a lantern and, cringing, beckoned Carnelian to follow him into the darkness.

Carnelian followed the small figure through a bewildering series of chambers whose frescoed walls gleamed faintly in the dark. After much walking they came to a hall into which fell shafts of red light regularly spaced off into the distance. Along the left-hand wall Carnelian could just see the archways staring blindly with their Lordly warding eyes. Within the nearest archway was a stone door, bronze-riveted, with niches empty on either side, presumably for guardsmen.

Accompanied by echoes, they walked past several more such doors until they came to one where the crescents of Vennel's banners told of his presence within. Some men came out from the niches with their sickles. The cipher gashed across their faces made them seem in awful mirth but their real mouths gave a different impression. Carnelian rushed by, even as they began prostrations, relieved to see his own House colors further down the hall.

"Master," came a cry of relief from up ahead. Then figures came rushing at him, dappled red, their faces only becoming familiar in the light of the slave's lantern. His men surrounded him, bobbing, touching the hem of his cloak. They spoke all at once and grinned and frowned alternately.

"Be quiet," said Carnelian. "Come on, quieten down. Do you want to embarrass me?"

The life went right out of them. They became so still, it alarmed him. The Legate's slave was gaping slack-eyed. He dismissed him before turning to his men. "Don't worry, I'm not angry." Their shoulders had a subservient hunching he did not like. "Let's get indoors."

They led him off to an arch and wrestled its door open. Some light spilled through, and something of the familiar smell of home. More of his people shuffled out to welcome him. Carnelian spotted Crail there among them, squinting, searching for something. When their eyes met, the old man's face crumpled into a crooked frown. Carnelian dropped his mask into his hand and glared at him.

"You were told to stay hidden. Out of harm's way."

The man scowled at him and Carnelian laughed. He took the old man's head between his hands and kissed it. There was a murmur of approval. The old man's smell was so familiar he wanted to hug him. Instead, he pushed him gently away.

He noticed Keal standing behind the others, trying to hide uncertainty, and gave him a smile. "Glad to see that you survived."

Keal rewarded him with a grin. "Many times I was sure we'd sink."

There were mutters of assent.

"In the future, let's try and avoid the sea," Carnelian said. Many of them beamed and nodded.

Keal pushed his way through. "The Master?"

"He'll be here soon and sent me ahead. Is everything ready?"

Keal grinned again, pointed at the wards on the arch. "These are proper Masters' rooms." He reached out to caress his hand up the jamb, and Carnelian saw where the veined marble had been clumsily painted with the chameleon glyph. "I did it myself."

"Neatly done," said Carnelian, wanting to be kind. He warmed when the other flushed with pride.

Keal indicated the banners, somewhat crumpled from the journey, their poles locked into bronze rings near the door. He reached out tentatively, took Carnelian's arm and drew him through the arch.

The people inside looked at Carnelian as if he were a fire in winter. Braziers had been lit. The balms the Master preferred were spiraling perfumed smoke up into the vault. Chameleoned blue canopies had been hung up to muffle the echoes. Mosaics had been polished. From somewhere they had managed to get bunches of irises and had sunk their purples and blues in vases of gold.

"It feels like home," said Carnelian loudly, meaning it, enjoying their smiles. He turned to Keal. "Where's Tain?"

"He's coming up with the rest of the baggage."

Carnelian nodded. "Have I a room of my own?"

"Certainly you have, Carnie. I'll show you where it is."

Keal left him. Malachite patterned the walls with the green of ferns in a dark wood. Smooth doors whispered open with a cinnamon waft. There were several chambers. One had a window paned with alabaster that softly lit a sleeping platform draped with feather blankets. In another, water ran waist-high in a channel from which various sinks could be filled. In that chamber the floor was incised with runnels.

Back in the sleeping chamber, Carnelian discovered shutters and folded them back. Warm green-scented air seeped in. The purple orange-veined sky made his eyes water. He fitted his face into his mask and stepped out onto the balcony. The balustrade was still warm but he dropped the mask when he found that the balcony was deep in shadow. It was an eyrie looking south. Half in shadow, the valley he had seen from the sea stepped its green terraces down from blue distance. Nearer, limes faded into dusty brown. Nearer still, a swathe of mudflats ran to a crisp edge of indigo sea. A causeway curved like the wingbone of a bird crossed the lagoon and wound the road it carried up into the terraces. Here it was already spring.

A sound from the chamber made him go back in to find Tain standing by the door, panting, leaning back under the weight of a trunk his arms barely managed to embrace. Ointment boxes hung from cords around his neck. Clothes tubes were strapped to his back like quivers. He gave a thin smile, then looked alarmed, bent sharply over as a tube slipped from his shoulder. He managed to catch its strap in the hook of his elbow as Carnelian rushed forward.

"Let me take some of those. Couldn't you have asked for some help?"

"I didn't want any."

Together they wrestled everything to the floor, then stood not looking at each other.

"Isn't this place enormous?" said Carnelian, trying to make conversation.

"Too big," his brother muttered.

Carnelian nodded. "There would be room enough in just these apartments for much of the household."

That was a mistake. Thoughts of the Hold soaked them both in misery.

Carnelian punched his brother's arm. "Come on, I want to wash." Tain started rummaging amongst the stuff on the floor. "What're you doing?"

"Finding the pads."

"There's no need for those," said Carnelian and began throwing off his clothes. Tain came to help but he pushed him away. "I'll undress myself. The way you smell you'd better strip as well."

Tain looked puzzled but did as he was told.

Carnelian's painted skin was moldering like old white-wash. He pulled the Little Mother amulet over his head, coiled the strap and put her down carefully. Then he went into the chamber he had seen earlier with its channel of water, Tain following with awkward steps.

With some experimenting and many accidents, Carnelian found out how to operate the various little bronze sluices. Soon he had created a number of criss-crossing waterfalls. Tain gaped. Carnelian crept behind him and shoved him in. Soon they were splashing round, screaming with the cold, letting the water spin rivulets through their hair. Both played with the sluices, pushing each other into any new deluge that erupted from above. They marveled at the way the runnels in the floor kept the surface underfoot free from puddling. Tain rubbed the paint from Carnelian's skin. When they were both shivering clean, he ran out and found towels. While he waited, Carnelian turned all the water flow back into the channel running along the wall. When Tain came up to dry him, Carnelian asked him to shave his head.

"Like the Master?"

"Like the Master."

"But what if I cut you?"

"Well then, do it carefully."

Carnelian knelt while Tain first cut his hair almost to the roots with a knife and then scraped his scalp with a copper razor. Carnelian watched his brother working, his tongue held between his teeth. "How are our people?"

Tain stopped, brushed a lock of black hair onto the floor, then gave him a sidelong glance. "They're afraid."

"Of what?"

"What's going to happen. And . . ."

Carnelian waited, looking down and playing with the hair that lay everywhere on the floor. He wanted to make it easy for Tain to say anything he wanted.

"The killings . . . the killings on the boat. Everyone's rattled."

"You as well?"

"What do you think?"

Carnelian relived the horror in his mind. The boy saw him grow pale and began nibbling the edge of his hand. "It was my fault, Tain."

"Maybe so. But there's other stuff. On the ship the lads heard things, sounds coming from the other cabins."

"What sort of sounds?"

Tain's face creased up. "Punishment sounds . . . other things . . . they're . . . we're afraid of the other Masters. And the Master, our Master, he's been behaving very strangely. The lads have even grown a little afraid of him."

Carnelian felt a twinge of anger that they should dare judge his father. "What can I do?"

"Keep an eye on them. You know they only live to serve you and the Master?"

The pleading in Tain's eyes melted Carnelian's anger. "I know they do. Tell them that I'll do all I can."

Tain beamed. "I told them you would, Carnie." He made to kiss his hand, but Carnelian grabbed him instead and gave him a hug. They let go of each other.

"Now get on with my head."

They stood together on the balcony watching the sparks light up in the black valley all the way up the road. "Like a river of stars," said Tain in wonder. He turned to Carnelian. "Did you see the Master of this place, Carnie?"

"Yes."

"Does he have a legion?"

"I'm not sure. Perhaps . . ."

Tain's eyes opened very wide. He reached out to touch Carnelian's arm. "Do you think there are dragons here?"

Carnelian shrugged. "I don't know." It made him wonder himself.

Tain went inside and drew back the feathered blankets to sprinkle perfume on the linen sheets. Then he took a blanket and began to make himself a bed with it on the floor. Carnelian told him he could sleep with him in the bed. "The floor's of stone. You'll have frozen to death by the morning and then what use will you be?"

In the darkness Carnelian nestled into his brother's warm back. He could feel the bumps down his spine. They had not slept in the same bed since they were infants.

"Do you think we'll see dragons?" whispered Tain.

"I'm sure we will," Carnelian replied. "Now go to sleep."

RANGA SHOES

The Chosen shall not set foot on earth, nor stone, nor any other ground outside Osrakum that has not first been purified in the manner prescribed.

—EXTRACT FROM THE LAW-THAT-
MUST-BE-OBEYED

Carnelian woke and had no idea where he was.

"The Master has sent for you."

It was Tain with an intense dark gaze. Carnelian sat up and swung his feet onto the floor. He rubbed his face, knuckled his gummy eyes, then stood up shakily. He lifted his arms away from his body and screwed up his face in anticipation of the cold touch of the pad.

Tain pushed Carnelian's arms down gently. "I was told not to clean you."

"Sorry?"

"You are to go as you are."

Carnelian stared at his brother, confused.

Tain chuckled. "Well, not *exactly* as you are. You're to wear this." His chin nudged a black garment draped between his outstretched arms.

Carnelian bent forward to allow Tain to feed it over his arms and head. Tain stroked it smooth then did up its spine of hooks. Carnelian yawned. He ran his palms down over the crusty brocades. "What sort of robe is this?"

Tain shrugged. Annoyance pushed its way through Carnelian's sleepiness. He lifted up some of the black cloth, peered at it, traced its patterns of glassy beads with a finger. He felt they must have some meaning but he had no idea what. He shook his head and let the cloth drop.

Tain led him out from his chambers. Carnelian felt unwashed, naked without his paint as he walked out into the great hall where the blue canopies were billowing. Doors were open, leading off in a long succession to the predawn sky. His people were face down on the mosaic. Tain joined them there. A door hissed open with an exhalation of lily. His father appeared, narrow, tall, his face fearfully white, clad in an identical black robe. Someone with eyes averted handed his father his mask and he hid his face like the moon behind a golden cloud.

"See," his father commanded.

Their people looked up and then rose to their knees. Keal and the other guardsmen began rising to their feet.

We go alone, his father signed, using the Lordly "we." He paced toward the outer door. Carnelian fell in behind him, scratching an itch on his head, startled when he touched stubbled scalp. He had forgotten the shaving. The hard edge of his mask pushed into his hand. He smiled his gratitude at Tain, put it on, then followed his father's back, watching the black samite bunch and loosen with each step. The doors rumbled open and they passed into the gloomy hall beyond.

They walked down the center of the hall. At the end was a tall door, before which flames leaping in braziers were the only guards. Silver ammonite shells embossed the door like startled eyes.

"My Lord, why would the legates use their legions against Osrakum?" asked Carnelian, feeling the need to almost whisper.

His father did not turn his head but kept his eyes fixed upon the door. "The legates and the commanders under them are all, naturally, of the Lesser Chosen. The God Emperor appoints them all and thus they serve the House of the Masks. It is their only source of wealth."

"Because they are excluded from the division of the flesh tithe as well as the taxes from the cities?" said Carnelian.

His father nodded. "Although they form no part of the Balance of the Powers, they hold in their hands almost all the military might of the Commonwealth."

"And it is feared that they will take with force what the Three Powers would keep wholly for themselves?"

They had reached the door. Flames flapped like hands in spasm. Carnelian glanced up. Flickers of their light were trapped in each tarnished spiral.

"Quite so. We have taken many precautions against them, chief of these being that we hold all they possess and care for within the Sacred Wall of Osrakum."

"But if they have the legions . . . ?"

"The Great have the double-strength legion, the Ichorian, and with this we hold the Three Gates into Osrakum."

"Would it not be safer to include the Lesser Chosen within the franchise of the Great?"

His father looked down at him. "Then the legions would be ours and the Balance would be broken."

"Could legates not be appointed from the House of the Masks itself?"

"No one of the Imperial Power can ever be permitted even to cross the Skymere to its outer shore. If ever that happened, and they managed to escape Osrakum, they could use the legions to overthrow us and again the Balance would be broken."

Carnelian gaped. "What you are saying, Father, is that

those of the House of the Masks are prisoners of the Great."

His father was eyeing the gloomy length of the hall. "Say, rather, hostages."

"The Great hold the God Emperor Themselves hostage?"

"As They in turn use their legions to hold us hostage in Osrakum. That is the Balance."

"And how do the Wise form part of this Balance?"

"They are the Law made flesh. Inside Osrakum they constrain the freedoms of all the Chosen. Outside, they maintain the roads with their watchtowers and the leftways with their couriers. Though blind, there is nothing in the Three Lands they do not see. Additionally, it is their ammonites that form a seal across the Three Gates. They keep the inner and the outer worlds apart and form the only bridge across the divide. It is only at their sufferance that we ourselves are permitted to be here, outside Osrakum."

"The Balance must restrict their power?"

"In terrible ways, but essentially the God Emperor's guardsmen, the Sinistral Ichorians, hold them hostage."

"And we, in turn, hold them all hostage."

"Rings, within rings, like the ripples on a pond."

"Moving outward from the God Emperor, a leaf dropped from the sky."

"Just so."

"Father, are these quaestors then the Wise?"

His father's hand flicked a dismissive gesture. "Of the Wise, Carnelian, but not a Sapient. Surely, if you noticed nothing else, you could see the quaestor still had eyes?"

"Of course . . . I was careless. What manner of . . . ?"

"An ammonite, but also a failed candidate for the Wise, though he came so close that I marvel that he kept his eyes. I was not able to examine his face fully but it seemed to me that he had passed many of the higher examinations."

"The numbers?"

"Their positions relate to the different lores, levels, domains."

"And what is the Privilege of the Three Powers?"

"It is a law that allows each Power the right to exclude

either or both of the other two from any matter that it considers internal to its affairs, unless this exclusion should be precluded by another law of higher rank."

"And so you included the Legate as the representative of the God Emperor while excluding the quaestor who is a representative of the Wise because you intended to overrule a law?"

Suth made a gesture of impatience. "You ask too many questions, my Lord."

"Knowledge is the best armor," said Carnelian with a flush of anger.

Suth looked down at his son, recognizing his own words. "There is something I must tell you."

The tone of his father's voice made Carnelian's stomach clench. At that moment there was an echoing sound of doors closing. Father and son turned to look down the hall and saw that the other Masters were walking toward them, hands and feet as pale as the dead. Three of them, shrouded in the same black robes, coming as for an entombing.

"What did you want to tell me, Father?" whispered Carnelian anxiously.

Not now, his father signed.

Carnelian was forced to stand silent at his father's side as they watched the Masters approach. When Aurum moved out in front of the others, Carnelian and his father made way for him. The old Master moved between them to strike the door. Each blow was answered by a deep vibration. "We are come because the Law must be obeyed," boomed Aurum.

Exhaling camphor, the door sighed open just a body width. One by one they rustled through the gap. A vaporing milky pool lay on the other side. Carnelian watched his father wade through, the hem of his black robe floating round him like a slick of oil. Already past the white lip of the pool, Aurum was moving off, leaving a glistening track.

Vapors spread chill up into Carnelian's nose. He lowered his right foot into the liquid. Biting cold washed over it. He put in the left foot, then he dragged his train across. As he splashed out the other side, he saw that his father ahead of him was using his hands to talk with Jaspar. Carnelian turned to see Vennel crossing, his narrow hands hitching up the skirt of his robe, revealing long marble legs, so white they made the pool look yellow.

Tall bronze lamps lit benches of stone, upon one of which Aurum had sat down. Sallow creatures appeared and fussed round him. Carnelian found a place beside his father. As he pulled up his soak-heavy robe it gave off a reek of camphor. Jaspar and Vennel were settling on other benches.

"You who are Chosen shall now make ready to leave this place." The words were spoken in Quya but did not have the rich timbre of a Master's voice. Carnelian located their source to be the quaestor in his purple samite. His face of polished silver had a mouth but only solid spirals for eyes. In his hands he held a cord like a bead necklace.

"You who are Chosen must take all precaution before crossing the Naralan and the Guarded Land," said the quaestor, counting the beads through his fingers as if he were using them for prayer.

The other Masters answered him, "As it has been done, so shall it be done, for ever, because it is commanded to be done by the Law-that-must-be-obeyed."

"The covenant you made with Him, the Dark One honors. In the hidden land of Osrakum He will not incarnate though His anima share the inhabiting of the God Emperor with His Brother. Beyond the Sacred Wall, all other earth unto the sea He has soaked with pestilence and plague. In these His domains you shall walk under the restriction of His Law as your fathers have done before you. This is His Law as it has been written in the Plain of Thrones."

Carnelian felt his father's warm hand stray over his own.

"The Chosen shall not stand within two fingers' breadth of unhallowed ground," chanted the quaestor.

All the Masters made the same response as before and Carnelian mumbled along with them. He turned his hand palm up to grasp his father's as one of the slaves, all bones and tallow skin, came to kneel before him holding a casket. Another gaunt slave leaned over to open it, her torso a basket of ribs. In place of an ear a snagging hook-rimmed mechanism of brass. She drew out the ranga shoes and placed them in Carnelian's lap with more care than if they had been painted with poison. Each was of wood lacquered black: a long and narrow platform for the foot, securing straps and, set transversally on its underside, three supports a few fingers' width deep—one painted black, one red, one green, presumably in token of the Three Lands.

"My shoes have been tampered with," said Vennel sharply.

Carnelian looked up. His father and the other Masters had also been given shoes. All had turned toward Vennel.

The Master held up a shoe. "The supports have been trimmed." He displayed it for all to see.

"The modification was carried out at my command," said Aurum.

"One cannot—"

"The full height would encumber us on our journey, my Lord. Quaestor, do they still meet the requirement of the Law?"

"They do, Seraph," said the silver mask.

Aurum turned back to Vennel. "Might we be allowed to proceed?"

Vennel made an affirmative gesture shaded with anger.

Carnelian felt his father's hand moving in his own. It escaped to sign, *Copy me*.

Carnelian watched his father search the hem of his robe. When he found a single embroidered glyph he pinched it up. A slave offered him a jar. With his free hand he broke its seal, ran the robe glyph round inside, then began to carefully anoint one of the shoes upon his lap with the pungent wax.

Carnelian found that his robe had the same glyph. Peering at it he saw that it was the double-ring annulus for death. He buried his unease and did everything that he had seen his father do. Several times as he anointed his shoe, he looked up to find the eyeslits of his father's mask angled toward him. A nod came from it when Carnelian was finished.

"The Chosen shall not breathe unhallowed air," the quaestor said.

The Masters gave the response.

Slaves with strange bright eyes came cradling bowls. They took tiny steps, afraid of spilling what they carried. As one came closer Carnelian saw fumes curling up from the bowl. He saw also the spiraled plaques that served the slave for eyes.

His father nudged him. Carnelian turned to see him laying his mask face down along the hollow between his thighs. His father then reached out, took one of the linen pads draped over the rim of the bowl, dipped it into the vaporous liquid, and pressing it over the nostril holes of the mask, he swiveled some little flanges to hold it in place.

Carnelian began the procedure. As he leaned forward the vapor from the bowl stung his eyes. He dipped a pad, squeezed it, poked it into his mask still smoking, then secured it with the flanges.

"It will protect you from the plague," his father's voice rustled in his ear.

Then the quaestor spoke one more time. "The Chosen shall not be touched by unhallowed light even unto the skin of the smallest finger." His hands dropped, the cord dangling in the left one.

At that signal, Aurum rose up to all his imposing height holding his mask in one hand, his ranga shoes in the other. Walking off toward an archway, he disappeared through it.

They waited. A blinded slave appeared in the archway. He looked small, fragile. Carnelian felt his father getting up. He watched his hand dart, *As the youngest, you must follow last.* Then he too crossed the chamber to the waiting arch.

So it was that one by one the Masters were swallowed by the arch until Carnelian was left alone with the quaestor and his spiral eyes. He averted his face from the fumes rising from his mask and looked at the quaestor uneasily. The man did not seem alive.

A muttering came from beyond the arch and Carnelian saw

the slave was there. He rose, walked to the arch and, after a moment's hesitation, passed under it.

Almost night. Vague sinuous movements like windows reflecting on dark water. Nudges guided Carnelian through the gloom. Fingers plucked at the hooks down his back and then his robe brushed away leaving him naked. Shapes solidified into men: yellow men, with dark whiteless eyes. Carnelian swallowed past the dry lump in his throat knowing he was wholly in their hands.

His fingers were prised open and his shoes and mask removed. He shuddered at the first cold touch on his arm. A melting snowflake. Then another and another, until he was the center of a blizzard of menthol swabbing.

Cool hands lifted one of his feet. He felt the wetness lick between his toes. Then it oozed along the sole. A hand cupped his heel and guided his foot down. Before it reached the floor it hit something solid. One of the ranga shoes. When the other foot was cleansed Carnelian climbed onto the second shoe.

He noticed the depression in the brass wall. It was as if a stiff-limbed man had detached from the wall, leaving behind his impression in the metal. The concave surfaces within this mold were ridged and whorled like fingertips. As he watched, one of the black-eyed men reached into the shoulder of the mold and, running his fingers delicately round the hollow, came back and transferred its designs to Carnelian's own shoulder. He squirmed at the tickle touch of the stylus. Others were reading the mold. Soon, ink was itching over every part of Carnelian's skin until only his face was left blank.

"That His servants might pass you by," one whispered.

They glazed him with sickly myrrh.

"That His breath might not corrupt your flesh."

Cloth bands darted through the air and spooled around his body.

"That His servants might be confounded."

The bandages stuck to the glaze as they wove into a tightening cocoon.

"That they might be lost in this labyrinth."

He grimaced as a bandage bound something hard and cold against his skin.

"Charms to shield you from their malice."

So it went on. He was the axis of their strange dance. Round and round they went, their whispers in his ears, until he dizzied and almost swooned.

When they stopped turning he fought the tightness round his chest and shoulder to raise his arms. His hands were there at the end of cloth wrists. He let them fall and sighed with relief as the pressure released.

A huge robe flapped over him.

"That they might be blinded by the night."

Hands flitted over the robe until it was hugging him. They shut him in behind his mask. His nostrils burned, then his lungs. His eyes watered. He did not even try to move until the burning had abated. Then he tottered out of the brass chamber by a doorway that appeared as a fuzzy glowing rectangle.

"Here you are permitted to remove your mask," his father said.

Carnelian did so with some relief. His eyes still watered and he was sniffing.

His father put a hand on his shoulder. Its whiteness was spotted with symbols. "The astringency will soon diminish, then you will bear it easily enough."

"And the tightness?"

"The bandages will stretch."

Carnelian heard Aurum say something about an "imminent departure."

Carnelian grimaced through his tears. "The Three Lands at last."

His father smiled grimly. "The Three Lands."

"I must make sure our people are ready: Keal, the tyadra,

the baggage. How much time is there, my Lord, before we all leave?"

His father's hand jabbed a sharp negation. "Surely you had understood that they are not to come with us?"

"My Lord?"

"They are an encumbrance we cannot risk. Their faces proclaim who we are."

Carnelian felt sick. "But I gave assurances."

His father's eyes narrowed. "Which you should not have given."

Carnelian opened his mouth to say more.

His father's hand flew up, *Enough!* "Whatever it is that you have said, it is my will to overrule. You may take Tain because he does not yet bear our mark. What little state you are allowed, he will keep."

"Will he be safe?"

His father looked at him, puzzled. "What?" His hand made a vague gesture. "As safe as you or I."

Jaspar came toward them, his ranga and bandaged legs lending him the gait of someone wading through water. He pursed his lips. "One fears this journey is destined to be exceedingly tedious."

Vennel raised his voice behind them. All four Masters turned to listen to him. "I shall go to make sure my household have made the preparations I commanded."

"There is no time for that, my Lord," Aurum said quickly.

Jaspar moved off toward them. "We must hold a conclave ere we leave this tower, Vennel."

As Suth turned to join them, Carnelian reached up to touch his arm. His father turned back. "What is it?"

Carnelian could see the irritation in his face. "Might I be permitted enough time to return to the household to bid them all farewell?"

His father frowned.

"And to ensure all arrangements properly made?" Carnelian added.

The other Masters were now involved in some kind of argument.

"If you must," his father snapped. "But do not dally. A guide will be there to bring our baggage to the gate. Let him lead you. I shall be going there immediately . . ." He looked over to the others. ". . . with the other Lords."

Carnelian walked as quickly as his ranga shoes would allow. Each step clattered echoes round the hall. When he reached their door the banners of House Suth no longer flanked it. He was wondering if he had come to the wrong one when he heard muffled voices. He flung his weight against the door. It gave way slowly, heavily. As he squeezed through the opening he trod on something and bent to pick it up. It was an iris, crushed, its bruised purple skin dusted with its own pollen.

Running up toward him, Tain stopped to look him up and down, no doubt startled by the strange clothes and the ranga shoes. "Thank the Gods you've come, Carnie."

He cast a quick, unhappy look around him. People were wrapping vases in the blue canopies. Someone cried, "The Master." People dropped to the ground. A canopy came loose and wriggled to the floor. Among them a single figure was left standing. It was Keal, his look so intense that Carnelian almost dropped his gaze. He felt shamed.

"You're not going," he said in a thin voice. It was difficult to squeeze the words out; his throat seemed to have narrowed. People were looking up at him from their prostrations. Everywhere he saw their bewildered eyes. Anger surged in him. He lumbered forward and slapped a stack of boxes. They crunched to the floor. A bowl rolled and shattered. "Why are you packing? You must all be stupid. You're not going, I tell you."

"We're being moved into the slave pens," said Keal. "When the arrangements have been made we'll be setting off after you along the road."

Carnelian noticed a man's back wearing the Legate's green. The stranger was the only one still prostrate. "You!" he shouted. The man trembled. "Yes, I'm talking to you."

The man looked up. The Legate's sign marred his face like a birthmark. Carnelian pointed at him. "Get out and wait for me outside." The man stumbled to his feet and cringed past Carnelian, who watched him slip out between the doors before turning back to his people.

Keal's eyes, Tain's eyes, so many eyes.

Carnelian removed his mask and bowed his head a little, giving in to its heaviness. "I did what I could. I can't see what more you could expect of me."

Keal nodded, but did not stop looking at him with pain in his face and something like an accusation of betrayal.

"Crail's gone," said Tain.

Carnelian turned on him. "What do you mean he's gone?"

"The Master left a command that we were to hand him over to the other Master's men. The ones with the tattoo," said Keal, running his finger from his forehead down the bridge of his nose to his lips.

Blood drained from Carnelian's face. His father had given Crail to Aurum. "When?"

"They came for him just after you left with the Master."

Carnelian stared blindly, chewed at his lower lip. "Maybe it's not too late," he muttered. He strode over to Keal. A pain of love passed between them. They embraced hard. "Look after them, brother," said Carnelian.

He felt Keal's nod against his chest. He disengaged, making sure he did not look into his face. Sniffing, he turned to the others, all standing now. "Don't fear that I'll forget you. Take care on the road. I'll be waiting to welcome you to our coomb in the Mountain."

He looked at Tain and saw he was struggling to hold back tears. Carnelian made his decision. "You're staying here."

Tain looked appalled. "But I'm supposed to go with you."

Carnelian shook his head. "It'll be too dangerous."

"Who's going to take care of you?"

Keal wiped his eyes and pointed toward a heap of carefully bound parcels. "Everything's ready. It would take ages to separate his things from yours."

Tain looked at Keal gratefully.

"He'll look after you for us," said Keal and there were several nods behind him.

Carnelian saw the tearful determination in their faces. "I've no time for this. Tain, come if you must."

As Tain scooped up the parcels, another boy that Carnelian did not know helped him. His face also was unmarked. Tain caught his brother looking at the boy. "He's new."

"For the Master's care?" Carnelian asked.

"Bought locally."

"Come on, then. Take one of those lanterns. We must hurry if we're going to have any chance to save Crail."

Once through the door, Carnelian tried to move fast, but the ranga resisted his efforts. He tripped and almost fell. He stopped to calm himself. The others stood nearby gaping at him. Carnelian bent down and undid the straps of the shoes. He stepped down off them, picked them up, then lurched off with long strides. Even through the bandages he could feel the cold stone of the floor. The hall echoed with the irregular footfalls the others made as they struggled to keep up with him.

When they had passed the door of the silver ammonites, Carnelian found three archways to choose from. He swung round to find the guide. The man was some way back, flustered, panting. His lantern wobbled its light across the floor and up and down the columns. Carnelian went back, tore it from his hand, then grabbed some of Tain's burden. He ignored his brother's protests at the impropriety and took some more boxes from the new boy, who stared with wide-eyed disbelief at the strange young Master.

Carnelian turned to the guide. "Which way?"

The guide pointed at one of the archways and Carnelian plunged into it.

Passages, gates, Carnelian blazed a trail for them through the blackness. It seemed a long time until they reached the stairway. The portcullis that led to it was raised. Above them its toothed edge just caught the light. Carnelian held his lantern up and saw the wide shallow steps going down. Looking back he saw Tain and the others. "I'll go ahead," he cried to them. "You lot follow as fast as you can."

Finding each step was difficult. Carnelian could hardly see them through the eyeslits of his mask. He put the lantern and the shoes down and removed his mask. Carrying it and the boxes in one hand and the lantern and shoes in the other, he raced down, taking the steps two at a time.

He descended flights that were straight and others that curved leftward out of sight. He came to a long landing. The portcullis that controlled access to it was up. His lantern found a grating halfway along the right-hand wall of the landing. It was a gateway closed against him. There was no way of knowing if it was the right one. He put down everything he was carrying and gave the bars a good shake. They hardly moved at all. He punched his fist into his hand. The scuffling sounds the others made came remotely down from the airy dark. He would have to wait for them.

He held his mask in front of his face as Tain appeared followed by the guide and the new boy, both looking scared. Carnelian grabbed one of the portcullis bars. "Here?" he cried.

The guide was breathing heavily. "This . . . this is only . . . the legionary stratum . . . Master. The West Gate lies . . . further down."

Carnelian did not wait to hear more, but was off down the next flight, cursing at the delay.

The stairway widened as he reached another closed gate. He hesitated for a moment. He could hear the noises of Tain and the others following him down. He looked through the grating. He made his decision. On he ran, finding the steps in the swing of lantern light. A glow welled up to meet him. He could hear the distinctive tones of Quya. The voices stilled. He put his mask up and rounded a bend.

Guttering torches revealed a line of guardsmen making a fence with their swords. All their anxious faces were disfigured by the Legate's mark. He walked down to meet them. Their swords and heads fell together. Carnelian looked over them, searching for his father. He spotted the tall shadows standing at the back. One of them came forward, breaking through the guardsmen.

"Carnelian." It opened its cowl to reveal his father's mask. "Hide yourself, boy." He was holding up Carnelian's salt-stained traveling cloak. He tensed. "By the blood, are you actually carrying baggage?" He looked down. "And where are your ranga?"

Carnelian looked at the shoes dangling from his hand on their straps. "To aid my speed."

His father leaned close, pushing the cloak into his hand. "Why do you persist in shaming me?"

Carnelian's cheeks burned as if they had been slapped. He sat down on the steps. His fingers were clumsy doing up the mask bands behind his head and strapping the shoes to his bandaged feet. It seemed to him that he could feel the eyes of all the Masters on him. He stood up on the ranga, threw the cloak around his shoulders, then, shoving his way through the Legate's guardsmen, pushed toward his father. The forbidding shapes of the other Masters loomed around him.

"We had thought you lost," said Jaspar.

"It would appear that we are all lost," said Vennel.

"Nobody is lost, my Lord," snapped Aurum.

"I still cannot understand why we could not bring our slaves to help us on our way," said Vennel. "It is distasteful to have to use another's tyadra, especially when they come from a Lesser—"

"We all feel naked," snapped Suth. "But what use is it standing here on this stairway discussing it? We must press on. Soon it will be dawn."

"One is forced to point out that it is your own son who delays us, my Lord."

Suth ignored him and set off down the stairway at a furious pace. The guardsmen scrambled after him, their torches painting everything with jerking shadow.

Carnelian walked beside his father. Aurum was on his father's other side. He had hoped the old Master would move away from them to allow him to talk freely. They passed under another raised portcullis. He looked round and saw Tain and the others coming into sight. There was no time. Carnelian turned back to his father. "My Lord?"

His father's mask looked sideways at him.

"Your old and trusted servitor, Crail—"

"Has been destroyed," said Aurum in a monotone. "The trauma of the amputations . . ." He waved his hand dismissively.

Carnelian felt a numbing spreading from his stomach. "By whose command was this done?"

"By command of the Law-that-must-be-obeyed and in the manner prescribed," said Aurum.

"You gave Crail over to him, Father?"

"He sinned against the Law. I did try to tell you earlier . . ."

"But . . . but you said . . ." His head was trapped in ice. "If he had to die it should have been with us, in our House, where he served us all the days of his life. We brought him with us to keep him safe." His father's impassive mask exasperated him. "Gods' blood, Father, he was your brother!"

"You stray into impertinence, my Lord."

"All this fuss over what?" said Aurum. "A worthless old drudge. The creature sinned against the Law, against me. You must never forget, my Lord, that the Law must be obeyed."

Carnelian regarded the Master's cowled head with a strange detachment. "But not, it seems, when it comes to our traveling arrangements."

Aurum's mask drew back. He raised his hand in a vague, unreadable but angry sign.

"You will be silent," said Suth in a dangerous tone.

"I will, my Lord," said Carnelian, "for now." His voice vibrated out from the frozen spindle upon which he was impaled. He let his body walk itself down the stairway. His mind was as clear as blue winter sky. What had happened there that day he determined never to forgive nor to forget.

THE
PURPLE
FACTORY

Evocation: What is this path of Law?

Response: It is the tangling labyrinth.

It is the roiling sea.

It is the spiraling shell of the

ammonite.

—PART OF THE RITUAL OF THE

APOTHEOSIS

Remotely, Carnelian felt the tugging on his cloak. It was a while before he reacted. He turned his head. Tain's face was there, anxious-eyed, desperate for some answer. Carnelian stared, not understanding what his brother wanted. Then he understood. Tain could not have comprehended the exchange in Quya. Carnelian moved his head once from side to side. As he watched the tears well up in his brother's eyes he wondered why he himself had none.

* * *

"Masters." The legionary knelt before them, head bowed. Behind him in formal prostration were ranged a number of black-skinned men.

Aurum gave the legionary leave to rise.

The man was tall for a marumaga, almost reaching Aurum's sternum even though the Master was wearing the ranga. His oily black cuirass had the blue wave cipher of his legion embossed on its chest. Typically, he was honey-skinned. "I would beg to know which of you, my Masters, will take possession of these auxiliaries?"

Aurum threw back his cowl to reveal his mask.

The legionary bowed and pushed his arms out, wrists together. As he straightened, he swept his arm round to indicate the prostrate men. "I come to give you these, Master."

"Twenty Marula?"

"Not so many, Master."

"Their collars have been removed?"

"Yes, Master."

Vennel pushed toward Aurum. "Marula? And why have their collars been removed, my Lord?"

"We shall discuss this matter at some more appropriate time, Vennel."

"How shall they be controlled without their collars? The creatures are notoriously feral."

Aurum made a gesture of annoyance. "The matter is well in hand. If my Lord will indulge us with a little patience, I think he will find that the water will soon run clear." He turned back to the legionary who was looking uncertainly from one Master to the other. "Have the creatures been given the treatment specified?"

"They have, Master." The legionary snapped his fingers. One of the shadow men rose up, black as wood, gleaming, finely made. He stepped forward with grace and overtopped the legionary by more than a head. Indigo designs marbled his skin. His forearms were turned white by bracelets apparently of bone. His slitted yellow eyes seemed to be searching for a direction in which he might find escape. Carnelian breathed in his animal odor. Vennel drew back as if he feared contamination.

The legionary barked a command. The black man gave him an insolent look but slowly lifted his arms above his head. The bracelets clinked as they slid down to his elbows. Carnelian saw the puffy patch just under his ribs just before the legionary stabbed it with his finger. The black man threw back his head, stretching open a red mouth rimmed with sharpened teeth. His fists were slow to unclench. Looking at the wound, Carnelian was impressed the man had made no sound.

The legionary turned his back on the black man. "They've all been bitten in the same place. Even now the poison works in their flesh. Without the proper medicine they will die. They all know this and are by this knowledge bound into my Master's service more surely than if they still wore their service collars."

"How long before the venom kills them?" asked Aurum.

The legionary shrugged. "That depends on each creature's strength, Master. Some will weaken in thirty days and be dead in forty. Others might survive longer."

Distaste came up through Carnelian's numbness. He pitied them.

Aurum walked past the legionary to stand before that gathering of shadows and said, in Vulgate, "Get up, slaves, so that you all may know those who are your Masters."

The Marula rose, unfolding their knotted limbs. Some dared to show their teeth. Carnelian was struck by their beauty. They were almost as tall as the Masters and had something of their poise and pride. They could have been Chosen reflected in a mirror of obsidian.

"Filthy brutes," muttered Vennel with his woman's voice.

Vennel argued with the other Masters the rest of the way down the stairway. Carnelian was remembering Crail and hardly listened. The gist of it seemed to be that Vennel felt that changes had been made in their plans without his approval. The Master could see no reason why they needed Marula or why their collars had been removed, however elaborate the measures taken for their control.

The stairway brought them eventually to a wide landing from which one last flight went down into a cave, cobbled like a courtyard, rib-vaulted, lit by lanterns hanging from chains. The ribs stood all along the wall. Between them, grilles flickered with the fires that burned behind and gates gave into dim rooms and corridors beyond. Carnelian saw all of this with a single glance, before his eyes were drawn to the creatures over to one side: graceful two-legged saurians, far taller than the grooms who held them.

The Marula swarmed down the steps. Carnelian remained behind with the Masters, Tain and the new boy.

"Where are the palanquins?" Vennel asked, an edge to his voice.

Carnelian knew the saurians must be aquar. He watched them, enthralled by their liquid movements.

"There are to be no palanquins, my Lord," Aurum said to Vennel.

Carnelian turned to look for Tain and found that his brother and the other boy had crept to his side and were following the graceful creatures with their eyes.

"Then how are we to travel?" asked Vennel.

"Is it not obvious that we are to ride, my Lord?" said Jaspar.

"Ride?" said Vennel. "What of the decision that was made in the Legate's hall?"

Carnelian watched the saurians' dancer's walk and their heads floating high above their grooms.

Vennel looked around for an answer. "And since when do the Chosen *ride*?"

"Would my Lord prefer to walk to Osrakum?" said Jaspar.

"First the collarless barbarians and now this. I must insist that these changes be ratified in formal conclave."

"Do you have any doubt, Vennel, that such a ratification

would take place?" The tone of contempt in Jaspar's voice caused Vennel to look round at him.

"At the very least I must have time to contact my household to make—"

"If you do, then we must leave without you, my Lord," said Aurum. "Even as we speak the tide comes in. Soon it will submerge the road we must take." He was watching the Marula move among the aquar.

"The wind made flesh," muttered Carnelian, recalling something his father had once said.

Vennel turned his long mask toward him. "Did you say something, my Lord?" He sounded livid.

Carnelian ignored him. He had no wish to speak to Vennel, no wish to speak to any of the Masters. Instead, he went down the steps towards the aquar, trailing Tain and the other boy after him.

Up close, the aquar had a dun surface, mottled, dull-gleaming. A groom held the reins. Carnelian followed these up to the swaying snake-scaled heron head, the narrow snout, the stone bit wedged into the angle of the jaws, the eyes' discs of green glass, as large as apples.

Plumes flared suddenly above the eyes like salmon-pink peacock fans. Its body lurched, giving off a strong animal musk. Reins tautened, straining. Carnelian stepped back. He was aware of the nervously clenching three-fingered hands, and of the scrape and thump of the clawed feet longer than his own leg. The groom wound his forearm into the reins, ran his hand along the sweating flank, made low whistling noises. As the creature calmed, Carnelian reached out. He expected its skin to be slimy cold, but instead it had a smooth-pebbled warmth. He was thrilled to feel the tremble of its heart.

"So beautiful," he sighed.

The groom grinned like an idiot and made a bobbing bow. "Master ride yes?"

The saddle-chair sat on the aquar's long back, held there

by the girth that passed under its belly. Carnelian stretched up to the chair rim. He ran his hand along the cracked barreling wood. He could not reach high enough to follow its curve right up. It narrowed to form a crude back. It was like a small round boat. Bone knobs and hoops bristled the sides. Some had broken off. Frayed knots of rope clung to others. The whole chair was grained with dirt.

Carnelian looked round at other saddle-chairs. Each had its own shape. One had a wider back, another had long staples instead of hoops, from yet another, tackle hung down like torn ship's rigging. All shared the same unkempt, patched and filthy look. They were hardly the seats of Masters.

"I have to go over there." It was Tain pointing. Carnelian had forgotten him. His brother pushed something hard into his hand and walked off. Carnelian opened his fingers and saw that it was Ebeny's Little Mother. He shoved the stone into a pocket, tucking its thong in after.

The groom was still bobbing and grinning. "Master ride yes?"

Carnelian saw that the other Masters were wandering among the aquar like shoppers at a fair. The aquar Carnelian was standing near looked to him as strong as any of the others. Its saddle-chair was no worse. He shrugged. He would take it though he could see no way to climb up.

He turned to the groom. "Master ride yes."

The groom showed a few stump teeth, then jerked the reins. The aquar shifted and adjusted its weight from one foot to the other a few times, then its legs hinged forward as it settled to the ground.

The saddle-chair now no higher than Carnelian's waist was a curved hollow padded with worn leather strips. Even through his nose filter, Carnelian detected something of the odor of its last owner. He conquered his disgust and gripped the chair rim. The groom gave an encouraging nod. Carnelian vaulted and fell untidily into the seat. He tried to slide into position even as the reins were being thrust into his hand. The groom whistled. With a sudden lurch Carnelian was pushed upward. It was the slide down the chair that choked off his cry. He panicked as he kept sliding. Then his buttocks slapped against something hard and he stopped dead.

Dazed, he saw the brown column of the creature's neck before him with his legs poking straight out on either side of it. The chair lurched as the aquar shifted. Eye-plumes rustled and quivered their pink above him.

"Put your feet in the stirrups, my Lord." It was his father's voice.

Carnelian managed to pull himself over in the direction of the voice. His father was hunched in a saddle-chair that was playing gently from side to side. He was guiding his aquar with small movements of his wrist. "The stirrup," he said, pointing.

Carnelian peered round his chair rim and saw the flattened wooden ring swinging. He stretched and managed to remove one ranga shoe. Then with some effort he managed to screw his bandaged foot into the stirrup. It was a tight fit but it gave him something to push against. He removed his other shoe and found the stirrup on the other side. With his feet secure he found it easy to push himself up the chair and settle into a sitting position.

"Once we get outside always breathe in through your nose pad. Do not forget, my Lord." His father's voice was cold and remote. He moved away.

Carnelian watched him go. He wanted to shout at him, how could you have turned Crail over to Aurum? His own remoteness was melting into tears. Grief sat like a stone on his chest. He concentrated on his breathing until the pressure lessened, then scoured around for a distraction. The ground seemed far below. Aurum and his father were near one of the lanterns. Eyes gleamed in its bronze, peppering their speaking hands with light. Jaspar and Vennel were sitting apart, each a massing of shadow adjusting into a saddle-chair. Vennel, particularly, was having problems. Ranged behind them were the slim shapes of the Marula, holding their aquar steady with skilled hands.

Carnelian looked for Tain. He found some other aquar,

eye-plumes all aquiver, which instead of saddle-chairs had frames on their backs to which were tied many bundles. Sitting on top of each pile was a boy. Carnelian counted them. Five, one for each of the Masters. One of them was Tain, slumped staring at the ground.

A Master's voice gave a command and aquar began turning to point in the same direction. Carnelian watched them forming into a column that was heading off behind him. His aquar shifted. He would have to turn it to join the others. He pulled hard on the right-hand rein. The aquar's long head lunged up and round. A huge green eye milked over with a blink. Plumes burst their pink almost in his face. The world spun round, then slowed to rest.

When he had stopped feeling dizzy, Carnelian pulled more gently. This time the creature turned slowly. The chair rocked to the right, then to the left. He let the reins slack and his aquar began to walk forward, rolling him smoothly from one side to the other. The other aquar were moving through a gate. Carnelian passed under a lantern. He felt unease at its weight hanging above him. Its rays seemed to riddle him with holes. Then he was among the others. He went through the gate and felt the shadow of the tunnel beyond slide over him. Rock undulated by on either side. He was deafened by the echoing scrape and clatter of claws on stone. The riders ahead alternated bright then dim as slaves trotted by holding torches.

Carnelian felt the breeze cooling his hand. He pulled his cowl down. Hidden, he lifted his mask a little. It was a relief to breathe unfiltered air. One deep breath. Another. There was a tang of the sea. He dropped the mask back. Through its eyeslits he saw the tunnel brightening ahead.

Everyone stopped. The riders in front were like a line of skittles. Beyond them torches were bobbing off toward a huge portcullis. Carnelian became aware of the voices just down to his right. A man was reaching into the wall and cursing. Another brought a torch to cast its light into the recess. The man reached in and grimaced as he struggled with a counterweight. Carnelian saw the cable running off from it in a groove cut into the rock. A beam recessed into the floor was slid out from the niche to let its counterweight hang free. A grating sound made him look ahead to where a few men were braced against the portcullis pushing up. It was rising smoothly and as it did so, the cables slid back along their grooves. With a rattle and clink the counterweights sank in the niches. More men rushed in to help lift the portcullis with poles until the whole mass of bronze-reinforced stone had been heaved up so that none of it could be seen. As the riders lurched into movement, Carnelian strained round to make sure the pack animals were close behind, then made his aquar follow.

They rode for a while along the passage and stopped for another gate. Its grating cut the sky into blue squares. After it had rumbled up they moved forward and under it. One by one, the riders ahead showed stark against the sky, then disappeared. Eventually, it was Carnelian's turn to ride out into the morning.

A vast sickle-blade of sand curved off into the west. Its inner edge was glinted by a creeping lip of sea. Its outer was defined by the cliffs into which, in the distance, a valley cut up from the beach. Carnelian's knuckles were colorless as his hands clamped to the chair. He was high up on a shoulder of rock that buttressed the Tower Crag. The rock jagged down to foam-laced pools. The sea was exploding white among the boulders.

Steps had been gouged into the rock. Aquar claws scrabbled and slipped as they were urged down. The stairway hugged the tower wall, its open side giving Carnelian too clear a view of the fall.

The last step gave onto a path grooved along a winding ridge of rock. They moved along it, riding parallel to the shore. Lime-green knuckled fingers of seaweed grasped the edges of the road. Channels carved across it, streaming water back to the sea. As they drew closer to the waves, Carnelian began to feel their thunder. Spume flecked the air. Sinking into the sand, the ridge grew flatter, allowing them to pick up speed. Carnelian was rolled around in the saddle-chair as his aquar took longer and longer strides. He found that if he pushed hard against the stirrups he could ride more easily.

The rocks ran into shingle which they crunched across. The sea charged them, frothed over the pebbles, weakening visibly as it neared. It almost reached them, lingered frozen, then began to hiss back, at first slowly, then with an increasing rush and roar.

The shingle quietened into sand. The riders ahead filed off along the margin of the sea, spurring their aquar into furious splashing speed. When Carnelian's time came, he did the same. He gave a whoop of excitement as the chair punched into his back and the wind whipped his black cloak up to flap around him. The aquar's diamond head cut the air. Its muscle-shudder pistoned up through the saddle-chair. Together, they crashed along the trail pool-pocked into the darker sand. Incredible speed. A wave slipped its glass across their path and they smashed through it. Then it whispered away wiping clean the printed sand. The salt air penetrated even the mask filter and Carnelian sucked at it as hard as he could. His eyes swam. The beach flowed as a brown spate on either side. He noticed it brightening. Behind him, over the cliffs of Thuyakalrul, the sun was rising and spreading its glow over the sand. The aquar all broke into song. Their voices were like reeded pipes. Carnelian and his aquar's joined shadow cast forward as they pelted along the crystal margin of the sea, buffeted by their own slipstream.

The stream bled into the sea, darkening the water, making the waves froth pink. Its artery-red channels fanned out across a stretch of beach, bruising the sand purple.

With the others, Carnelian had slowed his aquar to a walk. In the east the Tower Crag lay black beneath a rind of sun. Westward the sand stretched to the next bright headland. Carnelian looked upstream to where there was a wide gap in the cliff wall. Narrowing his eyes, he was sure that he could see the valley it gave into cutting upward to the land above. Sunlight had not reached into it. A powdering of birds flew up and caught fire in the dawn.

The reek of rotting was forcing itself even through his filter. Carnelian looked out across the reddened delta, wondering at the gulls that mobbed it. He watched them land with several hops, wings snapping open and closed, fighting, screeching, dropping soft sodden lumps when retreating.

The party milled around him. Aurum was marshalling the Marula into formation. Feeling a desire to lose himself in the morning, Carnelian urged his aquar into a jog. Soon the red sand was all around him. He was sure he was approaching a catch of fish left for days in the sun. He began feeling queasy as he came among the gulls and saw them tearing at hunks of flesh. Chunks clumped together, piling up into mounds like oozing gums around which the sluggish bloody waters flowed. Stained sand jiggled with sand-fleas. Mats of flies rustled up as his aquar's long shadow drove them from their feasts. Carnelian drew his cowl over his mask and fought nausea.

Voices thinned by distance rose above the rumble of the waves. Carnelian peered down the tunnel of his cowl. Further along the beach some scows had been dragged up onto the sand. Another was still in the sea, bucking amidst a slick of heads. He watched as it nudged closer to the shore with dark arms clinging to its sides. As its prow dug into the beach, the creatures dragging it came up out of the sea. They were brown jerking things like distorted men. He watched them strain together and the scow lunged up the sand to join the others. Around the scows, more of the distorted men were milling, each hunched under a basket. Carnelian watched them, curious, certain they must be sartlar. Naked, well-shaped men stood above them on the bows unloading something into their baskets. The burdened creatures then hobbled off to join the line wavering its way up the delta toward the valley in the cliffs.

Carnelian decided that he might as well take a closer look and was about to ride on when the air around him was sprayed with blood from the stream. He turned to see two Marula calming their creatures from the run. The gulls that had risen around them were hacking out their calls. One of the black men bowed but his act of subservience did not feel like one. Carnelian caught a flicker of yellow eyes and glimpsed their hatred. The man lifted his lance up and pointed back to where the party was formed up in good order.

Carnelian returned with a Maruli on either side. As he came closer to the other riders, he spotted Tain clinging to the top of their baggage, flushed and grimacing. Then he heard Vennel's voice, ". . . but I have been deceived. Why do we not ride for the road?" Jaspar replied that this was hardly the place to hold a discussion. They fell to arguing. Aurum signed with his hand. The sun caught his rings. The hand pointed and the Marula drummed off in a dark knot up the delta. The Masters and baggage straggled after them, their voices lost in the rumble of footfalls.

Carnelian watched the riders undulate away. It was a strange relief to be left alone with the buzzing flies. He glanced back to the Tower Crag where his people were. He might have fled with them if he had known a way to return to the Hold. He turned to the carnage. It seemed Crail's dismembered body that was clogging up the stream. He tried to remember the old man's face. He remembered that last kiss he had given him, that kiss of betrayal. The tears began trickling down the inside of his mask. Carnelian longed to throw it away, to fly along the beach, to have the clean sea-wind scour the tears from his eyes.

Far away the riders were flowing toward the valley. There was no returning. Carnelian cursed, sniffed, then lashed his aquar to race after them.

He splashed along the rivulets as they joined and deepened into browner streams. The triangle of the delta narrowed and he saw that he was drawing ever closer to the shambling file of creatures coming up from the scows.

The streams wound together until Carnelian was riding along the edge of a single channel. On the other side the creatures struggled with their baskets, which brimmed over with things like wheels. Whatever faces they might have had were hidden behind lank sheets of hair.

He reached the Masters where they had come to a halt. A stiff back betrayed his father. Height revealed Aurum. Vennel was precariously balanced in his chair. Jaspar's aquar was perched on the bank seeming to look across to the other side. Carnelian coaxed his aquar toward him.

They both looked down at the clots swirling in the purpled water. "What carnage is this?" Carnelian said and ground his teeth.

"A poetic term for such filthy commerce."

"Commerce . . . ?" The word was unexpected. Carnelian gazed across the stream.

"And a fitting occupation for the Wise."

Carnelian watched the creatures struggling on the other bank. "Are those sartlar?"

"Of course. Repulsive, neh?" He pointed an arm upstream. "No doubt we shall have to follow their stinking march through that."

Carnelian followed his finger. The valley was still in shadow but he could see that it appeared to be set with dark jewels. The stream came out of it through something that looked like a wall that stretched across its mouth.

With a motion of his hand, Aurum sent the Marula into the stream. As they crumbled the banks into the water their aquar stumbled, jolting their riders. Then they were wading up against the flow with the water foaming red against their legs. The baggage animals were next. Seeing it was safe, the Masters urged their aquar after them.

Carnelian followed Jaspar. He watched him sway as his aquar slid down the bank. Then it was his turn. He gripped the chair rim but was still thrown about and almost pitched forward into the eddying stinking water. Soon he was making his way up the channel with the others.

They reached the sartlar and pushed into their march. He

could see that it was spiral ammonites that filled their baskets. The aquar jostled the sartlar out of the way. Carnelian saw shells knocked out of the baskets being trodden into the water by the sartlar's spade feet. He wanted to see their faces but not a single one turned to watch them pass.

The wall was close now, so close Carnelian could see it was a scree. Little avalanches clinked down and he realized the whole slope was made up of fragments of ammonite shell.

He felt a change in his aquar's footfalls. Each impact was sharper. Peering down into the water he discovered that the channel was now lined with stone. Two buttresses rose up to hold back the hills of shells. Between them was a gap out from which the stream was flowing. Soon masonry had risen on either side. The other Masters were in the noisy space with him, being carried along by the sartlar tide whose burdens formed a mosaic that hid them from view. Carnelian saw a leathery hand fumble up to steady a basket. One of the sartlar became entangled in the legs of Jaspar's aquar and was knocked down. Its shellfish load pattered into the water like stones. Other sartlar bleated and tried to get out of the way. The aquar's plumes flared. It trumpeted. As it tried to keep its footing, its claws churned the sartlar's body into the stream. A gurgling shriek was followed by some crunching sounds that might have been crushing shells. Jaspar pulled his aquar back into control, then moved on.

Carnelian's aquar stepped around the floating mess. He glimpsed a face into which a spiral had been branded so deeply, the nose was in several chunks. He could not look away, even though he had to lean out dangerously to keep the corpse in sight. The baskets meshed and it was gone. He looked ahead, troubled, to find that they had come through the gap into a valley that was carved and gouged into a complex honeycomb awrithe with sartlar.

Jaspar affected a cough. "It is unusual to find oneself in a drain."

The channel swelled into a great sink whose walls were streaked abattoir-brown and pierced by many dribbling mouths. Gutter lips wedged into the top of the wall were disgorging thick dark jets. Meaty chunks made them spit and splutter. Carnelian watched a hunched sartlar using a paddle to brush a sodden lump over the edge so that it splashed into the pool below. That pool poured its bloody mixture past their aquars' feet. Carnelian pulled his cowl down over his mask and looked away.

Sartlar were hauling their baskets up a stairway that rose out of the channel. The Marula were sent to clear a way. With the other Masters, Carnelian urged his aquar up the steps.

As his aquar neared the top, Carnelian emerged into a red world, an amphitheater with tiers of cisterns, walkways, channels. The air hazed with flies. Everywhere there were piled ammonite shells. As each sartlar emptied its basket on a pile it caused a rattling avalanche. Sartlar sat surrounded by baskets like women at a market. They cracked the ammonites open on rocks, used their claws to scratch out the creatures inside and then discarded the empty shells. Other sartlar gathered these and shuffled off with them toward the rubbish wall, where, amidst a frenzy of gull wings and screeches, the shells were thrown away.

"Filthy industry," Jaspar cried above the clatter.

The Marula were trying to wave away the flies. As these spat against him, Carnelian became thankful for his mask and cloak.

A brown man was battering his way toward them through the sartlar, using the handle of a bladed whip. He made his hands into a tube and shouted through it, "You've come the wrong way."

The lances of the Marula pricked him out of their path. They started moving through, scattering sartlar, spilling baskets. Other overseers confronted them, shaking their whips, slapping the lance heads away from their faces. "Wrong way," they cried. "Wrong way."

"We should return," shrilled Vennel in Vulgate. "Clearly there's no road through here."

Suth said something to one of the Marula. The man advanced and lifted his lance to point up the valley. The overseers shook their heads and showed grimaces of brown teeth. Any sartlar that bumped into them suffered a crack on the head.

Aurum pushed his way through the Marula. "Show me the route." His voice carried even over the noise.

The overseers waved their whips and scowled at him. A whip handle clacked against Aurum's saddle-chair, causing his aquar's eye-plumes to flutter. The Master lunged forward. The men drew back, loosening their lashes ready to strike, but the beginnings of fear distorted their faces. Aurum slipped back his cowl to reveal his gold face. They sheltered and hid behind their arms. They cringed back, dropping their whips, tripping over baskets and sartlar. Aurum straightened, hid his face within the shadow of his cowl. The overseers cowered until he commanded them to approach. Then they fawned on him and strained to hear his every word.

Cringing guides led them up the valley. They wound through a maze of vats and channels. Carnelian watched sartlar stir a rot of shelled ammonites. Each stir gave off a stench and oozed out more yellow liquid that darkened as it flowed. Sluices let water in from above or allowed the liquid to filter down from one tank to the next. With each descent the color deepened. In one tank he saw it had become almost black but that its edges were the color of blood. He understood and looked around with wonder. The whole valley was a dyeworks for extracting fabled, precious purple.

A whole run of tanks was flushed clean by a flood released from higher up. Red to their waists, sartlar leaned against the current as they scraped at the rotting matter that was sticking to the sides. Carnelian knew this sewage would be channeled down to the sink from where it would stream red off to the sea.

* * *

"Do my Lords think it reasonable that I should now be given explanations," Vennel said over the scrabbling of aquar claws.

Carnelian was exhausted by the effort of keeping in his seat. During the long, hard climb his saddle-chair had been giving him a constant bruising. He would be glad to stop even for a while.

Aurum looked up at the sun. "We must be far from here before we camp tonight."

"Camp . . . ?" said Vennel.

"Aurum, we have almost reached the land above," said Suth. Carnelian saw his father turning round to look for him. "And it might profit us to rest our beasts before we go much farther."

"As my Lords wish," said Aurum with a tone of resignation. "I will seek out a suitable place to stop."

They continued to climb up the valley side. Carnelian strained to look over the juddering back of the saddle-chair and glimpsed the shimmer of the sea.

He was crossing a weir when he saw Aurum on the other side bringing his aquar to a stop. The Master set five Marula aside and divided the rest into two groups. The first he sent back down the way they had come. The second was sent ahead to spy out the land. Aurum made his aquar kneel, fastened on his ranga shoes and then climbed out of his saddle-chair. Carnelian bound on his own shoes. Aurum towered over the Maruli to whom he was handing his aquar's reins.

The river formed a lake below the level of the path. The aquar stooped to drink and the Marula bent down beside them, lapping like beasts. Tain and the other slaves stood apart from the Masters.

Jaspar struck a pose. "One is certainly relieved to have escaped that foul factory. Though not without cost." He pinched up his robe. "In civilized circumstances one would insist on having this immediately torched. This rag could not be sweetened by all the perfumes of Osrakum."

"The wind will cleanse it well enough," snapped Vennel.

"One fears the smell of those putrid mollusks will remain for ever in one's nostrils."

Suth looked at Jaspar. "The perfume of the road will make my Lord soon enough forget his putrid mollusks."

"At last," said Vennel.

"At last, my Lord?" said Jaspar.

Vennel's mask regarded him disdainfully. "We come at last to knowledge of our destination."

"Our destination has always been the same, my Lord," said Suth.

"But not the means by which we might reach it, my Lord."

"We all agreed we should proceed along the road disguised."

"I recall a mention of palanquins, of the Legate's banners."

"It has become necessary, my Lord, that we should adopt a different disguise," said Aurum.

"Why did the palanquins fall out of favor?"

"We can no longer risk using the leftway," said Suth.

"Why by the Two can we not, my Lord?"

"We have reasons to believe that were we to do so we should be attacked," said Aurum.

"These reasons were no doubt contained in the Clave's letter?" Vennel waited for confirmation but received none. "Do these reasons justify this preposterous choice of route?"

"Many eyes would have seen us leaving the tower if we had joined the road, there," said Suth.

Vennel pointed up the valley. "This will bring us up onto the road, no doubt?"

"It will, my Lord."

Carnelian could see Vennel's fury in the cast of his shoulders.

"What is this new disguise, my Lords, this wonderful concealment that will draw a veil of shadow over the eyes of our enemies?"

Aurum indicated the Marula. "We will hide ourselves among these barbarians."

Vennel looked at the Marula as if he were counting them. "These creatures are of a type rare within the borders of the Commonwealth. Do my Lords think it wise that we should attempt to conceal ourselves in such a conspicuous hiding place?"

"Marula are rare, my Lord," said Aurum, "but here, by the sea, black men from round the coast are not unknown. We shall masquerade as chieftains making a trade pilgrimage to the Guarded Land."

"One had understood the coastal blacks to be far more diminutive than these Marula."

Suth broadened his shoulders. "My Lord is not listening. Black men are uncommon on the road and thus few will know enough to make a distinction between their kinds."

Vennel nodded. "My Lords seem to have woven their schemes with some care. I can only wonder why I was excluded."

"I too have been excluded," said Jaspar, but Carnelian noted that his voice held no edge of resentment.

Vennel's mask turned its imperious gaze on him. "You seem not much concerned, my Lord."

"We are here now. It would seem foolish, not to say unpleasant, to return down this valley."

"The Ruling Lord Suth and I thought it more prudent that we should keep our own counsel," said Aurum.

Vennel made a gesture of exasperation. "This prudence was not, it seems, extended to the Legate of the Tower in the Sea."

"We needed his assistance," said Suth.

"A great quantity of it, my Lord, judging by our collarless and poisoned escort and these starvelings with their grimy chairs, not to mention the cut-down ranga. Tell me, Aurum, how did you persuade our dear Legate to give you so much assistance? Did you perhaps bind him to your cause with the promise of one of your blood-high daughters?"

Aurum closed his hands in a threat gesture. "Perhaps my Lord should consider choosing his accusations with more care."

Vennel turned away to look at Suth. "What of the much vaunted need for haste, My-Lord-who-goes-before?"

"There is still time enough to reach Osrakum before the election," said Suth.

"One more question, my Lord." Vennel leaned toward Suth. "Who are these enemies so terrible that they can force Lords of the Great to hide like thieves?"

"A conspiracy among the Lesser Chosen."

"To which, no doubt, our friend the Legate is totally immune?"

"Do you think we apprised him of all our plans?"

"And from all this caution can one conclude that these conspirators might dare to breach the Blood Convention?"

Aurum moved closer to Vennel. "It seems that they might indeed attempt our lives, Lord Vennel, and so it behooves us all to show great care. These are evidently very desperate people. You do understand, my Lord?"

Their two masks reflected each other's for a moment.

"Only too well, Ruling Lord Aurum," said Vennel.

Looking from one to the other, Carnelian could almost see the anger passing between them. He was sure more had been said than had been in the words.

Something touched his shoulder. It was his father. *Follow me*, his hand signed. Carnelian clacked after him though he was reluctant to be alone with him. Crail's blood flooded between them like a river.

Carnelian and his father stood on the weir looking down the valley to the sea.

"Behold Thuyakalrul," said Suth.

There it lay, beguiling like a ring: the Grand Harbor a paler region of the sea within its circle; the inner harbor of the tower a tiny winking jewel.

"This sea is a strange wealth," his father said.

Carnelian wrinkled his nose as he thought of the stinking purple dye.

Suth pointed to where the coast, curving round into hazy

distance, was inlaid with tiny mirrors. "There lie the pans in which the yellow-salt is made with which we buy soldiers from the Lower Lands. The sun's ardor distills it from the sea and the Chosen use its currency to buy barbarian blood. Is it not a paradox that a few holes in the ground should yield up such conquest?"

Carnelian played with his fingers.

"The Quyans came to these lands across that sea," his father said. "The Wise maintain it was the sea that was the mother of the Quyan race. They claim for evidence the colors of our Chosen eyes that constantly reflect her."

Behind them there was a mutter of voices. The aquar were shifting nervously.

His father looked back at the other Masters. "We cannot risk being divided, you and I."

Carnelian stared seaward but saw nothing. His eyes were searching inward, seeking a way out of the prison of his anger.

"I did all I could to save Crail," Suth said quietly.

"If you did, my Lord, it was evidently not enough," said Carnelian. The words were out before he could recall them. He felt his face burning against the metal of his mask. He could taste the venom in his words. He felt his father turn toward him.

"Henceforth, my Lord, always wear your gloves. A single pale hand could betray us all."

As his father strode off to join the others, Carnelian lingered, frozen by the coldness in his voice. He knew it was unfair to blame him but he could not help it. The bile rose in him as he told himself that it was his father's weakness that had consigned Crail to his sickening death.

The Marula had returned and were standing in the deepest shade. Apart from their outlines, all that could be seen of them was their amber sliver eyes. Carnelian watched his father move toward them. He could not hear his words but saw the way the black men quaked. They scurried out among the aquar and began to unbale baggage from one of them.

Carnelian walked carefully back on his ranga shoes, making sure to avoid his father. The Marula were tying all kinds of shoddy objects to the saddle-chairs. Carnelian came up to his chair and fingered the gourds, the filthy feathered bags, coils of rope, a wood harpoon.

"The barbarian has such a childish liking for clutter and whimsy," said Jaspar as he gingerly poked the objects hanging round his chair.

Carnelian watched him wipe his gloved hand against his cloak. Vennel was looking up the valley. His mask gave him a look of contemptuous detachment.

Carnelian managed a better vault into his saddle-chair than he had before. At his signal, his aquar rocked him back into the air. He made sure to see Tain scrambling back up into his place amongst the baggage.

As they set off Carnelian took a good look at the bracelets that covered the forearms of the Marula. After what his father had said, he decided that they were not bone but bitter salt.

THE
GREAT
SEA ROAD

A hundred days to the sea

Along the high white road

But I shall fly there with the wind

To leave behind this land of dusts.

—EXTRACT FROM THE "LAY

OF THE LORD OF THE SEA"

Shoals of people slipping past, scraping, scuffling. Dense rafts of bales, of poles and palanquins, floated in the flow. Wheels taller than men drove irresistibly round like mill stones. At Aurum's command, the Marula scrabbled down the slope, making the throng a shadow procession behind their kicked-up dust.

"Conceal yourselves," cried Aurum, "sit low in your chairs to disguise your height." Then his aquar was stumbling down into the rolling ochre air. In front of Carnelian, a cloud billowed up. He pulled his cowl forward as it broke over him. His aquar's plumes rustled as he urged it down into the haze. Every step jarred the saddle-chair. The grind and creaking grew louder with the babble of voices and the clatter of stone bells.

He broke through the dust and pulled his aquar up. The river had faces. He peered from one to another. Some were dark, some painted, some cried, some laughed. Across the eddy of heads floated a wreckage of wood and canvas held together with ropes. He watched it totter back and forth, waving above it a tatter of flags.

"Hey, you! Get on or get out of the way," came a cry from behind him in Vulgate.

Carnelian peered round the edge of his saddle-chair but could make no sense of what he saw. A huge wedge of bone swaying ponderously from side to side, tapering down to a cruel beak. Horn stumps curved out from the four corners of the wedge behind which, more bone fanned out in a fluted crest.

"Out of the way, barbarian, or by the horns I'll run you down."

A small man was creasing his belly against the mottled edge of the crest. A tarpaulined mound rose behind him, criss-crossed with thongs. The man grimaced as he shook his hooked goad at Carnelian.

There was an impact to the side of his saddle-chair. Carnelian whisked round just as the reins were snatched from his hand. The cowled figure of one of the Masters leaned back as he pulled Carnelian's aquar out of the way.

"Try and be more careful," his father cried.

Humiliation stung Carnelian to anger. A smell of malt distracted him from any outburst. He turned to see bronze hide flexing. His chair shook as he watched the monster lumber by. A wagon pole juddered past like a battering ram. Then the edge of a solid wheel of wood rolled into view, its splintered rim turning slowly. It lurched into a rut, causing Carnelian's aquar to flare its eye-plumes. He was shaken around in his chair as the creature recoiled.

Carnelian saw the other Masters nearby, waiting for the wagon to pass. He moved toward them, recognized Jaspar by his gloves and drew close to him. "Was that a dragon?" he shouted in Vulgate over the noise.

"What?" the Master shouted back. "No, no, no. Though a huimur, it is of a species far smaller than those used by the legions."

The movements of their aquar separated them. Suth was making the party form up. Carnelian was directed into place with curt gestures. Resentment burned up in him. His father was treating him like a child.

The Marula sculled a way into the throng with the hafts of their lances. The Masters and baggage animals waded in after them. The Marula dug a space in the middle of the road then fell back to shield the Masters with their bodies. The inexorable march swept them all in its tide off into the south.

Drab drifts of barbarians jabbering. Chariots studded with shell buttons snaking streamers. Strings of smaller half-feathered aquar carrying nests of clutter. Sawn-horned huimur clacking stone bells, their backs like upturned boats. Some had howdahs, some were snail-shelled with trussed goods, some pulled carts or painted wagons. Carnelian's mood brightened. He indulged his curiosity and looked at everything. It surprised him that the two streams of travelers slid so smoothly past each other along the road. One was going to the sea, the other coming from it, penetrating deeper into the Naralan. He peered to front and back to see their march swallowed at both ends by hazing horizons. Swarthy hawkers clamored at the edges of the road, waving their meager wares. Children threw stones, stared, pointed laughing. The sun-baked land behind was patterned with spaced trees. Boulder-bordered tracks scratched off into the hinterland. The land folded distantly into vague hills or crusted here and there into clusterings of hovels.

Carnelian wondered at the narrow track that ran alongside the road beyond a ditch. In some places this was paved but he saw nothing move along it. He deduced it to be the much vaunted leftway. It did not impress him much until he saw a tower up ahead with its stiff banners. As it came closer he realized it was a fort standing by the road. The banners turned out to be gibbets hung with the tatters of flesh and bone the birds had left. Behind the fort, churned earth spread as far as he could see. Charred spots and litter showed that the land had recently held a huge encampment.

The heat made him drowsy. He had grown used to the rocking of the saddle-chair and even found a comfortable way of sitting. The crowd noise became a rushing of water. The road flowed ever on, eating up all time, all distance.

At last the sky began darkening in the east. The traffic began streaming off the road onto a field of trampled earth. A few dust-grayed trees stood here and there among the ruts. A rush was on for the better sites in the stopping place. People were being absorbed into the hazy hem of the sky. Aurum passed back a message that they would press on. They would make better speed on the emptier road.

The air cooled. Nightfall slowed their progress. Wagons lit feeble flickering lanterns. These winking flecks sparked off into the distance, showing the windings of the road. On they went until the moon rose to silver everything. Carnelian drifted in and out of sleep.

He woke suddenly. The rhythm of his chair had changed. The stars covering the earth all round him outshone those in the sky. Wafts of roasting meat. Songs, night-thinned, nasal-voiced. He realized they had left the road. His reins were hanging loose but his aquar was following the others.

They found their way round fires and wagons, tethered beasts, tents, pavilions and all the other flotsam washed up by the road. Calls and curses came from every side as they blundered through the flickering night.

Aurum found them a sandy knoll on the edge of the camp where the Marula put up tents. Some of the black men were sent to fetch water from the wells, while others led the aquar off to find drinking troughs. Those who remained squatted in a ring around the tents, facing outward, their lances aslant against their shoulders.

The Masters sat in a circle unmasked, eating, each cross-legged on a low stool, their ranga shoes beside them on the ground. The air was wreathed with purifying myrrh. Around them flapped a canvas wall stretched over a ring of uprights.

"Are you sure it is high enough?" asked Jaspar, carefully unpeeling the leaf that wrapped a hri cake.

"Even a rider could not see over it," said Aurum.

"The Marula will protect us against intrusion," said Suth. "But still it might be wise if my Lords were to keep their masks close to hand."

Aurum put a crumb of the yellow porridge-cake into his mouth and nodded.

"It makes one uneasy to be so naked in the outer world," said Jaspar.

Vennel's eyebrows lifted. "But then, my Lord, does not such nakedness serve to hide us from the terrible eyes of our enemies?"

"Often the blinded see further than those with sight," said Suth severely.

Even though Vennel dropped his gaze, seeming to give all his attention to his porridge-cake, Carnelian had glimpsed the wariness on his face.

"I had expected the road to be more than just a dusty track," he said. He crumbled a piece of cake and put it to his lips. It exhaled saffron.

"We are still only in the Naralan, cousin," drawled Jaspar.

Vennel looked at Carnelian. "My Lord had better become accustomed to the dust." He gave the others a sour look. "It seems that we will be a long time journeying to the Guarded Land."

"Oh, the weariness," sighed Jaspar. He shook out a sleeve of his robe and clouded the air with dust.

Frowning, Vennel blew on his hri cake, brushed it clean

with a twist of leaf wrapping. "If our journey has become so wearying, my Lord, it is because of the choices that others have made."

Jaspar frowned. "It is true. Had one imagined the discomfort, one's ring might have voted for the faster way, whatever the risks. To travel with the common herd is hideous enough, but at their level . . . without perfumes . . . it is perfectly too much." He turned to Suth. "Alas, my Lord has been proved only too prophetic: one has utterly forgotten the mollusks."

Vennel looked round the circle of luminous faces. "Is it any surprise that we should pay a heavy price for the flouting of the Law?"

"We do not flout but choose to set aside in direst need, my Lord," said Aurum.

"Once one begins this business of setting aside the Law," said Jaspar, "one does begin to wonder where it will all end. Are we now to disregard the whole Law?"

Aurum's face became limestone. "Only the Law of Movement has been set aside. The rest of the Law remains sacrosanct."

"And yet there are other laws that our present circumstances will make it difficult to enforce."

"Such as, my Lord?" said Suth.

Jaspar smiled. "The various punishments that one might have to mete out to one's slaves, not to mention our barbarian escort. Surely, my Lords, the honoring of those laws would only serve to reveal who we are? It might be wiser to show mercy or to seek postponement."

"The Law, my Lord, does not allow for mercy," said Aurum.

Carnelian looked at the Master's face. It had the same hard look as when it had pronounced Crail dead. He went cold with fury. Though he pressed his lips together the words mumbled out. "No . . . not . . . mercy."

Aurum turned his Master eyes on Carnelian. "Did you say something?"

The unyielding face maddened Carnelian. "Only that my

Lord seems to have an unnatural appetite for inflicting punishment," his voice rang out.

A slow smile formed on Aurum's lips, humorless, intimidating. He turned to Suth. "Sardian, your son gives insult to my blood."

Suth looked sick as he focused his eyes off into the distance. Carnelian stared at him, willing him to confront Aurum in his defense.

"You will apologize to the Ruling Lord," Suth said, not looking at his son.

Carnelian looked at him in disbelief. He wanted his father to turn round. He needed to look into his eyes. The smile was still fixed on Aurum's face. Carnelian despaired. When he spoke his voice was hoarse. "No, my Lord Father, I will not apologize."

Jaspar lifted his hands in a gesture of peace. "Come, come, my Lords. It is not fitting that we should quarrel thus. The road has frayed our tempers. We should retire for the night. No doubt, the morning will bring its own distractions." He turned to Vennel. "Does my Lord know the sleeping arrangements?"

"There are only four tents," said Vennel.

"Obviously, the intention was that the Lord Suth should share with his son."

Carnelian was appalled. He had never slept in the same room as his father. At any time this would have been difficult; now that there was such bad feeling between them, it was unthinkable. "No," he blurted.

"No?" parroted Vennel.

Carnelian could feel all the Masters looking at him. The anger in his father's eyes only served to spur him on. "Surely it is unseemly that a Ruling Lord should share with anyone?"

Jaspar looked surprised. "You suggest, my Lord, that you and I share a tent?"

"The boy has a point," said Vennel, with a predatory leer.

Jaspar looked briefly exasperated, then shrugged. "So be it."

Such a swift victory made Carnelian uneasy. He looked to

his father but he averted his gaze. Aurum's eyes were bright with malice. Carnelian knew he had made this happen and now he would have to see it through. He put on his ranga and his mask, rose and left the enclosure.

Fire spangled the darkness. The smell of men and beasts mixed with the smoke of meat charring. The rising falling murmur of voices was pierced by flutes, rhythmed by tambours.

Two of the Marula had followed Carnelian to the edge of the knoll. They moved when he moved as if they were his shadows. Carnelian heard a sound behind him and turned. Against the faint light coming from the Masters' enclosure, a column of blacker night was drifting toward him flanked by the shapes of more Marula.

"Night is best to brood in, cousin." It was Jaspar.

Further up the slope the Marula had made a fire and were cooking something of their own.

"Their food smells better than ours," said Carnelian.

"But then of course it is unclean," Jaspar said, sounding regretful.

Carnelian turned to look at him, a shape cut into the starry sky. "From whom do we hide, Jaspar?"

"We Chosen hide from everyone, Carnelian, out of care, lest the radiance of our faces blast them to ash."

"It is the Empress Ykoriana who threatens us, is it not?"

"Lower your voice," hissed Jaspar. His silhouette consumed more stars and gave birth to others as he moved away. Carnelian heard him muttering commands. The Marula melted away and Jaspar returned. Carnelian felt the gold face sizing him up. "It is unthinkable," it said at last.

"Aurum and my father are thinking it, my Lord."

"It is this Lesser Chosen plot they fear."

"Tell me, Jaspar, are the Marula rare in the Commonwealth?"

"What does this—?"

"Humor me."

"They pay us no flesh tithe and only a handful of them enlist as auxiliaries in the legions."

"Then I would suggest that the Ruling Lord Aurum always intended us to return using them as our disguise." Carnelian could not conceal the smugness in his voice.

"I do not quite follow . . ."

"Does it seem likely to you, Jaspar, that the Legate would just happen to have more than a dozen of these rare creatures in his auxiliaries?"

"And so . . . ?" said Jaspar.

"And so, either Aurum brought them with him or he had the Legate obtain them. Either possibility makes it certain that the arrangements were made before you all set off across the sea. This suggests that Aurum knew my father would return with him."

"It is well reasoned." Jaspar's mask nodded. "Well reasoned," he said, his voice lower, as if he were speaking to himself. His mask became very still. "Why then was Aurum so despondent on the journey out?"

Carnelian deflated. The implication was that the influence Aurum had over his father he had not brought with him. If that were true then he must have found it on the island. Carnelian worried that Jaspar was moving toward the same conclusion and spoke quickly to ruffle the surface of his thoughts.

"By the same reasoning, it cannot be the Lesser Chosen that we hide from. Whatever was written in the letter, it could not be that."

Jaspar said nothing. Carnelian became disconcerted by the Master's mask floating its dead face in the night. "The Marula, my Lord, were already waiting for us."

Jaspar gave a slow nod. "Let us say, cousin, that you are right and we are hiding from the Empress. What then?"

"Why are we hiding?"

"Spinning pure conjecture, it could be that she intends to stop your father getting to Osrakum in time to influence the election."

"How could she do that?"

"She could set assassins searching for him along this road."

Carnelian went cold with fear for his father. "She could not . . . the Blood Convention . . ."

"She has already murdered her own daughter."

"Her daughter?"

"Flama Ykoria."

"Why . . . ?"

"Ykoriana was the first woman for generations to be born blood-rank four."

Carnelian almost gasped as he calculated it. "Her ring casts eight thousand votes. Nearly half as much as all the Great together."

Jaspar nodded. "Through her, Flama Ykoria inherited the same rank. Now, Ykoriana alone enjoys this distinction."

Carnelian was aghast. "But even she must fear the Law."

Jaspar laughed without humor. "She had already long before suffered all the punishments the Law can inflict on Chosen women: the purdah imprisonment, blinding."

Carnelian shuddered. "But not death?"

"We do not slay our women, they are too precious to us."

Carnelian realized Jaspar was not being ironic. "What other crime did she commit?"

Jaspar shrugged. "Some matter internal to the House of the Masks. That is in the past. It is the election that concerns her now."

"How will victory assuage her bitterness?"

"Nephron is his father's son, Molochite his mother's: a weak prince, a wallower in rare vices. She would wed him, encourage his corruption, then rule unfettered from behind his throne. Of course, if your father were to ensure Nephron's victory . . ."

"My father?"

"Then he would enjoy high favor at the new Gods' side and, should he choose, could wield oppressive power over others of us of the Great."

"My father would never abuse such trust."

"*He* might not, but what if he became an instrument in another's hand? Aurum's, for example?"

"Aurum?"

"You must have noticed, Carnelian, what influence he has over your father?"

Carnelian felt the sweat soaking the bandages on his back. "I . . . I really have no idea what you mean, my Lord."

"Are you certain that you have not, cousin?"

"Absolutely certain."

"Well then." Jaspar's mask was a dark mirror. "We have talked enough, cousin. One would not deprive you of much needed sleep. The days that follow promise to be wearisome, neh?"

Jaspar turned and walked back up the slope. As Carnelian watched him fade away, his heart seemed to be shaking its way out of his body. A scent of menace lingered on the night air. He told himself that really nothing much had happened. It amused his cousin Jaspar to frighten him a little, that was all.

When Carnelian was calmer he began to climb the knoll. The Marula squatting in the dark like boulders stood up silently as he passed and followed him.

Mattresses thick enough to satisfy the commands of the Law had been rolled out to form a floor in the tent. The air was weighed with incense. Carnelian jerked a nod at Jaspar. He frowned when he saw Tain prostrate with another gangly boy beside him. His brother looked up and twitched a smile.

"What a relief it would be to remove these accursed wrappings," said Jaspar, speaking from behind him.

The Master's comment made Carnelian aware of his own bandages.

"One fears we will have to stew in them until we reach Osrakum."

Carnelian gave the boys leave to rise. He registered the look of horror on Tain's face and could make no sense of it. The other boy slipped past him with hands held out. "Let your slave help you, Master," he said in a thin voice.

In increasing confusion, Carnelian watched Tain clasp trembling hands over his face. He turned and saw the other boy's small hands reverently coping with the weight of Jaspar's mask as it was handed down.

"My slave is not as pretty as yours, cousin, but he is a wonder with a brush," Jaspar was saying.

Carnelian felt sudden nausea as he stared at the Master's naked face. "You have destroyed my brother."

Jaspar started back and put on an expression of childlike innocence. "Cousin? Ah, you are being droll."

"You removed your mask."

"Indeed. Did you think I would sleep in it?"

"But the Law . . . he will have to be punished."

"He will have to be blinded."

"You did it deliberately?" Carnelian put his hand to his head. "I can't believe it," he said in Vulgate.

"All the slaves we brought with us will be blinded. Did you really think, Carnelian, that the Great would choose to suffer inconvenience merely to save the eyes of a handful of slaves?" He laughed. "It is *too* grotesque."

Carnelian turned back to Tain. His brother's hands hung limp at his side. He would not lift his eyes.

"One can see no reason for so much distress. What is this pretty creature to you, cousin?" Jaspar gave a knowing smile. "He will still be able to perform for you."

"He is my brother!" Carnelian said, aghast.

"That is a ridiculous word to use of one whose blood runs dull and cold." Jaspar reached down to his slave's hand and lifted it. The boy could have been a rag doll. Jaspar opened the boy's hand. "I might as well start claiming this one to be my nephew, or some such."

A green tattoo on the palm proved the boy had been fathered by a Master. Jaspar let the arm flop down.

"The procedure can be made painless. Besides, you can give him beautiful new eyes of stone. Turquoise would match his coloring. Give him sapphires if you wish to pamper him."

Carnelian gaped at Jaspar, then dug his chin into his chest and held his stomach. He dared not look round at Tain.

"Do not be cruel, cousin. Think on my loss," said Jaspar.

Carnelian looked up.

"Yours might at least preserve some of his uses while mine . . ." Jaspar took his slave's chin in a gloved hand, lifted it. The boy's enormous, dark, bruise-lidded eyes closed and trembled. "Without his eyes, this one will be of very little use." He pouted his lips, lapsed into Vulgate. "Isn't that so, little one?" The boy produced a tearful grimace that attempted to be a smile. Jaspar released the slave's chin and turned to Carnelian. "Feel at liberty to remove your mask, and then we shall be equally responsible for the damage of each other's property."

Carnelian shook his head slowly, seeing nothing. Everything was drenched with decay. His father must have expected this would happen and had done nothing to stop it.

Jaspar was all joviality. "You really will have to forget these peculiar sensibilities, Carnelian. They are so unbecoming in one of the Chosen."

Only in the dark did Carnelian remove his mask. Then he lay down, rubbing the edges of his face where the mask had dug in. He clasped his left hand over his blood-ring, the sign of his manhood. It was no charm. He felt like a lonely child. Tain was somewhere outside. Jaspar had insisted it was not fitting that a Lord should sleep in the same place as another's slave. Carnelian had said nothing to Tain. What comfort could he have given him even if Jaspar had not been there? His brother could not have understood the Quya, but he knew well enough what punishment would be his for looking on the face of a Master from another House.

Carnelian could hear Jaspar's slow breathing. He wondered why he felt no anger toward him. It was a terrible betrayal to feel no anger. With a peculiar detachment he considered the conversation he had had with the Master. He knew now that Jaspar's motives for talking to him had not been any attempt at friendship. Jaspar was no different from the other Masters. In that, at least, his father had been right.

Outside a voice was singing. Its sad sound failed to touch Carnelian. Everything seemed to be shut outside him. He wanted to die. What point was there to a life in which one felt nothing? His fingers found the mattress edge. They dangled over. Then, daring sacrilege, they pushed down to touch the unhallowed, corrupted earth. Carnelian expected something, a shock, a sting, but there was nothing, nothing but his fingers stirring dust.

Carnelian was woken by aquar song welcoming the dawn. His body ached all over. He sat up. He could hear the murmur of the camp. Jaspar was gone. Squatting in a corner, Tain was staring at the ground. As Carnelian stood up, his brother came over to help him dress. They adjusted Carnelian's riding cloak avoiding each other's eyes. Carnelian felt that if he were to stretch out his hand he would stub his fingers on the wall that had risen between them.

"I bet you thought those four-horned monsters on the road were dragons, eh, Tain?" He could hear the flat emptiness of his words.

His brother shrugged, bit his lip and continued to adjust the riding cloak.

Carnelian felt as if his bones had been removed. He put his hand on his brother's chest. "How are you feeling, Tain?"

His brother looked up, furious. "How do you think?"

Carnelian looked at those bright angry eyes and imagined them replaced with dead stone. "It's not my fault," he shouted. "It's not." The last word tailed off. He could see that Tain was close to tears.

"I'm sorry, Tain," he said gently. His legs felt too weak to hold him up. Reassurances were on his tongue but he remembered Crail and swallowed them. He reached out to touch Tain, but his brother drew away.

"A Master might see us."

Tain held out his mask. Carnelian took it, put it on, drew

the cowl over his head then walked out into the morning.

A dewy fragrance overlaid the smoky stink. Clinks and voices sounded sharp, seeming nearer than they were. The throng was shifting into motion.

Soon Carnelian was mounted with the other Masters and filing back through the camp. Tain sitting on the baggage found a smile for him. It hurt Carnelian as much as if his brother had thrown a stone. Men levered wagon wheels into turning. Pots clacked as they were stowed. Urine sprayed on embers made hissing steam. Laughter and the shrilling of babies pierced the swelling hubbub.

The Marula jogged their aquar onto the road. Mist hid the animals' bird feet. Another of the way-forts lay a little distance back with its sinister fence of punishment posts. Carnelian gazed out over the stopping place. Its brown flood of travelers was leaching toward them. A diamond-bright gash had torn between earth and sky. Chattering clouds of starlings flashed down from the trees. He turned, sensing the Masters moving off. Soon they were riding in among the trundling chariots, the creaking axles, the chatter of the women, heading southward to where the Naralan met the Guarded Land.

For days they rode with a relentless rhythm, pounding into endless dusty distance. Night brought hri cake, incense, weary hope. Carnelian looked across a chasm at his father. The other Masters were quick to anger. Their Marula cordon beat away the hucksters and the curious. Tain's eyes dulled as if they were already stone. Carnelian hid in his cowl, blood pulsing in his head. The thud and thump of huimur feet. Sandals scuffing, scraping. Wheel rims always rising always falling. Litters rocking. People dragging squalling infants. Hand-carts hard pushed to keep in chariot shadow. Swaying horned saurian heads. To kill time, people quarreled over trifles. Heat. Unbearable heat desiccating everything to chalk. Out from the haze far behind came an endless procession of travelers. Up ahead, it simmered away to nothing.

Carnelian sagged dozing, sometimes sucking furtive gulps of water in the shadow of his cowl, brooding, licking without caring the stone of salt that had been pressed on him as protection from sun madness. His legs, his back, his neck nagged aching. His head nodded, bobbing, keeping time with the rhythm of the road.

Tain was wasting as thin as Jaspar's boy. Carnelian had tried to make him eat, to comfort him. All this had to be done in snatches, for at night Jaspar was always there and in the day Tain was lost amongst the baggage.

Carnelian wore a face of patience over his anguish. He kept Tain away from the tent when Jaspar was there, hoping that the sin might be forgotten. Sometimes, when Carnelian had to undress himself, Jaspar would give him his indulgent idol smile. It was then that Carnelian's self-control wore thinnest.

Jaspar persisted in finding fault with his own slave. It had been agreed that there were to be no punishments on the road and so instead the Master amused himself by describing to the boy those that were waiting for him in Osrakum. Carnelian turned from the slave's sweaty trembling, bit his tongue, struggled for deafness. Their tent stank of the boy's fear.

Pulsing cicadas, buzzing flies, the sounds of the road, all were muffled by the lazy heat. Even in the shade of the cedar the air was stifling, but Carnelian was thankful for the tree. The throng shimmered along the road. Away toward the melting horizon the towers of Maga-Naralante danced their dark flames like a mirage. Vennel pointed toward it.

"My Lords, there we could find discreet comfort: a welcome respite from the road. We would resume our journey refreshed."

"Sometimes legionaries collect the tolls," said Aurum. "They might see through our disguise."

"The markets, the narrow streets," said Suth, "all would be inimical to secrecy."

Vennel muttered his discontent. His aquar echoed him with a rumble in its throat.

The shadow-dapple fused each Master and aquar into a single fantastical creature. Carnelian chewed his lip. Even though their saddle-chairs were almost touching, his father was beyond his reach.

"However much we may share your desires, Vennel, the risk must be avoided," said Suth.

Carnelian fixed his eyes back on the road. He was always on the lookout for Ykoriana's assassins.

"Again I am overruled," said Vennel, "and again I think the diversion will prove the more delaying choice."

"Does my Lord wish to have the matter put to the vote?" said Jaspar.

Vennel turned to him. "Would there be any point?"

"I would vote with you, Vennel. I have a notion to spend a night in something like comfort." He turned to Suth. "Whatever the risk."

"So be it," Aurum said sharply. "My ring I set against yours, Jaspar."

"And mine against Lord Vennel's," said Suth.

Jaspar looked at Carnelian. "It seems then that it is you, cousin, who is to decide the matter."

Even muffled by his cowl and mask, Carnelian could tell the Master was smiling his damned, self-satisfied smile. He surveyed the four Masters in their saddle-chairs. It occurred to him that if he voted with Jaspar it might help the Master forget Tain's sin. It would also bring the pleasure of voting against Aurum. The most important consideration, though, was that he would be voting against his father. His father was to be pitied. Every day that passed showed more clearly the power Aurum had over him.

"Carnelian," Suth said. "How shall your ring fall?"

It was the first time that his father had said anything to him for days. Carnelian looked at him, wishing he could see his face.

"Why do you delay, boy?" said Aurum.

"I shall vote with my father," said Carnelian.

"One is not surprised, my Lord," said Jaspar, "but a little disappointed. Now that you have come of age one did not think that you would so *blindly* follow your father's lead."

Carnelian started at the emphasized word. As they rode back into the crowds, he wondered if there was anything Jaspar would take in exchange for Tain's eyes.

They left the road within sight of Maga-Naralante's black gate. Rolling dust broke over them. Wheels rattled violently as they jolted into the ditches that criss-crossed the track. Foul stenches rose with the flies. Hovels all sticks and wattle leaned over into their path. When the air cleared a little Carnelian saw more of this debris sloping up toward the mud rampart of the city. There were too many vehicles squeezing along the track. A chariot snagged a hovel and tore it down. Its wheel collapsed, swerving the chariot into the path of a huimur. Bleating, the monster swung away, crushing into a crowd of travelers. The wagon it pulled tipped over. Bundles rolled into the gutters. Filthy urchins appeared and swarmed the wreck. The traffic built up behind. Annoyance swelled to anger then burst into riot. It was easy for Carnelian to imagine assassins in the crowd. Aurum must have shared his fears for he ordered the Marula to slay a path through the mob. People were cut down screaming. Carnelian stared into a face foaming blood, then he leapt his aquar over the wagon pole and loped off along the track after his father.

"Trouble comes often to those who are too cunning," said Vennel.

"It comes always to those who show no cunning at all," said Suth.

Aurum had his back to them. "The straightest road is not always the fastest." He had made the Marula put the enclosure up around an ant's nest. He had opened its belly with a knife, dropped in a firebrand and was using another to crisp the ants that sallied out.

"Blood burns brighter than oil," said Jaspar.

Suth and Vennel both turned on him.

He lifted his hands in apology. "I thought we were listing proverbs."

"I fail to see, my Lords, how our objectives were served by what happened today," said Vennel.

"What happened today is irrelevant," snapped Suth. Carnelian saw his father looking at him as if he were just out of reach.

"If we remained undiscovered it is due to fortune and not to any skill in planning on your part, my Lords," said Vennel. "I would hazard that the commotion and the violence of our escort did little to turn attention away from us."

"Violence is not uncommon on this road," said Suth.

"So you say, my Lord, so you say. But I do not think that creatures of the kind we mimic would show such élan for slaughter."

Carnelian searched his father's eyes. It was as if he were trying to say something to him. Carnelian rose and moved toward him.

Suth immediately stood up and looked down at Vennel. "My patience with this discussion is at an end, my Lord." He put on his mask, hid it with his cowl and left the enclosure.

Vennel looked at the other Masters as if surprised. Jaspar smiled enigmatically. Aurum looked bored as he lit the ants one by one like candlewicks.

On the thirteenth day after they had left the sea Carnelian noticed a darker southern horizon: a crack between earth and sky that could only be the rim of the Guarded Land. Next morning it looked closer, a ribbon of liquid blue dividing the world. That day and for the next two it was lost in the blinding white burning of the Naralan, but the day after that it formed a permanent smudging lilac layer in the haze. It crisped and browned, bubbling up so that when they camped that night it had solidified into a heavy banding of the darkening sky.

The eighteenth day dawned. That day the cliffs of the Guarded Land wavered up from the simmering plains as a dark forbidding wall.

The road climbed into a cutting in the cliff, its gradient so gentle that when it reached its first turn and doubled back, its corbeled edge was obscured by the flags of the chariots passing beneath. Its scar zigzagged up the rock seemingly all the way to the clouds.

"The road climbs to the very top?" Carnelian asked, incredulous.

"More accurately it descends it," Vennel replied.

"We had it built down from the Guarded Land so that we might reach the sea," said Jaspar.

"The city of Nothnaralan waits for us up there," said Jaspar.

Carnelian pushed his head back against his saddle-chair to try to see the sky city. "With what sorcery was all this wonder wrought?"

"Not sorcery but sartlar," said Suth.

Carnelian could hardly believe that his father was talking to him. "It must have cost many lives," he said, trying to nurse this little spark of intimacy.

"It is said that this hill is the knitted mounding of their bones."

Carnelian glanced back down the slope that carried the road to the plain. "So much death."

"The sartlar are a limitless resource."

"The world is as verminous with such creatures as slaves are with lice," sneered Vennel.

"Are they all enslaved?" asked Carnelian, resenting the Master's intrusion, aiming his question at his father.

Vennel turned his hood toward Carnelian. "Is that not what their name means?"

"Yet once they were free," said Suth. "When our Quyan forefathers scaled this cliff to the land above, they found the sartlar already there and—"

"And domesticated them," snapped Aurum.

Carnelian could have cursed him. Now that the Master had spoken, his father would say nothing more.

"Come, my Lords," the old Master continued. "We are not at some elegant reception." His hand lifting caused the Marula to rise up from where they had been huddled round them in a ring. "It is time that we rejoin the road and begin the ascent. Several days must pass before we reach the land above."

"One might forgive the creature's sin," purred Jaspar.

The words made no impression on Carnelian's mind. He was already exhausted from the climb and still they were only halfway up to the Guarded Land.

"You would of course have to pay me recompense," said Jaspar in a low voice. "For such a one to go unpunished . . ."

Carnelian turned blind eyes on the cowled figure.

"Do you toy with me, my Lord?" said Jaspar, warming to anger.

"My Lord?"

"What price will you pay to save his eyes?"

Jaspar came into hard focus. "You speak of my brother?" said Carnelian.

"Your slave, my Lord."

Carnelian frowned. He must not let his fury wake, nor his hope. "What price would my Lord ask for this act of mercy?" he asked coldly.

Jaspar turned away, gazing out into airy space. "If I were to forget that the creature had looked upon my face it would be more than an act of mercy, Carnelian." He turned back. His cowl framed an oval of blackness. "There is but one price, cousin."

Carnelian stared at him as the anger bubbled up in him. "Well?" he cried, boiling over.

"Hush, Carnelian. We would not want the others to learn of our negotiations, would we? It is a simple boon I desire from you, namely, I would know what hold Aurum has over your father."

"You would have me betray my own father ... for a slave?"

Jaspar chuckled. "Come now, Carnelian, look how quickly your brother has become your slave."

"It is unthinkable," gasped Carnelian.

"Perhaps ... and yet I think you would like your brother to keep his bright, animal eyes."

Carnelian shook his head. "I cannot do it."

Jaspar opened his hands. "Perhaps my Lord will change his mind. Think on it, but do not take too long. The day the boy sees the outermost gate of Osrakum could well be the last day he sees anything at all."

Jaspar pulled his cloak round him and hunched before slipping through the screens.

Carnelian watched him go, trying to see through his hatred the slim hope that lay in the offer. Some pennants jiggled like butterflies above the screens. The next push up the road was beginning. Carnelian turned for one last look out across the vast pale wash of the Naralan spread out below, then he left the parapet.

They were climbing into purple sky. The edge of the cliff above was jagged with tottering tenements, streaked green with the filth that ran down their walls. A sewage stench wafted on the torrid air. They walked their aquar up onto the lip of the Guarded Land. The end of the climb at last. The throng fanned out to carpet the level field that had been gouged into the plateau edge. It was like half a bowl sunk into the stone of the cliff. Its sides merged up into the towered mud ramparts of Nothnaralan, whose dusty sunset-rouged face was drilled with countless windows. The whole smooth curve was unbroken except at one place in the east where stony towers intruded to offer up a pair of doors, bloodied gates upon which the sun was embossing the twin faces of the Commonwealth in flaming gold.

"Thus does the Commonwealth attempt to close her doors against the night," said Suth in a melancholy tone.

The road had spread its tapestry all around them. They had managed to reach the eastern edge of the field near the gates. Aurum had not allowed them their enclosure, judging that it would not hide them from the windows in the walls above. The other Masters had all been too weary to protest.

Carnelian looked past the cordon of the Marula, out over the squatting masses, over the clumps of wagons and huimur, to where the city walls had already been claimed by darkness.

"I think I will retire, my Lords," said Vennel. The shadow in the loop of his cowl scanned them as if he expected some retort. When the Masters said nothing, he rose, hunched as they always did to conceal their height, and shuffled off toward the tents.

Carnelian glanced at his father's inanimate form and turned back to his vigil. He watched the shadow of the city creep over the camp, lighting fires as it went. Its blackness washed over him, lapped at the foot of the gates, then scaled them to the very top. The sky gave one last violent blush, then indigoed. With its windows now lit up, Nothnaralan formed a hem to the starry night.

Carnelian struggled to sleep in the clinging myrrhy heat. The bandages were restricting his breathing. Sweat crawled beneath the cloth. His heart would not quieten. Memories of his island home flashed into his mind. Every image had acquired a warm aura. He ached with the longing for friendly faces, familiar smells, a single lungful of cold clean wind that spoke with the voices of the sea. There were other darker visions. Tain eyeless, the empty sockets accusing him. He had made a promise to Ebeny to protect him. The thought of Jaspar's offer caused a rushing in his stomach. Carnelian fixed his mind's eye on the memory of the double-headed gate and felt a sweat of excitement. What wonders lay beyond?

Jaspar groaned in his sleep. Carnelian sat up. The camp was murmuring outside. With slow care he rose. He fumbled for his traveling cloak, found it, gathered it in. He tucked his ranga shoes under his arm, crept to the opening, put the shoes outside, stepped up onto them, covered himself, then pushed his masked face out into the night.

The moon was setting into a smoke-scratched blue darkness in which a hundred campfires flickered. The smells and sounds of beasts and men were gently settling. He looked over to the gate glimmered by moonlight.

He was searching for Tain when he noticed some moving shapes. A coalescing of the night. Lifting up, moving, merging, dropping down, disappearing. He waited. They rose again, came closer. He wondered if they might be Marula, but the shapes were too furtive. To see better, Carnelian dared to remove his mask. He turned it sideways so that he could still breathe through the nose-pad. Over its rim he scoured the night. The Marula were still round them like a ring of stones. Again the shadows slid into motion. Again they stopped and vanished. Cold sweat, fear and his eyes searching. He bit his lip, looked round and made his decision. He dropped down from his shoes. Half in crouch, half crawling, he moved forward, touching the earth now and then for balance. He reached one of the Marula and crept into the man's aura of stale sweat. His fingers touched the man's warm skin. As it jerked under his touch, Carnelian hugged the man hard against his chest and stifled a cry with his hand. He pushed his mouth into an ear. "I'm a Master," he whispered, and felt the burr of the man's hair and an earring moving against his lip. The Maruli tensed hard as wood. "Silence. You understand?" The woolly head nodded against his face. Carnelian released him. Saw the yellow eyes, watched them widen, then the man was cowering against his knees.

Carnelian grimaced as he understood. "My face," he muttered. He sighed, looked around desperately. He put the mask on again, bent down and, prising the man up, forced him to look at it. There was more yellow-eyed terror before he forced the man's head round. At first there was nothing to see but then the shadows moved again, very close. The Maruli clutched his lance. Carnelian released his head so that the man's frightened eyes swiveled back to his mask. Carnelian indicated the other Marula. The man struck his forehead on the ground then slipped into the night.

Carnelian retraced his steps. He was near the mounds of the tents. Cries broke out, so loud they stopped his breathing. He whisked round and saw a shadow dance. Screams. A swish of blades muffling into flesh. Growls. Two shapes broke from the fight and catapulted toward him. One fell forward, coughing, with a tall shape on it working a lance out of its back. The other veered away.

Carnelian saw where it was heading. "The tents!" he cried and sprang after it. Uproar was spreading. Through the eye-slits of his mask he could just make out the figure. There was the stuttering rasp of canvas rending. Carnelian stooped as he ran, grazing his fingers along the ground, scooped up a stone, then charged howling. He heard his father's voice crying out in alarm, then he crashed into the invader, clawing and hammering with the stone. He was enraged, keening, fearing for his father's life. The body slumped against him. He let it slide off him to the ground.

A light. Carnelian stared frozen. On the ground, his father was pathetically stretching out his fingers trying to reach his mask; hands, face, bandaged body black with blood.

WINDSPEED

Right hand, left hand

What has passed, what is to come

The green and the black

Earth and Sky

Two faces and the Mirror

But in truth they are all one

—FRAGMENT

"Douse that light," hissed Aurum, a tower of blackness in the night. The boy holding the lantern turned to stare at him, his eyes growing impossibly wide. The Master surged forward, snatched the lantern from the boy and dashed it to the ground.

The sudden disappearance of his father's bloody face brought Carnelian back to life. His eyes adjusted slowly to the dark.

Angry questions carried through the night with complaints about the noise, the lateness.

One of the Marula appeared and fell at Aurum's feet.

"Take your brethren and silence those voices with fear," the Master rumbled.

The man punched the ground with his head, rose and was about to go when Aurum spoke again.

"Take this thing," he said, lifting the boy squealing into the air. "Destroy it."

There was a coughing behind him. "He is . . . my body . . . slave," said Suth.

Aurum shoved the boy at the Maruli who received him with a grunt and loped off. The Master crouched down beside Suth. "Are you wounded, my Lord?"

Suth trembled his hand in the air. "The boy . . ."

"He saw your face, Sardian. You will have to make do without him. Are you wounded?"

Suth gritted his teeth as he held his side. "A cut in my belly."

Carnelian stared. "He is covered in blood."

Suth smiled up at his son. "Most of it is the assassin's."

Aurum peeled Suth's hand away from the wound and peered at it. He stood up. "It is quite deep but bleeds cleanly. The bandages resisted the blade. Do you think you can walk, my Lord?"

Suth jerked a nod and Aurum helped him up. Carnelian felt his father's wince like a stab. Suth pressed on the wound to keep it closed. The bandages looked black under his hand.

"Why are you just standing there, my Lord?" said Aurum to Carnelian with a flash of anger. Carnelian stumbled round to support his father's other side. "This wounding is unfortunate but at least it has drawn Ykoriana's sting. Now we must abandon secrecy."

In Carnelian's grip, the stone still nestled warm and sticky.

They gathered in the enclosure that Aurum had commanded the Marula put up around the corpse and shredded tent. He waved away Vennel's comment about the eyes from above and, by unmasking, forced the Master to remove his mask with the others. The light had gone out of Vennel's face. His colorless eyes turned reluctantly to Suth sitting stiff-backed on a stool. "These robbers have spilled your precious blood, my Lord. They would not have dared had they known you to be Chosen."

"These were no robbers," said Aurum.

With his foot he rolled the corpse's head to one side and drew its tunic down with his toe. A lantern on the ground revealed the red ruin of its face. Carnelian stared, clenching and unclenching the fingers from which Tain had had to prise the stone.

Aurum indicated the six-spoked wheel tattooed just above the corpse's clavicle. "It would be strange indeed if the Brotherhood of the Wheel were to send their men so far merely to rob some merchants."

Vennel was mesmerized by the tattoo. "What else?"

"Assassination."

Carnelian tore his eyes away from the tattoo to look at Aurum. Vennel also looked round and Carnelian could see the way his eyes were avoiding contact.

Aurum looked down. "These creatures meant to slay us all."

"All?" Vennel examined the old Master's face. "How so?"

"They are hired killers. They came at night. They could not know which tent was which. To slay one they had to slay us all."

"Which . . . which of the Chosen, however desperate, would thus dare breach the Blood Convention?" breathed Vennel.

Jaspar gave him a filthy look. "Your pretenses begin to wear parchment-thin, my Lord."

Vennel sneaked glimpses at the other Masters as if their sleeves might conceal daggers. "Even Ykoriana would not dare . . ." he said at last.

Aurum rounded on him. "You think not? Even after she murdered her own daughter within the very precincts of the Labyrinth?"

"That is an ugly rumor."

Suth's stormy eyes were gazing at Vennel. "Believe what you will, my Lord, but do not try to deny that your mistress lies behind this outrage. You should perhaps consider that your own blood would have soaked this ground had my son not raised the alarm."

Suth looked at his son. The warm pride Carnelian saw in his father's eyes melted him a little.

Vennel's face was ice. "Even the Empress could not hope to wash her hands of such blood as ours."

Suth indicated the corpse. "She wore these creatures like gloves that could easily be discarded. Who would dare accuse her as she pointed to her own emissary found among the dead?"

Jaspar nodded grimly. "Our disguise would allow the Wise to give interminable sermons on the price that must be paid by those who disregard the Law."

Carnelian's eyes had been pulled back to the corpse. "How many of the Marula were slain?"

"A handful," said Aurum, without turning. His mouth twisted with contempt. "She has used you for a fool, Vennel." He snorted. "And now you even confess complicity in a breach of the Blood Convention."

Vennel turned away to hide frantic, calculating eyes. "By all the huimur of the Commonwealth and on my own blood I swear that all I was party to was a temporary abduction, a delay that would ensure the election should go ahead without us, nothing more, no attacks, certainly not bloodshed . . ."

Jaspar was looking into space. "How can one believe that the Brotherhood would dare raise their hands against the Chosen? We have tolerated their activities for centuries. This single act invites annihilation."

"It is likely they knew not what they did," said Suth.

"How did they find us?" asked Carnelian.

"Well . . ." said Vennel. As they all looked at him, he floated his hands in elegant apology. "In good faith, my Lords, and bearing in mind that my blood is as much at risk as yours—"

Jaspar dropped his forehead into his hand. "Do we have to listen to this?"

Vennel flinched. "The Legate and I came to an arrangement. A message was sent to Osrakum."

Jaspar chopped a sign of contempt. "Do you imagine we did not know? Why else do you think we forwent the leftway where you expected us to be?" He turned his back on Vennel and addressed Aurum. "Do you think, my Lord, that any of these vermin escaped to carry word of their failure?"

"That is immaterial," said Aurum. He swung his arm round in an arc to take in the city wall. "It is certain the Brotherhood had eyes up there to monitor the attack."

Carnelian searched the wall, but it was as dark as the sky.

"When will Ykoriana know that they have failed?" asked Jaspar.

"Even by leftway courier, she could not have received Vennel's message much before the day that we passed Maga-Naralante, ten days after we set off from the sea," said Aurum.

"Surely not ten days," said Jaspar.

"You ignore the difficulty in getting the message secretly up from the City at the Gates to Osrakum and into Ykoriana's hand in her forbidden house."

"Assuming you are right, my Lord, that would allow her at most only nine days to get the assassins here."

Aurum jabbed the corpse with the toe of his ranga. "We are at least sixty days by road from Osrakum. This thing was already here."

"Not if it came here on the leftway," said Jaspar.

Suth shook his head. "That would be difficult without the complicity of the Wise. Besides, she would not risk being so easily incriminated. The traffic records for the leftways are meticulously kept."

"Either way," said Aurum, "it is probable that in a few days Ykoriana will learn that she has failed. Desperation will make her doubly dangerous. We must reduce the time she has to spin another web. We must use the leftway."

"On the leftway we will be exposed," said Vennel.

"Thanks to you, my Lord, we are exposed wherever we go," grated Suth.

"What of your wound, Lord Suth?" asked Jaspar.

Carnelian disliked the way Vennel's eyes turned to feast on his father.

Suth smiled. "A scratch."

Carnelian remembered how much blood there had been. He looked away, over the canvas wall, and saw above the gate a paler edge of sky. "Behold, the morning," he said, with wonder. He had believed the night would never end.

The clanging of stone bells could be heard all across the field. Beneath the city wall everyone stood waiting, looking toward the closed gates. Carnelian and the other Masters were formed up within the cordon of the Marula. He was anxious that his aquar as it shifted should not step on the flattened tents. Beneath the canvas the corpses of the assassins lay side by side with the Marula they had killed. Though it was their custom, Aurum had not allowed the Marula to burn their dead. They glanced furtively at the canvas, stroking the salt bracelets they had stripped from the corpses. One of them sat stiffer than the others. Carnelian kept noticing the red corners of his eyes and so knew the man was looking at him. When the black face angled toward him, gaunt with fear, Carnelian recognized it as belonging to the Maruli who had seen him unmasked the night before. There was no way he could reassure the man that he was safe, but Carnelian was determined to keep their secret. There was already enough blood on his hands.

A grinding grumble drew his eyes away to where a crack was widening down the center of the gate. As the faces on the doors swung inward to look at each other, the crowd murmur rose in pitch. Everything began to shuffle forward. A slow rhythm of huimur bells, axles and wheel trundle answered the steady ringing from the towers. Fully opened, the gates released a river of travelers from the city. The two flows sheared against each other with a continuous protest. Consternation spread outward from their meeting. Something fearful. The uproar hissed toward the Masters like flames across a parched fernland. From the chatter, Carnelian snatched the single, chilling word "Plague."

Aurum barked an order and the Marula dismounted round them to form a ring of spear points. It looked to Carnelian a frail defense. Still, when he looked for Tain, he was relieved to see him with the baggage inside the ring.

Carnelian watched Aurum's hunch lean down to one of the Marula. As the old Master sat back, his action seemed to jerk the man up into his saddle-chair. The Maruli strode his aquar off into the crowd and was consumed by it. When he returned, he spoke to Aurum, pointing his arm toward the gate.

When Aurum turned to shout something, Carnelian and the other Masters strained to hear.

". . . mere rumor carried here from . . . south. If plague exists . . . far away . . . might . . . burn itself out before . . . reach it. We go on."

Vennel straightened up. "Should we not consider remaining in Nothnaralan?" His high voice carried more clearly than the old Master's. "We could wait it out. Surely it would be foolish to ignore the peril."

"We shall go on," shouted Aurum. "If it is your wish . . . remain here."

Carnelian saw his father and Jaspar lift their hands in agreement. Aurum nodded, then commanded the Marula to remount. Aurum's hand punched more commands into the air. The Marula reversed their lances and began to bludgeon a path with the hafts. As the aquar cleaved into the flow their quivering plume fans showed their distress. The Marula jerked their reins tight and continued forcing their way through the crowd. Carnelian's chair was jolted continuously as he followed his father in their wake.

The crowd surged in waves against them. Carnelian grew tired. When he looked up, the gate seemed further away. The tide was against them. More and more people were pouring out from the gateway into the field. The buffeting was driving him to rage.

"This is unbearable!"

For a moment Carnelian fancied it was his own voice crying out, but his teeth were clenched, his lips pressed closed.

"Digging a ditch in water."

It was his father's voice ringing clear above the turmoil. Carnelian saw his shrouded mass unfolding to betray his height. His huge hand appeared and with a sudden motion, he pulled his hood back. His bandaged head was revealed and his mask that was a piece of sun. Carnelian was transfixed by that gold face, the serene center of the storm. He watched his father lunge forward so that his saddle-chair collided with one of the Marula. He watched his father grab the man's salt-bangled arm. The Maruli turned, lifting his lance in menace, stared wide-eyed at the mask, then down at the white Master's hand that held him. Suth shouted something before he let go and the Maruli bowed so low his head disappeared between his thighs. When he came up he was bellowing and holding his arm out as if he were cooling it from the Master's touch. The other Marula craned round, saw the Master's terrible mirror face, slitted their eyes and brayed battle cries as they turned their lance blades on the crowd.

"We are revealed Lords of the Hidden Land," boomed Aurum pushing back his hood. The crowd slid distorted across his mask as he scanned it. "Take care, this riot might conceal our enemies."

Jaspar gave a fierce cry and straightened in his chair as he too revealed himself. Vennel unbent more slowly. Carnelian watched his hand waver but then the Master followed the others. Carnelian was last of all. He glanced uneasily at the throng but realized it was futile to search it for assassins.

As the Marula's aquar strode forward, the crowd gave way grudgingly, snarling. Faces were turning to look, then a chorus of voices struck up. "Masters! Masters!"

The word spread panic more rapidly than had the rumor of plague. Swathes of people were collapsing to their knees. The Marula trampled ahead regardless, scything their lance blades before them. Carnelian watched the crowd, in flight, yawn a corridor all the way to the gate. Down this he and the Masters sped. On either side the gates flung up their walls of wood. He glimpsed the bronze sneers of the faces high above. He was clattering up a ramp into a screaming, echoing canyon. A continuous mass of beasts and men slipped by. His aquar loped on, dodging wagons. A mudbrick wall coursed past on his right with people flattened against it open-mouthed. Shrilling children dashed from his path.

The road ahead forked round a tower. As he rode into its shadow, he could make out windows, a parapet. There was a rush of noise. At the edge of his vision the Masters and the Marula were rearing back. Plumes flared as Carnelian's own aquar juddered to a stop. As he toppled to one side he yanked the reins, causing the world to sweep before his eyes.

"Toll, toll," coarse voices cried in Vulgate above the roar.

Carnelian's aquar struck something and there was a clatter of things hitting the ground. His world steadied. He saw a tinker's angry face. The woman behind him went bloodless. Her look leapt to the other faces looking up. People began bending, groveling, moaning.

Carnelian's hand strayed up to his mask. After so long hiding he had felt naked when they looked at him. He saw the toll-gatherers. Their high conical caps bore the city's cipher of the ladder and the sea. For a moment their faces showed fierce defiance but then the moaning spread to them. Their mouths gaped so wide they squeezed tears from the slitted eyes above them. Their billhooks toppled like scythed reeds.

"Make way," Aurum cried in Vulgate as he hung above them, vast and menacing.

People shuffled aside, bleating. A wagon was rolling out of the way. The road seemed carpeted with dead. The Marula moved forward between the toll posts and the Masters followed. Echoes flattened as they came into the open, into a marketplace, that swelled wide then narrowed in the distance almost to a point. The road was a loop raised around its edge upon which crowds were slowly circling the sunken center with its mess of stalls. As they rode nearer, chariots rolled their man-high wheels left to right across Carnelian's vision. Among their arches people ambled and the heads of saurians bobbed floating. It seemed an impenetrable flow.

Carnelian felt the rising anger of the Masters. Sitting tall and terrible in their midst, his father lifted his arm and with it sent the Marula crashing headlong. As their chevron cut into the crowd, the Masters followed them. Carnelian clung to his chair as if he were riding a small boat down rapids. They were picking up speed as they drove everything before them. Carnelian felt the power pistoning up through his saddle-chair as they blew along the road like a gale. A woman scrambled screaming from Carnelian's path. His aquar swung round a wagon that was turning ponderously out of his way. He felt the shatter of each dropped pot. Gourds rolled like heads. Someone slipped, tumbling crunched into a ball. Carnelian gritted his teeth as his aquar kicked and stumbled through the obstruction. The buildings on his right were wearing the first lurid colors of the sun. He had dizzy glimpses of the mudbrick façade with its porticoes and tiers in which cracks led down into alleyways. From the corner of his eye he had an impression that a storm was rising in the east. Looking off between the jumbled stalls, he saw the gloomy rampart that defined the other side of the marketplace. His aquar was slowing to a walk. He turned and saw that the road ahead was choked by a convoy of wagons. Beyond these there rose a thick stone wall behind which loomed a tower, a truncated pyramid pricked with windows. Spars grew up from the pyramid, as if some ship had run aground and rotted away leaving only its ribs; three on either side resembling the prongs of a fork. The nearest middle prong carried a plaque. When Carnelian screwed up his eyes he could make out a ring glyph and below it the two spots and three bars of the number seventeen.

One of the wagons was rolling free and the Marula were already streaming through the gap. Soon Carnelian and the Masters had fallen in behind them. It turned out that tower seventeen was set on the corner of a road that left the marketplace heading westward. The wall that hid the tower to the waist continued round the marketplace to two more identical towers.

Carnelian saw they were heading toward a monolith set near the tower corner close to the wall. As they came closer, soldiers appeared from behind it. Aurum rode forward while Suth formed the Marula into a cordon to keep back the throng. Carnelian watched the old Master ride into the soldiers as they were trying to kneel and edged his own aquar closer.

". . . bear a pass," Aurum was saying to one of the auxiliaries, who was a marumaga. He passed down a silver tablet ridged with spirals.

As the man took it, Carnelian could see that he had a brass collar inscribed at the throat with the ring glyph, on either side of which were his service and rank rings.

"This pass allows what you demand, Master, but I have my instructions from the legate of this city." He pointed across the marketplace to the black rampart.

"It is you and not the legate who are the keeper of this watchtower," Aurum rumbled. "This pass demands unconditional obedience."

The marumaga faltered and began chewing his quivering lip. "Although I am its keeper, this watchtower still lies within the jurisdiction of the local legate, my Master."

"Enough," cried Suth.

The marumaga took a nervous step back as this second Master rode his aquar toward him.

"Keeper, you've seen our pass. Now you have a simple choice: either you let us through or else you delay us. If you choose the latter I'll have a chair upholstered with the skin from your back."

The marumaga looked ill. His watery eyes flicked from one mask to the other. His head began nodding in an uneven rhythm. "Of course, Master, of course . . . the pass is entirely valid."

Jogging, looking back many times, he led them to the monolith where the Masters dismounted. Carnelian handed his reins to one of the auxiliaries as he saw the others do. Although the monolith lay very close to the watchtower, a passage angled behind it with space enough for the aquar to pass through in single file. Beyond, a doorway led into dank gloom.

Lantern light allowed Carnelian to see the doors that ran along one wall. A ramp angled up against another. As they began to climb he was deafened by the scrape of aquar claws and the clatter of ranga shoes. The ramp brought them up to another level whose flagstones were smothered with straw. The place stank of the aquar that could be seen in stalls.

As they climbed more ramps, Carnelian glimpsed machinery and the counterweights that spoke of other doors. Skeletal men with large eyes hid as they passed. Their thin fear reminded him of the massacre of the sailors on the baran. He disliked their cringing even more than the rings and seventeens branded into their faces.

At last they came up into a lofty hall, cheered by purling water. Squat columns held up a weave of heavy beams. Shafts let light in from the floors above. Ladders hung on the walls. Running down one side of the hall was a cistern filling from a spout. Men clambered up on either side of a portcullis to release the counterweights that allowed others to lift it. Carnelian led his aquar out past another monolith into the bright morning.

He walked to a parapet and saw the market's roaring seethe laid out below him.

"A leftway, at last a leftway," said Jaspar.

Carnelian turned. It was only then that he realized they were standing on a road that ran along the top of the wall he had seen from below. In one direction it crossed the west road by means of a narrow bridge. In the other, it curved off to the next watchtower.

As their aquar loped round above the marketplace, Carnelian saw that the tower ahead bore the number eighteen high in its ribs. He made a broad scan from the north, where the Guarded Land fell away into the sky, to the south where it ran flat to the horizon. Nothnaralan's half-circle seemed scorched into the land's rusty edge. He could see a wall running alongside the western road carrying the continuation of the same leftway along which he rode. If instead of coming this way they had turned to cross the bridge beside watchtower seventeen they could have ridden its pale thread through the city and out beyond it to fade into the hazy western sky.

As they drew closer to watchtower eighteen they came to a fork in the leftway. One branch crossed to the watchtower over a narrow bridge that spanned the southern road: the other turned south to run beside it.

"Here we leave the Ringwall," Aurum boomed as the Marula made the turn.

Carnelian looked up at the plaque, suddenly understanding its ring glyph. He stared in wonder at the leftway that continued over the bridge and past the watchtower into the east. Should he ride that way, in months or maybe years he would have made a complete circuit of the wall that enclosed the Guarded Land. He looked over the back of his saddle-chair. He would come from the west riding the top of the Ringwall round to that very spot. Giving the market and the fortress one last look, he turned his aquar's head south to follow the others.

They sped above a moldering chaos of mud walls, flat roofs, views down into alleys, stairways, balconies. Below them, a river of people rumbled along the southern road. They passed earth ramparts that were crumbling into a moat. Beyond, the poorer outskirts of Nothnaralan spread their shambling messy browns. Tumbled hovels squashed together into neighborhoods. Dust choked crooked lanes. They reached the city border ditch with its torn palisades. Beyond stretched a limitless rusty plain bisected by the line of the road.

Aurum shouted something into the scorching wind and the Marula surged ahead, black cloaks flapping. The Master lifted his hand, signing. A dove's wing flap.

Windspeed, read Carnelian. It was not difficult to guess the meaning. The aquar ahead were already slipping away. The rocking quickened as his mount leapt after them. He was thrown from side to side, each swing smaller than the last, then his robe was snapping up around him, the chair vibrating, the parapets pouring past. The wind dissolved the din of the road, pressed him back into the chair, slipped his hood off, then streaked his ears with half-heard cries.

The Guarded Land was tiled with brown squares that faded shrinking to every horizon. Its monotony was only relieved by wheels that dotted the fields, turning constantly. A heavy sky pressed the whole scene flat. It was only when he listened to the wind and watched the rushing parapet that Carnelian knew he was flying.

At some point he felt the motion of his aquar faltering. Its head trembled and the milky inner lids flickered across its eyes. Fatigue shuddered up from its flanks as its speed slackened. He disliked forcing the creature on, but had to make sure of keeping up with the others.

Ahead, a watchtower looked like a woman holding her arms up high in a dance. Carnelian was relieved as Aurum began to slow. The tower became a giant. He eased his aquar to a walk. The chair began jerking. His cloak fell lifeless. Clamor swelled up from the road. The air was pungent with peculiar odors. His aquar lifted its heron head and opened the fans of its eye-plumes. Every movement had become ponderous, heavy. Every step the creature took jarred him to the bone. Carnelian felt like a bird snatched suddenly from the sky.

The leftway ended at a narrow bridge. He crossed it with the others, riding past the counterweights that fanned out from its hinges to allow the bridge to be lifted.

Around him the aquar were folding their legs, sinking the Masters and Marula to the ground. Carnelian saw more aquar were waiting for them, larger than the ones they had been riding and as sleek and silver as fish. Their plumes were the color of poppies. Elegant saddle-chairs were strapped to their backs. Slaves held them while auxiliaries stood to one side. Beside them, sinister in their silver masks, two figures in purple brocade were watching everything. Carnelian wondered by what sorcery these ammonites had known of their coming.

A marumaga came forward and knelt before Aurum. Suth was still climbing out of his chair. Carnelian had accepted his father's assurance about his wound and was thus alarmed to see with what care he moved and, when he straightened, how he pressed a hand to his side. Other slaves ran forward to deal with the baggage. Tain was helped down. He looked round at Carnelian with a face so gaunt that Carnelian almost did not know him. His brother gave a thin smile that was very Tain. Carnelian remembered Jaspar's offer. The thought of betraying his wounded father put a knot in his stomach.

The Marula were already mounting the new aquar. Tain was rummaging through the baggage. He pulled some packs from it and then watched as the grooms began to carry the rest away.

A whining led Carnelian to look down to see a groom offering him one of the fresh aquar. He examined the man's face with its bloodshot, fearful eyes. The forehead was branded with the sea glyph and four bars. By the way three of the bars were grouped, Carnelian read all four together, as one hundred and fifteen. Craning, he looked up the tower to where its wooden ribs overhung the leftway like the branches of a tree. He found that the plaque attached to the middle rib bore the same number. Above this a man was hanging in a kind of cage.

The groom was still there below him, waiting. Carnelian gave his aquar the signal that made it lower him to the ground. He climbed out of the saddle-chair and pointed up at the caged man. "Punishment?"

The groom fell to his knees and bowed his head.

Carnelian nudged the man with his foot. "Well?"

"A lookout, Master, in a deadman's chair."

Carnelian left the man alone, and mounted the silver aquar that pushed him smoothly up into the air. He ran his hand along the oily black curving rim of his new seat. Adjusting himself into it, he found that it fitted him better. As he moved toward the other Masters he was surprised by the different rhythm of the aquar's walk.

Vennel moved his animal to block the way. "The speed is delightful, my Lord, is it not?"

Carnelian could not understand why Vennel was suddenly trying to make conversation.

"How frequently must we make these stops?" he heard his father say.

"I will try to keep them to a minimum, my Lord," said Aurum. "But it will serve neither of us if we lose speed."

The Master moved off to speak to the marumaga tower keeper. Carnelian made some polite noises and walked his aquar round Vennel's to approach his father.

"Are you in pain, Lord?" he asked quietly when he had come near.

"It will get better," his father replied. "It is just that the riding has opened the wound a little. Where is Tain?"

Carnelian looked round and found his brother sitting in between the legs of one of the Marula.

"Are we ready, my Lords?" said Aurum.

The Masters made signs of affirmation. Aurum lifted his hand signing, *Windspeed*.

On and on like arrows flying. Three watchtowers they ignored but, as the aquar were tiring, they stopped at the fourth; it was numbered one hundred eleven, from which Carnelian surmised they would pass one hundred ten more before reaching Osrakum. Again, exactly the right number of fresh aquar were waiting for them.

Carnelian felt a giddiness from stopping and the clammy hot clutch of the odored air. His problems returned, his unease. He hungered for the cool rushing oblivion in the mouthing wind. Instead there was the humdrum rumble from the road below, anxiety over the pain his father concealed, the sight of Tain being passed among the Marula like baggage. The changeover was faster this time and he breathed his relief when he was up again in the wind that washed everything away.

At watchtower sea one hundred nine, they paused again. Everything had been ready, and they quickly resumed their headlong speed. They had passed one more tower and the next one was just a peg pinning the thread of road down to the plain when it emitted a spark. Ahead, an aquar flared its plumes as if it had been startled and began to fall back. He saw its rider, Aurum, pulling on its reins, straining to look round. At first Carnelian thought that the Master was looking back at him but soon realized he was looking past him. Carnelian struggled to peer round the back of his chair. The watchtower they had just left was holding a star between its stretched up hands. This disappeared, then reappeared. He watched it flash on and off several times, then nothing. He sat back, rubbing the twisting out of his neck but froze when he saw the tower ahead giving an answering candle flicker.

The next time they stopped Carnelian tried without success to see what it was that was up on the platform held aloft by the six arms of the watchtower. As they set off he made sure to keep his eye on the road. Two flashes near the rusty horizon confirmed his suspicion. The watchtower ahead had been informed of their coming.

Two more watchtowers went by and a third was in sight when Carnelian saw it give a double flash. He was wondering what it could be responding to when they all began to slow. They had soon rocked to a halt. At Aurum's command, the Marula were dismounting and unhitching their lances from their saddle-chairs. He watched Aurum shape them into a cordon across the road, facing back the way they had come where there was a tower tiny in the distance. He began to suffer from the heat. His mask felt as if it was sliding off his sweating face. The Guarded Land's spicy odor hung heavy in the air. It had been there every time they stopped.

He gazed out across the land, a becalmed ocean of dust. He walked his aquar to the parapet to look down onto the road. The smell rising up reminded him of the weary journey from the sea. The road was too large for the traffic. Its glaring white was only half skinned over with people. He lifted his head high and sniffed the exhalation of the land. Musky earth, pungent hri fields, perhaps an undercurrent of human dung.

Near him the Marula were looking uneasy. Over their heads he saw a tiny figure melting toward them in the heat. Its little flame grew slowly larger until he could hear the rhythmic scratching of claws. At last the rider swept up on an aquar identical to the ones they rode, streaming behind him a banner of green and black. Aurum barked an order and the Marula lowered their lances. The rider seemed blind to the blades awaiting him, only at the last moment pulling up, so that the Marula were forced to fall back from the frantic flailing of his aquar's hands.

"Way," the rider cried, "way!" He reached forward to stroke calmness into his aquar's neck.

The Marula waved their lance blades in his face to force him to dismount.

"Let him through," said Aurum.

The Marula put up their weapons as they opened up a lane in their midst. Without looking at them, the rider thrust his reins into one of their hands and paced toward Aurum. As he came nearer, Aurum grew taller and the little man lost his swagger, bowing as far as his padded leather suit would allow.

"As you must know, Master, I'm a courier and none can stop me."

"What do you carry?"

The man looked horrified. "A . . . communication for the Mountain, Master."

"From Nothnaralan?"

The courier shook his head slowly, staring all the time. "The Master knows I mustn't speak."

Aurum put out his hand. "Give it to me."

The courier took a step away from the hand. He looked round him as if seeing the Marula and the other Masters for the first time.

"He speaks truth, my Lord," said Vennel in Quya. "His office is guaranteed inviolable by the Wise."

Ignoring Vennel, Aurum said to the courier, "You will give me what you carry or else I will have it taken from your corpse." He made a circling motion with his hands and Marula lance heads appeared at the man's throat. The man licked his lips as he looked into their pitiless yellow eyes. Trembling, he fumbled off one of his gloves and reached behind him to unfasten a packet. He looked at it, hesitated, then handed it to Aurum.

The Master took the packet and turned away. "Destroy him," he said over his shoulder.

"But, my Lord . . ." cried Vennel.

Carnelian watched the stabbing, blinking at every thrust.

"I will take all the responsibility," he heard Aurum say. The Master flicked his hand and the courier's gory body was hurled over the parapet, then he mounted and began to accelerate off down the road.

At the next tower they were met by consternation. As the changeover was made, Aurum secluded himself in the tower with its keeper. Carnelian looked in both directions for signals from the neighboring towers. Aurum returned and, saying nothing, led them off down the leftway. As he rode, Carnelian looked for and found the usual signal sent ahead to announce their coming to the next watchtower. This time there was more. A long and complex communication flashed from the tower they had just left. He wondered with some trepidation what message was being sent through the air to the Wise in Osrakum.

Thrice more they stopped and thrice more set off again, coursing down the white road that split the world in half. On and on they flew until the sky darkened to night and they slowed, almost blind, lured by a star that seemed to have fallen to the ground.

The star was a beacon that a watchtower held aloft. A belt of flames round its waist exaggerated its black mass and cast a lurid glow up into the undersides of its arms. Figures huddled across the bridge, dwarfed by the torso of the tower.

The Masters slowed their aquar and clattered them over the bridge. Carnelian gazed out over the light-apron of an encampment that spread round the tower. Beyond its glittering edge there was only night.

As they dismounted the keeper came toward them.

"Masters, we are unworthy," he said, as he and the auxiliaries behind him knelt.

Aurum swelled vast before him. "Everything is ready?"

"All your instructions have been precisely obeyed, my Master. I oversaw the cleansing myself."

Aurum swept past him with the others. Carnelian took one look up at the three huge ribs above him, then followed the others behind a monolith into the tower.

Carnelian let the quartz beads slide along the strings of the abacus. They made an annoying clink. He angled the frame the other way and grimaced at the sound. He was thinking about his father. His feelings were in turmoil. Clink. Clink. He put the abacus down with a *crack* on the table and lifted the lamp to look round the cell. It reminded him of the cabin in the baran though it was not so small. He stretched himself out on the sleeping platform and found that it ran out at his knees. The ceiling was formed by a long barrel of wood that ran diagonally across the cell. He guessed that it was the root of one of the wooden arms of the tower. He kept on seeing his bloodied father. Then he had felt such loss and had been unable to show it. Now the love he bore his father had cooled again and Crail's blood still trickled between them.

A knock on the door made him sit up and reach for his mask. He held it before his face. "Come."

The door opened and something like the ghost of his brother Tain slipped in. Carnelian dropped the mask and they looked at each other. Carnelian forced a smile. He could not bear to see him look so limp. He reached out and pulled him into a hug. He winced when he felt how thin his brother had become.

He let him go and blustered, "I should've expected it. Now that I'm free of the other Master, I can have you back." The reek of incense coming off Tain was stronger than that which still clung to the cell from its fumigation. "They cleaned you?"

"I had to be purified before approaching a Master," said Tain with no change of expression.

Carnelian nodded, searching for words.

"Is the Master well?" Tain said at last.

"He says so."

More silence.

"He has no one to tend to him," said Tain.

Carnelian remembered the boy that Aurum had handed over to be killed. "Would you mind . . . ?"

"No," said Tain, and turned to open the door.

"Please come back . . . after you've seen him . . ."

Tain nodded without turning, then left.

While he waited, Carnelian busied himself by rummaging through the cell. He found a small cupboard recessed into the wall that gave off a waft of ink as he opened it. The shelves inside were neatly stacked. Some folding parchments in a rack were crammed with geometrical figures, calculations, tables solid with symbols. A tube holding writing styluses stood beside jars of ink. Most curious of all were strange instruments, organisms of brass and bone, with hinged arms and shell edges filigreed with numbers. All these things confirmed Carnelian's belief that this was the cell of one of the watchtower ammonites.

He knelt on the bed to peer through a slit in the wall. His eyes filled with the glimmers of the encampment. He was in the upper story. There were two more below him, and then the entrance hall with its cistern. He pushed his face into the slit to breathe in the cooking smells, the warm stink of beasts that overlaid the cloying odor of the land.

The door opened behind him and he turned to see Tain looking ashen.

"Father?" Carnelian gasped.

"He's fine, the wound's not too deep, but the bandages that have soaked up the blood are rotting." Tain wrinkled his nose.

"I'll go to him," said Carnelian, crossing the cell.

Tain took his arm. "You'd better let him sleep, Carnie."

Carnelian reached up to trap his brother's hand. He examined the narrow face. His little brother had the look of an old man. Their eyes meshed. Carnelian searched Tain's, thinking about Jaspar's price. He wanted to say something but could not find a single word.

Tain gently pulled his hand away and walked over to the bed and started stroking out the creases. His hands looked painfully thin. Carnelian had to have some air and so he put on his mask and left the cell.

Three sides of the hall had wooden walls into which were set the doors that led into other cells. The fourth side was formed by the outer wall of the tower. Against its stone was the ladder they had pulled up after them when they had left the Marula in the dormitory story below. On either side dangled the counterweights that kept it in place. Perhaps as an attempt at humor, these had been shaped like men around whose necks the cables were attached. Other cables went down to the longer ladder they had climbed from the entrance hall, past the grooms' dormitory and into that of the auxiliaries below. Its counterweights were strung up with their heads touching the ceiling. The keel-beam ran over his head to bury itself in the opposite wall. The six ribs coming through the plaster embedded themselves in this beam, three to each side.

The floor boxed in by the wooden walls was formed into a cross by the four hatches cut into its corners. Carnelian went to the center of this cross and peered at the doors that lay at the ends of the arms. Each had an eye daubed on it but only one door, apart from his, had the chameleon. He crept close to listen but could hear nothing. The desire to see his father was tempered by a reluctance to disturb his rest. Besides, a meeting would be painful for both of them. An angry voice rang out. Though muffled, it was still clearly Jaspar's. Carnelian heard a slap and flinched. Maybe it was the attack that had made Jaspar lose enough composure as to actually strike a slave with his own hand.

Carnelian retreated. In the light flickering up through the hatches he spotted a ladder going up into the ceiling. He swung onto it and began to climb. When his head butted against a trapdoor, he fumbled around until he found the catch and opened it. He clambered up onto the tower roof.

The six ribs rose around him like the boles of trees. The air was thick with naphtha fumes. A flicker led his eyes up one of the ribs to where it held aloft a beacon. Cut black from the starry sky, a platform was suspended between all six ribs. He made toward the beacon rib, cursing as he stumbled over pipes, around machinery. Bronze staples formed a ladder up the rib toward the beacon flare. He stopped dead, hearing a scratch of voices. They were coming from where the keel-beam projected out into space pointing north toward the pinhead beacon of the next tower. A man-shape rose into view. Behind him, another was spread-eagled in the hoop of a deadman's chair which was fixed to the end of the keel-beam.

Carnelian decided to ignore these lookouts and began climbing the staples. The rib carried him out over the leftway. He passed a board twice his height bolted to the rib that he recognized as one of the plaques that advertised the number of the watchtower to the road below.

When he reached the top, he found that the end of the rib

formed a platform. At one corner, a pipe swelled up in a dragon mouth from whose jaws spluttered smoky flame. From this eyrie, Carnelian could gaze out across the night-black land. Below, the ribbon of the leftway faded off north and south where he could see the flares of the nearest towers.

A sound made him look down. Something large and black was coming up the rib toward him. It looked up, allowing the flare light to well in the hollows of its Master's mask.

"You have come to escape the odors below, my Lord?" It was Vennel.

Carnelian backed against the flare. "In search of solitude."

Vennel came up to join him, unfolding to his full height. "Prolonged proximity to the Great can be wearying. It is said, and truly, that the Chosen require the solitude of their coombs."

Carnelian felt that the Master's bulk would push him off into space.

"Behold the brutish masses."

Carnelian looked at the swathe of campfires twinkling at their feet. The murmur from the encampment blew on the warm night air with scents of smoke. He could also hear a persistent nagging creak.

Vennel coughed. "This will be quite a homecoming for you, my Lord."

Carnelian stared at him. "What do you mean?"

Vennel turned to face him. His ivory hands began to rub each other. "Only that my Lord must be looking with keen anticipation to returning to his coomb. That is, after being so long away."

This was the second time that day that Vennel had tried to be pleasant. "Yes," said Carnelian. It was the easiest answer to give.

Vennel's hands made a dry sound as they slid round each other. Carnelian stared out into the night. His finger traced the warm curves of the flare. He noticed the creaking again. "What makes that sound?"

"My Lord?"

"The creaking."

"The creaking? You do not know?"

"I would not ask if I did."

"Of course, my Lord. It is made by the wheels that draw water up to irrigate the Guarded Land."

Carnelian squinted into the darkness and thought perhaps he could just see them turning.

"Exile from Osrakum is the hardest burden to bear."

"What exactly do these towers watch for?" Carnelian asked quickly.

"Watch . . . ?"

"Barbarian incursions?"

Vennel opened a hand. "Sometimes, my Lord, but mostly they are used to anticipate rebellion."

"The sartlar?"

"Just so, my Lord. They are like locusts, singly innocuous, but when they swarm causing great damage. These leftways are a web spanning the land. If the local tower garrisons are unable themselves to quell a disturbance they can quickly summon a nearby legion."

"But there must be regions far from the roads."

"That is true, my Lord. The Guarded Land is a vast sea across which few venture. Away from the roads, unseen, the cancer of rebellion can spread unchecked for months. It is only the walls of the leftways that make sure the infection is contained within a province. Once detected, huimur fire will soon destroy it."

"It looks so peaceful."

"Often, so does the sea."

"The roads are like causeways . . ." said Carnelian, thinking aloud.

"My Lord?"

Carnelian waved his hand, *Nothing.*

"Outside Osrakum there is only wilderness."

Carnelian turned to Vennel, disliking the lurid reflections in his mask. "As you said before, my Lord, I am weary. I need solitude. If you would please move aside . . . ?"

The Master did not move. "It is hard to imagine what

reasons the Lord your father might have to stay so long out here."

Carnelian tried to gauge whether he might manage to push past the Master.

"Of course he was bound by blood oath."

"If you know about the oath, my Lord, then you have all the reason you require. My father is an honorable man."

"Most certainly, my Lord, most certainly, though such oaths when sworn before the Wise are enforced more by the Law than by honor. Even honor cannot explain why your father would insist on keeping an oath from which he had been released so long ago."

"So . . . so long ago?" said Carnelian, feeling as if he was trying to swallow a stone. "How long ago?"

"Oh, many years. Oh, I see . . . this is news to you?"

The stone was stuck in his gullet.

Vennel grabbed him by the shoulders. "What ails my Lord?"

Carnelian loathed the Master's touch, but the more he squirmed, the tighter Vennel held on to him. "It is nothing. I need to sleep. Please, let me go."

"But—"

"I bid you good night, my Lord," Carnelian said through his teeth, jerking free, almost falling from the platform before reaching the ladder. Vennel was speaking after him but Carnelian heard nothing, saw nothing. His hands and feet moved by themselves as he descended the rib. He could still feel the Master's fingers gripping his flesh. Vennel had frightened Carnelian, but far worse was the knowledge that his father had lied to him.

PLAGUE SIGN

Round and round the mirror

A teacher, ruler, giver

We kiss you, we kiss you

You all fall down

—NURSERY RHYME

Carnelian woke in another ammonite cell wearing a frown and for a moment did not know where he was. There was a face in the wall. He reached up to touch its stone-smooth swelling cheek. Really, it was only a bit of a face, clipped off where one block joined another. He sat up and found there were other fragments everywhere, chipped, worn, at angles. Each leaf, eye, hand on its own block in the jigsaw of the wall.

He fell back again and stared at the snake belly of wood that crossed the ceiling. A day had passed since Vennel had told him of his father's lie. A long hard day during which they had flown along the leftway deeper into the south. He had watched his father make the changeovers with increasing stiffness until his fear for him had become a constant ache but still there was the lie; and the lie had reopened the wound of Crail's death and gushed his blood between them. Though he cursed himself for weakness, Carnelian could see no way to cross over.

The previous night, Carnelian had sent Tain to tend his father. When his brother had returned ashen-faced, Carnelian had no need to ask questions. He had turned his face to the wall and struggled for sleep.

Now he could see through a slit the sky paling blue. The air was still cool and the sounds of waking were rising from the encampment. He would soon have to confront another day.

He heard the door opening and pretended to be asleep. Through slitted eyes he watched Tain creep in and wondered where he had been. His brother looked over at him, then, without looking away, his foot stirred the blankets on the floor. Where had he spent the night? A picture came unbidden to Carnelian's mind: Jaspar talking to Tain the day before as they were making a changeover. Carnelian had thought the slump in his brother's shoulders a result of one of the Master's threats. Cold flushed up from his stomach. There was another explanation.

"Where have you been?" he said. The cold had reached his throat to chill his words.

For answer his brother hung his head and Carnelian knew. Wrath made him dress with icy speed. He left the cell hunting for Jaspar.

He found him on the watchtower roof, standing near one of the corner ribs, gazing down into the encampment. Carnelian marched up to him and had opened his mouth to speak when he saw, past a winch that leaned out into space, a crowd milling below. People were streaming off the road back into the stopping place, their flight only stemmed by those already there. An incessant angry buzz mixed with the lowing of beasts. Wagons at the far edge of the encampment were flattening tracks off into the hri fields. Beyond, the flat umber plain was already crawling with sartlar amidst the lazy waterwheels.

"What is happening?" he asked.

Jaspar said nothing, but walking round the rib he gazed along the keel-beam, beyond the lookout in his deadman's chair, to the south. He lifted his hand to point.

Carnelian followed the finger down the narrowing road to the tiny prong of the next watchtower. Behind this he noticed a scribble over the dawn. He strained his eyes. "Smoke?"

Jaspar turned to him a face the color of the sun. "Plague sign."

Carnelian stood for a few moments, digesting the words. Then his sight cleared and he saw Jaspar's mask and the anger seized his throat so that he could hardly speak.

"My . . . my Lord . . ."

Light slid off Jaspar's mask as it angled to one side.

"You forced my brother to come to you."

"The creature came of its own free will."

"You promised him he could keep his eyes."

"Perhaps."

"Will you honor your promise?"

"One does not consider oneself bound by anything one says to a slave."

Carnelian fought down a desire to do him violence. "You will have your price for his eyes, I shall betray my father, but you will promise me on your blood never to touch my brother again."

Jaspar's beautiful hand rose and signed elegantly, *On my blood.*

The Masters gathered on the watchtower roof within the valley of its wooden ribs.

"Surely now we must go back," said Vennel.

"We are protected," said Aurum.

Suth had propped himself up against one of the ribs.

"Not so our servants nor the Marula," said Carnelian, giving him an anxious glance, sickened by planning his betrayal.

"What touching concern for your inferiors, my Lord," said Jaspar.

"In this matter each Lord must make his own choice," said Aurum. "I for one will go on." He turned to Suth. "And you, my Lord?"

For a while it seemed that Suth had not heard the question. Then he nodded. ". . . with you," he said with effort.

Carnelian withered witnessing this proof of his father's worsening condition.

"Then it is decided," said Jaspar. "We shall all go on. Unless the Ruling Lord Vennel wishes to set up palace here, by himself?"

Vennel scanned the circle of gold faces. "No doubt nothing I can say would make my counsels prevail?"

"No doubt," said Jaspar.

The world distorted through his tears. With the others, Carnelian had applied fresh unguent to his mask filter. Aurum was having to threaten the Marula who eyed the distant signal with alarm. They knew how dangerous a crack it was in the sky. As they mounted, Carnelian noticed for the first time their weakness. They had a look of plants in need of water.

At the next watchtower they all stopped in eerie silence. The air weighed down with increasing heat. Carnelian saw his father wilt against the wall. He wanted to go to him but could not, and rationalized that it was better not to draw attention to his father's distress. When Aurum moved to support him, Carnelian felt as if he had already betrayed him. He walked his aquar toward the parapet, hunched in self-disgust. The bone-white road was empty; its travelers were huddled at the margins of the stopping place or scattered in pockets through the hri fields. Chariots and wagons were ranged like barricades. The only sound was the creaking of the waterwheels buckling in the heat shimmer as they turned.

Then they were off again. As they drew nearer, the black line in the sky split in two. Clearly, both were rising from a watchtower Carnelian could not see. They slowed. Suth fell back so that his aquar came close to Carnelian's. He was sagging in his chair, his head resting on his chest. "Wind your robe tight . . . the Black Lord's Dance."

"Father . . ." Carnelian began but his father urged his aquar on and it loped forward to join Aurum up ahead.

The smoke swelled into a pair of wavering ribbons. Motes danced in the air above like swarming flies. The aquar were jogging. The Marula were cringing in their chairs. Guiding his aquar near the parapet Carnelian could see the road was no longer white, but flecked with corpses. As they continued, these dark signs of death grew denser, in places spilling off the road far out into the fields. He saw a huimur wandering, dragging a broken chariot, ploughing furrows through the dead.

Carnelian could see the watchtower with its horns of smoke.

"Windspeed," cried Aurum.

They all accelerated. Remembering his father's warning, Carnelian wound himself into his cloak. This melted out some of his love for his father who, though suffering, could still care for his son.

From its upheld arms the watchtower was pumping smoke into the sky in a rolling boil. They crashed over the wooden bridge. The watchtower rushed by, its door monolith daubed with tar. The parapet opposite was set with half-charred animals skewered on poles. As these were being left behind, Carnelian realized with horror they were sartlar. His nose filter could not mask the fetor from the road. Above, scavengers were screaming, floating on the air like ash. Fingers of plague were feeling for them across the plain. Carnelian struck his aquar to make it run faster. Other smoke columns rose off to the left wafting a sickening cooking of flesh. Along the road, corpse mounds were smoldering. Hunched sartlar were building more. Mounted overseers rode through them, with whips or carrying fire. One looked up as they hurtled past. He had no face but only funereal windings of brown stained cloth.

All day they sped into the furnace south. Each changeover was made hurriedly. Slowly, the road below began to fill again with people, although only with those who were going toward Osrakum. Carnelian sank back into the chair, closed his eyes, rolled with the smooth pistoning of his aquar. The net of roads and sartlar kraals went slowly by, lulling him into a pounding stupor.

Carnelian became aware of the sun's gory eye bloodying all the clouds. Gilded land slipped past unfocused. Mounds resolved on either side of the road, defined by strokes of shadow. He began to see patterns: immense sweeping rings of red earth, straight edges, terraces; the houses and streets of a vast and ruined city. It was in a watchtower nearby that Aurum decided they would spend the night.

Carnelian stared at his father lying on the bed. They had all crammed into his cell because he was too weak to rise.

"The Marula are failing," said Jaspar.

"The poison is killing them," said Aurum.

Vennel was rubbing his hands together. "How can we be certain it is not the plague?"

"If it is, the boys will also be tainted," said Jaspar.

"It might be prudent to have the boys and Marula all destroyed," said Vennel.

Carnelian jerked round in horror.

Jaspar winked at him. "Aesthetic perhaps, Lord Vennel, but certainly not prudent. You find me reluctant to destroy the only servants and guards that we possess. Besides, there is the practicality of whom one would use to do the destroying."

"It will suffice that we keep them away from us," grated Suth from the bed.

"Even our servants?" asked Carnelian, alarmed that there would be no one to tend to his father.

"Especially our body slaves," Aurum replied. "With their every touch, they threaten our ritual protection."

Vennel looked like a column of iron. "Has it finally come to this? Are we now, my Lords, to be stripped of these last shreds of comfort and of state?"

He looked round but none there gave him answer.

Tain and Jaspar's boy seemed to have hardly the strength to hold their little packs. In among the Marula they could have been infants with uncaring parents. Aurum waved them all away with a gesture of dismissal. The Marula looked uncertain, sickly. Aurum made the gesture again with a harsher hand. The Marula began to shuffle off, back the way they had come, over the bridge. Carnelian watched Tain walk off, head drooping as if his thin neck had snapped. Carnelian hated himself. What use was his impotent wrath?

They ate on the platform held aloft by the six ribs of the watchtower. It was cooler and the air was free of the staleness of the cells. The Masters had dismissed the lookouts from their deadmen's chairs and even the ammonites who tended the signal flare. With their own hands the Masters had laid out the circle of incense bowls. Once they were lit they could for the first time that day remove their masks. There were sighs of relief all round. Fingers rubbed at mask-grooved skin. Suth's face was sallow; his eyepits looked kohled. He had used what little strength he had climbing the ladders. He breathed in, making a hacking sound. "Ah, the beauty and comfort of the night," he sighed.

Vennel still wore his mask. "Are we certain that it is safe up here?"

Aurum looked north. "The plague rages far away from here, my Lord. The creatures who might carry it are down on the road and forbidden to come near us on pain of death.

There is a reasonable margin of safety." As he looked at Suth, worry creased his face.

Vennel unmasked.

Carnelian was nibbling crumbs from his hri cake. He was sick of purified food. The Masters were just so much animated marble. Only his father's sweat-glazed face betrayed the possibility of Chosen mortality. His mouth twitched sporadically as if a needle were darning his flesh. He was seated a little away from the others, leaning against one of the turning-handles of the strange mechanism that stood in the middle of the platform. Carnelian had examined its square mirror of louvered silver strips attached to pivots at each end; the long handles to turn and dull the strips; the toothed arcs that allowed the whole mirror to tilt; the turning board that allowed the machine to swivel round. A heliograph, Aurum had called it, the means by which the ammonites turned the rays of the sun and sent them glancing to the neighboring towers carrying messages.

Carnelian gazed at his father bleakly. Perfume could not entirely smother the rot of his bloodied bandages. The continuing discomfort had been forced on him by Aurum invoking the support of ammonites against his father's plea to be washed. The old Master had insisted that, however unpleasant, the bandages were necessary to give Suth protection against the plague. His father had been too weak to fight him.

Thoughts of the treachery he was planning made Carnelian turn away, but also fear, and embarrassment that he should witness his father thus. Out past the rising bars of myrrh smoke, past the empty hoop of the deadman's chair, out beyond the glimmers of the stopping place, the night was patterned with lozenges, patchy ovals, a suggestion of lines.

"What are all those tumbled walls?" Carnelian said at last, just to say something.

"Ruins," said Aurum.

"One of the Quyan cities," said Jaspar.

"There are many such . . . many . . . scattered across the land," his father said in a throaty voice.

"All ruined?" said Carnelian, keen to encourage any life in his father.

"All. The last book of the Ilkaya tells of their fall."

"The Breaking of the Perfect Mirror," said Carnelian, naming the book.

"Pah! Children's stories with which the Wise seek to cow the Great," said Aurum.

"Stories? Perhaps . . . though even a pearl . . . needs a grain around which to grow," said Suth.

"By the blood! My Lords, you speak lightly of holy scripture," scolded Vennel.

". . . do not deny spirituality . . . but . . . even Wise hold its truths metaphorical," said Suth.

"There is nothing metaphorical about those ruins there," said Jaspar, "and they have a look of hoary age."

"That city was there ruined . . . long before this road was built," said Suth.

Carnelian turned to him, remembering the faces in the wall of his cell. "Those ruins were plundered in the making of this road."

His father nodded.

"Such antiquity commands awe if not reverence," said Vennel.

"I see no reason why the living should revere the dead," said Aurum.

"Is it not reason enough that the dead have built the world into which we were born?"

"Did the Gods have no part in that, my Lord?" asked Carnelian.

"I meant of course, the initial creation, but the latter part also of course under divine . . ." As Vennel closed his mouth, Carnelian resisted the temptation to smile.

"Certainly, gratitude is due the Quyans for bequeathing us their treasures. One possesses many perfectly exquisite pieces from the period of the Perfect Mirror," said Jaspar.

"So do all but the meanest Houses," snapped Vennel.

"And, my Lord, you would know all about the meanest Houses," returned Jaspar.

"I dislike your imp—"

"What does my Lord think is the grain lying at the core of the scriptures?" said Carnelian quickly to his father, feeling that the heat of the arguments was wilting him. Carnelian sought for him the healing there is in telling stories.

"Conjectural, but . . ." Suth grimaced and held his side.

Carnelian became alarmed that he had coaxed his father into wasting his dwindling strength.

Suth closed his eyes and then opened them, smiling crookedly, his eyes as brilliant as jewels. ". . . the previous book describes a long period during which the Quyans prospered." He breathed in heavily. "They achieved harmonious balance . . ."

Carnelian had heard his father speak thus before. "Between the two Essences?"

The bright eyes regarded him for a while, making him uneasy, until his father nodded.

"I thought that esoteric doctrine defunct," said Jaspar.

"Its precepts . . . are the foundation of all the creeds," said Suth. ". . . it is merely a matter of emphasis."

"An emphasis that once caused schisms among the Great," said Vennel coldly.

"You prefer the literal interpretation in which their lords fell into evil ways and so led their people into the worship of false gods?" said Aurum.

"That is what is written."

"If one stands on the wording of the texts then one should apprehend it *exactly* as written," said Jaspar. "It is written 'false avatars.' "

Vennel stared. "You are a fundamentalist?"

"I believe that the Lord Suth's Two Essences form the matrix of creation and that each has a number of centers of divine sentience that manifest as distinct avatars."

"Avatar manifestations . . . ?" said Carnelian.

"Jaspar believes . . . that there is not a single united pair of twins . . . but many . . . like reflections in facing mirrors." His father stopped, showing gritted teeth between his parted lips.

Carnelian flinched. "If this is too painful?"

"Perhaps you should heed your son, my Lord," said Aurum.

His father waved his hand in negation. He looked at Jaspar. "How does my Lord interpret . . . the choosing of the Chosen?"

"Divine favor. As it says in scripture, the Twins came to Osrakum in dreams to certain of its lords, to show the shape Their wrath would wear. Osrakum was commanded to close her gates lest Their wrath find its way into her hidden land."

"Implausibly, I find myself agreeing with you, Jaspar," said Vennel.

". . . their dreams came from within," said Suth.

"You deny the agency of the Twins?" said Vennel.

"I say virtue . . . virtue is that agency."

"You hold then, my Lord, that the Chosen survived through higher virtue?"

"Harmony with the Essences, or virtue . . . yes."

Jaspar smiled. "I had always understood that we gained our empire through conquest."

"Perhaps," said Suth, "but we hold it by maintaining . . . the various harmonious balances . . . Reeds bend with the wind yet can be woven to make shields."

"Disharmony lost the Quyans their empire?"

"Each city put ripples . . . into the Perfect Mirror of their commonwealth." Suth shook his head. "Until it could reflect no divinity . . . but only fragments of themselves."

"Nonsense," said Aurum. "They weakened themselves with internecine strife and were then annihilated by the plague they had themselves stirred up among their sartlar."

Jaspar's mouth twisted with distaste. "Even now, the plague appears among those creatures as spontaneously as maggots do in meat."

"Certainly, Lord Aurum," said Vennel, "but from whence did the plague come if not from the Black God?"

Jaspar looked pained as he shook his head. "It is the breath of the Lord of Plagues, an avatar whom the Wise unify with all the others into the Black God: a hotchpotch deity, convenient only because He is a concept small enough to squeeze into the minds of the barbarians."

"But the plague did come to Osrakum?" said Carnelian.

"It was burning across the land," said Jaspar. "The fire-breaks of our quarantines were not yet in place. Is it any surprise that the plague entered? When the desperate came from the dying cities, we let them in."

"The affliction would soon have spread to the whole of Osrakum had not the Obedient Ones, who later became the Great, cast out the polluted refugees," said Vennel.

"That was foolishness," said Aurum. "Our forefathers would have done better to destroy them. Letting them return to spit their poison of resentment into every ear . . . pah!"

"And they gathered up their ruined strength and came to Osrakum with vengeance in their eyes," said Vennel.

"And we came out and were defeated and so on and so on . . ." droned Jaspar. "And how was it that this defeated rabble were able to overwhelm the pursuing Quyan host so that the Skymere became a lake of their blood?"

"The Black God with dragons came—"

"The Lord of Mirrors," said Jaspar, "the divine Lord of War . . ."

"Inspired by virtue," said Suth, "our forefathers found a strength hidden in themselves . . ."

"Was it virtue that in the Valley of the Gate turned their host to stone? Did virtue inspire the gift of fire that the Lord of Mirrors gave the Chosen with which then and now we make victorious war?"

"Naphtha burns whatever hand, Chosen, marumaga or barbarian, ignites it," said Aurum. "Flame-pipes are mechanisms through which the naphtha is driven by pressure. It is wisdom not divinity that has given us these weapons."

"And our blood, our burning blood?" said Vennel. "Does my Lord deny the source of its fire to be divine?"

Aurum frowned. "I cannot deny what I myself have felt. Besides, it is self-evident that we are as far above other men as are the stars above the earth."

"The Twins were our first Emperor. In mortal form, They

put the fire in our blood, and through Apotheosis all subsequent God Emperors inject more."

"That orthodoxy . . . is a childish conceit," said Suth. "Through alignment with the forces . . . that move the world . . . we achieved the Commonwealth."

Jaspar laughed. "And they all lived happily ever after."

Suth's eyes blazed. "And they lived plagued by blood intrigues, squabbling among themselves, lectured at by the Wise and sapped by their own vices of greed, pride and levity."

"Particularly levity," said Vennel.

Jaspar looked at Vennel with raised eyebrows.

Carnelian saw his father had sagged back against the heliograph. He lurched to his side as his head fell forward. The Masters rose with a rustle. Carnelian leaned close, relaxing when he heard him breathing. "Father," he said gently.

The weight of his father's head stirred and lifted. "I must rest . . ."

"Not here," said Carnelian.

His father's lips twitched a smile. He gave an almost imperceptible nod.

Carnelian turned and saw Aurum and Jaspar showing something like concern; Vennel, something like hope. "He needs help."

As Aurum and Jaspar began to move, Carnelian was buffeted by his father standing up. Suth waved the Masters away. "My son is all the help I need," he croaked.

Together they shuffled over the narrow bridge to the rib with its naphtha flare. Carnelian was wedged into the hinge of his father's arm. Its weight lying along his shoulders forced Carnelian to look down at the terrible distance they might fall. His father's breathing roared its moisture in his ear. The rot of the blood wafted with each step they took.

Carnelian helped remove his father's cloak and then laid him down on the bed. Suth was trying to hide the pain but a twinge near his eye betrayed it. His side was a single black stinking stain. The smell creased Carnelian's nose. When he saw his father noticing his disgust, he was forced to speak.

"You cannot continue like this, my Lord."

"It is better this way . . . Aurum and the ammonites were right . . . the ritual protection . . . above all, the Law must be seen to be obeyed."

"We have both seen lapses in the Law's operation," said Carnelian, "and, this mess cannot be better."

"But I could not allow Tain to . . . besides, now he is forbidden me."

Carnelian reached out to touch the black bandages. His father's hand tried to brush his fingers away. "You . . . defile yourself."

Carnelian took his father's hand and gripping it firmly folded the elbow up and forced the hand down on his father's chest. "Your blood is my blood, Father, how could it defile me?" He reached out again, felt the wet touch of the crusted bandages and winced when they cracked. He shook his head.

"This must be cleaned," he said, before his father could say anything. He found some cleaning pads and unguents. He threw off the encumbrance of his own cloak.

His father sat up with a look of horror on his face. "What . . . ?" The effort was too much. He fell back with a groan. "This is not for you to do."

"There is no one else, Father."

His father closed his eyes, breathing heavily. Carnelian took this for acquiescence. He surveyed the stain, made his decision, picked up a knife and then gingerly began to cut the bandages around it. Having done this he took one strip and peeled it back. It stuck in a few places. He grimaced each time he had to give it a tug. At last he had it off and dropped it on the floor in disgust. One by one he pulled the strips off while his father lay like a corpse, the only sign of life the twinges as the strips caught. To reduce his suffering, Carnelian began cutting bits away.

"We must talk," his father hissed through clenched teeth.

Carnelian peered at the ridged fleshy mass his work had revealed. He went blind. What if he killed his father? His sight returned. In as level a tone as he could muster, he said, "You are too weak, my Lord."

"Because of that . . . I might die."

"Don't say that," snapped Carnelian. Instinctively, his hand flew up toward his mouth, as he remembered to whom he was speaking.

His father smiled, shook his head, reassuring him. "About Crail . . . my hands were tied."

The grief welled up in Carnelian's eyes. He concentrated on the wound, seeing it distorted through tears, sniffing. He pulled one more strip.

His father groaned, chuckled. "Are you trying to hurry me from this world?"

Carnelian saw his father's lopsided grin and grinned back. Their eyes met, smiling. The promise he had made to Jaspar was an ache in the marrow of his bones. Tain and his father were tearing him in two. Both were of his blood. This blood, he thought, looking at his reddened hands.

"My son . . . you look unconvinced."

Carnelian shook his head. "No, it is something else." He looked his father in the eye, seeing something of Tain there, then blurted out, "Did you know Tain would be blinded?"

The puzzlement in his father's face forced Carnelian to describe the events in the tent the night Tain had seen Jaspar's face. Horror glazed his father's eyes.

"Then you did not know this would happen?" said Carnelian.

"Of course I did not! How could you even . . . think that? . . . Tain is my son."

Carnelian felt he was a bow being unstrung.

Suth was embarrassed by the emotion that came over his boy's face. "Does he ask for . . . something?"

Carnelian blushed.

"Is there a price for Tain's eyes?"

Carnelian squared up to his father. "Knowledge of what power it is that the Lord Aurum has over you."

"He did it on purpose . . . to trap you."

Carnelian gaped. "On purpose?" He shook his head, unable to comprehend such wickedness.

Suth closed his eyes, thinking.

Carnelian poured the unguent into the bowl, dipped in a pad and concentrated on cleaning the blood away. He felt the need to confess everything. "Vennel told me that our exile was long ago rescinded."

Suth opened his eyes, saw the boy's pain, closed them again. "That one looks at me . . . with vulture eyes. But he spoke truth. I will try to explain." His eyes opened once more to look at his son. "The man that later became God Emperor . . . Kumatuya . . ."

"My uncle."

"We shared love."

Carnelian's eyes grew round.

"His sister, Ykoriana . . . coveting all his love, resented me. When their sister . . ." Suth closed his eyes.

"My mother . . ." suggested Carnelian.

Suth nodded.

Carnelian resumed the cleaning, waiting for his father to muster enough strength to continue.

Suth went on. "When she died . . . Ykoriana's resentment turned to hatred. At the last election . . . she threatened to use her votes against Kumatuya unless . . . unless I swore on my blood to quit Osrakum."

Carnelian frowned. "She blackmailed you."

"Without her eight thousand votes . . . Kumatuya would have died." There was a long pause. His father stared at the ceiling. "By the time that I was released from my oath . . . other factors had come into play."

"And these other factors lie behind Aurum's influence over you?"

Suth nodded, then seeing the doubt returning to his son's face, he added, "They are not shameful . . . but cannot be discussed. Will you trust me over this, my son?"

Carnelian looked into his father's eyes and was moved by their appeal. He jerked a nod.

"Good," his father sighed.

Carnelian resumed the cleaning. He had found the slack mouth of the wound. He cleaned carefully around its swollen lips as his father trembled with the agony of it. Carnelian stopped and wiped away the sweat that threatened to blind him. Then he looked round, thought for a moment, checked to see his father was not looking, bent down and began to release the bandage from around one of his ankles. It gave and he unwound a length up to his knee and cut it off, as quietly as he could. He took another length from his other leg and then began to wind them round his father's body to cover the wound.

"And Aurum?" he said as a distraction.

"He thinks me weak . . . I let him believe it . . . but I will cheat him yet," he looked at Carnelian, "with your help, my son.

"You see how they have exploited our disunity . . . cleave to me. When we enter Osrakum . . . I will be taken into the Labyrinth . . . but you must go to our coomb . . . I will write a letter . . . there might be trouble there . . . I have been too long away . . . if I should die .. . ."

Carnelian began an emotional protest but his father's hand raised to stay him.

". . . find Fey . . . let her advise you . . ."

"Aunt Fey? Brin's sister?"

His father gave a nod. "Beware of the other lineages . . . and my mother . . . she knows nothing of the reasons behind my exile . . ." The last words were sighs.

Carnelian could not bear to look at his father's pain-crumpled face. He busied himself with his handiwork. The bandages over the wound were already blushing.

"We . . ."

"You are squandering your strength, Father."

"We must save Tain's eyes."

Carnelian looked at him with hope.

"If Jaspar wants you to . . . betray me, then betray . . ." His fingers hooked in spasm. "Tell him of the oath . . . the blood oath I swore to Ykoriana . . . best to stay close to the truth . . . Tell him it was the oath that kept me in exile . . ."

"Will he know nothing of its rescinding?"

"He might know of the oath . . . but not of . . ."

"Rescinding."

Suth lifted his hand. "Take it . . ."

Carnelian gripped his father's hand. He could feel the pain in its trembling. "But—"

His father's hand squeezed. "There is more." He took some ragged breaths. "God Emperor and Aurum found a loophole . . . in the Law. Oath was made as a Ruling Lord . . . not as He-who-goes-before. As long as I hold that post . . . I am free to return . . . but . . ."

"But Aurum controls the Clave and thus your appointment to that post and can at any point strip you of it and force you back into exile."

Carnelian felt his father squeeze his hand.

"I understand, Father. Please rest now."

Suth gave another squeeze. Carnelian carefully laid his father's hand down on the bed and disengaged his grip. He scooped up the filthy bandages and turned to leave. His father's hand grazed his. Carnelian looked round at him.

"Make sure . . . bind him with a blood oath."

Carnelian leaned forward to kiss his father's forehead. "Sleep, Father, I will do everything as you say."

The next day his father put on a show of strength. Carnelian rode beside him and helped him make the changeovers. At first he was surprised when Aurum did not challenge his new place. Then he realized how fearful the Master was that his most important piece might yet be snatched from the game. He would allow anything that would help keep Suth alive.

"My father will die," said Carnelian, hoping to cheat his fear by speaking it.

"If we can get him there in time, the Wise will heal him," said Aurum.

They hurtled down the channel that centuries of couriers had worn in the leftway. Although they maintained a furious pace, it seemed to Carnelian they were not moving at all. Each time they stopped they were in the same place: a watch-tower amidst a simmering plain.

That night his father began to burn with fever and had to be carried up to his cell. Carnelian made a bed on the floor beside him. He hardly slept. He cooled his father by smearing water on his face and sprinkling it over his bandaged body. The wound had already stained the new bandaging. Carnelian dabbed the blood with water to soften the crust. His father moaned. Carnelian looked down at him bleak with fear. He could not understand how quickly the Master of the Hold had been stripped of all his granite strength.

Morning found them already slicing through the wind. Another long, long day melted past. Carnelian nodded in a stupor, trying to snatch some sleep. He had still found no chance to be alone with Jaspar.

The horizon had been thickening for a while before he noticed it. His mask eyeslits reduced the glare enough to see there was a definite smudging along the lower sky. His stomach tightened. Although he knew what it was he dared not name it, but watched it grow as they rode a few more stages down the road.

When next they stopped he saw all eyes looking in that direction.

"My palaces, my treasures, my slaves," said Jaspar with greedy delight.

"To be rid of these filthy wrappings," said Vennel. Carnelian watched the Master's mask move round just enough to bring his father within reach of its eyeslits.

The Marula were squinting with hatred at Osrakum. All day they had lolled in their saddle-chairs. At the changeovers they moved with the slow, careful deliberation of the aged. Like his father, they were dying. He could see what Osrakum meant to them but what did she mean to him? The end of this cursed journey? Tain's blinding? He looked over at his father, slumped lifeless. For the hundredth time, Carnelian reassured himself that he was only asleep behind his mask.

"We shall not enter her crater today," said Aurum.

Carnelian swung round. "In the thousand names of the Twins why not, my Lord?"

"Because it is too far."

"What is that there?" Carnelian pointed a stiff finger down the road to where the umber was burned into the edge of the opalescent sky.

"Can you not see how low is the sun, my Lord? There is still a long ride to the City at the Gates."

"But my father—"

"We would not reach the gates themselves before nightfall. We would be forced to lodge in the city. It would do the Lord Suth little good to spend a night breathing the vapors of the Gatemarsh. In the morning, we can finish the journey refreshed."

"We must think of the Lord Suth," said Vennel. He waved a hand. "The vapors . . ."

"It is hard to see, my Lord Aurum," said Jaspar, "how one could find spending a night in another stinking shed at all refreshing. But, no doubt, anticipation will make the reaching of one's coomb all the more delightful." He turned to Carnelian. "One finds that pleasure is so often enhanced by the delay in its consummation, neh?"

It was all Carnelian could do to stop himself ripping away the Master's mask to punch the dirty smirk off his face.

Watchtower sea three rose near the edge of the Gatemarsh: a vast mirror scribbled over with mud calligraphy. The City at the Gates lay in its midst like a half-rotted golden starfish. Causeway threads pulling out through the marsh formed its arms. A gilded mold grew in the angles. Behind rose the Sacred Wall of Osrakum, as if the sun had been hammered flat to make a frieze for the darkening sky.

Carnelian stood, stirred by fear and hope for his father, for his brother, but he also felt a yearning that had the taste of the silver box. Near the city there was a fissure in the

Sacred Wall. His heart beat against his ribcage. That fissure could be nothing other than the beginning of the canyon that led up into Osrakum. It seemed unbelievable that he would walk in her crater before the next setting of the sun. It was easier to imagine entering the Underworld.

Carnelian struggled under his father's weight to the watch-tower door. While he was getting his breath back, his eyes were drawn back to Osrakum. Aurum was a black spindle around which the Sacred Wall vibrated its gold. He was talking to a Maruli from whom he kept his distance. He threw something that landed on the ground between them. Grimacing from the pain, the black man bent down to retrieve it, hesitated a bow, crawled into a saddle-chair and sped off. Carnelian watched him shimmer away to nothing against the gold, then heaved his father into the watchtower.

The Masters had locked themselves away and so Jaspar was out of reach. Carnelian knuckled patterns of light into his eyelids. Beside him, his father was restless, hot, stuttering half-words, sighing. He was the voice of Carnelian's despair.

The babble stopped. Carnelian came awake. He stood up and saw the moonlight catching his father's open eyes. His lips moved. "Forgive me."

Carnelian took his hand. It was cold and heavy. He touched his lips to his father's brow. It felt as if he were kissing stone. He prayed to the Twins, Their avatars, the Two Essences, but all were deaf. He kneaded the Little Mother in his hand and promised her anything if she would save his father. He found the bundle with his clothes and rummaging in it felt the roughness of Ebeny's blanket. He tugged it out and burrowed his face into it. For a moment he could believe that she was there with them. He pressed it harder to muffle his sobs. When he had done, he stood up and spread it over his father, pulling its edge up so that his father could smell her too.

"Sleep now," he whispered and his father obeyed him. Carnelian felt for his hand through the blanket, squeezed it and then lay down.

He jerked awake panting. His blanket was soaked with sweat. Above him, his father was muttering some fevered incantation. A scent of horror smoked around the edges of the cell. He was reluctant to return to the red face smiling in his dreams. Standing, he swayed a little and stared at the thing muttering on the bed. He did not recognize it and felt it to be something malevolent he had to escape.

Robe. Mask. Cold stone under his foot. He went out into the silent hall. All the other doors were closed. Moonlight fell in columns round him. He climbed the ladder to the roof.

Through the copse of the ribs he glimpsed a sky filled with stars. He edged across to the inverted arch between the northernmost ribs. The keel-beam ran out from the edge of the roof to the lookout in his deadman's chair. He walked out toward him. The man turned. Imagining his stare, Carnelian wobbled. He walked further out. Below, the leftway ran its dim canal.

"Master?" said a fearful voice ahead.

"I will take your watch for a while," Carnelian said.

The man hesitated, then swung himself up onto the beam into a crouch.

"Wait on the roof."

The man ducked past with a waft of stale sweat.

Carnelian took a few more steps forward. A cylinder pushed out from the end of the beam. The hoop formed a halo around this. He reached out, grasped the hoop, then swung down onto the cylinder. It rotated, almost throwing him out into space. Trembling, he used the hoop to pull himself back into balance. He shuddered. Now he understood why it was called a deadman's chair. At least the fright had brought him some relief from the foreboding. He looked out.

Down on the road the Marula's fire had gone out. The land spread away textured with shadow lumps. The snuffling of animals and some voices seemed eerily close. In the direction of Osrakum, the starry sky fell into a gulf of darkness. The heart of the city glowed dimly beneath it. Faint traceries showed the causeways. The land between seemed to be adjusting. He strained to hear something, some human sound that might come to him from the metropolis. There was only the rasp of frogs and, intermittently, the cries of creatures stalking the marshes. He closed his eyes. Breathed deep the sweet air.

He heard a cry, nearby, muffled. He craned round and saw a yellow light in one of the top-story windows flicker, then go out. His father. He scrambled back onto the beam and sprinted along it to the roof. The hatch formed a glowing rectangle. He found the rungs of the ladder and began descending.

"It wields a dagger." A woman, voice raised in anger. No, it was Vennel.

Carnelian looked through the rungs down into the hall. Vennel loomed, with Aurum coming up holding a lantern. Behind them both stood Jaspar. The three formed a frozen tableau of immense black figures, their gold faces smoldering against the deathly white stripe of their throats. All the masks were half turned away, peering off into a dark corner. Aurum lifted the lantern high, so that its edge of light pulled up the further wall. On the floor was the tight hooked figure of a man. A black man. A Maruli shaking, with sliding slitted eyes and a blade like a fang in his fist.

As Carnelian slipped down into the room, the Maruli turned, hearing him. Carnelian knew his face. He saw it twisting, the lips drawing back from feral teeth, hissing.

Aurum took a step forward. "Abase yourself before your Masters, slave." His voice filled the hall.

The black man flinched but his face remained hard with defiance.

Aurum unmasked to reveal his cold white anger.

The black man cowered away, almost closing his eyes. The blade trembled in his grip.

"Kneel!" boomed Aurum.

The black man closed like a hinge.

"Hold these," Aurum said quietly, thrusting the lantern and mask into Vennel's hands. Shadows slid this way and that as Vennel fumbled, then they steadied.

"Come, kneel, it'll be better that way. It'll be better," coaxed Aurum.

The black man's knees cracked against the floor. He bowed his head, his arm still out to one side, stiff clutching the knife.

Aurum took a few strides toward him, bent down, grabbed the man's curls, yanked back his head. In the glare of the Master's face, Carnelian saw the amber eyes strain round with terror. There was a glint at the black man's throat, a slicking sound. He gurgled, then grimaced. Aurum kicked his body away with a snort, wiping his hand down his robe. The black man twitched, face down on the floor, a black halo spreading round his head, his fist still gripping the knife.

Vennel was frozen. "It tried to kill me."

Jaspar circled the corpse as if it were diseased. After surveying it he moved in, placed a ranga shoe on the wrist, crunched it down against the floor. Using a fold of his robe, he stooped down and worked the knife out of the dead man's grip. He held it up. "A kitchen knife?" He sounded amazed. He flung it away with a clatter that made Carnelian jump.

"That it should dare threaten one of the Chosen," said Vennel. "It is quite, quite, quite unbelievable."

"It was attacking you?" Jaspar demanded.

"It sought my life."

"It was me he was trying to kill," said Carnelian quietly.

Two masks and the old man's face snapped toward him.

"Explain yourself," said Aurum.

Carnelian looked down at the man lying in the blood. "He saw my face."

"What do you mean?"

"That man lying there, he saw my face. The night we were attacked, he saw my face."

"You little fool," said Vennel, lunging toward Carnelian.

Aurum overtook him. He caught Carnelian by the shoulders and shook him until his mask was askew. "Why did you say nothing at the time?"

Carnelian tore free of Aurum's hands and stared back into his cold eyes. He tried to slide the mask back into place. "I did not want him to die. Not when his sin had come from the saving of our lives."

Jaspar coughed a nervous laugh. Carnelian glared at him. He was close to blurting out that not only he but also Jaspar had been guilty of the same sin. The same sin, except that at least Carnelian had demanded nothing for his silence.

Suddenly, he was shoved round so that he was looking at the man bleeding over the floor. He looked away.

"Look at it," Aurum said. "Look at it, I say."

Carnelian obeyed. The gash was a slack-lipped smile opening a mouth in the corpse's throat.

"That thing could have spilled your precious blood." Aurum's fingers dug into his arm. "The Law of Concealment must be obeyed. It is not some arbitrary nonsense. It is meant to stop that!" His finger jabbed at the corpse.

"Look," shrilled Vennel, "look." He pointed at Carnelian's feet. "He does not even wear the ranga."

Aurum released him, turned away.

"One would have thought the boy would have learned something from the debacle on the baran," said Vennel.

Hatred of the Masters overpowered Carnelian. He remembered Crail. He remembered that they had opened the chasm between him and his own father, whom even now they were expecting to die. He remembered Jaspar using Tain's eyes to bait his trap. He opened his mouth to spit his bitterness at them but at that moment his father's ravings came from behind the door, and he felt his anger seep away.

"Now we see the consequences of all this secrecy," said Vennel. "If we had traveled with our guardsmen this would never have happened."

Aurum turned an icy face to Carnelian. "Go and sleep."

Carnelian went to his father, remembering what he had

said. Before he closed the door, he heard Aurum say, "We had better hide the carcass . . . Yes, with our own hands. Everything must be done to avoid this contagion of rebellion spreading to the others. They will all have to be destroyed."

CROSSING
THE
WHEEL

Facilitate commerce, encourage avarice, allow the widest variation in rank and wealth: let our subjects find enemies amongst themselves. The slave who is thrown the leavings from his master's table will not have the stomach for rebellion.

—A PRECEPT OF THE WISE,
FROM THE DOMAIN OF
TRIBUTE

Carnelian had his back against the bed. He so wanted to sleep but he would not give up guarding the embers of his father's life. His father's hand was ice in his grip. All night Carnelian had held on to him to stop him being tugged away. His muscles ached from the effort. Each time death pulled, his father would grow fevered, raving ever more loudly, then cool until the sweat was beading on his skin. Silence would then come so suddenly that each time Carnelian thought him gone. A whisper of breath, a tiny trembling in a vein would turn his grief to anger. He would stare at the fevered face, grinding his teeth, wanting to rail at his father, to blame him, to tell him that it was not fair to leave him alone to shoulder all the burden. Afterward, when he had managed to pack the anger back in somewhere, he would dry his father's face and rewrap his body in the covers he had thrown off. Drowsing over him, Carnelian had sometimes become aware that his hand was stroking his father's head or his lips were mumbling one of Ebeny's healing songs. Once he wondered if it was perhaps their charm that stoked the fire inside his father's shell until it glowed red again and the babbling came hissing out. He had stood watch over him as long as he could, then had slumped to the floor, his head a hollowed stone in his hands.

Now his father was sleeping quietly and it seemed that the fever had passed into Carnelian. Tremors moved across his skin as if something were burrowing under it. He was desperate to sleep, to escape the numbness, to dull the pain.

Sounds were coming through the wall. One of the Masters was stirring. He swiveled his head round. A window slit showed a shade paler than night. The morning. A sigh deflated his body. Osrakum. Today, Osrakum. He opened his mind to receive the vision. He waited, then closed it when nothing came in. Was this to be the day his father died?

Something heavy struck the door. Groaning, Carnelian stood up, to put his body up as a shield between the door and his father's face. He fumbled his mask up to hide his own. The door opened to frame a darkness in which an oval floated like a summer moon. Aurum came in stooping, trapping the whole room in the mirror of his mask. It fell away to reveal his Master's face creased with dismay. That look sharpened Carnelian's own fears.

"Take this," Aurum said and pushed his mask onto Carnelian so that he had to let go of his father's hand. The old

Master leaned over Suth and bent to touch the dangling veined marble of his hand.

"His blood still burns." Aurum's face smoothed as he pulled his hand back over his gray stubbled head. "Perhaps there is still time."

"Perhaps. . . . ?" Carnelian's stomach curdled. "Why should there not be enough time? Surely, we are only a few stages away from the Wise?"

Aurum's eyes were dulled, looking at some inner landscape. "There is much that can happen along those few stages."

"You mean Ykoriana?"

Aurum's eyes ignited. "Bite your tongue. Just make sure you do what you can to keep your father alive. The rest is not your concern."

The cistern wobbled sinuous patterns across the rafter-latticed ceiling. The Masters held their aquar themselves. Aurum had dismissed the grooms so that they would not witness Suth's weakness. Jaspar clucked his impatience to be gone. An aquar was made to sink. With Aurum's help, Carnelian wrestled his father's body into the saddle-chair. They ignored Vennel's question about his health. Carnelian took the reins and held them as he and the others mounted. He tied them to his chair.

Outside, it was cold. Lazy sounds came up from the encampment. Carnelian felt the unease around him. Vennel's mask could not decide whether it wanted to look at his father or at the Marula. Jaspar's maintained a constant oblique angle to the Marula. The barbarians were clumped a little way off, already mounted. Their heads hung as if they slept in their chairs. They had turned their backs on the road ahead as if by not seeing it they could make it go away. Behind them, beneath an indigo sky, Osrakum's wall was a gloomy island rising from the sea of mist that submerged the city.

Carnelian looked for Tain among the Marula. Wearied almost to tears, already grieving for his father, Carnelian knew he must find the energy to buy back his brother's eyes.

Mist fingered the grim sleeping face of the land as they rode. It reached into Carnelian's cloak to chill his skin. Its breath smelled damp and moldy. The vague shapes of the Masters floated near him. The scratch of claws on the road seemed far away. Ahead, the Marula were wading through the twilight.

The sky paled, the blur cleared a little and Carnelian saw that they were riding along a causeway through a land of folded mud. Tarnished silver mirrors lay along the folds across which furtive creatures were spreading rings. Ridges bristled with reeds. Cranes lifted languidly into the air and flapped their angled silhouettes off, trailing their legs.

Ahead on a rutted mud shelf moored to the road like a raft, another encampment was coming alive. Air fuzzed blue with smoke. Muffled voices worried the silence. The edges of a watchtower contrasted with the liquid curves all around it. It grew huge and so solid that it made the fen look like a painted backcloth.

Then it was dropping behind and for a while Carnelian dozed away his misery, only vaguely aware of the mottled dull-mirroring rush on either side. Mounds began curving up from the mud, some with hovels on their backs, others caught in patches of netting. Carnelian sat up. Runs of gray water slipped around the mounds. Huts stood everywhere on legs. Boats lay half out of water, hiding behind tarpaulin skirts. Then he saw the edge of the city ahead. A mud bank textured with houses and shrubby trees was like the carcass of some immense monster rotting on the marsh. A stench was floating on the wind. Their aquar drummed along the leftway. The buildings ahead were rising higher. Soft-edged canals branched off into the marsh patinated with scum, littered with boats like dead leaves. Here and there pimpling the mud in the distance little citadels of trees hid buildings.

The stench of the city was wafting stronger. The channels

Carnelian could see were matted with filth. Two towers with sagging walls formed a kind of gateway through which the city received the road. They flashed between them and in among the mess of tenements. The angles of walls and alleys jagged his eyes. He could not make out a pattern. It was like a termite mound cut open and exposed to a rain that had melted everything together. Now and then he would see a flight of steps winding down to a canal hemmed in by rickety warehouses, along which long punts were sliding.

Then they came to a more prosperous region where the tenements wore blistered whitewash. The stench was ever-changing, like music. The mud walls heaved closer, riddled with passages, spined with the ends of beams that betrayed the anatomy of floors within. Dusty gardens crammed into corners. A single fig tree roofed a courtyard with its branches. From the midst of this riot rose another watchtower.

As they slowed, the city's perfume thickened: moldering mud, frying, the tang of slimed alleys, the dull odor of stagnant water, the vinegar reek of men.

Aurum had reached the monolith guarding the watchtower door. The aquar swung their heads from side to side as they slowed from their run. Aurum commanded the Marula to dismount. He used his aquar to herd them behind the monolith and disappeared. Carnelian was intent on the saddle-chair that held the huddle that was his father. He leaned close, desperate for some sign of life. His father's aquar adjusted its feet and the huddle gave a groan that let Carnelian breathe again. "My Lord?" he whispered but there was no reply. He looked round at the others.

"Where has Aurum gone?" He did not even attempt to mask the anger in his voice.

Jaspar motioned with his head.

Carnelian turned his aquar and saw that Aurum was there, his gold face peering from his hood.

"Why do we stop, my Lord?" Carnelian demanded.

"To leave the leftway and descend to the road."

Jaspar's hands expressed surprise. "Into the herd?"

"We cannot do that," said Carnelian.

"There is no choice, my Lord," said Aurum.

"There must be. The delay, not to mention the commotion, will kill my father."

Aurum rode up to him. "Last night I sent a messenger to the gates to announce our coming along this leftway. For that very reason we must leave it. This road leads only into peril."

"You anticipate another attack, Aurum?" asked Jaspar.

Carnelian noticed that the Master's voice lacked its usual note of amused detachment. "Surely we do not know for certain there will be another attack."

"There will be another attack," Aurum said darkly.

"Even if there is, how can my Lord be certain where it will occur?"

"The messenger, my Lord, the messenger," snapped Vennel.

Carnelian turned on him. "Does my Lord not think it possible that his mistress will see through Lord Aurum's subterfuge?"

"You are impertinent, my Lord."

"Nevertheless, Vennel, my cousin makes a reasonable point," said Jaspar.

Aurum lifted his hands. "I have taken all this into consideration. Our enemies will see in the messenger our attempt to hide our intention to leave this leftway. It would be unlike them not to see through this deception. Thus, they will expect us on the leftway. We shall thus do the unexpected by in fact leaving the leftway."

"In other words, my Lord, you have no idea whatsoever where our enemies are looking for us," Carnelian said. "For all we know they will be waiting for us on both routes. Since this is possible it behooves us to take whichever one will more quickly bring my father to his healing by the Wise."

Vennel gave him a nod. "On the contrary, if there is danger both ways we would be better in the marketplace of the Wheel where we would be as invisible as fish in the sea."

Jaspar squeezed his hands together. "Let us not forget the

filthy Marula. It would be prudent, cousin, if we were to find them work to do. The crowds will distract them."

Carnelian felt that the situation was slipping away from him. "Since when are the Chosen fearful of such animals?"

"Since, my Lord," sneered Vennel, "they are poisoned near unto death and know that we slew one of their number and, no doubt, will soon find a way to slay them all."

"If we move down to the road a greater distance will be put between them and their antidote. This will endanger them as much as it does my father. Surely they will know this and so become more dangerous."

"They will know nothing," Vennel said scornfully. "Did you not yourself say that they are animals?"

Carnelian cast around him. "My father still has his vote."

"Would you use up the last of his strength?" said Aurum.

Carnelian hesitated and looked from one mask to the next.

"Lord Suth should form no part in our calculations," said Jaspar. "It is unlikely he will live."

Aurum's hand darted up to cut short Carnelian's outrage. *Enough.* "If we three vote together we will carry the decision."

Vennel and Jaspar nodded.

"It is decided then. We will descend to the road." Vennel made no attempt to conceal the note of triumph in his voice.

Carnelian went cold with anger. "If my father should die . . ." he said through gritted teeth.

"You will be elevated to Ruling Lord."

"A privilege rare in one so young," said Jaspar and turned his aquar away.

As the others filed into the watchtower, Carnelian gazed down the leftway that narrowed off into a hazy crush of towers dwarfed by the dark mountain wall. The entrance to the Canyon of the Three Gates had widened into a narrow valley. Standing guard on either side of it were manikins almost hidden in its shadow. The mass of the city between served to cut them off at the knees. Carnelian shook his head, making no sense of their scale. What was certain, however, was that there was still a long ride to the gates and through the crowds it would take much, much longer.

He rode into the tower in despair, pulling his father's aquar after him, muttering under his breath, over and over again, "He'll hang on. He'll hang on."

In the gloom he could make out the immense shapes of the Masters on their aquar. In his anguish he had almost forgotten Tain. He tied the reins of his father's aquar to his own saddle-chair and then joined the Masters' line. When his turn came he turned his aquar onto the first ramp and his father's followed after. Halfway down one of the ramps he managed to get close to Jaspar. He forced his pain aside, his anger, his hatred and reached out to pull the Master's sleeve.

We must talk, he signed when he had Jaspar's eyes. The Master pointed inquiringly at Suth. Carnelian shook his head. They let the others move round the landing and begin descending the next ramp. Carnelian moved his hands into the light of a lantern.

If I pay your price, he signed, *you will forget my brother's sin?*

Your slave will keep his eyes, signed Jaspar with eager fingers.

"Swear on your blood."

"You challenge my honor?"

"Swear!"

Jaspar protested but swore the oath.

Carnelian signed the lie his father had given him. He hoped that a Jaspar would interpret the tremble in his signs as guilt rather than subterfuge.

Moving out onto the road was like walking into a crowded room. Carnelian resisted covering his ears with his hands lest their brightness should betray them. He ground his teeth. All around, people were packing up and getting ready to move on. Feet were smudging fires to smoke. Uneven walls shoved in on every side, echoing the clatter.

Aurum ordered the Marula forward through the encampment. They sat their saddle-chairs like dummies. The general commotion was getting Carnelian's aquar agitated. He looked round to see his father's shy away from some children and almost cried out when he saw his father slump over. More and more people were gathering to look at them. Soon they would be revealed as Masters. The news would pass all along the road and choke it. Their attackers would know where they were. Seeing the danger, Aurum moved into the Marula and woke them with his anger. Their uncurling seemed as slow as ferns. The Master's hand flashed a jab into the ribs of one of them. The man jerked up and threatened the Master with his lance. Aurum grew larger in his chair. The man withstood his menace for a moment before bowing his head and going to join the others.

The Marula began pummeling their way through the crowd. Their stiff arms rose and fell as they cleared a path for the Masters. People grumbled out of their way. Some fell, losing their bundles to be trampled by the aquar. Others were pushed onto those behind and came to blows. Anger rippled out into the crowd. Carnelian could see the Marula were wasting what little strength they had left. Their hands lifted less frequently, less high. In one place a Maruli was driving some men back against a huimur whose driver struck at their backs with his goad. One man turned to fight. Another was shoved forward by the stump of the huimur's horn as it tossed its head. His companions turned on the Maruli, shouting, threatening him with sticks. The black man's aquar shied back, plumes jittering, as he struggled to control it. Two of his brothers raised a baying in which Carnelian could hear weary desperation. Their mouths stretched in a fixed gape. They gleamed with sweat and pain and anger. They began a feverish stabbing. Throats in the crowd pumped out cries of panic as people fought to escape. Carnelian watched one of the Marula breaking his lance in a woman's body. Her face registered surprise as she plucked at the wood poking from her breast before slumping into the arms of the people around her.

"They are out of control," Vennel cried over the roar.

Jaspar backed away and his posture suggested he was looking for some direction in which to flee.

It was Aurum who rode forward into the carnage, his shrouded figure serene in the midst of fury. His huge hands pulled the Marula back. Carnelian looked on nervously as the Marula mobbed him. Aurum's cowled head looked around at them. The Marula hesitated and their mouths' rictus slacked. When Aurum came back through the roar the Marula were about him, obedient, menacing only those who came too close.

As the Marula angled their lances up, gore ran down the shafts. Carnelian turned his face just enough to see their eyes darting and the way their faces twitched as under their cloaks the poison ate into them. When they scowled and showed their teeth they appeared to be demons but mostly they just looked like old men.

The Masters percolated through the crowds following the Marula. Campfires and wagons forced wide detours. Each delay made Carnelian despair. His father's time was running out. He was letting go of what little hope he had left when a clamoring of bells drifted from somewhere up ahead. The crowd began to drift along the road in groups. Their exhalations overpowered the stench of the city. Wheel-creak, footfalls and chatter drowned the bells. As they picked up speed an ache of hope returned. Carnelian searched ahead for the dawn. The sky above the dark wall of Osrakum was already blue but the sun still hid behind her rampart. The light that filtered down into the canyon only served to reveal the contempt with which its guardians were looking down on the toy towers of the city.

Visions of the termite city interwove his weary vigilance. Yellow mottled walls. The tunnel of an alleyway; glimpsed shadowy doors; a brilliant flutter of doves; light slicking on a scum-fringed canal. Bridges swagged everywhere and the faded bunting of clotheslines. Tenements rose higher, opened shuttered mouths and breathed out the perfume of a thousand rooms. Carnelian glimpsed the face of a girl looking down at them. A child swung on a beam end. People melted off into alleyways. Once, the dirty curtain of tenements parted and he saw the long, faint mound of another road rising away across the hut—pebbled mirrored fen, angling toward them so that he guessed that they converged somewhere up ahead like the spokes of some gigantic wheel.

He was startled by a swell of sound, as if a door had opened nearby. A width of steps cascaded the crowd down to a harbor jostling with punts. Water lapped the lower steps where barefoot, half-naked people were unloading barges. He darted his gaze over the bobbing heads on the road about him, looking for assassins. He peered round past the mesmerizing circling of spokes, the pendulum palanquins, to see his father's chair. The body sagging in its curve looked already dead.

Barbarian voices crying out made Carnelian raise his eyes, see fingers pointing ahead and follow them to a pale rectangle flanked by two massings of shadow. As he drifted closer he began to hear a sound like swarming bees. The carpet of their march dragged slowly on. The shadows solidified into two gatehouses standing guard upon the road. The buzzing had become a distant roar. He passed the last tenement whose sharp edge defined the beginning of airy space. Voices broke out around him in excited exclamation. From the babble he gleaned the single word, "Wheel."

Carnelian's eyes widened with wonder as he reached the threshold of a moat canal. A bridge carried the road across to the gatehouses looming to receive it. These gave entrance to a plain; a vast roaring marketplace; a seething mass grained with countless heads whose sluggish currents carried toylike palanquins and the stalks of aquar heads. Skinned with crowds, the Wheel stretched off to vague distance, half of it in the shadow of the Sacred Wall.

As he drifted slowly across the bridge, Carnelian could not help drinking in the thrill bubbling up around him. His eyes flitted from one bright face to another until they stumbled on some that looked sick and grim. In that carnival, the Marula had the faces of mummies. Only their eyes showed any life as they scrutinized the wall of Osrakum. Carnelian followed them there and he too grew troubled. Its slope filled the lower sky like a storm. The sun rising above was burning a halo round the head of the leftmost gatehouse, making its shadow fall across the bridge as a cold diagonal. Light bathed the other inner flank and spilled out onto the bridge and along the wall that carried the leftway up to the gatehouse. Its face was studded with the cipher the five-spot quincunx. Carnelian wondered what the device might mean. His eyes slid down to where the gatehouse tenoned into the rock of the Wheel plateau. The plateau edge curving away in each direction was fringed with cranes that leaned over to dangle their lines down into the moat. On the water below, a barge was being poled while others were moored receiving goods from above. The outer wall of the moat rose to support a cliff jigsawed together from the buildings of the city that crowded up to its edge. This cliff followed the curve of the Wheel and was boned with wood, quoined and buttressed with brick. Mouths opened here and there where sewer throats and alleys broke through to vomit their rubbish into the moat. Filth streaked down from the sores of countless windows.

A scratching trumpet blast made Carnelian whisk round. One of the Masters was looking up to the leftway. The trumpet shrieked louder, closer, and one of the gatehouse towers answered it with a clanging bell. When the air stopped reverberating other bells could be heard sounding from the further reaches of the Wheel.

Carnelian saw the messenger flash past above. He searched the black huddles of the other Masters for some reaction.

One of them was forming signs, made clumsy by his gloves, . . . *as expected. She will soon know that we are somewhere in the Wheel.*

The gatehouses loomed up on either side. A double arch passed a leftway between them. One of the inner walls was snagging sunlight. Carnelian held the edges of his cowl and craned up to see that the gatehouse was sheathed with brass almost to the top. He was aghast at such profligate use of metal. The sun smoldered the wrought surface. Ledges trapped blue from the sky. Carnelian could not at first believe there could be so much metal in the world. Faces in the brass were larger than wagons, with eyes like wheels. Only when he saw the hinges, and the rollers as tall as men that lined its lower edge, did he realize that it was a gate.

He looked away and saw his wonder on other faces, but there was only fear on the faces of the Marula. They reminded him of his own misery and of the danger. The sun beat full upon their sweat-gleamed skin as they looked fixedly at Osrakum's dark wall. The focus of their terror was plain to see. Off a little to the left, the Wheel squeezed the slurry of its crowds into the funneling canyon. Standing flanking that funnel throat were the guardians, the two Gods of the Masters, each a quarter of the height of the mountainous Sacred Wall.

Beyond the towers the carriageway fanned out to meet a cordon of toll posts. They had to wait their turn. Holding their billhooks upright, the toll-keepers looked out from under conical wooden helmets into which the five dots of the quincunx were inlaid in bone. Their leather jerkins bore the glyphs, gate and sea.

Aurum sent a Maruli forward to drop a pouch into a toll-keeper's hand. The black man then leaned back to take in the whole of their party with a gesture. Nodding, the toll-keeper emptied the pouch out and began to count the bronze double-faced coins off against the Marula and the Masters. While he was doing this, one of his companions nudged him and pointed up at the Maruli whose face was slick with fear. The toll-keepers narrowed their eyes and began shouting at the Maruli, gesturing with their billhooks that he should dismount. The man looked back at the Masters, begging instruction; his brothers' lance blades were lifting. The billhooks were now clattering against the Maruli's saddle-chair. "Get down!" cried one of the soldiers.

The Maruli's aquar sank to the ground and he was dragged out of the chair groaning. More toll-keepers had come up. One was barking questions. Hunched, the Maruli slapped the man back only to find the billhooks shaking around his head. The Marula around Carnelian were growling. Nervously, he scanned the crowd beyond the toll cordon.

Aurum surged forward. The toll-keepers drew back from him with their billhooks lifted like cobras. Aurum's glove beckoned one. The man came reluctantly. The Master leaned over and opened a slit in his cowl so that the man could peer in. The man's face turned to clay. As he began sagging to his knees, Aurum grabbed the billhook to hold him up. They exchanged a mutter, then the toll-keeper fled back to the others who all began nodding, almost bowing as they opened up a way and let them pass through, between the posts of brass and into the roaring crowd.

They were forced to wait while some man-drawn carts rolled by, then they swam into the shifting currents of the Wheel. A tinker clinked earthenware on a branched pole. A party of northerners lumbered past on muzzled, large-headed aquar, each saddle-chair holding three or four of them, skin marbled with dirt, matted hair pebbled with amber.

As the Marula thrust a way into each new current they looked back with questioning faces. Each time Aurum shook his shrouded head. At last they came to where a river of people was flowing along a black paved road. Aurum gave a nod and the Marula led them in.

While all the time searching for enemies, Carnelian reeled in his father's aquar. It was as if they were in a boiling cauldron. Faces, hand-clasped bags and sacks and pouches, fruit-filled baskets, all were rolling in and out of sight. Mottled beasts rose here and there loaded with panniers, yoked to wagons, to chariots or swinging palanquins like soft humps. He saw painted eunuchs; women in gaggles or swaying on carried chairs, some swollen with child, their menfolk trying to make way for their bellies. Toll-keepers rode through like lords at a fair. Merchants marshaled their caravans with whips and bellowing. Urchins ran, weaving in and out, screaming, playing hide-and-seek among the angling thickets of legs. The roar never ceased. The air was never free of the bristle of poles, the slap and billow of canopies, of swagging ropes. The ground rarely showed its slimy mush of peelings and feathers, of flowers and dung.

Tortuously, they worked their way round the Wheel on the black road and then, abruptly, turned in toward its center to climb a wide ramp. Through a gap in the crowd, Carnelian saw a snatch of its balustrade where an old woman sat amongst a rot of melon rinds, offering up trinkets, her toothless grin tracking passers-by.

At the summit of the ramp a roar of water drowned out the crowds. Over the balustrade Carnelian saw a wide channel thrashing white, rushing water round in a wide arc. The water spilled out from the channel all along its length into cisterns mobbed by people.

When he looked up he realized the whole vast mosaic of the Wheel was laid out around him. He twisted to look back. The gatehouses they had come through now looked smaller than his hand. Behind them was the irregular rim wall. He followed that round and saw another pair of gatehouses at a greater distance, then round to another pair further still, and to where yet another gateway touched the canyon edge. On the other side of the canyon he found one more gate to close the ring. The quincunx cipher made sense to him. Not counting the way into the canyon, the Wheel had five gates in all.

The shadow of the Sacred Wall was still dulling colors

over half the Wheel. Where the sun had reached, delicate patchwork stretched its hues off toward the moat. Far away it was stitched together from tiny lozenges; closer it resolved into neat rows of vendors sitting among their baskets and their blankets, green-heaped with herbs and all manner of vegetables and fruit. Dark cuttings toothed the Wheel rim, showing where channels cut into it from the moat. A ring shearing in the human flow showed the road they had left. Inside that, the water channel and its cisterns formed a glittering circle. Six ramps crossed this. Five of them lay on one of the spokes that led to a pair of gatehouses. The sixth led to bridges over the moat and on into the canyon and the crater of Osrakum.

As they descended into the inner Wheel, Carnelian was beginning to believe they had managed to elude their attackers. He could hear music. Flags proclaimed the trades of the bonesmith, the featherer, the copper-beater. The weavers were there with their cottons, the pigmenters with their dyes. Lacquered boxes rather than baskets held every kind of precious commodity. One man was rolling out rippled leathers and another was displaying cylinders of ivory as thick as his arms. Among them strolled buyers, their face tattoos proclaiming them the servants of the Masters. Behind them swung chests with their treasure of coined bronze.

The music of horns and cymbals was coming from somewhere up ahead. Carnelian tried to see round the riders blocking his view. They were nearing the ring of poles that defined the hub of the Wheel. From each pole hung strange fruit. The fetor of decay swelled with the carnival music. Carnelian could see dancers cavorting between the poles, snaking yellow ribbons through the air. People were poking sticks into the things hanging from the poles. Squinting, he was appalled to see that they were men dangling in the air, spread-eagled on diagonal crosses. As he came closer, Carnelian flinched away from one man's agonized face. A hawker was selling makeshift spears to his tormentors. Carnelian had to pass so close to the crucified man that he could smell his sweat and the excrement that streaked his legs.

The hub of the Wheel was fenced in by these crucifixions. Carnelian was looking round in disgust when his aquar began to be jostled. The crowd was milling. One Maruli's aquar was shoved into his. Angry voices were drowning out the horn. His aquar's plumes flared. Carnelian maneuvered his father's saddle-chair as close as he could, then stretched over to grab its rim. His father jigged like a sack. A surge was rushing toward them across the mass of heads. When it struck, Carnelian was almost unseated, but he still managed to keep hold of his father's chair. Aurum's voice was shouting commands over the riot. Carnelian watched the Marula stabbing at faces with their lances. Panic was ripping gaps in the crowd as Carnelian watched hands reach up to one Maruli's saddle-chair. The black man had a sword out and was chopping at them. For each hand that let go, two more grabbed hold. The chair was toppling. The aquar was struggling against the bodies pressing round it. Suddenly the Maruli was yanked into a surf of hands and disappeared. For a moment he resurfaced, bloodied, then the crowd closed over him. Carnelian looked round in shock and saw another Maruli being dragged to his death. He tried to edge his aquar and his father's round to shield him. His own chair lurched suddenly to the left and he saw the hands grasping its rim. He was forced to let his father's chair bob free. Faces grimaced up at him as he fumbled for one of his ranga shoes. He stamped at their fingers and heard bones crack but still they clung on.

Masters' voices crying out in wrath made Carnelian look up. They were revealing themselves, huge and golden-faced. He threw his own hood back. Instantly most of the hands released their grip as if his mask were shooting flames at them. His chair righted a little, but fingers still clung on like grappling hooks. The faces over the rim showed doubt as round them the crowd was falling to its knees. Still they pulled, gnashing their teeth as he struck repeatedly. His chair was leaning further. Soon he would fall out. He could see enraged men waiting below with flint knives.

A voice boomed so loud it made the crowd seem quiet. "Brothers of the Wheel." The assassins looking up at Carnelian faltered. He was jolted to one side as his saddle-chair was released. He looked round and saw the gold-faced figure sitting tall in his father's saddle-chair. "I am the voice of the Masters."

Carnelian stopped breathing. His father had come back to life. The crowd stilled.

"The Mountain knows who you are, Oh Brothers of the Wheel, and what . . . you do here . . . today. Slip . . . slip . . ." His father crumpled.

A voice could be heard giving commands in thin Quya but Carnelian could see the blood lust returning to the eyes below. Fingers curled slowly over his chair rim. Carnelian watched them, his ranga shoe held high. He allowed his arm to sink and put the shoe across his knees. He lengthened his back, lifted his chin. He moistened his lips. "Slip away." He felt his mask quivering with the words. "Slip away, Oh Brothers of the Wheel." His voice was finding its strength. "Slip away now and this sin will be forgiven you." He felt the power. He was a spindle of iron. He raised his hand to point up at the sky. "Persist and you may be certain that as surely as that sun will set tonight, so shall the vengeance of the Masters find you, exterminate you root and branch even to the remotest of your kin."

His words had turned the crowd to stone. A lone voice warbled a command. Carnelian saw his attackers fleeing, chasing the ripple of prostration that was spreading away through the crowd. Around him the marketplace might have been a plain of ferns flattened by a whirlwind. A murmur came from those distant parts of the Wheel that the silence had not reached. As Carnelian looked round he felt the power drain away. An aquar was wandering with what was left of his father crumpled in its saddle-chair. The moaning of the crucified was a wind through winter trees.

THE
THREE
GATES

Three lands

Three gates

And three tall crowns

—NURSERY RHYME

"Suth has killed himself," shrilled Vennel.

Jaspar's mask was surveying the further reaches of the crowd. "I had thought him already dead."

Aurum rode to stoop toward Suth's cloak.

Vennel looked at Carnelian. "Grieve not, my Lord, your father's death was not in vain. He saved us and now you are the Ruling Lord Suth."

The reins sagged in Carnelian's hand. His aquar began ambling.

Jaspar looked round. "We must ride on to the gates. This is no place to linger."

Carnelian was numb.

"He still lives."

They all turned to Aurum.

"He lives, you say?" cried Vennel. "Are you sure?"

Aurum straightened. "Though his blood grows cold."

Carnelian pulled his aquar back into control and moved to his father's side. He reached over to touch him. His father's cloak could have been stuffed with clay. No sound of breathing came from behind his mask. Carnelian rummaged in the cloak for a hand. He lifted the lank flesh and placed his finger to the blue cord bridging the wrist. There was a flutter like a taper flame. He sighed and stroked it, before replacing it in the folds. He felt a shadow fall on him and looked up. It was Jaspar. "Are we safe?"

Aurum's mask seemed to melt and flame as he nodded. "The danger has passed for now. Her web is torn a second time."

"And the Marula?"

The crowd had ebbed away, stranding the corpses of three of the black men in their own blood. Aurum ignored the question and began barking commands at those still alive. Carnelian's eyes lingered on their pinched faces. They seemed not to have heard. Their red eyes slid sidelong to their fallen comrades.

"On, I say, on!" cried Aurum.

Marula eyes glanced off the mirror of the Master's face to stare up to the faces of the Gods sneering down at them from the throat of the canyon.

Aurum swept his hand round to indicate the encircling crucifixions. "If you don't want to end this day hanging on a cross, you'll move on."

The Marula hunched reluctant, then first one and then the rest urged their aquar forward toward the prostrate edge of the crowd. Their lances lifted as they coughed battle cries and began to pick up speed. There was a screaming scramble as people scurried out of their way.

Aurum looked over at Carnelian. "Come, my Lord."

Carnelian tied his father's aquar to his saddle-chair, then, with a lash of his reins, he crashed after the Marula, pulling his father and the other Masters in his wake.

The feet of the colossus appalled the Marula. Great wedges of scabrous stone. Toenails like the roofs of houses. An instep that was a cave. Each foot narrowed up several stories to an ankle thicker than the gatehouses of the Wheel. The legs barreled up their leprous towers, leaning toward each other, swelling toward the knees that were bending the mountainous thighs toward them. They shuddered, imagining the kneeling avalanche of so much stone. The waist and belly seemed a more remote and solid part of the mountain. A fist supported an arm that in turn buttressed the slab of a shoulder. Strangely, the head looked no bigger than a human head. The head of the other colossus leaned close as if they might be talking together, oblivious of the ant world milling at their feet. The eyes of the Marula were forced to scale further up the Sacred Wall. Crag piled on crag up the slope. The whole skyful of rock leaned out as the canyon walls came together. The black men stared unblinking at the narrow ribbon of blue nipped between them. It was like tottering on the edge of an abyss in whose remote depths a brilliant river ran. They could imagine falling. They squeezed their eyes closed, dropped their heads, dizzy, their nails gouging a grip on the rims of their saddle-chairs.

Wind acrid with smoke blew hard against Carnelian's mask. He felt his aquar slowing. He could make out that the ramp he had been riding up from the canyon floor ended abruptly in a promontory. His aquar's narrow head angled up and back, flaring plumes, as he yanked it to a halt. The plume fans folded and he saw the gloomy nave of the canyon. Its slope milled with traffic. Far above, the sky was an improbable painted ceiling.

The scrape of claws made him turn to see the Masters racing toward him with Aurum at their head.

"I will take responsibility for the Lord Suth."

"You will not," Carnelian said.

Aurum came very close to tower over him. Carnelian straightened his back and faced him. Aurum flicked the air in anger and turned his aquar, all the time bellowing the commands that sent the Marula hurtling past and onto the road grooving off along the left-hand canyon wall.

Jaspar came up. "Why have we stopped, my Lords?"

"The Marula are the danger now," said Aurum, the eyeslits of his mask following the black men as they grew smaller and smaller in the groove road.

Carnelian glanced up the length of the canyon. The sound of water made him look down to see the canal. "A river," his voice said.

Jaspar snorted. "The vermin in the city below call it the River of Paradise. We call it the Cloaca, for it is the sewer of our hidden land."

"We ride to the Green Gate." Aurum left the words behind as he launched into motion, leaving Carnelian and the other Masters to chase after him.

Rock was hurtling past his head. The canyon narrowed into the distance where, in a gloomy haze, it turned abruptly southward. All the way to this bend, the floor was a dusky swirl of wagons and people divided in two by the groove of the Cloaca. A scraping scuffling shook up the canyon walls and set Carnelian's teeth grinding. In the wind, his cloak became like a trapped bird. Up ahead he glimpsed the bladed edges of the canyon reaching high enough to graze the sun. It seemed impossible that any light should ever find its way down to the floor.

As they sped round the bend of the canyon, Carnelian watched the next stretch coming into view. Billows of smoke rolling toward them engulfed the Marula, then broke over Carnelian until he was riding blind. He choked on the gray air. The clouds thinned enough to show the insect crowds below. Coughing, eyes welling, he tried to peer through the murk. He swam out spluttering as the smoke dispersed like morning mist. They had come to the prickling edge of what appeared to be an impenetrable forest.

"The Green Gate, at last," cried Jaspar.

Staring, Carnelian realized the forest was made of bronze, a bladed hedge shaped into a fortress wall that filled the canyon from side to side. Before it, the canyon floor was striped and chevroned with wagons covering these patterns in ordered files. The Cloaca had sunk into a chasm spanned by bridges.

Carnelian could see no way through the bronze hedge. Tall banners burned red among the thorns. Other flames appeared and became figures shrouded in vermilion. Some were as small as children. All were enveloped in cloaks that brushed the ground.

As Aurum's mask looked back, Carnelian followed its gaze and saw that the Master was studying the Marula who had fallen behind them in close escort. Their faces were wooden with fear. Mouths hung open as if they were panting. Their eyes fixed on their hands. Slight, unblinking, Tain sat like a doll between the legs of a Maruli.

Dread began stirring in the pit of Carnelian's stomach as he watched the vermilion figures forming into a crescent. He looked at their faces. Each was the same, each divided, half skin, half black. He drew back into his chair as they threw back their cloaks. All wore legionary collars of gold. Their leather armor was baroquely textured on the same side as their faces were black and on the other side as smooth as their skin. On each chest was a red flower like a flame.

"Ichorians," he breathed. All his life, he had heard tales about these half-tattooed men. The Red Ichorians, guardians of the Three Gates.

One of them stepped forward lightly, like a dancer. He stood smiling before Aurum's aquar and then performed an elegant prostration.

"Surely you are Masters," the man said, rising to his knees, "though you wear no ciphers, no banners, nor are you guarded by tyadra. And those," the Ichorian stabbed his black-tattooed hand toward the Marula, "those creatures defile this road."

Aurum pulled back his cowl to reveal the mask beneath and as he did so all the Ichorians knelt except the one in front of him who rose, still smiling.

"You're correct, Ichorian, in all you say," Aurum said. "We've come far through many perils and have had need of these disguises. Now we'll happily discard them."

"We've heard that a party such as this accompanies the Master, Our-father-who-goes-before?"

Aurum lifted his hand in the affirmative and the Ichorian searched eagerly among the shrouded riders "We expected you on the leftway, my Masters. Are you desirous to pass swiftly through the Three?"

Aurum repeated the affirming gesture. "But first there's one matter you must attend to, centurion."

There was a clack as two Marula chairs struck together. Aurum's mask turned slightly to one side as if he were listening for more collisions.

"We aren't yours to command, my Master, unless you wear the Pomegranate Ring."

In answer Aurum pushed his white hand out of his sleeve and splayed it. The ring was a huge wound in the heart of his palm.

"Father," the Ichorian cried and fell before him onto the pavement. The cry was taken up by the other Ichorians. The centurion rose up again to his knees. "Forgive the children that didn't know their father."

Aurum turned his aquar so that he was looking back at the Marula. Carnelian followed his lead. Hunched in their saddle-chairs, the black men were huddling their beasts together. One of them who dared to raise his eyes had the shy look of a child expecting punishment.

Aurum lifted his hand and pointed. "Destroy those animals."

"Destroy them," chorused Vennel and Jaspar.

As one, the crescent of Ichorians swept forward, passing quickly between the Masters to face the Marula. The black men's faces creased with panic. One of the guardsmen lifted his tattooed hand. He had in his grip a bird of bronze winged with blades. He released it into whistling flight around his hand. As he let out its leash its blurring circle widened with the eyes of the Marula. Their lances wavered out in front of them as they backed their beasts away. The bladed bird began to keen. Other Ichorian arms were whirling similar weapons. Their keening modulated together into an eerie discordant chorus. The Marula began raggedly wailing as the first blade hurtled through the air. A Maruli slapped into the back of his chair, the blade deep in his throat, his lance angled lifeless. The line that held the blade yanked back and the Maruli's head lolled forward, bounced on the dead man's knees and thudded to the ground, arcing blood. The air was sliced by more blade flights. The Marula ducked frantically but there was no place to hide. The aquar made cries like tearing metal as their plumes were scythed. A shielding hand flew off. Screams were choked to gurgling. Carnelian looked down with horror and saw heads thudding to the ground like overripe fruit. When he looked up, the headless trunks were jerking as the aquar milled bleating, blood welling in their saddle-chairs and spilling down their flanks.

Carnelian remembered Tain with a gasp. Quickly untying his father's reins from his saddle-chair, he threw them over to Jaspar and then forced his aquar into the maelstrom. Cries of warning from the other Masters seemed remote. Everything was moving as slowly as curling smoke. As he slid his eyes round, Carnelian saw one of the Ichorians, only a boy, tugging twice on a line; it bellied back dragging its blade. Blood flicking off it across Carnelian's hand was pleasantly warm. His aquar's steps pumped him lazily up and down. He saw Tain sitting stiff and bloody, eyes squeezed shut, clamped in the arms of a headless black and red man. An Ichorian placed himself in Carnelian's path mouthing something, but he urged his aquar on, forcing the man to jump out of his way. He lifted his gaze, saw Tain, leaned precariously out and pulled him from the corpse. As he fell back into his saddle-chair, his brother's weight crushed out a grunt.

"My Lord! Carnelian!" Aurum's outrage blared.

Carnelian looked down into his brother's face, felt him for wounds, prised a reddened eyelid open. His brother's dark eye rolled to white. "Carnie," he gulped and burrowed his head into Carnelian's armpit.

Carnelian turned his aquar to face Aurum and the others.

"What in the thousand holy names, do you think you are doing?" Aurum boomed. "You could have been slain."

The golden frieze of the Masters' faces were judging him, but Carnelian ignored them, hugged Tain tighter and pushed his aquar through their line. He rode towards the thicket of thrusting bronze. A vinegar odor reeked off its mossy rust. Carnelian's eyes became trapped in all that curving and wandered lost. He found he was looking up through its bristling where his gaze had found the top. A vast height of canyon wall rose to a faraway sky.

He dropped his head into Tain's warmth, rocking him, crooning so that neither of them heard the hedge clank its thorns as a part of it began to open up in front of them.

When Carnelian lifted his head, he saw silver faces floating in the gloom. Lamps glowing like stars lent vague substance to the walls. Masters' masks streaked reflections. Looking round, Carnelian could not locate the doorway they had come through. Tain stirred against his chest as if awaking. Carnelian felt him tense as ammonites drifted near. Carnelian tried to make his aquar back away but one of them touched a hand to the creature's neck and it sank down.

"Give the slave to us, Seraph," one of the ammonites said in Quya.

Carnelian clutched Tain.

Ranga shoes clacked toward them.

"You must give them the boy, my Lord."

Carnelian turned on Jaspar. "Curse you, I paid your price."

Jaspar backed away. "Calm yourself, cousin." He glanced round to see if any of the other Masters were paying attention. He leaned closer. "The boy's eyes are safe, but he must pass through the quarantine with the others." He pointed. "Look, my Lord, we are all handing them over."

Carnelian looked and saw Jaspar's pallid blood-smeared boy creeping into the waiting hands of an ammonite. He turned back to Jaspar. "How long?"

"Before he is returned to you?"

Carnelian nodded.

"Thirty-three days."

"A month," Carnelian cried in disbelief.

"Twenty cells lie between here and the Blood Gate and there are another thirteen beyond. He will have to spend a day in each before he is allowed to pass through the Black Gate."

"Promise me on your blood that he will not be harmed."

Jaspar shrugged. "My Lord cannot expect one to vouch for everything. If the child is found to have plague . . ." The Master put his wrists together in a sign of powerlessness.

"He does not," said Carnelian, more emphatically than he felt. He nudged Tain. "Come on, we must talk," he said in Vulgate.

Tain clambered over the edge of the saddle-chair. Carnelian fumbled on his ranga shoes and then climbed out beside him. He waved the ammonites back and walked a little way from the others, beckoning Tain to follow.

As he looked down at his brother, Carnelian saw his own bloody handprint on the boy's face. He touched his mask. "I wish I could remove this thing."

Tain looked back at him with huge bruise-rimmed eyes.

"Tain, you'll have to go with them."

His brother looked fearfully back at the ammonites. "Will they let me come back . . . back to you and the Master once . . . once . . . once they've blinded me?"

Carnelian threw his head back and moaned. "Oh, no, no, Tain, it's not that. I've sorted that out. It's not that."

Tain was still gazing at him.

"No, really, I promise, I swear on my blood, your eyes are in no danger, but . . ."

"But . . . ?"

"You must be kept apart from us for a month until they're"—Carnelian indicated the ammonites—"sure that you're free of plague."

"Plague," nodded Tain.

Carnelian noticed the ammonites gathering around one of the kneeling aquar. "Please go with them. I must see to Father. Trust me, Tain."

"At the end of it, they'll send me to where you are, Carnie?"

"I promise." Carnelian gave his brother's arm a squeeze. There was nothing to grip but bone. Tain looked stuck to the ground. Carnelian pushed him gently away. "Go on, pull yourself together, endure it, you're strong enough." He remembered something. He fished out the Little Mother from a pocket and pressed her into Tain's hand. "She'll look after you."

Tain gave a watery smile and hid her in his fist. Carnelian watched him turn, hesitate, looking at the ammonites with their sinister silver faces, then pace toward them. Carnelian turned away and strode off to where ammonites were crowding round his father. Aurum was standing looking in over their heads. Carnelian heard the tearing sound. He pushed through them and saw they were ripping through his father's cloak like a crab's shell to expose the yellow-white body inside. One of the silver masks leaned so close that it caught a twisting reflection of the wound-stained bandages.

The creature straightened up and looked round at the gold masks. "Seraphim, these bandages have been tampered with."

Aurum leaned over to see. "Perhaps his slave . . ."

The ammonite whisked round, looking off toward the boys who were undressing. "Which is he? He must be destroyed."

"It is too late for that; he was one of the Lord Aurum's numerous victims," said Carnelian bitterly.

Aurum's mask looked down at him.

"Besides," Carnelian continued, "it was I who cut the bandages."

"Indeed, my Lord," said Aurum. "Now we see why he is dying."

Carnelian flared up. "How dare you accuse me of that? I did it with his agreement. The bandages were rotting . . ."

"The Law—"

"Does my Lord speak of the same Law which he has seen fit to break at his every whim?"

Aurum's mask angled a little to one side. "This impertinence—"

"Are you then, my Lord, He-who-goes-before? You must be since you wear his ring."

"The boy makes a hit, my Lord, a veritable hit," said Vennel gleefully.

"I think, Lord Aurum," said Carnelian, "it would be better if the ring was returned to him to whom it legally belongs."

Aurum seemed to grow taller, more menacing.

"The Law must be obeyed," said the ammonite.

"I merely borrowed it to protect He-who-goes-before when he could not protect himself," grated Aurum. He put his hand out and opened it to reveal the muted flame of the Pomegranate Ring.

Carnelian reached out and took it. The ammonite began to protest, but stopped when Carnelian lifted his father's hand, threaded the heavy ring onto the middle finger and closed the hand around the gem.

Vennel turned to the ammonite. "This matter will have to be reported to your masters."

"Perhaps, before he does that, he should first attempt to save the Ruling Lord Suth's life, or would you both rather have him die," said Aurum icily.

Vennel pulled back like a serpent ready to strike.

The ammonite lifted his hands. "Seraphim, this behavior is unworthy of your blood."

"His life, ammonite . . ." hissed Aurum.

"It . . . this wound, it is beyond my skill, Seraph. Only my masters can save him."

"Then, ammonite, do you not agree that we had better make haste to get him to your masters? I promise you, your skin will not long remain your own if they find that you have let him die."

Ammonites led them up a flight of stairs to a hall where the Masters were divested of their riding cloaks. Their long slim bodies were revealed wrapped in bandages sweat-stained yellow. New ranga were brought and jade-green robes spiraled with ferns. Their old cloaks and ranga shoes were gathered up with tongs and burned in a brazier.

As Carnelian came back down, he clenched and unclenched his hands, which were sticky with Marula blood. He watched his father being moved to a bier and then covered with one of the green robes. Tain was a little way off, naked with the other boys, just skin stretched over bones. His head was in an ammonite's grip being turned this way and that as the creature's silver mask peered at him. His shoulders and back were painfully bruised. Carnelian could guess by whom. Another boy whimpered as he was folded for examination. Carnelian turned away, knowing there was nothing more he could do for Tain.

As a bright rectangle opened in the further wall, Carnelian strode after his father's bier. The green silk was heavy as he lifted it with his knees. The new ranga were taller than the old ones. He had to swing his feet. It was like walking on stilts.

He clacked out onto the road with the other Masters. The air had grown hot. Chariots stood amid kneeling rows of Ichorians. His father was being carried to one whose wheel rims rose above the heads of the people round it. Carnelian followed. The back of the chariot was a dull mirror of gold from which a Master was surfacing as if from a bath. Ammonites reached up to the handles with hooks and halved the Master by pulling open the doors. Others lifted the bier, rested its edge on the chariot floor, then, careful to touch nothing, fed his father in.

Carnelian watched Jaspar climbing into another chariot nearby. He saw that it was yoked to a pair of pale-skinned aquar. Naked half-colored men held their halters.

"Fetch riders," Aurum said to an Ichorian.

Three ammonites converged on him, protesting.

". . . too slow," Carnelian heard Aurum say, and, "The Law . . ." one of the ammonites responding.

Aurum muted the man with an angry gesture and flowed toward Carnelian like a column of green water. He pointed over Carnelian's shoulder. "Your chariot awaits."

"I will travel with my father, Lord Aurum."

The Master said nothing though a slight curling in his fingers betrayed his anger as he strode past Carnelian.

One of the chariots was already being led off at a jog by an Ichorian as Carnelian climbed the steps into his father's chariot. There were three chairs set side by side. His father lay on the floor between two of them. Carnelian chose a chair next to the wall. He had hardly sat down before the doors closed him into the perfumed glimmering gloom. With a lurch they were off. Carnelian leaned over the arm of the chair, slipped his hand under his father's shroud, found his hand and held it.

His father's hand was so like wax that Carnelian feared he might melt it with his grip. On the floor, his father could have been a corpse wearing a death mask. Though Carnelian could hear the wheels sighing and the clink of harness, the chariot seemed hardly to be moving. Leaning close, he could detect no sound of breathing coming through the metal face. He sat up and rested his head against the quivering wall. He was alone. They had taken everything from him and left him entombed in this gold box with his father. He wanted to cry, to rage, to bellow. He centered himself. This was not the time for emotional indulgence. He looked back down at his father's body. If the Lord of the Underworld was not there he was very close; Carnelian could smell his myrrhy breath. To survive, he must free himself from Aurum's hope. He reminded himself that all the Master wanted was a puppet. At least in death his father would be free. Carnelian could do nothing for him. His duty there was ended. He stretched his hand down to his father's chest.

"Forgive me," he said, and felt the water begin to spill from his eyes. "Duty," he growled and clenched his eyes closed to dam the tears. He still owed his people duty. That was something to cling to. He had promised Tain that he would be there waiting for him and there were the others making the long journey up from the sea. There would be no more Crails. He must make the Suth palaces in Osrakum safe for them. Besides, his father had told him to go there. He looked down again. It was one of the last commands he had given. Carnelian would go to Coomb Suth and alone. Alive or dead, Carnelian knew that Aurum would not allow him to take his father home. The thought of leaving him in the old Master's hands was sickening. Even dead, Aurum would find some political use for him. With thoughts of Aurum came false hope. Were there limits to the sorceries of the Wise? What if by some miracle his father did survive? Then he would have to go to the Labyrinth to play his part in the election.

Carnelian crushed his ear against the wall and let its panels cut his mask into his skin. It was a distraction. He spotted the catch, lifted it and found that he could slide a panel back. He peered through the window out into the canyon twilight. Its wide empty floor was cracked in two by the Cloaca. He narrowed his eyes when he noticed the red square. Marching Ichorians. He could smell blood in the color of their cloaks. He slapped the panel back over the window and reached down to squeeze out what comfort there was left in his father's hand. Metal edges bit into his fingers. He lifted the hand to look at it. The Pomegranate Ring on the middle finger. On the little finger, above the blood-ring, sat the Ruling Ring of House Suth. Carnelian chewed his lip staring at it, then worked it off with his free hand. He would not give Aurum the chance to defile his family ring as he had the ring of He-who-goes-before, even if this meant despoiling the dead.

* * *

The chariot stopped and he waited for it to move off again. The Ruling Ring was the warm heart of his fist.

"Seraph?" said a voice muffled by the doors.

Carnelian adjusted his father's mask, then found the handles on the doors and opened them. He glimpsed the ammonites' silver masks as they bowed their heads and knelt. Then he saw behind them a tidal wave of bronze that made him flinch. He searched the bronze for an edge and found one, a bloody tower to one side. As he put his ranga shoe out onto the first step he saw the sister tower on the other side.

He hovered round the ammonites as they pulled his father out.

Aurum swept up. "Hurry, hurry."

"You make them clumsy, my—" Carnelian stopped, looking past him, feeling vertigo as the world began to shift. Dull thunder rumbled the air. At first Carnelian thought it was an earthquake and braced himself against the bier, but then he realized it was not he but the wall of bronze that moved. A crack appeared in its green-blurred firmament. He narrowed his eyes anticipating its titanic collapse. Then he saw tiny figures walking into the crack and realized it was a gate.

As he followed the bier through the opening, he trailed his hand along the edge of the gate. Peering behind it he saw its thick wheels taller than those of the chariot and the brass ruts curving in the ground in which these ran. There were chains and pulleys and the engines that made the gate open and close. At no great distance another gate rose as massive as the first. The walls on either side were filled with doors, tunnel mouths, with galleries growing brighter as they climbed. Far above, the canyon walls held a river of sky.

Ichorians stood everywhere in the shadows. More ammonites crowded round his father's bier. "Seraph Suth," they whispered, "returning for the election."

"Where are the Wise?" said Aurum and his voice played the gates like mountainous gongs.

The ammonites lifted their hands in mute apology. "They could not come so far, Seraph. Purity. During divine election, the court needs them all."

"Pah!" cried Aurum, flinging up his arms, scattering the ammonites into kneeling clumps.

"Shall we then proceed to the Halls of Returning?" said Jaspar. "It might be pleasant to have these stinking bandages removed, neh? But perhaps my Lord Aurum would prefer to remain here terrorizing ammonites?"

Portcullises lifted to let them into one of the tunnels. Carnelian kept close to his father. A hissing made him turn to see ammonites ladling blue fire over the path upon which they had just walked. He watched the flames sprint and die across the floor. More fire was being poured in front of them, and when it had gone out Carnelian removed his ranga as he saw the others do and walked across the still-warm stone. As he came into the hall he lifted his foot and saw its sole was black.

Arches gave into other halls whose floors were spangled with pools. Ammonites carried lanterns aloft on poles. Some swung feathers of thick smoke into the air from censers.

"Come with us," they sighed. "Come with us."

Carnelian protested as he felt his father's bier slip away under his hand. He struggled to think. Another wreath of smoke swagged down from a censer. He did not understand what was happening. His head was swelling. They took his hands. They led him down into the water. Fingers fluttered at his ears and he felt the pressure in his head relaxing. He sighed with relief as the mask peeled away from his face. Smoke curled round him like acrobats in a dream. He touched his face in alarm at what harm its nakedness might do. Their stone-blind eyes reassured him. The soaked weight of his robes pulled away from him, leaving him light and bobbing in the water. He sighed as he felt their hands on him, unwinding. Strip by strip his body was released. Ah, the sensuous arousing pleasure. Their hands were everywhere caressing him, pressing, exploring his openings with their fingers.

At last, they drew him from the pool and dried him. He looked at their faces, confused. Tain? Was that Tain shaving his head? Sharp menthol swabbed cool tracks over him. Once it stung and he scolded Tain. He tried to snare the sinuous smoke in his fingers but his hands were caught like butterflies. His skin was aglide with silk. When he looked down his body was ridged with brocade scars. They put him on low ranga, placed the sweetened mask over his face and pressed something into his hand. They coaxed him along passages out into the morning, slowly, so that his eyes would become accustomed to the glare.

He saw a vast smooth-floored ravine, along one edge of which the Cloaca cut its chasm. The walls rose near-vertical, scarlet, ridged with galleries up to impossible heights on either side. Their skirts were filigreed with brass machinery. He tried to focus his eyes. "Where . . . ?"

"The Red Caves, Seraph."

The stables and barracks of the Ichorian Legion. Carnelian guided his vision carefully to a black dike blocking the canyon where its walls flared up mountainously, drawing away from each other to reveal a liquid blue vision of sky. His eyes were trying to focus on something solid when he was walked up into a chariot and shut inside its box.

He sat in the gloom feeling the quiver of the chariot, wondering what was happening to him. Poppy? This was different, another drug. Something hard nestled in his hand. He hinged his fingers open and saw that his palm welled with blood as if it had been pierced with a nail. He brought the redness closer. A stone coin. Red carnelian, his name stone. It was too dim to see it clearly but he could feel the vague pips of glyphs set around its motif of a halved pomegranate. He closed his fist and rubbed it over his other hand, whose shape seemed unfamiliar. A swollen knuckle. No, a ring. His father's ring on his hand. The strangeness of it made him laugh, then remember, then search the floor to find his father gone. It was difficult to think. Where had he lost him? The clinking harness fell silent, the chair stopped quivering, then the doors opened.

"Resurrection," a voice intoned. "From the Dead Land to the Everliving."

The silver-faced creatures had extracted Carnelian from the chariot, prised the stone coin from his hand and brought him into a world of mirrors where he was a thousand times reflected.

"My father . . ." Nobody listened to him.

"Leave the debris of the other world behind. Those grave goods. Those shrouds. Cross the water. Live again."

A single voice sang with many tongues. Silk slid off him. Lilies. Fields of lilies crushing out a wall of perfume. His skin burned hot, then cold. Long licks of paint enstriped him. He gulped thick, lilied air. He opened his eyes and saw that he had been transformed into a pillar of ice existing in many worlds.

The moon ray of his body hid behind a green cloud. Then he was pacing through the night, a void beneath his feet. He watched them dart out from under the robe. His mask was kissing his face all at once. Gold faces blew toward him like luminous kites.

"The Black Gate," sighed Jaspar as if something were appearing to him in a vision.

Carnelian followed him to a little arch standing all alone. His fingers reached out to stroke the faces inhabiting it. Worn, indistinct, like half-forgotten memories. Then he was through it and each of his footfalls was shaking the air. He stopped walking, desperate to silence the thunder of his tread but the air still shook. A bell. He had been pacing in time to the tolling of a bell. Just then a vertical crack of sky swelled in front of him and swam him out into its coruscating furnace glare.

A
STRANGER
IN
PARADISE

How high then must we build the wall

Around the fields of Paradise?

—FRAGMENT,

ORIGIN UNKNOWN

They smiled and he smiled back, black angels rising up into
the glorious sky on columned smoke. Carnelian put his foot
on the honeycomb pavement and could feel its scorch even
through his shoe. He stepped carefully from one cobble to
the next, recalling that he must not touch the cracks. He
played the game in time to the clanging of the bell. It brought
him to one of the columns; not smoke, but lichened stone. He
tried to embrace it but it was too wide for his arms. He
frowned, then hooked his fingers into a horizontal joint.
There was another above it, and another, each defining a

block. The blocks were piled one upon the other like stone bowls. As he looked further up the stack he smiled again seeing the angel carved into its summit. Its face was vague, clay left in the rain, but it had his father's smile.

His father. Where was his father? He whisked round and saw the bier in among the poppy-red Ichorians. Carnelian pushed through them. He took slower steps as the bier came into sight. There was a flash in the corner of his eye. Two creatures were approaching, fish-scaled, gleaming, crowned with summer rain. Each carried a standard. Carnelian stepped back, narrowing his eyes against the dazzle of their armor as they knelt beside the bier and bent to kiss his father's hands.

Jaspar was there beside him. Carnelian had to rummage in his mind to find his voice. "Who . . . ?"

"The lictors of the Ichorian Legion, the shadows of He-who-goes-before."

Carnelian looked up at their standards. The rayed eye of the sun was surmounted on one by the lily and on the other by the pomegranate, both wrought with emberous stones. The guardsmen round him all had the fruit embossed on their cuirasses, halved to show its bellyful of seeds. All had the half-black face and body of the Ichorians.

As the bier began to move, Carnelian walked beside it. He looked over the helmets down the widening valley and his eyes threatened to burst the limit of their sockets. He could not breathe. He feasted on the blue, richer than any sky, until he began to fear that his eyes might forever lose their ability to see that color. He forced his gaze to follow a causeway across the water. This swelled into a triangle that attached itself like a handle to a vast green-mottled mirror. No bowl of jade held up to the sun had ever filtered such emerald. Jutting into this region was an island, a turquoise ridge that swept up into a narrow peak. Beyond lay more of the blue lake, the color faded enough by distance and molten air to no longer hurt his eyes. Round the outer shore of this lake was a purple vapor of mountains that the wind might have streamed out in an arc from its mouth to wall this heaven in.

Carnelian remembered to breathe. He gulped the crystal

air. It was a perfume of such richness that he had to close his eyes else be overwhelmed. One breath, another. He strained to hold its vibrant burn in his lungs and felt it swell him like a bud to flowering. He stumbled and felt a hand supporting him.

"My Lord?"

Carnelian gasped his eyes open and saw a face of gold. A Master's mask. Jaspar.

"You reel, my Lord."

"The . . . the air . . ." Carnelian managed to say.

"You mean the smoke," Jaspar said, laughing like a child, indicating with his head the way they had come.

Carnelian wrenched his head round. The pleated stone of the Black Gate concertinaed between the hands of the Sacred Wall.

"The ammonites used lotus smoke to free our minds, to detach them from the bodies that had to be . . . shall we say, intrusively cleansed. Enjoy your flight; soon mind and body will be reunited."

Preoccupied with breathing and walking, Carnelian hardly heard him. "The air," he sighed, "the perfumed air."

Jaspar breathed deep through his mask. "The exhalation of thrice blessed Osrakum. This air . . . it is unfouled by the lungs of the creatures beyond our mountain wall."

"Like . . . like . . . like breathing the sky," said Carnelian. Two new bells were tolling together in the Black Gate. He looked back over his shoulder at the wall. "Those bells . . . ?"

"Announce the entry of four Lords of blood-rank two. Those chimes tell Osrakum that we are here."

A deeper voice rang out. Carnelian could feel it coming up from the ground, vibrating him, then fading enough to free his feeble heart to beat again.

"The bell for He-who-goes-before," said Jaspar as Carnelian fought the intoxication of the air.

Curbs contained the river of the road. Beyond, hexagons raised up giant stairways, tables and dikes, or speared skyward their shafts tipped with angels. In places columns were formed wholly of angels standing one upon the other. Angels? He concentrated. Not angels, but the host of the Quyans turned to stone. He tried to make out their battle-lines but was distracted. Through the thickets of knuckled stone, he glimpsed the indentations in the crater wall burning like shards of jewel-stained glass.

The valley widened its sky-seeking walls and Carnelian noticed that every stone Quyan had two faces. The one gazing back up at the Black Gate was joyful, but the other looked grieving down toward on the lake. Following that gaze he was snared again by the blue addiction of the water. His heart trembled when his eyes fell on the Isle with its single peak for he knew that somewhere, melted into that vision, were the tombs and palaces of the Gods, the Labyrinth.

The Ichorians formed themselves into a wall that Aurum breached and walked through. Further down the road, Carnelian could see a silver house. Tarnished, windowless, eyed with stars, nail-gouged with moons. Doors opened in its gray side and a procession came out pushing glittering crescents aloft on poles. Rising behind them was a spindle figure walking with the aid of a staff whom a child was leading by the hand. The pair came up the road fringed by standard-bearers. Aurum met them and gave a curt bow. Carnelian was made uneasy when he saw that the purple figure with the child was more than a head taller than the old Master.

Aurum came back, bringing with him the child, the purple figure and their procession. For a moment all were absorbed into the Ichorians so that Carnelian could see only the silver crescents waving in the air. The child emerged from the guardsmen first, leading the purple being whose face was a long oblong of silver. The right eye was just a crease. The left eye appeared to be cataracted with ice and spilled tears down the silver cheek. From the brow of the mask a crescent moon curved up like horns.

As this apparition poled its staff toward him Carnelian withstood a compulsion to hide. He looked sidelong at the child. It had the body of a boy but the wrinkled face, the eyes, the thin compressed lips of an old man. Carnelian watched this homunculus release the hand of the apparition, take the staff and, with both hands, plant it with a *clack* before them both. The apparition peeled off gloves to reveal hands so pale they seemed hollow alabaster. Each middle finger and knuckle had been removed so that neither hand could help making the sign of the horns. The hands articulated as if boneless. The homunculus reached round and with a practiced movement took first one and then the other, forming them into a loose collar of fingers around its throat. The fingers coiled, meshing around its larynx, and then began to flex.

"We are not used to being kept waiting," the homunculus said. Its voice was high, beautiful but unhuman.

Carnelian stared at the fingers playing the throat like an oboe.

"Seraphim, you have gone beyond the bounds we permitted you in the outer world."

Vennel came forward, nodding a bow, his hands making the vague shape of surprise. "You have come yourself, Grand Sapient Immortality, from the sickbed of . . ."

As he spoke the homunculus muttered an echo to Vennel's words.

"I wish to wash my hands of all responsibility."

The homunculus was repeating those words when the fingers at its throat choked it quiet. They trembled more instructions into its neck and it said, "Seraph, the Empress expects your immediate attendance at court."

Vennel bowed lower.

Carnelian looked up at the tearful silver mask. This was one of the Wise. He was trying not to imagine what kind of face the mask concealed when the cloven hands turned the homunculus' head toward him. Carnelian had the feeling that it was not the homunculus but its master that was scrutinizing him through its eyes. As the fingers began to shift at its throat, Carnelian winced, seeming to feel their movement inside his head.

"You are that son of Suth for whom we recently made a blood-ring?"

"Suth Carnelian." The words were squeezed out of his mouth like pips from a lemon.

The homunculus repeated the two words. Its finger collar flexed. The homunculus pointed at the bier. "It is the Ruling Seraph of your House that lies there?"

Carnelian nodded eagerly. One of the cloven hands detached itself from the homunculus' throat and blurred pale instructions. Ammonites swarmed forward and the Ichorians moved away from the bier as if they feared even the touch of their shadows. Their purple robes huddled over Suth, producing many fingers that they touched to his neck, his wrists, his chest. They began rattling out words. "Pulse. Five. Soft. Tallow threefold. Lipped blade. Two by three deep."

The homunculus echoed everything they said. Carnelian found his eyes drawn to the final on the staff it held. A limpid green jewel larger than his hand carved into the form of a man who wore upon his head a crescent blade.

The ammonites straightened, silent, waiting, looking to the Grand Sapient.

"Salve edge, blue vaporing, soft white bind," the homunculus said.

The ammonites opened boxes, unstoppered vials, pulled lengths of cloth and bent over Suth.

"Seraphic Aurum," said the homunculus, "it is your disregard for the Law that has imperiled this life."

"I told him—" Vennel began.

The homunculus spoke over him. "This matter will be examined fully."

Aurum stood very still. "Will he live?"

Carnelian held his breath. Vennel's mask inclined so that it was focused wholly on the homunculus' mouth.

"Perhaps," it said after a pause. "We shall bend our skills

toward the healing. We must haste back to the Isle where we have the requisite resources."

"It is customary for He-who-goes-before to seek formal ratification in the Clave before he should begin his duties," said Vennel quickly.

"Does my Lord wish the Ruling Lord Suth dead?" said Jaspar over the homunculus' muttering.

"Custom is not Law," it said.

"Then I shall accompany the Ruling Lord on my way to court," said Vennel.

"As you wish."

Sapient Immortality's hands uncoiled free of his homunculus' neck.

Carnelian took a step forward. "Sapience . . ."

The homunculus reached up to touch the retreating hands and they slipped back around its muttering throat. "Proceed."

Carnelian stared at the long mirror face, swallowed. "Is there not a risk that my father will die unless you heal him now?"

"Do you presume to greater wisdom than the Wise?" the homunculus said severely.

Carnelian was unable to respond.

"Good, then we shall proceed to the Labyrinth."

"I won't go with you," said Carnelian, lapsing into Vulgate.

Aurum whisked round. "Why will you not, my Lord?"

Carnelian closed his eyes to find composure. "I wish to go to my own coomb."

"You would desert your father?"

Carnelian looked at the old Master. "I would follow his command."

"This command must have been given you some time ago. Much has changed since then, my Lord."

"Nevertheless."

"This is outrageous. Immortality, you must stop this."

"The matter does not concern us," said the homunculus.

Aurum's mask bore down on Carnelian but he refused even to flinch. The Master swung round on Jaspar. "Since it seems Suth Carnelian's mind is made up perhaps my Lord would condescend to accompany him."

Jaspar snorted. "And why, pray, should one wish to do that?"

"Because you would find me grateful."

Jaspar turned to Carnelian, saying loudly, "The gratitude of House Aurum is a prize to be devoutly desired, neh? One's coomb is near your own, cousin, so there would be only a little inconvenience. Besides, we might even manage to amuse each other on the way."

Carnelian was in no mood to be amused or to oblige either Master, but nor did he want to be left alone in this strange new world. He lifted his hand in agreement.

Jaspar held Carnelian back when he made to move toward his father. Carnelian shoved his arm away.

Jaspar flared his palms. "You misunderstand, my Lord. Our way lies along a different road."

"But I thought . . ." Carnelian's resolve crumbled. He had not expected to have to part from his father so soon.

Aurum turned to Jaspar. "My Lord, your father must come to the Labyrinth immediately to represent his faction."

"That will not be possible. The Lord Imago will take several days to prepare himself." He waved a vague gesture. "One will have to inform him of our . . . our mission, a household will have to be readied to accompany him." He sighed. "My Lord knows well what tedious arrangements one is required to make before planning even the briefest sojourn at court."

"Make sure that he is there in three days," said Aurum and turned away.

"My Lord Aurum?" said Carnelian.

The Master turned back.

"Will you send me word if my father improves, or if he were to . . . ?"

Aurum's hand snapped agreement, and he strode away.

Carnelian knelt at his father's side. He glanced at the metal face and then found the hand and cursed the mask that stopped him kissing it. He stood back as the bier was lifted and mournfully watched it move away with the Grand Sapient, the Masters and the others.

"Alas," said Jaspar beside him.

Carnelian turned to him, surprised. "You share my pain to see them go?"

Jaspar laughed. "On the contrary, it is a blessed relief. One was bemoaning the necessity of more walking. It is customary to send ahead to one's coomb for suitable transport and an escort of one's tyadra." He pretended to look around him. "As you can see, cousin, we shall have neither convenience."

The Master's flippancy angered Carnelian. "We will get nowhere unless we move on."

Carnelian looked for his father and was dismayed to see him being carried into the silver house. A protest was on his tongue when the whole edifice lurched into movement and he noticed its skirting of wheels and realized it was a chariot. The thought of his father locked inside with the Sapient and the homunculus made him shudder.

"Will the Wise heal him, Jaspar?"

"Grand Sapient Immortality is guardian to all the lore of his Domain. Short of divine intervention there is no power in all the lands that can do more for the Ruling Lord Suth than he."

Fearing hope would unman him, Carnelian said quickly, "Which is our road?"

Jaspar pointed out an avenue running toward the lake.

Carnelian saw the silver chariot veering off to the right, disappearing into the forest of stone.

"Our road is the straighter." Jaspar sauntered off.

Carnelian watched the last silver panel of the chariot wink out and almost ran after it. He felt as trapped as the Quyans in their stone. Their dimple eyes saw through his flesh. They mobbed the road all the way down to the lake. He strode after the only companion he had left, his enemy, Jaspar.

*　　　*　　　*

"Curse the sun, it makes me sweat!" growled Jaspar.

Carnelian threw a fold of his robe over his head to stop his mask heating. The sun was splitting his head in two. He squinted past the ache. Ahead, a burning barricade appeared to be set across the road. He was sure that he could feel its waves of heat beating against him. Soon he saw that its flames were really a hillside of carved and gilded columns that divided the road. One fork was edged by a narrow rind of shadow.

When they reached this shade, they stopped to rest, pressing their backs against the cool gilded stone. The air still burned Carnelian's lungs. His robe clung to him. He pinched some of the cloth to peel it off his skin and wafted it. Jaspar was panting.

Carnelian turned to the column he had been leaning against and saw that it was the shins of a narrow Lord. Hundreds more crowded up the slope. The carving was unlike the angels. It was sharp and fresh and the curving golden limbs seemed almost alive.

"The Clave," said Jaspar, looking at Carnelian. He lowered his head and fanned it with his hands.

"Where the Great . . . meet?" said Carnelian.

They walked round, rubbing against the cool legs of the golden crowd, keeping in their delicious shadow. They came to where a stair of snowy marble wound up between the giants.

"Is it cool up there?" Carnelian asked.

Jaspar shook his head. "The Clave is a bowl in which we meet only when the sun is behind the Sacred Wall or sometimes at night. Now, it will be incandescent."

They passed several more stairs before they reached the edge of the shadow. "One longs to linger here, but alas we must go on . . . it should be cooler by the lake."

Carnelian watched Jaspar stand there for some moments as if he were gathering up his courage, then the Master stepped out and was burned up in the glare.

* * *

Jaspar swung the bronze clapper on its ropes. Then the heart-stone bell seemed the only stillness in a trembling world. Carnelian did not hear it peal. He had lost every sense but sight. The Pillar of Heaven was there, a filament from the Singing Turtle's heart, where it had been since the creation, a mountain holding up the immense weight of the sky. The Sacred Wall was set about its axle like the rim of a wheel. Around the Pillar spread the terraces and water meadows of the Yden, the Gods' own Forbidden Garden floating in the midst of the Skymere.

"They come," a voice said remotely in his ear, waking him.

Carnelian followed Jaspar's pointing finger and saw a needle detach itself from the Yden's rim and dam a white stitch into the perfect sapphire of the lake.

"We shall wait up here in the shade," said Jaspar.

Carnelian looked down the flight of steps that fell precipitously to the water's edge. Carvings of stone flanked it all the way. He put his hand out to touch the nearest one, in whose shadow they sheltered. The flow of years had smoothed it but still he could see it was a turtle. He looked out across the lake, daring to be possessed again. He ran his eyes round the outer wall of the crater bowl. It had folds all along its purpling length which were the coombs of the Chosen.

Carnelian's gaze settled back to the mirrors of the Yden and the strip of earth that moored it to the cliff upon which he stood. There along that causeway a fleck of light caught his eye. It seemed a signal. He stretched his hand out as if he would pluck it from the distance.

"The Grand Sapient's chariot," said Jaspar even as Carnelian had guessed what it was.

"My father . . ."

"With Aurum fretting," said Jaspar and Carnelian could hear the smile in his voice. "And our dear Lord Vennel." He chuckled. "One does not envy him the meeting with his mistress."

Thoughts of his father brought back Carnelian's headache.

He waited for each tiny flicker as if he could read some message from it. He narrowed his eyes to examine the causeway. It looked like nothing much except that it was a road across the Skymere, a lake deeper than the sky. Mountains had been crumbled and fed into that lake so that chariots could roll their wheels across its water. "Sartlar numberless as leaves . . ."

"My Lord?" said Jaspar.

Carnelian looked at him. "Something my father once told me about the building of that road."

Jaspar looked off toward the causeway. "It is said that its stones were mortared with sartlar blood."

"Then it is another of their tombs."

"Hardly, cousin. The Law insists their carcasses be removed from Osrakum. It is true that when we need labor we bring them in from the outer world. But then, those that do not die in the work are slain. The Law forbids that they should return alive from paradise. But be assured, my Lord, that what is left of them is returned. This holy land must not be polluted by the impious dead."

Carnelian's wonder was souring. He had looked altogether too often on death's face. The boat was nearing the quay below and so he left the shadow of the turtle and went down to meet her.

The ferryman's robe confused his eyes. Whether it was a white pattern on a black ground or a black pattern on a white, Carnelian could not tell. He stared at the man's ivory mask, the face of a dead Master locked into a right profile. Half a face with a single eye staring out of it. It was like those ill-omened faces in the glyphs that encoded sinister words. Carnelian stopped his head turning in unconscious mimicry. The ferryman wore a crown in which the turtleshell sky glyph was the body of a nest of bony limbs that could have been the remains of a crab bleaching on a shore.

The pattern on the ferryman's robe moved, entangling Carnelian's eyes so that it took him a while to notice the outstretched whitewashed hand. Carnelian looked at it, not knowing what to do.

"The kharon asks for his fee," said Jaspar.

Carnelian watched the Master pull off a ring that he dropped onto the ferryman's hand. The man did not close his hand but brought it back to Carnelian who looked at his own hands. All he had was his rusty blood-ring. He turned to Jaspar. "Can my Lord lend me some gold?"

"The kharon take only jade." Jaspar twisted another ring from his finger and handed it to Carnelian, who took it and made to give it to the ferryman.

"The other hand, my Lord, the other hand."

Carnelian did not understand what he meant.

"If the jade is given with the left hand the kharon will only take you across to the Isle. Put the jade in your right hand."

Carnelian did as he was told. The ferryman's whitened fist closed around the rings as he moved back from the bow. Jaspar reached out to clasp one of the posts rising from the gunnel and pulled himself aboard. Other than Jaspar and the ferryman, there was no one the length of the deck. The whole boat was yellow-white, patched together from rods and roundels. An ivory boat. Carnelian reached out to grasp the post. Its knobbed shaft slipped smoothly into his hand. Its carving was picked out in brown. He realized what it was. Quickly, he heaved himself onto the deck and let go of it in disgust.

"Is anything the matter, cousin?" said Jaspar.

Carnelian stared at the cobbled deck that narrowed up at either end to posts as pale and slender as beech saplings.

"Come, sit here, cousin." Jaspar rested his hand on the back of a chair. There were three of them under a dark canopy.

Carnelian walked across the cobbles as carefully as if they were eggshells. "Bones . . . there are bones everywhere."

"Of course," said Jaspar. "This is a bone boat."

Carnelian looked round, aghast. "But human bones . . . ?"

"Sit down, cousin."

Carnelian walked round and sat in a chair beside Jaspar. He craned his neck round. The ferryman was there, looking as if he were a carved part of the stern post, holding the handle of a steering oar in each hand. The boat began to turn away from the quay. Soundlessly the oar heads spooned the water on either side.

"I thought it a fairy tale."

Jaspar chuckled and tapped the arms of the chair. "If you look under your arm, cousin, you will see that even these chairs are made of bones."

Carnelian lifted his arms, saw the chair was a mosaic of finger bones. Here and there was the tell-tale green pinprick of a copper rivet.

"This deck," Jaspar was tapping his foot, "skulls."

Carnelian could see how the cobbles were of ovals of different sizes, fissured brown. He gave up trying to estimate how many had been used to make the deck. "Generations . . ."

"Since the Twins raised up the Sacred Wall," said Jaspar. "Our dear ferryman," he glanced back at the stern, "and all his brethren rowing beneath our feet, will one day add their own bones to this very vessel. These boats are the tombs of their race."

"Tombs," muttered Carnelian. The ache in his head intensified. He rested it against the back of the chair and closed his eyes. Tombs. And what of his House tomb? He imagined consigning his father to its everlasting night.

He opened his eyes. Beyond the sapphire water the Yden spread its meres as a floor of varied jades. Something winked on the thread of road that ran along its stony margin. At that signal the crystal air shattered as flamingos rose in a red blizzard. Carnelian watched for the sparking on the road that showed where the silver chariot was making its progress beneath their cloud. He closed his eyes to trap their tears and choked down the voice that was telling him he would never see his father again.

*　　*　　*

Carnelian longed to kite away on the breeze but his heart was too heavy. Its beating echoed up into his head. He was being smothered by the sweaty shell of his mask.

"Behold your coomb, my Lord," said Jaspar.

Carnelian looked up blearily. Crags. He pushed his head back, and further back, until at last he had to narrow his eyes against the sky glare as his gaze reached the jagged edge of the Sacred Wall. He dropped his eyes, dizzied, appalled by the scale of it.

"You really will have to do something about your palaces, cousin."

Carnelian gaped at him. "Do something?"

The Master waved his hand, shook his head. "It is all so old-fashioned." He indicated some scaffolding. "There something is being done, but not enough, not nearly enough. The overall lack of decoration positively reeks of past times. Where are the pierced roof combs, the tortured friezes? Look at those meager columns. They are like starved girls and those domes are as flat as their breasts. But I forget, cousin, you have been so long away and can have little notion of what canons are fashionable among the Great."

Carnelian turned back to gaze at the lean, elegant symmetries.

"Especially when you are possessed of so much space," Jaspar added, with a twinge of envy.

Carnelian saw that they were moving toward a quay set to one side of the coomb. There was a rustle beside him as Jaspar began adjusting his robe. Carnelian's ears still rang with his patronizing tones and now the Master was readying himself to disembark with him. He peered back at the coomb. Those façades concealed other Masters of his House. His guts were telling him that this was not his home. That was lost, far away, in a different fairy tale.

"I might as well accompany you, cousin," drawled Jaspar.

"There is no need."

"Ah, but, Carnelian, you forget that one is still striving to earn the gratitude of House Aurum."

"It will be difficult enough . . . I know nothing of my kin."

Carnelian clutched the air for words. "This new world . . ." He was feeling so many emotions. He stood up, walked to the bow rail, blinked until he could see again. The bay swelled up into the middle of the coomb where the water extended its colors up into a pebbled beach. He went toward the stern, aware of the skull cobbles, steadying himself on the rail. The ferryman was a sinister doll. The only living parts of him were the hands that stroked the handles of the steering oars.

"I would have you leave me on the beach," Carnelian said to the ivory mask, seeking the brightness of an eye behind its single slit. He clenched his fists. Did the creature even have ears? He was lifting his hand to point when he saw the ferryman's fingers urge the steering oars to the right and he felt the boat veer to port. Turning, he saw that her prow was now pointing into the bay.

He walked back to where Jaspar stood waiting, his hands on his hips. "Why have we changed course, my Lord?"

Carnelian's hands made warding motions that he could see Jaspar was trying to read, then he was past him and the Master's protests became nothing more than seagull cries. Carnelian reached the prow post, embraced its elaborate fluting of thighbones. The crescent of the beach was rushing toward him, the water turquoising as it shallowed. The boat slowed. He could see that if she were to go much further she would run aground. Looking back, he saw that Jaspar was closing in on him, hiding everything behind his vast shape. Suddenly, Carnelian could not bear to have a Master near him. He swung himself round the prow post, let go and fell. The water sucking up to receive him squeezed out a gasp. He found his feet and fought his way toward the shore against the drag of his robe. When the water was around his knees he swung round panting and saw the boat already turning, showing her bony length and the gradient of her oars. Carnelian glimpsed Jaspar who had a flash for a face, then the boat had swung about to hide him with her stern and was sliding away, stirring the wake with her shoulder-blade steering oars.

* * *

Carnelian heaved his robe out of the water and crunched up the pebble beach. One last tug caused him to stumble. He fell onto his hands, cursing. He pulled against the weight of soaked cloth and sat up. His palms felt contours in the pebbles. He picked one up that was as blue as the Skymere. A fish twisted round on itself in the lapis lazuli. Its tiny scales snagged the end of his finger. Its gills were delicate fans. He put it down carefully and picked up another pebble. A piece of flawed jade, carved into a fern spiral. He looked round him. All the pebbles were carved. He stared along the sweep of the beach, his hand stroking the spiraled jade. So many pebbles. He tried to imagine the labor they represented, but he might as well attempt to count the stars in a night sky.

A movement caught his eye. He straightened to see a man up the beach, frozen. As Carnelian clambered to his feet, the man yelped and fled. Carnelian attempted to run after him but his feet scooped pebbles as his robe pulled on his shoulders like chains. He gave up and watched the man lope up some steps and disappear into trees.

"Let them find me," he muttered. He tucked the jade pebble into a pocket and stooped to remove his shoes. He gathered up his robe and wrung some of the water out of it. His feet looked very white. He worried that the water might have washed off their paint. He shrugged. What could he do if it had? He hoisted the train of his robe over one arm and sauntered up the beach feeling the pebbles' carvings with his toes. Something was whirring in the air. He turned his head slowly. A dragonfly was hovering in the blur of its wings, the size of a dagger but more exquisitely enameled.

Voices across the beach wafted it away. A familiar clink of armor made him turn. Perhaps a dozen guardsmen were filing toward him. Carnelian almost cried out when he saw their chameleon tattoos. He dropped his robe to wait for them. They looked at him uncertainly, rounding their shoulders. He searched their faces, then cursed his stupidity at trying to find one he knew. Their commander plunged his knees into the pebbles and in threes and fours the others followed him.

Carnelian did not know what to say.

"Master, please take no offense," the commander said without lifting his eyes, "but our Masters have given us no warning of your visit. If you'd please go, Master, go"—he pointed—"back to the quay and wait with your tyadra, someone appropriate will come down to greet you . . . Master."

Carnelian shook his head. "There's no tyadra." He lifted his arms from his sides. "I'm here as you see me."

"Of course it's not my place, but . . . the Master shouldn't be here."

"Don't worry, I'm not trespassing . . . what's your name?"

The man looked up fearfully. "M-Moal, if it please you, Master."

"Well, Moal, I'm your Master's son returned."

Others were sneaking looks at him. Moal chewed his lip. "Our Master's son's well known to us."

Carnelian had to think about that for a moment. "No, not the Master you have here. I meant *the* Master of this House, who's long been away."

Several of the guardsmen forgot themselves enough to stare, but quickly ducked their heads. Carnelian watched their hands fussing with their weapons.

"Is there someone I can talk to?"

"If it pleases you, Master, someone will be here soon," mumbled Moal.

So Carnelian waited, eventually turning his back on them because he did not want to see their groveling. He reached down to squeeze more water out of his robe, all the time feeling their stares.

"Master?"

A woman's voice. He turned and instantly a weight of tears stiffened his face, It was Brin. He squeezed his eyes closed several times. He gritted his teeth. She was still there. He examined her more carefully. His shoulders sagged; it was not Brin. This woman was younger, though she was very like his aunt.

The woman bowed. "Master, why are you come to Coomb Suth?"

Carnelian squared his shoulders. "It's my coomb. I'm Suth Carnelian."

The color left her face in which Carnelian could see his father's eyes.

"You're Fey, aren't you?"

The woman flinched, nodded slowly. "Yes, Master, steward of this House, Master. Please . . . I don't understand. Forgive my confusion, Master, please . . ."

Carnelian gazed at her eyes. It was almost as if this woman had stolen them from his father. He paused a moment, thinking, and then reached back to release his mask.

Fey threw her hands up in horror. "Master, would you blind us all?"

"But we're all of one House . . . I'm Suth Carnelian." He realized that the woman might find his face no proof at all. Suddenly he made a fist and cried, "Look." He thrust out his hand so that the woman could see the Ruling Ring on his hand.

Fey leaned forward, choked a cry and crumpled into the pebbles. "Master," she said from Carnelian's feet, "Oh, Master."

Carnelian crouched down and, putting his hands round Fey's shoulders, lifted her gently. It was only then he saw the tears striping her face.

"Are you so happy, Fey?"

"Of course happy, Master, but also I grieve for our Master, your father."

Carnelian shook the woman. "When did the news come? When did it come?"

"News . . . news?" spluttered Fey. "The ring, Master, the ring."

Carnelian let her go. He looked at the Ruling Ring on his finger. Would that finger soon be its proper place? He held his head at his stupidity. There had been no time for any news. "I'm a fool," he said aloud.

Fey was dabbing tears from her eyes. The guardsmen

looked miserable. These strangers were also his people. He was forgetting his duty to them.

"I'm sorry, Fey. You misunderstood me." He removed the Ruling Ring. "I don't have the right to wear it. It's a long story. My father was ill when I parted from him in the Valley of the Gate. The Wise will heal him and then we'll have him back here with us."

His confidence visibly cheered the guardsmen. Fey looked uncertain.

"I hope I didn't hurt you? When I shook you? I forgot myself . . ."

Fey stared.

Carnelian put his hands up to his mask. "Now, if you don't mind, I'd like to remove this thing."

"Master, your will is our will."

Carnelian removed the mask, rubbed at the grooves in his skin, smiling at Fey, allowing her to search his face. "You see my father?"

Fey looked hard at him then nodded unconvincingly, giving a thin smile. "Yes, Master."

"I'd rather you cut that out, Fey. My name's Carnelian."

Fey frowned, shook her head. "It's forbidden me to soil a Master's name with my tongue."

It was Carnelian's turn to frown. The thought of his next question made him grimmer still.

Fey spoke first, with evident concern. "Master, your robe is sodden."

"Never mind that. Where are the other Masters, my kin?"

"In the Eyries, Master." Carnelian must have looked uncertain because Fey turned to point up the Sacred Wall.

Carnelian scanned the craggy heights. It took him a while before he saw the scratches of balconies halfway up to the sky.

"More than fifty days ago our Masters went up there to avoid this heat. I'll make immediate preparations for you to join them, Master."

Carnelian was still looking up. "Perhaps tomorrow, Fey. Tonight I'd like to stay down here."

Fey looked aghast. "That's impossible, Master."

"Why?"

"These halls have become unsuitable for a Master. Work-men are everywhere . . . the Master must understand that we always carry out restoration work when the Masters go up to the Eyries . . . furniture's been stored away . . . Master, there is no accommodation suiting of your rank."

"You'll find me easy to please, Fey." He silenced any more of her protests with his hand and eventually, accepting that she was not going to change this strange young Master's mind, Fey led him off into the palace with the escort of the guardsmen, some of whom carried his soaking train.

Carnelian and the escort were a thread pulled by Fey's needle. There was a hall like a wood, its sultry air nuanced with odors. The day was only a glowing band in the distance. He felt more than saw the eyes in the mosaics. Murals had the colors of concealed jewels. Wisps of voices ribboned between the columns. A door closing seemed an echo still lingering from the day before. Floors rainbowed like oil on water. Sometimes he glimpsed courts whose colors were more vibrant than any dream. Awe infected him so that, when he saw the eye and dancing chameleon ward on the lintels of a door, he sighed his relief that they were leaving the echoing grandeur of the public chambers.

At Carnelian's request, they left the guardsmen behind. Against Fey's protests, Carnelian insisted on carrying his wet train in the crook of his arm. Steps took them down into a courtyard carpeted with the petals that were drizzling down from magnolias. They kicked their way through the drifts, walking round the urns that held the trees. At the edge of the courtyard there rose a gate of white wood warded with eyes.

As they walked past the gate Carnelian reached out to touch Fey's shoulder. "The halls of a subsidiary lineage?"

The woman blushed. "The halls of the first lineage."

"But then why . . . ?"

Fey bowed her head. "They have long been occupied by the secondary lineage. There have been changes, Master."

Carnelian looked up at the white doors. "Have there?" he said, and not wanting to make trouble for her, he allowed her to lead him away.

More gates and courtyards brought them to a door in a wall. Fey pushed against it and Carnelian leaned over her to help. They walked into a small courtyard around which ran raised porticoes. Water slid round its edge in a shallow channel. In one place its lip had crumbled and water oozed down, greening the marble, running into a puddle. Some dull bronze troughs held dry, brown-leafed trees in balls of parched earth that had pulled away from the sides. Dust grayed the precious inlay walls.

"This quarter hasn't been used in a while," said Carnelian, trying to hide his disappointment. He would not allow Fey to kneel. She grimaced as she looked round her. "These were some of the halls of the third lineage, Master. They now occupy the quarter traditionally belonging to the second, who—"

"Who now occupy my father's halls," said Carnelian heavily.

Fey cringed a little, as if she were expecting a blow.

"As you said, Fey, there have been changes."

The woman went over to one of the withered trees, touched its plug of soil, shook her head. "This shouldn't have been allowed." She looked back at Carnelian. "You must believe that I did everything I could, Master."

Carnelian walked up to Fey and put his arm round her shoulders. The woman went so tense that Carnelian immediately pulled his arm away. "I do believe you. Now come and show me where I can wash away this paint."

They walked together round several more courtyards until they came to an echoing suite of chambers whose lofty vermilion walls were mosaiced with slender waving lilies and soaring birds.

"For one night, perhaps, these chambers will be adequate for the Master," said Fey, opening tall blue rectangles of sky in a faraway wall.

Narrowing his eyes against the glare, Carnelian crossed the marble mirror floor to stand beside Fey in the flooding sunlight. Below, a pebbled cove smeared its green into the azure of the Skymere. Further off was the fiery emerald vision of the Yden with the Pillar of Heaven towering up from its heart. Carnelian closed his eyes and drew in the perfume of Osrakum. "Miraculous," he sighed.

When he opened his eyes Fey was smiling at him. "You *are* like your father, Master."

Carnelian felt a twinge of guilt as he looked at the barrow of the Labyrinth mounding up from the Yden. How could he feel joy when his father might be there, already dead?

Fey saw his frown. "To wash, the Master will need slaves. I'll send them to attend you, and to clean up this mess. If the Master would allow me to guide him . . ." She waited to see him move, then bustled out through another door.

Carnelian followed her on a long walk to a chamber of yellow marble. One whole wall was so thin that it glowed as it filtered daylight.

"It's like being inside a sea shell," Carnelian said in delight.

Fey walked to the door. "I'll go and fetch body slaves."

Carnelian touched her arm. "I'd rather be alone."

Fey looked startled. "But who will wash you, Master?"

"The Master will wash himself."

Fey's eyebrows lifted and creased her brow. "As the Master wishes, so shall it be done."

As Carnelian slipped the damp robe off, something cracked to the floor. Crouching, he picked it up. It was the jade pebble. He frowned when he saw that its spiral had cracked in two. He put the pieces inside the hollow of his mask and put that, face down, on the robe. He went to the water wall and rearranged the gold sluices set into its channels. At last he managed to braid the water into a single splashing waterfall. He gasped as he slid into its envelope, tensing in the cold. It roared over his head. The paint leached away down his legs. The water pooling round his feet was like milk, but soon ran clear.

AT HOME

A rose watched withering

Waits forgotten

In this forbidden house

Youth's blush frowned gray

Perfume faded

Left only her thorns

—FROM THE POEM

"BEYOND THE SILVER DOOR"

BY THE LADY AKAYA

Although the Pillar of Heaven was already crowned with gold, the twilight was only thinning at its feet. Osrakum still slept. The narrow arc of the crater's faraway wall was still black. Only its glowing edge showed where the sun was beginning to set the sky alight. The lake was cataracted with mist. The Yden was gray. Carnelian inhaled sweet vaporous morning. As he rubbed his cheek on the blanket, its hummingbird feathers bristled and changed color along the folds. He had climbed out onto the roof. His sleep had been troubled; that first gleam on the Pillar, and the paling sky, had drawn him with the hope of a new day.

The indigo above was going blue. Carnelian looked south-west to where a mountainous buttress of the Sacred Wall hid the next coomb. He followed the sweep of the wall round to the Valley of the Gate. There he watched turquoise begin to seep into the edge of the lake as if the color were flooding out from the valley. The brightening crept across the lake to the Ydenrim and then up to reveal emeralds sparked with amber. Sunrise now lit the Pillar to its foot and was spearing its shadow back across the lake. Fire spread over the Laby-rinth mound. The sun's disc melting up from the Sacred Wall forced him to quit the roof for fear of it tainting his skin with its gold.

Carnelian grew solemn as he climbed back into the cham-ber knowing that soon he would have to face his kin. The smell of sleep was coming off his body, but he did not feel like braving a shivering waterfall. Besides, the day's meet-ings were bound to require a formal cleansing and that required servants. He looked round for something to throw on. He wandered through several chambers but they were empty of everything but the echoes of his footfalls. Even-tually he was forced to return to the small chamber in which he had slept in preference to the vast bedchamber Fey had given him. He removed the broken pieces of the jade spiral from inside his mask. When he lifted the hollow face he saw the letter that had been put under it. He stared at the perfectly folded, creamy rectangle. He picked it up and smelled its rich waft of attar of roses. Its wax seal bore the circular impression of a blood-ring. He broke it open. The parchment had only two panels. At first the glyphs looked strange. They were unlike the ones he or his father would make. He used the faces to gauge the differences in the style as his father had taught him. Soon the pictures were forming the sounds in his mind.

Sardian, you are returned. Your mother's eyes are impatient to behold you though they have so patiently waited out the years. Come, mount the steps. There is much that you must know.

He looked again at the ring of glyphs and numbers in the wax. There beside the Suth chameleon was the glyph "Urquentha," his grandmother's name. He frowned. What had led her to believe that he was his father? He read the letter again; then, folding it carefully, tucked it into the mask. He picked up the green robe. Its odor of lilies made him hurl it into a corner. Instead, he secured the feather blanket round his waist, picked up the mask and walked off to open the outer door.

A procession of pillars held back the shadow from an avenue that led off to an archway through which he could see a courtyard. He stopped to listen. Only birdsong embroidered the silence. He stepped into the hall, enjoying the feel of its cool stone. He walked toward the gray courtyard.

When he reached its edge he looked across the fish-scale cobbles to the distant gates. The raised portico running round it was still in darkness. A flight of steps that led down to the cobbles was flanked by tripod urns of mossy bronze. He noticed a figure hunched on the end of one of the steps and padded toward it. When he was near he stretched out and touched it lightly on the shoulder.

The figure jumped to its feet and whisked round.

"Master . . ." it gulped. It was Fey, eyes wide, her hand pressed over her chest.

"Forgive me, I didn't mean to startle you," said Carnelian.

Fey shook her head, panting, made uncomfortable by the apology and the glare of so much white skin. "Master, I was waiting for you. I've taken the liberty of having some breakfast prepared." She indicated a low table set between two columns, overlooking the courtyard. "I've also sent for servants of all the different kinds so that the Master might choose a household for himself."

"My own people will form my household."

She darted a look of hope at him. "Did you bring them all back with you, Master?"

Carnelian remembered them blanketing the quay as he sailed away. The memory seemed from someone else's childhood. As he shook his head free of it, he noticed Fey looking at him anxiously. He smoothed his frown and even found a smile. "We were forced to leave most of them behind. Ships will already have been sent to fetch them."

"Ships . . . ?" Fey stared off as if she could see their sails tiny in the distance.

Carnelian frowned. "Are you telling me that you didn't know where we were?"

Fey pulled her eyes back into focus. "There were rumors, Master."

Carnelian pondered this.

"Those you did bring with you, Master, will take more than thirty days to come through the quarantine. Until they come through . . ."

Carnelian imagined Tain, frightened and alone, and Keal and the others somewhere on the long, long road coming up from the sea.

Fey gave an uncertain smile as she again indicated the breakfast table. "I'm getting old and foolish, Master. I should have brought some servants with me, garments . . ." She looked confused. "I don't really know why I came alone." Her eyes dropped to her feet.

"Did you want to talk to me, Fey?" When the woman looked up at him he could see her need for news. He walked round her toward the table. "It was thoughtful of you to arrange this. I'd very much like to break my fast while the air's still cool."

He stood in front of the table on which dishes and bowls were like inlays. He thought of his people on the island, abandoned to famine. Fey positioned a stool and he sank cross-legged onto it, putting his mask down carefully on the floor. Fey knelt beside him and began to serve him. Carnelian put a hand on her arm to stop her. "This is beneath you . . . aunt."

She ducked her head to hide a blush. "You're the son of . . . of the Ruling Lord," she said through her hair. "Nothing that I can do for you is beneath me."

"Then you'll eat with me."

Fey looked up with her jaw hanging.

"There's no point in looking like that," said Carnelian, trying to make her smile. "It'll give me no pleasure to eat while you fuss around me. I'm not used to it."

Fey looked at him as if she could not understand what he was saying.

"Sit there," Carnelian said gently. "I'd like your company." He looked away when the woman sat down awkwardly, trying to save her more embarrassment. Carnelian picked up a box, opened it and offered it to her. Fey hesitated, looked up into his face and then carefully took one of the wafers of bread.

"Where will my father be now, Fey?"

"But, Master, you told me yourself that he was with the Wise."

"Yes, but where would they have taken him?"

"To the Isle."

"The God Emperor . . . he's gone to see the God Emperor."

Fey made the sign of the horns and ducked an obeisance. "The Gods are in the Sky." She gazed up between the columns.

Carnelian frowned, not sure what to make of the awe on her face. "In the Sky?"

His expression brought her back to earth. "The Master will have climbed the Pillar . . . the Gods have gone up there to the Halls of Thunder, as your brethren, the other Masters of this House, have gone up to the Eyries."

"You have my father's eyes," said Carnelian.

Fey turned away as if trying to hide them from him. "The better half of me is sister to the Master."

"He told me to trust you."

The words put tears in Fey's eyes. She dabbed at them. "Please, Master, where's Brin?"

"Your sister had to be left behind."

Fey's mouth twitched. "Crail? He must be an old man by now?"

Carnelian looked down at his food, trying to find the words. He looked up at her. "He's dead."

Fey's face crumpled. She snatched a glimpse at his eyes. "Grane?"

"We had to leave most of them . . ."

Carnelian could see by her face that she saw something of the conditions in which they had been left. She nodded slowly. "Ebeny too?"

"She wouldn't come," said Carnelian, biting his lip, hearing his voice betraying pain.

"Her boys, Master?"

"Keal's on the road, coming here. Tain's in the quarantine."

"With others?"

Carnelian shook his head. Fey lifted a bowl of filigreed turquoise and offered Carnelian its peaches. Carnelian took a fruit, bit into it. He was vaguely aware of its sweetness.

"Our orchards are famous," said Fey.

Carnelian looked at her and then the fruit. "Yes . . . it is delicious." He put it down. Fey lifted a ewer and poured water over his hands to clean them. Carnelian watched her put it down on its three legs. Each had a human form. Carnelian ran his finger over one of them.

"A Quyan piece, Master, and very rare," said Fey.

"I promised my people that I'd make this place ready to welcome them," said Carnelian. "There won't be any problems, will there?"

She stretched a smile over her lips.

"Do the other lineages resent my return?"

Fey looked at her hands.

"I see that they do."

She looked up. Her face in anger was so like his father's that Carnelian started. "It's not their place to resent you,

Master. If you demand the Seal, they'll have to give it to you."

The words were hardly out before she clapped her hand over her mouth. Carnelian could see her eyes expecting punishment. He gently peeled her hand away from her face. "You've not spoken out of turn."

She regarded him as if he were a creature come alive out of a story.

"Please, tell me about the Seal," he said.

Her eyebrows showed a flicker of surprise. "Whoever holds it rules this coomb."

"But my father . . ." Carnelian thought about it. "It controls all our wealth?"

Fey gave a slow nod.

Carnelian suddenly understood their poverty in the Hold. "But why did he leave it behind?"

"Without it here the coomb wouldn't work."

"And you're trying to tell me that my father left all this power in the hands of the second lineage?"

Fey compressed her lips, shook her head erratically.

"Fey . . . ?"

"The Master left it with the Mistress."

"You mean my grandmother?"

"The Lady Urquentha," said Fey, using the Quya.

Carnelian frowned. "I've had a letter from her." He watched Fey go yellow as she dug her chin into her chest. "What's the matter, Fey?"

Fey refused to look up at him. She jerked back from the table, slapped her hands down on the floor and cracked her forehead down between them. Her abject prostration angered him.

"Get up, woman."

Fey looked up with blood smearing above her eyes.

Carnelian winced. "Look what you've done to yourself." He reached up but she pulled away. He dug the letter out of his mask and held it up. "This isn't for me, Fey, but for my father."

"The Mistress must have received garbled news, Master

... the forbidden house ... it's closed against the world ... she's not allowed to see anyone ..."

Carnelian examined her eyes as she rambled. "Fey, what's the matter? Why are you so frightened?"

She hid her face again. He was trying to think what he could do when a deep clanging made them both look across the courtyard to its gate.

"By your leave, Master."

He had hardly had a chance to nod before she was fleeing down the steps. Carnelian watched her recede. The sun was painting color into the porticoes on his left. Friezes carved into their lintels animated their crowds of tinted marble in the morning sun. A pyramid rose behind from which faces were staring out. Beyond reared the striped green sky of the Sacred Wall.

Fey was laboring back toward him looking flushed and distressed. "The Masters come."

"The second lineage? Down here?"

She gulped. "Yes, Master."

Carnelian's heart sank. "Here?" He looked at the courtyard with its dead trees and then down at his body wrapped only in the blanket of feathers.

Fey shook her head. "The Master will want to meet you on nonlineage territory ... probably the Great Hall of Columns."

Carnelian spread his arms and grinned. "Shall I go dressed like this?"

She smiled. "By the time we're finished, Master, you'll look every bit the angel."

In a chrysalis chamber he stood naked while they painted him with camphor. Its evaporation left him shivering. Fey supervised the shaving of his head and then the polishing of unguents into his skin. In their shimmering perfume, Carnelian outshone the glowing circuit of the alabaster wall.

Robes of gauze swam through the air to engulf him. Layer after layer the robes grew heavier, the threads of their weaving more discernible, although the cloth was still so delicate that it would not hold folds but only, and temporarily, flakes of light.

"Do we really need more robes?" he said at last.

Fey looked horrified. "The Master must put on an outer robe." She clapped her hand to have them paraded. Each, carried by two servants, was an elaborate piece of furniture. Some were paneled brilliantly with feathers. Others were sculpted into ridges of brocade climbed by ladders of ivory and spineled jewels. In honor of his father, he chose a somber one of raven plumage flecked with bird's-eye opals. His father's ring lay warm against his chest where he had hung it on a chain.

Fey had them bring Carnelian masks so fine that it seemed as if he held nothing but sunlight in his hands. He chose one whose face might have been stolen from a boy gazing out over a summer sea. Fey nodded her approval as they bound it on.

She surveyed her work proudly. "All that is needed now is a crown."

"A crown?" Carnelian's exasperation vibrated the gold skin of his new mask. "I broil and the woman wants me to wear a crown."

"You must wear a crown, Master, when you meet them."

His head drooped. He had almost managed to forget the meeting with the Masters. He brooded as crowns were shown to him, many-tiered, like towers or ships, inlaid with precious cious leathers, haloed, startling with iridescing feather fans. He would have none of them. He overruled Fey and settled for a simple diadem of black jade. She herself climbed on a stool to put it on his head.

"Beware the father," she whispered in Quya and then stepped down.

Carnelian thought to ask her what she meant but he saw the servants all around them. "Thank you," he rumbled and they all fell flat upon the floor.

Fey ordered a door to be opened in the alabaster wall. Beyond Carnelian could see only gloom. His robes were stifling. His skin felt as if it were being pricked with needles. He lurched into movement. The robes were heavier than armor. He had to breathe slow and hard to lift them with his chest. After a few steps he steeled himself but the tug of the cloaks never came. He turned his head as far as he could and glimpsed some of the children carrying his train. He looked back to the lamp-striped corridor and putting one foot before the other began to journey along it.

At first Carnelian thought they were a guard of diamond men, but as he drew closer he found them to be blocks of ice. It seemed strange that such vestiges of winter should be found in this land where it was always summer. He passed through their cordon into cooler air, then through another of lamps and saw the two towers of sculptured silk awaiting him. Slabs of samite stiff with jewels joined by barreling brocade. High in these structures, surrounded by coronas of quetzal plumes, was the gold of their disdainful faces.

As he stopped, he felt the mass of his robes settling round him. The green coronas inclined. He returned their bow. Sweat was soaking into his robes.

Facets flashed as one of the creatures began to move. A long white hand gleamed into being. *Shall we be alone?*

Carnelian lifted his arm against the weight of his sleeves and made a gesture of affirmation.

The other's fingers shaped a sign of dismissal. There was an impression of movement in the shadows. Carnelian felt something pull at his shoulders, looked round and saw the children arranging his train in folds over the floor.

"We have come to see if you are indeed who you claim to be, my Lord," said one of the Masters. The voice was so deep it seemed to come rumbling down the avenues of columns.

"I am Suth Carnelian."

"So you say," said a different voice.

Carnelian was angered by the Master's tone, but he calmed himself. He was coming to dispossess them. It was natural that they should resent his claim and reasonable that they should seek proof. It occurred to him that he might show them his father's ring, but he realized that was lost beneath the layers of his robe.

"My blood-ring," he said aloud.

He steepled his hands together and took it off. As he moved forward his cloaks' drag made him feel as if he were yoked to a cart. If that inconvenience had been the Masters' intention in sending away the children, Carnelian was not going to allow them the satisfaction by acknowledging it. When he was close enough, he held out the ring. One of the Masters took it and held it up to the light. His gold face scrutinized it before returning it. The Master backed away, reached down the slopes of his robe, took hold of some brocade and pulled on it like handles. His robes billowed up as his jeweled torso began sinking. The silk subsided sighing as Carnelian realized the Master was kneeling.

"House Suth rejoices in your return, my Lord," the deep voice said.

The other Master looked down at his companion, his hands moving uncertainly over his robe, but then he too knelt. When they removed their masks, their faces were snow reflecting a winter dawn. Carnelian unmasked as they were rising. Their beauty was much alike and bore no resemblance to his father's.

"I am Suth Spinel," said the elder of the two in his deep voice. Carnelian recalled Fey's warning as Spinel's hand arced elegantly towards the other Master. "This is my son, Opalid."

Carnelian bowed his head as much as his diadem allowed.

"And what of the Ruling Lord, cousin?" asked Spinel.

"He has gone to the Halls of Thunder."

"As He-who-goes-before?" said Opalid.

Carnelian answered with his hand.

Opalid shook the green dazzle of his head. "We never believed he would—"

His father slashed him silent with his hand. "When is the

Ruling Lord intending to return to the embrace of his family?"

"You are likely to know that better than I, my Lord."

"Cousin, I become confused."

"Surely you know why we have returned?"

Spinel regarded him with cold eyes. "To take back what is yours."

Carnelian was surprised. "That is far from being our prime concern. We have returned because of the election."

"So, the Lord Aurum has once more outmaneuvered his enemies." Spinel's tone was conversational but his eyes were sharp.

"That remains to be seen," said Carnelian, "although my Lord might recall that my father has always been of independent mind."

Opalid flickered a frown.

Spinel fixed Carnelian with his eyes. "This delay in his return, though regrettable, does give us time to make all the required preparations."

"You will quit those first lineage halls that you now occupy?"

Spinel's face became a cake of salt. "Yes, my Lord, though you will appreciate this is something that cannot be effected in a moment."

Carnelian nodded.

"In the meantime, perhaps, my Lord would condescend . . ."

Carnelian gave the Master an expectant look.

". . . to occupy the halls of the third lineage in the Eyries?"

"For the moment."

"In less than a month we shall make the journey to the Halls of Thunder to vote in the election."

"Am I to understand that my grandmother is up in the Eyries?"

Spinel gave him an enquiring look and a slow nod.

"I intend to meet her today."

Spinel shaped a barrier gesture with his hands. "The Lady

is old now and frail and receives no visitors . . . the shock of this sudden appearance . . . not to mention—"

"My grandmother already knows that I am here."

Spinel frowned. "How could you know this, my Lord?"

"I have a letter from her."

"A letter? I see." Spinel put on a jovial smile. "It seems then there is no problem whatsoever."

Carnelian felt like a jeweled doll as they put him into the palanquin. His arms and legs were folded into place and his train was fed in after. The door slid closed and then he was hoisted into the air. The swell of the carrying poles damped away to stillness, then, with a sway, they were off. He breathed his hot, humid perfume slowly and did what he could to loosen some of his robes. He found a grille that he could open to let in some air. Walls and gilded pillars, glimpses of courts, manicured trees, all slid past in bewildering procession. He slumped back and turned his blood-ring round and round his finger, watching the play of light that the grille was freckling over the satin wall. He tried to ignore the heat, to think about his grandmother. His guts churned. What was he going to tell her about her son?

At some point the palanquin angled up and the pressure of its wall slid up to his back. He could hear a watery tumble and hiss.

A mossy smell greened the air. He drowsed during the long climb up the Sacred Wall, as he was cooled and heated in alternating rhythms.

It was the palanquin settling to the ground that woke him. Carnelian sat up and put on his mask. He listened but could hear nothing. He slid back the door and saw the guardsmen kneeling in a half-circle. They helped him climb out into their midst. When he straightened, he saw a columned hall running deep into the rock. Hugging the cliff, a wide stair with many landings wound down from where he stood, past galleries and colonnades, under balconies, round gargoyled buttresses. The whole cliff seemed to have been carved. When his eyes strayed to the open side of the stair, he reeled, gripping the balustrade that was all that lay between him and an infinite realm of air. The Skymere below might have been a sea seen from the clouds. The rim of the Yden traced its circle into vague distance, barely containing its emerald world that was all atremble with slivers of sun. In all that melting world the only solidity was the Pillar of Heaven. Carnelian leaned over the balustrade and saw rock plunging down and further down until he saw the roofs and courts of the Lower Palace like a border of ivory plaques sewn into the edge of the Skymere.

The air was cooler than it had been below. He drank it in so deeply that he felt his lungs were dragging him forward into flight. He turned his back on the sky and its beckoning fall and took some steps into the shelter of the columned hall. His train was lifted without need of his command. He reached out to touch one of the columns. His hand slid up and round the twist of its cabled stone, which was of a piece with the ceiling and floor.

As his eyes adjusted to the gloom he began to make out the guardsmen and the door that lay between them, which had molded upon each of its leaves the womb glyph. As he walked toward them, the guardsmen knelt. The door was of silver flecked with red and was stitched down the middle with several enormous locks. One guardsman rose and struck the door three times and then returned to his knees. Carnelian tried to lift them to their feet with a sign of command, but it only put more strain into their backs, and set their heads to ducking in apology, muttering, "It's forbidden, Master, forbidden . . ."

Carnelian examined the door. Its silver was a white garden, sinuous with flowers, pendulous with fruit, into whose riotous growth embedded rubies and amethysts drizzled their blood rain. He looked down the hall to where its last columns framed the glaring sky. He fidgeted with his ring.

"How long will I have to wait?" he asked at last.

The guardsmen shrugged, hunching.

The door was struck from its other side and then Carnelian heard mechanisms operating. The guardsmen rose and a few of them lifted fishbone keys to the locks. As the door began to open it breathed out an odor of mummified roses.

Carnelian walked through. More guardsmen awaited him but these seemed to have had their chameleons painted on their faces with blood. Though as tall as men, they had the shape of boys. It had never occurred to Carnelian that eunuchs might wear his cipher. A silver-faced ammonite came through them, and then another, both wearing purple. They bowed.

You were expected, one signed while the other lifted his hand shaping the sign, *Close*.

Carnelian felt the shudder in the air as the door shut behind him. On its other side, the guardsmen were resecuring the locks.

Seraph, all the standard procedures are to be observed.

Carnelian lifted his hands. *I do not know the standard procedures.*

The ammonites moved aside and indicated the wall behind them. In the stone, glyphs burning with jewel fire read:

THE WISE CERTIFY THIS HOUSE APPROPRIATE TO THE SEQUESTERING OF FERTILE WOMEN OF THE CHOSEN. TO ENSURE BLOOD LINE INTEGRITY, ALL CREATURES WHO ARE FULLY MALE ARE FORBIDDEN ENTRY. CHOSEN MALES ARE PERMITTED VISITS TO THE SEQUESTERED UNDER THE FOLLOWING, SPECIFIC CONDITIONS:

FIRST, BEFORE THE VISITOR IS ADMITTED TO THIS HOUSE, THE SEQUESTERED SHALL BE PLACED IN A CHAMBER OF AUDIENCE TO WHICH THE VISITOR SHALL THEN BE ADMITTED ACCOMPANIED BY TWO AMMONITES;

SECOND, THE VISITOR MUST SUBMIT THROUGHOUT TO SUPERVISION BY THE AMMONITES;

THIRD, THE VISITOR MUST NOT TOUCH THE SE-

QUESTERED UNLESS SUCH TOUCH IS SANCTIONED
BY CONJUGAL RITE;

FOURTH AND CONCURRENTLY, THE VISITOR AND
THE SEQUESTERED MAY MAKE NO EXCHANGE OF
ANY KIND UNLESS THAT EXCHANGE HAS BEEN DE-
CLARED LEGAL BY THE OBSERVING AMMONITES
AND RECORDED, SAID RECORD TO BE SUBMITTED
TO THE WISE;

FIFTH, BEFORE THE SEQUESTERED IS REMOVED
FROM THE CHAMBER OF AUDIENCE, THE VISITOR
MUST HAVE QUIT THIS HOUSE;

ALL THIS BY ORDER OF THE LAW-THAT-MUST-
BE-OBEYED.

The words chilled Carnelian to the bone. One of the silver
masks angled to one side. *Shall we proceed, Seraph?*

Carnelian broke his immobility with a nod. The slicking
of bolts made him look to see them finishing the locking of
the door.

"Seraph?" said one of the ammonites in a strange voice.

He turned to follow the creature's narrow back into the
gloom. He could feel the other padding behind him carrying
his train. He climbed a stair. On his right side, tunneling slits
were glazed at their further end with the brilliant colors of
the crater. On his left, the stone was pierced to form screens
behind which there moved a world of shadows.

They came to a door inlaid with red stone. The ammonite
ahead of Carnelian scratched it. A woman's voice gave them
leave to enter and the ammonite crept in.

The Lady Urquentha was the first Chosen woman Carnelian had ever seen. Her beauty lit the chamber. A jeweled
halo that framed her face took all its glimmer from her skin.
The rest was in darkness.

Urquentha's face thinned to fragile alabaster. "You are not
my son."

"Lady," said Carnelian and made a clumsy bow. "Did they not tell you?"

She gazed at him. "Who would tell me? It has been my fate to know of the world only as much of it as I can see through windows. Rumors are the only communication to penetrate this house."

"But your letter, my Lady, it came so swiftly."

She frowned a little. "That was delivered by my keeper ammonites. But how came it into your hand, my Lord?"

"I am the son of your son."

For a moment, Urquentha lost her wary expression. Her hand began sending a series of quick signs to the ammonites which Carnelian could not read. He turned to see the creatures nodding, and when he looked back Urquentha was gently beckoning him. He went as a moth to her flame. When he was in range, she asked permission with her eyes before reaching out to catch his chin. Her fingers were warm. He returned her gaze. Her eyes were windows onto a violet sea. She turned his face with her hand as if she were checking it for imperfections.

The hand released him and receded into a pearl-crusted sleeve. She looked sad. "I can see nothing of my son in your face."

Carnelian blushed.

She smiled. "That at least is his. The rest is wholly your mother's. I should have recognized her beauty when you came through that door. Who else could you be but Azurea's son?" Her smile warmed him. "Have you been made comfortable?"

"Yes, my Lady."

"You may call me Grandmother, child." Her eyes darkened to purple. "You have spoken with the second lineage?"

"Lord Spinel came down to meet me, Grandmother."

"Did he indeed," she said, souring, showing the cracks in her marble face. She chuckled without humor. "I would very much have liked to witness that fish floundering in the net he knotted for himself."

A movement caught the corner of Carnelian's eye. He

glanced round at the watching ammonites. With their numbers and fixed expression, their yellow faces could have been cast tallow.

"Where is my son?"

Leaning close to his grandmother, Carnelian whispered, "Could we not be alone?"

"You wish to be free of my chaperons?" She turned a thin smile toward the little men.

Carnelian nodded.

She laughed like a girl. "I more than you have wished to be free of those jaundiced faces, but it is forbidden by the purdah. But do not worry about them, Carnelian; they may have eyes but they have no ears." She smiled at him. "We were talking about your father."

"My father, Lady . . . Grandmother . . ."

His grandmother used her hands to tease out his words.

"He has gone to the Halls of Thunder."

Her lips narrowed as they pressed together. The jeweled structure around her head rustled and glimmered. She sighed. "It seems it is always to be thus?" She looked through him as if her eyes were seeking the edge of the sky. "Always it is the Masks that win the greater part of his affection."

"He was hurt."

Fear washed across her face.

"Wounded."

"Will he die?" The words were flat and lifeless.

Carnelian could see the pain in her violet eyes. "The Lord Aurum is confident the Wise will save him."

Urquentha threw open her hands. "Of course, that one would be in this."

Carnelian was a little dazzled by the flower of her fingers. He tried to find a thread to pull, some way to unravel their journey for her, but she seemed almost to have forgotten him.

"Is it not enough that he should have my daughter to lock up in his coomb but that her brother should also conspire in his intrigues? My son has always been a fool."

"His honor—"

"Ah, yes," she said, angling back the halo behind her head.

"His honor. Fifteen years this House has suffered for his precious honor. He told me he would be but a little time away. His honor demanded that he leave Osrakum before the Apotheosis: that he remain in the outer world long enough to give the new Gods time to consolidate Their reign free from the entanglement of Their love; the very same entanglement that another, less honorable man would have turned to his advantage. His honor. What of the honor of this House and its first lineage? Fifteen years we have been a pale power among the Great. For fifteen years at the dividing of the flesh tithe we have had to stand at the end of the line, lost there without distinction among the Lesser Houses. For thirteen long years I have been imprisoned here . . ." Urquentha subsided, looked forlornly around the chamber as if seeing it for the first time. "In his absence, I was to maintain the ascendancy of our lineage in this House. He left me the Seal . . ."

Carnelian nodded.

"He told you that?"

"No, Fey did."

"Fey." Her eyes narrowed. "When my son went off into the wilderness, I begged him to leave you with me. What kind of life can the bleak outer world provide a scion of the Great? Besides, with you and the Seal together I could have ruled. Without you my hand was weak enough for Spinel to snatch the Seal away. Your father said that he would leave Fey to be my support. It did not take more than two years for Spinel to bring her over to his cause. I was told that House Suth would fall even lower if we did not participate in the festivities and masquerades of the Great, and that in such society men were essential. Men will always claim this and it is always a pretext. It was nothing but greed and power-lust that made Spinel take the Seal." One of her hands crushed the other. "If that usurpation was not enough, he buried me here in this house, though my womb had long been an empty husk."

She looked up and the smile that came through her tears allowed Carnelian to see the girl that she had once been. That girl had a look of his father that put a stone in his throat.

"But now you are here, Carnelian. The damage will be difficult to repair but not impossible. It might not be too late for us to secure for you a worthy blood match. She will be a child destined for years to remain barren to your seed, but what matter that? You are as youthful as the morning." She smiled a cold smile. "Spinel had begun to believe that you would never return. He thought his usurpation all but complete. He and the Lords of the third lineage support the Empress in the election. She has made sure of gathering about her all the lower orders by making extravagant promises of the blood and iron she will give them once she rules through Molochite. I suspect Spinel actually hoped to have the Imperial Power aid him in becoming the first lineage in this House.

"Now, whether Ykoriana triumphs or not, it is all over for Spinel and his hopes. With my aid, Carnelian, you shall rule until my son returns. Together we will push Spinel and his sycophants back into the shadows where they belong. With the Seal in our hands, House Suth is ours. Tell me quickly, what arrangements have you made to have the Seal returned?"

Carnelian opened his hands in something between apology and a shrug.

His grandmother's eyes lost their color. The light coming from her skin dimmed. "But why?"

"I did not think it appropriate to act without my father's sanction."

"But without the Seal, we can do nothing. I will have to stay here."

She bent visibly under the weight of her years. Carnelian could see the tears she tried to hide. He reached out, took her hand, stroked it as if it were a dove. The ammonites stirred in alarm.

"On my blood, Grandmother, I will get the Seal, then end your imprisonment."

* * *

Carnelian would have preferred to return without the aid of the palanquin, but his cumbersome robes made this impractical. He was carried down the stair. Through the grille he watched the sculpted cliff glide by. When the palanquin was put down, he climbed out. Guardsmen formed an escort up some stairs. He walked between them to reach a platform and passed through a door into an atrium where he was greeted by servants, and the purling of fountains. He was led into the cliff, through chambers paneled with malachite and purple porphyry, lambent with lamps, filled with bronzes, feather carpets and tapestries.

He chose a chamber cooled by a waterfall, one wall of which was windowed with glaring sky, where his attendants released him from his robes and mask. He took a few steps away from them in the delight of almost floating. He whisked round to thank them. "Now I know the pleasure a snake must take in discarding its skin."

The smile waned on his face as he saw them all standing their eyes fixed upon the floor. The moult of his robes hung heavy in their arms. "Does the Master want anything else?" one of them said without even lifting his head.

"No," said Carnelian and watched them creep away. The hiss of the waterfall echoing off the lofty cold mosaiced walls made him feel lost in a cave. The windows with their sky seemed far away. He felt utterly alone.

Carnelian composed the letter carefully in his mind before drawing the glyphs on the parchment. He was trying for forcefulness without discourtesy. When it was finished he read it several times. He was unhappy with some of his glyphs but told himself to stop being so precious and made to seal it. He removed his blood-ring. He chewed his lip, then returned the ring to his finger. He pulled the chain that was round his neck over his head and dangled his father's ring before his eyes. To use that was almost to admit his father dead. He reminded himself of his grandmother in her captivity. This had to be done. He inked the Ruling Ring and pressed it down firmly on the parchment. He folded the letter, placed a sealing frame over the join, melted wax into it and printed that with the ring. He sent for a servant and was surprised when Fey appeared.

"I need someone to deliver this."

"I'll do it, Master."

"You?"

She bowed.

"To Lord Spinel then," he said in Quya.

"Does the Master have any further instructions?"

"If you would please wait for an answer."

"As you command, Master." She bowed again and walked away.

Carnelian went to one of the windows. At his feet, the mosaic of the crater spread out its vast circumference. He waited there for a long while drinking in the view. When his sight was all bleached out he went to explore the shadowy halls. Soon he was beyond the chambers that had been furnished for him, wandering among half-seen wonders. Gradually, the echoing emptiness of the halls began to oppress him. The sounds of water haunted the gloom with voices. Loneliness stole the colors from his mind like winter graying the land. He made his way back hoping to find Fey returned, but she was not there. He went to the window, seeking its vision of summer, but shadow swamped the crater, and the Pillar of Heaven had become the heart of the encroaching night.

He woke and waited. He watched the morning creep down into the crater. Servants came with rare foods on plates of white jade but when he asked them they told him they had not seen Fey nor knew where she was. They bathed, painted and dressed him and he waited standing at the window watching the movement of shadows, the play of color in the world below.

It was afternoon when Fey returned. He felt angry with her. "Where have you been?"

She knelt and bowed her head.

"Where is it?"

"Where is what, Master?"

"The Seal?"

She shook her head.

"A letter then?"

Fey showed him her empty hands.

"Nothing at all?"

"The Master Spinel bade me say that the Master will have his response soon."

"Soon . . . how soon?"

Fey shook her head.

"I will go to him."

Fey looked up with pain creasing her face. "Master, if I might presume . . . ?"

Carnelian asked for her words with his hand.

"To go visiting would diminish you, Master."

"What should I do then?"

"Begging your pardon, Master . . . you could wait."

Carnelian frowned. "I promised my grandmother."

"The Mistress has been confined for many years . . ."

"And a few more days will make no difference?"

Fey's head dropped.

"To wait?" Carnelian muttered to himself.

"The life of a Master is filled with pleasures."

Mirrors were aligned to bring the blue of the sky deep into the palace. As the chambers lit up like lamps, Carnelian found trees growing up in the walls and through their arches mysterious landscapes glowed and fabled creatures stood startled or sliced cloudscapes with their jewel-mosaic wings. Sluices opened, gushing water down channels, sparking the air with diamonds, frothing in feathering falls, trembling their sheet crystal down rilled slopes.

For a while he forgot everything as he walked through this enchanted garden. Only when the daylight started to fail and the naves began to fill with shimmering lamps did melancholy settle its leaden cloak about his shoulders. Then Fey had them bring him books, some so small their oblongs could not cover the palm of his hand, others large enough for him to need help to lever their covers back. There were story-books so brilliantly illuminated they cast their colors on his face. He opened others like windows and peered through them into miraculous lands.

Even these wonders began to pale. The night seeped in around him and he went away to hide himself in sleep. His dreams were troubled and he woke before daybreak in a world peopled with guttering flames. A carving in the wall became Fey. He asked her for news but she told him there was none.

"Nothing from court?"

"Nothing," she said and coaxed him off to a pool into which mirrors were pouring the colors of the dawn. The air seemed more rippled than the water as he slipped in and swam its length and depths. He floated spread-eagled on his back, watching light ribboning over the vaulting and snag-ging the faces in the walls. He brooded on the life that he had lost and on the pleasures of this new, Chosen existence. He had to squeeze the grief for his father down into the pit of his stomach. Images of Crail, of Tain striped with blood, came unbidden to his eyes. He felt crucified on a slick of their blood. Where were his other brothers, Ebeny, all his other people? And when they came, how could he rule them all? He was not ready to rule. He hated his father for doing this to him. He hated his father for bringing them here. He hated him for dying.

Evening was carried in on an intertwining of nasal-voiced reed pipes. Their aching melody closed his eyes with a wast-ing melancholy. Morning opened them again and he eased his anguish by floating in the pool or standing in waterfalls until he was completely washed away. Sometimes he found himself at a window but the world outside was too soft a mirage. He rejected the slipping colors, preferring to hide himself in the coruscating caverns where he would stroke faces in the walls, dive deep into books or linger over foods and wines or music that wafted like perfume.

Night would always return like a mood and then he had
them wreathe the air with incense smoke until the tears were
running down his face. Often he would see Fey watching him
with his father's eyes and turn away to find sad rapture from a
lute whose strings took their delicate vibrato from the player's
own pulse. Carnelian would sleep wherever he was and wake
when he did. His only notion of time came from whether it
was the mirrors or the lamps that were the brighter.

Carnelian had languished on the marble floor until its chill
soaking up through his bones had turned him to stone. He
felt a tremor in the floor. He opened his eyes and saw one
of the lighting mirrors was filled with stars. The floor tre-
mored again. He turned his head. Footfalls coming toward
him stopped. The sound of hurried, terrified breathing. He
located the creature. A woman, gaping at him, visibly shaking. He saw her bucket, her scrubbing brush. He smelled her
body and her fear. He imagined how vast and luminously
white he must seem to her, a Master stretched out as if dead
upon the floor. His eyes were turning her to jelly and so he
closed them and turned his head away to let her flee. He
heard her scurry, a click, then silence.

His ears searched for other sounds as he waited for his
body to thaw. He rolled over to wedge his hands under his
chest and then pushed himself up, groaning at the stiffness,
bending limbs, rubbing muscles. He stood up, scanning the
gloom. Off in the distance glowed a glimmering jeweled
world where a hall had been lit with lamps. There was no
sign of the woman.

He loped off, hunting her, stooping as if he could smell
her footprints, and came quickly to a wall. Its bas-reliefs
grimaced as they caught some light. He could hear creaking
close but muffled. When he pressed his ear against the wall,
the sound grew clearer. He slid his hands over the reliefs
until his fingers found a straight edge. He searched for a
handle and was on the verge of giving up when his thumb
slipped over a hole. Probing inside, he felt a lever and tried

to work it. With a click, a small door opened and the creaking grew louder.

He hunched, then fumbled his way into the darkness. Rough stone grazed his skin as he moved along a narrow passage. He ignored his dislike of confinement. Water was gulping up ahead. The air was stale with sweat and frying. Light welled bright enough for him to see. Curiosity drew him on. He could smell wet rock. He came into a cavern in which a huge rotating drum carried wooden scoops from which water dribbled and spluttered over the floor. As he went nearer the floor fell away allowing him to see the cistern from which the drum was lifting water. Leaning allowed him to see another drum further down, and another further still that closed off any further view. His eyes rode up with a scoop and he saw that there was another drum turning in a higher cavern.

The drum shuddered and squealed as it turned. A narrow ledge ran round one end. He edged along it, crouching under the grimy axle, and saw the creatures walking in the treadmill of the hollow drum. He could hear above the din their wheezing. One looked up and Carnelian gaped. The face was not sartlar but the remnant of a man's that bore the chameleon tattoo. He was horrified and was waiting for the wretch to notice him when the guttering light revealed eye pits into which Carnelian could have poked a finger.

When Fey appeared before Carnelian his glare made her fall prostrate on the floor. He made her rise, oblivious of how she was withering in the face of his wrath.

"I couldn't help it, Master . . ."

"Help it?" He tried to clear his mind.

The tears were running down her cheeks. "As the years passed and we'd no news of you, I crumbled . . . the Master was unrelenting . . ."

"Spinel?"

"Forgive me, Master. I betrayed you." Fey collapsed and hid her head under her arms.

Carnelian felt tears coming to his eyes. "We Masters are all monstrous. The fault's not yours."

Fey sobbed. Carnelian crouched, touched her gently on the arms. "Come on, it's fine. I forgive you, and my father will too when he comes. He's not cruel."

She looked up. "You don't understand, Master, even here." She shook her hands at the chamber. "I've conspired with them to cheat you of your rights. Seduce him with luxuries, they said. In exile he'll have had no experience of them and will succumb to their temptation." She sobbed. "I betrayed you to them, Master, I betrayed you."

He put his arms round her. "It doesn't matter, I tell you. If as a Master I showed such weakness, how can I expect more strength from you?" He rocked her until her sobbing slowed to groaning. He kissed her wet forehead and whispered, "You're of my blood. Now please, get up."

Fey rose shakily, leaning on his arm, wiping her face, flickering red-eyed looks at him.

"Come on, let me see you smile."

She managed a crooked one and gently, let go of him.

"That's better. I'd already intended to do something about this, and now . . ." As he described the treadwheel she saw the haunted look in his eyes.

"Once they were put there as a punishment, but for years now it happens to those the Master . . . Master Spinel can find no further use for."

Carnelian's eyes were burning. "But why?"

"At this time of year, Master, there's not enough rainwater in the Sacred Wall and so it must be lifted from below."

"Not enough . . . ?"

She pointed to the waterfall that formed one of the walls of the chamber. She watched him go deathly pale and fought the desire to hide her face.

"Close the sluices," he said in a level, dangerous tone.

"But they cool the air, Master."

"Damn the air, I said close them."

"As you command, Master."

"After you've done this you will please go to Spinel. Tell

him that if he's not here with the dawn, with the Seal in his hand, he'll regret the day he ever laid eyes upon my face."

Fey stared.

"Say it just like that. I've had enough of these Masters, of all Masters."

Fey opened her mouth to speak, closed it, then opened it to say, "As you command."

Amidst tyadra and others of his household, Carnelian sat on a throne watching the approach of the Masters of the second lineage. Each was a jeweled spire pulling behind him a train carried by many boys. Behind them, among their guardsmen, walked Fey. She and Carnelian exchanged a look of understanding.

The Masters stopped in front of him, their faces impassive marble.

"You are welcome, my Lords," Carnelian said and waited for their obeisance, but all they gave him was a nod.

"Have you heard the news, my Lord?" said Spinel.

"News?"

"Rebellion . . ."

"What rebellion?" Carnelian said, exasperated, wishing to come immediately to the matter of the Seal.

"In a nearby coomb, a Ruling Lord has been most heinously done to death by"—Spinel sketched disbelief in the air—"apparently, by one of his slaves. Such a singular event shakes one's world to its very foundations."

"What concern is this of ours?"

"It will affect the election and that is the concern of all the Great."

"The election?"

"The Lord Imago was—"

"Imago? You speak of the Ruling Lord of that House?"

"Just so, my Lord."

"And you say his murderer was a slave."

Spinel threw his hands up. "It is entirely beyond comprehension."

"Will the Lord Jaspar now lead his father's faction?"

"He will if he has the courage to put on the mantle of his father's power along with the Ruling Ring of his House." Spinel looked at Carnelian expectantly. "He was your companion on the road, was he not, my Lord?"

"He was, but you were not summoned here, my Lord, so that we might discuss politics. You will surrender the Seal to me."

"My Lord, the Seal is your father's."

"My Lord might have noticed that my father is not here. Until he returns, I am the head of the first lineage."

"Still, the customs of this House do not sanction what my Lord requests."

Carnelian was determined to break the stony resistance in the Master's eyes. "To spare your grief I have kept something from you."

Spinel's eyes narrowed.

"When last I saw my father he was mortally wounded. For all I know he might now be dead."

"We suspect otherwise," said Opalid.

Spinel gave his son a sharp look, then reached into his sleeve and pulled out a letter. "Then who is this from, my Lord?" The Master beckoned a servant and gave him the letter to take to Carnelian.

Carnelian hesitated, then took the parchment and brought its seal close. In the wax, a pomegranate showed its seeds. The letter began to tremble in his hands. It could only be the seal of He-who-goes-before. Carnelian looked at the letter, reluctant to open it.

"My Lord?" said Spinel.

The look Carnelian gave Spinel made the Master flinch. "How came this into your hand?"

Spinel's hands were apologetic. "I rule this coomb . . ."

Carnelian broke the wax, unfolded the parchment and read:

My son, I have sent this letter sealed with the Pomegranate because my ring has gone, none knows where.

Leave the House Seal in my mother's hand. Avoid disrupting the flow of power in the coomb. Have a household prepared and send it to me here. Include a letter from yourself. I am making a fair recovery and will come to you as soon as I can.

Your father, in the Halls of Thunder.

He should have felt joy instead of unease. He examined the glyphs. They were not in his father's hand, though they were very like. The look of the faces proved to him the letter had been written by someone else. He could feel a corner of his mind steeping in dread. Was this one of Aurum's schemes? He felt sick. What if his father was dead and Aurum had arranged this whole charade to conceal it?

"Is our Ruling Lord well?" asked Spinel.

Carnelian looked at him, striving to keep the misery from his face, trying to gauge the man's intentions. "Apparently, he is recovering."

Spinel's face was blank but Opalid's betrayed disappointment before it set like plaster.

"I must go to join him in the Halls of Thunder." Carnelian heard the emotion breaking into his voice and saw that Spinel could hear it too.

Opalid framed a questioning gesture. "It is forbidden, my Lord."

"By whom?"

"The Law, my Lord."

Carnelian stared, not understanding.

Opalid read his face and his lips took on a sneer. "Surely you know that at this time only Ruling Lords are permitted at court? It is—"

"It is part of the Balance," Spinel broke in. "Intended to take away from the House of the Masks the temptation to take the Lords of the Great hostage, or worse."

Carnelian fought a frown. He could see that Spinel was thinking furiously. The Master took a step forward, trying a smile. "However, if my Lord feels it essential that he join his father, there might be a way."

"What way, my Lord?"

"The Ruling Lord Imago, now sadly deceased, was expected at court. It is almost certainly the Lord Jaspar's intention to go there in his father's place. The Law insists that he will have to accompany the body to the Plain of Thrones for its embalming. It is likely that he will go from there straight up to the Halls of Thunder. He might be worked upon . . . but of course I am neglecting to take into account his grief."

"Finish your thought, my Lord."

Spinel opened his hands. "I was just thinking that perhaps the new Imago might be worked upon to take you with him, my Lord . . . passing you off as one of his minor kin. It is unusual to take a companion, but then Imago Jaspar is not yet fully a Ruling Lord and in the electoral negotiations he might well desire to lean upon the experience of an older Lord."

"You propose that I deliberately break the Law?"

Spinel shrugged. "It is a minor infringement, my Lord. The penalty would not be above a little wealth."

"And Jaspar?"

"He could pass it off as an amusing jape. He might do it for a friend."

Carnelian thought about it. "We know each other well enough. It might not go amiss if I were to pay him my condolences personally."

"Such an act of compassion would be . . . eccentric, but then—"

"Imago Jaspar is well used to my eccentricities," said Carnelian.

"My Lord could join his father, and return here with him once the election is over. Meanwhile, in the time we still have before we ourselves shall go to court, we could continue to prepare the coomb for your return."

Carnelian nodded. "I will go to Coomb Imago."

Spinel smiled. "My Lord will have need to plan his journey." The Master bowed. "We shall return to our halls and immediately resume our labors." He began to turn away.

"My Lord, you have forgotten something."

Spinel turned back, his eyebrows arching.

"The Seal?"

Spinel's nostrils flared. "But I had understood—"

"I will have the Seal."

Spinel's hands clenched. "How shall we make all the necessary changes without it?"

"The time has come for my Lord to be relieved of the burden of rule that he has borne for so long. On behalf of my father, I thank you for your stewardship of our House, but now it is time for another to bear that weight."

Opalid stared at Carnelian. "Surely you do not mean . . . ?"

"Urquentha," said Spinel, his voice as dull as his eyes.

"Yes. I feel my grandmother has been locked away for long enough."

There was a pleading look in the eyes that Spinel turned on Carnelian. "It was done for a reason. She is a dangerous woman."

Carnelian gave him a cold smile. "Perhaps she has been made so. Dangerous or not, I intend to give her the Seal."

"Did you see their faces?" said Carnelian, grinning. He was weighing the Seal in his hand.

"I saw them, Master," said Fey, looking at the Seal with a doleful face.

Alarmed by her expression, he reached out and took her shoulder. "Are you all right?"

Fey straightened, smiled, nodding. "I was thinking that the Mistress Urquentha has been much wronged. It is only just that she should have the Seal again."

Carnelian ran his hands over the carvings on the block of jade, over its handle, its tassels. "Here, take it."

Fey put her hands out and he put the Seal into them. "Please, go now. Take it to her with my respects. Come back as quickly as you can. I'd like you to help me make arrangements to go to Coomb Imago. If I leave it to anyone but you I'll get a lot of fuss. All I really need is a mourning robe."

INTO THE
LABYRINTH

Crucifixion is a punishment capable of infinite refinement. A spectrum of pain effects can be readily achieved. With judicious care, the agony can be extended for long periods without peril of accidental fatality. The technique is particularly useful as an object lesson to the inferior and has, besides, an element of aesthetic display.

—FROM "OF THIS AND THAT" BY
THE RULING LORD KIRINYA
PRASE

Fey struck the smallest heart-stone turtle. Its chime rippled off across the water. Fey struck it again. The second vibration dulled away to silence. The crater seemed to be an ear listening to the sky. The further curve of the Sacred Wall could have been a crack in the world. Carnelian's red mourning robe looked gray. He turned to gaze along the quay, up past the towers of the Lower Palace to the Eyries. While waiting for Fey, Carnelian had tried to sleep, but he had been unable to quieten the arguments in his mind. At last he had given up and gone to a window from where he could see the Pillar blotting milky swathes of stars. He had reread the letter that Spinel had given him many times, until he was able to convince himself that it had come from his father. Fey had returned at last, alone, as Carnelian had asked her to. She had helped him put on the mourning robe. Then, together, they had made their way down the stair with guardsmen carrying lanterns to light the steps.

On the quay, as he searched the darkness for the kharon boat, Carnelian felt the sky begin to redden. Twilight still filled the crater right up to its brim. Mist seemed to be teasing out from the bobbin of the Pillar. A thin birdsong stirring only thickened the silence. The Yden's lagoons were reflecting some murky alien sky. Beyond, the Labyrinth seemed a burial mound. Carnelian shivered though he was immersed in the hot humid breathings of the lake. He began to ask Fey about the crater mostly to feel breath moving in the cavity of his mouth, to bring his world back to a scale in which he was more than just a sliver of fleshed bone. He drew answers out of Fey but then paid no attention to them.

Suddenly, Fey turned to him. "Please tell the Master that though I failed his trust I never betrayed his love."

"You can tell him yourself when we both return," said Carnelian.

Fey would not look at him. Carnelian felt he was being judged.

"We'll come back, Fey. We will, and when we do, we'll put right all the wrongs."

Fey put her hand on his arm. "You've already put things right with your forgiveness."

He put his hand over hers. As they watched the pallid boat ruffling the fiery mirror of the lake, Carnelian checked to make sure he had brought the jade rings he needed for payment. He looked down at Fey. "When Tain's finished his quarantine, will you see if you can find a way to send him to me?"

"Of course, Master."

The bone boat was slipping along the quay, a ferryman at her bow, his one eye spying out her way. Carnelian squeezed Fey's hand and let it go. There were tears in her eyes.

"It'll take a few days to get a household to you. I'll make sure to include a court robe."

"That's good."

They looked at each other.

"Goodbye, Fey."

"Goodbye, Carnelian."

He stood for a moment, unsettled by her use of his name, then climbed aboard. As the boat sighed away he looked back at her. She was a forlorn stump on the quay. For a moment he was sure he could hear a wind keening over the lake. He shuddered, not understanding where the feeling came from. Perhaps this parting reminded him too much of sailing away from the Hold. He told himself it was not the same at all, lifted his hand and waved.

The bone boat rippled the shadowy reflection of the Sacred Wall as, far above, its edge caught fire in the dawn. Sunlight burned quickly down the buttresses and deep into the coombs. Carnelian watched it reveal palaces and the jeweled colors of the gardens.

They rounded a promontory, into a coomb bay that gouged deep into the wall. He looked along the blazing deck, wondering where the ferryman was taking him. He could see no palaces, no gardens. One more outcrop swung past the starboard bow, allowing him to look into an inlet whose upper reaches were filled with a dazzling avalanche of sculpted stone. Terrace piled on terrace. Spires and towers frowned and stared with faces. Giants stood impaled, disemboweling balconies, their skin riddled with windows. Where terraces came out over the water they were held up by man-shaped buttresses up to their waists in the lake.

The boat was nearing a white caryatid colonnade. The figured columns looked down, their faces desperate, enraged as they bent under a mountainous piling of balconied halls. As the boat came to rest, Carnelian squinted into the cavernous atrium framed by their shins. He used the bone post to swing himself onto the quay, and swiveled round into the blinding sun. He could feel his mask aflame. His sight was slow to return. Like an Ichorian, the crater was half in shadow, half in light. The division of the two vibrated along the ridge of the Labyrinth mound and up the flank of the Pillar of Heaven. Into this vision the kharon's bone-patchwork stern was shimmering away.

Carnelian turned to peer into the atrium. He walked round a lichened foot and column leg. For a time there was nothing but blackness. Then from the gloom there emerged a wall of crowding Masters, tall as trees. He discovered in their midst a doorway that even they could have entered without stooping. It opened onto a flight of steps flanked by oily mosaics. He ran his hand over the amber and jade. Hearing footfalls, he looked up the endless stair. Men were coming down looking smaller than his hand, their faces crossed with dragonflies.

He waited until they were close before he stepped out into the light. "I've come to visit your Master."

His words produced a hunching commotion on the stair. He moved back to give them space to kneel. Their faces were so tight with fear it narrowed their eyes and made them unable to close their mouths. He was lifting his hands in reassurance but they were throwing glances back the way they had come. Carnelian looked up the stair expecting to see the horror that was stalking them.

"Your Master . . . ?" he asked gently.

They shook their bowed heads erratically. "Sorrow, sorrow . . ." one of them began.

Another looked up, eyes popping from between the wings of his dragonfly tattoo, brown blood smearing his forehead. "Expected?"

"Well," Carnelian began, but stopped when the guardsmen

started squashing themselves against the stone. Carnelian could feel their shaking. Silk was sighing down the stair. A Master was descending, wrapped in the flame of a scarlet cloak, his mask smoldering in his cowl. The guardsmen backed away as if the Master were a furnace, and as he planted his bright foot among them they began to thud their heads bloodily on the stone.

Carnelian lost his voice watching that reddening.

"You trespass," said the Master with Jaspar's voice.

Carnelian gestured appeasement, found words. "You know I have some understanding of your grief, Jaspar."

"You are mistaken, my Lord, I am not he," said the scarlet Master.

"Then who . . . ?"

"You are the stranger here, my Lord. It seems hardly appropriate that you should interrogate me. Who are you that dare intrude upon our grief?"

"I regret the intrusion, my Lord, but I am come as a friend . . . a friend of Imago Jaspar."

"Even at a normal time your demeanor, my Lord, would invoke suspicion. Is it your habit to appear naked like a beggar at the door of a Great House? What is your rank, my Lord?"

"As high as yours," snapped Carnelian, feeling he was twisting in a trap.

Up in the palace somewhere, a shapeless voice swelled a moaning song then faded away.

"I see," said the Master. He inclined his head and his mask rushed with reflections. "Tell me what it is you have come to say and I will make sure my brother hears your words."

"Your brother? Then we are cousins."

Jaspar's brother's head straightened and he gave a humorless laugh. "You are Suth Carnelian?"

"I am."

"My brother has told me all about you."

The Master's mask sneered at him but Carnelian stood his ground.

"Very well, my Lord, I shall accede to your request though

I cannot imagine what you want here." He turned and began to climb the stair. He stopped, turned, chuckled. "Be warned. My brother is grown dangerous with grief."

Carnelian followed Jaspar's brother through a multitude of somber halls, his footsteps echoing among the scuffling of their escort. Several times the inhuman wailing broke out far away. Each time shivers ran up Carnelian's back.

At last they came to where a door opened into a chamber walled and floored with shifting rainbows. As Jaspar's brother passed through, yellow filaments moved across him edged with orange and turquoise. The chamber was cool and damp. From somewhere there came a continuous hissing. Carnelian located the sound, a waterfall windowing the chamber, made brilliant diamond by the risen sun.

"He is there, my Lord, if you have the courage to approach him," Jaspar's brother said beside him.

Turning, Carnelian saw an immense and shadowy stair climbing with many landings up to remote heights. Each landing was flanked by a pair of idols around whose feet light pooled. On the first landing stood a being like a column of blood.

Carnelian began to ascend the steps. Sensing he was alone, he looked round to see Jaspar's brother below him. "You will not accompany me, my Lord?"

The Master's mask smeared color as he shook it.

Carnelian resumed his climb, keeping the blood-red giant in the center of his sight. The figure shifted and Carnelian saw Jaspar's face, a shell cameo imbedded in the welter of mourning red. He was holding to his nose a pale mottled orchid. Carnelian saw a frown begin to crease the perfect face.

"It is Carnelian, cousin," he called up to Jaspar, giving him a little bow. Although the air was laced with incense, Carnelian's nostrils caught an incongruous whiff of foulness.

Jaspar moved back to give him space to come up onto the landing. The orchid drooped away from his nose. "Has the smell of holy blood drawn you, dear cousin? One little expected that you would be the first of my father's scavengers."

"I came in sympathy."

"Another of your curiously barbaric emotions?"

"I know what it is to fear one's father dead."

"Suth has recovered, then?"

"Well, yes . . . at least, I have a letter from him in which he claims recovery."

"So. Your *sympathy* then does not seem well grounded. Your father is not dead; nor, if one recalls correctly, was he struck down by one of his own filthy slaves, neh?"

Carnelian looked round and saw the fragile look of the attendants, the queasy guardsmen clinging to their blade-winged dragonfly halberds, some painted boys huddling together and a woman playing the lute, its body against her chest where a breast had been cut off.

"Was it really one of your own people that slew your father?" asked Carnelian.

"I will not rest until I have bled this murderous conspiracy out of them."

Carnelian followed Jaspar's eyes. In front of a horned altar stood a cross in the form of a youth with legs and arms outstretched. A living man of flesh was spread-eagled on its bronze, his dragonfly tattoo creasing into the agony of a face that seemed frozen in hysterical laughter. Carnelian looked along one arm and saw its yellowing extremity. Wire creasing into the elbow was hung with weights in the form of apples. The end of his other arm was also being slowly pruned. Nausea almost caused Carnelian's knees to buckle.

Jaspar clapped his hand on Carnelian's shoulder. "Come, cousin, one must show you the craftsmanship in these frames."

Carnelian yielded to the pressure from Jaspar's arm. The Master lifted up an icy hand and ran it down the green-brown thigh of the metal youth. "These are exquisite pieces. Can you see it is a single casting?" He reached above the crucified man's agony to the metal face hovering over him. "Have you ever seen such a beatific expression? Scandalously, the whole set has not been used for years." Jaspar ran his finger along under the man's bloodless forearm. He held his finger up to show Carnelian its red. "See, the channel carries the blood away so that there is no spillage . . ." He pointed to where a bowl was set into the bronze youth's foot. ". . . and collects it there. From whence it may be fed to the avatar."

Jaspar pointed to the altar on which Carnelian could see many such bowls. Carnelian turned his back on it all but was unable to free himself from the odors of blood and excrement and sweaty fear that the incense could not mask. He saw the people kneeling, staring at the crucifixion, the cross of their dragonfly tattoos a sinister reflection of its shape, their eyes, wounds oozing tears, the noses of the children dribbling mucus down to their quivering lips.

"Why do they watch this?" Carnelian said, horrified.

Jaspar sniffed his orchid. "Because if they do not, they themselves shall end up on the frame."

"How could all these poor creatures be responsible?"

Malice cooled Jaspar's eyes to ice. "They are all responsible. How can my House make claim to leadership among the Great when it cannot control its own slaves? Before any of their filthy hands should be raised against me, I would nip all their arms off at the shoulder."

Carnelian took a deep breath. "My father too was struck with a knife, Jaspar, but was it really the barbarian's hand wielding it?"

Jaspar turned to stone. "What you suggest . . . is inconceivable."

"That is what you said on the road, and yet my father bled."

"But here . . . within the Sacred Wall . . . it is simply inconceivable."

"My Lord seems to have forgotten to whom he attributed the death of the Lady Flama Ykoria, who died not only within the wall, but in the Labyrinth itself."

Jaspar crushed the orchid and let it drop from his hand.

"How many of your people have you crucified?"

"Many," Jaspar waved his hand, "notwithstanding the cost."

"And have you found even a whisper of a conspiracy or of rebellion?"

Jaspar regarded him. "Under excruciation they confess to all the fanciful plots their animal minds can conceive, but none have rung true . . . so far."

"What will you believe once you are left only with limbless slaves, my Lord?"

"Is this all you came to tell me, my Lord?" Jaspar's voice sounded flat, emotionless.

"I had hoped that you might intend to take your father's preeminent place among the Great."

And if I did? signed Jaspar.

Then you would be going to the Labyrinth?

All the other Ruling Lords are there.

Could you take me with you?

"To join your father?" asked Jaspar.

Carnelian nodded.

"You ask me to break the Law, my Lord."

"It is not so great a sin, cousin. You could pass me off as one of your kin."

"An outrageous request, Carnelian, although one is heartened that at last your machinations are acquiring a Chosen hue." Jaspar looked away, thinking. Carnelian could hear the blood dripping into the bowls. "Perhaps I will accede to your request, although one can hardly see why you felt the need to manufacture these elaborate notions of conspiracy."

"But I believe—" Carnelian began, but was distracted by a clamor of bells and moaning that came wafting down the stair. Jaspar looked up toward it.

"One will give the matter some thought. But now my father begins his journey to the Plain of Thrones. One's decisions will be made there. If my cousin wishes, he could form part of the somber procession."

"I would be honored to attend the funeral," Carnelian said.

Jaspar turned back to look at him. "Funeral?"

"I thought . . ."

"Do you really imagine that the entombment of a Ruling Lord of the Great is an occasion that can be organized in a few days? The Houses have to be invited, the grave goods prepared, and"—he gave Carnelian a patronizing smile—"it is customary to have the body embalmed. You would not have the vessel of my father's blood perishing to dust like the cadaver of some slave, would you?"

Carnelian lifted his hands in apology. "I meant no offense."

Jaspar made a dismissive gesture. Before he could turn away, Carnelian reached out and touched his arm. "Perhaps in view of what I have said, cousin, you might consider putting an end to this torture."

Jaspar jerked his arm free. "You presume too much, my Lord. This is a lesson that I will brand deep into the memory of my slaves. Since his guardsmen did not care to die to save his life, they will die so that my father's ghost might have their blood to sup on as he descends into the Underworld."

The moans and pealing grew deafening. Carnelian looked up the steps with increasing unease. The idols of the avatars leered down at the crucifixion frames standing beside their altars. A procession was coming down the steps between them. Sapients, horned and wearing the moon's face, drifted hand in hand with their homunculi. Behind came ammonites chiming heart-stone bells or waving moaning silver mouths aloft on poles.

Carnelian was forced to move aside to draw closer to the tortured man. Water oozing in Carnelian's mouth anticipated vomit. He closed his eyes and prayed that he would not retch. Taking his mask off would bring even more death and mutilation to the household Imago.

A heavy waft of stale incense made him open his eyes. The Sapients were upon him, their bead-crusted purple samite swinging like plates of armor. Each carried a staff capped with a manikin of green-rusted copper crowned with a scything crescent moon.

My Lords of the Domain Immortality, Jaspar signed, then bowed.

The Sapients worked their staves backward and forward as they slid past. The moaning was a peopled gale. Carnelian saw the silver-faced ammonites striking their stone bells, compelling his heart to their dirgeful rhythm. Floating between them was a slab of ice like smoky quartz. Upon this a Master lay, reeking of myrrh, encased in a green robe as stiff as wood, the cloth darkening where it sucked up meltwater. The robe was spangled with tiny spirals that might have been the heads of nails hammered through into the flesh. On the chest lay an annulus of mirror obsidian in token of the Dark Water over which the dead cross to the Underworld. The gold mask was a face in which the world slid reflected, like the memories of the dead man's life. Leaning in toward each other, the ammonites gripped their burden with blue hands.

Jaspar pushed into Carnelian and forced him to retreat further until he could feel the arm of the cross digging into his back. He shuddered, feeling the pain-tremor in the frame. A Chosen woman, her face sagging yellowed marble, stopped to allow Jaspar his place behind his father's bier. Carnelian was glad she did not look to question his own presence there. More than a dozen scarlet-clad Masters followed, some throwing frowns at him as they passed.

Carnelian was hoping for a place at the end of the procession but the Imago guardsmen bringing up the rear, resplendent in azure-feathered cuirasses, heads hanging, waited for him to join the other Masters. As he hesitated, one of the guardsmen looked up as if waking from sleep. Gashes that had been cut down from each of his eyes were weeping tears of blood.

Several kharon boats were waiting at the quay, the sun gleaming on their bony curves. Guardsmen knelt and cried their blood onto the stone. Carnelian was standing with Jaspar when his brother came toward them, his hands signing, *Why does he come with us?*

"Because I will it," said Jaspar.

Jaspar's brother turned the eyeslits of his mask on Carnelian, who looked away to see the bier being presented to some ferrymen standing in one of the boats. The creatures did not look like men at all as they inclined their bone-crowned heads. One lifted the dead Master's pallid hand from which he removed a ring. The Sapients and their homunculi were already standing on the deck. Under their instruction, the bier was loaded onto the boat.

First Jaspar and then his brother gave rings to a ferryman and stepped aboard. Carnelian pulled a jade ring from his finger, remembered to offer it with his left hand and pulled himself onto the cobbled deck. The other Masters of House Imago followed him. Feeling out of place, Carnelia watched the other boats being loaded with the people and baggage that were streaming out from the palace.

His own boat was the first to turn her prow toward the lake and move off. Carnelian felt sad for the old Chosen woman left standing off to one side, alone on the quay. Swinging more freely on their poles, the silver mouths summoned up for them a wind of keening that seemed to carry the bone boats across the water with only the merest effort from their oars.

Jaspar sat on the middle chair with his brother on his right, and Carnelian on his left. The other Imago Lords stood behind them. Carnelian kept his back as stiff as the chair and tried to shut out the bells and moaning. Before him the corpse of Jaspar's father lay on the ice like a fish waiting to be gutted. Although the ammonites held a canopy over the body, the sun was still low enough to slip under it. Rivulets ran down the ice, sparkling indigo, pooling on the skull-cobbled deck.

The corpse looked so much like his own father had done in the Ichorian chariot that Carnelian warmed with sympathy for Jaspar and for his brother. But his stomach reminded him of the crucifixions and he grew cold.

On the water, the bone boats turned toward the slope behind which lay the Plain of Thrones. In its green wall there was a cleft that came slicing down to the water's edge.

"The Quays of the Dead," murmured Jaspar's brother.

Carnelian was sure he could hear grief catching at his throat.

The boats began nestling into the quay. Ammonites carefully unloaded the corpse as the other boats began disgorging their passengers. Carnelian watched a Sapient disembark leaning his bulk on his homunculus. The Sapient sank into the quay; his homunculus stooped among the purple skirts of his robes, reached inside and came out with ranga. Carnelian looked back across the Skymere to where the circling cliff of the Sacred Wall crimped with coombs and realized that even there the ground was too profane for the Wise to walk on without ranga.

Guardsmen unfurled banners as the embalming procession formed up at the foot of a stair. Carnelian followed Jaspar and his brother and felt the other Masters walking behind him. The Sapients were already moving up the stair.

The climb was long and arduous. At landings, they stopped just long enough to allow the ammonites to transfer the burden of the corpse among themselves.

They came up onto a larger landing whose outer edge was lined with stumps. Carnelian felt a touch on his shoulder.

"One would speak with my Lord," said Jaspar. He nipped off the beginning of his brother's protest with a sign and sent him and the other Masters up the next flight of steps after the procession, accompanied by the majority of the guardsmen, all the women and children and the porters with their burdens. Only a few guardsmen remained, hanging their banners above them like parasols. Carnelian saw that the cuts down their cheeks were healing brown.

"Perhaps, cousin, you would explain to me how my slaves

might have been prompted into committing murder?" said Jaspar.

"Have you had visitors? A message from court?"

"Some Lords came to conclave . . . but from court . . . ?" Jaspar shrugged a no.

"Perhaps their entourages . . . ?"

"My Lord's arguments tend toward a certain circularity, neh?"

Carnelian had to agree. He used his foot to scrape earth from a ring shape on the ground. "Are you sure that no person whatever came from court?"

Jaspar's mask regarded him as if from a great height. "I suppose there is always the regular traffic in ammonites."

"Ammonites?"

Jaspar fluttered a gesture of disbelief in the air. "If you draw ammonites into your fantasy then their masters are sure to be close behind."

"Why should the Wise not conspire with Ykoriana?"

"Enough! You would have me believe that two Powers work in concert against the third." He shook his head. "If that were so, first the Balance and then the Commonwealth would be destroyed."

Jaspar dropped his cowled head as if he were deep in thought. So as not to interrupt him, Carnelian looked down at the ring his foot had uncovered. It was of bronze and had a hinge at one end. A mooring ring. He looked out over the blue waters spread out below. He glanced from side to side along the landing and wondered if in some ancient time it could have been a quay. He felt Jaspar move away. "Well?"

Jaspar turned. "I must follow my father this one last time." He sighed. "And, as Funereal Law demands, on foot."

Carnelian followed Jaspar, sensing victory. He noticed that the steps had several times been recut deeper into the rock. The dirgeful bells came echoing distantly from above. Striped walls of stone rose up on either side. As they climbed, Carnelian became uneasy, convinced he was being watched and then discovered that the walls had in them an impression of a crowd. When he squinted, he could make out their faces, vague from uncountable years of rain, furrow-mouthed, scratch-browed, noseless, with pits for eyes.

"The Plain of Thrones," announced Jaspar.

Carnelian gazed at the walled plain that widened round then narrowed again in the distance to where the wall looked no higher than the thickness of his arm. Behind it rose an immense blackness that overwhelmed him. As the pealing of the bells struck him with its hammer blows, Carnelian was again clinging to the deck of the baran. His mind's eye widened looking down into the gyring horror of the well. He blinked. Before him was the plug that would have filled that pit in the sea. It was only motionless rock, he told himself, the flank of the Pillar of Heaven, narrower from this side. The pressure of the bells was fading. He let his gaze slip down to an arrowhead, a hollow pyramid cut into the wall of the plain, a buckle in its belt. He realized the stone on either side of it was pricked with windows, ribbed with balconies, striped with colonnades. Below stood a line of shadowy men. He turned to follow them round. Standing one beside the other, they hemmed the wall for fully half its circle. In the west they stood revealed by the sun as solemn stone.

The funereal pealing and moaning was pulsing round the plain. Remembering his father's stories, Carnelian snatched his eyes back, searching. There, beneath the pyramid hollow, he found a space wedged between two of the stone men and knew that it must hold the Forbidden Door, the entrance to the Labyrinth.

Carnelian was walking along a road that ran straight as a shadow toward the Forbidden Door. For a while he had been noticing a group of people conclaving in the center of the plain. It was only the heat shimmer that had lent them movement for as he came closer Carnelian discovered they were actually stone monoliths set in a ring.

"My Lord," said Jaspar, in the silence vibrating between two peals.

Carnelian turned to him and saw the Master's hands begin to sign.

Soon I will leave this procession and go into the Labyrinth. If you still wish to accompany me you must do as I say, agreed?

Carnelian agreed and they continued on their way.

Inside the outer ring of monoliths and close to its center were two more rings, one within the other. Most of the monoliths were the black of a stormy sky but those forming the innermost ring looked as if they had been painted with blood. All the ground within the outermost ring was slabbed, mosaicked, ridged or spotted with cobbles. The road they were on divided to curve round the flanks of the stone circle, then joined up again on the other side. Along the left fork Carnelian could see another procession moving with banners. The Sapients took the embalming procession along the right. A quarter of the way round, a new road branched off toward the northwestern edge of the plain. At this junction the procession came to a halt and Jaspar and his kin began to argue using their hands. Carnelian looked away, not wishing to intrude further into their grief. The Sapients waited beside a pair of monoliths that lay a little distance out from the circle. Although only half their height, the Sapients bore some resemblance to them. Jaspar glanced over, then chopped an angry sign that caused his kin to bow and move away.

Carnelian watched Jaspar walk to his father's bier and kneel beside it, then rise and come toward him. His heart warmed to see Jaspar showing affection.

"It must be very hard to lose a father," he said when Jaspar returned.

"Terrible." Jaspar's hand went to a chain at his throat and drew a Ruling Ring out from his robe. He dangled it. "But still, there are compensations, even for such a loss. Long have I coveted this . . . to wield its power. . . ." He sighed in a kind of ecstasy. "I cannot count how many times I have wished him dead."

"Dead? But . . . I thought . . ."

"What did you think, my Lord?" said Jaspar, as he fed the ring and its chain back into his robe.

"The crucifixions . . ."

"You thought I did that from sentiment?" He laughed, shaking his cowled head. "How rich. Really, you are too peculiar, cousin dear. It was done for revenge, but, even more, for future security. Could one have conceived a better way to inaugurate one's reign? Admittedly, it is a profligate waste of flesh wealth, but exactly because of that the lesson will live long in the memory of my slaves. If fortune is not unkind to me, it will never have to be repeated."

Carnelian was glad of the mask that hid his distaste.

Jaspar made a gesture of dismissal. "Enough. This is neither the place nor the time for social banter. I have a gift for you, cousin." Jaspar held out his hand and waited for Carnelian's to move under his before he dropped something into it.

Carnelian looked at it. "A blood-ring?"

"Hush! Put your hand down." He turned until one of his mask eyeslits could see the procession that was already moving down the northwestern road in the Sapients' wake.

Carnelian obeyed him, concealing the ring in his fist. "Whose is it?"

Jaspar grabbed his shoulder. "Come, my Lord, let us proceed. The sun begins to grow oppressive and we still have a long walk to the Forbidden Door."

They journeyed round the circle of monoliths, and as they passed the kneeling guardsmen and retainers Jaspar motioned for them to follow.

"One would have thought it obvious that the blood-ring in your hand is from a Lord of one of my lesser lineages. Khrusos, to be precise," said Jaspar in a low voice. "You must wear it instead of your own."

Carnelian's hands lifted in protest but Jaspar swatted them down.

"You asked that I take you with me, my Lord, as one of my kinsman. That is exactly what I am doing."

Carnelian's eyes wandered between the outer monoliths to the inner ring. After some thought, he carefully removed his own ring and replaced it with the one that Jaspar had given him.

"Good. Now you are my inferior," said Jaspar.

Carnelian could hear that the Master was speaking through a smile. Carnelian was not happy. The new ring felt unnatural on his finger. He distracted himself by counting the monoliths. He noticed that the red inner ring was completed with two green and two black stones.

"What are those stones, my Lord?"

"The Dance of the Chameleon."

"A calendar?" said Carnelian, since that was the only meaning the words had for him.

"In a manner of speaking. Does my Lord see the innermost ring? Well, he will also see that there are twelve stones of the same colors as the months."

"Your inferior still does not understand."

Jaspar's mask flicked toward him. "It is a machine, a sorcerous engine that the Wise use to predict the coming of the Rains and all other temporal matters that provide impetus for the actions of the world."

"I see," said Carnelian, seeing nothing but stones. He waved his hand. "But these others?"

"The calendrical stones also have inscribed on them the Law-that-must-be-obeyed."

Carnelian realized he had known this but still he gaped in wonder. "The Law itself!"

Jaspar nodded, taking his utterance as a question. "And these other stones are commentaries and amendments. The markings on the floor link the whole corpus in some manner unfathomable to any but the Wise."

Carnelian was walking blind, stroking his new blood-ring, working through what he would say to his father if they should actually meet. An acrid charcoal tang made him see again. The road ended at an edge of sooty stone. Looking up he saw the charring stretching away towards the wall of the plain.

"Why do you linger, my Lord?" said Jaspar.

"This burning . . . ?" said Carnelian, pointing.

"Yes, it has been burned," Jaspar said impatiently. He waited but Carnelian did not move. He sighed. "It is here at the ceremony of the Rebirth that our tributaries kneel to worship us"—he pointed up at the pyramid hollow—"up there."

Carnelian surveyed the black field and tried to imagine it covered by a vast and groveling throng. "But the burning . . . ?"

"Carnelian!" Jaspar sounded aggrieved. "Do you really think that we could allow the pollution they bring with them to go uncleansed, here . . ." He lifted his arms. ". . . here at the very center of our hidden realm? The flame-pipes of the Ichorian Legion sweep this whole space with fire and then . . ." He pointed the blade of his hand back the way they had come. ". . . all the way along that road, down to the quays, round the Ydenrim, over the causeway, through the Valley of the Gate and all the way up to the Black Gate."

Carnelian saw the dragonflied faces round them hanging miserably and lost his curiosity. "This is all the burning I have seen."

"Sometimes, Carnelian, you are like a child. Do you really believe that the Chosen would leave the route black so that our servants might walk around leaving their footprints all over Osrakum?"

"A vast labor of cleaning," said Carnelian gloomily.

"There is a sky full of rain to help them."

Carnelian looked at the charred stone. "How do we cross?"

Jaspar made a sign of exasperation. "That way, my Lord." The Master was talking through gritted teeth. "That way, past the Cages of the Tithe."

Carnelian saw that the road went round the edge of the black field and that along its southeastern side there ran a fence.

*   *   *

When they had reached the bronze fence, Carnelian walked slowly along it gazing through the bars. He realized that, through Ebeny's words, he had seen this place before. He looked over to the other side of the road, at the black field. She had told him about a hearth, wide enough to cover half the world and there it was. He gazed at the plain. It was here that Ebeny's people had brought her to pay their flesh tithe. She had told him of the walls that were like the blue mountains she had seen on the migrations of her people. The sky had been filled with thunder. Its blackness had been dragged down to the earth in a monstrous funnel. At its base a jeweled fire burned. He could see her hands making the triangle. He looked at the pyramid hollow and felt the ache around his eyes. Her words were making him a boy again, a homesick boy. He recalled the look of terror in her face as she told him of the whimpering, of her people unmanned, gaping at the jewel triangle that was the angry core of the sky. She had talked of giants hemming them in and, most terrible of all, the dragons. A wall of them on either side. Like the glorious creatures the Sky Father had made to thunder as free as a storm over her people's plains. But these were muzzled, their thunder caught in chains, their backs profaned by the terrible machines the Masters forced them to carry. It was this that had broken Ebeny's bravery. She had admitted to pleading with her people. A few of them had clung to her but others had torn her from their embrace and shoved her toward the dragons. She was carried off in a tide of children. The reek of magic fire tainted the dragons' animal scent. There beneath their mountainous bellies she had been examined by a purple demon that had the same water-mirror face as the childgatherer that had chosen her. The demon had prised open her fist to read the picture tattooed on her palm. Its talons had squeezed her skull and probed her mouth with a bronze thorn. It had torn her clothes and touched her everywhere. Even on the island Ebeny would never look in a mirror from choice and she loathed the color purple.

When the examination was over, she was herded into a cage. Carnelian looked through the bars. He recalled Ebeny's descriptions of her life in the cage. The misery. The endless moldering rain. The feeding. The cruelties the children visited on each other. Carnelian could almost smell the fear behind the bars. He saw stains on the clay floor and had some notion about what might have made them.

"I loathe this flesh tithe," Carnelian said.

"Why so?" said Jaspar.

"It is not just."

"Is it just that we should pay it too?"

Carnelian turned to look at him. "Pay what?"

"A tithe on our own flesh. Are marumaga not appropriated from our Houses to be turned into the Wise? Besides, the barbarians are pitifully poor. They have nothing but their children with which to pay our tribute. Your loathing is hypocrisy, my Lord. From where do you think your own household came?"

The marble guardians looked imperiously down. Each stood astride a heart-stone door, the crack between its leaves sealed with a disc of red clay. There was one guardian and one door for each House of the Chosen. The doors led into tombs.

"We honeycomb the rock like termites and fill the cavities with our pupating dead," said Jaspar.

Carnelian shuddered, imagining the chambers beyond lodging their embalmed Masters.

"Each year our forefathers' ghosts rise up from the Underworld to feed on the worship of all the peoples of the Three Lands."

Jaspar was looking up. Carnelian leaned back to see one guardian's empty eyes and gaping mouth, holes giving into a chamber into which the dead might climb. He could almost see his father's ghost peering out. "Where is the tomb of my House?"

Jaspar pointed off along the wall of the plain.

Carnelian would have made off in that direction except that Jaspar touched his arm. "This is not the time to take in the sights. We are being observed."

Carnelian saw a palanquin and, beside it, a Master waiting with a host of his attendants.

Jaspar's hands made a furtive gesture of annoyance. "There is no way we can avoid him. One had hoped he would have passed through the door well ahead of us." He kept walking, muttering, "This Lord was of Aurum's faction but will have been one of the first to defect to Ykoriana."

They were now close enough for Carnelian to see the Master's autumn-plumaged robe and the cloud glyphs tattooed on the faces of his people.

"Greetings, my Lord Cumulus," said Jaspar.

"Is that you, Imago Jaspar?" said Cumulus.

"With one of my House."

"He accompanies you to the door?" Cumulus sounded surprised.

"To the sky."

"Indeed." Cumulus examined them for some moments before lifting up an enormous hand to make the sign for grief. "All the Great share the sorrow of your loss, my Lords."

"Alas, our time in this world is brief," said Jaspar.

"Still, none should be hastened unlawfully to their tomb. I am not the only Ruling Lord who has carried out precautionary reprisals among his household."

"My Lord is very wise."

Cumulus made space for Jaspar. "Perhaps we can walk together."

"The Law only requires that the mourners walk, my Lord."

"Then, with your indulgence, and for a while, I will become a mourner."

Carnelian saw Jaspar making covert signs to him. *Behind us.*

He fought resentment but did what he was told, taking a place behind the two Masters.

Cumulus' guardsmen formed up on one side while those of House Imago formed up on the other. The households merged into a mass behind. Carnelian watched the men with cloud tattoos look over warily at the blood-crusted faces of Jaspar's men.

Cumulus' gold face turned to Jaspar. "Is it not somewhat unusual at this time for a Ruling Lord to go to court accompanied by another from his House?"

"These are unusual times," said Jaspar. "Besides, I am not yet fully become a Ruling Lord."

"One can see that your father's mantle would be a heavy burden to bear alone, especially when it has fallen upon my Lord's shoulders so unexpectedly."

"One's father carried it alone and he was aged. One expects his son might carry it lightly enough."

"And has his son decided to carry *all* his burdens?" asked Cumulus.

"Tell me, my Lord, why are you come so late?" said Jaspar. "The other Lords will already have been gathered in the sky for many days."

Cumulus attempted other lines of enquiry but Jaspar refused to say whether or not he was intending to hold together his father's faction. Carnelian grew weary of trying to follow their word games and watched another tomb door pass. He allowed his eyes to climb its guardian. Above it, the pyramid hollow gaped cavernously. A stair climbed to a pitchy apex. The spines coming off its backbone held tiers of thrones. On either side of the hollow, the cliff was cut with long terraces.

It was the sounding of his House name that brought Carnelian's attention back to earth.

". . . it is true, he is returned," Jaspar was saying.

"To support Aurum?" asked Cumulus.

Jaspar answered with one of his elegant shrugs.

"If Suth were to support him, Aurum would no doubt be once more a power to be feared."

"No doubt," said Jaspar as he looked away. "Behold, my Lord, we are arrived at last."

Two guardians stood among the others but neither had a tomb door between its shins. Instead, the door they guarded lay between them.

Jaspar glanced back at him. "Come."

Carnelian made no sign that he had heard.

"We must prepare to pass through the Forbidden Door, neh?"

Carnelian stared at the door. Its plain green-black heart-stone and modest size made it seem like nothing more than the entrance to just another tomb.

One of the marble giants guarding the door had an archway cut into its ankle. From this ammonites emerged and then a homunculus behind which a Sapient towered with his hands around its throat. The creature and its master stood themselves before the door.

When Carnelian and the other Masters had drawn close enough, the homunculus put out its hand. Jaspar allowed Cumulus to be the first to give his blood-ring over for examination before he pulled his own off and gave it to the creature. Its rheumy old-man's eyes flickered along the rim of the ring, then it glanced at Carnelian before turning to Jaspar. "Imago Jaspar, at this time only Ruling Seraphs are permitted at court."

"I am not yet a Ruling Lord, Sapience."

Muttering, and then with the Sapient's fingers playing its neck, "We had not thought your succession was in doubt."

"Still, one is inexperienced, Sapience. I have brought Imago Khrusos to help me take my first shaky steps at court."

Jaspar moved aside and the homunculus extended its hand. Carnelian hesitated, removed the ring Jaspar had given him and put it on the hand. The creature examined it, muttering. The Sapient uncoiled a hand from round its neck and flashed out a series of commands. A while later an ammonite put a string of beads in the Sapient's translucent palm. The Sapient freed his other hand and holding one end of the string dropped the rest to the ground. Its beads shone and tinkled. Carnelian watched the Sapient's fingers descend the cord feeling the beads as they went. The hands returned the cord to the ammonite before returning to strangle the homunculus. For a while, the Sapient's long silver mask froze, then his fingers twitched and his creature said, "Very well, Seraphim, the door shall open for you."

EARTH
AND SKY

> Even the sky's heart of thunder
>
> Is silenced
>
> By the darkness under the trees
>
> —FROM *THE BOOK OF*
> *THE SORCERERS*

Carnelian was disappointed. He had expected some wonder to lie behind the door but all he could see was a plain tunnel cut through the rock with niches carved into the walls long enough for one of the Chosen to lie in. He became uneasy. He seemed to be standing in the entrance to a tomb.

"We shall meet again in the sky, my Lord," said Cumulus.

"No doubt," said Jaspar.

Carnelian watched the Lord Cumulus climb into his palanquin and slide its door closed. The box was lifted and slipped into the tunnel, pulling after it the Master's attendants.

Jaspar flourished his hand in front of Carnelian. "After you, my Lord."

Carnelian walked into the tunnel, Jaspar followed him and

the Imago guardsmen and the procession fed in behind. In the stone walls, narrow passages could be seen running off on either side. The scuffling seemed to make the air too thick to breathe. Their many-headed shadow stretched longer, moving away from them as if it were being sucked into the gloom ahead. The door closed behind them with a dull clunk, plunging them all into sudden night.

"How do we see?" blurted Carnelian among the mutterings of fear.

"We still have the Lord Cumulus' radiance to guide us," said Jaspar.

Carnelian saw, some way off, lanterns hovering around the dark cocoon of Cumulus' palanquin. They carried on. Carnelian could hear Jaspar's heavy footfalls, and the clink and patter his people made following on behind.

"Is this then . . . ?" He stopped, startled by how much his voice reverberated. "Is this then the fabled Labyrinth?" he whispered.

Walking beside him, Jaspar made no reply and so Carnelian dropped the matter and they continued in silence. On and on they went with nothing ever changing so that only the movement of his legs convinced Carnelian that they were going forward at all. A dusty odor floated round them that might have been ancient, faded myrrh. Jaspar's people were clearly terrified. Carnelian sensed their trembling in the air. He himself was fighting a growing conviction that they were descending into the Underworld.

The lanterns up ahead gradually lulled him into a kind of stupor from which he was only slowly released by a vision of a forest. The tunnel was coming out into a clearing among twilit trees. It was their appalling immensity that brought Carnelian fully aware. When he looked for Cumulus' palanquin he saw it among the mossy trunks, moving off up a hill accompanied by shadow men. With each step, the vision widened, brightening to a brooding gloom. As he reached the end of the tunnel, Carnelian was able to see deeper in among the columned trees. He followed the trunks up and further up to find the canopy of their branches, but when he reached it his eyes could make no sense of what they saw. The branches joined the trees to each other with soaring arches through which he could not see even a glimpse of sky. Angling his head to one side, he found a hole, a scallop-edged disc of blue whose aching incandescence forced him to look away. Wandering high in the half-light, his gaze fell upon a face. Beneath the vaults of branches, one of the trees had a face. It was such a face as a god might have, serene, seeing past all horizons, with thoughts that were clouds in a sky of mind. Peering, Carnelian found that every tree had a face. Focusing on the nearest trunk, he saw it was jointed and that it rose in tiers. It was only then he realized they stood not at the edge of a forest but on the threshold of an endless hall of carved colossal stone.

An Ichorian melting out from the gloom seemed still to carry its stain of shadow all down his left side. There were other signs that this was not an Ichorian of the gates: his collar was of silver, he was armored with bosses of green bronze and the cloak that fell about him could have been tar smoke. This was one of the God Emperor's own Sinistral Ichorians. Green and black together were the heraldry of the Gods.

"Where do the Seraphim wish to go?" the Sinistral said in Quya, lifting up his tattooed left arm and pointing upward. "To the sky?"

"To the sky," answered Jaspar.

"Then we shall bear you there, Seraph."

Jaspar turned to Carnelian. "Is this fabulous enough, cousin?"

Carnelian turned to him in a trance. When he looked back, the Sinistral had disappeared. Only Jaspar's people were there, huddling together like lost children, looking to their feet as if ashamed.

Carnelian's eyes drifted up to roam the vast volumes between the branches where the stone trees had their faces. By changing the angle of his view, he discovered that some had faces on two sides, one looking to the Plain of Thrones, the other in the direction of the Pillar of Heaven, into the southwest from where the Rains came. He remembered that the Labyrinth was built over the birthplace of the Two Gods.

"Do these all represent the Twins?" he asked, keeping his voice low as if he feared he might wake the stone colossi.

"Rather, they are the sarcophagi of God Emperors a thousand years asleep, of their sons and daughters, of their Empresses." Even Jaspar had lowered his voice and Carnelian could hear in it a tinge of awe. Jaspar opened his arms. "This columned hall stretches from here to the Pillar, and on either side almost to the shores of the Skymere."

Carnelian gazed off, hoping to see some distant glimmer of the lake. "Where do we get this obsession with death?" he murmured.

"My Lord?"

Carnelian had difficulty focusing on something as close as the Master's mask. "Let us go on, my Lord."

Jaspar shook his head. "If we were to go in there unguided we would certainly be lost for days, perhaps indeed for ever."

Carnelian's eyes searched and found many paths winding off into the twilight. He could not begin to calculate the labor in the building of such a place. His imagination was not large enough to grasp the measure of it. It oppressed him. He felt he was trapped somewhere deep beneath the earth. He longed for a single ray of sun to reach him through the vaults.

He jumped, startled when he saw their Sinistral guide had returned. The gloom between two towers was dewing more of his kind. Some were carrying chairs, one of which they settled on the floor beside Carnelian. He sat himself upon it and was himself lifted up beside Jaspar. Trailing the latter's people, they marched into the column forest.

Craning round, Carnelian soon lost sight of the tunnel mouth. For a while he could still catch snatches of the dark outer slope that walled off the Plain of Thrones. Then the chair leaned forward and he had to brace himself against its footboard. Past the two files of their left-tattooed heads he saw the steps his bearers were descending; the towers' roots formed buttresses on either side. Between their trunks he glimpsed meandering avenues, or he found himself looking up into valleys from which paths and stairs came tumbling like streams. Leaning his head back he saw a flock of birds flying their tiny crosses against the vaulting. The faces up there awed him with their disdain, causing him to lower his gaze, forcing him back to his proper level at their feet. Their presence pressed down like the unbearable anticipation of thunder from a stormy sky. This was a place where mortals must creep or else be trampled underfoot. This was the Gods' sepulchre. The deathly stillness was making the air too heavy to breathe. Wherever he looked, constantly shifting perspectives ensnared his eyes. When he tried to escape by closing them, the rise and fall, the shifting angle of the chair, made him seem always on the verge of falling.

Deeper and deeper they wound their way into that forest of stone. It was an underworld meagerly lit by a rind of moon he searched for but could not find. They came into a region where the Gods were reflected in a black tarn. Once, he was sure he spied through a faraway edge of the forest the Yden: an alluring string of slivered emeralds hanging in the gloom. Lost in the terrible twilight, Carnelian found it harder and harder to believe that he had ever been anywhere else. Only the rasping rhythm of his bearers' breathing, and the sight of Jaspar's chair, reminded him of who and where he was. Then, for moments at a time, he was able to cling to the faith that one day they might find their way back into the living world above.

Miraculous light was seeping toward Carnelian through the trees. He could hardly believe that it might be the forest ending. As it grew brighter he looked around him as if he were coming awake. The trunks' grooved drapery folds reminded him that they were not trees but gods, and then only gods of carved stone. As they passed between the last of them into the clearing, the nightmare was already lifting.

His chair stopped, suddenly, shockingly. He had learned to know all its rhythms save stillness. Half-black faces looking back past him made him crane round. Stooping, Jaspar's people were stumbling out from the columns that faded away behind them into impenetrable darkness. "Just a building," Carnelian said, but his shudder betrayed the lie.

Jaspar came alive in his chair. "My . . . Lord . . . cousin?"

Carnelian focused on the Master. "The Labyrinth . . . it is only a building." He tried to force conviction into his voice.

Jaspar's mask stared at him for some moments before turning away. "The stair." His voice sounded dreamy.

Carnelian looked and saw the green cliff rising all around them.

"The Pillar . . . of course," he muttered, daring to lift his eyes.

They were in a fissure of the Pillar rock that opened raggedly to the northwest. Up it funneled, shadow-mottled, filled with heads and limbs. The fissure was all carved. His gaze floated higher and higher. The rock turned black but still it climbed and Carnelian's eyes could find no end to it. He gaped, stunned. This mountain dwarfed even the cliff edge of the Guarded Land, yet it was carved all the way to the sky.

"The Rainbow Stair," said Jaspar.

Carnelian's eyes came clambering back down the crags. They took a while to grow accustomed to the nearer scales. He could see nothing like steps, only, in the shadows, rills of water winding down among the mossy men. The ground was sodden, with a road crossing it. He narrowed his eyes to look out through the open side of the fissure. He blinked several times. The stone forest of the Labyrinth fell away down a slope until over its green undulating roof he could see the Yden's melting emerald spreading out to meet the Skymere. His gaze crossed the causeway to where the wedge of the Valley of the Gate was cut into the girding mass of the Sacred Wall.

"We have waited for them long enough!" cried Jaspar, his anger stinging their chairs into movement.

Carnelian hung over the arm of his chair, reluctant to disengage his eyes from the glorious vision of the crater. After the Labyrinth its airy freedom was a salve for his eyes. The moldy smell of the Pillar's stone drew him to peer at the creatures that lurked in it. Like ferns, they grew up from the boggy earth, uncurling their limbs and frowns over the heartstone. He saw the stair. Steps, striped with red chalcedony and amber, gold, jade, turquoise and lapis blue, and, where they touched the Pillar's wall, bordered by a band of amethyst. Among the green spiraled men, the rainbow ribbon of the stair climbed as far as he could see.

They climbed the Rainbow Stair into the sky. The Labyrinth's roof stretched below as a vast scrubby plain merging its edge into the emeralds of the Yden. Beyond was the blinding blue of the Skymere. Humid air rose carrying hints of perfume that mixed with the wafting sweat of the bearers. The sun was withering them. Carnelian was glad of his cowl to hide in.

The stair darned its way back and forth across the fissure. They kept to the red and amber bands so that if on one flight they were walking close to the carved wall of the fissure, on the next they would be near the edge where Carnelian would be able to see the precipitous fall. Parties of ammonites and Sinistrals passed them, returning to earth.

When the floor of the fissure looked the size of a shield, doorways began appearing among the carved men. The rock became riddled with windows, with stairs as steep as ladders. Hanging banners proclaimed the presence of Masters whose retainers huddled up the steps. Tattooed faces turned to watch them pass as Jaspar's party picked its way through them.

They came to a long landing. On one side the Pillar's rock rose carved with avatars all pierced with openings. On the other a narrow pool ran alongside the rainbow paving. Jaspar had his chair put down and Carnelian, observing him climbing out, took the chance himself of stretching his legs.

The pool ruffled with sunlight. Its furthest edge was a bone of rock beyond which was the vast fall. Carnelian saw that Jaspar's people were hoisting chests up a stair to one of the apartments cut into the cliff. Two of them were feeding an Imago dragonfly banner over a balcony.

Carnelian went up to Jaspar. "Are you planning to stay here?"

"This is as good a halfway house as any to spend the night."

"The night?"

Jaspar's mask regarded Carnelian with contempt. He sighed. "It is customary to spread one's journey up the stair over two days."

"Why?"

"Because, my Lord, otherwise one can be afflicted by the sky sickness."

"My Lord?"

Jaspar looked up and his mask mirrored the sheer cliff of the Pillar they still had to climb. "Up there one breathes the sky. Even the Chosen must accustom themselves gradually to such purity."

Carnelian gazed. The mountain lodged its thorn in the infinite depths of the heavens. "One recovers from this sky sickness?"

"In time."

"A day or two?"

Jaspar's hands made a gesture of exasperation. "Sometimes three."

"I am young, my Lord, I will take the hazard. I intend to see my father today."

"It is unlikely they will let you see him."

"Nevertheless, I will go, my Lord."

Jaspar stood motionless, looking up the next flight of the stair. He shook his head. "I will not come with you, my Lord."

"I will gladly go alone."

Jaspar gave a snort. "Even the least of the Lords of the Lesser Chosen would not appear at the Skygate without an escort."

"I was hoping my Lord would see fit to lend me some of his people."

"You did, did you?"

"Currently, I am one of the Lords Imago. As such, I would not wish to bring shame upon your House."

Jaspar's mask regarded him.

"If I have to, I will go alone."

"Oh, very well! If you will insist on this ludicrous course of action I will not stop you." Jaspar clapped his hands and one of his guardsmen came instantly to throw himself before his Master. Jaspar arranged an escort, then turned to Carnelian. "You will need a household."

"For one day I can do without one."

"One day, my Lord?"

"A household is being sent up from my coomb."

"Indeed, my Lord, and you expect it to be up there with you so soon?" He made a fist. "They will not."

"But Jaspar, how can I use your people?"

"Ah, the delicate sensitivity shows itself again like the horns of a snail. My dear, I will give you blinded slaves who will suffer no punishment whatsoever should you appear before them unmasked. Does that assuage your scruples?"

Carnelian nodded.

"Well, let us give thanks that at least we have managed that."

Carnelian sighed his relief as the Sinistrals carried him away from Jaspar. Behind him came dragonfly-faced guardsmen leading two blind slaves. Once they were out of sight of the pool, Carnelian settled into the gentle rhythm of his chair. They had to pass other halfway houses with their encampments of retainers. When at last they had left these behind, Carnelian was isolated in the rushing wind, watching the graven gods slip by or gazing out over vertiginous views of the crater.

The air grew progressively cooler until Carnelian was forced to pull his robe tightly round him for warmth. The crater had become a remote floor. Several times when the stair doubled back at a landing facing north, he glimpsed the disc of the Plain of Thrones. However high they climbed, there always remained a vast mass of the Pillar looming above.

In a keening gale, they came to the last step of the Rainbow Stair. Towering up behind it, the Skygate was an immense oblong of bronze studded with turtleshell sky glyphs. Carnelian's Sinistral bearers put him down and backed away to allow his Imago guardsmen to flank him as he climbed out of the chair.

Carnelian felt a surge of euphoria. Strangely, even the thought that his father's death might soon be confirmed did not darken his mood. More Sinistrals appeared wrapped in flapping cloaks of green and black. Collared with tarnished silver, eyes averted, their half-black faces looked out from horned casques.

Carnelian was about to shout to them over the wind when they opened a path in their midst leading to the gate. Bending to keep his cowl from blowing off, he walked along it trailing Jaspar's men. He struck the gate and waited. Glancing up he saw one of the sky glyphs hanging over him as large as a chariot. The Skygate gasped open and a thick perfumed exhalation streamed past him. He walked through. The ground shook as the gate closed behind him, cutting through the tongue of wind like a knife.

A cavernous hall ran off into shadowy distance. The air, which carried a tang of lilies, was pulsing. Carnelian thought he was hearing his own blood, but when he pushed his hand to his chest he found his heart was beating faster. Concentrating, he thought perhaps it might be a drum playing somewhere in the faraway shadows.

"Seraph Imago, you were not expected until the morrow."

The voice made Carnelian start. He turned to see the silver face of an ammonite beside him. He could not think what to say.

"Which of the Seraphs Imago are you?"

For answer Carnelian removed Khrusos' ring and handed it to the ammonite, who examined it and gave it back.

"Will he that is to be Imago be joining you, Seraph?"

"Tomorrow."

"Fortunately, chambers have been made ready to receive you, Seraph. If the Seraph would deign to follow."

Carnelian reached out to stop the man turning away. "I must see the Ruling Lord Suth."

The ammonite's silver mask regarded him. "Seraph, even if you were Imago, it would take days to arrange an audience with the Regent."

"The Regent? He is well, then?"

The ammonite clasped his hands. "Seraph, I do not understand."

"I assure you that he will want to see me."

The ammonite made vague gestures but would not look up at him. "Seraph, perhaps I should go and fetch one of my masters?"

"No," Carnelian said, feeling a stab of fear. The Wise must not be involved. Carnelian thought furiously. "If I had something that I wished to give the Regent, could you make sure that he received it?"

The ammonite took a step back. "My masters, perhaps . . . ?"

Carnelian reached into his robe and pulled out the chain with his father's Ruling Ring. He snapped the chain to unthread the ring. "This should be given to the Regent. It belongs to him."

The ammonite hesitated. Carnelian grabbed his hand and forced the ring into it. The silver mask regarded the hand.

"Give it to your masters if you must, but get it to the Regent."

The ammonite put the ring away into his robe, bowed, and

then led Carnelian and his Imago guardsmen down the hall. He found a door down the left-hand side. The Sinistrals who guarded it stood aside and the door opened into a corridor of more human proportions that curved out of sight, its left wall regularly set with doors. As they walked down this, Carnelian soon gave up counting them.

At last the ammonite stopped at one, opened it a little, jerked a bow and rushed away. Carnelian pushed the door fully open. It gave into a long narrow chamber that had steps at the end rising to another door. He crossed to open it and found another similar chamber. Seven such chambers brought him to a flight of steps leading up to a more imposing door. He climbed to open it and walked into a bedchamber. Over the rattle of shutters, he could hear the wind careening through the sky outside. He returned to the door and urged the Imago retainers to make themselves comfortable, then he closed the door and went to sit on the bed to wait. The distant heartbeat was the loudest sound in the chamber. He listened to it with the taste of copper in his mouth, wondering if this was a symptom of the sky sickness.

SYBLINGS

My reflection was my brother

Wheresoever I did go

He was bound to follow

—CHOSEN NURSERY RHYME

Carnelian skimmed sleep like a flying fish. Beneath its waves nightmare shadows slid, driving him to struggle out of the water and up into the air. He longed for their mouths to swallow him and end the nausea of fear, but still with a slap and a flick he managed to evade each lunge and fly free, winnowing the wind, frantically rowing the air. He would see the fire in the chamber, perhaps his stone fingers, the gloom pulsing with his heart, and then first his head and then his spine would suck back into the sleeving sea.

He was shaken awake. All he could hear was his beating heart. "Carnelian."

Impossibly, his father's voice, his father's face quivering with the beat of Carnelian's heart. It was his father sitting on the bed in the flickering firelight clad in some peculiar close-fitting garments. Carnelian reached out for him and they clung to each other.

Suth pushed him gently away and looked at him. "Why are you here?"

Carnelian's head throbbed. He reached up to feel for the spike hammering into it. "My heart," he said, not understanding how this could rhythm his father's words.

His father frowned, looked puzzled. He turned his head to one side, listening. "No, not your heart, the God Emperor's." His face darkened. "Why are you here, my Lord?"

"I came to . . ." He saw the Ruling Ring on his father's finger and pointed. "Good, they gave it to you."

His father looked at his ring, frowning. He rubbed his finger over its cipher and showed Carnelian the ink stain on his skin. Carnelian felt that his father's eyes were seeing into his head. "This is not the time to examine what has transpired in the coomb, but be assured, my Lord, that you will have to provide me with a full account. Now, why did you come?"

The ache in Carnelian's head made it difficult to think. "Your letter—"

"Contained nothing about your coming here."

Carnelian began shaking his head but stopped when it increased the hammering.

The look in his father's eyes softened. "Are you in pain, my son?"

"Just an ache . . . The letter you sent purported to be from you but was written in another's hand."

"I should have explained that in the letter. The drugs the Wise have been giving me—"

"Your wound, Father!" Carnelian felt sick that he had forgotten it.

"Do not concern yourself. Under their supervision it heals well enough." Suth lifted trembling hands. "But you see how it affects me?" Carnelian stared at his father's hands. They looked so frail. His father rested them on his knees. "What did you hope to achieve by coming here?"

"To discover if you were still alive. To make sure that Aurum was not using your . . ."

". . . corpse?" His father snorted a smile. Then his face hardened again. "What part has Jaspar played in this?"

"How do you . . . ? Of course, his people outside. Are they suffering like me?"

His father made a dismissive gesture. "Not as much as you. Why are they here?"

Carnelian grimaced. "It was the only way I could think of getting to court."

His father's eyes narrowed. "Who put this idea in your head?"

Carnelian considered it. "Spinel, I suppose."

"Did he indeed. Was it also his idea for you not to come as yourself?"

Carnelian nodded.

His father rolled his eyes. "What price did Jaspar ask for aiding you in this farce?"

"None."

"Do you really believe the Lord Jaspar would do this from kindness?"

"His father's murder made him my natural ally."

"What do you mean?"

"Ykoriana murdered his fath—"

Suth slapped his hand over Carnelian's mouth. "You must not make such accusations," he hissed. "Here, you must take care even when speaking that name." He looked round as if there might have been ears lurking in the shadows. "We are in the very heart of her power."

"Still. You can see what I mean, Father?"

"What you suggest is utterly impossible."

"Ammonites . . ."

"No. The Wise would never give her the leverage to topple the Balance."

"Surely you could not imagine that any of Jaspar's household would have dared such an act?"

His father shook his head. "There is another suspect."

"An enemy among the Great?"

"Someone much closer to home."

Carnelian thought it through. His jaw dropped. "His own father . . ."

Suth nodded slowly, giving his son time to let it sink in.

"While we were crossing the sea, she gained control of Imago, and with him their faction."

"But to kill his own father . . . surely he will be punished."

Suth made a sign of doubt. "If there were proof, the Wise and the Clave together would send him for ever into the outer world . . . but he will have left no proof."

Carnelian saw again the crucifixion. "Even now he washes away his guilt with their blood." He shook his mind free of the nightmare and looked at his father. "Why did he bring me, then? To curry favor with you?"

"No, to make me vulnerable through you."

Carnelian sagged and his head felt close to exploding. "Then I must return immediately to the coomb."

"That would change nothing. The damage is done, but perhaps we can still turn this to our advantage. Whether you stay or go you must remain here at least until you have recovered from the sky sickness."

"Jaspar did warn me of that but I chose not to listen."

His father smiled. "It is better to be free of him. Besides, by tomorrow it will have gone." As he stood up, Carnelian noticed that he was clutching his side. Suth caught his look. "I have a spasm sometimes, that is all."

Carnelian reached up to touch his father's arm. "I would rather stay."

"We would hardly see each other. The machinations of the election are interminable and alas, I am at their center."

"I would find ways to amuse myself."

"That is what I am afraid of," his father said through a crooked grin.

Carnelian did not recognize the mask his father put up to hide his face. Its right eye sprayed sun rays over the cheek and forehead. Wearing it, his father appeared to be an angel peering down indulgently upon the world of men.

"Give me the Imago blood-ring."

Carnelian realized he was still wearing it. Gladly, he took it off and gave it to his father.

"I shall return this to Jaspar and shall dismiss his men and leave some of my Ichorians in their place to make sure you are not disturbed. They will attend you. In their presence you may remain unmasked. While I am He-who-goes-before they perform the function of our tyadra. It might take some time to sort this matter out with the Wise. To avoid difficulties, please, do not leave this chamber until either I come myself or send a summons. Will you do that for me, my son?"

Carnelian nodded, smiling, but his smile crumbled as he watched his father's painful walk across the floor. Turquoises and iridescent blues streaked across the opening door. For a moment Carnelian glimpsed the two half-black men standing guard outside wearing the lictors' golden fish scales, then the door closed. As he lay back, his head felt as if it were being nailed to the bed.

Carnelian found that if he paced about, the pain became more bearable. The shutters drew him with their fevered shaking. He ran his fingers up the bright crack where they met. The smooth wood led his touch up to a cold mechanism. Bringing his fingertips to his nose, he could smell bronze. He brought a lamp to see the handles, then yanked them down. The lock clicked and the shutters slapped against his hands. As he opened his arms, air and light broke over him in a wave. For moments he was blind and blinking but then a round shape formed in the glare and he realized he was looking down at the Plain of Thrones. Beyond lay the Sky-mere's fading blue. The looser curve of the Sacred Wall hardened up from its edge. Over the wall, the Guarded Land was a patchy lilac layer squeezing away under a colorless sky. He was so high that he imagined his outstretched arms were wings lifting him soaring above the crater of Osrakum.

Next day, Carnelian was fretting. He had thrown off the last of the sickness as he slept. With his vigor fully returned, he regretted the promise he had made his father. He felt caged. He climbed out of bed and was putting more wood on the fire when there was a knocking at the door. Eagerly he grabbed his mask, hid his face and bade whoever was outside to enter.

A two-headed monster came into the chamber. Carnelian backed away, looking round for something to use as a weapon. The monster kneeled on its three legs and bowed its heads. "Seraph," two voices chorused in Quya.

Carnelian pressed his mask to his face to see the creature better through the eyeslits. His head jerked up as another of the creatures entered. This was four-legged and its two abdomens each had a head. It was carrying a long box with the outermost of its four arms.

"Seraph?" said the monster still kneeling in front of him.

Carnelian looked down. It was offering him a letter in its tattooed hand. He reached behind his head to tie on his mask and then he took the letter gingerly. Keeping an eye on the creature he turned the letter and saw that it was sealed with his father's Ruling Ring. He broke it open and read:

Carnelian. Hopefully, you will have recovered. I have sent syblings to prepare you and then to convey you to me.

He heard the door closing and looked up to see that the second monster had disappeared, leaving the box in the middle of the floor. He looked down at the first monster, still kneeling. "Please . . . please rise."

As the creature rose up onto its three legs it looked up at him and in the firelight he saw it had a pair of beautiful girls' heads. One was tattooed and had eyes of jet like wet tar; the other was unmarked marumaga honey with bright living eyes. They might have been two girls of heated wax pushed together so that their waists and touching legs had melted into one. The left one of the pair was all tattooed. Tiny glyphs poured their ink down from her head, swirled her shoulders and arms, one leg and half the one she shared with her sister. Under her gleaming tattoos the continuation of her sister's golden skin showed like cracks in a glaze. The eyes of the unmarked girl moving down his body made him aware of his nakedness.

He blushed behind his mask. "You . . . you are syblings?"

Their heads inclined together. The living-eyed one flashed her pearl teeth in a grin. Her jet-eyed sister frowned. "Why yes, Seraph."

"I had heard of you . . . in fairy tales, but . . ."

"Fairy tales?" The living-eyed sybling giggled.

Her sister hesitatingly touched his hand with hers. "See, we are flesh and blood, Seraph."

"You are . . . ?" said Carnelian, still feeling the fading warmth of her touch.

"We are the Quenthas."

"Both of you?"

"I am Right-Quentha," said the living-eyed sybling. She slipped an arm around her sister's shoulders and smiled. "And this is Left-Quentha, my better half."

Left-Quentha gently worked her torso free of her sister's arm. "Will the Seraph allow himself to be prepared?"

Carnelian managed a nod.

The syblings walked round their middle leg to turn to face the chest. They knelt. Their outer arms pushed back its lid while the inner ones began fishing inside. Carnelian gaped as all four arms began taking objects out, laying them in a crescent on the floor. Their movements reminded him of a spider walking. They stood up and turned. Right-Quentha had a smile on her lips. "Would the Seraph be so kind as to stand here?"

Obediently, Carnelian moved to the spot her golden hand suggested. She produced a copper mask green with verdigris and carefully placed it on her face. One of her sister's hands helped her tie it on. As all their arms rose up to remove his mask, Carnelian was relieved to see the copper mask had no eyeslits. He looked from one to the other as they cleaned him. It would have been difficult to believe they were anything other than two girls standing close together, except that their arms moved with such a confounding coordination.

"Are there many . . . people like you, here?" He blushed again.

Left-Quentha jerked her hand back from his cheek as if she had felt its burning. "Does the Seraph mean Ichorians?"

Her sister's copper mask turned to her. "I think he means syblings."

The other frowned. "You must not speak about the Seraph as if he were not here."

"I was asking about syblings," Carnelian said quickly to make it clear he had taken no offense.

Left-Quentha unstoppered a jar that exhaled sickly myrrh. Carnelian groaned. "Do we have to use that?"

"The Law demands it, Seraph."

Carnelian submitted and they began painting him with the gum.

"We form four cohorts, Seraph," said Right-Quentha.

"Of attendants?"

"Of blood guards, Seraph. We also are Ichorians," said Left-Quentha, touching the silver collar at her neck.

Carnelian looked at their delicate melded body showing the first sweet swellings of womanhood. "But . . . you are women, and . . . and . . ."

"And one of us is blind, Seraph?" said Right-Quentha, as they bent together to pick fans up from a cloth they had laid out on the floor.

"Well, yes," he said, grimacing at his clumsiness.

They wafted his skin with the fans.

"I might have given up my flesh eyes at birth, Seraph," said Left-Quentha, "and have always been in darkness, but ears and skin are their own sight."

"Besides, Seraph," said Right-Quentha, "we share much more than just our body. I have access to many of my sister's sensations and she to mine."

When Carnelian's skin was dry, they carefully held his mask over his face while at the same time tying it on. Right-Quentha removed her copper mask and then they began to dress him in undergarments of pale padded silk that Carnelian recognized as similar to the ones his father had been wearing when he visited.

"But why is it necessary? The blinding, I mean?"

"Mortal eyes would be blasted if they looked on the face of They," said Left-Quentha. She clinked her stone eyes with her nail. "These can behold Them unblinking." Her face was proud.

"Then you are handmaidens to the Gods?"

"Mostly to Their sons."

"Nephron and Molochite?"

Right-Quentha smiled warmly. "Most recently, to the Jade Lord Nephron."

"But also Molochite?"

The sisters became expressionless. "He also was our master," said Left-Quentha, smoothing the leggings over his thigh.

"We prefer the Lord Nephron," said her sister.

Left-Quentha swung round. "Hush! You will ruin us."

"Nonsense! This Seraph is son to the Regent who supports our Lord."

Left-Quentha turned her face away from her sister as if her stone eyes were searching the silk on his leg for wrinkles.

Carnelian grinned behind his mask. He liked these syblings. "And what of their mother, the Empress?"

The girls' faces froze together. His hand made a fist. He congratulated himself on his subtlety. They moved away to the chest and came back holding either end of an elaborate belt from which dangled bony hooks and loops. There was a hardness in their faces that did not invite any more of his questions. They asked him to raise his arms, and when he did they wrapped the belt round his waist, let it slip down to his hips and secured it.

"Does the Seraph find that comfortable?" asked Left-Quentha.

Carnelian looked down at his body, puzzled. He ran his finger round inside the belt. "I suppose so."

They brought straps and rods of brass and attached these to his belt. They returned to the chest and each pulled out a wooden contraption with many straps and hollows and an unhuman articulation. The girls carried these and, kneeling, placed them carefully on end, a little apart, on the floor in front of him. Carnelian watched their long fingers making adjustments.

"If the Seraph would please climb onto the ranga?"

Carnelian could see no shoes.

Left-Quentha pointed at the contraptions. "The court ranga, Seraph."

Carnelian stepped forward and lifted his foot. Two of their hands fed his toes into a gap halfway up the shoe. The smooth, comfortable hollow swallowed his foot. Then the girls rose and braced his arms to allow him to step up. His other foot was guided into the hollow in the second shoe. Putting his weight onto it he found that he was standing, well balanced. The syblings knelt below him and began clicking levers, tightening ivory screws. At first there was slack in the hollows but soon they were a snug fit.

"I feel ridiculous."

Left-Quentha's stone eyes looked up at him. "If the Seraph would please try walking."

Right-Quentha gave him a wink. Carnelian laughed surprising her sister. He lifted a leg, expecting the shoe to be heavy, but it was so light his knee came up too fast and he overbalanced. The syblings managed to catch him and prop him back up. He took another more careful step. The shoe put down first a ridge of toes then a heel as it settled to the ground. Soon he was walking comfortably around the chamber. He stopped and beamed down at them. "What next?"

"Would the Seraph please kneel."

Carnelian looked at Right-Quentha. She nodded. Gingerly, he bent his knees. The shoes folded in half and for a moment he felt he was falling, but they locked, leaving him kneeling, his shins supported in long ivory grooves. He tried to straighten his knees and found the shoes slid him back to standing.

Carnelian turned to the syblings. "Why . . . ?"

Left-Quentha looked startled. "Surely, Seraph—"

Her sister turned to her. "He has been away in exile all his life. How do you expect him to—"

"Sister!" Left-Quentha stared, appalled. Her sister's hand flew to her mouth.

"No harm done," said Carnelian and he held up his fingers in a smiling sign.

Still frowning, Left-Quentha turned to him. "Kneeling on the ranga allows the Seraph to make the robe support its own weight."

"What robe?"

Right-Quentha gave him a sheepish grin. "We shall have it brought in, Seraph."

The syblings walked to the doors and drew them open.

At first Carnelian thought it was a Master who was coming glittering in to fill the chamber, but then he saw the figure had no head and that several sybling pairs, half hidden in its skirts, were carrying it. As the suit came into the light it seemed to ignite. It was a column of brocade densely woven from gold in which a tall and narrow panel running from neck to floor was a window into a heavenly realm. A verdant garden blossomed, each leaf a cut peridot or emerald. Roses petaled with spinel rubies. Orchids, opals. Creatures ran among the foliage, the mottle of their hides, blemished bloodstone. Sapphire rivers foamed diamond spray. Jade trees filtered the light from iolitic skies. Rainbows formed ladders up to a storm among black coral and moonstone clouds in which fire topaz lightning flashed. As the robe came closer he put his hand out to touch the miraculous mosaic.

"But this looks like Earth and Sky, the heraldry of the Masks."

"The Regent petitioned the House to have his son adorned thus," said Right-Quentha.

"The robe has been adjusted for the lower ranga the Seraph is entitled to," said her sister.

Carnelian wondered if the heraldry was a disguise but he thought it better to say nothing. He watched the suit begin to spin slowly round until his fingertips were grazing metallic threads. He was surprised they did not make the sound of a harp. The suit opened to reveal its internal reinforcing frame of tiny bones.

"Please, Seraph, would you walk into the robe and then kneel," said Left-Quentha.

Carnelian did so. They closed its hinged ivory collar around his throat.

He fumbled blindly at the frame.

"The bones of birds and the smaller saurians, for lightness," said Right-Quentha, who must have seen his fingers move. She coaxed his arms down into the sleeves. He felt the robe closing behind him.

"With care, would the Seraph please slowly stand to try lifting the burden of the robe?"

Carnelian tried to straighten his knees and at first met so much resistance he could not. More adjustments were made and at last he found he could stand, supporting the robe.

He knelt again and they began to build a crown upon his head. First a diadem of misty jade from which fell tresses of beaded tourmalines. Over this they set a helmet of jewel-ribbed leather that flared behind his neck like the hood of a cobra. Above this they placed a final coronet that spread a jeweled halo behind his head, upon whose summit sat side by side a face of jade and one of obsidian.

They produced two Great-Rings. "My own?" he asked, surprised.

"Come from the Three Gates," they answered and urged him to rise again.

He lifted the robe, took a few tentative steps and was amazed when the whole mass moved with him. The syblings scurried around below, clearing obstacles from his path. Before Carnelian left, Right-Quentha bullied her sister into setting up a mirror, angling it so that the Seraph might see how he had been transformed into a towering, glimmering apparition.

*　　　*　　　*

The syblings formed a ring at whose center Carnelian paced slowly along the curving corridor, pumping the hinges of his knees open and closed in slow rhythm. His breathing roared inside his mask. The court robe swung languidly. He felt mountainously tall. A precipice of gold fell away toward the floor, casting glimmers on the faces of the syblings.

The corridor opened into a blaze of light. Carnelian narrowed his eyes and walked into the glare. When he tried to turn his head, the neck flares of his crown resisted him. He discovered it was easier to move his whole frame round in the direction he wished to look. He saw a sky of flame, pulsing in time to the Gods' heartbeat. Against this, the syblings seemed to be put together from charred sticks. It took Carnelian a while to realize that he stood before a mosaic of amber rising to such heights it made the window appear narrow.

"Is that the sun?" he gasped.

"Does the Seraph refer to the door?" asked Right-Quentha.

"The door? What door?" He followed her eyes and saw to the right of the window, smoldering in its lurid glow, a door in whose gold the sun's rayed eye was wrought.

"No, what I meant to ask was whether it is the living sun that is shining through that window?"

"It lends the amber its fire, Seraph."

Carnelian began a nod but stopped when he imagined his crowns toppling from his head. He carefully turned his back on the light. "Which way?"

Both Quenthas pointed. "Down the nave, Seraph."

The incandescence flooding over his shoulders could not reach the end of that cavernous space. Distantly, a dim mossy column rose like the rotted trunk of some immense tree. It was from this that the beating of the God Emperor's heart seemed to be coming. Its pulsing drew him. The syblings followed in a cordon round him. There was something flickering in the corner of his eye. He peered sidelong through his the slits of his mask. It was one of the lictors, his armor set alight by the window. Carnelian had forgotten them. He watched the uneasy glance the man cast over the syblings.

He himself was surprised how quickly he had accepted their strangeness. He looked around him. One pair were barely joined. Another pair were melted so close they had only two legs between them and but a single, wizened arm squeezing out from where their shoulders joined. Every pair seemed to have two living eyes and two of stone. Their bronze armor looked as if it had been cast directly onto their flesh: the left half baroqued with spiral inlays, the right smoothly imitating the contours of the skin beneath. Several dragged green and black tessellated cloaks. As his eyes fell on one of their halberds, they widened behind his mask. Its black blade could only be iron. He looked and saw that all their weapons were made of iron. It was a display of fabulous wealth.

This discovery made Carnelian hungry for more wonder. As the light from the window waned, he found he could see better. The Quenthas walked in front with a fluid three-legged gait, arms about each other's shoulders. A breeze laced with strange perfumes was blowing. Away ahead, the gold spindle of a Master was moving amidst a retinue of guardsmen. Carnelian felt more than heard a strange flapping like birds in a dream. He peered into the gloomy stillness of the colonnades that flanked them on either side. More columns marched off as far as he could see. The slow continuous beating of immense wings was unnerving him. He searched above the colonnades where the carved stone rose sheer. When his head was angled back he saw the furtive movement of shadowy banners wafting like unbrailed sails.

His crowns wearied his neck and forced his head down. They were entering an even wider cavern where the Gods' heartbeat was putting tremors in the air and floor. What had appeared to be the trunk of some vast tree was a curving wall of green rusted bronze almost filling the center of the cavern and ringed by a mirror moat. A bridge crossed over to a gate in the bronze. For a moment, staring at the dense interweaving of branches, Carnelian was convinced that he was peering into the secret darkness of a forest and remembering the Labyrinth, he shuddered.

He leaned towards the sybling sisters and pointed across

the bridge, whispering, "Is the God Emperor in there?"

Right-Quentha smiled up at him. "Only Their heart."

"Within lies the Chamber of the Three Lands, Seraph," her sister added, "where the Seraphim cast their votes in divine election."

Carnelian turned to look back toward where the window was glowing its tall oblong flame. "And this vast hall?" he whispered, his eyes catching in the languid movements of the banners high above.

"The Encampment of the Seraphim."

Right-Quentha reached up to take his hand and the sisters led him along the edge of the mirror moat. They passed two more bridges that crossed to gates in the bronze wall. Opposite a third, a crowd of guardsmen spread. All were turned to an opening in the outer wall of the cavern into which climbed a flight of steps that might have been the foothills of a mountain. Carnelian gazed up over the heads of the guardsmen. By their color, the steps had been hewn directly from the Pillar's heart-stone but these were jammed between two rows of giants, on one side of translucent leaf-green stone, on the other of black glass. All were avatars of the Two Gods, their heads vague in the high shadows. This then was the inspiration for the stair in Jaspar's palace, though in comparison that seemed fit only for servants. A glinting on the slope caught Carnelian's eye. He focused and saw a filament of gold, a Master halfway up the stair.

"You must climb, Seraph," said Left-Quentha.

Carnelian regarded the crowds that lay between him and the first step. Both Quenthas lifted their chins and swept forward. The guardsmen parted, and as Carnelian paced between them they knelt. He saw they were marshaled according to the ciphers on their faces. Each retinue had its uniform: feathered cuirasses, bronze-banded armor and chain mail, breastplates of striped or spotted leathers; he saw spears, tridents, swords curved and straight. A familiar heraldry drew his eyes. Chameleoned faces. He would have gone to them except that he was supposed to be a Lord of the House of the Masks.

He turned to the Quenthas. "My father will be glad to have his own tyadra again."

"Seraph, they cannot mount the Approach," said Right-Quentha.

"Though Seraphim may climb, the seeing must not follow them," said her sister.

Carnelian looked round, counting the different kinds of guardsmen. "So many Houses, so many Ruling Lords." He looked uneasily up the steps between the glassy colossi. The Master had almost reached the summit. Carnelian regarded his people. He wanted to please them and his father by giving them to each other. "Could they not be blindfolded?"

The syblings looked identically shocked. "Seraph, the Stairs of the Approach lead up to the Thronehall of the Gods Themselves."

He looked over at the grim lictors. "They stay here too?"

The Quenthas nodded and he walked with them to the stair. They showed him the handles that allowed him to pull up the skirts of his robe, and, lifting one of his court ranga onto the first step, he began the climb.

It was a relief to be nearing the summit. His head rose high enough to see a landing aglow with Masters. A few more steps and he was standing on its edge. He paused to regain his breath and his composure. At the feet of the looming avatars, the landing was a bloody swirl of red and purple mosaic upon which dozens of Masters stood in their court robes, their backs to him, motionless gold towers. Beyond them Carnelian was surprised to see rising another slope of steps. On both sides, from the edges of the landing, other narrow stairs ran up between the column legs of the avatars.

Left-Quentha's stone eyes looked at him. "You must discard your pomp, Seraph. The Law of Audience requires it."

"But they . . ." Carnelian stared, seeing that the Masters were all headless. The court robes could have been the discarded moults of angels. He gazed up the next stairway, almost expecting to see ethereal beings floating up them.

A mass of ammonites came weaving their way toward him through the forest of court robes. Soon they were all around him, reflecting him in their eyeless faces of silver, touching him, guiding him. When they found a clearing among the robes he was asked to kneel. He obeyed, sighing with pleasure as the yoking weight of his robe lifted off his shoulders. His head seemed to float free as they removed his crowns. He rolled it to release the tension in his neck. Ammonites carrying screens began to build an enclosure round him. Right-Quentha threw him a smile before the screen wall shut her out.

The ammonites trapped inside with him removed his mask and prised his court robe open. He walked free of the robe. When he climbed down from the ranga, he felt smaller than a child. They stripped his hands of everything save his blood-ring. They put a new robe of unbleached hri-fiber over his padded underclothes. Feeling its coarse weave, he could hardly believe they had meant to dress him in it. He looked for a samite robe but they were already dismantling the screen wall. He made a sound, nearly crying out, his hands almost over his face, but then he saw that his sybling escort had all donned eyeless masks.

Puzzled by the crudeness of his dress, feeling cold, he allowed the Quenthas to lead him through the maze of empty robes to the next stairway. Framed against the legs of an avatar, another Master attired like he, was climbing with a staff. Carnelian turned to the steps. Free of the encumbrances of court robe and ranga, the ascent was easier. Conversing, two Masters passed him, coming down, each with a staff topped with his House cipher, each wearing a robe of unbleached fiber. They stopped to look at him, their eyes haughty sapphires. The beauty of their faces and limbs was made even brighter in contrast to their coarse-weave. He realized he was staring, gave them a bow and climbed on.

The second landing was a pavement of jade enclosed by throne-daises and standards. Here were gathered more Masters in coarse-weave robes, all Ruling Lords, all facing something Carnelian could not see.

He leaned toward Right-Quentha's copper mask. "Is this the Thronehall?"

The sisters shook their heads. "That lies at the top of the final stair."

He looked and saw where the landing ended a third stair rising up into darkness. On his right, flanked by oily black, winged avatars, steps led up to a flinty door in whose center was a tearful eye. Carnelian stared for a moment, remembering the opium box. The sisters touched his hands and walked toward the Ruling Lords with sure steps, though they were both blind. The Lords did not seem to notice them. Some were in groups talking with their hands, but Carnelian noticed that most seemed focused off beyond the thrones to where another stair ran up between two colossal youths of quartz. At their feet he could see what appeared to be a narrow window opening onto a bright meadow. As Carnelian walked, he kept glancing at the oblong of emerald light and realized that toward the top it held a luminous Chosen face.

"My Lord."

The Master approaching had a familiar woman's voice. He turned. "Vennel!" The Master's eyes were like water welling on a cake of salt. They looked at each other. Vennel tried a little nod of his head. Carnelian said nothing, realizing he had been discovered.

"The Jade Lord has requested that you approach him." Vennel curled a hand back to indicate the emerald figure.

"Tell my Lord that I hasten to a meeting with the Regent."

Vennel gave him a frosty smile. "I had forgotten how little you know. When a Jade Lord makes a request it is really a command."

"Perhaps, Vennel, you have also forgotten that the Regent outranks your Master."

Vennel smiled. "I will be pleased to convey your refusal to the Jade Lord."

Another Master joined them. Jaspar. He looked at Carnel

ian and indicated Vennel. "Is this creature bothering you, my Lord?"

Vennel moved forward. "The Jade Lord—"

"Has asked me to correct yet another of your mistakes."

Vennel's face seemed brittle enough to shatter.

"You might as well return to your place beneath his feet." Jaspar used a sign of dismissal whose shape was close to that used for servants.

Vennel hesitated, then struggled to free himself from his frozen stance. They watched him walk off with ungainly steps.

"That one has been reduced to his rightful size." Jaspar gave one of his cold smiles. "You have seen your father, cousin?"

Carnelian made a nod, hearing in his mind the word *patricide!*

"I trust that he has fully recovered from the little unpleasantness on the road."

Carnelian jerked another nod.

"One has put it about that you were summoned to court by the Regent."

"My Lord is kind but my father has himself taken this matter up with the Wise."

Jaspar cleared the subject away with a sweep of his hand. "The Jade Lord Molochite wishes to meet you."

"Well, I do not wish to meet him."

Jaspar's eyebrows lifted. "He is not one to be slighted casually, Carnelian. Nothing raises him more than the whim to wreak revenge."

"I do not fear him."

Jaspar shrugged. "Why give him one more reason to hate your father?"

Carnelian frowned. Jaspar flourished his hand to offer Carnelian the lead. He took it, walking through the Ruling Lords, ignoring their stares, his eyes fixed on Molochite who was framed between two staves held by his entourage of syblings. Carnelian stopped as the Jade Lord pulled himself up on the staves, and only then realized the Lord had been kneeling. As his green flame came burning toward Carnelian, the Great bowed out of his way. Carnelian waited, clearing his face of expression, his view filling with Molochite's wall of faceted emerald. His eye was level with the Jade Lord's waist.

"Why, cousin, will you not let us see your eyes?"

Carnelian looked up fiercely, refusing to be appalled by the Jade Lord's height, but when he saw the white face he forgot himself and gaped. Gazing down at him was the most beautiful being he had ever seen. Molochite's eyes were spring. The smile on his lips was summer. Carnelian felt the light going out as Molochite turned away, replacing the radiance of his face with the smolder of his green-jeweled crowns.

"Imago, you spoke truth, he has the beauty of the Masks. Our blood breeds true however it is tainted." Molochite's eyes turned their depths back on Carnelian who felt he was looking into the Yden. "Son of Azurea, you are welcome to our court."

Carnelian bowed to free his eyes. "My Lord." He tried to find a shred of composure, then looked up.

"Would you then like to stay with us a while?" Molochite swept an exquisite hand round loaded with four Great-Rings. "However worthy, these Lords weary us with the endless business of the election." His smile was a window letting sunlight into a dark chamber.

Carnelian struggled to unhook his eyes from the glorious face. "My . . . my Lord is very kind, but I must go . . . to see my father."

The window closed. "Well, run along then. We must not keep the Regent waiting, must we?"

The emerald angel moved away leaving Carnelian in confusion.

Halfway up the third stair, Carnelian began to frown. He could not believe what he was seeing coming into sight.

"A gate . . . a skymetal gate."

"The Iron Door, Seraph," said Left-Quentha.

"Inconceivable . . . riches." He was breathing heavily.

Right-Quentha fumbled a hand out to steady him. "The Seraph should rest." He was touched by the concern in her voice.

"You seem to be right," Carnelian said, squeezing her hand. Her sister's stone eyes looked at his hand as if she could feel its touch.

"It must be the sky sickness still diminishing my strength."

While he caught his breath, he turned to look back down the steps. The Great were there like pieces of torn parchment. Molochite was a narrow prism of emerald in their midst. At that distance Carnelian found it hard to understand the power the Jade Lord had exerted over him.

He resumed the climb, his eyes fixed on the Iron Door. He stroked his blood-ring. He knew that iron hailed from the sky in nuggets, but surely so much iron must have fallen as a mountain.

As he came up over the brow of the stair he glimpsed Masters standing with their staves and as he surveyed them he found himself looking into Aurum's face. The old Master stared at Carnelian as if he were watching him rise from a tomb. He pointed the horned-ring finial of his staff at Carnelian. "What are you doing here?"

Carnelian lost his speech. He had forgotten the compulsion of those misty blue eyes. Aurum repeated his question. Carnelian found his tongue. "My father, I have come to see my father."

"Do you know this boy, Aurum?" one of the other Masters demanded. All the cold blues and grays of their eyes settled on Carnelian. Aurum's stare had moved to the syblings spilling up round Carnelian from the stair.

Aurum impaled him with his eyes. "Does your father know you are here?"

Carnelian grew angry. He had had enough of being treated like a child. "Are you blind, my Lord? Does it seem likely I would have such an escort if the Regent himself had not summoned me?"

Aurum flinched and looked from the corner of his eye at the other Masters, who were showing a certain amusement at his discomfiture.

"You will have to wait your turn, my Lord," said a voice Carnelian recognized as belonging to Cumulus. "All here seek audience with the Regent."

"If it please the Seraphs," said Left-Quentha, "the Regent commanded us to bring Suth Carnelian to him without delay."

The Masters looked shocked. Aurum was the first to move aside, a smile carved on his marble face. Reluctantly, the others opened a way through to the Iron Door. Carnelian ignored Aurum's eyes and the statements of outrage that the other Masters made as he walked between them.

The door was like a frozen wall of smoke. He dared to reach out, to touch its iron. It was icy cold. He brought back his fingers and smelled bloody rust. Left-Quentha lifted one of her tattooed arms, struck the door and knelt. All the syblings began kneeling round him, bowing their heads. Carnelian's robe pulled taut across his chest and flapped behind him as the Iron Door breathed open.

GODS' TEARS

These are the four substances of a god:

Flesh that is earth,

Ichor that is fire,

Seed that is rain,

Spirit that is the breathing sky.

But there is a fifth substance, tears,

And that is a memory of the first sea.

—FROM THE *ILKAYA*, PART

OF THE HOLY SCRIPTURES

OF THE CHOSEN

Carnelian stared at the two faces set on a single neck, Master's faces, joined so that when one spoke its jaw dragged down the corner of the other's mouth. One face regarded him with gray eyes and seemed to be trying to determine what manner of creature Carnelian might be; the other had black diamonds for eyes. Eyebrows on the face that had spoken rose expectantly as the other face frowned.

Carnelian cleared his throat, unable to stop staring. "Lord, Carnelian . . . Suth Carnelian."

"I see," said the blind face.

"If the Lord Carnelian would follow us," said the frowning face. The creatures lifted their right hand, beckoning, and Carnelian noticed the two blood-rings, one above the other. As they turned away he saw their double-lobed head. He watched them walk off toward a jewel fire, a window blazing far away in the gloom.

"Seraph," said Left-Quentha as she and her sister rose from their knees. "You must follow the Seraphic Hanuses."

Carnelian started a bow, remembered their blindness, reached out to touch both their shoulders and thanked them. The sisters inclined their heads together. Left-Quentha smiled as they bowed. Two coughs made him turn to see the Masters, the Hanuses, waiting for him, both faces now frowning. Carnelian went toward them and they led the way.

The hall was a black tunnel gouged through the rock to the sky. It was so vast that he could see nothing of the walls or ceiling but only syblings standing in faraway rows on either side, three and four legs astride, holding halberds and billhooks, crusted in black armor, tracking him with stone eyes.

As he drew nearer the window, its hues erupted visions in his mind. Light through new leaves. Cobalt blue. The red of splattered blood. The topaz of an eagle's iris. The whole, a rainbow, first shattered, then reassembled to show the creation. The Turtle's rending, its shell torn apart to form earth and sky, its eyes the sun and moon, drops of its blood, the stars. The Twins stood in the blood rain, among the creatures They had shivered into being with Their ecstasy at the first rainmusic. The heart of the design showed the raising of the Sacred Wall, the flooding of Osrakum and, in culmination, the making of the Chosen. Carnelian marveled. It was as if the world's jewels had been fused into a single lens through which was pouring the light of every sky.

The Hanuses bowed, revealing the dark center of the win-

dow: a black throne set upon a pyramid. Eight figures were
ranged below, Sapients, narrow posts squeezed narrower still
by the colors coruscating round them. Above, framed by the
throne pyramid, a bar of gold was set on end, a Lord in a
court robe seemingly crucified between two staves held upright by the syblings crouching at his feet. The arms detached
themselves. White hands framed the sign, *Wait*. The sign had
a flavor of his father's hand speech.

As the Hanuses walked past Carnelian, their right face
gave him a predatory look.

His father was speaking. ". . . when the collations are complete, Rain."

As he drew closer, Carnelian began to hear the mutterings
of homunculi. Although their masters had their backs to him,
Carnelian could see they were unmasked. A morbid curiosity
made him creep round until he could see their faces. White
leather, pleated tight to a mean, lipless mouth. They had neither ears nor nose, only a nostriled hole. Jet almonds gleamed
for eyes. The foreheads were a fan of creases as if the skin
had been upholstered tight to the nose hole rim. Between
their eyes, the horned-ring of divinity had been branded deep.
All eight stood in robes of moonless night, each apparently
in the act of strangling a child with a silver face.

Carnelian became aware again of his father's voice. ". . .
are correct, Gates, it is better that we should wake the huimur."

The homunculi whispered, the quiver of their lips hidden
by their masks. Each held before it a staff, like a silver tree
upon which flowered the cipher of its master's Domain.

"If my Lords would please leave me a while. I have need
of rest," his father said. "Grand Sapients Gates, Cities and
Tribute, I would ask that you keep yourselves ready for my
summons. We must complete the arrangements for admitting
the tributaries into Osrakum."

The muttering continued a little longer and then, eerily,
stopped. Carnelian became convinced the Grand Sapients
were surveying him with the black malice of their eyes. Their
hands unwound from the necks of their homunculi. They put

on their cloven gloves, their tearful masks. They took back their staves, then bowed. Each Sapient took his homunculus by the hand and, in a column, slowly, they came drifting toward Carnelian. He was trapped, staring up into the mirror of their leader's face as he came on relentlessly, pulling his homunculus like a child. Its unslitted silver mask made the creature as eyeless as its master. The blind leading the blind, thought Carnelian. Just in time he leapt out of their way and watched the beaded slopes of the Sapients gliding past and disappearing one by one into the darkness.

A clatter whisked him round. He cried out and ran to where his father had fallen on the steps. The whole gleaming length of him, struggling like a fish, his elbows digging back, rasping their brocades, trying to find a grip. Carnelian pushed through the blind syblings, causing the staves they carried to waver erratically. They made noises of panic that he could hear spreading down the hall.

Carnelian ignored everything but his father. He grabbed him, enduring the snagging on his hands and arms, and managed to wrestle him into sitting. He made sure his father was steady before he himself stood up, smeared the blood from his palms down his hri-fiber robe, then pushed in to sit some steps higher, reaching over his father's crowns to free him of his mask.

His father's eyes rolled red and confused in their sockets. His yellow lips opened and closed. Carnelian gaped, appalled, not knowing what to do. "Are you hurt, Father?"

His father's eyes anchored themselves upon his face. "My son." His hand clawed up to Carnelian's shoulder and pulled him close. "Reassure them," his father said almost in his ear. A strange odor staled his breath.

Carnelian became aware of the commotion the syblings were making. "Celestial, Celestial . . ." they were saying, evidently distressed.

Carnelian stood to face them. "Calm yourselves. The Regent has merely fallen."

"Is he hurt?" It was the Hanuses. The syblings opened their ranks to let them through.

"I think he slipped upon the steps."

"We should help him rise," they said.

Carnelian looked from one face to the other. "I think it better that he rest awhile, my Lords."

The right face narrowed its eyes. "As you wish." The creature turned and began to herd the syblings away.

Carnelian turned back to his father, who lifted a hand. The effort was too great. It shook down, and jammed as the crusted volume of its golden sleeve caught. Carnelian lunged forward to free the sleeve from the angle of the step, and taking his father's hand, he sat down beside him stroking it. He saw how prominent the sapphire cords of its veins had become. The limp fingers made him search his father's face in fear. He was relieved to see him blinking. Carnelian dropped his gaze, not wanting to stare. He felt the need to say something. "Why do the dragons need awakening?"

His father tore his hand free and looked malevolently out from under his brows. "Do not call them that," he hissed. "You are not a barbarian."

Carnelian's heart stopped. Suddenly, he did not recognize the vast broken creature hunching there. The colors of the creation window beat on him like a migraine. The black tunnel of the Thronehall was contracting. The syblings ambling away looked like colorless crabs in a cave.

Seeing his son shrinking back from him, Suth found the strength to lift a hand and put it on his head. "Forgive me. I am so weary."

Carnelian rewarded him with a watery smile.

"The huimur of my Ichorian Legion . . . of the Pomegranate and the Lily . . . they must be made ready for the Rebirth." He went back to staring, then with a visible effort came alive again. "The Wise feed them a drug . . . it makes them sleep . . . while they dream we cheat time, preserve them . . . they live long beyond the years of their kind."

"Is this the kind of drug the Wise have given you, Father?"

No, No, his father signed with a fluttering hand, and quickly, "Time is everything. Soon the legates will be recalled, leaving the gates open in the Ringwall."

Carnelian could see that his father did not want to discuss his condition and was just glad that he had become recognizably himself. ". . . so that the barbarians might plunder the Commonwealth."

"It is essential," his father said, brightening, as if a cloud shadow were leaving him.

"The sun already burns the Guarded Land. If the God Emperor is not reborn, the Rains will not come and the Commonwealth will perish with the old year. The tributaries are massing outside our gates with the flesh tithe and the thousands of wagons carrying the coined taxes from the cities. When the time is right, we will bring them into holy Osrakum. The tributaries must all be there, in the Plain of Thrones, when the Rains arrive."

"When will that be?" said Carnelian, wanting to feed his father's resurrection.

"The Wise will soon know."

"What sorcery do they use to reveal the very intentions of the sky?"

"It is a sorcery of sorts. Daily they gather reports from all their watch towers. In a chamber far from here they receive the flashes of light that have come from the furthest edges of the Commonwealth. They collate the reports and compare the results with their almanacs. Eventually, by this procedure, their collective mind determines the day upon which the storm clouds will dash their water against this mountain. On that day the world will be reborn."

Carnelian looked up as if his eyes might pierce the shadow and massing rock to behold the distant sky.

"The Rebirth is in itself a mighty labor to arrange," his father said. "But combined with Apotheosis . . . ?" He raised his hands. Carnelian thought he could see light filtering through their parchment but at least they were steady. "Soon the Chosen will gather here for the sacred election. Their coming cannot be sullied by the tributaries, and yet they too must be there." His father inclined his massively crowned head. "There is so little time."

Carnelian frowned. "How can you be so sure there will be

need for an election before the coming of the Rains?"

"The Wise are sure." His father motioned. "Make them bring the staves."

Carnelian understood his father's meaning. He maneuvered the syblings to prop their staves in front of his father. He saw that these were really standards. One carried the wheelmap of the Commonwealth he had seen many times in his father's books: a black disc within a red within a green, the whole jeweled roundel surmounted by the horned-ring of divinity. The other staff bore the jade and obsidian faces of the Gods, each crowned with the horned-ring.

His father groaned as he tried to push himself up and failed. Carnelian leaned in to shoulder one of his father's arms. He hoisted it until his father had grasped one of the staves and then did the same for the other hand. Holding on to him he rocked him back up onto his ranga. His father suddenly stood as tall as Molochite. As he came down the steps holding on to the staves, Carnelian saw the dent in the woven metals of his father's court robe. Once he had reached the floor, he tentatively let go of the staves and took a few steps without their help. He told the syblings to stay where they were and wait for him.

"Come, Carnelian, lend me your strength."

Carnelian gave his father his shoulder to lean on. The warm, heavy pressure filled Carnelian with a love for his father that stung his eyes. Suth pointed out the way he wished to go, and they set off.

"Are you, as Regent, responsible for all this?" asked Carnelian, ignoring his father's weight.

"For this purpose, the Regent is, in everything but name, God Emperor."

"Then who now is He-who-goes-before? Who speaks for the Clave? Aurum?"

The shaking of his father's crowned head vibrated them both. He opened his hand to reveal the red eye of the Pomegranate Ring.

"Surely then, Father, you direct two of the Three Powers?"

"That is so."

"There must be those who object to this concentration of might?"

He felt his father's mirth trembling down his arm. "Indeed there are."

"She of whom we must not speak?"

"She most of all. The God Emperor made me Regent and while They live I am secure."

"And then . . . ?"

"The Regency will pass to her until a candidate is elected."

"Still, she will be safely locked away in her forbidden house."

"Not so. She will be let out, brought here to wield the power of the Masks."

"Will that not endanger us?"

He felt the shaking again. "Why should it?"

"Why then did you set your lictors upon my door?"

"They cannot enter here. I had no other use for them."

"And the escort of syblings, today?"

"You are a Lord of the Great, Carnelian, and my son. I would not have you appear before the Ruling Lords without proper state."

"There is no danger, then?"

"Not now."

"Then, my Lord, your worry is at an end." Carnelian glanced off toward the Iron Door. "Out there . . ." He stopped. The faces of the Hanuses were both gazing down the length of the hall at them.

"Go on."

Carnelian screwed his head round to look up at his father. "I saw some of our people . . . and the Jade Lord Molochite. He spoke to me."

"Did he? What about?"

"Nothing . . . he saw my mother in my face."

"She is there, in your face, in your eyes."

"He is the most beautiful being I have ever beheld."

"Even in a House that breeds so much beauty, Molochite is an emerald among jades."

"He was amiable enough."

"Is that not what you once said about Jaspar?"

Carnelian thought about this. "Where is the other Jade Lord?"

"Nephron? With Aurum to espouse his cause, he has no need to show himself. Only Molochite is forced to bend his pride to canvas for his own votes."

"His mother cannot help?"

"She suffers the full purdah. Although I suspect that even if she were free, she would not stoop to going out among the Great. It must gall her that she has no one in her party whose blood the Ruling Lords respect enough to deal with. It is necessity that has made her resort to sending her own son to negotiate for the block votes."

"Of course," Carnelian said, thinking aloud. Into a ballot, a Ruling Lord could cast all the rings in his House save for those worn by adult males. This was another reason why they had come up to court alone. Their block votes would play the major part in the election.

Carnelian looked up and saw that they had reached a door. It was barred by huge billhooks, each held by the four hands of the sybling pairs on either side. The burden of his father's weight grew lighter as he straightened up. Carnelian let him go reluctantly. They took some steps towards the syblings. The billhooks clinked as they uncrossed.

Carnelian stopped. "My Lord." He waited for his father to look down at him. "Did you know that there are many Lords waiting outside your door?"

His father gave a nod.

Carnelian looked at the syblings and saw that they were either blind or wearing eyeless masks. *Aurum is among them*, he signed.

Let him wait, his father responded.

He was angry seeing me here.

So, he is always angry.

I was rude to him.

His father made a dismissive wave and beckoned Carnelian to follow him through the door. The hall beyond was walled with opals so that as they moved through it, they were followed by iridescing waves. The floor was a mosaic of different-hued pearls. Feather rugs changed colors like flitting hummingbirds. The furniture was all spired ebony and jade.

As they passed another sybling-guarded door, Carnelian asked, "Is the Lord Hanus really of the Chosen?"

"The Lords Hanus. They are two beings, and yes, they are Chosen."

"But they are syblings."

"The Wise teach that the Chosen are all conceived as twins. The rarity of twin births they put down to fratricidal conflict in the womb. They use this to explain our predatory spirit and even the love yearnings that we sometimes feel for one another."

"These syblings are then the natural offspring of the Chosen?"

"Of the God Emperor, Their sons and Their Lesser Chosen concubines."

"Is that because the Twin Essence is so hot in imperial blood?"

"Perhaps, though I suspect the drugs the Wise feed their mothers might make some contribution."

Carnelian considered this. "Still, they are two in one, just like the Gods."

"Their joining is imperfect, demonstrating all the ways in which a man can be wedded to his reflection in a mirror. Unlike the Twins they are not complementary beings. Even when they are born entirely unjoined, they are merely a reflection of each other."

They reached a door and passed into another chamber that was mosaiced with clouds of amethyst. His father stopped him there. He turned to him and stooped to hold Carnelian's face in his hands, then kissed him on the forehead. "Did you think your father had forgotten your birthday?"

"I had forgotten it myself," Carnelian said in surprise. "Is it already the thirty-third day of Jalod?"

Suth nodded.

They had left the island in the last few days of the ninth

month and here they were at the end of the eleventh. Perhaps seventy days in all. Those seventy days seemed a memory of years.

His father smiled at him. "You are fifteen, a ripe old age." He straightened up, looking away off into his memory, regaining for a moment something of his familiar beauty. "I have never told you before that the day of your birth was also the day when the last God Emperor died. Birth during the broken mirror days of an imperial interregnum has momentous astrological implications. The first such day has particular significance. The Wise prophesied that fateful consequences accrued to your birth." His eyes focused back on his son. "At least your birthday has come before another such interregnum." He frowned. "What are those stains upon your supplication robe?"

Carnelian looked and saw the blood streaks. He looked up at his father and showed him the grazes on his palms. His father grimaced, glancing down his own gold brocades, and made a sign of apology.

"There is no pain, Father."

Suth jerked a nod. "Come, let us hurry. I cannot afford to be long away from my responsibilities."

"Where are we going?"

His father's sad face managed a smile. "You shall see soon enough, my son."

The echoing apartments grew colder and gloomier. Their wall mosaics became dark shifting nightmares. Everywhere there were doors and more doors, each guarded by its complement of syblings.

"Is it safe, my Lord, to wander thus unmasked?" Carnelian asked his father.

"Here there are no seeing eyes but ours," Suth replied.

Carnelian longed to reach up and grasp his father's hand, but he was no longer a child.

At last they came to a door beside which a Sapient stood

among a brood of homunculi whose silver faces could have been snatched from dead children.

As Carnelian and his father came closer, one of the homunculi moved into the Sapient's cloven embrace.

"Who comes to the door of the Dreamchamber?" it said, eerily, a dead child speaking.

"The Regent," said Suth.

The Sapient reached out and tweaked the necks of the homunculi one by one. Carnelian recoiled as they crept forward feeling for his father with their hands. He watched them pull the crowns one by one from his head, then peel him free of his court robe. He stepped out of it, pale, narrow. When he climbed down from his ranga he became once more mortal. He turned and offered his hand. Carnelian could not read the strange, sad expression on his father's face but took the hand gladly.

The Sapient turned and with his fist stroked the lintel of the door. It rang with a sound like a cymbal and after some moments began to open.

Myrrh misted the chamber. Ferns frothed up from the floor, curling, pushing up a giant, sleeping. Sagging down from the ceiling was another huge figure, like a man hanging face down in a hammock of spider's silk. Apple-green jade formed the circular floor that sloped up to the sleeping giant. Sapients squatted around the walls, their bleached skin straining tight, their jet eyes staring, their lipless mouths valving open and closed from which a dirge was oozing, a grating, grumbling chant that rose and fell as wordless as a gale. Somewhere a bell was being struck with a rhythm slower than Carnelian's breathing.

He followed his father toward the giant and saw that it was formed of the same jade as the floor. His father released his hand. He felt the ceiling pressing down ominously and gazed up at its black turmoil. Close up, it seemed a giant stuck to the ceiling with thick tar who gradually, under his weight, was dragging the whole sticky mass down.

Busy with this obsession, Carnelian did not at first register the feeling against his side. Then he gave in to its nagging, its brushing against his leg. There was someone prostrate on the floor. For a moment he thought it one of the Wise who had slipped by him as quietly as a shadow, but then saw it was his father. The sight of him lying there caused a shiver to run down Carnelian's back. He dared to look up at the jade giant even as he felt the chilling realization seep into his head.

It was his father's grip on his coarse-weave robe that pulled him down to the floor and then a while later back onto his feet. Together they crept forward and began to climb the sloping jade. Carnelian's heart was louder than the chanting. As his line of sight rose higher he saw that the jade giant was a kind of bed and that lying on it was a man, or something with a man's shape, whose face was mirror-black obsidian.

"Deus," said his father, his head bowed. "I have brought my son at Your bidding."

Carnelian gaped at the Gods. Horror floated on the chanting of the Sapients. He saw one of them standing behind the giant's head that was a pillow for They. The Sapient was leaning forward so that his fingers were touching the Gods' throat. Carnelian saw the thin yellow arm laid out along the giant's arm. Another Sapient, kneeling, had his cloven hands pressing on a vein running down the yellow arm as if he were preparing to play it like a flute. Yet another of the Wise was holding the wrist, and also striking the heart-stone bell.

"Even now, child, they use Us as an instrument to probe the sky for its Heart of Thunder."

The voice rumbled from nowhere. Carnelian's eyes searched for its source.

"Later, when We shall dream, they assure Us that they will be able to chart its movement up from the sea."

The plural pronouns registered. Carnelian stared at the Mask's obsidian lips and waited for it to speak again.

"The other one, child, waits for a sign of Our dissolution. The moment of Our death will form a crucial part of their astrological calculations," the Mask said. "Release Us, Immortality."

The Grand Sapient's noseless face frowned as he relinquished hold of the Gods' throat.

"Child, are you as mute as they?" the Gods said.

Carnelian swallowed several times, moistened his lips, breathed his voice to life. "Perhaps . . . Deus . . . perhaps You will cheat them."

The glassy face began a chuckle that came apart into coughing. "We shall soon be occupying Our jade suit. A new column in the Labyrinth gapes ready to receive Us into the second waking." There was more labored breathing. "Sardian, the Mask impedes Our breathing."

Carnelian watched his father's long fingers reach for the Gods' face.

Suth glanced first at Immortality and then at his son. *Close your eyes*, he signed.

Carnelian obeyed him, squeezing them closed, preparing himself for the blast of light as the Gods' face was revealed.

Carnelian heard the tempo of the bell increase a little. The tone of the Sapients' chanting changed as they reacted to its vibrations. He jumped when a hand touched his face.

"Kiss Their hand as a token of love," whispered his father in his ear. "As much as They are Lords of Earth and Sky, They are your uncle."

Suth's hand guided his face. Smelling myrrh, Carnelian anticipated the scald of the Gods' skin. He cried out as something snagged and tore his lip; his eyes opened. He saw the narrow hand, the sharp ring, the blood pooling on the yellowed skin. His eyes snapped closed.

"Kiss," whispered his father insistently.

Carnelian pushed his lips forward to kiss the slick of blood he had spilled on the Gods' palm. He drew back, licking the saltiness from his lips, muttering, "Forgive, forgive . . ."

"It is only a little blood, child. What is a little blood between an uncle and his nephew," said They.

The bell was ringing very fast in Carnelian's ears.

"Come, nephew, let Us kiss your hand. We will not meet again."

Still tasting salt, Carnelian stretched out his hand, trembling for the touch of the Gods' radiant face. Cold fingers grasped his and drew his hand further. Carnelian flinched as the lips touched his hand. His thumb strayed onto other skin. Wetness. A thread of it under his thumb. Touching the tear track made him numb with terror. He withdrew his hand and stood back as his father and the Gods exchanged a muttering of words. He struggled to make sense of the sounds.

". . . you must save my true son," the Gods were saying.

Carnelian tasted his thumb. It seemed miraculous that Their tears should be as salty as mortal blood.

THE MOON-EYED DOOR

Without wings

He soared in the sky

But when he fell

He fell like a star

> —FROM THE MYTH
> "THE TALE OF THE
> THREE GODS"

His father had Carnelian move openly with his new household deep into the Sunhold. From the nave of the Encampment of the Seraphim, they passed into a guardroom between two bastions that lay to the right of the sun-eyed door. They traversed passages lined with loopholes and several double sets of portcullises before they reached his new chamber with its ambered walls.

It was there that he sat hunched, squinting at his thumb,

hardly believing that it could be whole. He was outraged that its whiteness bore not the least stain to show where the divine tears had touched it. He remembered the gaunt yellow hands of the Gods: he had expected starlight diffusing through a membrane of adamantine. He remembered the weary voice from behind the Mask: he had expected it to shake the Dreamchamber as thunder shook the vaulting sky. The air had not thrilled with the ozone tang of lightning, but had been wreathed heavy with funereal myrrh. Inside the withered body, the divine blood had at best fluttered, a candle flame in a pavilion of stained parchment.

Was that a scratching at the door?

"Enter," he said, had to repeat the word more loudly.

The door trembled open to show a man holding a box. The familiarity of the chameleon on his face made Carnelian smile. The face froze, making its tattoo look like a gecko startled on a wall.

"Well, come in then," said Carnelian. He had sent for one of his new household to clean him. It was a pretext. In truth, what he desired was to build a bridge over which he might cross to his new people. He needed friends.

The man was standing there as if the floor between them were strewn with blades.

"Come on, I don't bite. Are you intending to clean me from the other side of the room?" He intended this as a joke, but it only made the man more frightened. The wretch shuffled nearer, his shoulders curved, and, with maddening care, made sure to place the box soundlessly on a rug.

Carnelian stood up.

The man flinched.

Carnelian tried to smooth the frown from his face by smiling.

The man crouched and began to unpack the box onto the rug. Carnelian watched his short brown fingers with increasing irritation. He forced himself to wait. The man stood up with a pad, and looked Carnelian over as if he were some tower wall he had to whitewash.

"How are the lads?" Carnelian said.

The man stared at him.

Carnelian nodded, sculling his hand, trying to scoop some words out of the man's mouth.

"Master?" the man said, as yellow as a corpse.

"The tyadra, the guardsmen, you know, the people outside with the weapons?"

"They are . . . doing their job, Master."

Carnelian was afraid that if he pushed for more the man might vomit. "I see," he said, and tried to stand perfectly still as the pad crossed the distance between them. It settled on his skin as lightly as a butterfly. Carnelian fought a grimace as the pad tickled lightly over his skin. He was unable to suppress the laughter for long. He struck himself repeatedly in the chest to quell it as the man stepped back with a look of horror.

Carnelian pointed at him. "Gods' fiery blood, man, what . . . *are* you doing?"

The man's knees struck the ground with a crack that made Carnelian wince, and then he hunched forward in a clumsy prostration. Carnelian stared, shaking his head. "Get out. Come on, leave me. I'll clean myself."

The man began to shuffle backward.

"Stand up, and get out," said Carnelian, not managing to keep the anger from his voice.

He watched the man leave, the door close, then sat heavily on the bed still staring at the door, shaking his head. He wanted to cry or smash furniture. They would all have to change. "I couldn't bear it if they didn't," he muttered. He imagined himself in Coomb Suth surrounded by fawning slaves. The chameleons on their faces seemed counterfeit. He gave himself a reassuring nod. His own people would bring change. He felt himself lighting up as he thought of them. Ebeny, Keal, Brin. "Even Grane," he sighed. At that moment he would have given anything for one of his scoldings. Tain. Tain would soon be through the quarantine. The light dimmed. The first image of his brother that had come into his mind was of a vague face with blood running down it like lank hair.

"No," he cried, stood up and walked about. There was no point in thinking about that yet. Time would come soon enough to count the cost. For now, he would allow himself to believe that his people would bring something of the warmth of the Hold back into his life.

The arrival of the Quenthas was announced to give him time to put his mask on. The syblings walked into the chamber and knelt. He strode over to them, pulled them up, easily managing to span both their shoulders. "I cannot tell you how happy I am to see you." He stood back to look at them. Left-Quentha had her head bowed but Right-Quentha was grinning at him all bright-eyed. He gave them both a bow. "What brings my Ladies to this humble prison?"

Left-Quentha raised her stone eyes. "Prison, Seraph?"

"The Regent has sent us to amuse you," her sister said.

"He did?" Carnelian frowned.

Right-Quentha shook her head. "Oh, not like that, Seraph." Then she smiled coyly. "Though . . . ?"

Her sister turned to her, frowning, then back to him. "We have some skill with instruments, we sing and play a fair game of Three."

Carnelian noticed the sword hilts appearing above their shoulders. He pointed at them. "And can protect me?"

"That also, Seraph," they said together.

"I will allow you to stay on one condition."

Left-Quentha angled her head back, a little anxious. "And what is that, Seraph?"

"That you call me Carnelian."

For several days the sybling sisters strove to amuse him. They produced an instrument that had many strings, and frets and a gilded gourd at either end, and squatted with it on the floor. Their outer legs would have been called crossed if they had not been so far apart. Their middle leg folded under them. The instrument sat across their thighs. Two arms were under the neck, two over the strings. Their long fingers plucked and strummed all at once, coaxing cascades of sound, arpeggios, complex percussion. Sometimes they interwove their voices into the melodies, singing harmoniously, one voice sometimes chasing, sometimes shadowing the other. They also played reed pipes. As one blew a continuous drone, the other would waft over it rich, heart-rending melodies.

Carnelian became addicted to a strange game they called Three. It was played on a circular board with a black center within two concentric bands of red and green. The three sets of pieces each took one of the colors. The sisters always chose the jade and the obsidian sets, smiling conspiratorially, saying the colors of the House of the Masks were naturally theirs. He acquiesced. After all, the red pieces were made of his name stone. He assumed they would ally against him, but instead he was ignored as they fought each other to destruction. He became tired of winning. Losing his temper, he insisted that they fight the game fairly and try to defeat him. They shrugged, grinned, and in the games that followed overwhelmed him. He rejected their offer that they should begin the game with fewer pieces. Slowly, he began to learn strategy from his defeats. The games became tortuous, subtle, merciless wars in which his red pieces began more and more to triumph.

Often, as they played, he would try to talk to the Quenthas about the election, the candidates, their factions. They met his questions with elegant deflections. They grew positively sullen if he ever strayed close to mentioning Ykoriana.

"No more music," said Carnelian, adding quickly, "though you play like the rain."

Left-Quentha reached for the Three board.

"Not that either." He stood up, stretched, groaned. "My body aches from inactivity." He frowned, locked his hands together and tried to tug them apart. "I know," he said brightly, looking at the syblings. Right-Quentha was wearing her green copper mask. At his insistence, she and Carnelian took turns at being masked. "You girls can give me a tour of these Halls of Thunder."

They both made evasive gestures with their hands. "We would have to put you in your court robe, Carnelian," said Left-Quentha. She glanced at it, an intruder gleaming in the corner.

"You might well come across other Seraphs," said Right-Quentha.

"And then again, it might not be wise that we three should be seen together," said her sister.

"It certainly would look strange," said Right-Quentha.

"Strange," echoed her sister.

Carnelian sank cross-legged to the floor. He propped his face up with his arm. "You confirm what I have suspected. My father has sent you to keep me imprisoned here, in the Sunhold."

The sybling sisters looked blindly at each other. "There is nothing to stop us giving you a tour of the Sunhold."

Carnelian brightened, leapt up, grabbed his mask. "Come on then."

They sallied out into the passage where they gathered up an escort of his tyadra. In the chamber set around with doors, the Quenthas pointed out the portcullises that they told him led off down long passageways to various gates giving into the Encampment. Between these were other doors which they said led into barracks. At his insistence they opened one and lighting a lantern they all went in.

"Soon this warren will be filled with a cohort of Red Ichorians," said Left-Quentha and both sisters frowned.

"Apart from the side on which they are tattooed, how do they differ from the Sinistrals?" he asked them.

"In every way, Carnelian," Right-Quentha replied indignantly. "They belong to the Great and we to the House of the Masks. We live in different worlds."

"Worlds . . . ?"

Left-Quentha fixed him with her stony gaze. "We can no more be in the same world than my sister and I can be on the same side of the mirror as our reflection."

Right-Quentha chuckled. "Ours is a dark, looking-glass world." She made them both dance a little.

"The Halls of Thunder and the Labyrinth," added her sister, forcing their three feet firmly to the floor.

"Theirs is the world of the sun, across the Skymere."

"And yet, on occasion, you permit them to come here into your world?" Carnelian said.

They both looked at him. "It is a concession the House of the Masks makes to the Great," Left-Quentha began.

"And only during such dark days as these," her sister continued.

"And even then they have to lock themselves in here, within this fortress, from fear of us," said the other, fiercely.

Carnelian smiled indulgently. They had taken on a poise that he could see was making an impression on the nervous faces of his guardsmen.

With a grin, Right-Quentha became a girl again. "And would our dear like to see the chambers that will be his father's?"

Carnelian nodded and they led him back into the chamber of doors and across it to a golden mirror that showed the sybling sisters to themselves. This was a door that brought them into an atrium where the sisters said the tyadra of He-who-goes-before could defend their Lord. The guardsmen peered into the quarters leading off it that their fellows would occupy. Another gold mirror door was opened and Carnelian's eyes widened as he looked in. He followed the syblings into the chamber. The thick gold of the walls was molded into wheels, rayed eyes and huge ruby-seeded pomegranates. The floor was fossiled stone-wood ribbed and lozenged with carnelian. Gorgeous apartments opened off on either side, every wall and door and ceiling a piece of jewelry.

When Carnelian had marveled at everything, the Quenthas announced that it was time to see the Hall of the Sun in Splendor. They returned to the chamber of doors whose marbles seemed to Carnelian suddenly drab. A double portcullis was opened, allowing them to walk down a tunnel into a vast columned hall. This too was paneled entirely with gold. Carnelian saw they had entered it through a side door. At the far end of the hall, with their sun-eye, were the huge bolted doors that opened into the nave. Opposite them, behind a dais at the other end, the wall held a glowing mosaic of rosy gems that Right-Quentha called the Window of the Dawn.

"On that dais, your father will kneel to give audience to the Seraphim."

Across from where they stood, down the long side of the hall, ran a series of tall and narrow amber windows. Carnelian walked toward one. He touched its mosaic of molten gold. The window formed the image of a man in flames; only the eyes of watery gray diamond suggested this might be a representation of a Master. Carnelian walked along the line of windows. In the terrible burning beauty of their faces, their eyes were such cruel winter.

Carnelian's foot stubbed against something on the floor. He turned to look down at it. "A trapdoor?"

"It is nothing, Seraph," said Left-Quentha.

"Surely it must lead somewhere?"

"A flight of steps down to ancient halls." Right-Quentha made a gesture to take in their surroundings. "Precursors to these. Ruined now a thousand years."

Carnelian imagined these ancient dusty wonders. "Could we not go and see them?"

"They are decayed, Seraph," said Left-Quentha.

"Lightless," her sister added.

"Filthy."

Carnelian made a smiling sign with his hand. "Just a peek?"

Right-Quentha could not help a smile.

"We must not," her sister whispered to her.

"Just a peek," said Right-Quentha. "Where would the harm be in that?"

Left-Quentha turned away, blinking her stone eyes, pursing her tattooed lips. Her sister forced her to bend when she herself bent down to lift a handle in the trapdoor. Left-Quentha gave in. They crouched, took the handle with all four hands and pulled. The cover stone grated open, spilling light down the steps.

"The Seraph should send his guardsmen ahead," said Left-Quentha.

Carnelian turned to his men and saw with what terror they were peering down into the depths.

"What's the matter with you lot?" asked Carnelian in Vulgate.

They began to kneel. He focused on one and grabbed his shoulder to stop him. "Well?"

"Master . . . it's said this whole mountain's hollow." The man stared, slack-eyed.

"And so?"

"The Gods and the Masters walk the higher levels but in the lower they keep . . . you keep . . ." The man's voice tailed off, then he whispered, ". . . monsters."

Carnelian threw his head back and laughed. He turned to the syblings. "It seems they are afraid."

Left-Quentha regarded them imperiously with her stone eyes. "Slaves are always afraid. Soon enough we will have them trotting down those steps." The syblings rose, both stone eyes and living fixed menacingly on the guardsmen.

Carnelian lifted his hands. "There is no point in forcing them. I do not want to be deafened by the chattering of their teeth. We will go alone."

The syblings frowned. "As the Seraph commands." They walked round Carnelian, scattering his guardsmen. Each sister reached behind her shoulder and drew a sword.

"I will go first," said Carnelian.

"We will go first, Seraph," they said together, their sword blades catching the light.

Carnelian could see that they would brook no argument and stepped aside to let them lead the descent into the darkness.

*   *   *

Left-Quentha carried the lantern and Carnelian followed behind, peering between their shoulders at the steps revealed by its jiggling beam. Although the steps were smoothly cut, the walls were roughly hewn. The stair wound from side to side, and several times passed places where a porthole fed in a ray of daylight.

At last they reached the bottom and the Quenthas moved out into black echoing space. They lifted the lantern and spread its light across the floor to find the further wall.

"Behold the first Hall of the Sun in Splendor. No He-who-goes-before has stood here for a thousand years," they whispered together.

Carnelian turned. The stair was a ragged rupture in the corner. "Where is the gold?" he whispered.

The wall grew brighter as the Quenthas came up to him. Left-Quentha slid her hand over its stone and found something. Her sister caught Carnelian's hand and drew it to replace Left-Quentha's. He could feel a hole deep enough to stick his finger in.

"The plates that were attached here were carried up there." Left-Quentha pointed at the ceiling.

They wandered off across the chamber. The floor was moldy with dust. The Quenthas showed him the dais and the blocked-up hole where the ancient jeweled Window of the Dawn had been. Carnelian walked down between the grim pillars to the door. Through its gaping maw was utter darkness. He called the syblings to his side. The three of them stood together in the door mouth casting light out into a nave. Although this was on a smaller scale than the one above, it still ran off further than their light could reach.

Carnelian looked round him. "Was this, then, the original sun-eyed door?"

In answer the Quenthas stood on tiptoe and reached up to touch half a hinge of twisted dull bronze.

"Please, let us go a little further," Carnelian whispered.

The sisters turned to each other as if they were having a silent conference. Brandishing their swords, they took some steps into the nave. Carved columns ran off on either side.

All together, they walked on, and however far they went their lantern found more columns.

At last their light showed a narrowing end to the nave, another doorway, its gates long ago torn from its jaws. Beyond, more darkness spread without apparent limit. They crept into this.

"The ancient Chamber of the Three Lands," whispered Left-Quentha.

"See," her sister hissed as she tapped the floor with her foot.

Carnelian leaned over but could see nothing but an age-pitted floor. He shook his head.

"Walk with us, Carnelian," said Left-Quentha.

However lightly they put down their feet, their footsteps produced echoes. The syblings were feeling their way with the lantern beam.

"There," muttered Right-Quentha and they rushed forward, keeping the beam anchored to a spot on the floor. They crouched and he joined them. He could see that the floor had two different tones divided by a black line. "You see?" Right-Quentha tapped the nearest zone, "Green," and then the further zone, "Red."

Carnelian stood up, whistling his breath out. They cast the light round for him to see the curve. "A wheelmap," he hissed. They both nodded. They took him to the center of the design where there was a third zone, a black disc inside which was inscribed a turtle. On the wheelmap, they now stood at the center of the Commonwealth, in Osrakum. The syblings slipped the lantern shutter round to produce a narrower, brighter beam. They played it about to show him the faraway curve of the outer wall, and stopped at a gap. "The House of the Masks' door." Round to another. "The Gods' door." Round one more time. The beam sparked on an oblong of ice. Carnelian narrowed his eyes. Not ice, silver. As he made to walk toward it, they touched his arm.

He looked at their stiff spider silhouette. "I only want to see it close up." He sensed their annoyance but he went anyway and they followed, afraid to lose him in the darkness.

As he approached he saw it was a door of silver in the center of which stared a huge crying eye. "A moon-eyed door," he muttered and remembered the other he had seen on the Approach.

"It is here as it has always been. The entrance to the labyrinthine chambers of the Wise," the syblings whispered.

"Can we just take a look?"

The Quenthas became a statue. "It is forbidden, Seraph."

He considered wheedling but decided he had pushed them far enough already. "The other doorways?"

"Lead to the Forbidden House." They had gone cold on him.

"Shall we go back?" he said gently.

"That would be advisable, Seraph."

As they walked away, Carnelian snatched a regretful look back at the moon-eyed door, already a fading glimmer in the night.

When they returned to his chamber, they played a game of Three, but Carnelian's attention wandered. After two more disastrous games, he told the syblings that he was tired and wished to retire early to bed.

He lay in the darkness, his mind's eye bewitched by a ghostly image of the moon-eyed door. It haunted his dreams so that when he awoke he was still tired. For breakfast, the Quenthas brought him peaches, fluffy hri bread and an aromatic paste made from honey and the tongues of hummingbirds. They played their pipes, they sang. He brooded.

It was afternoon when one of his tyadra came knocking at the door. The Quenthas answered it. There was muttering and then the syblings both turned to him and said, "The Red Ichorians are come."

They dressed him and together they went out to meet the new arrivals in the chamber of doors beyond the double portcullis that guarded the access to his chambers.

A number of Ichorians were there waiting for him. As they removed their scarlet-feathered helmets and tucked them under their arms, Carnelian could see by the number of rank rings on their gold collars that they were all officers. One of them came forward, and as he knelt before Carnelian the others knelt behind him. The Ichorian touched the two zero rings and three bars on his collar.

"Master, I am the commander of the third grand-cohort of the Pomegranates. I have come at the bidding of our father with a detachment of its third cohort to garrison this hold."

Carnelian could see the fruit jeweled into his armor. "I too am here by order of He-who-goes-before."

"We've been instructed to protect you, Master."

Carnelian watched the commander narrow his eyes at the Quenthas and said quickly, "They too are here at his command."

The commander and his officers were all shaking their heads in disagreement.

The Quenthas looked at Carnelian. "Seraph, if they are here we cannot be."

Carnelian could see it would be pointless arguing; the sisters had taken on their warrior stance. The Ichorians were squaring their shoulders in response.

"We shall leave now, Seraph," the sisters said. They both smiled. "We would not want to have to hurt them."

"You must not forget your reed pipes," he said.

Left-Quentha frowned a little but her sister allowed herself the slightest curving smile. Carnelian followed them back to his chamber and closed the door behind him, watching them pick up their instruments.

"I will see you again," he stated.

They both looked up, expressionless. Right-Quentha shook her head. "Perhaps, Carnelian," her sister said.

Carnelian had a stone in his throat. "I'm sick to my stomach of losing friends," he said, in Vulgate. His words put sad expressions on the sisters' faces. "Right-Quentha, please close your eyes. I am going to unmask."

The sybling reached for the mask hanging around her waist.

"No, just close your eyes."

They obeyed him. He went over to them, held the shoulders of each in turn and kissed her. They left him, Left-Quentha wearing a murderous scowl that scattered the Suth guardsmen, her sister dabbing at her eyes.

For a while, Carnelian moped, missing the sisters. He went out to see the Ichorians, but the chamber of doors was empty. Only one pair of portcullises was lifted. He went to look through into the curving passage beyond. He remembered the guardhouse that was at its end, the same one he had passed through when he had first come into the Sunhold. Its gates were near the sun-eyed door. Remembering that golden door put him in mind of its silver sister in the shadow world somewhere beneath his feet.

What did he have to say to the Ichorians anyway? He returned to his chamber. He made patterns with the pieces of Three. He wrapped himself in blankets and went out onto the balcony.

He watched indigo soak into the sky until the color had grown so deep it was freckled with stars. His eyes became mirrors. The image of the moon-eyed door seemed to be hanging over the crater. He shivered. It imbued him with a longing that reminded him of the opium box.

He made his decision and came back into the warmth. He had his men bring him a sword, a lantern and a tinder-box. He made sure the lantern was well filled with oil and that its shutter opened and closed smoothly, and spent time honing the bronze blade of the sword.

He rose with the moon, clothed himself, then left the chamber quietly. He silenced the question of the three guardsmen outside with an imperious hand and told them that they should not worry about him. If anyone came to see him, he commanded them to say that their Master was sleeping and refused to be disturbed. The eyes of one fell on the hilt of the sword. They could all see the lantern.

He left them to their conjectures and crept into the darkness of the chamber of doors. It was silent, with only a trickle of light and conversation coming from the Ichorians in their guardhouse. In front of the first portcullis that led to the Sun in Splendor, Carnelian carefully put down the sword and lantern. He slid the restraints from under the counterweights, braced himself against the bronze grille and, using the strength in his back and legs, lifted it a little. He pushed the sword and lantern under it and slipped through himself. He pushed the portcullis down and then opened and closed the second one in the same way.

The Sun in Splendor was pale with the moon that was a vague red eye peering through the Window of the Dawn. He stole across to the trapdoor. When he ground its cover back, he winced at the noise. He listened for Ichorians but they did not come. He crouched to light the lantern, shuttered it to produce a narrow beam, played this over the steps, then began his descent.

It seemed to take much longer than before to reach the first chamber. He raked the blackness with the light. "This is madness," he hissed, frightening himself with his own echoes. For a moment he considered going back, then steeled himself and made for the gaping doorway.

The timbre of his steps changed as he moved into the vast sepulchral void of the ancient Encampment. He stopped several times along its nave, waited until the echoes fluttered away and listened.

At last he reached the chamber with its moon-eyed door. Only when he was halfway across it did he dare to lift the beam of light. The huge eye flared, irised with white fire. It was cut down the middle. For a silly moment, he thought that his light beam had sliced through it. He chided himself. The door was slightly ajar. He drew closer, close enough at last to touch its cold silver. He reached up to run his hand along the rim of the eye's lower lid to where it overbrimmed to spill tears the size of fists down the door.

He closed the lantern shutter a little more, took a deep breath and threaded its narrowed light into the gap between the leaves. The chamber beyond was crowded with jeweled people and the ghosts of other lights. He snatched his head back, trying to still the betraying hammering of his heart. He waited for footfalls, a challenge. The only sounds were his heart, his breathing. He smothered the lantern in the lurid blood-red of his robe and dared to put his head through again. Perfect silent darkness. He uncovered the lantern to release its light and used it to impale one head. There was another beside it and another, as regular as sentinels. With a jerk, he realized a light was moving on the other side of the chamber. He lifted the lantern and it lifted too.

"Only reflection," he breathed.

He squeezed through the door, trying to keep the light fixed on one of the heads, and reassured himself that its apparent movement came from his own wobbling. A bench, friezed with silver spirals, was the foundation for the glittering stumps he had thought were people. He stepped closer. Each stump was composed of three orbs set one above the other. He reached out to touch the glittering surface. It was cold and lizard-skinned. He peered closer. Beads. Bead necklaces wound onto wooden reels. He reached up to touch the spindle that came up through their centers. Three reels impaled like pumpkins on a spear. He moved to the next three. Then there was an empty spindle followed by two more reel stacks. He walked round the bench and saw there was a second row of spindles behind the first. He played light over the bench. On its side were four bronze loops from which hung short lengths of rope. He scooped one up, ran its beads through his hand.

He stood back, opened the lantern a little more, then held it up to look around the chamber. Twenty benches spaced out in a grid. The walls were the burnished heart-stone of the Pillar itself. He walked toward an archway. To one side hung a tapestry of glass, which he found was made of beaded ropes fixed to a row of loops set into the wall. He fingered one of the ropes, wondering what its function might be.

He shone light through the archway, then crept into the next chamber. This was very much like the first. It too had twenty benches with their spindles and reels, its near-mirror walls, its bead-rope tapestries. He wandered through another archway, another chamber, more arches, more chambers, each with its complement of benches. He wanted to find something that might make sense of it all.

He turned in the middle of a chamber. An archway opened in the center of each wall. He could not remember which one he had come through. He closed his eyes, turning, trying to feel for the direction he had been facing. He opened his eyes and walked back to an archway. The next chamber looked much like all the others. So did the next, and the next. He grimaced. "Fool, fool, fool." He shook himself. Why had he not taken some precaution? Now he was utterly lost.

Carnelian began his search for the moon-eyed door. Only the pulsing of the blood in his ears and his scuffling steps gave time shape. His path threaded the chambers as the cords did their beads. Neither made sense to him.

Huge whiteness reared up in front of him. His lantern clattered to the ground. He cried out and swatted at something with his sword.

"Gods' blood!" exploded a voice.

A blow made him drop the sword with a clatter. Falling to a crouch nursing his wrist, Carnelian stretched for the lantern that was angling its beam up to the ceiling. He felt the lantern being snatched away. Its beam sliced the air like a spear, then steadied to come down to run him through.

"Stay where you are," the voice hissed.

Carnelian put an arm up as the light climbed to his face.

"What have we here?" said the voice as Carnelian tried to back away.

The lantern clunked down onto a bench and opened to expose its burning heart. Carnelian blinked and saw the shape standing behind it. Long, pale Master feet stepped into sight. Carnelian looked up. The face reflecting the light made his eyes hurt. He narrowed them and saw a Chosen face, its beauty only marred by a birthmark on the forehead that

ooked like the impression of a kiss. The eyes were diamond
nails pinning the face to the darkness.

"Are you going to get up?" the face said, offering Carnelian a hand.

It was a boy not even his age. Carnelian slapped the hand
away. "I can stand without your help."

The boy's eyes moved over him as if he were reading
glyphs inscribed over Carnelian's body. It made him feel
uncomfortable.

"You surprised me," said the boy, now scanning Carnelian's face.

"You were the one lurking in the blackness like an owl.
What by the burning blood were you doing?"

The boy's nostrils flared. "Reading."

Carnelian stared into his eyes, fascinated. There was something familiar about this boy. For some reason, Carnelian
became embarrassed.

"In the dark?" he said, affecting a derisive snort.

"In the dark."

Carnelian frowned, wondering if the boy was making fun
of him. The boy's eyes moved elsewhere, allowing Carnelian's shoulders to lose some of their tension.

The boy stooped to pick up Carnelian's sword. He angled
the blade, weighed it in his hand, looked up. "Hardly a
princely weapon, my Lord."

Carnelian blushed.

"What did you intend to do with it?"

Carnelian felt silly. "Protection."

The boy raised his eyebrows. "From?"

"How would I know?" Carnelian said loudly.

The boy turned the sword round and gave its hilt into
Carnelian's hand. Carnelian laid it down along the edge of
the bench. "What were you reading?" he asked, to say something.

"This." The boy held up a necklace that sagged off into
the gloom. He pulled, making more of it appear. He offered
it to Carnelian who took it in both hands. The beads felt like
teeth.

"Beaded rope?"

"Beadcord."

Carnelian held it closer. Stone and shell and pink coral, all carved into different shapes. "The colors?"

The boy raised an eyebrow. "In the dark?"

Carnelian grimaced. "The shapes, then?"

The boy nodded. "Run your fingers along it. No. Without looking at it."

Carnelian closed his eyes and rolled a bead round in his fingers. "A little ridge."

"And the next one?"

Carnelian moved his fingers to the next one. "Another ridge."

"Feel again."

"Three ridges," said Carnelian, feeling round the bead.

The boy nodded approvingly. "The first one is 'earth,' the second, 'flower.' "

"Jewel?"

"Exactly."

Carnelian gaped at the beads. "This is a story?"

"Rather a historical treatise."

"Then we are in a library of the blind," said Carnelian, looking round him at the reels on their spindles.

"Of the Wise," corrected the boy.

"Are they here?" Carnelian asked, suddenly alarmed, searching the darkness.

The boy's eyebrows lifted. "Bound to be, somewhere." He waved his hand. "But there are many, many chambers and the Wise are preoccupied at present."

"I shouldn't be here," said Carnelian, lapsing into Vulgate.

"No," the boy said in the same language, with the beginnings of a smile.

"And you?"

The boy looked amused. "I'm as elusive as an owl."

"I should leave."

The boy shrugged, turned round and sat on a chair that was in a niche in the wall. He draped the beadcord over his knee and began counting its beads through his fingers.

"I think I'm lost," said Carnelian.

"Yes, you would be," the boy said without looking up.

Carnelian grew angry. "If it would not incommode you very much, my Lord, I would appreciate it if you were to show me back to the moon-eyed door."

The boy looked up and hooked Carnelian with his eyes. Carnelian withstood their brilliance with some difficulty. "Give me your lantern," the boy said.

Carnelian obeyed. He watched the boy walk off between the benches in a ball of light that was fringed with the glitter of beadcord. He followed him. They passed through seemingly endless numbers of chambers with the boy a black shape always in front of him haloed by the light. At last, they reached a door, its silver scarred with locks.

"Your moon-eyed door," the boy said.

"Thank you," said Carnelian.

The boy gave a nod.

As he was turning away, Carnelian reached up and touched his shoulder. The boy looked at the hand and Carnelian quickly withdrew it, blushing.

"I was wondering . . . ?"

The boy gazed at him.

"Would you consider teaching me to read the beads?"

The boy frowned. He stared down at his hands. They were long-fingered, clever hands. They looked so like marble that Carnelian was startled when a finger moved.

The boy was gazing at him. "Be here at the rising of the sun and forget the sword." He gave Carnelian the lantern, turned and disappeared into the darkness.

As Carnelian came back up into the Sun in Splendor, he felt as if he were returning from the Underworld. He looked back down the steps. The meeting with the boy seemed almost a dream. What had possessed him to arrange to go back and see him? As he made his way back to his chamber, Carnelian realized that he did not even know the boy's name.

BEADCORD

Fingers will read what eyes cannot see

With hands the deaf shall hear

Mutes shall speak with borrowed tongues

When the storm clouds draw near

—A CHOSEN RIDDLE

Before dawn, Carnelian lost hold of the edge of a dream and woke. He rose, cleansed himself, dressed, put on his mask and went out from his chamber. The watch guardsmen looked up at him with weary eyes. He stopped them kneeling with a gesture. They began to shuffle together an escort. He told them he had no need of them. When they sneaked glances at each other, he gave assurances that he would be safe.

He encountered no one on his way to the trapdoor. He lit the steps with his lantern. Removing his mask to see more easily, he made his way down and then along the dark nave. All the way he kept telling himself that this was madness.

The moon-eyed door was closed. He widened the lantern beam and raked the shadows with it looking for the boy. No one was there. As he lowered the lantern its light washed around his feet. The huge eye on the door stared tearfully over his head into the dark chamber.

"Well, that's a relief," he lied, as the disappointment washed over him.

The silver trembled as one of the leaves angled away, slicing the eye in two. Someone came out through the gap. It was the boy. His bright face made the silver of the door appear to be lead. For a moment they gazed at each other. Then, saying nothing, the boy turned and disappeared. Unease blew out of the gap like a draught but still Carnelian followed him.

Through the mazing library Carnelian followed, watching the boy's white feet tread the edge of his lantern light. They stopped between a beadcord bench and a wall where a niche cut back into its stone. Lifting his light, Carnelian saw one of the curious chairs on which the boy had sat the previous day.

The boy took the lantern from Carnelian and indicated that he should sit on the chair. Carnelian sat. He fingered the spike that rose from the end of the left arm of the chair. The boy put the lantern down and turned to face one of the bench spindles. He took hold of its topmost reel, lifted it free and then threaded it down onto the empty spindle next to it. He did the same with the second reel from the original stack. The third he lifted and turned with it in his hands. It could have been a human head wrapped in a jeweled cloth. Hoisting it, the boy impaled it on the chair arm spike.

"What are you doing?" asked Carnelian.

The boy's hands were moving over the beadcord on the reel. "Hush!" He saw Carnelian's frown. "In a web, a single vibration can bring the spider."

"You mean the Wise?" whispered Carnelian.

"Do not look so fearful. I would know if one of them was near."

"I am not fearful," protested Carnelian, glancing over the boy's shoulder to scan for any movement in the chamber.

"Aha," the boy muttered with satisfaction as he found the

end of the beadcord. He pulled at it and the reel turne
smoothly, glittering.

"First, we must teach you the basics. This is the mos
elementary beadcord I could find." His fingers slid alon
from the end until they reached a faceted ring of bronze
"This bead is where the text begins."

Carnelian peered at it.

"No, close your eyes. It is your fingers that must see."

Carnelian held it then closed his eyes.

"What do you feel?" whispered the boy.

"It is angular, regular."

"And?"

Carnelian shrugged.

"Is it not also cold? That shape with coldness will alway
tell you that you are at the beginning.

"This here is the title of the reel."

Carnelian opened his eyes to see the boy running his finge
from the bronze bead along the twenty or so beads to th
end of the cord. The reel rattled as the boy yanked a lon
length of it, hand over hand. He coiled it up in his left, fel
along it with his right.

"Here." He offered Carnelian another bead to feel. "Thi
bead marks the beginning of a section and can be used t
move accurately and rapidly backward and forward along th
cord." The boy pointed down to Carnelian's feet. "You ca
respool the cord with that treadle." Carnelian could see noth
ing, so he felt around with his toes until he found a plate
As he pushed, it gave way and the reel beside him turned
little, sighing some beads through the boy's hands.

"Here, take it." The boy gave the loops of beadcord t
Carnelian who pushed down with his heel then with his toe
and as he did so felt the cord spitting out of his grasp as i
wound onto the reel.

"It is like a spinning wheel," Carnelian whispered, smiling

The boy nodded, all the time watching the reel. Reaching
forward, he closed his hand over Carnelian's, lifting an
dropping it in a smooth rhythm. "Move it up and down s
that it winds back evenly." He examined the reel. "If it i

one untidily, a Sapient would know that someone unau-
orized had been reading it."

The soft warmth of the boy's hand contrasted with a hard-
ess at its edge. As the boy took his hand away, Carnelian
aw the blood-ring. He had thought him too young to have
ne.

"The bones of the beadcord," the boy whispered, once the
ord was again taut and Carnelian had hold of nothing but
s end, "are the syllable beads." He found some examples.
Carnelian tried to memorize their shapes as the boy sounded
em for him. "Any text could be coded just with these, but
erhaps to speed up reading—though I suspect more for se-
recy—many words are represented by a single, special
ead."

"Like glyphs," whispered Carnelian.

"Very much like glyphs. I have chosen this reel because
is composed mostly of syllabic beads. You must learn these
efore you progress on to the more esoteric ones."

"Were you taught the beadcord by the Wise?"

The boy smiled enigmatically. "You think that likely?"

Carnelian shrugged.

"Well, I taught myself."

"They allow this?"

The boy looked up at him with raptor eyes. "They cannot
orbid what they do not know. It is one of the arts the Wise
eep jealously to themselves." He rotated his hand to take in
he surrounding gloom. "I have counted more than six twen-
ies of these chambers. Each has an average of twenty
enches. Each bench can hold two dozen reels on its spin-
les. There is enough beadcord here to weave a garment that
vould clothe Osrakum's crater."

Carnelian touched the reel. "Each of these is a book?"

The boy wavered his hand. "Three or four together can
orm a book. In contrast, a single reel can contain a dozen
eports."

Carnelian tried to imagine it all. "A vast accumulation,"
e sighed.

"The exquisite distillation of millennia of dreaming an analysis."

"And you can read all of it?"

The boy shook his head. "If only I could. Much is hidde from me. This blind reading is a deep art. Some of the bea cord is snake-smooth." He displayed his finger ends. "The ten are like the eyes of fish in a muddy pool. The eight the Wise see further than eagles. I have read a reel claimir that only the blind can see past the bright, false and shiftir mirages of our mortal world into the immortal and immutab truth of the divine. It is said that the Wise do not only se what has been but what is yet to be. As in the glyph th represents them, they look over their left shoulder into propl ecy."

"Are they born blind?"

"No. At first they are like you and me, though of imperfe blood. They rise up from the flesh tithe that the Wise then selves impose upon the impure, marumaga children of th Great. After gelding, the candidates begin their studies the Labyrinth. Those with winged minds soar up into th rarefied regions of the Wisdom. At every height there a those who can climb no further. Failing, they fall. They be come the quaestors, the higher ammonites, the eunuchs the Forbidden House."

"Blinding seems a poor reward for such a struggle. I ha thought it punishment."

"You are not completely wrong. The mutilations were im posed long ago when one of the Wise betrayed his trust. Th imperial Commonwealth has her foundation in their silence

"They are mute?"

"They have only a single sense. Touch."

"Surely they can taste and smell."

The boy shrugged. "It is rumored that they retain a fain capacity to taste bitterness. That aside, they are in our work only by their skin. When they have achieved the highe wisdom that is allowed to those with eyes and ears, they a locked away. Each eye is sliced out like a stone from a peac The red spirals of their hearing are cored from their heac and the fleshy shells shorn off. Caustic inhalations burn away their organ of smell and afterward the useless meat of their nose is discarded. Their tongues are drawn out and harvested like the saffrons of a crocus. Once these mutilations are complete, a Sapient is left only feet and hands as the primary organs of his perception. Remote from seductive sensation, they can be entrusted with the deeper secrets. In the caverns of their cool uncluttered minds they are made capable of measuring the currents of our vast world minutely."

"They have their homunculi," whispered Carnelian, seeking some salve for his pity, his revulsion.

The boy nodded. "For each Sapient, his own, unique homunculus is a bridge to the outer world that if removed leaves him as isolated as a rock in the sea."

Carnelian looked off, understanding. "No treasure chamber could be made more secure."

The boy gazed at him, then snapped his eyes away to look at the beads. "I thought you wanted to learn touch reading."

Carnelian flinched at the harshness in the boy's voice. He took the beads and, slowly, they continued to work through the bead shapes. Concentrate as hard as he might, he still had to go back many times. His fingers became as raw as his mind, but the boy was relentless and Carnelian swallowed his complaints.

At last, the boy moved to the lantern and closed its shutter. For a while Carnelian could still see him standing there, but with each blink, his ghost image dimmed until Carnelian was in perfect darkness.

"Why . . . ?" he whispered.

"Here in the library, darkness is the beginning of true seeing."

Carnelian fumbled on through his lesson, coaxing words from the beads until he began to hear them speaking in his mind as if the beads were calling up through his hollow fingers.

"The lesson is at an end," said the darkness.

Carnelian was in a dream. As his fingers lost hold of the

beads their voices went silent in his mind. "But I have learnt so little," he whispered.

"You can learn more, tomorrow. Wind the cord."

When he pushed the treadle it gave an alarming rattle. Carnelian stopped.

"Why have you stopped?" whispered the dark.

"The noise . . ."

"Our voices and not the treadle are alien here."

Carnelian worked the treadle until he felt the end of the beadcord in his hand. Something brushed his finger and the cord was gone. He heard the reel being replaced on its spindle and then the other two being slipped down over it.

Carnelian felt another's skin touch its warmth to his.

"Take my hand," whispered the boy.

Carnelian closed his fingers over the hand as carefully as if it were a throat. "The lantern . . . ?"

"I have it," whispered the boy, firming the grip.

Carnelian was pulled off the chair. He became a ship being towed through a starless night. At first his steps were tentative, anticipating collision, but after a while they grew confident in the boy's impossible ability to see in blackness. Their footfalls dulled as they passed each archway and swelled again toward the center of each new chamber.

The boy loosed his grip. Carnelian felt adrift, frightened. The lantern flared to life. He hid his eyes until he could bear it. With his free hand, the boy opened the silver door. Carnelian followed him out into the vast circular chamber. The boy held out the lantern and Carnelian took it.

"The same time tomorrow?" Carnelian said quickly, as the boy turned away.

The boy looked back, nodded.

"I am Suth Carnelian," Carnelian said before the boy could turn away again.

The boy gazed into the distance. Carnelian could see his reluctance to give up his name. "I am of the House of the Masks," the boy said at last.

They looked at each other, Carnelian willing him to say his birth name. The boy lowered his eyes. What shame was there in coming from the God Emperor's own House? Unless . . . ? It came to Carnelian then. He realized whence the resemblance that had been nagging him came. He looked at the boy's face and imagined another identical beside it, sybling-joined. The likeness to the Lords Hanus was unmistakable.

"You have a twin?" Carnelian asked, letting the boy know that he knew what he was and did not mind.

The boy looked up. He raised an eyebrow. "I do."

Carnelian gave him a smile. Although the boy was an unjoined sybling, his blood-ring proved that he was Chosen. His behavior suggested that he was ashamed of his low blood-rank. In spite of having been fathered in the House of the Masks, his concubine mother must have badly tainted his blood.

"Can you not guess what my name is, then?" the boy said, both his eyebrows rising.

Carnelian shook his head, frowned. "Should I?"

A slow smile spread over the boy's face. "I am Osidian."

"I am honored to know you, Osidian." Carnelian knew that blood pride should make him keep his distance from the boy but he did not care.

"Tomorrow, then," Osidian said.

"Tomorrow."

The boy went back through the door, and as he closed it behind him he healed the cut in the moon's eye.

The next morning, Osidian was waiting for Carnelian as he had promised. He said nothing as he led Carnelian into the Library of the Wise. The lantern light revealed the rich jewel seams of the beadcord as they moved through the chamber. At last they stopped at a beadcord chair. Again, Osidian urged him to sit down and going off came back with a reel that, in the dark, with his help, Carnelian began to read.

First they reviewed the syllabic beads but quickly moved on to more complex ones. Fluted spheres like coriander seeds. Glossy shapes like beetles. Beads with the texture of cold skin that Carnelian guessed were amber, others he knew were metal by the way they drew warmth from his fingers. Pumice, rough but floatingly light. Wood, waxed and un-waxed. Each was a word, an idea. Fumbling them, Carnelian was reminded of learning his glyphs. Haltingly he whispered the meaning of each bead. Whenever he stopped, Osidian's fingers would take the bead from him, and read it. Some-times, Osidian would run his fingers back along the beadcord to find one they had read earlier and, squeezing it into Car-nelian's fingers, would point out the similarities in shape or texture that reflected a similarity in their meanings. Thus, Carnelian discovered that each bead that represented a crea-ture had a nipple head. That smooth curving often implied liquid; lightness, air; corners, something made by craft. The same shape with different temperatures often determined a spectrum of emotion.

Bead by bead, a story began to unspool in Carnelian's mind. Obsidian-faced, a God Emperor issued forth from Os-rakum, riding in some fabled chariot of iron so huge it was honeycombed with chambers. With towered huimur They had gone southward across the Guarded Land. Every being They saw They slew, being the incarnation of the Black One, the Plague Breathing, the Lord of Death.

"This is a story?" he whispered.

"History," hissed Osidian. "Read on."

The annal continued. Somewhere along the southern edge of the Ringwall, the Gods descended with Their host down to a vast plain teeming with herds. The Chosen host cut a swathe through this crowding flesh until the earth had been stained as red as the Guarded Land. Barbarian villages, rude, enclosed with wicker walls. The Gods' black tide lapped their ditches, igniting the palisades like the dawning sun. Carnelian bit his lip anxious for the next bead, impatient with himself when he could not decipher its meaning. As each squeezed through his fingers, he felt the earth shake, he was as blinded by the huimur flame-pipes as the barbarians. The beads let him look down from the vantage point of a huimur tower and watch the barbarians flee before their fire. Remembering the ants Aurum had torched on the road, Carnelian shuddered. Huts and children trampled by thunder. Their world turned to ash. The Gods swept, unsated, seeking new victims beyond the smoke-clogged horizon.

Osidian brought him other reels. More campaigns. They studied the dates. The days they spoke of were more than a thousand years dead.

"So much carnage," Carnelian said at last. The beads were becoming shapeless, their voices muffled.

"Even barbarians cannot be brought under a yoke by persuasion," said Osidian. "Anciently, they were proud. We broke their will with terror. Once, through fear of the Twin Gods, all the world paid us tribute."

"Of children?" Carnelian asked, bringing his knees up to his chest, hugging them, seeing Ebeny.

"Not just children, but all the fruits of the Three Lands."

"Is this necessary?"

"If beasts are allowed to come into a garden will they not trample it?"

Carnelian forced himself to consider this.

"Do you wish to read more?"

"No. My fingers can no longer hear the beads."

"Perhaps it is best. My blood afflicts me."

"It burns?" asked Carnelian.

"In my bones."

Carnelian worried that he had never felt it.

"Rewind the cord."

Carnelian slipped his feet down to the treadle. There was a rattle and a quivering in the chair and then silence. He waited. He could hear nothing. His eyes were making shapes in the dark.

"Come, I will take you back to the door."

The voice speaking suddenly beside Carnelian made him start. He grew angry. "How do you see in the dark?"

"See?"

"You find your way—"

The darkness chuckled. There was a fumbling. Sudden

light stabbed Carnelian's eyes and made him wince. "You could have warned me."

"Sssh!"

Carnelian saw Osidian's eyes were the purest jade.

Take off your shoes, he signed.

What? Carnelian chopped back.

"If my Lord pleases, his shoes . . ."

Grumbling, Carnelian stooped and took them off.

Osidian urged him off the chair. The light receded as he walked away, backward, still hooking his finger at Carnelian to follow.

Carnelian did so, grinding his teeth, wanting to hit him.

And?

Carnelian opened his hands, not understanding.

Your feet. Do you feel nothing under your feet?

Carnelian became aware the floor was textured. He looked down, crouched. *Bring the light closer*, he signed. As the floor brightened, he saw it was carved. He touched the embossed surfaces. Osidian's white hand strayed across some patterns.

"All of these are paths," he whispered. "You follow them with your feet. North Door, South Door." He stroked one pattern after another. "East Door, West." Still crouching, he rocked himself a little way off and pointed down. Carnelian followed his finger, touched the eye carved into the floor.

"The path to the moon-eyed door."

"Exactly." Osidian stood up. "Will my Lord care to try for himself, this seeing in the dark?"

Carnelian straightened, smiling even as the light went out. He found the eye with his toe. He took a step and after sliding his foot around a bit found another eye. He took another step.

"Like stepping stones," he muttered, finding the measure of the stride that took him smoothly from one eye to the next.

He followed the path, at first certain that he was about to walk into a bench or a wall. After a while he grew more confident and soon was moving comfortably through the darkness.

He seemed to have been walking forever when suddenly he stepped forward and found that there was no eye under his foot. He stopped and Osidian walked into him. Carnelian clutched him to avoid falling. The body under his fingers was like warm stone. He could smell Osidian's skin. "My Lord, forgive me." He stepped back.

"Hide your eyes," Osidian said.

Light flared. Carnelian squinted until his eyes were able to see again. Looking round, he saw they were standing near the silver door. He began putting on his shoes.

"Will you come again?" Osidian asked.

Carnelian looked up at him, nodded.

As he walked back, Carnelian caught a scent coming off his shoulder that he recognized as Osidian's.

Carnelian smiled when he saw Osidian waiting for him. "Will we be able to go together in darkness?" he asked.

Osidian shook his head. He pointed at the floor. "Which path would you follow?"

Carnelian looked. The stone was marked with trails.

"There are paths here leading to various points in the library but none going to the chamber I want to go to."

Carnelian deflated. "Then one must know where the chamber lies in the library maze?"

Osidian lifted his hand in the affirmative. "A labyrinth can be a better defense than the strongest gate. Still, we can go through the darkness like children." He offered Carnelian his hand.

Carnelian looked at it, embarrassed, shook his head. "It would be easier to use the lantern."

Osidian took back his hand and frowned. "As you will." He strode off stiff-shouldered.

Cursing himself, Carnelian followed.

* * *

All that day Carnelian read the annals of God Emperors whose column sepulchres, Osidian told him, were some of the first put up in the Labyrinth. Carnelian came to realize that once long ago the Labyrinth had been only a processional way. He was reading faster and hardly had to ask Osidian for help.

Later, when he had grown weary of the interminable descriptions of conquest, he told the darkness that he wanted to leave. He found Osidian's hands as they fumbled with the lantern and gripped them. "There is no need for light, no need for you to come. I will make my way back to the door myself."

"And tomorrow?" said the darkness.

Carnelian felt as if he were in a dream haunted by the voice in the beads.

"We could try something different tomorrow, if you want."

"Like what?"

"Well, there are chambers filled with the reels of the Law and its commentaries, with the *Ilkaya* and other mystical works. There are technical treatises on just about any topic you could imagine. The records of the flesh tithe, tribute, taxation of the cities, censuses of the barbarian tribes. The *Books of Blood*—"

"Where the blood-taints of the Chosen are kept?"

"Every Chosen who has ever lived."

"The *Books of Blood*, then," whispered Carnelian, and, taking the unlit lantern, he strode off along the path of eyes.

The following day, Osidian was waiting for him. The walk through the library seemed longer than usual. They reached a chamber that smelled of freshly spilled blood. Uneasy, Carnelian lifted his lantern. It was a chamber larger than the others with many benches. All the beadcord he could see was dull and black. The reels were only as thick as his wrist. He took the lantern close to one, ran his fingers over its beads, then smelled them. It was as he had suspected. "Iron."

"These *are* the *Books of Blood*," said Osidian.

Carnelian looked round, trying to calculate the value of such treasure.

"Look here," said Osidian, touching the tip of a spindle.

Carnelian came to look. Carved into its top was the cipher of a Chosen House.

"Your reels will be over there somewhere, with the rest of the Great," Osidian whispered near his ear.

Carnelian walked away in the direction indicated. Spindle by spindle they searched for the chameleon, moving from one bench to the next.

"Here," hissed Osidian.

Carnelian joined him and saw the chameleon carved dancing into the spindle tip above the six stacked reels. *How many people of my House?* he signed.

Osidian shrugged. "Your House is as ancient as the Commonwealth." The beads clinked like chain mail as he ran his fingers down the stack. "The reels are fat. The blood-taint of maybe," he shrugged again, "eight twenties of generations."

Carnelian took hold of the topmost reel. He could feel the beads shifting under his hands. He lifted the reel carefully off the chameleoned spindle. It was as heavy as a stone. Osidian pointed out a chair. Carnelian carried the reel against his chest and impaled it on the chair spike. He was glad when Osidian closed the lantern shutter. For some reason, the rusty blacks of the reels were reminding him of massacres.

The beads soon absorbed him. They were simple to learn. Most of the beadcord was made up of the numbers one to nineteen, with a bead like a berry for zero. It was strange to feel the first name he came to was his own. He ran the cold, rough beads through his fingers again and heard them say his name, *Carnelian.* The beads after that were his blood-taint: zero, zero, one, nineteen, zero, nine, fourteen, sixteen, nine, thirteen, fifteen. The next name along the beadcord was his mother's, Azurea, followed by the first few beads of her blood-taint: zero, zero, zero. He ran the beads through his fingers again. Three zeros. Blood-rank three. Such purity. It made him proud. He read the next numbers almost trying to feel something of his mother in them. Two, one, three, nineteen, nine, sixteen, seventeen, ten. There was nothing there but cold iron. Beyond the separator bead was Suth Sardian, his father, and the numbers: two zeros matching his and then a three, fifteen, nineteen, fifteen again, ten, three, two, ten.

He read on, finding Spinel's blood-taint and the others of his House's second lineage. Next came the third lineage. Then he found his grandfather's name, his grandmother Urquentha's, the parents of Spinel and so on, further and further back in time. His father's father's father. Numbers and strange names rolled through his head as he wound them up from the ancient past.

He released the beadcord, sat back bewildered, awed by the tale of years, feeling he was like the Pillar of Heaven holding up a skyful of ancestors.

"I have had enough," he whispered. He had forgotten Osidian. Convinced suddenly that he was alone, Carnelian felt around. His hand found him.

"I am here, Carnelian. Where else do you think I would be?"

"Looking up your own bloodline."

There was a long silence.

"I know my blood," Osidian said.

"I did not mean—"

"It does not matter," whispered Osidian. "Can you find your own way back?"

"Well, yes . . ."

"Farewell then," said Osidian and with a waft of air was gone.

Later, in his chamber in the Sunhold, Carnelian was wondering for the hundredth time if he would ever see Osidian again. He had replayed those last few words over and over in his mind. Each time he had felt a stabbing in his guts. Why had he so carelessly offended him? His stomach ached as the words circled round in his head like carrion crows.

He went to bed early and ate nothing. Sleep would not

come. When it did, it brought dreams. All night he fumbled blindly over a stony beach seeking the pebble that would whisper to him its answer.

Carnelian awoke feeling tired. Sullenly, he determined he would not go to the moon-eyed door. He told himself that he did not want to. Eventually he had to confess he was reluctant to go in case Osidian should not be there. He turned his anger on himself until fear of never seeing Osidian again made him leap up. He rushed through his dressing, cursing. It was already morning.

He took less care going to the trapdoor than usual. Halfway down the steps he found that he was counting them, swore and stopped, though each footfall was like a bead slipping through his fingers. He thought he had prepared himself for the disappointment but when he reached the moon-eyed door he found its blank gaze withering. Osidian was not in his usual place. That was the end of it. Still, he could not bring himself to turn away. He heard the clink and saw it opening. Osidian walked out and Carnelian lurched a few steps toward him then stopped. "Osidian." Relief thinned his voice.

The boy's eyes were summer sea. He twitched a smile. "What shall it be today, my Lord?"

Carnelian tried to think through the blood pulsing in his head. He ran through what he remembered Osidian had said the day before. "History?" he suggested.

Osidian showed surprise. "I thought you did not like history."

"There is more to history than conquests." He racked his mind for a topic. For some reason he recalled the Masters arguing theology that night on the watchtower roof.

"The beginning."

"The creation?"

"The beginning of the Commonwealth. The Quyans. The Great Death. Does the library contain reels going that far back?"

Osidian's brow creased. "I have never sought such antiquity. What you speak of is more religion than history. Still . . ."

Carnelian grew calm watching Osidian thinking. There was so much he wanted to know about this strange boy but he feared to make even the smallest enquiry.

"There is one place to find out if such a reel exists."

"Let us go there, then."

Osidian made his hand into a barrier sign. "Less haste. We will have to be careful of the Wise. Most of them are busy calculating the Rains' arrival, arranging the Rebirth; that is why we have seen nothing of them. But what you seek lies at the heart of the library, the very center of their web. Many will still be there and they will detect the slightest vibration. We must be as silent as shadows."

Carnelian nodded, his pulse quickening again.

Carnelian crept into the library after Osidian, who was holding the lantern up to light their way. After a few chambers, Carnelian reached out to touch Osidian's shoulder. The boy turned round, raising his eyebrows.

The lantern? Carnelian signed.

Osidian grinned. *Yes, it is one.*

Carnelian made a face at him. *It is very bright.*

Here the only eyes are ours, replied Osidian, constructing complicated signs with his free hand. *The light will help you avoid bumping into anything.*

Carnelian gave a snort and they went on.

He soon lost count of the chambers. They were moving between the benches of another when he almost ran into Osidian who had come to a sudden halt. Carnelian followed the direction of his gaze and saw a Sapient with his pleated waxy noseless face, the black almonds of his eyes alive with malice. He came round the bench toward them. When he was between two benches, he stretched the four fingers of each hand out to either side. The fingertips settled on the benches and tensioned like exquisite traps. The Sapient stood motionless, a spider waiting.

From the corner of his eye, Carnelian caught a tiny white movement. He turned his head slowly, keeping an eye on the Sapient. Osidian, his eyes round, signed with his free hand, *Not a blink. His fingers feel everything.*

The Sapient's hands jumped up from the benches. Carnelian focused fully on the creature as he came treading toward them, long feet sucking to the floor, fingers swimming, sensing currents in the air.

Carnelian looked desperately for an escape. The coldness of the floor was making his feet ache but he dared not move. Sweat was trickling down the gutter of his spine. Some was oozing down his nose. He feared that it might collect in a drop and fall, betraying them. He drew his shoulders back, his head further still, drawing away from the four-fingered hands. The Sapient stopped between two new benches. Again, he deployed his hands then froze. Carnelian looked from the cages of fingers to the black insect eyes. He could smell the Sapient's musty odor.

The hands lifted and Carnelian turned his face away. He suppressed a shudder, anticipating the touch of those moist fingers. He might have fled, save that just then the Sapient turned and swiftly returned to where he had been. Carnelian watched him reach down to a bronze ring and pull at the tail of beadcord hanging from it. The beads slipped through his fingers. Then both his hands rose to lift the topmost reel off the spindle above. This was swiftly transferred to the empty spindle beside it. The hands returned to pluck up the second reel. Cradling this in his arms, the Sapient slid through a door and disappeared.

Carnelian gulped in a breath, another. He found that Osidian was grinning at him. Crookedly, Carnelian grinned back.

Do you want to go on? signed Osidian.

Carnelian's nod was rewarded with a look of approval.

*   *   *

They encountered more Sapients. Mostly they were folded into the niches on spinning-wheel chairs, caressing words from beadcord. Sometimes Osidian would lift the lantern high and pull its hem of light up the dark, brocaded robe to find the leather of a Sapient's face and put a fierce glint in the jet eyes. Each time Carnelian recoiled, distrusting the blindness, certain that the Sapient must feel the light tickling over his flesh. But the Sapient would continue reading undisturbed, looking as if he were busy spinning jeweled thread.

They came at last into a chamber in which their light flashed among tall screens that seemed hung with colored water. Osidian entered boldly. Carnelian was reluctant to follow but did not want to appear afraid. He looked back. The way they had come was utterly black. He shuddered, imagining returning blind through a darkness infested with the Wise.

He caught up with Osidian whose hand was playing through the jeweled shrouds.

He must have heard Carnelian for he turned. *Hold this*, he signed and pushed the lantern onto Carnelian, then continued reading.

Carnelian saw the screens were like huge folding books whose pages were strung with beadcord. As he watched Osidian's fingers stroking across the strings, Carnelian almost expected to hear music. Osidian shook his head and padded away. Carnelian followed him, holding the light of the lantern over them as if he were carrying a parasol. He tapped Osidian on the shoulder.

What is this place? he signed, having to resort to difficult one-handed signs.

The Master Index, signed Osidian.

Carnelian followed him deeper into the bead partition maze of indices. Sometimes through one crystal wall Carnelian would see a Sapient moving past or racing his hands over the surface of an index.

Suddenly, Osidian shot him a grin and made a triumph

gesture. After he had read down a beadcord he signed, *Come,
I know where to go now*.

Carnelian touched the cord he thought Osidian had been
reading. There were words, numbers, but he could make no
sense of them.

He was glad to leave the Chamber of the Master Index,
following Osidian back into the smaller rooms of the library
proper. They had to creep through a fearful region filled with
the Wise. Gradually the chambers became free of them and
Carnelian relaxed enough to risk more solid footfalls. Exhaustion sapped him as he released the tension in his muscles.

Osidian stopped at a doorway. "This should be the place."
He was fingering something to one side. Carnelian played
some light on it. A tapestry of beadcord hung on the wall.
Osidian muttered something and nodded. "The reels are here
as the index said." The chamber appeared to be much the
same as any other. "Put the lantern on a bench and help me
look."

"What are we looking for?"

"I am not sure. The index did not give the names of the
works, only that they were written Pre-Commonwealth."

Carnelian moved to the nearest bench. His fingers found
a bronze ring with its title beadcord. He began to feel his
way down the beads. They were smooth and of no distinctive
shape. He moved to the next cord. It was the same. And the
next. As he held the first bead, he concentrated all his mind
on his fingertips. He took the weight of the cord with his
other hand so that he could lighten his touch on the bead. It
was not smooth. There was the faintest whisper of a ridge,
but he could not hear what it said. He let the cord go. He
looked up and saw Osidian's shadow body away off across
the chamber. He picked up the lantern and went to join him.
Osidian had a beadcord title clenched in his fist.

"What are you doing?" Carnelian whispered.

"Heating the beads."

Carnelian blinked.

"Sometimes, heating them makes them speak. Pah."

"Nothing?"

"Not enough." Osidian reached up to the nearest reel. He found its end, rubbed a few beads between his fingers. He shook his head.

"Perhaps time has worn them smooth," said Carnelian.

"No." He took in the chamber with a sweep of his hand. "It is just that the Wise have made absolutely sure that the beadcord here can only be read by their fingers."

"I see," said Carnelian, disappointed, looking at the reels.

Osidian grinned at him. "I know a thing or two. We shall return." He saw the question on Carnelian's face. "You will find out what I am talking about, but only tomorrow."

"What is it?" whispered Carnelian.

Earlier, when he had found Osidian waiting for him by the moon-eyed door, the boy had given him an enigmatic smile and then led him to the chamber they had been in the day before.

Carnelian looked at the phial Osidian was holding up. It was a helix of quartz with a hinged silver cap. Within its murky worm body he could see a yellow liquid.

Osidian smirked. "It is something the Wise drink. It has . . . let us say, some useful effects."

Carnelian looked at Osidian's green eyes. He did not like the idea of acquiring any habit from the Wise. He wondered at Osidian's mood. Carnelian almost asked him to drink first, but he did not want Osidian to think that he thought it poison.

"How much?"

"A sip will do."

Carnelian flipped open the cap and sniffed it cautiously. Its iodine smell nipped his nose. He looked at Osidian who gave him an encouraging nod.

"Do you think I would try to poison you?"

Carnelian answered him by putting the phial to his lips and letting some of its liquid trickle onto his tongue. Its bitterness forced a grimace. He swallowed quickly, sucked his tongue, then licked his teeth to try to rid his mouth of the taste.

Osidian took the phial from his hand and drank. Carnelian was pleased to see his face scrunch up. "It really is foul," said Osidian, glaring at the phial.

"And now?" whispered Carnelian.

"Now, we wait." Osidian shuttered the lantern. In the darkness, Carnelian felt the bench shudder as Osidian, sitting down, threw his back against it. Carnelian slid down beside him. He tried to make conversation, to ask what they were waiting for, but Osidian answered every question with an irritating, "Wait and see."

The tingling grew as if coming from far away. Carnelian adjusted his position. Against his back the bench seemed to have become the trunk of some vast tree. His back ran up it for a great length. Carnelian found himself wondering if the yellow potion had made him grow into a giant. His legs had stretched so much they must have pushed his feet into the next chamber. He lifted his hand and it swung up like a crane. He fingered the air, half believing that he would find the ceiling of the chamber just above his head.

"Do you feel it?" asked Osidian's breath. Carnelian could feel its wet heat catching in the folds of his ear. He turned his head and was momentarily disorientated by the thick currents of air that he ruddered into motion. His lungs seemed as large as the sky. He breathed in all the winds.

"My lungs are the Turtle's shell," he said.

Osidian's chuckle was a shunting of machinery. "You feel it all right."

Carnelian felt the earthquake of Osidian rising.

"Stand up," came Osidian's words, tumbling down from above. Carnelian felt the fingers fumbling into his as an avalanche of pillars. They kept sliding round and through his until they locked closed. Even lying naked on a rock, Carnelian had never felt such a vast expanse of his skin touching the world. Their hands were a jumble of warm stones in whose crevices lay thrilling moisture.

Suddenly the whole meshed mass of fingers were flying

skyward. Carnelian's forearm followed, then his elbow, then his upper arm, all straightening like the links in some monumental chain. The whole mass of him unfolded up and up, faraway joints opening until he found himself standing.

"We should release each other's hand," rumbled Osidian.

Carnelian struggled. Their flesh seemed wedded together at the hands. When they managed to wrestle their fingers apart, Carnelian was left feeling as if part of him had been cut away. It was all he could do not to flail the night to recover it.

"Take some beadcord in your hands."

Carnelian had to wait for the loss to fade before he ran a finger along the wooden wall of the bench. It had been smooth before. Now it was pitted, gnarled, scored with ruts. His finger ran into something that at first he though must be a skull. He felt the heat radiating from Osidian's fingers touching the other side of the curving ball of bone.

"Can you read it now?" asked Osidian.

Carnelian was startled when he realized he was only touching a bead. He allowed his fingers to explore its landscape. They found the ridges, the sensuous curves. Cool regions, warm strips his mind told him must be narrower than a hair. "I do not recognize it," he said.

"Let me."

Osidian's fingers resumed contact. Carnelian felt as if his skin was drinking from Osidian's. He let his hand climb down from one bead to another until it was a safe distance away.

"Untouchables," said Osidian.

Carnelian could feel the vibration in the cord. Something was coming down it. His hand escaped further down, bead by bead.

"Removing the Blood . . . no, the Liver," said Osidian.

A whole earthful of flesh brushed past Carnelian and set his entire skin quivering like a bell's bronze.

Osidian had moved to the next title cord. "Preserving the Viscera in Canopic Jars."

Through the floor, Carnelian could feel the quake as Osidian moved further along the bench.

"Hooking out the Cranial Organs."

"What?" said Carnelian.

"Pah!" said Osidian. "These are nothing but manuals of embalming."

"Is it a secret art?" asked Carnelian, with a sour taste in his mouth.

"One of the most secret."

"Not something I desire to learn," said Carnelian, not bothering to hide his disappointment.

"Nor I."

Carnelian felt suddenly angry. "Is that it then?" he asked loudly. A fleshy door closed over his mouth.

"Hush!" whispered Osidian and took his hand away.

"If these are the most secret books in the Library of the Wise," whispered Carnelian, "then, my Lord, I am grown weary of their tame marvels."

A heavy silence fell. He listened for and found the breeze of Osidian's breathing. "Does my Lord challenge me to find for him a diversion that is less tame?" the darkness said through a smile.

"Well, if—"

"Tomorrow, come to the usual place but wear warm clothes and heavy outdoor paint. Tell your people not to expect your return for three days."

THE LADDER

I touched with eye

Right hand speaking

But all the while, the left

Was sowing the whirlwind

—FROM THE POEM "THE

BIRD IN THE CAGE"

BY THE LADY AKAYA

Carnelian looked through the robes Fey had sent him. They were all delicate silks, clothing suitable for wearing in his chambers, not for whatever expedition Osidian had in mind. And what was that? He was plagued with speculations. Outdoor paint? Where could Osidian be planning to go that required outdoor paint? For three days? It had to be some region of the Halls of Thunder exposed to the sun. That would be it. Nothing more than an extension of their exploration of the Library. Still, he was nagged by the knowledge that he was going against his father's wishes.

"I must," he said. He knew no way to get a message to Osidian to tell him that he was not coming. How could he just not turn up? He smiled thinking about him. There was still the problem of the robe. He knuckled his forehead. At last, with a sigh, he went to pick up the only outdoor robe he had. He shook out its scarlet mourning brocade, laid it out, then went to the door to call a servant. When the man came he sent him off to fetch bodypaint.

"Bodypaint, Master?"

"Bodypaint."

The man was soon back with a jar and pads. Carnelian put up with the timorous painting. Once the paint had dried, he put on the mourning robe and finally, his mask.

Outside his chamber, he told his guardsmen that he would be spending three days away from them. He gave them assurances that he would be all right. He had to ignore the pleas in their eyes for explanations. After all, he himself did not know where he was going. Their looks of fear made him swear a silent promise that, should it become necessary, he would put himself between them and the Master's wrath. This did not stop him from feeling selfish and hazardous of their care.

Osidian was waiting for him. His eyes widened as Carnelian came closer. "Is that a mourning robe?"

"It was the only one I had."

"It is hardly the best omen for our expedition."

Carnelian did not like Osidian's unfocused stare. "Where are we going, then?"

Osidian seemed to come awake. "Down to the Yden."

Carnelian stared at him in disbelief. "The Yden? Down the Rainbow Stair?"

Osidian shook his head. "There is another, more ancient way."

"Another stair?"

Osidian's lips formed an enigmatic smile. "More a ladder than a stair. The descent is harrowing. Do you feel you have the strength?"

The challenge fired Carnelian up. "If I do not, then at least

I shall have the long pleasure of falling into the Yden like a star."

Osidian's brow darkened. "This is not a children's game, Carnelian. You speak lightly of what you do not know."

Carnelian was stung to anger but before he could say anything Osidian threw his hands up in appeasement. "Forgive my tone." He grinned. Carnelian could not help grinning back. Osidian lowered his head and looked enquiringly at Carnelian.

Carnelian forced solemnity into his face. "I am certain I have the strength."

"Well then, let us make haste. When night falls it will not bode well for us should it find us on the Ladder. First we must put on our disguises."

"Disguises?"

"It would be unwise"—he smirked—"to go deep into the chambers of the Wise as ourselves."

Osidian slipped out of the lantern light and returned carrying two packs. As he offered one, Carnelian remembered the Tower in the Sea and his father's anger at him carrying burdens. He realized that Osidian was angry too.

"Does my Lord consider it shameful to bear a pack when I did not consider it so to bring them both here?"

"No, not at all." Carnelian grabbed one and swung it round onto his shoulder. He was adjusting its straps when Osidian threw him a bundle. Carnelian turned the thick purple silk in his hand. Osidian had already unrolled his and flung it over his back, concealing the pack under it. Carnelian followed his lead, but worried about the hump the pack made. He shrugged when he saw Osidian was unconcerned and pulled the cloak round him, securing its bony hooks. Smoothing it, he touched beadcord. He looked down and saw the panels. He closed his eyes and began to read with his fingers, out loud. "The heart of thunder is the locus of the rain-heavy sky. It translates along the ritual axis, from the sea. It can be—"

"These cloaks are reserved for near-Sapient acolytes. They are a study aid," said Osidian. "Come."

"Our masks?"

Osidian shook his head. "We must be free of their encumbrance."

He led them through the moon-eyed door into the library. He opened the lantern, blew it out, then put it on the ground, out of the way against a wall.

"Will we not need it further on?" asked Carnelian.

"Let us hope not," replied Osidian.

Carnelian reached out to take a grip of Osidian's cloak. He felt his hand being disengaged.

"It will be faster for you to follow your feet," said the darkness.

Carnelian felt Osidian's cold foot nudging his across the floor to where it was embossed.

"Read it," said Osidian.

Carnelian used his toe to feel around the shape. "A face . . . a horned-ring above . . . a circle below . . . bisected thus a sky glyph, thus Sky God." He returned to feel the face. Its eyes were closed, its mouth open. "Blowing," he said. "It reads as, wind?"

"Indeed," said Osidian, his voice fading into the blackness.

Carnelian followed the wind glyph trail blindly through the library. For a while he had been hearing a whistling up ahead. He bumped into Osidian who gave a groan.

"Hide your face deep in your cowl."

Carnelian was doing so when a smudging brightness opened in front of them. As he stumbled after Osidian, a gale took hold of his cloak. Carnelian squinted both ways. They were standing near the edge of a ravine. On its further side a smooth heart-stone wall rose up into blackness. Sunlight flowed in from the right, where the ravine turned a corner. Left, it narrowed off to a ragged eye-aching blue hole. Here and there narrow bridges arched the drop.

With his hand, Carnelian clamped his cowl onto his head. "What is this?"

"The Windmoat," cried Osidian and turned into the blast.

They strode leaning into the wind. On their left the stone was sieving light. Rays blinked through the holes as they walked past. A murmur came through as if from a crowd at prayer. Carnelian paused to glue an eye to one of the holes and saw a tunnel running off into the distance. All the way down one side it was peopled from floor to ceiling with squatting, tallow-faced ammonites. He found the angle to see the other side of the tunnel. Stone sloped up to a ledge on which something was sitting in a chair. He could make out a voice, a homunculus, droning, "Compare cords twenty-five to thirty, Ba-Ta process result spindle for five computations . . ." He pushed his cheek into the stone, trying to see more. Almost in darkness, the mummified face of its Sapient master hung above the homunculus, his fingers operating its throat.

Osidian pulled him away.

"What . . . ?" Carnelian said, pointing at the fretted wall.

Ammonite arrays, signed Osidian's hand. *Calculating the approach of the Rains.*

They passed one of the bridges, a simple arch without a parapet only wide enough for a single man. It crossed over to a postern gate sunk deep into the heart-stone wall. Carnelian glanced up and saw, high above the gate, a few isolated holes that might have been windows. It looked like a prison.

He pulled Osidian's sleeve. He pointed at the gate. *Where does that go?* he signed.

The Forbidden House.

Carnelian stared up at the windows and then pulled his cowl down and held it tight over his face by pressing his chin into his chest. He had a silly fear that Ykoriana might be up there looking down.

They went along the ravine edge as it widened to sky. Carnelian glimpsed the blue spread of the crater and then he saw Osidian had found some cracked ledges that led down into the ravine and begun to descend. Carnelian peered down to where its sheer edges were snagging morning light. For the first time he considered the reality of where they were going. He remembered the long climb of the Rainbow Stair, and that Osidian had described this Ladder as being harrowing. He shrugged. There was no turning back now. Chewing his lip, Carnelian started down the precarious steps.

The ravine squeezed down to a narrow cleft. The steps continued out through its end seemingly into the sky. Osidian had wedged himself between the walls. His cloak flapped desperately in the wind as he compressed it into a ball, which he then wedged between the small of his back and the rock. He swung his pack round into his embrace and inserted his hand into it. He looked away with narrowed eyes as he rummaged. With a triumphant grin. He brought forth a jar, that he gave to Carnelian. He fished out another. Carnelian watched him open the jar, then pull up the corner of his robe and rub it round inside. It came out white and oily. Osidian bent his knee to bring his foot toward him, leaned over and began to rub it with the paint. After a few strokes he looked up, holding his foot with one hand, the whitened corner of the robe with the other.

"Are you just going to stand there watching?" he cried over the wind.

"Are we going barefoot?" Carnelian accented his words with gesture.

"Naked feet provide a better grip as well as a sensitivity to the movements in the rock." Osidian resumed the daubing of his feet.

Carnelian wriggled himself into a stable position. Tentatively, he lifted one foot and kneaded his toes, rubbing dust from between them. "And the paint?" he shouted.

"It will not come off. It will protect the paleness of your feet."

Carnelian dipped a corner of his robe into his jar and rubbed some on. The paint reeked of turpentine. It was sticky and gleaned coldness from the wind. He began to apply it over his foot up to the ankle.

"Take it higher, at least up to your knees." Osidian hoisted the skirt of his robe. His long strong legs were so white they made the paint seem yellow.

When his feet were done, Carnelian began to spread the stuff up his legs.

"It is only paint," cried Osidian, grinning. "From your face one would think it was dung." He made a lunge with the corner of his robe. Carnelian grazed his arm trying to dodge, but it landed anyway. "You had missed a bit," said Osidian. "Now do the soles." He folded his feet up into his lap one at a time as he painted them. When each was done he waved it in the wind to dry.

"You look ridiculous."

Osidian's eyebrows rose, making Carnelian look at himself. They both laughed. Osidian touched his foot gingerly to the floor as if he feared the paint might glue him to the rock. When he was standing firmly on both feet, he began to wriggle out of his robes.

Carnelian stared in amazement as Osidian pulled layer after layer over his head and pushed them under his feet. The last two robes were merely a mist concealing his body. Soon, he was dazzling, naked against the rock. Carnelian looked away.

"You too," cried Osidian, through chattering teeth.

Carnelian tried to turn his back on him but the effort threatened to tumble him into the crack of the ravine. He cursed as he began to struggle out of his robes. He winced when his elbow struck rock. "Is this really necessary?" he cried.

Osidian jabbed a finger out toward the sky. "Out there, these robes would make us kites."

"Could you not have found a better place to change?"

"Would my Lord prefer to expose himself above to the eyes of the Forbidden House?"

Carnelian grumbled. He turned when he was wearing only a single almost transparent robe. He could see his goose-pimpled legs and the dull, discoloring paint. "It is cold. Perhaps I should keep this on."

Osidian made a face at him. "I promise you that feeling

the cold will be the least of your problems. Take it off."

Carnelian pulled the last robe over his head, aware that Osidian was looking at him. He blushed. Osidian pulled neatly folded bundles out of his pack and threw them at Carnelian. They turned out to be a padded tunic and close-fitting trousers. He put them on as quickly as he could. "This is hardly the attire of the Chosen."

Osidian flashed a smile and then shouldered the pack.

They stepped out of the ravine into a blinding churn of wind and sun. Carnelian clung to the rock until he could see again. He clung harder when he realized how narrow was the shelf they stood on. Beyond was a world of air remotely floored by the turquoises of the crater. The ground was impossibly far away. His fingers tried to force their way into the rock to anchor him.

"How long will it take us to go down?" he shouted, stunned. He looked up when there was no answer. Osidian was standing away from the rock leaning into the wind with his back to him, his head up and very still. Carnelian released his hold and carefully moved to his side. The wind roared in his ears. Osidian looked so solid that he had to fight a desire to grab hold of him. Osidian's eyes were piercing the southwest. Carnelian shaded his eyes and squinted. Dazzling blue sparked off to a dip in the Sacred Wall above which the pearl sky was tainted darker.

"What is it?" cried Carnelian, swallowing wind.

"Rain," cried Osidian, not looking round.

Carnelian looked again. It made him remember his father organizing the Rebirth. What if his father had need of him? He put the thought out of his head. He had made his decision.

Osidian was saying something. Carnelian turned and saw him mouthing sounds. He shook his head and pointed to his ears. Osidian took him by the shoulders and leaned in toward him. "Do not worry. We have time." Carnelian felt Osidian's lips brush his face and was aware of the hands gripping his shoulders. "It is still more than ten days away," said Osidian in his ear.

As he was released, Carnelian put his hand up to stop the warmth of Osidian's breath from escaping. Slowly he relaxed the tension in his other hand and, daring to trust to the wind, braced himself against it to look down. He mastered his terror of that airy gulf. He was more determined than ever to follow Osidian down, whatever the consequences.

The steps were cracked, treacherous with scree, an uneven, narrow flight ablaze in the sun. On one side rose a chaotically jointed wall of slabs. On the other, a vision of falling. It was a height vast enough to daunt a hawk.

Carnelian felt Osidian looking at him and saw that he was frowning. *We had better go back*, he signed. *The wind is too violent.*

I do not fear, signed Carnelian, with shaky hands.

You are still weak from the sky sickness.

That was days ago.

The wind, the sun—

I am fine, chopped Carnelian. He pointed at the steps. *I will go first. I do not want to take you with me if I fall.*

Try not to be a fool, flashed Osidian's hand. *Do you know the way?* He stormed off down the steps.

Carnelian watched nervously, terrified that he had stung Osidian into a perilous anger, but when he observed how carefully his heels were finding the angles in the steps, he decided that he would do better to worry about himself.

Carnelian was already struggling with the steps when they came to the first ladder. Osidian crouched on the edge. Carnelian snatched at him as he slipped over and out of sight. He leaned out with cold fear expecting to see him falling and saw instead Osidian's face grinning up at him. Carnelian's eyes lost their focus on that face. It became a speck in limitless blue. Carnelian wobbled, cracked to his knees.

Clutching the edge made him feel that he was pivoting on his wrists, into flight. The vertigo would not even allow him to close his eyes.

"Carnelian." His name cried on the wind. He took a deep breath and managed to wrench his eyes back into focus. Osidian was already some way down wedged into a crack. His mouth was moving. Carnelian caught only the merest scratches of words. He shook his head then gaped as Osidian released a hand to sign. Carnelian slapped the rock repeatedly until Osidian resumed his hold. Osidian grinned then grew concerned.

Carnelian scowled at him. *I see the handholds*, he jerked with his fingers. Osidian shook a puzzled face. Carnelian repeated the signs more slowly, sketching them larger, then added, *You go down first, I will follow.*

He ducked back and crammed his body into a cleft. It was the furthest away he could get from the edge. Eyes closed, he pressed his head back against the rock until it hurt. He rasped breaths in and out, his heart rattling his chest. At last he forced his eyes open. The cold wind on them made him blink. He looked up the steps, yearning to go back. In front of him was the terrifying edge.

"Gods' blood," he grumbled. "Gods' flaming, fiery blood."

Osidian was down there. What would he think of him? He was behaving slavishly. Nodding his head, spitting curses and encouragement, Carnelian scraped his way on hands and knees to the edge. For a moment he saw nothing but a whirling drop. Then his eyes focused on a tiny shape floating on the air below. A bird, not Osidian falling. Carnelian felt he was tying his friend to safety by making his eyes follow the line of the ladder down. Osidian was waving.

Before fear could overpower him, Carnelian turned and let himself over the edge, feeling the sheer face with a desperate foot. It found a crack. He wriggled his toes into it as if it were a shoe. He released some of his weight onto it to allow his other foot to feel down. He touched another fissure like the corner of a mouth into which he slipped his foot. Slowly he trusted his weight to the cracks. He felt for the next one and saw another near his face. Slowly, one hold at a time, he descended, always pressing his cheek against the cracked stone, never looking down. He tensed when he felt Osidian's hands on him.

"It is very hard, the first time."

Carnelian could only growl at him.

It was as if he had become trapped in a falling dream. Ledges led to flights of steps, then handhold ladders, then to more steps, in an unending, grueling succession. They had been cursed to squeeze down the rock with the sun always burning its stare into their backs. Carnelian longed for each rest stop, but every time they reached one, he found the waiting for the next leg a torture and would hurry Osidian on. Here and there a cave had been cut back into the jointing between two slabs. He feared their coolness more than anything else. Each time they crammed in, he was not sure he would find the courage to come back out.

"Halfway . . . down . . ." said Osidian, panting.

Carnelian fanned himself. He tried to loosen the tension in his throat enough to speak. "Have you . . . done this . . . many times before?"

Osidian lifted his hand up to perhaps the height of a man's waist. "Since I was that tall."

Carnelian gaped. "You dared . . . as a child? Who . . . showed you the way?"

"I found it for myself," Osidian's eyes were sun through leaves, "and always, before, alone." He closed his eyes and rested his head back on the rock.

Carnelian smiled at the compliment. His eye traced the curve of Osidian's throat up to his chin, over his lips up to the beautiful jutting of his nose. In the gloom his birthmark was like an open eye.

*　　*　　*

The sun was rifling down its rays, withering Carnelian with their onslaught. He craved release from his tunic, lusting after the cold caress of the wind, but fearing for his skin, he did not even loosen it.

He felt his head and shoulders cooling. He looked up, through his fingers, expecting to see some cloud momentarily blinding the sun. Instead, the burning eye was impaling itself on the Pillar's black spear. As Carnelian watched, the sun melted away until there was only a smoldering rind, then that too went out and the Pillar was holding up a smooth blue sky.

"Look," cried Osidian below him.

Clinging hard, Carnelian dared to look down the Pillar's craggy narrowing plunge into the ground. Its shadow was beginning to creep out over the Yden. He closed his eyes, hugged the rock, rejoicing at their deliverance from the burning tyranny of the sun.

His rejoicing was short-lived. The wind blowing up from the Yden abated until it became a gentle breeze. It grew steadily colder until he was pressing himself against the rock to suck up what he could of its fading heat.

Down they climbed and ever down, the passage of time measured by the Pillar's shadow-creep over the Yden.

Its coming was like a tidal wave. Carnelian looked south and saw the black horn of its crescent. He stopped for a moment watching as shadow engulfed the Sacred Wall, a coomb at a time.

Osidian came scrabbling up toward him. "I have miscalculated." His eyes squeezed almost closed with each pant. He shook his head, swallowed. "We will not make the Yden."

Carnelian looked down. The Yden had become an immense expanse of trees. Its air clung to him like sweat. Its further edge tattered into glimmering emerald water that was eventually hemmed by Skymere blue. It did not seem that far away.

"It is," said Osidian, as if he had heard his thoughts. He looked up, judging whether they could make the climb back to the last cave.

"There must be some place further down," said Carnelian.

Osidian made a face. "There is, but it will not be to your taste."

"Why not?"

Osidian shook his head. "There is no time for discussion. You will see." In the east, the Pillar shadow was already fumbling up the Sacred Wall. "If we do not get to where we are going before nightfall, we shall either have to spend the night here," he indicated the windswept wall of stone, "or risk stumbling down, blind."

They hurried on, Osidian leading them down into the thickening humid air. The shadow of the Sacred Wall washed over them and began rippling off toward the east. It seemed no time at all before it had covered the Yden and was pouring its ink into the lake. Carnelian reached the bottom of one long ladder to see the shadow lapping against the faraway wall, then fill the crater up to the very brim with darkness. All the light they had then came from the sky. As flames engulfed it, Carnelian began to notice movements out of the corner of his eye. Monstrous shapes lurked here and there in crevices and ledges. He saw a pickaxe head lifting and, hearing a flapping, turned to see enormous bat-wings opening and folding back.

He caught up with Osidian and grabbed his arm.

"Gods' blood," cried Osidian.

The air rustled and squealed. The monsters shifted round them. Carnelian came to a halt as Osidian hugged him back against the stone.

"If we raise them they might knock us off the ladder," Osidian hissed in his ear.

"What . . . ?"

"A sky-saurian roost."

Carnelian scrunched up his nose. "It stinks of fish."

"Just be glad there is no saurian nesting in here," snapped Osidian.

"Ugh!" grimaced Carnelian. The floor was an oozing paste.

Osidian's hand grabbed his arm and dragged Carnelian after him, deeper into the cave.

"Do you have a light?" asked Carnelian, wincing at each moist footfall. There was no answer. "I said, do you—"

"I have not grown suddenly deaf. The answer is no."

"But—"

"I did not think we would need it. We could have brought a bed as well, if I had thought of it, but perhaps my Lord might have also complained at having to carry that down the Ladder."

Carnelian decided it might be better to say nothing more. The noisome walk ended at a low smooth wall.

"Jump up," said Osidian.

Carnelian felt him lurch past. He slid his hands up over the top of the wall and could feel a damp ledge. He brought his fingers near his nose. They smelled of nothing worse than must. He pulled himself up and found that he was sitting on a narrow shelf. He could feel a column backing it, an ankle of stone, with another beside it. He slid his hand up to the knees.

"Will you stop fidgeting! Lie down and sleep," said Osidian.

Carnelian lay down. His tunic and trousers clung to him. The air was as moist as breath. "What is this place?"

There was no answer, just the sound of Osidian breathing. He supposed there was no point in telling him that, fishy stench or no fishy stench, he was hungry. Carnelian waited until he could hear Osidian's breathing slow and then he shifted closer to him, buried his nose in the sweaty-smelling cloth of his back and quickly fell asleep.

FORBIDDEN FRUIT

Clutch my warmth

Until day comes

For then we must part

—FROM THE POEM "THE
BIRD IN THE CAGE"
BY THE LADY AKAYA

The raven hopped into the air, flicking open its fan-feather wings. Carnelian tried to catch it, his fingers shredding the air like its black pinions. The other distinct half of him was there without a face, touching the whole surface of his skin. He clenched the anchor grip of their hands but its fingers were squeezing to blood. The raven's eye stared white as an egg. A red tear leaked from the corner with each blink.

"Flee with me away from here," the raven screeched. Its beak was the pin holding everything together.

But Carnelian would not abandon the faceless half of him. Looking round, he tumbled falling. The red earth caught him. Grit in his eye. Sinking. He struggled to stay perfectly still. Every movement trembled pebbles and scratched his skin deeper in.

"Away from Her."

The earth brimmed over him like honey round a stone. Warm pulsing red darkness. Buried alive. Opening his mouth to scream let dust pour into his stomach, into his lungs. Drop by drop, moisture sucked out of his husk until his organs rattled inside him like seeds.

Carnelian jerked awake to see a creature hovering over him, its wings splayed like hands to grab him.

"What is wrong?" said the creature. Carnelian recognized Osidian. As his friend crouched, Carnelian saw the idol of stone behind him, a winged man, looking as if he had only at that very moment descended from the heavens.

"The Black God," he breathed.

As Osidian looked up, his shoulders relaxed. "The Wind Lord."

Carnelian could not stop staring. Terror lurked in the empty eye sockets of the idol. From the left, tears ran down the stony cheek. "An avatar of the Black God."

Osidian shook his head. "A false Quyan deity. The only true gods are the Twins." He smiled. "Besides, our friend here poses no threat. Has he not given us the comfort of his hospitality?"

"The comfort . . . ?" Carnelian said, stretching the stiffness from his arms, arching his back. Osidian was gazing toward the entrance. The narrow shrine with its corbel vault ended in a triangle of morning so bright it hurt his eyes. Its sloping walls were stiff with the carved wings of wind creatures. Filth clotted the floor. "Do we have to wade back through that?"

"Unless, in the night, my Lord has been gifted with a sprouting of wings," said Osidian. He made a pantomime of looking for them.

When Carnelian slapped his hands away, Osidian grinned. Carnelian was embarrassed by the look in his eyes.

As they slid down to the floor, the ooze came up to their ankles so that it seemed they stood on the stumps of their legs. They exchanged looks of disgust and began to squelch off to the entrance.

When they reached it Carnelian glanced back. The winged god appeared to be a great raven. He realized something. "His altar was our bed."

"You would agree that it was better than the floor," said Osidian. "Do you think he begrudged us it?" He did not wait for an answer but walked out into the morning.

Remembering his nightmare, Carnelian looked back into the shrine uneasily, then followed him.

He stopped. At their feet was a tangling forest. "Thorn trees," he said, his voice loud with disappointment. He had expected the Yden to be more lush.

The air tore with screams and something like a shaking of many blankets as the cliff of the Pillar came to pieces round them. He ducked with Osidian as a vast shape wafted over them. He glanced up to see the air screeching with leather kites.

"It seems you have woken our fishy friends," cried Osidian. "Come on."

Half crouching they fled, laughing, down the wide steps crusted white, through a shimmering stench of ammonia and rotted fish. Above them, the creatures circled on fingered wings, slicing the air with their pickaxe heads. Soon the white on the steps was only a splatter, the air cleared, cracks became jagged with weeds.

The trees formed a wall of thorns. Through their knotting branches, the sky was a blue mosaic. Looking back, Carnelian could see nothing of the steps. Gazing up the cliffs, he found the nodules of the sky-saurian nests and perhaps, though he could not really be sure, the Ladder's zigzag. The Pillar soared up to fill the sky. Somewhere up there were the Halls of Thunder.

Carnelian came back down to earth. Osidian was walking

off clothed to the waist in dust clouds. Carnelian followed him, frowning. Here and there an angled paving stone showed where a road lay under the dark earth. Peering into the thorns he saw the cracked carvings running along its edge. The road curved off to the north but Osidian turned off it and ducked into the thicket.

"Hold on," Carnelian shouted after him.

Osidian's head poked out from the thicket.

Carnelian pointed. "The road goes this way."

Osidian smiled. "So it does, into the Labyrinth. We, however, go this way." He pointed into the thicket. "Be careful of the thorns," he said with a grin and vanished.

Carnelian frowned when he reached the place where he judged Osidian had gone in. After much squinting, he managed to spot him moving away through the tangle along something like a tunnel. Carnelian gave the road one last envious glance before ducking in under the branches.

The tunnel forced him to bend his back. Thorns snagged his clothes so that he often had to stop to unhitch the cloth. Several times, mockingly, he muttered, "Be careful of the thorns," and then growled.

He struggled to catch up with Osidian, wanting to berate him, but when he began Osidian turned and lifted up his hands to show his own red scratches and Carnelian had to give him a grudging smile and close his mouth.

At last they came to a lofty wall. Its massive blocks were irregularly shaped but fitted together with remarkable precision.

"What now?" asked Carnelian, exasperated.

"We climb over," Osidian replied and slipped sideways, hugging the wall, going down the gradient, in the wedge of space that was free of thorns.

Carnelian followed. Osidian found a way up using the edges of blocks as footholds. Carnelian watched him climb higher and higher and then, with a vault, he was sitting astride the wall, waving him up.

Muttering, Carnelian began the climb. Some handholds he had to stretch for. He missed one, slipped and grazed his arm. Osidian offered him his hand and grinned when it was refused. Carnelian insisted on scrambling his own way up. He made sure he was secure, then turned to Osidian.

"You are—" He fell silent, gaping at the view. Below them spread a terrace of black earth divided neatly into plots. Further down the slope there was another terrace and further down from there, another and another, until he had counted almost twenty in all, the most distant of which looked like chequered cloth. Beyond, a forest stretched for a great distance, turning at last into polished jade and then the purpling turquoise of the Skymere.

Osidian touched his shoulder. "It gets better."

They slithered down, dropping the last bit into a thick bed of giant cabbages that squeaked and snapped as they fell in among them. The musk of wet earth and the green bruising smell of the leaves filled the air. They clambered out onto a path and wandered along a maze of them, each walled by vegetables. Here and there Carnelian glimpsed a glitter of water running in stone channels. They crossed several by means of little bridges. Every so often the vista would open out and he would see the terraces again.

"A kitchen garden?" he asked at last.

"For the court," Osidian answered him, pointing at the black craggy cliffs of the Pillar.

As they strolled, Carnelian asked Osidian the names of everything. Osidian always had an answer and even added what he knew of their uses or plucked some for Carnelian to smell or taste.

Carnelian glimpsed movement and found himself scrabbling for his mask. Osidian's hand restrained him.

There is no need, he signed. *Here we alone can see.*

They walked out into a clearing in which a number of creatures were harvesting leaves with sickles, or turning the rich black earth with hoes. Carnelian tried to see what kind of beings they were. Nut-brown, with spade hands and feet, but not tall enough to come up to his knee.

They move as if they had eyes.
The sylven have keen ears and well-honed touch.
They look like little men.
Animals. "Let me show you," said Osidian. As he spoke the sylven stopped their work and turned their wizened heads. Osidian clapped his hands. "Attend me."

The sylven came, forming round them, their heads bowed, their huge ears sticking up like horns.

Osidian crouched and took one in his hands. The little wizened creature flinched and whimpered. Carnelian began protesting even as Osidian cooed and said, gently, "You will not be hurt."

He held the creature's little brown head carefully. Carnelian crouched to stroke it. Osidian angled it back to reveal a tiny face. A wide gashed mouth, a nose flat and splayed. Osidian squeezed apart the wrinkles that closed its eye. In the pit there appeared to be the raisin of a pale grape. Osidian let the creature go.

"It seems very much like a tiny man," said Carnelian.

Osidian shrugged. "The world is filled with manlike creatures. What is a man? Are these men? Are the sartlar?"

"The barbarians are men."

"Perhaps, but if so, not like you or me."

"I suppose, then, that you would claim that we are angels."

"Is that not what the Wise teach?"

They wandered further into the garden, seeing sylven everywhere. The sun was beginning to pour its fire into the day when they came to a region where each tree was inside the square of a low wall.

"Aha," said Osidian. He leapt onto one of the walls, and reaching up into the branches of its tree he plucked a fruit. He turned and offered Carnelian its red-streaked gold. "Smell it."

Carnelian did so and closed his eyes as he drew in its perfume. He bit into it. Its flesh was creamier than a peach, filled with seeds that had the flavor of almonds. Osidian beamed at his reaction. Carnelian took another succulent bite. "Why the wall?"

"It reserves the fruit for those who are of the House of the Masks."

Carnelian stared at the forbidden fruit. His sin was there, cut into its flesh. He felt its juices dripping down his chin.

"Who will know?" said Osidian. He took a bite of his own fruit. "Come on, finish it. Have you ever had a better breakfast?"

Carnelian ate it, quickly, swallowing every last bit of it.

Osidian widened his eyes dramatically. "Maybe we should consume the whole tree. It might be perilous to leave any evidence."

Carnelian made a face at him and they both laughed.

The terrace took them round the Pillar until they came at last to another wall in which there was a gate. Through its frame lay a another garden. In the morning shadow of the Pillar of Heaven there were as many terraces but these were arranged in a design so complex that it confused the eye. It appeared to move, rotate, like some fantastic mechanism. The patterns were bewildering and on every scale. The whole glinted darkly, chinked and shimmered.

Osidian was smiling at him, reading his face. He jabbed his thumb back in the direction of the gate. "My Lord thought that was the Forbidden Garden of the Yden, did he not?"

Carnelian had to admit that he had.

"Well, let me show you the real one," said Osidian and strode through the gate.

Carnelian walked by his side. He fingered his mask hanging at his hip. "Will we come across anyone?"

"Perhaps more sylven but none of the Chosen. This late in the year, we will have the garden to ourselves."

Carnelian allowed himself to be carried along by the gleaming, iridescing pavements. They wandered down avenues of dragon-blood trees that looked like upturned brooms, their trunks striped with bands of jasper and carnelian. They dangled their hands in pools in whose green water white, gold-patched carp slid, each larger than a man. Osidian pointed out their mouths and fins all pierced with silver rings. Other pools had tiny fish that glistened hither and thither like sun flecks on the sea. The pools poured into each other through great spouts, sometimes arching water over their path so that they could feel its flash and mist on their skins. Everywhere the walls were carved into grotesques, grimacing or pouting gargoyles spitting fountains or bristling with trees. A pavilion of salmon-striped green marble tempted them into its murmuring recesses. Steps banistered with cascades led down to the next terrace. They dallied in other pavilions. Those of heart-stone, quarried from the Pillar of Heaven itself, Osidian told him, were rainhalls, their roofs and pillars contrived to convert rain to music. Others had walls so thin they could make out the vague languorous shapes of the trees beyond. In places the air darted with parrots more brilliant than butterflies. Quetzals shuttled emerald between trees. Screeching their cries, peacocks pulled trains of staring feathers.

It was the vast and somber pillared hill of the Labyrinth that brought them back to earth. Its mound ran along the edge of the terraces, tumbling its frowning façade down into the distance. Where the Labyrinth and the Pillar met, the latter folded into a crevasse that rifled all the way up to its dark and brooding summit. Carnelian searched there and found the jagged line.

"The Rainbow Stair," he said.

Osidian appeared to be looking for somewhere to hide. "We have come too far round. Come on."

He took them down a stair and another and so they descended the terraces, running for pleasure through the perfumed air. At last they reached the last terrace, which ended at a high glistening wall. They turned to look back. The garden was a colossal staircase rising up to where the Pillar stood like the Black God Himself, hefting the blue of the sky upon His shoulders.

They explored along the wall until they found a bronze trellised gate through which they could see a shadowy world under the trees. Carnelian was surprised when Osidian produced a key. He thrust it into the center of the gate, turned it, and then using the weight of his body he swung it open and beckoned Carnelian to go through.

Trunks were spaced like the pillars of a ruined hypostyle hall. Here and there the canopied roof had collapsed into a clearing. They wandered into it as if they were afraid of waking the trees. Scented air encouraged slumber. Soft mulch muffled their steps. Birds flitted across the corners of their vision. Several times they saw saurians, two-legged, as small and curious as children, that when approached slipped away like memories.

This shadowy world was terraced too. Every so often they would descend a shallow stair, then behind them they would see a wall of rough-hewn stones. In some places this had burst, allowing the red earth to spill down and revealing the black layer beneath.

They did not talk. Something about the forest encouraged silence. A resinous breeze wafted constantly in their faces. It grew even hotter. Peering ahead, Carnelian had the impression a fire was burning toward them. The tops of the trees around them burst into flame. Light shot over their shoulders from above, growing ever brighter, and suddenly it was stabbing all around them. He turned and saw the shadow of the Pillar of Heaven ebbing away from them as the sun melted up out of its black brow. He was struck by how much it looked like a Master in a court robe.

They walked in the hazing air. It grew torrid, humid, thick with an odor of moldering. They were by this time following a trickle of water running in the bottom of a crumbling channel. The brightness showed them that the trees were filled with fruit, and it seemed to Carnelian that they walked in an orchard long ago abandoned. Then he noticed the spaces between the trees were all aglitter and he saw, against the band of the Sacred Wall, the blinding sheets of the lagoons stretching to the Skymere.

Osidian clasped his shoulder. "Behold, the mirrors of the Yden."

Carnelian watched Osidian sleep in the stultifying heat. Even hiding in the deepest shade they had found no coolness. Through the trees he could see the alluring shimmer of the lagoons. Their glaring silver was animated by the scratches of flamingos wading. There was a lazy buzzing of flies. Everything seemed to be pulsing in time to his slow heart. Osidian had told him that they must wait out the heat of the day. Even with their paint, the sun, in the last month of the year, was a danger to their skin.

Carnelian licked his lips, remembering the delicious melting sweetness of the forbidden fruit. He looked up into the branches that were their parasol. The apples there were as brown and wizened as the stony fruits that they had cleared to give them space to lie down. He wanted something succulent. He rose, his tunic sticking to his skin. Osidian swatted a fly from his face.

Carnelian pulled one of the purple cloaks from a pack and draped it over his head. Creeping from shadow to shadow, he searched the glowing dappled world for fresh fruit. His skin prickled. He felt the need to scratch himself everywhere. He made sure to look back every so often so as to know where he had left Osidian.

It was the red that drew him to the grove. A low wall ringed it. In many places its stones had tumbled into the weeds and were almost lost from view. Some of the trees had red flowers. He recognized the pomegranates nestling among the waxy green. He jumped the wall and, reaching up, felt the pregnant tautness of the fruit. He plucked one and then another and two more. Their skin was hard but it gave a little when he squeezed.

He returned with his treasures and woke Osidian. He cut one open and offered half of it to him.

Osidian frowned. "Where did you get these?"

Carnelian gestured vaguely.

"The fruit here are bitter, poisonous."

Carnelian looked at the womb of the pomegranate, melting with juicy rubies. He sniffed it. "Are you sure?"

"It is forbidden to eat from the trees outside the garden wall."

"As it was forbidden to eat the golden fruit?"

Osidian had to smile.

Carnelian looked into the moist jeweled fruit. He could not resist it. He scooped up some seeds, licked them off his fingers, sucked them free of pulp and spat them out. "Sweet nectar," he sighed.

Again, he offered Osidian the pomegranate half. "I sinned for you."

Osidian's eyes smoldered like emeralds hidden from the light. He took the pomegranate and slowly bit into its juicy heart.

Osidian woke him when the shadow of the Sacred Wall had washed over them. He grinned. "Come on."

The sky was a cooler blue. Carnelian walked into a clearing and looked back. The Pillar of Heaven was spouting its fiery wall into the sky. He turned to follow Osidian off through the trees.

The ground began to soften. He could feel the delicious moisture squeezing out under his feet. He saw a circle of plate-leafed water lily. At its center a column thrust up from the water flaring into a pink trumpet. More lilies spread their carpet off into the lagoon. Between the shore and the first pad lay a narrow strip of dark water. He saw Osidian hesitating, then in one swift movement leap across. The ridged leaf buckled a little but held. Osidian turned to grin at him. "They still bear my weight. I was not sure, but they do." He leaned over to grasp the flowering column and, holding on

to this, walked round from pad to pad. He stepped onto another plant further into the lagoon. It was larger and held
·him more steadily.

Carnelian jumped across. His feet bent a leaf rib like a
bow. He followed Osidian, stepping from one pad to the
next, the flower stalks waving above his head with each step.
Slowly they moved away from the shore. The air cooled
delightfully. Up ahead he saw that Osidian had stopped. As
he drew closer he saw that his friend was at the edge of the
lily pad floor. Beyond, clear unrippled water mirrored the
sky. Carnelian reached a pad next to Osidian, who was looking off to the distant Sacred Wall. Its upper edge was still
glowing with the sun. Osidian turned to Carnelian.

"You know, I have never even seen the world beyond that
wall?"

Carnelian nodded.

Osidian's eyes searched the Sacred Wall as if he were
counting its coombs. "Even those—I can see but never visit."
His jade eyes fell again on Carnelian. "Is it not paradoxical
that the Skymere should be more difficult to cross than your
sea?"

Carnelian could think of no answer.

Osidian's melancholy left him and he grinned. "I will
teach you to swim."

"I already know how."

Osidian looked puzzled, then smiled. "In the sea?"

"Since I was a child."

"Last one in is a mud worm," cried Osidian.

Carnelian watched him as he began to tear off his clothes.
For a moment the flashes of Osidian's cool white skin froze
him, but then he yanked off his tunic. When he looked up,
Osidian was standing on the pad edge naked. Laughing, he
dived into the water and disappeared. Carnelian was left
rocking on his leaf. He watched the ripples fade away and
the smashed reflection re-form.

"Osidian," he cried in alarm, then grinned as the edge of
his leaf began folding into the water under the grip of ten
white fingers. He tried to keep his balance, but he toppled,

crying out, and the water slapped him cool in the face and he felt it envelop his body. He kicked around, found the surface, pushed up through it to gulp at air.

"Mud worm," he heard, and then a hand on his head pushed him under. He struggled, feeling the vice around his chest, wriggled free, undulated away, opening his eyes and seeing the shadowy shapes, rose to the surface. He gasped air. His trousers clung to his legs. He searched and found the white head floating on the water, looking for him. He emptied his lungs, filled them, then went under. He swam strongly, peering until he found Osidian bright among the reeds. He rammed into his body, clasped it, yanked it downward caught the shoulders and, shoving, threw himself backward onto the surface. He was rewarded by Osidian's startled face erupting out of the water. Seeing Carnelian, Osidian laughed, then sank for another underwater attack. Soon they were wrestling in and out of the water, drinking it, spluttering, until Osidian lifted his hand and cried for a truce.

Carnelian dragged himself up onto a pad and helped Osidian onto the neighboring one. They lay back over the ribs, still laughing, coughing.

"Who is . . . a mud . . . worm," Carnelian managed to say and the pads trembled with their laughter.

Back on shore they hung Carnelian's trousers up to dry. Carnelian was aware that he was noticing Osidian's body too much and hid his blushes in the twilight.

Osidian pointed. "You still carry vestiges of your paint."

Looking down at his chest, Carnelian saw a patch dulling the gleam of his skin. Osidian too looked like the moon passing behind tatters of cloud. He watched him walk away. His eyes slipped down his tensing and untensing back. Osidian had taint scars only on the father's side. He watched him crouch over one of their packs. Could he be marumaga? No, he had a blood-ring. He watched Osidian rummaging. Perhaps his sybling brother carried their mother's taint on his back. Carnelian decided it was time to ask Osidian who he was. He was coming back, a jar in one hand, a red lacquered box in the other.

"What are those?" Carnelian asked, his question ready, his heart quickening.

Osidian did not answer or look up until he was standing near enough for Carnelian to smell his body. This time he could not hide his blush even though he looked away. Osidian's hand took his face and turned it back. Carnelian watched him kneel down, open the jar, open the box and bring out a pad. He dipped it in the jar and stood up with it. Carnelian looked at the pad held at the ends of his fingers. He looked into Osidian's eyes. They swallowed him. He felt the pad moving toward his face. The sight of it freed him. He snatched Osidian's wrist and held it firmly.

"What are you doing?" he asked in Vulgate, his heart beating hard enough to make him shake.

"Your skin—it's still streaked with paint," Osidian replied in the same language, smiling tentatively through a frown.

Carnelian shook his head. "But . . . you can't. Not you."

"I want to." Osidian brought up his other hand to release his wrist softly from Carnelian's grip.

Carnelian let his arm drop. He closed his eyes and flinched as the cool pad touched his forehead. It slid first to one side and then to the other, each time moving further down. Carnelian opened his eyes. He watched Osidian's careful concentration. He closed his eyes as the pad moved into the hollows of his eyes. He opened them again when it moved out over his swelling cheeks and the ridge of his nose. Sometimes, at the end of a stroke, their eyes would meet. Osidian's would gently disengage and he would continue with the cleaning. The pad slipped up and over Carnelian's lip. It came back up and along the hollow between his chin and lower lip. It slid back finding the valley between his lips. Its pressure made them open so that he felt it brushing his teeth and could taste its bitterness. The pad moved away. Osidian came closer until his eyes were all that Carnelian could see: his warm breath all he could feel. He closed his eyes as their mouths met and then allowed Osidian's tongue to open his lips further.

They swam again in the night-black water, slipping like ripples until they found a little stream by its bright gushing. They clambered up over rocks and found a pool. The moon rose to show them the fish darting their silver. At first their attempts to catch them were all splashing, curses and laughter, but eventually they settled down to hunt them slowly, with guile, slipping their hands round them and scooping them out onto the shore where they beat their shapes into the mud. They took them back, gutted them and ate their flesh raw with more pomegranates and some of the sweet little hri cakes that Osidian had thought to bring.

That night was a wonder of stars. Carnelian lay with Osidian in his arms on the bed they had made from rushes. Osidian's skin touched his all along his side. He moved his head so that he could feel Osidian's breath on his cheek. He gloried in his smell and would have kissed him except that he did not want to disturb his sleep. He propped himself up on an elbow to feast his eyes on moonlight made flesh. Then he lay back, not wishing to drink too much joy. The next day it would be there for him, and the next, and a few days more, and then what? He tried not to think of it. The worry about his father was a dull ache. He clutched Osidian, who moaned and rolled away.

The morning woke them with glorious birdsong. The sun gleamed on the faraway curve of the Sacred Wall. Osidian's kiss on Carnelian's shoulder turned into a bite. Carnelian growled, Osidian ran away laughing to plunge into the lagoon. Carnelian gave chase, dived, came up shrieking from the chill, but soon he was pursuing Osidian's flash through the weedy shallows. They played like eels until they saw the fire of the day had reached the edge of the Yden.

They returned, rubbing the water from their skins. Carnelian stood quietly while Osidian painted him, kissing his hands whenever they came close enough. Afterward he painted Osidian, caressing him with the brush, their eyes igniting passion.

When the sun grew tyrannous in the arch of the sky, they hid from it, leaning their smooth skin against the rugose bark of trees. Panting, eyes closed, half dreaming under canopying branches, limbs intertwining, they waited for the cooler afternoon.

As the shadows began to spear eastward they stirred, trusting to their shielding paint. They took their bundles and ran, exploring the wilder thickets of the Yden. Pale creatures dressed only in the dappling shadows of leaves, they slipped through the steaming afternoon. Their eyes flashed like dragonflies as they searched out each new wonder. They cast covetous glances on pools and fingers of the flamingo lagoons in which they did not dare to swim lest it should strip away their paint. As the crater darkened they dared to swoop across the water meadows, using lily pads as stepping stones. Then, when the Sacred Wall had drawn its shadow over them, they slipped sighing into a pool, burying their flesh in its heavy folds, scrubbing each other free of paint, undulating through the waters that were so filled with fish they could feel their silver against their skin.

At night they ate the food that they had found as they had found it. Fire seemed a sacrilege. They cleaned each other as if it was something they had always done. They made love. They slept together with only the moonlight for a blanket.

The next day they made a raft, and hidden beneath an awning they improvised from their purple cloaks, they paddled among the stilted flamingos to explore the islands lying in the lagoons. On one of these they sheltered from the greatest heat of the day. All day long they heard the waft of birdcalls and the delicate sculling of water as the flocks fed. Stick legs crossed and recrossed like a passing of spears before the scintillating textures of the water.

In the early evening they ran across the mud waving their arms and sending a pink drift up to hide the sky so that they stopped, gaping at the color and the rushing surge of it.

"This must be what it's like to receive Apotheosis," muttered Osidian.

Seeing the serious, fixed wonder of his face, Carnelian crept away and kicked water over him so that Osidian grew angry and chased him. They wrestled their patterns across the mud and, thrashing, rolled into the shallows. They rose panting, their laughter gashing white their muddy faces. The deepest pool they could find only came up to their waists. They washed each other. Osidian stopped Carnelian when he would have had more play. He seemed remote.

"What are you thinking?" Carnelian said, as lightly as he could.

Osidian turned to him, as beautiful as a marble god. "This morning we used up the last of the paint. I didn't expect that we'd stay down here so long."

Carnelian gazed at him, aching with a longing to engulf him so intense it almost made him cry. Instead, he grinned outrageously and slapped the ridging of Osidian's belly. "What of it? We'll have to hide out the day in the shade. The night will still be ours."

"But how shall we return?" Osidian turned to look back at the Pillar of Heaven, a thunderous mass against the mauve sky.

Carnelian looked at it, tried to see where the Halls of Thunder were, remembered his father with a pang. He had forgotten him and that his people would be expecting him back.

Osidian's somber looks stopped him passing it all off with a jest. It would have been hollow anyway. They went back together, gouging the mud with their toes, so close that often their shoulders and elbows touched.

"One more day?" Carnelian asked at last.

Osidian looked sidelong at him, and gave the slightest of nods.

Carnelian sat up. Something had woken him. He stood up, cursed under his breath as he tottered, waiting to see if he had woken Osidian. When there was no stirring at his feet, he ducked out from under the sheltering branches. A miraculous vault of stars dizzied him. The moon had set. The Pillar of Heaven was a hole cut out from half the sky. He was sure he could see some tiny flecks of light floating there near its top. He shook his head. It must be illusion. The Halls of Thunder were too far away. A sound. A faint, creaking sound. He turned to look across the Yden. Stars snared in its mirrors. Beyond, the pale, mountain wall stirred its reflection into the thick black Skymere. There it was again. A creaking and, perhaps, floating above it the tickle of faraway bells. He saw the lights. A necklace of tiny diamonds stretching across the crater's black throat. People were moving along the Ydenrim.

Something brushed his arm. He cried out.

"Hush," hissed the shadow, grabbing hold of him.

"I'm sorry I woke you," said Carnelian, fitting his head into the space between Osidian's neck and shoulder. He could feel Osidian's heart beating through his tense body. By the shape of his profile, Carnelian knew he was watching the lights. Another set had appeared, off to the south. "What are they?" Carnelian whispered.

He waited and was going to repeat the question when Osidian said, "Processions of the Chosen." He had returned to Quya for the first time in days.

"What does it mean?"

"That we must return to the sky."

Carnelian tried to get more out of him, unsuccessfully. He let him move away.

"Let us grab what sleep we can before daybreak," said Osidian.

Carnelian felt a twinge of irritation. With his resumption

of the Quya, Osidian was turning himself back into a stranger. Carnelian's stomach knotted. Was he regretting their lovemaking? Carnelian followed him back. Crouching under the branches, he lay down, fighting his desire to touch him. He lay for an age, miserable, bound on the rack of the worries he had put aside, until sleep released him into a fitful dream.

THE
SILENT
HEART

Better a sword thrust

Than a wounding silence

—PROVERB,

ORIGIN UNKNOWN

Reaching out for Osidian and not finding him, Carnelian awoke. He sat up and saw through twigs and leaves the morning bright on the faraway Sacred Wall. The Skymere smiled its alluring blue. The waders stirred the glimmering lagoons.

He crept out from under the branches, stretching, delighting in the warm caressing air. He looked for Osidian. The Pillar of Heaven was a slab of night auraed by the sun. From it came shadow that washed over him and out to narrow a dark road across the lagoons and the lake and up the Sacred Wall.

Osidian was nowhere to be seen. Carnelian followed a trail

of footprints to the water's edge. A few ripples creased the silk lagoon. He waited for a head to surface. He dipped his foot. He walked in, enjoying the coolness as it came up his legs. He allowed his knees to fold and sank. He swam as languidly as the fish, enjoying the weight of water on his limbs. He came out when he saw Osidian coming down to the shore. He seemed unnatural clothed.

"Have you bathed?" Carnelian said, rubbing the water off his skin.

Osidian gave him a nod.

"Why didn't you wake me?" Carnelian used Vulgate in an attempt to coax Osidian back into intimacy.

"The day ahead will be best met with you fully rested," Osidian replied, in Quya.

"Kiss me," said Carnelian with a grin.

Osidian looked at him without emotion. He came closer, leaned toward him as if over a wall, touched a kiss to Carnelian's cheek. Carnelian watched him stand back, feeling how closed Osidian was to him, how dry his kiss. "Is anything the matter?"

Osidian looked over his shoulder at the Pillar. "Without paint we must return always in its shadow. Though it will ebb slowly we must still allow time to gather fruit."

Keeping in the Pillar's shadow, they paddled across the lagoons, sometimes having to heave the raft over spits of mud. Eventually the water began to crowd with water lilies. When they became dense enough to snare the raft, they abandoned it and wound off across the pads. The pools narrowed and clogged with reeds until they were mostly walking on land.

When they reached the wild orchards, Carnelian looked back. The Pillar's shadow had retreated from the Sacred Wall across the Skymere and was now defending the Ydenrim against the morning.

They wandered up through the terraces, plucking apples and pomegranates from the trees and slipping them into their packs. Hearing water, they found a stream that they followed until it brought them to the wall of the Forbidden Garden. They walked along this until they found a gate that Osidian opened with his key.

The jeweled colors of the garden were dulled by the Pillar's shadow. The terraces staircased up to its dark sky-seeking cliff. Barefoot, they wandered paths in the oppressive perfume exhaled by trumpet-throated lilies. Staircases of jasper and mirrored granite were ice under their feet. Carp hung their gold motionless in pools. Trees stood like mourners. Carnelian felt he was trespassing.

At last they found a pavilion through which water percolated in a thousand twisting rivulets that made the air humid and filled it with melancholy music.

"We must wait until the sun passes overhead," said Osidian and laid himself out on a ledge so that Carnelian could hardly believe him not carved from its lifeless stone. He tried to wash away his loneliness with the sacrament of the feeling from the sound of rain. As the shivers coursed up and down his back he tried to focus on how with this ecstasy the Twins had brought into being all living things.

Osidian woke him wearing a solemn face. "It is time."

Carnelian watched him tearing strips from the hem of his purple cloak and winding them round his feet and hands. Osidian looked up. "Do as I do. The sun will be at its highest. Exposed skin will taint instantly."

Carnelian copied Osidian. When they were ready, they stood at the door of the pavilion with the rain sounds behind them. Outside, the garden burned fiercely with hardly a shadow. They ran out into the sun-ray downpour. Soon they began to feel the heat through their hoods and through the silk shoulders of their cloaks. They moved quickly, pausing only wherever they could find shade. The kitchen garden gave welcome relief along its narrow half-shaded paths. The wall of the garden had to be climbed with some care. Several times, Carnelian winced as a sleeve fell away to reveal the blinding whiteness of his arm. The scorch of the sun seemed to threaten a blistering burn.

At first they were glad when they dropped down on the other side into the thorn forest. But the canopy was thin and brown. The thorns snagged their cloaks, trying to pluck them off and expose them to the shriveling glare of the sun. Each time a cloak snagged, it had to be worked free with tedious care. Imprisoned in their cloaks they broiled. At last they reached the shadow that the Pillar was casting toward the east. It was as deliciously cool as the water of a mountain lake.

Osidian drove Carnelian up the Ladder as if they were being hunted. Up and further up they climbed. Carnelian hardly dared to look out across Osrakum. When he did, he had to cling hard to the rock, feeling that the wind was trying to pluck him off, to send him soaring down into the turquoise world below. Each time, he would see that the Pillar's shadow had stretched further out over the Yden, angling slowly toward the south. It was exhaustion that made him stop looking. When his hands had walked their way up to the next handhold, he pressed his cheek against the rock, one eye left free to make sure he was not falling. When they reached each rest cave, he would flop into it, his breath rasping, mute, waiting with increasing resentment for Osidian's next demand that they press on.

They were sitting in such a cave when Carnelian refused to go any further.

"But we can make the next stop if we push on," Osidian pleaded.

Looking out, Carnelian could see the tide of shadow was already close to flooding Osrakum's floor. He was weary. His limbs were trembling. He let his head hang forward. He would not go any further.

"What is wrong with you?" cried Osidian.

Carnelian looked up and saw disturbing flickerings in his eyes. "Nightfall is near."

Osidian snorted, saying haughtily, "My Lord has quickly gained expertise in judging time."

"If you wish to go on, my Lord, go. I am remaining here."

They ate the fruit they had brought in sullen silence. The sharp, sweet pomegranate juice awoke in Carnelian memories of joy. He glanced at Osidian and felt his anger melting away. The stubble on his head made him seem less a Master. He tried to find a way to his side. "Osidian?"

"What?" said Osidian, his voice, his face, his eyes, all granite.

Carnelian turned away thinking that perhaps the Yden had been nothing but a dream.

The morning sun found Carnelian's face with a single ray. He smiled in his dreams, then woke with a start and edged away into a shadow. He could see an arch of sky bright enough to stab pain behind his eyes. Osidian was sleeping in the gloom. He crept close to him and looked into his face. Even in sleep he was frowning his birthmark. Carnelian leaned close, thinking to kiss him, but pulled back when he stirred.

"When do we continue the climb?" he asked, as he watched Osidian wake.

"When do you think?"

It was like a slap. Carnelian hid his hurt in silence. Sometimes he would catch Osidian looking at him, his lips parted, and he could see that the boy had something he needed to say. But the words would not come out and Carnelian would lean his head back against the rock, close his eyes and try to make his mind as blank as a drizzling sky.

*　　*　　*

The moment they felt shadow come, they left the cave and teetered on the edge of the sky in a wind that came scorching up from the land. Above them, the Pillar's head still showed the halo of the sun passing behind it. They resumed the climb. The rock that at first had been almost too hot to touch cooled slowly. The wind grew turbulent. As they struggled on, Carnelian nursed his resentment, ignoring the little voice reminding him that Osidian had warned him how terrible the climb would be.

Even as the sky was darkening, they dragged themselves up into the throat of the Windmoat ravine. Once they had rested a while, they put on their robes, their shoes, their masks, covered themselves with the purple cloaks and climbed up to the ledge. There was only enough breeze to ruffle their cloaks. The heart-stone screens of the ammonites were filtering light along the whole length of the ledge. In contrast, on the opposite side, only a handful of lit windows pricked the gloomy face of the Forbidden House. Osidian went ahead, his shape defined by the light freckling through the screen. Through its holes, Carnelian glimpsed the long crowded galleries. Their hive mutter was more insistent than it had been those few days before.

The library swallowed them into its black silence. It seemed a refuge and Carnelian's heart sank as they reached the moon-eyed door and removed their masks. "So we part here?" he said, wanting to make it a joint decision.

"No," said Osidian. "I will come with you at least some of the way."

Carnelian was more cheered than he would admit to himself. He led Osidian off along the familiar path back to the Sunhold. After the perfumes of the Yden and the rushing currents of the sky, the air was oppressively stale and lifeless. "Like a tomb," Carnelian muttered.

Osidian grabbed his shoulder and yanked him round. "What do you mean by that, my Lord?"

Carnelian blinked at him. Osidian's eyes held bladed light.

Carnelian felt rage building up inside him. "I meant nothing at all. Do you not find this place grim in comparison with the Yden?"

Without answering him, Osidian launched off into the blackness. Carnelian felt as if a knife point had been taken away from his throat. It made him feel violent.

They walked in silence until at last they reached the stair that led up to the Sunhold. They were more than halfway up when Osidian stopped. The narrow space was filled with their breathing.

"What are we waiting for?" Carnelian asked, exasperated.

"Hush!" hissed Osidian. "Listen."

"I hear nothing," Carnelian whispered.

Osidian nodded vaguely, his eyes looking far off through the stone.

The feeling of being shut out made Carnelian's anger flare. "Please let me pass. My Lord evidently has a need to be by himself."

Osidian frowned and his eyes came back to focus on Carnelian. "What?"

Now that Osidian was looking at him, Carnelian felt he was behaving like a petulant child. He was incapable of apology so he gave way to coldness. "Let me pass."

"Come on," said Osidian, urging him to go down the stairs.

Carnelian stood his ground. "Why?"

Osidian's porcelain perfect face looked down at him. "What are you waiting for?"

"Explanations."

Osidian jerked his finger upward. "Your father is up there and the trapdoor is closed. Do you want to go and knock on it and then appear before him and whoever else might be there, dressed as you are?"

Carnelian thought about it. Why would his father have returned to the Sunhold? "How do you know this?"

Osidian's head dropped as if he were dealing with a stupid child. He looked up again. "The pulse of the Emperor's heart has stopped."

Carnelian listened for it. Osidian was right. The pulse was gone. His hand came up to his head. He ran it over the stubble. The God Emperor was dead. His father was no longer Regent. The God Emperor was dead.

"Will you go down now?"

Carnelian let Osidian squeeze past and stood for some moments, dazed, as the light receded down the stairs. When he caught up with Osidian, he touched his shoulder. "You knew before we came here?"

"Did you not know when you saw the processions of the Chosen moving along the Ydenrim?"

"The election," said Carnelian in sudden realization.

"Of course the election," snapped Osidian.

They reached the bottom of the stairs.

"But how will I get back?" said Carnelian.

Follow, commanded Osidian's hand. He walked them to the edge of the nave and into the column forest beyond. As they walked along the back wall, Carnelian could hear Osidian sniffing the air. He lifted his nose and detected the tang of urine.

When the smell had grown very strong, Osidian lifted the lantern and showed Carnelian a narrow staircase. "Up there. Guardsmen of the Lesser Lords sometimes use this old construction stair when they have need to make water. It comes up into the Encampment."

"Where there are tyadra, surely there will be Chosen."

"They will be in the nave observing the Great selling their votes. You should be able to slip through unnoticed to one of the Sunhold's postern gates."

"We part here, then?"

Osidian jerked a nod. Their eyes locked. Each could see that there were words the other wished to say.

"Goodbye then," Carnelian managed at last.

"Goodbye," said Osidian. He handed Carnelian the lantern and disappeared into the darkness.

* * *

In spite of his efforts to cover the nostrils of his mask with the edges of his cowl, Carnelian found the urine stench grew overpowering as he climbed the steps. He reached a landing whose walls were arched with stains. He hitched up the skirt of his cloak in disgust and walked toward a dim doorway. He stared. Pavilions had been put up everywhere. Perfect rows of them, each made by stretching jeweled cloths between columns. Some were dark but others were lit from within like paper lanterns and glowed the colors of their heraldry. A path narrowed off across to the faraway wall of the Sunhold. But this was no easy route. Along its length it was lit by many filtering pavilions and glimmering along it were Masters moving with their guardsmen. To left and right were the beginnings of many more such paths. He would have to trust to luck to find his way to the other side unseen.

As he came out from the shelter of the archway, he heard the murmuring and searched for its source. Where the column forest opened into the nave of the Encampment, a brilliant river streamed like a pouring of stars: the thronging Masters in their court robes.

He shook his eyes free of the wonder and crept into the shadow pooling round an unlit pavilion. In the breeze, its cloth walls trembled off a lily scent. He touched its jeweled brocade and bumped his finger along the tail tip of the serpent that doubled back and forth upon itself until its jaws spat out its tongue high above his head. As he came to the column that was the corner of the pavilion he heard voices. He peered round it and saw guardsmen huddling round a brazier. Their faces carried the same cipher as the wall of the pavilion they guarded. He risked it. As he walked out, they fell silent watching him. Carnelian ignored the seductive glimmer of the nave in the corner of his eye and breathed more easily once he was between the next pair of pavilions.

Gradually he made his way across the Encampment, taking a route that avoided the brighter pavilions. He could not avoid them all. Quya came from one whose cloth wall was showing a gigantic shadow play. Others were more sinister, filled with subtle movement, as if they were chrysalises in which vast butterflies were dreaming.

He was passing near some tyadra when they surged suddenly to their feet. They opened a flap, allowing Carnelian to see an interior like a jewel casket. Two Masters came out crowned with subdued fire, in court robes so massive that their guardsmen's heads hardly reached their waists. Carnelian drew back, ducking his head so that the cowl would fall to hide the betraying mirror of his mask, pulling his hands up into his sleeves. He heard the lilt and exquisite enunciation of Quya syllables sounding among the footfalls of the men. He saw the golden dapples around his feet and dared to look up enough to see the Masters smoldering past. He waited some moments. He looked to see them framed by the shimmering nave, then continued on.

When at last he reached the Sunhold's wall, he walked along it, keeping in the shadows. Recessed into its barbican the first postern gate had its portcullis down. Through it he could see another gate and a passage curving off. When he struck the bronze some Ichorians came from a side door. Their half-black faces peered out at him.

"Ammonite?" said one.

Carnelian opened his cowl so that their light could reflect off his mask.

They bowed. "Master."

"Open this," Carnelian said.

"We cannot, Master."

"I'm the son of He-who-goes-before."

"We can't open this gate under any circumstance, Master," they said and shook their heads as they retreated.

He was in a cold sweat. What if all the doors should be closed against him? How could he appear in the nave dressed as he was? He would humiliate his father and his House before the majesty of all the gathered Great. He leaned back against the Sunhold's wall cursing softly. His gaze wandered among the pavilions wondering if, with the election upon them, the Chosen ever slept.

"The commander of the Ichorians," he muttered. The man

might have the authority to let him in. If not, he would have to be coerced into going to get permission from He-who-goes-before. Carnelian grimaced imagining the consequent confrontation with his father.

He skirted the next postern gate and came to a region where crowds of tyadra had gathered to stare into the nave. Carnelian kept as close as he could to the wall where there were some shadows. The wall swelled to form the bastion of the last gate. He slipped round it, had a glaring impression of the nave and then ducked in toward the gate. The Ichorians there would not let him in either. Putting all his authority into his voice, Carnelian demanded that they go and fetch their commander.

As he waited he looked out and saw the gapes on the tattooed faces. The guardsmen could have been staring at a city burning. Patches of glimmer slid everywhere, stretching and contracting, finding their faces in the gloom. There was such wonder in their eyes that Carnelian could not resist edging out to see what they were seeing. He was forced to squint against the dazzle. The nave was hung with suns beneath whose showering rays slipped the vast shapes of angels sheathed in starlight. Some were jeweled sculptures. Others opened like exquisite mechanisms, spreading their arms to display sleeves that were falls of sunlit water. White hands fluttered signs. He searched and found their masks, faces carved high into the golden towers where each swelled into a huge crown.

The grate of the portcullis lifting drew him back into its shadows.

"You are the Master, Suth Carnelian?"

It took a breath or two for Carnelian's eyes to adjust enough to able to see the grand-cohort commander. Carnelian removed his blood-ring and offered it.

Eagerly, the commander took it in his tattooed hand and held it up to the light. His whole frame visibly relaxed. He gave Carnelian back his ring. "The Twins be thanked, Master. Our father has been searching for you."

Carnelian almost groaned. "When . . . how long ago?"

"He found my Master gone when he took up residence in this place, yesterday, when the sun still shone through the Amber Window."

"I must go immediately to my chambers."

"I will escort you, Master."

"Master. Oh, Master."

The desperate relief in his guardsmen's voices alarmed him. The commander's eyes were examining him, perhaps noticing for the first time that he was wearing a dirty, ammonite robe.

"Thank you for your escort," Carnelian said to him.

The man bowed but seemed reluctant to go. "Your father, Master."

Carnelian opened his arms so that the commander might clearly see his purple robe. "Shall I go like this?"

The man's eyes blinked brightly in his half-black face.

"Once I'm properly attired I'll go to him." He made a sign of dismissal. "Now go, Ichorian."

Carnelian turned his back on the commander, waiting to hear him walk away before unmasking and surveying his guardsmen. "What is it?" he said, not managing to control the irritation in his voice.

They thumped to their knees.

"Stop groveling," he said dangerously. "I'm in no mood for it."

His anger only caused them to fall flat on their faces. "Gods' blood!" he spat, throwing his hands up in exasperation. "I know the Master's been here. What did you tell him?"

When none of them spoke up, he jabbed one of them with his toe "Get up, man. Tell me."

The guardsman looked up, his face twitching. "Craving your pardon, Master, but . . . we had to tell him . . . he is the Master."

"And . . . ?"

"He demanded to know where you were, Master. We told

him we didn't rightly know . . . we had to tell how long you'd been away . . . that you'd gone away before." The man cowered.

"And he was very angry?" Carnelian asked.

The man looked up, tearful. "He's going to crucify us all."

Carnelian felt the blood draining from his face.

The man must have seen this because his eyes darted out of sight.

Carnelian squatted down. Touched their heads, saying gently, "Now look at me." He waited until he had their eyes. "I won't allow even one of you to be put upon a cross." He nodded into each face. "Not one of you." He stood up. "Now get me some people. I need to be dressed, and quickly."

As one of them scampered off, another looked up.

"Master?"

Carnelian looked at the man expectantly.

"Master, the other Masters of our House . . . ?"

Carnelian frowned. "The other lineages?"

The man nodded. "They've sent word that they're here and want to meet you, my Master."

"I've no time for them," said Carnelian as he moved toward his chamber. Once inside, he let the ammonite cloak slip off his shoulders and hung his head. Now his father.

"The Master wishes to be formally attired?"

Carnelian whisked round to see a servant, head bowed, others kneeling behind him. He was sure that they were not part of the household he had left behind.

"You've just come from the coomb?"

"That is so, my Master."

"Why?"

"We were sent to bring the Master a court robe." The servant indicated the golden suit standing against a wall. Carnelian walked over to it. It was similar to the suit he had worn before but it had different heraldry in the panel running down its front. He touched the chameleons writhing on a field of jades, emeralds and other green stones. Under his fingers their skins were a mottle of pearls. Their black opal eyes blinked. They looked more alive than geckos on a wall.

It occurred to him that Fey had talked about sending him such a suit with the first household. He wondered why it had been so long in coming.

"If the Master will allow, I'll coordinate his dressing?"

Carnelian turned to the new servant. "As fast as you can." He lifted his arms from his sides and they ran in to disrobe him. "What news, *coordinator*?"

"The return of the Master and his son is longed for," said the man without the slightest movement of his chameleon tattoo.

"Has the servant Tain arrived from the gates?"

"An unchameleoned boy, Master?"

Carnelian grabbed the man's shoulders. "You've seen him?"

The coordinator went waxy soft in his hands, melting away as Carnelian released him. "Y-yes, Master. Yesterday, he was being prepared to come here."

Carnelian smiled, longing to see his brother's face. He hardly noticed the cleaning, the putting on of the belt of hooks. He climbed onto the ranga and then they locked the court robe round him. They masked him. They built a crown upon his head. When they knotted a scarlet sash around his left wrist he was reminded that all the Chosen were in mourning for the God Emperor. He allowed a few more adjustments then, gigantic, he strode from his chamber to face his father.

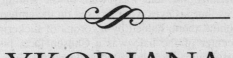

YKORIANA

Often I heard her speak

With a voice of angels

Words barbed and dripping poison

—EXTRACT FROM "THE
VOYAGE OF THE
SUNCUTTER"

The grand-cohort commander was standing with other Ichorians at the entrance to the Sun in Splendor. He looked at the heraldry on Carnelian's court robe and let him pass. The hall was smoldering gold, its walls and pillars catching their light from somewhere round the dais. The pillars blocked his line of sight to the dais itself. He stopped, closed his eyes to find composure, then, opening them, left the shelter of the columns. He moved into the center of the hall and turned to face the dais. On it and beside it were two Masters; three more faced them like frozen flames. These three rose slowly, pivoting round, the skirts of their robes slightly rising. Each face seemed transfused by a beam of light. They could have been angels caught in the act of forming from fire.

Carnelian walked toward them, timing the placing of each ranga to the heavy swing of the robe. He could feel their eyes watching him and was aware of the shining ovals of their faces, but his eyes were focused on the enthroned being rising behind them, haloed by a corona of flickering flames. At the center of the halo was a Chosen face, his father's, alarmingly gaunt. A hand lifted a sleeve that was a slab of mosaiced gold.

Is that you?

The question brought Carnelian to a halt. He watched the hand fall. His father glanced at the other Lords, and Carnelian saw it was Aurum beside him and that Imago Jaspar was one of the three. The other two Masters Carnelian did not know. Each nodded to him and he responded vaguely, his eyes already returning to his father's wary hope.

"I am come, my Lord, at your summons," his own voice said and almost choked on the words when he saw the bright relief fill his father's face.

"Your father is glad to see you, my Lord son."

Carnelian remembered to unmask, and when the metal face was off they exchanged tiny smiles.

Please wait for me there, his father's hand signed and pointed to a place near Aurum. Carnelian paced to the spot, turned to face the dais and sank to his knees as he saw the other Masters doing.

"Excuse the disturbance, my Lords. Shall we continue?" his father said.

The Masters all bowed and began to speak with hands. Carnelian made a point of ignoring Aurum. Jaspar's fixed, cold-eyed smile forced a twitch of recognition from Carnelian before he focused on his father's face. The hollow cheeks and recessed eyes appalled him. His father had become an aged man. His hands, when they were not signing, clung for support to the staves that were planted on either side of him. Sun-rayed eyes stared from the staves and their tops burned red with the ciphers of the pomegranate and the lily.

Carnelian noticed some ammonites squatting on the floor. Three more were in the shadows; before the dais, Aurum and himself. For as long as he watched, they sat hunched, doing nothing.

His father glanced at him setting anticipation of the coming conflict grinding in Carnelian's stomach. He tried to distract himself by following the Masters' talk but it was all blood transactions, bride-prices and iron. Carnelian gave up trying and let their talk flow over him. His mind strayed to the Yden. The vision lost its brightness as he remembered how they had parted. He and Osidian had made no arrangement to meet. Carnelian looked over to where a pillar concealed the trapdoor. That way was closed. He looked down the hall to the sun-eyed door and imagined the glittering host out there. Even if he knew where to find Osidian, how could he ever hope to get to him?

Dapples of gold flickering round him made it seem he was among breeze-ruffled trees. Carnelian lifted his head and saw the crusted masses of the Masters grow taller and then turn toward the distant door, like sails into a wind. One of them remained. The Ruling Lord Aurum. He raised his hand. *There is now no need for you to go and see her?*

Carnelian looked at his father who seemed blind to Aurum's signs.

If you go, I shall go with you.

Suth's hand stirred into motion. *If I go, I go alone.*

Aurum's face became stiff with anger. He stabbed Carnelian with his eyes before glimmering away.

Carnelian felt the opening of the doors as a change of pressure in his ears. They let in a perfume wind and the roar and glimmer of the throng. Carnelian watched his father. The doors came ponderously together and Carnelian was left alone with his father in the glowing golden gloom.

"Leave us," said Suth.

Carnelian's eyes were drawn downward by movement. He had forgotten the ammonites. He watched them creep over the floor and slip down into a hole over which a lid closed silently. Something like tumbling fire jerked Carnelian's head up. His father's head had fallen forward. He appeared to be nothing more than a golden puppet. Alarmed, Carnelian opened the angles of his knees and lurched towards the dais. The sunburst crown presented its teeth to him so that Carnelian could not see his father's face.

"Father." The word came strangled from his throat.

The spiked halo rose, lifting the limestone of his father's face after it, sighing, "Where have you been?"

That close, Carnelian could not avoid seeing the sallow skin, the thinned lips, the eyes deep in their pits all shot with red. Those eyes were on him. He sought their familiar stormy gray but found only pale drizzle. "Exploring," he said.

"For . . . five . . . days?"

Carnelian could admit nothing without admitting it all.

"You were alone . . . saw no one?"

Carnelian blushed. "There was someone with me." He withstood the probing of his father's eyes.

Surprise dawned in his father's face. "So it is that way. The sybling Quenthas?"

"A sybling, but a divided one." He watched his father's yellow forehead creasing. "He wears a blood-ring."

"Does he?" There was a long pause during which his father's red eyes turned to glass. "His House?"

"The Masks." Carnelian watched the eyes close. Sepia welled in the eye pits and round the corners of the mouth. Looking at that yellow mask, Carnelian could hardly believe to whom it belonged. "You look tired, Father."

The eyes opened, brightened. His father gave a chuckle and his lips wore something like a smile. "You could say that."

"Your wound?"

His father gave the merest shrug with his eyebrows. "This is no time for convalescence."

"Does your wound still bleed?" Carnelian took a step forward.

His father's head made the slightest movement side to side. He looked into Carnelian's face.

"Be not concerned. Once this matter is resolved . . . I will abdicate to Aurum the power that he craves, then I will have all the time I need to rest."

He went deathly sallow. "They who were the mirror to divinity are no more. We are left to live through these broken mirror days. The Commonwealth must be given a new heart lest she should perish."

Carnelian remembered what the dead Emperor had once been to his father. The need to tell him of the Yden was burning, but it was not the time for such confession.

"The gates in the Ringwall are open. The barbarians will be coming in, riddling the Commonwealth with their cancer."

"And the election?"

"In five days."

"Goes it well?"

"Very well." His father smiled raggedly. "The new Imago, our friend Jaspar, has brought his faction behind Aurum's. At every conclave I buy more votes with imperial blood and iron. The towers of the major blocks are all in place, we merely need to build the curtain walls between them. Barring some unforeseen intervention, Ykoriana and Molochite will be defeated."

"She is quite given to interventions, Father."

The cores of his father's eyes showed indomitably. Carnelian felt something of their usual power as they settled on him. "That is why you must promise me that until the election you will not leave the Sunhold save with me."

Carnelian yearned for Osidian. Vague plans, imagined meetings. As it was, the election had come between them. Once it was over, he would return with his father to their coomb. The gulfs of the Skymere and the Labyrinth would lie between them. Carnelian knew that if he made this promise he might never see his lover nor feel his touch again.

Suth's hand jumped to his son's shoulder like a grappling hook and drew him in. Carnelian stared into the yellow red-veined eyes. His father's words began with a hiss in which Carnelian could smell the illness the strange odor of some drug. "The tighter she is caught in my trap . . . the more desperate will be her efforts . . . to . . . break . . . free."

Carnelian rocked back as he was released.

"Your oath, my Lord."

Seeing his father locked into those weak, ravaged remains, Carnelian could not deny him. "On my blood."

His father closed his eyes, nodding, breathing heavily. Bleakly, Carnelian put all thoughts of Osidian from his mind.

He remembered his duty to his people. "My Lord has threatened my guardsmen with crucifixion."

His father smiled at him. "Fear for you made me wrathful. Rest assured they will suffer no further punishment." His face lost color. "You and I will go and have some words with your aunt, now Dowager Empress and Regent."

"Me?"

"I need your strength. Besides, now that I have you back I find myself reluctant to let you out of my sight." He looked away down the length of the hall to its doors, growing older as he did so. "I do not relish wading through that sea outside, so I shall take a boat."

He turned to look down at Carnelian. "I am afraid you will have to swim in its wake."

Carnelian did not understand.

"Put on your mask," his father said. Carnelian obeyed. His father masked himself with some difficulty and then motioned with his hand toward one of the staves. "Lift this thrice and each time bring it down hard."

Carnelian shuffled closer and then, with both hands, lifted the staff with its sun-eye and its pomegranate and cracked it down. A ringing tone reverberated round the hall. Twice more he lifted the staff and twice more brought it down. His father's lictors dewed out from the shadows.

Summon the forty-eight, his father's hand signed.

The lictors went off into the dark and then came back with more Ichorians, in groups carrying poles, their half-black bodies concealed only by their golden collars. Carnelian took some steps back as they collected round the sides of his father's dais. A pole was lowered almost to the ground and then pushed into a hole in the edge of the dais. Carnelian watched the pole feed in and its head appear at the other side. Other poles were being pushed through the dais. When they were all in place, the Ichorians moved in between them.

They bent like rowers to their oars, strained, and the dais and his father rose slowly into the air.

The dais was a raft drifting through the gloom toward the doors. The lictors walked ahead of it carrying the two staves of He-who-goes-before. Carnelian walked behind between files of Ichorians. On his right their shoulders and faces had the hues of barbarian skin. On his left these hues were clothed in swirling black tattoos. His father was a pillar of gold from whose apex rayed the sun disc that hid fully a third of his height. Carnelian watched the doors ahead opening. The elegant hubbub of the Great wafted through with their lily perfumes and the shimmer of their court robes. Around Carnelian, the Ichorians lifted shawms to their lips and began a ragged braying. Floating on this, the dais carrying his father slipped burning into the light, parting the Great before it. Carnelian angled his head so that his mask would shield his eyes from the glare as he too came into the nave. More Ichorians appeared pumping more volume into the pulsating fanfare of the shawms. The Great loomed like towers in a fortress wall that were hung with the mirror shields of their masks. Carnelian narrowed his eyes further against their dazzle. Incense puffed up in clouds into a region where lanterns larger than men hung ablaze. Higher than these flapped banners that carried all the heraldry of the Houses of the Chosen. The weight of his crowns forced Carnelian's eyes down to look along the avenue of the Great. Between flashes he caught glimpses of his father reflected in their masks: an idol being carried aloft in a sacred procession. The music shrilled on. The Great spoke with flickering hands. Trying to read the signs made him dizzy. He locked his eyes to the ambered rubied edge of the dais and concentrated on the opening and closing of his knees.

The wall of the radiant Great fell suddenly away as they came among the Lesser Chosen. On his taller ranga, Carnelian overtopped even their Ruling Lords by a head. He could see two banks of them running all the way down the nave.

Carnelian reached the bronze wall of the Chamber of the Three Lands in a dream. His eyes took a while adjusting to the lack of summer gold. The Emperor's heart no longer caused the massive doors to tremble. The shawms frayed with echoes as they left the nave to follow the bronze wall round. When the Approach came into sight, Carnelian saw that syblings were crowding its lower steps in the midst of which a figure in glimmering black was descending. The dais broke through the sybling tide and washed up onto the first step. Carnelian walked round it, watching his father for signs of life. Syblings took the staves from the lictors and held them upright before his father, whose gold mass flickered and flamed as he rose. His sleeves hinged up, his hands caught hold of the staves and he seemed to be pulled by them onto the first step.

The Ichorians stopped Carnelian pushing through to his father's side. Arms outstretched, his father seemed crucified between the staves. One hand uncurled to beckon Carnelian through the half-colored men.

Now I will, the hand flickered. It recurled itself around the stave and slid down to rest upon its sun-eye. Carnelian saw it move. He wanted it to speak again. It detached and began signing, *Stay close. I will have to find the strength to climb these steps.*

Looking up, Carnelian saw the vast black Lord was almost upon them. Syblings covering the steps around him appeared to be an extension of his raven-jeweled court robe. Others carried a pair of court staves before him bearing the jade and the obsidian masks. His own gold mask was the sun peering through a pillar of smoke that his crowns threatened to eclipse.

A porcelain hand appeared. *Sardian, I was coming to see you.*

"I must meet with your mother, Celestial."

The black Lord turned his vast head a little as if he could hear someone calling for him down the stairs. *She will not welcome you, my Lord.*

"Nevertheless."

Have you strength enough to climb these steps?

"I will find it, Celestial."

I shall go among the Great. The black Lord made a gesture to hook Carnelian's eyes. *Take good care of him, my Lord.*

Carnelian stared, then inclined his head as the Lord swept past and began to move off toward the bronze wall.

"Molochite?" Carnelian asked, puzzled.

"His brother, Nephron," his father replied. "Now, let us begin the climb."

For both father and son, the climb was an ordeal. At first Suth managed to keep up a reasonable pace but after a while it was obvious that he was spent. They stopped. Carnelian could hear his father's labored breathing. Looking down the steps, the floor seemed far away. Above them, the summit seemed further.

"Can you not be carried?"

His father stretched open his hand. *The Sun cannot be carried. It would be as much as admitting that I am unfit to wear the Pomegranate Ring.*

"But Father, why must you do this at all?"

His father's hand trembled, *There is no one else.*

They resumed the climb a step at a time. Even for Carnelian, lifting his ranga was an effort. He could imagine what it was costing his father, whose ranga were besides much taller. He leaned close and tried to help push him up. In front of them, the syblings carried the staves that his father clung to. Carnelian waited for the clack of each shoe, chewing his tongue, fearing that one would not find its step. The last few steps, when they could look onto the landing, were the worst. Rasping each breath, his father climbed them. When he reached the top he sank down in among the empty court robes that forested the landing. As the disrobing syblings came, Carnelian tried to mask his father's breathing with his voice as he told them to attend to his father first.

"He-who-goes-before is the embodiment of the celestial

nature of the Seraphim and as such is permitted to retain his pomp."

Carnelian looked with horror at his father, whose robe seemed as empty as the others standing round. He looked to the next flight, a hill of steps, and higher up he knew there was yet another. He drew as close as he could to his father and whispered to him. "This ascent will kill you."

"No," said the mass of gold. "By the time . . . you are disrobed . . . I shall have found more strength."

Carnelian allowed himself to be taken off by the syblings who removed his court robe and attired him in coarse fiber. His father had risen when Carnelian returned. Without his ranga, Carnelian hardly reached his father's waist. They walked together to the next stair. Neither of them looked up it but just began to climb.

Somehow, his father managed to reach the second landing, which swarmed with Masters in their supplicant robes. Cries went up of "He-who-goes-before." As they flocked toward them, Carnelian commanded their sybling entourage to form a cordon. Within this protection, his father slid on seemingly unaware.

The third and final stairway was almost more pain than Carnelian could bear. More of the Great wandered up and down on either side, and for the sake of appearances his father dug deep and moved up the steps steadily. Tears of bitter anger trickled down behind Carnelian's mask. He knew the climb was consuming his father's life.

When they reached the final landing they found many of the Great waiting before the glowering Iron Door. Carnelian expected his father to sink and rest but instead he commanded the syblings to take away the support of his staves and strike them both against the door, crying, "He-who-goes-before seeks audience with the Regent of the Twins."

Once the dull thunder reverberated to silence, the door opened to show the Hanuses, who bowed.

"I have come with the Regent's nephew to speak to her."

The syblings lowered their double head in a deeper bow and the door closed. Carnelian felt the gleaming mass of his father turn to look back down the stairs and he went to stand beside him.

"Do you remember standing on the weir gazing down at the sea?" Carnelian asked in a low voice.

His father's sun-haloed head shot with fire as he nodded. To both that morning was already a lifetime away.

The Iron Door rumbled open and a Ruling Lord came out walking with a staff, followed by other Masters of his House. He gave Suth an angry look before he and his companions inclined their crowns and stood to one side.

Carnelian's eyes were drawn away to where the Hanuses had one face turned obliquely to him, the other hidden. The syblings' hand beckoned them to follow. Preceded by his staves, Suth slid glimmering into the Thronehall and Carnelian followed. After a few steps he moved to one side to see past his father's brocaded trunk. Red braziers painted a bloody road across the night to a bonfire in whose heart something like a blade was standing.

They followed the syblings down the road between the braziers, in whose lurid light Carnelian could just make out the sybling guardsmen on either side. Moonlight pierced the Creation Window and fell around the throne. A black fence edged the lamp-lit clearing below its pyramid. The palings turned and Carnelian saw they were Sapients with their hole eyes and scar mouths.

Suth took hold of his staves and the syblings that had been carrying them walked away. "My Lords of the Wise," he said, with a nod.

The Sapients bowed and turned back to strangle their homunculi, gazing blindly up into the light toward a welter of red like a blooded sword. This scarlet figure stood between two court staves. Curled at its foot was an exquisite carving of white jade, a youth crouching.

Carnelian felt as much as saw the rustle of his father's robe settling. Even kneeling, Suth's chest was at Carnelian's eye level. Carnelian stood uncertain, only falling to his knees when his father touched his shoulder.

The red figure lifted a slim long-fingered hand that had two Great-Rings on it and released a veil. A gold angel face appeared like the sun at dawn. When the other hand rose Carnelian saw that it too had a pair of Great-Rings and then he knew beyond doubt that he was in the presence of the Dowager Empress, Ykoriana. The hand kept rising and pulled a chain that in turn uncurled the white youth to his feet. By his height, his blue eyes and the perfect pallor of his skin he might have been Chosen. The youth's nakedness, however, displayed his mutilation and when Carnelian looked more carefully he saw his eyes were sapphires.

The scarlet mass slid down a little as Ykoriana knelt on her ranga. Her gold face bent toward the youth's ear.

"Sardian, have you become so decrepit that you must needs use your own son as a stick?" The youth's voice was honey-smooth. Homunculi mutterings echoed it.

"The Regent must know how long and perilous a journey I have had returning to Osrakum," said Suth.

"We have heard something of it," said the melodious voice. "Do you come here as He-who-goes-before or as Suth Sardian?"

"That is in your choice, Celestial."

Every word was repeated by the homunculi.

"I would talk without the Wise."

The Empress flicked open a hand like a fan in a gesture of dismissal. The Sapients released the muttering throats of their homunculi who, hand in hand, fled away into the darkness.

"Must their masters stay?" asked Suth.

"You forget, my Lord, that though I am Regent the rigor of my purdah must still be observed," said the melodious voice.

"It is not only you, Celestial, who have suffered seclusion."

"Did you then suffer much those long years you spent in the wilderness?" purred the youth.

"Do you mock me, Madam?"

"Perhaps a little. We have led parallel lives."

"You chose the suffering for us both."

"Thwarted love is the charioteer of vengeful deeds."

"Tell me, Ykoriana, have your acts of vengeance brought you joy?"

"Vengeance is a pale creature in comparison to joy, but still, Sardian, she is brighter than darkness."

"A darkness of your own making."

Laughter rang out from behind the golden mask, making the youth turn round and gaze up at it.

"Sardian, I do think you could take a little more pride in your handiwork," said the Empress in her own, rich voice.

"This was no work of mine."

"Was it not? My husband, now sadly deceased, told me I could buy my eyes with your release."

Suth shook his head. "I was horrified when I heard what had been done to you."

"Spare me your pity."

"Outrage rather than pity, Ykoriana. Such mutilation was without precedent."

"The Wise found that it was not, my Lord. When I would not bend to my husband's will, he asked them to enforce an ancient form of purdah. Oh, they put me into the dark gladly enough. They envy others the life of sensation that is denied to them."

"You cannot hate all the world, Ykoriana."

"Do not presume to lecture me, my Lord, on hatred. On that subject I am as learned as the Wise."

"Let go your bitterness, Ykoriana, lest it should consume you with its fire."

She chuckled. "Do you know he never stopped loving you? All I achieved by sending you away was to make you even more permanent in his heart. The Wise claim that embalming makes the dead live for ever. I thought if I brought you back from your tomb in the sea, your faded beauty, your bitterness would poison the memory of the youth he clung to. It was this that made me release you from your blood oath. But you cheated me even of that small hope. Tell me, Sardian, why did you not return then?"

"I feared what you might do to my son."

The Empress braced herself on the youth. Her head fell. "You know how much I loved Azurea. How could I ever harm her son?"

"You really think you did not harm him, forcing him to grow up outside in the *wilderness*?"

Ykoriana sat back. "Have you forgotten the offer I made you long ago? My quarrel was never with the child."

"Perhaps I misjudged you."

"It is too late for apologies, Sardian, too late for regrets."

"Is it too late for him to know his mother's sister?"

Ykoriana turned her mask away. "Have him speak that I might hear his voice."

Suth urged his son forward. Carnelian obeyed him and found himself staring up at the Dowager Empress in her widow's robes.

"Speak then . . . nephew," she said.

Carnelian licked his lips. "Celestial . . . I do not know what it is that you wish me to say."

The Dowager Empress's mask nodded. "Perhaps there is something of her in your voice. Sardian, does he look like Azurea?"

"Very much."

A sound of footfalls made Carnelian turn to see a pillar of green jewel fire sweeping toward them from out of the dark. He saw the mask floating high above and the horned crowns.

"Celestial, I did not expect . . ." he heard his father say, then Suth bowed his sun-crowned head as the Jade Lord swept past trailing a quetzal-feathered cloak.

Carnelian knelt, watching the cloak slide past. The faces of the Sapients had turned toward the Jade Lord. With his staff, one of them rattled out a rhythm on the floor. The Jade Lord loomed above the Sapient. Carnelian imagined he could feel his hot anger. The homunculi were streaming back. As they folded into their masters' embraces, they began to mutter, first one, then another, until all had murmured the word *Molochite*. The Sapients bowed and then opened their fence to let the Jade Lord through. He climbed the steps toward the Dowager Empress, who put out a hand which he caught and folded into his own. Carnelian watched their hands flow in each other's lasciviously and saw that the homunculi were watching too, murmuring, relaying every touch back to the hands at their throats.

"Jade Lord Molochite, I was talking to the Regent," his father said.

"Well, now you can talk to us both who shall soon be wed."

"Does the Regent wish that I should speak before her son and the Wise? What I came to say would be better said to her alone."

Ykoriana leaned toward the youth who said, "It matters naught to me. Say what you came to say in the hearing of my son, and of the Wise too."

Suth glanced down at Carnelian. He lifted both his staves and brought them down again with a clack.

"Then, Celestial, you force me to speak as He-who-goes-before."

Molochite stood beside his mother, holding her hand like a child. "Well, get on with it."

"When I wear the Pomegranate Ring I am become merely the lens through which the Clave focuses its will. I am acting in a similar capacity for your other son. Nephron bade me say to you that should you cease your opposition to his election he would give you thereafter such freedoms as you have been deprived of. I stand here witness to his blood oath."

The Dowager Empress threw back her crowned head and laughed like a girl. "What gift is it to a bird to open its cage once it has forgotten the freedom of the sky? Besides, even the Twins cannot give me back my sight."

"Sacrilege, Celestial, you come close to sacrilege," shrilled one of the homunculi.

She laughed again, then looked at Suth. "Still, you and

Aurum have built about me a wall of votes that I can see no way to breach."

Molochite tore his hand out of hers and came to the edge of the dais to look down. "By my burning blood, Suth, I swear that when I become God Emperor, I shall bend all my power to pursuing your House to ruin."

Carnelian felt his hackles rising.

Ykoriana's hand let go of the youth's chain and reached up to tug upon Molochite's sleeve. He turned the malice of his eyeslits on her. For moments, Carnelian was convinced that he would strike his mother, but then he moved back to stand by her side. She stroked his hand.

"It is Aurum who is its architect. Once the election is over I intend to retire to my coomb to live in quiet retreat with my son. I am not your enemy."

"Perhaps that is so, Sardian."

Carnelian watched the three masks looking at each other.

Ykoriana's was the first to turn away. "But I will not abandon my beloved. Several days have yet to pass before the House of the Masks and the Great meet in the Chamber of the Three Lands, and only then will this be decided. Until that time, my son and I are content enough to leave our fates entirely in the hands of the Chosen."

"I will take this answer back to Nephron. Be certain, Celestial, I shall do what can be done in urging him to free you, notwithstanding your response."

"Until the election, then. But lest your faction should become too proud, My-Lord-who-goes-before, remember that even the sun is bound by earth and sky."

Suth's mask looked at her a while. "I shall remember."

Ykoriana terminated the audience with her hand. Suth bowed his sunburst head. Syblings appeared to relieve him of his staves and he turned away. Carnelian walked beside him all the way back to the Iron Door where the Hanuses awaited them. The syblings bowed but when their head came up their eyes, living and stone, lingered gluttonously on Carnelian's face. It was only with the closing of the door that Carnelian was free of them.

* * *

In the gloom of the Sun in Splendor the Ichorians lowered his father's dull fire to the ground. Carnelian stared at him. The journey back down the Approach had been even harder than the climb. Somehow his father had avoided falling. Somehow he had managed each one of the myriad steps. But when they reached the waiting Ichorians and the dais, his father stopped and would move no more and Carnelian had begun to think that he had died and that it was only the stiff robe that was keeping him upright. At last, he had had to have him carried onto the dais. There, the knees of his ranga had bent, though Carnelian had no way of knowing whether it was his father who had knelt or simply that his ranga had collapsed. All the way back, dazzled by the throng, deafened by the storming shawms, Carnelian had had to follow fearing that at any moment his father would topple to the ground.

Once they were alone in the Sun in Splendor, Carnelian found the courage to step up onto the dais. Each step he took made his father tremble. He stopped when he was standing very close. With his father kneeling, and him on his ranga, they were of a height.

"Father?" he said.

It seemed quite natural that the huge, golden puppet should make no response. Carnelian became desperate to look inside to know if the suit had become his father's sarcophagus. He reached out to run his fingers down the edges of his father's sun-eyed mask. Finding the bands, he followed these back over ears that seemed to be made of leather. His fingers traced the bands into narrow channels that burrowed round into the sculptural mass of his crowns. His fingers came together at a knot. They struggled to undo it, then, carefully, he removed the mask. He stifled a cry as he exposed the closed eyes. The face had the texture of weeping wax. He moaned as he stroked it. He thought the sighing was his own until he saw a quiver in the pale lips.

"Father, O Father?"

"So . . . tired," said the lips.

Carnelian kissed him. "We'll soon get you to bed," he whispered in Vulgate.

He carefully replaced the mask and walked away with many glances back. He raged through the tunnel into the chamber of doors, scattering Ichorians. He demanded that they go and find their commander and then went to his father's apartments and dug out House Suth attendants. They were in his train when he met the grand-cohort commander. He had the man send for a Sapient from the Domain of Immortality and made him remove all his Ichorians between the Sun in Splendor and his father's chambers. When the commander hesitated, Carnelian said, "He is dying," in such chill tones that the man immediately did his bidding.

With some of his people, Carnelian returned to the Sun in Splendor where, towering over them, he directed them as they freed his father. He watched as they disassembled his sunburst crown and opened the shell of his robe. He shouted at them to be careful as they lifted the sagging body down from the huge ranga. He had them shield it as they carried it in its underrobes to his father's chamber.

As he waited, Carnelian removed his father's mask. He watched every breath from on high, fearing to look away even for a moment lest doing so might let the chest stop its rise and fall. When the Sapients came with ammonites they drove him out of the chamber. He stood outside its door and did not leave until a homunculus came to tell him that his father would recover.

He took the last few heavy steps into his chamber, and even as he heard the door behind him close he bent his knees and groaned as his robe settled its weight onto the floor.

"Master."

The voice came from somewhere behind him. For a moment he thought it might be an assassin sent by Ykoriana, and he was glad. "Come round in front of me," he said wearily.

A small figure moved into his vision and fell on its knees. There was too little light to see it clearly.

"Look at me."

A small thin face gazed up.

"Tain!" sobbed Carnelian. "Tain, Tain, Tain." He opened his knees, lifted the burden of his robe and lumbered forward. He slowed, fearing he might topple onto his brother. He fumbled with his mask; it cut into his jaw as he wrenched it off and flung it away. "Tain, stand up, let me hug you."

Tain rose unsteadily. He took one step forward and then another. When he was close enough, Carnelian reached down. He had to stretch just to touch Tain's head. Tain looked up at him as if from a pit.

BROKEN MIRROR DAYS

Apotheosis transforms the candidate into a mirror that in trapping a reflection of the Twins, fixes aspects of Their Duality at the heart of the Three Lands. From this center emanates with decreasing strength the mandate of the Chosen and the power of their Commonwealth.

When the vessel of grace, our Lords the God Emperor, die, this mirror breaks, cutting the umbilical link between Earth and Sky, the Chosen lose their mandate, the Commonwealth its power. Disharmony and chaos are endemic to these Broken Mirror Days.

—FROM A THEOLOGICAL CODICIL
  COMPILED IN BEADCORD BY THE
  WISE OF THE DOMAIN OF LAW

To escape the pain of silence, Carnelian told Tain it was time to sleep. Saying nothing, his brother found the darkest edge of floor and huddled down. This made Carnelian unhappy but he said nothing. He laid himself out on his bed and waited, listening to the rasp of Tain's breathing. When its rhythm had slowed he rose and crept over to him. He crouched and peeled his brother carefully from the cold stone. Tain twitched a little but did not wake. Carnelian stood up and winced, finding that his brother weighed nothing at all. He carried the skin and bones over to the bed and arranged them on it carefully. As he put a blanket over Tain, he had the feeling he was covering a corpse.

He chose to lie upon the floor, telling himself it was because he did not want to lie beside his brother and risk disturbing him. The floor was cold and hard and would not let him sleep. He lay awake remembering the promise he had made to Ebeny that he would look after her sons.

Carnelian woke and lit a lamp. In its light the face in the bed was an old man's. He watched a bead of sweat run down the cheek then slip into the spiral of the ear. Tain had the sky sickness. Carnelian realized that the signs had been there the night before, although he had seen only the sallow ingrained fear.

So as not to wake his brother, he did not call for servants but dressed himself. He closed the door quietly behind him as he left, instructing his guardsmen to make no noise and to let no one enter. He refused an escort and left them.

In the chamber of doors, Ichorians stood before the entrance to his father's chambers. They looked at him warily as Carnelian walked close enough to see the spirals in their tattoos.

"I wish to see my father."

They bowed and one said, "He-who-goes-before is being made ready to give audience."

"You must be in error. He was too weak . . ."

"Every night our father's weak but morning always finds his strength returned, Master. Surely that's as it should be."

"Should be?"

"He is the Sun who goes before."

Carnelian took some steps away and turned his back on them. However long it took, he would wait to see his father miraculously risen from his sickbed. The grand-cohort commander appeared from a tunnel. He gave Carnelian a bow before going to speak to the guards, then he too stood waiting.

Both turned when they heard the doors opening. The commander and his men fell to their knees. Golden light flooded out and it seemed indeed to be the sun that was moving out between the prostrate Ichorians. Carnelian narrowed his eyes against the coruscating glare of the figure's sunburst crown. He peered, trying to see if this tower of gold was really his father.

"You are recovered, my Lord?"

The figure lifted a white hand, *Quite recovered.*

Carnelian still feared that this was an impostor. "But you seemed beyond such quick resurgence, my Lord."

"All that was needed was sleep, my son."

Carnelian relaxed. It was his father's voice. "Still, it might be convenient for my Lord to have me beside him during the business of the day."

His father's head shake cast rays among the Ichorians. "It would be tedious for you, Carnelian." His father seemed to notice the commander for the first time. "What news?"

"The Lords of your House, Great Sun, are at one of our postern gates craving audience with you."

Suth's hands made a gesture of irritation. "Not again. I've no time to deal with domestic matters." He turned to Carnelian. "Perhaps you, my Lord, might convey my apologies."

As Carnelian hesitated, his father was already moving away. "As my Lord commands," he called after him in Quya. Hearing the doors begin to close, Carnelian looked through them into his father's chambers. There among the prostrate

Suth tyadra stood two Sapients of the Domain Immortality looking like charred posts.

Carnelian allowed the commander to guide him down the tunnel. He was only vaguely aware of the flecks of light moving over him as he passed the loopholes cut into the walls.

The commander stopped. His hands made embarrassed gestures in Carnelian's direction.

Carnelian looked down at himself and understood. "I'm not suitably dressed to be seen by the outer world."

The commander smiled gratefully and then walked off. Carnelian waited concealed from the postern gate by the curving of the passage. A clatter of many ranga preceded a golden glowing that was coming along the wall. Nine Masters appeared bright and gleaming, towering over the commander and an escort of Ichorians.

"At last. Is that you, cousin?"

Carnelian saw the Masters each had chameleon heraldry dancing up their court robes. Ivory plaques in their crowns bore the glyphs of their names. He looked to Spinel and gave a nod.

"Good, my Lord, you have gained us access. These Ichorians have been impertinently attempting to keep us from our Ruling Lord."

"At our Ruling Lord's express command."

"Surely you do not mean to say, cousin, that this command is intended to include his kin?"

"We are in now," said Opalid.

Carnelian saw the commander's unhappy face. "This far you have come, my Lords, but no further. My father is too busy with the election to meet with you."

"It is on a matter pertaining to the election that we are come."

"My father's commands are not made to be broken," Carnelian said severely. He watched their vast heads turning, snagging light as they looked in at their center where Spinel stood very still.

"We came, my Lord, to proffer fealty to our Lord," said one whose crown glyph read *Tapaz*.

"I have not been introduced to my kin, Spinel."

The Master's mass flowed with light as he slowly turned. "You know my son, cousin." He extended a pale hand upon which two Great-Rings were the only marks and began to point at the various Lords. "These are Emeral and Tapaz, also of my lineage."

Fire ran up then down their crowns as they bowed.

"Berillus, Onyxor, Koril, Veridian and Amethus: the third lineage of our House."

Carnelian returned their bows. "Be assured, my Lords, that I will let my father know of this visit. Your loyalty is gratifying to us both."

For a while they simply stood there looking down at him. Spinel was the first to bow. He turned. The others inclined their heads and then followed him glittering away.

Carnelian returned slowly to his gloomy chamber. Tain was still sleeping. Carnelian tried to distract himself with a book. He paced. He made sure that Tain was well covered. The day dragged on into evening. Outside, the Great were determining the fate of the Three Lands while he was locked away like a woman in a forbidden house. As he lay down on the floor to sleep, he imagined his father imprisoned in his court robe, weighed down by his crowns, sustained by unnatural strength. Carnelian remembered the Sapients he had seen in his father's chambers and had a suspicion whence such strength came. He tried to dislodge his unease with memories of home, but he would more easily have lit a fire with sodden kindling. Unbidden, it was a vision of the Yden that flared bright before his mind's eye. Dreamily, Carnelian relived his freedom among the shimmering lagoons. He saw Osidian, beautiful in the dusk and burned with the delirious fever of their loving. He quashed a dark fear that threatened to quench the flames: the fear that he would never see Osidian again.

An indistinct horror hung in Carnelian's dream. He lurched awake as he had been doing all night. He sat up, groaning a little as he pushed his stiff body up from the floor. A small black figure was obscuring the morning-bright crack between the shutters. It was Tain. Carnelian could feel his gaze.

"You shouldn't have given me the bed."

"You shouldn't be up."

"I feel fine."

Carnelian grinned. "You look as thin as a stick." He regretted the words the moment they were said.

"I didn't eat well in the quarantine."

Carnelian stood up and walked round Tain, pretending he was finding something to wear, trying to find an angle from which to see his face. When he found it he stared, trying to recognize it. "Do you want to tell me about it?"

Wearing a flickering frown, Tain looked down at his hands as they wrestled each other. He looked so small, so damaged, that Carnelian instinctively reached out to embrace him. Tain jerked away as if scalded. His eyes warned Carnelian not to touch him.

Carnelian retreated.

"You watched them strip me?"

Carnelian freed his head enough from the tension to give a nod.

"They took us down into a maze of halls filled with half-black soldiers. In a courtyard they threw buckets of water at us. The blood washed off. They put us in among a crowd of naked men. We boys stuck together. Creatures came in silver masks—"

"Ammonites."

"Yes, ammonites. They ran their hands over me. Everywhere over and into me. They took the Little Mother . . . smashed her to pieces on the ground." His mouth twitched.

"They took us to a chasm. Any comment, any step out of line brought a cudgeling. A stair led down into the chasm. We descended to a shelf. We crossed to a bigger shelf. They swung the bridge away. Some ammonites were there with us. It was crowded. On one side was the chasm wall, on all others, a drop to darkness. The biggest men took the space near the wall. We had to make do with the edge. "I looked over . . ." He stared as if he were there again. He shook his head, narrowed his eyes. "Sometimes a little dimple of paleness showed the water far, far below. Hardly any light came down to us. Our blankets of sacking were stolen from us. We huddled together for warmth. Cold and fear of rolling over the edge kept us always awake. In the morning, the ammonites checked us again then herded us over a bridge to the next shelf."

Carnelian saw Tain's lips moving but no sound came out. "Was this new shelf the same as the last?"

Tain nodded slowly. "One shelf after another, after another . . . for more than twelve days."

Tain's eyes made Carnelian's mouth almost too dry to speak. "Were you . . . did they hurt you?"

"Those who weren't protected by others of their House were victimized. We found protection where we could." Tain's face became very bony. "Those who didn't want to starve paid for their protection."

"Maybe we should forget this." Carnelian thought his voice sounded very loud.

Tain's eyes defied him. "Every day the chasm deepened. There were whispers that it went down as far as the Underworld. One day we came round a corner in the chasm to see a brown tower rising in the distance. Each day brought it one shelf closer. Each day it grew redder until it looked like a freshly butchered bone. The chasm forked around its bloody roots. The last shelf was down the left fork. In the shadow under a high bridge, stone doors led to new shelves. Thirteen of them. Colder. Darker. Under a skyful of shadow, Death's Gate, Nale fell."

"Nale?" asked Carnelian.

"The dragonfly Master's boy."

"Jaspar . . . Fell, you say?"

Tain glanced at him. "He threw himself into the chasm."

Carnelian shuddered, remembering the punishments Jaspar had promised the boy.

"Stone doors took us onto a path."

Carnelian was being numbed by Tain's lack of feeling.

"The chasm widened, letting in more sky. The air was dank. We came to a place of chains and deafening waterfalls. More gates, some tunnels . . . then we came out into . . ." Tain was staring at nothing.

"Heaven?" suggested Carnelian.

Tain gazed on as if he had not heard. Carnelian felt that if he were only to look close enough he would see a vision of the crater reflected on the boy's eyes. "I felt that wonder too."

Tain's face turned to him the eye holes in his skull. "I was sure I had died."

Carnelian felt the cold seeping up from the stone upon which he sat.

"The beating soon taught me otherwise. They took us up a stair to a cave floored with water. They demanded the names of our Masters. They put me on a boat, under its deck, where one-eyed monsters rowed. We arrived at Coomb Suth. They fished me out and put me on the quay. They rang a bell. I had the feeling I was in a story. The blue lake was not real. The island with its mountain. The vast, vast fencing wall. And there, at its foot, the coomb. So beautiful with its stepped gardens and gleaming palaces. Crail told me about it but I hadn't believed."

For a moment Carnelian thought Tain might smile. He yearned for it as if it were the dawn after a night of despair.

"A man came down for me. The chameleon on his face fooled me at first, but he wasn't one of our people. He was a stranger and spoke to me as a stranger. As I followed him he rattled off my duties, warned me that I should forget the ways I was used to. The coomb was ruled by the Master's mother and she wasn't a Mistress to be trifled with. Then I saw the hanging woman."

Carnelian felt a twinge of nausea. "Hanging . . . ?"

"Sagging off a frame . . . arms wire cut . . . above the path to one side . . . stinking."

"A crucifixion," said Carnelian.

"The wall behind her was stained with blood and shit. Her knees were swollen as big as her head. What was left of her arms looked barely in their shoulders. Her belly was red, distended—"

"Enough!" said Carnelian. He felt he was on the verge of remembering something. He was panting. Water was oozing in his mouth. "Did . . ." He swallowed. "Did he tell you her name?"

"Her name was Fey."

The sound of that name punched the contents of Carnelian's stomach all over the floor.

Carnelian helped Tain clean up. He felt the need to give him an explanation. "She was Brin's sister."

Tain seemed to age a little more. Carnelian ducked his head, cursing, scrubbing the floor so hard he made his fingers raw. When they were finished he looked at Tain. "I must know . . ." Tain's face was a blank. "What else did you see happening in the coomb?"

"I left shortly after arriving to come here."

"Were there any other signs of slaughter?"

"I didn't see any more . . . crucifixions."

Carnelian bit his hand, looking at his brother.

"There was an atmosphere of fear."

Carnelian's eyes went out of focus. "It seems to be the way the Masters celebrate their assumption of power."

Tain gazed at him.

Carnelian still felt queasy. "I must go and make father aware of what I have done."

* * *

Carnelian quickly found that Tain was unable to dress him in his court robe and so he had to summon servants. When he was ready he went immediately to see his father, but the Ichorians guarding the entrance to the Sun in Splendor would not let him pass. Towering over them he used all his powers of coercion but this only served to reduce them to quivering. One of the cohort commanders came to see what was happening.

Carnelian swung round to look down at the man. "They refuse to let me pass."

"He-who-goes-before himself barred this gate, Master."

"I have urgent need to speak to him."

"Our father is in a meeting with the Jade Master Nephron."

Carnelian calmed his anger. "Please tell him as soon as you can that I must talk to him."

He began the journey back to his chamber. The storm he had unleashed upon Coomb Suth, only his father could abate. No doubt he would conclave well into the night and then return to his chambers exhausted. Even if the commander managed to get his message through, there was no assurance that his father would pay it any attention.

A plan occurred to him. Carnelian turned slowly on his ranga and returned to the door of his father's chambers. After some discussion, the Ichorians there allowed him to enter. The Suth guardsmen in the atrium greeted him with surprise. He ignored the questions in their eyes and passed through into the chamber beyond. There he had them remove him from his court robe and ranga. When they were finished, he sent them away. For a moment, he stood gazing at the walls with their wheels and eyes and pomegranates, but then he crossed the stone-wood floor to a couch on which he settled down to wait.

A movement of air woke him. Carnelian opened his eyes and was transfixed. An angel was coming across the floor in an aura of gold. Two mortals walked beside it. It seemed miraculous that its furnace robe did not consume them with its fire. The angel lifted a hand and the men fled toward the door and were soon gone.

The angel slid toward a wall. It wavered a white hand out to touch the gold. Its whole shimmering bulk leaned forward, its fiery head clinking against the ruby seeds of a graven pomegranate.

Thus propped up, the angel raised both hands to its face. The fingers disappeared trembling into the fiery crowns. The gold mask detached to reveal a pallid face beneath. His father. The next moment Carnelian was jarred as the pale fingers lost hold of the mask and it fell flashing, like a sky-stone, clattering, then screeching along the floor.

Carnelian's gaze had been pulled after it but when it stopped making sound or movement he looked back in time to see his father raising an object to his face. He watched him sink his nose into the square spoon. Two sharp snorts, a groan, and then breath hissing out through his gaping mouth as the spoon dangled from his fingers. Even as Carnelian watched, it was as if his father was a withered tree drawing young sap up from its roots. He slowly straightened, his shoulders broadened, his face grew brighter. His eyes opened and he saw Carnelian.

"My Lord," he said, appalled. His face jumped into fury. "You spy on me?"

Anger disappeared as his father's face sagged. Carnelian stood up, stooped to pick up the fallen mask, went to him. He could see the mucus running down from his father's nostrils and the head hanging with shame.

"You knew . . . the Wise . . . their drugs sustain me."

"You mean, they keep you alive," Carnelian snapped. His father was a man trapped in a slab of gold. Carnelian could not be angry with him. "Please, Father, let me remove some of this . . ." His hand pointed up at the sunburst crown, the stiff slopes of the court robe.

His father frowned and Carnelian could see the protest forming on his lips, so he reached up, fitting his fingers up into the elaborate metallic folds. "Not there," his father sighed. "Round the back . . ."

Carnelian skirted him and stood on his toes to reach, found the catches, pressed and was thrown back as the sunburst fell into his arms. He walked with it and leaned its disc against the wall. He returned to lift down the upper crown, the lower, the sunstone circlet with its jeweled beadcords, the ear flanges, until the long dome of his father's head was revealed. His father moved it from side to side, grimacing, releasing the tension in his neck.

"Ah. That does feel better . . . thank you, my son."

"Let me remove the robe." Before his father could forbid him Carnelian had unhitched the shoulder pole with its cloaks. He unhooked the robe from the floor up. As its carapace came apart it released an odor of myrrhed sweat. Carnelian prised the suit open like two doors. His father's long narrow body was revealed in its underclothes, kneeling high upon enormous ranga that were attached to heavy belts. Carnelian squeezed into the robe, stooped and began to undo the shoes. As he worked he was bothered by a fetid, familiar smell. As he helped his father climb down he saw a raised area blushing red through the silk. When Carnelian leaned closer he could smell the rot of old blood. He groaned. "It has not healed."

"The drug gives me strength but at a price. The wound remains open but it hardly bleeds at all."

"And pain?"

His father shrugged. "A little." He smiled. "From long companionship, it has become a friend."

Carnelian felt a trembling anger. "The Wise . . . they are embalming you alive."

"It was my choice. Without their drugs I would have become an invalid long ago."

"The wound will heal, then?"

His father rolled his hand. "When I have time." His face grew immeasurably sad. "After the election."

Carnelian tried not to see how much his father was resembling Crail. "Something has happened."

His father's yellowed eyes fell on him. "I suppose the news will soon be widely known."

Carnelian watched him, urging him to speak.

"Jaspar has betrayed us."

"Jaspar . . . ?"

"He has gone over to Ykoriana."

"With his faction?"

"It is too early to tell . . . some will follow him." He affected cheerfulness. "I did not ask why you came here, my son."

Carnelian looked up, saw his father's bleary look. It was the fear of continuing massacre in the coomb that made him speak. "Tain is here."

"Good, good. Has he come through the ordeals of the road and quarantine unscathed?"

"We are none of us unscathed, Father."

"No, I suppose not."

"Tain brought with him terrible news."

His father's eyebrows squeezed wrinkles into the top of his nose.

"Fey is dead."

His father blinked at him, not understanding. "Dead?"

"Your mother had her crucified." Carnelian watched his father's face crumpling. He saw the tears oozing out. "Father, don't," he stuttered in Vulgate, horrified. He rushed to catch him in his arms and held him, feeling the racking in his body. "Don't, don't cry," he mumbled, touching with his lips the dry skin of his father's neck. "I . . . was a fool."

Carnelian could feel the words begin to rattle up from his father's chest. He squeezed harder but the words still escaped. "We should never have returned. I have lost. I have lost it all."

Carnelian pushed him away so that he could see his face. He forced himself to look on all the evidence of its ruin. "It was my fault," he said. "My fault."

His father looked at him with flickering red eyes. Carnelian stared back. His father's trembling had stopped. He seemed suddenly of stone. "Your fault?" His voice seemed to be coming from somewhere else in the chamber.

"I killed her. I gave the Lady Urquentha the Seal."

His father became flesh again. "The Seal?" He looked as if it was the first time he had ever heard the word.

"The coomb was not as you left it. Spinel had taken the Seal and forced the Lady Urquentha into the forbidden house."

His father gave a slow nod and narrowed his eyes.

"She had been long imprisoned."

"And so you gave her the Seal to set her free?"

Carnelian grimaced. "It was done as much from a dislike of Spinel."

His father opened his hand. "And so? It was your right, you are higher than he."

"But Fey was crucified."

His father looked down, his eyes unfocused. "Why did my mother do this?"

"She believed that Fey had conspired against her with the second lineage."

"And had she?"

"In a manner of speaking."

"Then my mother did what she had to."

Carnelian gaped. "Had to?"

"What Fey did was unforgivable."

"But she did it for you, for us."

"Nevertheless."

"You mean she was only a slave."

His father's eyes flashed. "She was my favorite sister. I trusted her . . . I loved her, even."

Carnelian slumped. "Then why . . . ?"

His father put his hand on Carnelian's shoulder. "My son, when I chose exile, I knew that I was choosing suffering for many others apart from myself. I could not take all the household with me. Fey asked to be left behind. Even if her actions were carried out from love of me, she betrayed my mother. No servant, however loved, can be allowed to live after betraying one of the Chosen."

"She knew," said Carnelian, holding back tears. "She knew and yet she said nothing. I made her put the Seal in the Lady's hands."

"She was always brave."

Carnelian felt a tear run down his face. "She asked me to tell you that she had always loved you. I had forgotten."

They stood for a long while sharing their misery. It occurred to Carnelian that it was not the news of Fey's death that had made his father cry. What then? The election. "You believe the election lost," he said at last.

His father rubbed his forehead. "Yes."

"Jaspar has taken with him many votes?"

His father's hands fluttered. "If it were only that. Such a breach in our wall of votes we could hope to repair, but he also took with him much knowledge of how that wall was built. We are defenseless."

"Surely you can do something."

"Aurum has thrown his last daughter in to plug the breach, but the whole wall is fatally compromised."

Carnelian turned to ice, remembering the threat Molochite had made to his father. He gritted his teeth. "Rebuild it then."

His father glared at him. "Just like that. We have two days to build a second wall when it took almost a month of weary labor to build the first."

"Surely fear of Ykoriana can be exploited. Will the Great not fear Jaspar triumphant more than you and Aurum? They have before their eyes evidence of how little he can be trusted."

His father frowned.

"I assume that the last wall was built carefully, with an attempt to minimize the concessions to the Great?"

His father nodded.

"What will iron or high blood brides matter to Nephron if his brother wins the Masks? Let him spend all the wealth of his House if needs be to throw up another wall."

Carnelian closed his mouth and saw that his father was thinking. He began shaking his head. "It could not be done with audiences alone. I would have to also go into the nave. I cannot be in two places at once."

"Send Aurum out into the nave while you remain in the Sun in Splendor."

His father shook his head. "Aurum has to be at my side to witness the agreements."

"Could no other Lord do that?"

"There is none that we could trust. Whoever we chose would be unable to resist the Ykoriana's bribes. We would suffer another betrayal."

"Could I do it?"

His father narrowed his eyes and opened his mouth to speak. He shook his head once. "They might not accept a witness from my own House."

"Do you put your own seal on the agreements?"

"I use Nephron's."

"With the mark of my blood-ring beside it, the two would not be of the same House."

His father was still frowning.

"What would we have to lose?"

Suth paced away. He stopped and ran his fingers round a pomegranate graven into the wall. He turned, grimly smiling. "Go and rest, Carnelian. Come with the dawn to attend me in the Sun in Splendor."

A knocking woke Carnelian. Before he was fully awake, Tain had gone to the door. The door opened, there was a mutter of talk, the door closed. Tain came up to him.

"One of the half-black men. He says someone's come to see you and it's very urgent."

Tain helped him dress and bound on his mask. Carnelian opened the door and looked out.

One of the cohort commanders was there. "Master, I waited to disturb you until the time you asked me to wake you."

"What is it?" asked Carnelian.

"A Master from your House needing to see you urgently."

"Who is he?"

The commander shrugged. "He came alone."

"Please bring him to me." Carnelian closed the door. He asked Tain to help him put on his court robe. Standing on the ranga he watched his brother struggle with the straps and screws. Every time Carnelian tried for intimacy, Tain responded like a slave. Carnelian was kneeling inside his court robe when there was another knocking on the door. It opened when he gave leave and a massive shape slid in. Its gold face looked down at Tain.

"Though he does not wear our cipher, my Lord, he is one of ours."

The Master spent some moments gazing down disdainfully at Tain before he reached up two white hands to remove his mask.

"My Lord Opalid, what a pleasure it is to see you. You have come with your father?"

"I have come alone, my Lord."

Carnelian raised his eyebrows as the Master fell into silence. "Well?"

Opalid frowned. "I was waiting for your minion to finish here so that we might talk alone."

"My 'minion' is more kin to me than you, my Lord, so please tell me what you came to say."

Opalid looked horrified and stared at Tain as if he were trying to blast him with his eyes. Tain seemed oblivious as he stood on a stool to do up Carnelian's robe.

"Very well," Opalid said. "I come, my Lord, on a delicate matter."

"Indeed?"

"I come to offer your lineage my fealty."

"It is welcome, my Lord, but this hardly seems to me to constitute an urgent matter."

Opalid produced some pantomime gestures of distress. "I came to tell you that my father has betrayed you."

"Go on."

"He has pledged his vote to Molochite."

"Publicly?" Carnelian said, rising, lifting the robe. There was a cry behind him. He had forgotten his brother. He sank down again, saying over his shoulder in Vulgate, "Sorry, Tain."

Opalid did not hide his distaste too well.

"How many of your lineage have defected?"

Opalid made a shrugging gesture with his hand.

"And you will, I suppose, know nothing about the intentions of the third lineage?"

"Nothing, my Lord."

Carnelian regarded him silently until the Master could not bear his scrutiny any longer, and looked away. "I will convey to my father your words of loyalty, my Lord."

Carnelian dismissed the Master and made sure he was escorted out of the Sunhold. Then he and Tain hurried through what remained of the dressing. He did not wish to be late for his meeting with his father.

The Ichorians let Carnelian into the Sun in Splendor. The hall was filled with gusts, and dark save for some braziers set in a circle round the dais. In their violent flickering, Carnelian saw two ammonites beside a beadcord chair. Of his father there was no sign.

Carnelian walked toward the ammonites, who knelt as they saw him approaching. "He-who-goes-before?"

Both creatures pointed off into a corner where Carnelian saw a pale rectangle open in the wall. As he walked toward it the wind beat against him. He reached the doorway and saw that it gave onto a narrow promontory jutting out into the sky. At its tip a glimmering figure was bracing itself upon a post of brass. A cordon of these ran all the way back to where Carnelian stood.

He reached out for the first post and used it to pull himself forward a single step. The wind buffeted him mercilessly. Pulling himself from one to the other he at last managed to reach the figure. It turned a little and lifted its hand making the signs, *My son.*

The wind flowed over them. They were two rocks in a torrent. His father's hand formed, *Behold*, and then the sign dissolved into pointing. Carnelian saw the indigo vastness of the crater laid out below. They seemed to be standing on the prow of a ship sailing into a dark sea. He could make out the curve of the Sacred Wall, the shore of the Isle, the closed circle of the Plain of Thrones twinkling like a puddle of stars.

Carnelian lifted his hand into his father's view and made the sign, *Tributaries?*

For answer his father pointed to the Plain of Thrones and then slid his finger out and slowly round. Carnelian saw that it was tracing out a sparkling gossamer thread. His father's hand made the signs, *They come in, night and day,* and then continued round until the thread disappeared into the black gullet of the Valley of the Gate.

The Rains are near, and soon—his father's hand pointed back at the Plain of Thrones—*we shall go down there for Apotheosis and Rebirth.*

Carnelian sieved the wind through his fingers as he prepared himself to give his news. He leaned on the wind to allow him to lift both his hands. *Father.* Suth looked at the hand. *Opalid, Spinel's son, has just been to tell me that his father has gone over to Ykoriana.*

Carnelian watched his father's hands stiffen then sign, *Why did he come to tell you this?*

I suspect his father sent him to curry favor with us in case the election should go our way.

Suth made a smile with his hand. *A childish stratagem.*

Spinel must be very certain of Ykoriana's victory or else their roles would be reversed.

Fear of my wrath must play its part in his calculations. When you took the Seal from him you left him without means to remove the evidence of his usurpations in the coomb.

How will Ykoriana victorious make any . . . ? Carnelian stopped to think. *Could she make him Ruling Lord?*

With enough blood and iron everything is possible. The new God Emperor will have much of both.

We are doomed then.

Suth looked at his son. *Hold on to your faith. It has become my strength.*

But surely if this defection becomes public many others will follow Spinel's lead?

It will become public. That is why Ykoriana has wooed him.

Will that not be disastrous for us?

Not necessarily. If other subsidiary lineages are encouraged to revolt against their Ruling Lords her strategy might well rebound on her since—

Since all Ruling Lords would be threatened and should then be forced to oppose her for their own preservation. Carnelian could see his father nodding and then looking off to where the sky was growing pale.

Suth lifted his hand again, *We must move inside and begin our work of masonry.*

The ammonite took Carnelian's blood-ring and pressed it into the clay. When he pulled it out, Carnelian could see the bead now bore a circle of his name glyphs and the numbers of his taint. The bead the ammonite had made from Nephron's jade seal was the first, Carnelian's was now threaded onto the cord to be the second.

"The first two stones in our wall," his father said.

Carnelian looked up to his father, a golden obelisk on the dais. He looked back and saw the two ammonites sitting beside each other, each with his trays of beads. In front of them a third was sitting with his back to them. All three wore eyeless silver masks.

Carnelian walked round the dais to take his place as witness at his father's right hand. At his feet facing him was a fourth ammonite. Between them was a low table upon which there was an ink sponge and beside it Carnelian's blood-ring. In front of his father a fifth ammonite sat with a table, ink and Nephron's seal. A little further away knelt a sixth. Carnelian could only wonder what his function might be.

His father turned to him. "Are you ready, Carnelian?"

Carnelian knelt on his ranga. "As ready as I can be, my Lord."

* * *

The first Masters that were let in were from one of the highest Houses of the Great: three of them, haughty, proud, come to tell He-who-goes-before that they would support him without condition. More followed, with their heraldry wrought in gems upon their smoldering robes.

"These are the towers of our new wall," his father said as they waited for more.

For those Houses that were rich enough already in blood and iron, flesh and treasure soon ran out. It was then that the negotiations began in earnest. Some Houses wanted gifts, blocks of white jade from the eastern mountains, black pearls that had been found in the sea. Sometimes it would be a piece of porcelain a thousand years old or a half-dozen chrysalises containing butterflies recently discovered, whose wings spanned a shield but would crumple at the merest touch of breath. Suth, as Nephron's proxy, promised these rarities from the House of the Masks' fabled treasury. Precisely worded, an agreement would be dictated to the two ammonites with the bead trays who would each quickly thread it onto a silver cord. The two cords would then be put, one into each hand of the ammonite who sat before them. Holding his arms out, this ammonite would quickly pass them through his fingers, presumably to determine they were identical. One cord he would then hand back to be added to the lengthening record of which the clay beads were the beginning. The other would be threaded through a hole in the floor. The Masters would wait, making conversation about the Rains, their hopes for beauty among the children in the flesh tithe, their anticipation of pleasure and distraction in the new season's masques. From the floor would emerge a piece of rolled parchment onto which the beadcord had been transcribed. Suth would read this before passing it to his son. Carnelian would check the glyphs, then return the parchment to his father. It would be rolled out over the table at his father's feet where Nephron's seal would be appended. The seal of Carnelian's own blood-ring would be added next and the document taken by the sixth ammonite for the perusal of the Masters. The negotiation complete, they would exchange formulaic greetings and the Lords would leave and allow the next party to replace them.

The negotiations became ever more intense as the rank of the Houses fell. In the case of a stipulated number of children, the Imperial Power ceded its rights to choose from the flesh tithe first or gave the child freely without exchange. Portions of the imperial revenue from the cities were assigned to the petitioning Houses for fixed periods of years, or a House would gamble, receiving it only for the duration of the next reign. Eyes were covenanted, the iron coins that were equivalent to ichorous blood. Suth confided in Carnelian that they did not have the time to make the complex arrangements in which the House of the Masks ceded rights to a House on the condition that that House should in turn cede rights to other Houses. The sky was already darkening when they began to barter imperial blood. Brides both living and yet to be born were promised from the imperial forbidden house. In some cases the marriage was restricted to a fixed period, in others it would remain in force until a child was produced.

Carnelian had hardly the strength to hold his head up when his father whispered that the doors were closed until the morrow. He managed to rise, and, with care, maneuvered his father to his chambers.

"It was good," his father croaked. "We have built much today. Tomorrow we will try to finish it."

They parted and Carnelian dragged himself back to his chamber. Tain brought him some food and put him to bed. His brother said nothing and Carnelian had no energy to find words himself.

The following morning, election's eve, Carnelian came into the Sun in Splendor to find his father with Aurum. He watched them for a while. They were alone, speaking with their hands, the slopes of their robes gleaming only on the side that faced the single brazier. Carnelian was reminded of that time long ago on the baran when he had seen them talking about Ykoriana. As he walked toward them, they turned.

"My Lord Carnelian," said Aurum, inclining his crowned head. The old Master regarded him for a while, making him feel uncomfortable. "It seems that I am in your debt, my Lord," he said grudgingly.

"It is nothing, Lord Aurum."

Aurum smiled coldly. "A nothing on which the future of both our Houses depends."

Suth distracted them with his hand. He looked at his son. "The Ruling Lord has come to tell me that there are rumors of more defections."

"Among the subsidiary lineages?" Carnelian asked.

"Ykoriana builds upon the betrayer within your own House," said Aurum. There was a tone of accusation in his voice.

"My son and I expected this," said Suth. "I think this strategy she has chosen could very well be her undoing."

Aurum rose as he straightened his ranga. "I will see what I can do." He bowed to each of them in turn. "My Lords." He turned and began the journey to the doors.

I dislike being allied to that Lord, Carnelian signed with his hand.

No more than do I, his father replied. *But a chameleon would be wise to make common cause with a raven when both are being harried by an eagle.*

Carnelian nodded and took his place at his father's right hand. Suth lifted and let fall one of his court staves and immediately the hole opened up in the floor before his dais and began to disgorge its ammonites. Before it closed again, Carnelian saw a flicker of light coming up. It reminded him. He looked over to where, concealed by pillars, the trapdoor lay that led down into the ancient halls, the library and Osidian.

The day progressed very much as had the previous one. Later, Ruling Lords arrived who admitted that they had agreed to vote for Molochite but were uneasy about the promises Ykoriana was making to the lower lineages. Their own third lineage made an appearance. As they offered him their loyalty, Suth remained aloof and only said that they had taken their time. Still, their votes added some more beads to the tally cord.

The agreements passed through Carnelian's hands in a constant waft of parchment. In every case he endeavored to make sure that the glyphs had caught the words his father spoke. He grew weary, then exhausted, until the glyphs began to swim before his eyes. Still they went on and he marveled at the reserves of strength the drugs gave his father. Night fell and still they carried on. More and more his father was husbanding his words. When he spoke, it was with visible effort.

The moon had risen before the flood of Masters became a stream and then a trickle. Then there was a heavy pattern of gongings on the door.

"Is that it?" Carnelian asked.

His father let out a long, long sigh. "Yes. I must rest . . . a while." Carnelian watched his father sag and waited, glad beyond measure that the election was almost upon them. Win or lose, he wanted to take his father home.

Suth roused himself and turned a little to catch Carnelian in his eye. "Mask yourself." Carnelian did so and watched with what painful care his father lifted his own mask to his face before he said, "Ammonites, see again."

Before him and at his side, all the ammonites removed their masks. Their faces were parchment written all over with numbers. More appeared out from the hole before the dais. His father sent one off to fetch Ichorians. Carnelian watched the others follow their fellow's movements with fearful eyes. One brought the beadcord of the agreements wound onto a reel and placed it at his father's feet, while another put a length of beadcord in his hands. Carnelian could see with what violence the man's hand trembled and became alarmed. Fanciful thoughts scrambled through his mind, of murderous plots against his father. He rose on his ranga and stood, indecisive. His father could clearly see their fear, they were just in front of him, and yet he showed no reaction.

His father only looked up when he heard the footfalls. The ammonite came stumbling back leading a file of Ichorians. Carnelian watched the ammonites line up in front of his father in obedience to his hand command. "You have performed your service well. He-who-goes-before thanks you."

The ammonites all fell into the prostration.

Suth turned to the Ichorians waiting behind. "Take them. Destroy them painlessly."

"My Lord," cried Carnelian.

His father's hand jerked up, *Silence*.

"But . . ."

"They have heard too much. They knew this was their fate. It is done today as it is always done."

Carnelian watched the Ichorians leading the little men off. Only when they had disappeared did his father drop his mask. He hung it on his robe and then looked down at the beadcord in his hand. Carnelian rose and walked to stand in front of him.

His father looked up. "I hold in my hand our wall of votes. I almost do not dare to count them."

"Let me do it, Father."

His father frowned. "You would have to know how to read the beads."

"Teach me quickly, Father. It does not look too difficult."

His father showed him how many votes each bead or combination of beads was worth. Carnelian could think of no way to explain that he knew their meaning well and so he pretended to be taught. When his father was finished, Carnelian took the cord. The beads were large, crude, made for insensitive fingers. He began to pay them through his hands, counting.

He ignored the distraction of the sun-eye door opening. He was aware of the clack of ranga coming nearer.

"He counts our votes, my Lord," his father said to the visitor.

Carnelian counted on, glancing up to see that it was Aurum. "Eleven thousand nine hundred and eighty-four," he announced.

His father's eyes closed. "It is not enough."

"I might have missed a few."

"No matter. It is almost a thousand short."

"We are closer than I expected," said Aurum. "Let us not indulge in despondency; there will be time enough for that if we lose."

Suth looked at him with narrowed eyes. He snorted. "If we lose, Aurum?"

"Once they are in the Three Lands, many Lords will shift their votes."

"By a thousand?"

Aurum made a dismissive gesture. "In the nave, I put a rumor about that Ykoriana intends to extend the franchise to the Lesser Houses."

Suth smiled a crooked smile. "That should put some unease in the hearts of the noble Great."

"Does My-Lord-who-goes-before wish to go and tell our Lord Nephron of this count?"

Suth smiled again. "I am without strength for the journey. Besides, my Lord, I am certain you would wish to tell him the good news yourself."

Aurum frowned and took his leave of them.

Carnelian waited until he was gone before asking, "Do you share his hope, Father?"

His father shrugged his hands. "All that can be done, we have done. The result, only the morrow will reveal." He groaned as he lifted himself up. "Come, my son, help your weary father to his chambers."

THE
ELECTION

Love came

I was its fool

There was joy

There was sorrow

—LOVE ECLOGUE,

AUTHOR UNKNOWN

Carnelian woke in such perfect silence that until he made a sound he feared he might have gone deaf. Even the shutters were still, as if the sky was holding its breath. A lingering memory of the Yden evaporated like dew. The day of the sacred election had finally arrived.

His fingers remembered the beads of the vote count. As he rose, he tried to cling to Aurum's optimism. He closed his eyes, trying to imagine what might be within the Chamber of the Three Lands. The Masters would all be there with their wintry eyes, Ykoriana and Molochite, Jaspar and Spinel. He glanced back at the bed recalling a tatter of his dream. He smiled. "Osidian," he breathed, wanting to feel the name on his lips. His heart began hammering. Surely, he would be there too. He had to be. All Chosen males of an age to wear blood-rings would vote in a sacred election.

He crouched to wake Tain. He had to shake his brother so long that he was relieved when at last his eyes opened. They snapped closed again as if dazzled by Carnelian's white body. He walked away frowning, wanting his brother back the way he had been.

"Master," Tain said.

Carnelian saw him standing there with eyes averted. He looked as if he were hanging from strings. "Please, Tain, would you clean me?" He watched the boy go for the pads and unguents. "Today is the day when the Gods will be elected."

Coming toward him, Tain gave a nod. He began cleaning him.

"You know what that means?"

"No, Master."

"That soon the Rains will come and we'll return to our coomb."

Tain gave another nod.

"Soon things will return to the way they were, you'll see. Ebeny will be here, Keal and Brin and Grane and . . ." Carnelian stopped, unable to put Crail into the list. He went on. "They'll all come up from the sea and we'll make a new Hold here."

Tain gave a nod. Carnelian looked at him. Cold clutched his stomach. What if all of them were like this when they arrived? Carnelian went to open the shutters to let in some light. He stared for a moment at the dawn sky. Its colors promised a new day, but they also looked like blood.

He turned his back on the sky. Tain was still there, waiting with his head hanging. Carnelian returned silently to stand in front of him and comforted himself with the hope that he might see Osidian, even if only from afar.

*   *   *

Carnelian sent Tain to see who was rapping at the door. The boy opened it a crack, then bowed deeply as he shuffled backward to open the door wide.

"My Lord," said Carnelian seeing who it was. His father had to stoop to come in and seemed to fill the chamber with his gold and rubied robe. Tain had fallen to his knees.

Looking down from his great height, Suth spoke. "Rise, child."

Tain rose, head still hanging.

"Come, look at me." Tain looked up. Carnelian watched his father's mask survey his marumaga son from on high. "We are glad to have you back with us, Tain."

Tain mumbled something.

"Now go and prepare people to come and dress your brother."

Tain slipped out and Suth removed his mask. His face was troubled. He threw a glance to the door.

"I told you he had not come through this unscathed."

His father nodded. "You will have time enough to heal his hurts. Now we must give thought to the day ahead."

Carnelian withstood the intensity of his father's eyes. He had not felt the pressure of that gaze for an age.

"I have sent commands that the Suth Lords of the other lineages are to come here and take you with them into the Three Lands."

"I thought, my Lord, I would be there at your side."

"Even if I were not today He-who-goes-before, I would be sundered from you. At elections, Ruling Lords keep with their peers."

"What makes my Lord think Spinel will obey him in this when he defies him with his vote?"

Carnelian was glad that the wrath that appeared in his father's face was not turned on him. "That Lord will one day give me account for that. How he votes is his business, but I am still his Ruling Lord." The wrath passed from his face like the shadow of a cloud. "Come here, my son."

Carnelian took the steps toward him, feeling his nakedness.

Although his father knelt on his ranga, Carnelian's head only reached his chest. His father took it in his hands. Carnelian looked up into his eyes. He did not see their yellow bloodiness but only the fierce love.

"You know, you are my heart."

Carnelian's tears distorted his father's face. With a groan of effort, his father managed to bend down to kiss Carnelian's forehead. He let go and rose so that Carnelian's eyes were level with his waist.

He took some steps back and hid his face with his sun-eyed mask.

"Today all our fates shall be decided." Carnelian could hear the sorrow in his father's voice. "Perhaps, even now, we shall be victorious."

"Aurum said—".

His father cut his reassurances from his mouth with a scissoring motion of his hand and left.

When Tain returned he came with others and Carnelian was forced to hide his distress behind a stony face. He could not rid himself of the harrowing conviction that his father had come to say goodbye.

As they put him into his court robe he bit his tongue to stop himself from spraying them with bitter words. He could not bear to look at Tain's remote expression. When they were finished he almost snatched his Great-Rings from their hands and, ordering the door open, he strode through it so fast he almost toppled over.

The Ichorians lifted the portcullises for him. Carnelian walked through into the nave and was suddenly among giants.

"Cousin Carnelian," said a voice he recognized as Spinel's. Carnelian saw him there with the others, the nine Lords of House Suth with their chameleon-ciphered court robes. Carnelian looked past them to the gleaming Great. Beyond, the nave ran empty to the closed door of the Chamber of the Three Lands.

Carnelian bowed his head. "My Lords. My father told me you would be here."

"Then you have spoken to him today, cousin?" asked one of the Lords.

"I have . . ." Carnelian read the name glyph on his crowns, "cousin Veridian."

The Lord bowed. "At the service of your lineage, cousin."

"I am heartened to receive it," Carnelian said.

"Does our Ruling Lord anticipate victory for his party?"

Carnelian shrugged his hands. "It hangs in the balance and why should it not when even those of his own House betray him?" He looked at Spinel.

The Lord lifted his right hand to show his blood-ring. "This is no mere bauble, my Lord. I will cast its votes as I will. That is my right."

"And you feel no duty whatever to your Ruling Lord?"

Spinel opened his arms to take in the gleaming concourse. "Only when we vote does the tyranny of our Ruling Lords lift enough to let us for a moment into the light. Like many others here, I will not be persuaded to walk back into the shadows merely by some rhetoric about family loyalty. Are you making me an offer for my votes, cousin?"

Carnelian controlled his anger, tried to think of something. "My father is a fair man." He turned to the other Suth Lords. "He will treat you as you treat him."

"I see," said Spinel. "So on the basis that your father is a 'fair man,' you would have me declare myself apostate before all the gathered Great and make the new Gods and Their mother my foes." He shook his crowned head. "I think not. I shall honor the agreement I have made with Molochite and we shall see what transpires."

A Ruling Lord appeared towering at the edge of their group. Carnelian saw the House Imago dragonflies on his robe.

"Internecine conflict within the House Suth, tsk, tsk," said Jaspar. "Not that one can own to much surprise, to judge from the lack of care with which its Ruling Lord is wont to treat its interests."

"My father's interests are his own, Jaspar."

Looking at Jaspar, Spinel pointed at Carnelian. "Lord Imago, my kinsman here was attempting to detach me from my agreements."

"Indeed. That would be foolish, Suth Spinel. One should not lightly abandon one's commitments."

"Spare us your threats, my Lord," said Carnelian. "My kinsman is already determined in his act of treachery. He had better only hope that when this election is over, Ykoriana will be able to protect him from my father's wrath."

"Carnelian, you should not concern yourself overmuch with that. Once Molochite wears the Masks he will reward his friends and, no doubt, become an inconvenience to those whose lack of foresight led them to number themselves among his enemies."

"We are not afraid—"

Carnelian was interrupted by a chime that shook the air all the way from the Chamber of the Three Lands.

"Ah, cousin dear, we must discuss your fears some other time. You are summoned into the chamber."

Another chime rang out. Carnelian waited for its reverberations to dull. "In spite of all your treacheries, Jaspar, the victory will be ours."

Jaspar laughed at him through his mask and walked off, dragging a train like a sunset sky.

Carnelian stood rigid, feeling set about with enemies as the pealing shuddered over him. He felt a pulling at his sleeve. He looked up to see his own mask reflected in that of one of the third lineage Lords.

"Come, cousin, we must obey the call of the Turtle's Voice."

Leading the Suth Lords, Carnelian made his way along the nave as the pealing rang out. The nave was filling with the processions of the Great like an armada of sails. The bronze trees of the chamber wall rose menacingly ahead. The moat caught their sinister reflection. The Great did not sail across the bridge, for the northeastern gate was shut. They curved toward the southeast, making the gloomy journey to where Carnelian eventually could see the eastern doors were opening, releasing a flickering flood of light. The jeweled oblongs of the Great began bunching as they crossed the bridge accompanied by a shadowy reflected host moving in the black depths of the moat. As they passed into the doorway they smoldered and then caught fire.

Carnelian slowed with the others, feeling the dazzle falling on him. A chime hit him with its wave. He began crossing the bridge and saw before him that the interior of the chamber was filled with the Lesser Chosen from which there rose an island fenced about with lantern posts. A wall feathered with fire hedged the Lesser Chosen in. Its whole flickering circuit was breached only where he saw a door open in the north and by the eastern door through which he was entering. Naphtha dragon odor wafted in the swell of the pealing bell.

He looked for the source of all that sound. A mound rose on the low island lying in the midst of the Lesser Chosen. Above this something floated like a summer moon. As he walked toward it down the avenue between the throng, he saw a hammer wielded by syblings hit this moon. It gave out a ripple of sound as if at that moment it had fallen from the sky into the sea. As the vibration rolled over him he faltered and, reestablishing the rhythm of his steps, he became aware of the void above his head. The chamber was open to the night sky. Looking upward, his eyes could find nothing to see. Fathomless darkness, a dead sky unlit by stars. He felt its emptiness pouring into his mind through the holes of his eyes and, dropping his gaze, he reminded himself how deep inside the Pillar's rock he was.

He was glad to reach the blood-red stone of the island. He had disliked seeing himself twisted in the metal faces of the Lesser Chosen. Steps climbed between the lantern posts,

which were tall and slender and grew six branches, each
holding aloft a light. He saw the resemblance they bore to
the watchtowers he had seen on the road and as he climbed
past them he had a notion. The island he had come up onto
was a perfect red circle inlaid with a network of silver lines.
This was the Guarded Land with its roads. The lantern posts
were set around its edge in the positions of the Ringwall
cities. The floor of jade and malachite that the Lesser Chosen
were thronging represented with its greens the encircling
lands of the barbarians. The platform that rose at the center
of the chamber seemingly of black glass was fenced by posts
carrying the horned-ring of divinity. That was surely Osrakum with its Sacred Wall. The carved stone bell that hung
above it in the black air was the Turtle's Voice, and, like the
Pillar of Heaven, a connection between earth and sky. The
chamber was a wheelmap made stone, the Commonwealth
become geometry, the Three Lands captured within a ring of
fire.

As the Great began to cover the platform of the Guarded
Land, Carnelian led the Suth Lords along its rim, until he
found the post in the northwest that represented Nothnaralan.
From this the silver line of the Great Sea Road ran toward
the Osrakum platform. Carnelian leaned on the lantern post
and saw the road run down to be lost among the Lesser
Chosen. He found Maga-Naralante, a spire rising in their
midst, and against the flaming wall, Thuyakalrul's post.
    "What are you doing, my Lord?" asked Tapaz.
    Carnelian had forgotten the other Lords. "I was looking
for my past," he said. Around them the Great were obscuring
the red stone with their gold. Already he could not see over
their heads to the avenue he had come along but only the
upper part of the eastern door.
    The Turtle's Voice fell silent. A muttering seemed to be
coming from the Chosen but as Carnelian listened it grew
into an insistent modulating grumble. He realized that the
slow, sonorous song was coming from behind the firewall.

The rumble of the chanting slid up to a peak, down and up again and took his heart with it.

When the other sound started he gasped with shock. A whining tearing into a braying, ululating cry. More shawms joined their voices to it, interweaving, fraying into great vibrating surfaces of sound. He saw the mirror faces round him turning to the northeast to where a black doorway was opening in the firewall. Out from the darkness came a light, a flaming apparition. A green path opened up in front of him. The shawms slid in a shrilling pitch, shredding the air as He-who-goes-before came coruscating, towering through the Lesser Chosen. His lictors walked before him, holding up his standards like glowing coals. Carnelian worried that their support was out of his father's reach, but his progress was as relentless as a comet through the sky as he pulled a flaming tail of the Ruling Lords of the Great with their lightning crowns.

Then his father was hidden. Carnelian could still follow the red eyes of his standards above the heads of the Great. As his father climbed onto the Guarded Land, the opaque pulsing brilliance of the shawms swelled louder. The sunburst of his father's head rose into sight and slid across Carnelian's vision and then, preceded by his lictors, moved up and through the horned-ring fence to stand facing the Turtle's Voice.

Carnelian felt the Great turning around him and, following their gaze, saw the Ruling Lords were moving along the edge of the Osrakum platform. A ripple of bowing accompanied their movement as one of them was being bowed to by the Great. A stone grew heavy in Carnelian's stomach. He knew it was Jaspar to whom they were already paying the homage due a victor.

A myriad crashes of breaking glass made Carnelian imagine for a moment that around him the Chosen were splintering into shards. His father stood as motionless as an idol. Behind him, in the south, a door was opening. Among a hailstorm of cymbals and crotala, Carnelian noticed the Chosen turning to look into the west. There too a door was opening and in it a pale pageant was appearing, of creatures far taller than the Lesser Chosen who moved back to let them through. The Grand Sapients' row of icy pinnacles slid along a curve withershins through the Chosen. Each wore the horns of the crescent moon and an icicle crown. Each was preceded by a pair of glittering standards that appeared to be moving of their own volition. All were clothed in a flash and fold of moonlight. Carnelian counted all twelve Grand Sapients and saw they were leaving behind them a gleaming track of smaller Sapients. He watched their pavane move into the southeast until all he could see of them over the crowned Great was a twinkling froth like the wake a ship might leave upon a moonlit sea.

A while later he saw another procession of the Wise churning toward him through the Lesser Chosen. The angle of their approach suggested they formed part of a long spiral feeding in from the southern door. Their course brought them right to the edge of the Guarded Land, close enough for him to see the starry glisten of the tears upon their blind masks. With sistrums trembling they slid past, walking with their staves and homunculi, winding their procession tight around the Guarded Land.

Then, above the cymbals, Carnelian heard a hiss that made him turn. Under the Turtle's Voice the crowns of the Grand Sapients were drifting thistledown. The tail of their march had formed up around the edge of the Osrakum platform. As the tinkling music abated, Carnelian saw the horned-ring posts begin to melt and waver, then turn into smoke that grew up into the starless night. This slowly blossomed into vast ghostly trees that hung their serpent branches over the Chosen and showered them with attar of lilies.

Carnelian's crowns lost their weight. His robe became no more burden than air-thin silk. He looked up and saw the white smoke uncurling in the air. Rain was falling in the distance. He watched the smoke weave its tendrils into a misty ceiling and realized it was drugged. The Great around him buffeted him as they moved toward the center of the chamber, casting glances to the south-west. He lifted a hand to touch the landscape of a jeweled robe.

"What . . . ?"

"The coming of the House of the Masks."

He let the Master go and found himself following him, lifting his ranga shoes with ease, feeling pleasure in his liquid motion. The thrumming was not rain but drumming. A pounding of a heart as massive as the Pillar of Heaven. Lighter rhythms pattered long patterns that took his mind with them even as he crushed in with the brocaded wall of the Great, gazing off to see the door in the southwest opening. The massive heart quickened its beating, making the air rock with its excitement. When the doors were fully open, Carnelian could see the three stairs of the Approach running seemingly as a single stairway all the way up into a remote distance where the Iron Door seemed a window onto a thunderous sky. The screaming began, grumbling, tearing metal, rasping into harshness even as the door began parting. More trumpets were bruising the air with fanfares as the Iron Door fed an incandescing procession onto the stair. Down the steps it poured like burning tar. The anger of the music shifted into an ever more frantic fraying until Carnelian was convinced that it would split him from crowns to ranga shoes. He stared appalled, grinding his teeth, as the procession bubbled down its syblings, carrying with it a gory eye, a bloody gathering of knives, Ykoriana and the other women of her House.

He let his gaze fall to the sybling vanguard of that march as they reached the chamber and carried tall flames into the Lesser Chosen. Ykoriana came on behind, floating into the chamber on a gale of horns and trumpets. Folded across her chest, her hands were sheathed in the jade of her four Great-Rings. Before her went the staves of the Regent with their horned-rings, their targets of the Commonwealth. Beside her paced four smaller amethystine women. Around them blood-eyed, bone pale eunuchs faced outward to display their mutilations. Behind came the Lords of the Masks, scores of them with jeweled nest crowns and the faces of angels reflecting sunrise: Chosen syblings, as wide in their robes as chariots, their brethren flanking them in greens and blacks, with iron casques and masks, with poles bearing faces of jade and of obsidian.

Amidst the imperious tumult, Carnelian gaped as the glorious mass broke against the Great and shattered, sending syblings to outflank the platform of the Guarded Land. The core broke free, climbing onto the Osrakum platform, surrounding it, filling it up so that Carnelian saw his father was engulfed.

Then the whole world shook to its foundations as one by one the doors slammed shut. Ripples ran along the firewall that seemed to shower the Lesser Chosen with sparks. The trumpets boomed, then grumbled silent. Carnelian could feel the resonant humming of the Turtle's Voice die away. His gaze followed the firewall round and found it was complete. The Chosen were all trapped within its fiery ring. With a rustling the Chosen lifted their hands to their faces and removed their masks. Carnelian was slow to follow, shivering, startled by the winter of faces. He looked up and saw his father, clean and bright like an unsheathed sword. Facing him on the other side of the bell, across the Grand Sapients, still masked, Ykoriana looked like an instrument of murder.

"The Jade Lords," murmured voices.

"The twins," sighed others.

"Nephron," said Spinel. Carnelian followed the nervous flicker of his eyes past the Turtle's Voice, to the southeast where high in the firewall there stood a man of black diamond. Spinel turned a frown to the northwest. "And Molochite."

In that direction stood an emerald man. Carnelian looked around in time to see his third lineage snatch their eyes away from him. One looked down in shame. Carnelian felt again his robe and crowns dragging him down. Were they all going to vote against his father? His foreboding seemed to be leaching out from him into the air. The grumbling chanting was coming again out from the firewall.

"You who are the Lords of the Earth," the homunculi of the Wise broke out in chorus, "who even now stand upon the Three Lands in power, as you do upon this floor, shall now make ready to choose as once you were chosen."

"As it has been done," the Great broke into thunderous voice, "so shall it be done, for ever, because it is commanded to be done by the Law-that-must-be-obeyed."

The chanting had grown stronger, more insistent.

"He that shall be chosen by you will be raised as a cup to the sky and thrust as a scoop into the earth that in truth are two but one. Thus he shall receive the double Godhead so that They might once more take Their place here, at the center of this realm, within the embrace of the Sacred Wall that They flung up to conceal from profane eyes this place of Their transcendent birth."

The Great answered the Wise, "As it has been done, so shall it be done, for ever, because it is commanded to be done by the Law-that-must-be-obeyed."

"As the Law ordains, this choosing shall be determined by the casting of blood-rings into vessels of jade and of obsidian."

The syblings below him raised up bowls in time to a growling of trumpets.

"Molochite of the Masks by virtue of primogeniture shall be the green candidate, Nephron of the Masks shall be the black."

The trumpets hung several ragged notes above in the swirling incense.

"The candidates are of the same blood, dewed from the Gods Kumatuya and brought forth from the womb of Ykoriana Four-Blood. Their taint is zero, zero, zero, zero, six, thirteen, ten, five, fifteen, four, thirteen, fifteen."

The trumpets grazed each number into the air.

"Let all be aware that any blood-taint zero, zero, zero,

three, zero, twelve, eleven, seventeen, two, three, fifteen or lower shall be forfeit at the Apotheosis that shall be held in four days' time."

The horns and trumpets began a slow crescendo and were joined by the oscillating calls of the shawms and a shimmer of cymbals. The voices rose deafeningly, pulsed, collapsed, rose again to shrillness, the trumpets playing a ragged ululation over which the shawms brayed a lilting counterpoint. They fell echoing silent.

"Choose!" cried the homunculi.

The forest of gold around Carnelian shimmered into movement. He took hold of Spinel's sleeve. *It is not too late.*

The Lord gave him a look of contempt as he pulled his sleeve free. Carnelian glimpsed the guilty faces of Tapaz and others as they turned their backs on him and began moving toward the syblings standing under the lantern posts. Around the edge of the Osrakum platform, the Ruling Lords were casting their votes. Carnelian saw one as he waited his turn, twisting his blood-ring into a loop that held a bunch of others. Carnelian's eyes were drawn to a white oval, Jaspar's face. Carnelian turned away from its look of triumph and went to cast his own vote in despair.

He stood in line with other Lords until it was his turn. The iron masks of the syblings stared eyeless. One held an urn of jade, the other of glassy obsidian. Carnelian removed his blood-ring, held it over the mouth of the black urn and dropped in its paltry twenty votes. Then he turned and waded a little way off into the golden robes.

Carnelian allowed his mind to float on the chant. He had searched the faces of all those who had come to the edge of the Osrakum platform to vote and he was sure Osidian had not been among them. Still masked, Ykoriana was a doll gazing at his father. Hopelessness seemed written on his yellowed ivory face. Carnelian refused to resign himself to defeat.

A hubbub of excitement made him turn to see gaps opening everywhere among the Great. At their edges, crowns leaned together as the Lords watched something passing below them. Then he saw the syblings filing up onto the Osrakum platform, each pair carrying two voting urns.

"Now for the result."

Carnelian glanced round at the speaker and recognized Tapaz. Spinel was there, Opalid, the other Suth Lords. Only Spinel dared look at him. A delicate shimmering chime was drowned by rustling as the Chosen everywhere sank on their ranga. The House of the Masks had knelt too, revealing the Grand Sapients with their homunculi looking out from under the bell. Carnelian watched the syblings lifting the urns up to the Wise. He realized he alone was still standing and quickly bent his knees.

Without any preamble the homunculi began in a rapid and random sequence to announce the votes. Chosen names rattled from their throats, each named Lord assigning a single vote to Molochite. Carnelian listened carefully, hoping to hear Osidian mentioned. He realized that he did not even know which way his friend might vote. Hearing that all the votes were going to Molochite, Carnelian thought at first Nephron's would follow after. The announcement of a vote for Nephron followed instantly by another for Molochite cheated him of this hope. He dug his nails into the palms of his hands and reassured himself that these were after all only the results for the individual Lords of blood-rank one.

"Suth Veridian for Molochite, one vote."

Hearing the name, Carnelian looked instinctively for that Lord and found him gazing fixedly away. Carnelian's eyes were drawn to Spinel. The Lord's lips were moving as he added up the votes. He looked round as if he had felt Carnelian's gaze and smiled at him. After that Carnelian tried to show no reaction whenever another Suth Lord's vote for Molochite was called out. Notwithstanding their promises, all five Lords of the third lineage had voted against his father.

His heart jumped when he heard, ". . . of the Masks." It was now that he would hear Osidian's name. He listened to each as it was called out. There were more than thirty of them and almost all were voting with the Dowager Empress. Carnelian frowned when the homunculi began announcing the votes cast by rank two Lords. The only names he had recognized from the House of the Masks were the Hanuses who had each voted for a different candidate. Carnelian could not believe Osidian could be higher than blood-rank one, but still he listened attentively. At least now more votes were being cast for Nephron, perhaps a half of what Molochite was receiving. Among the results, the Aurum Lords had declared for Nephron, all from Houses Vennel and Imago for Molochite. Carnelian had to endure Emeral, Tapaz and Spinel all being declared defying their Ruling Lord before the Chosen. As each was announced, he watched his father having to hold his head up in plain view of all. Carnelian smiled bitterly as he heard Opalid's votes going to Nephron. His own twenty votes soon joined them. Almost thirty House of the Masks' Lords were called out, but once again Osidian's name was not among them. When the block votes began being announced Carnelian gave up any hope that Osidian was in the chamber. He tried to fight the doubts and conjectures forming in his mind. His friend had stolen or borrowed a blood-ring. In spite of his white, jade-eyed beauty, he was not Chosen. Osidian had never claimed to be Chosen. Carnelian wondered again about the taint scars that Osidian had down only one side of his spine. He watched one of the Grand Sapients reading the rings strung on a necklace with his cloven hands. He knew without a doubt that he would never see Osidian again. The emptiness spread out from his core and seemed to fill the whole chamber.

As the block votes droned on, Carnelian became aware that the majority were now going in Nephron's favor. When the size of the blocks suddenly jumped it was obvious that the voting of the highest Houses was being declared and these too seemed to be going predominantly Nephron's way. Houses Vennel and Imago cast their block votes for Molochite, but Nephron received the endorsement of many others among whom were Aurum and Cumulus. Hope awoke in him and he tried to feed it by looking up at his father. They were winning the election. He wanted to shout it up to his father. They were winning. His father was concealing his misery but Carnelian knew him well enough to see it. He followed his father's fixed gaze to Ykoriana and his hope blew out. There she stood among her kin whose votes had not yet been announced. The highest of the Great had been able to cast only a few hundred votes: in her own right, Ykoriana had eight thousand.

He felt the buzz of excitement.

"House Suth Who-goes-before for Nephron, six hundred and ten votes," cried a homunculus.

The Chosen seemed to be quivering. The result was near.

"Lady Tiye of the Masks for Molochite, four hundred votes," said another.

"Lady Nurpayahras of the Masks for Nephron, four hundred votes."

"Lady Nayakarade of the Masks for Molochite, four hundred votes."

"The Regent and Jade Womb Ykoriana for Molochite, eight thousand, two hundred twenty votes."

The voice fell into a deep winter silence. Nothing moved except the feather flicker of the firewall.

"With his own ring added in, the total of the votes cast for Molochite of the Masks," said the homunculi in eerie chorus, "twenty-one thousand, one hundred ninety-two."

An excited murmur ran around the chamber. Carnelian caught the look of horror spreading over Spinel's face.

There was a commotion around Ykoriana. Rumor burned across the Great and spread down among the Lesser Chosen. "She is demanding . . ." Carnelian heard and strained to hear more. "She is demanding a recount."

"With his own ring, those cast for Nephron of the Masks, twenty-one thousand, two hundred and eight."

Carnelian saw his father turn to him, his face transfused with triumph. Carnelian swallowed, feeling his back buckling with the euphoric relief.

"Nephron is chosen by a margin of—"

The rest was lost in the swell of the Chosen rising as they turned to face Nephron in his niche.

The Wise were all turned to him. "Behold," their homunculi shrilled. "He that will be They, Lords of Earth and Sky."

The beautiful faces of the Great swam before Carnelian's eyes. Some frowned, others laughed. Spinel and the other Suth Lords looked ashen and their eyes would not hold his gaze. Jaspar was smiling at him. He started smiling back then froze as he felt the Master's eyes peeling him skin from bone. A cacophony of trumpets broke him free. He looked out across the Lesser Chosen throng and saw the snow of their faces focusing back over his shoulder. He saw the black angel coming through the Great. For a while Carnelian saw the face he expected, a face twinned to Molochite's. Something black on the forehead began his frown. His gaze snatched down to the jade eyes, searching. They saw each other as the Turtle's Voice set the Chamber of the Three Lands trembling. The whole world was coming to pieces around him but Carnelian could do nothing but stare into Osidian's smiling eyes.

JUST ONE MORE DAY

The cruelest traps are baited

With the heart of the lotus

—FROM THE "TALE OF

THE LITTLE BARBARIAN"

When Carnelian came back Tain was like something dead, an uninterested stranger helping him with his crowns. Though he kept telling himself that Tain did not know, could not know, it was all he could do to not to shake him.

"Go away," he said.

"You need help with the robe," said Tain.

"Go!" cried Carnelian. He watched Tain sullenly move away. The click of the door closing unleashed Carnelian's rage. He struggled to free himself from the robe. He swore. The bird-bone frame was snapping like twigs. He tugged at the ridged cloth, growling curses until at last he had tumbled down from his ranga, falling like a cut-down tree, crumpling the brocades, rending samite. He lay chuckling mirthlessly with the bone frame jabbing into him. He shuffled out, a snake discarding its skin, and when he was free he kicked the glimmering golden shell aside and went to stand upon the balcony in his underclothes until the wind had numbed even his bones.

Carnelian wrestled a nightmare in and out of sleep. The sweat that chilled him was the cool shell of his anger. He groaned awake and Tain stirred upon the floor. He had crept back in. "Do you want something?"

Carnelian could not make his tongue work. In the dark he could see Osidian's eyes mocking him. The lamp flared. Tain turned to face him, accusation in his eyes.

"Is something wrong?" the boy said.

"You tell me," growled Carnelian.

Tain closed his mouth, stared through him.

Carnelian sat up. "Blood and iron! I'm sick to my stomach of you moping around."

He saw fire flicker in his brother's eyes as if he were seeing distant lightning.

"I don't know who you are any more. If you've something to say, say it!"

"Do you really want me to speak, Master?"

That last word was the lash of a whip. Carnelian glowered. "Let it out, curse you, just don't *stand* there."

"Fine, I'll speak and you can have me punished afterward."

"Punished—?"

"You let them slaughter him."

Carnelian narrowed his eyes, his anger cooling under Tain's icy stare. "What . . . ?"

"Have you forgotten Crail so quickly, Master? Of course, I'm forgetting, he was just a slave."

"What? He was . . ." Carnelian felt the pain again. "I did what I could . . . even Father couldn't save him."

"You're all the same. He lied to us, all those years he lied to us. There in his hall pretending to be an angel, our people believing he controlled the sky, the seasons and the sea. Then he left, discarding the Hold like an old shoe, and when it came down to it he couldn't even save one . . . old . . . man."

"There are things you don't know, things—"

"There are always things we don't know, matters beyond us that only you Masters can possibly understand. You're no different. Don't tell me you had no idea what might happen to us boys on the road."

"I didn't want to take you—"

"What he did to me . . ." Tain's voice broke. "How could you let the Master do *that* to me?"

"I didn't know, Tain, on my blood, I didn't know." Carnelian was crumbling to tears. He was too tired to fight and could put up no defense.

"You let them hurt Father." Tain was crying.

Carnelian shook his head, licking the tears from his lip.

"You let them take me," he sobbed, "on the road, then into the . . . quarantine." His face grew dark. "I didn't really get a chance to tell you the worst that happened, did I?" He shook his head, staring wildly. "Do you want to know? Do you? Well, do you?"

Carnelian shook his hands up, wanting to look away.

Tain was shaking. "Why did you let them come . . . to bring us here to this evil place?" He was shouting now. "You're evil, you're all evil . . . you pretend to be gods but you're a disease. I hate you." He kicked at a jar and it smashed against the wall. "I hate you." There was a knocking on the door. Tain ignored it. "I hate you, I hate you all."

The door opened and one of the tyadra peeked in. "Master. Is everything—?"

"Get out!" Carnelian's bellow slammed the door shut. Tain's eyes were like coals. Carnelian felt empty. He bowed his head. "You're right, Tain. We failed you. I failed you." He could no longer hold back the misery. Sobs shook him. "I'm sorry." The sobbing choked him. "I'm so sorry." Arms embraced him, Tain's arms, his face pressing against Carnelian's neck.

"I know it wasn't you, Carnie." The words vibrated into his neck. "It wasn't your fault."

Carnelian hugged his brother and they rocked each other until they ran out of tears.

A knocking woke them. Carnelian had told Tain that he could not bear to see him spend another night on the cold floor and so they had shared the bed.

Tain leapt up, lit a lamp and went to see who it was. He opened a chink in the door, nodded and looked back at Carnelian, making a face. "It's the Master," he mouthed. They both looked at the chamber, shards scattered over the floor, boxes everywhere, Carnelian's court robe toppled broken against a wall.

Together they furiously cleared what they could of the mess and then they found him something to wear. "This will have to do," said Carnelian at last. "Show him in."

"If you're sure," Tain said and grinned, then went to open the door.

Suth entered. "What, are you still abed, my Lord?" He stopped. His mask surveyed the chamber. "A storm?" He saw Tain. "Open the shutters, Tain, let in some light, some air."

"As you command, Master," said Tain.

"It is such a beautiful morning." Light flooded progressively around the chamber as Tain folded back one shutter after another. "You should both have been up. You have missed the blushings of the sky."

"Neither of us slept well, my Lord."

His father was wearing a simple robe, the color of lapis against which his hands and feet were flakes of ice. "The excitement, no doubt."

"No doubt," said Carnelian.

Suth dismissed Tain. When they were alone he removed his mask. "Ah, but it was a wondrous victory . . . not that one should savor it too much," he said, throwing Carnelian a glance. "Still, it has quite put the fire back into my blood."

"It does me good to see my Lord so happy," said Carnelian, smiling. Though still haggard, his father looked a little more like himself.

"Tomorrow, we shall descend the Rainbow Stair together to the Labyrinth. You have participated in an election but you have still to witness an Apotheosis." His father's eyes gleamed. "In four, maybe five days Nephron shall be made into the Gods."

Carnelian flinched at the name. The chamber seemed to have gone dark again. "There is still time for Ykoriana to do something."

His father raised his brows. "I think not." He smiled. "Nephron has assumed the powers of the Regent and the Great are deserting her like an ebbing tide. Her wings are broken and she has already been put back in her cage." Carnelian saw his father's face become infinitely sad. "She chose this for herself and yet I find myself pitying her."

"So Aurum has won?"

His father nodded heavily.

"He is then already become the core of power among the Great?"

"He is welcome to it." Suth made a face. "I am sick of its taste." He made an elegant gesture in which something solid became smoke and then clear air. "But let us not worry ourselves with that. The Rains are near and soon the lands and the Commonwealth shall be simultaneously renewed. And you and I shall be able to return to our coomb and begin our new life. Soon we will have restored the palaces; perhaps we might build some new halls to celebrate our return. We shall organize such masques as will dazzle even the Great." His eyes lit up as he gazed at his son. "You will see, my son, I shall show you such wonders."

"What about Spinel and the others, Father?"

Suth frowned deeply. "They will reap what they have sown."

Carnelian was alarmed by his father's dark looks. "Perhaps the best way to celebrate our return would be to usher in an era of mercy and coexistence."

Suth smiled at him. "Yes, perhaps." He became pensive.

"First, we must attend Apotheosis and receive the tribute and the flesh tithe."

Carnelian wondered how he would cope with watching Osidian become the Gods.

His father came to stand near him, and crouched down so that Carnelian could look into his gray eyes, still tinged with red. "What ails you, Carnelian?"

Looking into his father's eyes Carnelian almost confessed, but then he saw the winter sky, the Hold and his people empty-eyed and gray upon the quay. It was time he bore some pain by himself. He cracked a smile. "It is lack of sleep, Father, just lack of sleep."

His father leaned forward and kissed his forehead. "I know how hard it has been for you," he said in a low voice. "We will establish a greater Hold here in Osrakum. You will see, Carnelian. Soon you will call Coomb Suth home. And there, with all our people, we both shall begin a healing."

He stood up. "Get your household ready. With the next rising of the sun we will return to the earth below." His father started walking to the door. He came back. He smiled. "I almost forgot to give you this." He gave Carnelian something small and hard. Carnelian looked in his hand. It was his blood-ring. He clutched it as he watched his father leave, tighter and tighter until he could feel it cutting through his skin.

Carnelian put the ring on when Tain returned. He could see his brother had something in his hand. "What's that?"

"A letter." Tain gave him it.

It had been sealed with a blood-ring. He saw the two-face House cipher, the name glyph "Nephron," the blood-taint with all its zeros. He stared at it.

"What's the matter, Carnie?"

Carnelian looked up, thinking to send him away. His brother's face was filled with concern. Carnelian would do nothing to damage their delicate reemerging intimacy. "Let me read it and then I'll tell you."

He broke the seal. The paper bore only three glyphs: "I must see you." Carnelian read them over and over again.

"Perhaps you'd rather be by yourself," said Tain warily.

Carnelian put out his hand to take his wrist. "No, stay with me. It would help me to talk about it."

Carnelian told Tain of his meeting with the strange boy in the Library of the Wise, their expedition to the Yden. Tain could see the brightness of the lagoons in his eyes as Carnelian told him everything. The tale brought Carnelian and Osidian back to the Halls of Thunder and the long days of separation.

"And you hoped to see him at the election?" asked Tain.

Carnelian nodded.

"Did you?"

Carnelian's glower made Tain flinch. "Oh yes, he was there."

Tain waited for the words to come.

"He is the one we chose to become the Gods."

Tain gaped. "The actual, the very Gods?"

Carnelian shook the letter. "And now, he writes that he *must* see me."

"Do you want to see him?"

"No," cried Carnelian. "I won't be his plaything again."

"Carnie, are you sure that's what it was?"

Carnelian glared at him. "What else?"

Tain lowered his eyes and played at interweaving his fingers. He kept snatching glimpses at Carnelian's face until he could see that he had sunk back into sad introspection. "There's one thing you should think about, though, Carnie."

Carnelian impaled him with his jade-green eyes.

"Once he becomes the Gods, you'll never see his face again."

Carnelian's eyes went out of focus; his head shook. "So be it. I can't see him. I'll never see him again."

Something was tickling his lips and Carnelian brushed it away. The tickling returned. He opened his eyes, irritated, and looked straight into familiar green eyes. He lashed out, punching bone, pushing himself away up the bed.

Osidian was there as tall as the sky and as beautiful, even as he grimaced holding his face. "You hit me."

"What did you expect?"

"Anger, I suppose."

It welled up so strongly in Carnelian that all he could do was glare.

Osidian took a step back, his palms in front of him in a sign of appeasement. He looked so funny that Carnelian had to frown hard to stop himself from smiling. Osidian's hands dropped slowly. For some reason, that made him the enemy again.

"What do you want, *Nephron?*"

"To explain," said Osidian, dropping into Vulgate.

Carnelian crossed his arms and continued to glare at him.

"You aren't going to make this easy, are you?"

Carnelian glowered more darkly.

"Don't look at me like that." Osidian scratched his head. "I meant to tell you."

"When?"

"Several times. Before the election I even thought of sending you a letter, but . . ."

"But what?"

"You were deep in the Sunhold. I was reluctant to give it to your father and afraid to give it to the Ichorians in case it should fall into my mother's hands."

"It wouldn't have made any difference even if you'd sent it. By then it was already too late. You had plenty of time to tell me."

Osidian looked at his hands, then up again. "I did tell you my name. Well . . . one of them."

"Am I supposed to be grateful?"

Osidian's face darkened. "You could make a vague attempt at seeing it from my point of view."

"Your rank, you mean, Celestial?" asked Carnelian, returning to the Quya.

"No," replied Osidian, grimacing.

Carnelian could feel his anger cooling. "What then?" he said, trying to reheat it.

Osidian grew taller, thrust out his heavy-sleeved arms. "Everyone has always known who I am." He let his arms drop to his side. "When you obviously did not . . . well, I went along with it."

"Playing with me."

Osidian's chin dropped to his chest. "No," he groaned. He looked at Carnelian. "No. No. No. It was that . . . that you allowed me to forget who I was . . . to forget the election."

"The election." Carnelian thought about how close the result had been, how even now, Molochite was under sentence of death. He lost his grip on his anger and let it leak away.

"Then we went down to the Yden," said Osidian, light seeming to shine from his face.

Carnelian saw again the glittering lagoons, the smell and touch of him.

Osidian looked at him with longing. "After that, the fear of losing you was greater than my fear of losing the election."

"You were so cold when we were coming back," said Carnelian.

"My father was dead," said Osidian, a note of pleading in his voice.

"I didn't know that."

They were both measuring the space between them.

"You know it now." Osidian looked at him with hunger.

"But . . ." Carnelian was overwhelmed by grief.

Osidian came closer. His hand touched Carnelian's shoulder.

Carnelian looked up at him. "But you're to be—"

Osidian interrupted him by covering Carnelian's mouth with his own. He lay down on top of him. The sharp brocades of his court robe scratched into Carnelian's skin but Carnelian did not care. Osidian pulled up to look at him. His eyes and breath were fire. Carnelian buried his face in the small part of Osidian's neck that was exposed. He drew him closer, gasping as the metal brocades bit deeper into him. He pulled him closer still. It was an exquisite pain.

When Osidian saw the weals his robe had gouged, only Carnelian's smiles allayed his remorse. "I would bear much worse for you."

Osidian kissed the pain away from each wound. Then he straightened up and began to struggle out of his robe. Propped up on his elbows, Carnelian looked on entranced. "Are you just going to watch?" grimaced Osidian with his head caught.

Carnelian grinned and nodded. Osidian looked like a white butterfly pulling itself from the crusty prison of its chrysalis. Once free he unfolded his arms like wings. Carnelian sighed as Osidian slipped his warm alabaster skin past his.

They intertwined, firm and hot against each other.

Osidian lay in Carnelian's arms as peaceful as a sleeping child. Carnelian touched his body with wonder, examining the vessel that would hold the coruscating energies of the Twins. He shuddered at the thought, and Osidian nuzzled closer. Carnelian ran his hands over him as if he were feeling the pale yielding marble for hairline cracks that might allow the ichor to weep through.

Carnelian stroked Osidian's birthmark. "It really does look as if it was left by a kiss."

"Some of the Wise have argued that it made me unsuitable for the double Godhead."

"Unsuitable?"

"They said that it was the mark of the Black God."

"And the God Emperor must be both Twins and not favor one above the other."

Osidian nodded.

Carnelian lay back. "How did you come here?"

"I came to see the Lord Suth, to thank him for his help."

"You mean, to see me."

Osidian lifted his head and looked at him solemnly. "I owe your father the Masks and will not forget it."

"You came as yourself?"

Osidian grinned. "I came disguised as one of the Lesser Chosen of my House."

Carnelian bit him. "My Lord seems much given to passing himself off as someone else." He looked over at Osidian's discarded robe. He should have noticed the lack of ranga. "Why the disguise?"

"I didn't want to be mobbed by the Chosen."

Something occurred to Carnelian. "You did come with guards?"

"The Quenthas. They're outside your door now."

"Two girls?"

"Girls? Those girls could fillet a half-dozen of your best guardsmen without breaking into a sweat."

"I do like them."

"They like you too. There was a boy."

"My brother Tain."

Osidian raised an eyebrow. "Brother?"

Carnelian tensed. "Do you have a problem with that?"

Osidian adopted an expression of appeasement. "Brother it is."

Carnelian relaxed. "He's been through a lot. We've been close since we were children." He reached up to smooth the frown from Osidian's forehead. "I know it isn't worthy of one of the Chosen, but there it is."

Osidian squeezed him, kissing him passionately. "You could do nothing that was unworthy."

Carnelian smiled. "You think not?"

"You've even chosen the Gods for a lover," said Osidian, grinning.

Carnelian put his fingers to Osidian's lips.

Osidian kissed them and lay back. "Who did you think I was?" When Carnelian said nothing he turned to look at him. "You blush, my Lord," he said in Quya.

Carnelian could not look him in the face. "I thought you were . . ."

"Who?"

"A sybling."

"A what?" cried Osidian. "How did you work that out?"

Carnelian hid his eyes with a hand. "Well . . ." He peeped at Osidian. "You look a bit like the Lords Hanus . . . ?"

Osidian looked horrified. The expression softened. "I suppose . . . my grandfather sired them . . . but a sybling?" He made a big show of feeling his shoulders. He blew out. "I didn't think I had a second head."

Carnelian blushed again. "I know it's stupid, but when you told me you had a twin . . . and you seemed embarrassed about telling me who you were . . . well, I put two and two together—"

"And ended up with a sybling." Osidian chuckled, shook his head. "I see . . . no wonder you asked no more questions." His face went very serious. His eyes looked deep into Carnelian's. "And even then, you went with me . . . the Yden . . ."

"You're beautiful," said Carnelian and it was Osidian's turn to blush. "Besides, I loved you for who you are."

"Love?"

Carnelian looked away. "What am I supposed to call you?"

Osidian pulled Carnelian's chin back. His eyes were a furious green. "Whatever you want."

They lay wrapped in each other's sweat. Osidian's arm lay over his eyes. Carnelian was staring at the ceiling.

"What about your taint scars?" he said suddenly.

"What about them?"

"You only have them down one side."

Osidian lifted his arm off his face and looked at him with one eye. "Even you must have realized by now that I was fathered by a God Emperor?"

Carnelian punched him and Osidian laughed.

"But the blank side is on your left, the mother's side."

"The God Emperor's paternity goes on the left because of the sinistral nature of Godhead."

"I see," Carnelian said and resumed his staring. A little while later he sat up. "Can I see your blood-ring?"

Osidian lifted up his arm again. "Does my Lord need proof that I am who I say I am?"

Carnelian growled and showed his teeth.

Osidian affected fear. "All right. All right." He removed his ring and gave it to Carnelian who peered at it. Four zeros. He whistled. Blood-rank four. He held it up to the light. Even the fifth number was low, a five. He gave it back to Osidian.

"It surprises me that I can't feel the heat of your fiery blood from here."

Osidian smiled at him. "Are you sure you can't?"

Carnelian turned and hugged him so hard he cried out. He relaxed the circle of his arms, buried his head in Osidian's neck, nibbled it. His hands slid down his spine. He could feel the taint scars with his fingers.

"This is your mother's taint?" he said into Osidian's neck.

"You know it is."

"Do you love her?"

Osidian pushed him gently away so that he could see his eyes. "She's my mother."

"But do you love her?"

Osidian frowned. "I've seen very little of her. Mostly, I fear her."

"So do I. You know she tried to have us all killed?"

Osidian nodded slowly. "She slew my sister who would have been my wife."

"That is rumored—"

"That is fact!" Osidian cried, making Carnelian flinch. "She knew that Flama would have voted for me."

Carnelian put his hand out and stroked Osidian's head. "I'm sorry."

"We loved each other since we were children. When I am the Gods . . ."

Carnelian shivered when he saw the chill look of anger

that came into his face. "Does she know you feel like this?"

"How could she not? Her eyes are everywhere."

Carnelian looked around the chamber.

Osidian laughed. "Not literally."

"And your brother?"

Osidian's mouth showed his distaste. "Molochite will be taken from her. He's always been her creature." He shook his head. "His cruelties . . . There are many in the House of the Masks who will breathe with relief when my crowns are painted with his blood."

"Will many others die?" Carnelian asked, almost whispering.

"Some." The green fire in his eyes went out. "My sons . . ."

"Your sons?"

"Only syblings, but I feel something for them." He smiled a pale smile. "There are always children from the House of the Masks slaughtered at an Apotheosis."

"Why then did you make them?"

"It's one of my duties to make blood for ritual."

"I must go soon," said Osidian.

They clung to each other more tightly.

"Must you?"

"I've already been away too long." The shutters rattled a long tattoo.

"When I'm the God . . ."

"Let's not talk of that."

Osidian slid his hand to squeeze the nape of Carnelian's neck. "We must."

Carnelian closed his eyes.

"Our love will be difficult," said Osidian. "But if we both really want it to, we can make it work."

"But they'll put your face for ever behind the Masks." Carnelian could feel that Osidian's body had grown wooden.

"Yes. But we can still talk. The Wise will not know it if we touch hands."

"Will we touch like this?"

"Perhaps yes, perhaps even that."

Carnelian did not believe him. He knew the Wise would be always there. "I can't bear it," he said. Osidian silenced him by pulling his face into his chest. Carnelian could feel the beating of Osidian's heart. He pulled himself away. "How much time do we have?"

Osidian said nothing, but stared up into the shadowy ceiling.

"How much?" Carnelian demanded.

"There is no more time."

Carnelian felt his heart become a stone. He felt it spreading numbness up into his head, down to his groin. "No." He shook his head. "No."

Osidian touched a tear from Carnelian's eye. "We have to face it."

"My father said that there are four days, maybe five until they do it.".

"Yes, but the rituals, the preparations . . . they're endless, inescapable."

"But you've to go down to the Labyrinth?"

Osidian looking at him, nodded.

"Couldn't we go there another way?"

"What other way?"

"Through the Yden."

Osidian stared. Carnelian watched Osidian's eyes lose their focus as he calculated the possibilities. "No," he said at last. "I couldn't do it."

Carnelian fixed him with his eyes. "Even one more day like this. Just one!" He could see the cracks appearing in Osidian's resistance. "So we'd cause consternation. What of it? You'll have your whole reign to appease the Wise."

Osidian was crumbling. Carnelian could see the boyish hope peeking through. "We'd have to let them know . . . tell them something . . ."

"We could leave my father a letter. In all this world he at least should understand."

Osidian nodded slowly. "He won't quickly forgive us for forcing him to stand alone against the Wise."

"He bore thirteen years of exile for your father's sake. He's stood against your mother and won. He speaks for the Great. Are the Wise so terrible?"

Osidian looked at him with round eyes, as much as to say, you have no idea. "As you say, we'd have all my reign to make it up to him."

"Then you'll come?"

Osidian smiled a crooked smile. "How could I not?"

Carnelian gave a whoop and threw himself on him. They wrestled violently until they fell onto the floor and rolled apart.

Osidian sat up panting, grinning. When Carnelian began to move toward him, he put up his hand. "I submit. I submit."

Carnelian embraced him. They leaned their heads together.

"Will you write the letter?" Osidian asked.

Their ears rubbed together as Carnelian gave a nod.

"I'll still have to return to my household, give them instructions."

He disentangled Carnelian's arms gently, stood up. They managed to get him back into his robe. "Meet me before sunrise at the usual place." They grinned at each other, they kissed and Osidian left.

Carnelian slumped onto the bed. He gathered up the sheets and wrapped himself in them. Doubt surged in his stomach. He frowned, wondering if he was making a mistake.

Carnelian sat cross-legged, with the parchment on the low table in front of him a narrow rectangle in the lamplight. He drew the glyphs carefully with the pen as his father had taught him. Several times he stopped, angling the pen so that it would not drip ink onto the parchment, then looking off into the darkness. His lips moved as if he were speaking but he made no sound. He was trying to explain to his father how he felt. How could his father not understand? But if he did not, no matter. Carnelian knew with a deadly certainty that he would withstand his father's fury a hundred times if that was the payment demanded for this last day of freedom with Osidian.

Carnelian let Tain in when he scratched at the door. His brother stared at the nest of sheets, the table in the middle of the floor, and at Carnelian's white-flaming weary happiness, his haunted look, the way he danced a little when he walked, the way he looked at him but saw another.

"Did I do right to let the Master in?"

Carnelian grabbed him, hugged him, kissed him. "Never have you done so right."

Tain smiled uncertainly. "He gave you joy?"

"Joy, yes, and . . ." Carnelian stopped, his limbs seeming suddenly cast from lead, ". . . despair."

Tain could not understand it at all. It seemed madness.

Carnelian read his face. "Yes, it is a kind of madness." He smiled sadly. "Such consuming fire . . ."

Tain brought him food, and cleaned him when he stood still long enough. He tried to chat and sometimes Carnelian seemed to listen, but then he would narrow his eyes and look away. Tain made a bed for himself upon the floor. When he turned off the lamp, he could almost feel Carnelian staring into the darkness.

Tain could not wake Carnelian. He shook him, a wail beginning to escape through his gape. Suddenly, Carnelian came alive, gulping as if Tain had just drawn him up drowning from the depths of a well. His arms locked around the boy, squeezing.

"Carnie! Carnie!" Tain cried as he struggled to free himself.

Carnelian kissed his neck with passion. "Terrible, terrible, terrible," he muttered.

Tain was scared. "Carnie, Master, please let go."

Carnelian opened his eyes impossibly wide. His arms lost

all their strength and Tain fell out of them. Carnelian put his hands to his face. "Sorry, I didn't . . . it was . . ." He sighed, shaking his head, backing away up the bed. "A dream . . ." His mouth gaped, his eyebrows twitched.

Tain stared for moments, then, "Today . . . we must get ready to leave today."

"Today," echoed Carnelian. He remembered the letter. He stumbled off the bed and found it where he had left it. He stared at it, knowing he must tear it up. His mind saw his hands tearing it but instead they gave it to Tain. Carnelian turned to focus on Tain standing gripping the letter. It was already out of reach. He felt suddenly free, as if he had escaped from a court robe of stone.

He smiled at Tain. "I'll not be coming with you."

Tain frowned, looked nervously down at the letter in his hands and back up at Carnelian.

"I've been a little distraught, Tain. Don't worry about it. I'm going away but will join you in a day or two. Please, give that to the Master this evening. Don't give it to him earlier. If he asks tell him that I commanded you. Once he reads it, he'll understand."

"But Carnie . . . where are you going?"

"That doesn't matter. You'll do as I say?"

Tain looked miserable, but he gave a hard nod.

"That's good. Now let's get me cleaned up a bit."

As Carnelian said his farewells to Tain, he assured him that he would see him in the Labyrinth the next day, the day after at the latest. Then he left the chamber.

The corridor was a flurry of packing. Guardsmen dropped what they were doing to escort him but he sent them back to their work.

The Ichorians at the mouth of the tunnel into the Sun in Splendor were more difficult to persuade, but eventually they too gave way and opened the portcullises.

The air in the Sun in Splendor was rosy-hued. He crossed to the trapdoor and opened it. He lit his lantern and hesitated for a moment looking down into the darkness, then went quickly down. After the commotion above, the silence was eerie. Doubts came crowding in with the blackness. He stopped and could just hear faint sounds coming down the stair. He lifted the lantern to push back the gloom and reveal more steps below him. He imagined Osidian waiting for him at the moon-eyed door. That thought quickened his heart. He laughed at the darkness. Osidian was a bright beacon.

He walked through the midnight halls. Unusual brightness swelled ahead. His steps faltered. He shuttered the lantern. Soon it was bright enough for him to see his way without it. He listened for voices. He drew closer and looked into the great round chamber. Lamps had been hung all round its wall. The door to the library was gaping open. Arranged before it, like sarcophagi washed out by a flood, were rows and rows of chests. Hearing nothing, Carnelian crept into the light. He looked at one of the chests. It was long and narrow and had five rows of paired golden nipples on its top. Its side was studded with silver spirals. Nearer the floor, a long carrying pole passed through several rings of brass. He realized it was a beadcord bench closed for transport. The Wise were taking their library down with them to the Labyrinth. He heard footsteps and saw light swaying through the silver door. He looked round desperately, stomach churning. What if Osidian had not come?

"Carnelian." His name strained from the gloom behind him. He looked wildly at the light shaking out through the moon-eyed door. He peered round into the dark. Something pale rushed out.

"Osid—" he began joyfully but his arm was yanked as he was dragged off into the shadows. A hand clapped across his mouth. He leaned back into the warm body. He could feel Osidian's breath on his ear. He pushed back harder.

"Stop it," was hissed in his ear but followed by a kiss. Carnelian watched as ammonites appeared with a chest hanging in the air between them. He could see their faces, disfigured with numbers. They negotiated several chests until they found a space in which to put their burden down. They filed back into the library. Carnelian turned in Osidian's grip and sank his weight into him. They kissed, then moved apart. Osidian offered his hand and Carnelian took it. He let himself be led through a doorway. Deeper and deeper into the darkness they went until Carnelian could see nothing and was stumbling. Osidian stopped and pulled him close. Carnelian felt Osidian's face with his lips. Osidian pushed him gently away, chuckling. "This is neither the time nor the place."

Carnelian tried again.

"I'm serious," Osidian said firmly.

Carnelian pulled back.

"Are you sure you still want to do this?"

"More than ever," said Carnelian, burning with need. "Will we have to wait until they've cleared the library?"

"That will take days."

"What can—"

"There's another way." Osidian fumbled their hands together.

"Don't you think it's funny that the Gods-to-be should be creeping around in the blackness?"

"I don't," Osidian said through a smile. "Now walk carefully, and by the blood, keep quiet."

They felt their way through the darkness with their feet until they came through a door into the Windmoat. They walked along it toward the morning sky. The heart-stone screens on their left were dark. No sound came from behind them. The windows in the wall of the Forbidden House were blind. They descended into the ravine. In its gullet they prepared themselves with the thick paint as they had done before although this time they helped put it on each other with much biting, mock anger, laughter.

Then it was out into the morning. From the east the crescent shadow of the Sacred Wall matched the curving Ydenrim. Between the two was the gleaming scythe of the Skymere. They turned their faces into the southern wind. Carnelian stared. The sky was brooding black. The Rains could not be more than a few days distant. They looked away, saying nothing, their joy subdued.

The descent was long and hard. There was time for nothing but the next foothold, the next weathered flight of steps. The sun rose higher and higher into the sky and scorched them. The crater was a seductive mirage, with its gleaming arcs of precious blues and greens.

When the sun slid behind the Pillar's gleaming head they were suspended between earth and sky. Above and below them the Pillar narrowed. The screaming wind soon turned their relief to shivering. They wrapped themselves up as best they could but still they had to cling with numbing fingers to the rock. Down and down they climbed and the earth never appeared to be any closer. Only the shadow of the Pillar jutting out below and the increasing ache in their muscles told of the passing time.

By late afternoon they were among the rookeries of the sky-saurians. Carnelian had a notion to go and rest in the shrine but Osidian urged him on.

The shadow of the Pillar was already nosing its way across the Skymere when they reached the ground. They took a short rest, some water and a little hri cake, but Osidian drove them on. They scratched through the thorn forest to the wall of the Forbidden Garden. Sitting astride its stones they saw the shadow of the western Sacred Wall was already slicing through the heart of the Yden. The lagoons lay in its night.

They dropped into the garden and made their way as quickly as they could down through its terraces to the outer wall. As Osidian was opening a gate the shadow of the Sacred Wall was already coming up through the trees. In the orchard, twilight pulled over them like a blanket. Shadows grew rosy from the reflected fiery reds of the sky. Night had fallen before they reached the first lagoon.

They waited for the moon, each locked in the prison of his own thoughts. This was not how Carnelian had expected it to be. He looked sidelong at Osidian's face. It was too dark to see its expression. How could Osidian be thinking of anything other than his Apotheosis? He should even then have been at the heart of his household, being carried down in the midst of the pilgrimage of the Great.

Stars were dusting the mirror lagoons. Frogs were rasping. Mosquitoes were sewing the air with needle flight. This was the last night of his freedom. Carnelian was filled with a desperate longing, but Osidian was a tower invulnerable to assault.

"What're you thinking?" Carnelian asked.

The tower moved. "Of many things."

"Apotheosis?"

"Not just of that."

"Would you have preferred to be now in the Labyrinth?"

The tower loomed close. Carnelian felt Osidian's arms encircling him, drawing him close. He rested his head in the angle between Osidian's neck and shoulder. Their clothes were masking the passion in their skins.

"I would possess you," Carnelian whispered.

"You do," breathed Osidian on his neck.

They tightened the circles of their arms as if they wished to merge their flesh.

"Your bones are my bones," breathed Carnelian.

"Your skin my skin," said Osidian.

"My heart is yours."

"My blood runs in your veins."

At that moment they felt the moonlight falling round them. Carnelian lifted his head and looked into Osidian's dark eyes and was consumed by a fierce, terrible joy. He kissed Osidian as if he sought to swallow all the breath from his lungs. He disengaged. "Shall we swim?"

"Like fish," said Osidian and laughed.

They broke apart, tore their clothes off. Carnelian was free first. He raced off down the moon path toward the water. He could hear Osidian's footfalls hammering after him. Lily pads clustered at the shore like boats. Carnelian did not check his speed. He ran across the pads, felt them buckling, ran faster, lost balance, two more steps and then he was rifling through the air. He saw himself mirrored in the surface, smashed it and went under. The water was as warm as blood.

Carnelian came up first into the wafting warm perfume of the air. He turned to see Osidian rising from the pool like a spirit forming from the foam.

He heard something or sensed some movement. He tried to pierce the shadows under the trees with his eyes. Black shapes. Men. He tensed. It was like the night they had wounded his father. He had half turned his head to give Osidian warning, when the air was ruffled by footfalls.

"What . . ." Osidian said near him.

They crept into the moonlight. Swarthy stunted men, eyes round as if they were seeing demons. They lifted cudgels as they closed their crescent round them.

"The Twins," cried Osidian as he dashed his white body into them.

Carnelian groaned as he watched them blur his brightness with their squat bodies. Their cudgels rose and fell like hammers. It was the cries of pain from Osidian that freed Carnelian. He crashed forward clubbing them with his fists. Each blow hurt his hands but he would not stop. Their attackers pulled back, exposing Osidian. He was on one knee staring at his hand.

Carnelian moved toward him, turning round and round as he went, seeing their attackers closing, their cudgels lifting. He reached out behind him. His fingers found Osidian's shoulder. "Get up," he said.

Osidian did not move.

Carnelian whisked round and grabbed him. "Get up!" he cried, yanking Osidian to his feet. He put his back to Osidian's. He glared at the little men. He felt the stickiness in his hand. He brought it to his mouth, tasted it. "Blood . . ." Osidian's blood. Rage surged in him. After that he could see nothing. He was clawing through their flesh. He was smashing his head into their faces. Their rancid smell was smearing on his skin with their blood. Their grappling-hook hands dug into him. Blows fell on his back, his arms. They were hanging off him. He swung, dislodging some. He was weakening. They were slowing him with their weight, with pain. A wall crashed into his head and their cries thinned to blackness.

FUNERARY URNS

To achieve Doubling the poison must be administered not later than ten days from conception. The initial dosage should be the size of a pigeon's eye. Thereafter this should be increased daily by an additional dose, this regime to be followed for at least sixteen days. The poison may lead to various levels of morbidity in the mother but rarely to death. One in three offspring will be lost. The level of separation of the product sybling cannot be predicted.

—EXTRACT FROM A BEADCORD
MANUAL OF THE DOMAIN OF
IMMORTALITY

A knife was stabbing into Carnelian's head, over and over again. His body was bludgeoned meat. He tried to move his hand up to his head but it would not budge. His eyelids felt as thick as his tongue as he opened them. He saw a glare that pulsed with each throbbing in his head. He squeezed his eyes closed, breathing carefully until the pain lost its ragged edge.

A flapping like trapped birds. He carefully reopened his eyes. Shape-changing light patches seared. He swiveled his head to angle the hammering and his sight into a dark corner. He found he was able to open his eyes wider. The shadows found their hard edges, straightened, became lines and curves.

When he moved his body, waves of nausea surged up from his stomach. He tried to pant them away. His ears were hearing a linking counterpoint of lifting rising Vulgate in different voices. He turned his head gingerly to look at the light shapes. Bones of light, twisting. Water undulating morning in its dimples far off down a tunnel through ribbing. Wooden ribs. A sequence of them seeming to rock the water in their cradle. The ribs held something long and sleek and tooth-yellow, like a huge discarded arm. He focused his eyes on its skin. A clinker-built surface of ivory shards. Bones. It was a bone boat leaning toward him, her prow post like a tree over his head, her bow swelling off in the wooden cradle of ribs.

Men were growling Vulgate. Carnelian recalled the attack. Their blows were still drumming on his skull. He walked his eyes back from the water, a rib at a time. He ground his head round carefully as if he were afraid to dislodge the ache balancing on top. He saw Osidian, the marble of his face ruptured red near his eye. His lip as livid and bloated as an earthworm, twitching. Bruises like ink infusing alabaster. The eyes opened and they saw each other. Carnelian saw Osidian rising to the surface, shared his pain, bewilderment, watched the firming brightness of realization in his eye. Osidian opened his mouth as if to speak, but obviously became aware of the men talking behind him and narrowed his eyes as he listened.

"Hey . . ." he groaned.

Carnelian tensed as he heard the conversation stop.

"Hey, you, come here," Osidian said in an imperious tone that made Carnelian cringe, and set the pain twisting its blade in his head.

"Shut up," said a voice.

"Come here," said Osidian, his swollen lips slurring his voice.

Carnelian could hear them getting up. He fought the ropes but they only burned his wrists. The rib he leaned against shuddered under someone's weight, then a foot came down beside him. He looked up the dark leg to the leather skirt. He could not see any more of the man but could certainly smell him. The man crouched. His face was like raw meat. Carnelian found the tiny eyes, the gray stumped teeth. He recoiled from the stench of the man's breath, from the animal intensity of the eyes looking at his unmasked face.

"How dare you look at me," Osidian cried in outrage.

"How will you stop me looking, Master?" the man said.

His words sprayed saliva onto Carnelian's cheek. The rib shuddered again and as it released, another man jumped down. Both men stood back. They were monstrously alike. Carnelian saw that the new one refused to look at him and was trembling.

"Do you know what will be done to you for walking here, on holy ground, for laying your hands on a Master, for seeing our faces?" Osidian said.

Carnelian could see both men flinch. The second man's shoulders were beginning to hunch.

"You filth came in with the tributaries, didn't you?"

The second man's chin dug deeper into his chest as he nodded.

"You do know that you won't be able to sneak out that way, don't you?"

"Our employer's made arrangements to get us out," sneered the first man.

"Your employer will not be able to protect you from my wrath. I'll find you and all your kin. Each death will entertain me for twenty days."

"You'll not be finding anyone where you're going," said the first man.

"And you think your 'employer' will let you live after what you've seen, what you've done?"

The second man was trembling so much he was shaking against the first.

"What're you afraid of?"

"They're Masters, Rud. We oughtn't ever to have looked at their faces. We oughtn't to have come here . . . this place isn't meant for us. They have powers . . . we're—"

"Look at them!" said Rud, stabbing his finger. "Can't you see they bleed blood, not fire?"

"But look how much damage they did to us. They killed Nar, and Pleyr, and roughed the rest of us up. They're too big to be just men, too beautiful."

Carnelian could see the fear lurking in Rud's eyes.

"You'll envy your dead friends once I get free," said Osidian.

Rud bent toward them and whipped a slap across Osidian's face. Carnelian jumped as Osidian's head lashed round. He saw the disbelief in Osidian's face. Neither of them could believe the sacrilege.

"You shut up. Just shut your mouth!" spat Rud.

Carnelian could see the second man staring and that his spine had regained some stiffness.

"They don't look all that godlike now. He takes a slap like a woman, he does." Rud pushed out his chest. "Come to think of it, he looks a bit like a woman. Maybe I should take a knife across his face and then we'd see how beautiful he'd look." He nodded gluttonously. "Maybe I'll just cut something off him, a bit of his milky flesh, a finger, an ear, a little memento of our visit to 'paradise.' " Rud pulled out a flint-bladed knife and took pleasure in showing them its scalloped edge. As he leaned forward, Carnelian tried to shove his body in the way. With a thump, two more feet landed in front of him.

"You know they're not to be touched," said the newcomer.

"But, Skame, we could hurt them where it doesn't show,"

said the second man, grinning his stump-rimmed mouth.

Skame turned on him. "Do you want to die here? Well, do you? Who's going to get us out if we don't keep our end of the bargain?"

"I say we cut them," said Rud, with a filthy grin.

Skame slammed into Rud, who hit the rib like a sack of sand. He straightened up shakily.

"We were just trying to get them to keep quiet," said the second man.

"Well, gag them then," said Skame.

Carnelian saw the venomous look that Rud shot Osidian as he moved off.

The sun was turning the boathouse into an oven. Through the holes gaping in the hide roof, fire poured down over the earth floor, caught in the rib curves and bleached the ruined bone boat. An edge of heat reached slowly toward their feet. They tried to move out of its way but could not. Carnelian felt it begin to roast his feet. He looked over and saw Osidian's face. The gag gaped his mouth. His eyes were squeezed closed. Sweat beading on his face made his birthmark glisten. Carnelian forced himself to look at that battered face, making its silent scream. Osidian had not opened his eyes since he had been gagged.

Down where the boathouse ended, there was water that was white-hot silver. A breeze belched up a stench of mud that told of the lowering level of the Skymere. But there was another smell. The reek of rotting flesh that he was sure was coming from their reddening feet.

Heavy footfalls woke Carnelian. He groaned, adjusting his painful spine.

"Put it there," said a voice in Vulgate. By its timbre, it was a voice accustomed to speaking Quya.

A lantern settled brilliant as the sun in front of him. One of their captors' shapes moved away from it. Carnelian squinted sight into his eyes and saw the ranga, the jewel-brocaded hem of a Master's cloak. The ranga shoes walked to stand beside the bronze lantern. Carnelian looked up at the huge shrouded figure.

"No doubt my Lords never expected to find themselves in such squalid surroundings?" said two beautiful voices together in Quya. Two white hands, each blood-ringed, opened the shroud to reveal a double mask of gold.

". . . an. . . . yus," blurred Carnelian through his gag. He strained to see Osidian staring out from his bruised, gagged face.

The double mask turned on Skame. "You were told not to spill blood." The syblings' voices were flat and deadly.

Skame hunched. "They fought like demons."

The double mask lingered a while and Skame appeared to grow smaller. The mask turned back. "No greeting from you, Celestial?" said one of the syblings. "Ah, but I see they have stopped up your divine mouth." Their hand made a lean, smiling gesture. "We would remove it ourselves but no doubt you have been fingered by the hired brutes . . . and they are thoroughly unclean."

He motioned to the shadow behind him. "Ungag them."

The man came, Skame, his thick, grubby fingers worried at the knots and the gag came away from Carnelian's mouth.

"The other, the other," said the syblings, jabbing their finger.

Carnelian watched Skame leaning over Osidian. The man stood up, gave the double mask a fearful look. The syblings made a gesture of dismissal.

Skame jerked a bow. "Your assurances, Master . . . ?"

"Do not provoke us. Bring in the urns. Take care that neither you nor any of your filthy band look upon our faces."

Skame hesitated, narrowing his eyes, then ducked a bow and lurched away.

"Repulsive creature." The Hanuses reached up and carefully, slowly, removed their mask. Freed, their alabaster faces looked around. "We will have to arrange a fiery accident for this noisome shed." The living eyes looked down on Osidian and then Carnelian. The blind left face smiled bleakly.

"My Lords are wondering what has brought us all to this less than salubrious spot, eh?" said Right-Hanus. "Your silence denies nothing. I can see the curiosity in your eyes." He looked at Osidian. "Your divine mother sends you greetings, Celestial."

"You think I did not know she was behind this?" said Osidian.

The Hanuses gave a little bow.

"But this is sacrilege," cried Carnelian.

"Let us not concern ourselves with niceties of terminology," said Right-Hanus.

"It is merely political necessity," said Left-Hanus.

"You have lifted your hand against the Gods," Osidian said.

"The almost-Gods, to be precise, and when Jade Lord Nephron does not appear, the burden of the candidature will fall inevitably on his brother."

The rib rattled as Osidian struggled to free himself. The Hanuses stepped back, left face looking alarmed, the other glancing toward the door. Their hands lifted their mask almost to their faces. As Osidian stopped struggling, oily smiles oozed back over both.

"The Empress assured us that her hirelings were dependable," said Left-Hanus.

"One is gratified to see that this is true," said Right-Hanus.

"They are of the Brotherhood of the Wheel?" asked Carnelian.

The Hanuses' faces looked surprised. "Why, yes, my Lord," they replied.

"Why would the Brotherhood risk so much?" asked Osidian. "If they are discovered, not only they but all their kind will be exterminated even if it became necessary to lay the city waste."

"The price they asked was the City at the Gates," said Left-Hanus.

"She cannot intend to give it to them." Osidian was incredulous.

"She would pay any price."

"But you distract us, Celestial," said Right-Hanus. "Now, where was I? Ah, yes, the Empress bade me say to her son that she bears you no more malice than you do her. She knows that if she allowed your accession you would move against her."

"She prefers that the son who wears the Masks should be her creature," said Left-Hanus.

"And what place has she made for you?" asked Carnelian.

The Hanuses both beamed. "We have been promised power," they choroused.

"You think you can trust her? She has killed her own daughter and now . . ."

"Her son?" suggested Left-Hanus.

"It is said that there are carnivorous saurians that when caged will devour even their offspring. Yet these same creatures will allow tiny birds to pick ticks from their gums," his brother said.

"She will consume you."

"We have taken precautions," said Left-Hanus.

"The very act of making us her instrument has made her vulnerable to us," said Right-Hanus. "If news of this crime were ever to reach the Great and the Wise, both Powers would rise against her."

"Against them both not even she could prevail," said Left-Hanus.

"So now you come to spill our blood yourselves?"

The Hanuses looked shocked. "Not so, my Lord, not so," said Right-Hanus.

"We merely came . . . to gloat," said Left-Hanus.

They brought their faces very close to Carnelian. "We have waited long for our revenge," they said together.

"Revenge? Revenge on us? On me?"

The syblings made vague gestures. "The Chosen, the House of the Masks . . ." said Left-Hanus.

". . . even the Empress," said Right-Hanus.

"Look at us . . . we are an abomination," said Left-Hanus.

"You cannot imagine the unending horror of our lives," said his brother.

"But this was done to you by the Wise."

"Pah! They are machines," said Left-Hanus.

"Blind instruments wielded by Chosen hands," said Right-Hanus.

"You too are Chosen. Look, you wear a blood-ring."

The faces sneered and spoke together. "We are freaks, merely symbols of the Twin Gods created as a decoration for the court, nothing more."

"I have always treated you with respect," said Osidian.

"Ah. Certainly you have talked to us . . ." said Left-Hanus.

". . . but with respect?" said Right-Hanus.

They shook their head, lips pursed up to their noses. "Not respect . . . most certainly not respect."

"Now, condescension . . ." said Left-Hanus.

"But we prattle on. We must have your blood-rings." The syblings gathered up their cloak and robes and, crouching, tucked them into their lap. Their faces grimaced with the effort, causing the flesh joining them to ruck. "You are very bloody, my Lords," said Right-Hanus. They both looked frightened. "The barbarians have played with you?"

"They did not cut you, remove any flesh?" demanded Left-Hanus.

"No matter." They frowned, and came close enough for Carnelian to see the pores in their white skin. He felt them fumbling his fingers. His ring was tugged off.

"Ah," sighed the syblings, as they sat back holding the ring.

"My father will punish you," said Carnelian.

"Even now, He-who-goes-before searches frantically," said Right-Hanus.

"He will find nothing," said Left-Hanus. "Then it will be he that will be punished."

Carnelian remembered Molochite's threat and shuddered.

"And now yours, Celestial," said the syblings as their bulk engulfed Osidian. When they had Osidian's ring, they sat back. They put the rings carefully away. "The Empress demands proof." They were about to heave themselves up.

"One last matter, Celestial," said Left-Hanus.

The syblings brought their faces close to Osidian, who strained to turn away. Both spat. Right-Hanus watched the spittle running down the side of Osidian's face with a sigh of pleasure that was almost sexual. They stood up.

Osidian's eyes came up dark fire.

"Put away your oh so terrible glare, nephew. Your days of power are over," sneered Right-Hanus.

"We do not fear you now. Soon you will be dead," said his brother.

"Nothing will ever be found to put inside a tomb," said Right-Hanus.

They snapped their fingers.

"It will be as if you had never been at all," said Left-Hanus.

"Alas, you will be quickly forgotten," his brother said.

"You would not dare spill his blood," cried Carnelian. "The very earth of the Isle would cry out."

"It will not be done here. The Empress was most insistent on that."

"You will both be taken out beyond the Sacred Wall and there, in the polluted outer world, you will die," said Left-Hanus.

"How can you hope to get us through the Three Gates unseen?" Carnelian asked.

There was a grinding sound behind him. The syblings looked up and covered their faces with the mask. "Soon my Lord will see." They stood up and walked out of sight.

Carnelian could hear one of the syblings' voices speaking Vulgate. He heard many feet coming back. He saw Skame, Rud and others of the Brotherhood. They crowded him and lifted him.

"By the horns, they're heavy," said one.

Carnelian was half lifted, half dragged round the wooden rib he had been leaning against. The Hanuses stood, a shrouded immensity. On either side of the syblings stood two huge earthenware pots as round as pomegranates, daubed with red ochre, eared with many handles. Both pots were tall enough to come up to the syblings' waist.

"Your palanquins await you, my Lords," chorused the Hanuses' voices.

"You are going to put us in those," said Carnelian, staring with horror.

The double mask inclined its rightmost eyeslit to one of the pots. "I need hardly tell you how difficult it was to procure two funerary urns large enough."

"Alive?"

"Oh yes, my Lord, very much alive," said Left-Hanus.

"You cannot hope to gag us so that no sound will be heard," Carnelian said in quick desperation.

"My Lord should not worry about that. He will be drugged," said Left-Hanus.

"In his urn, my Lord will dream like a fetus in a womb," his brother said.

Carnelian was set on the edge of the urn. The lip of the urn bit into his spine and thighs as he was leaned back. Supporting his weight, his captors took his ankles and folded his legs up against his chest so that his chin jammed between his kneecaps. He was hinged closed, then packed into the urn. Its glazed cavity pressed over more and more of his skin. The feeling of being trapped was squeezing a scream out. The cruel satisfaction in his captors' eyes made him swallow it.

His buttocks touched the bottom of the urn. His spine fitted into its curve. His knees speared into his chest. He could just manage to see over the urn lip. He strained against the urn but it was as if he had been built into a wall. He took swift shallow little breaths, trying to control the panic.

The Hanuses hovered above him like a thundercloud. The curtains of their cloak parted and their gleaming double mask descended, coming close enough to almost lean its two chins on the rim of the urn. Right-Hanus' whisper came from behind the gold. "The Empress bade us tell you that even if you had not been involved in the destruction of the Lord Nephron, she would still have found a way to encompass your ruin."

"This she has done for your mother's sake," whispered Left-Hanus.

"The flame of your life was lit from hers before you blew it out. The loss of freedom, the colors of this world, were as nothing to losing her sister."

As the mask began to rise like double suns, Carnelian found enough breath to say, "How . . . ?"

The mask paused in its ascent. Its two eyeslits turned to look down at him. "How . . . ?" said the gold. "How were you taken?"

Carnelian closed his eyes and opened them again instead of a nod.

"It was you yourself that gave us victory. Once Imago brought you to us . . ." The syblings made a grabbing gesture, the sign for capture.

"Jaspar?" Carnelian gasped, and dizzied, struggling to suck in breath.

"Imago Jaspar, yes, it was he. He told the Empress that you might bear watching, that you were the Lord Suth's fatal weakness. We saw you in the library, we saw you in the Yden."

The syblings' hands made an obscene gesture.

"We saw everything," said Left-Hanus.

"It was the most inconceivable folly that you should both come down here again, but she had hoped for that and you did not disappoint her." The mask began pulling away. "Pleasant dreams, my Lord."

"Tomorrow you die," his brother said.

The syblings receded, their hands remaining behind only long enough to make a summoning.

One of the Brotherhood appeared. He brought a cane over the rim, a spear questing for Carnelian's face. Carnelian tried to move his head but his knees held it like a clamp. The cane impaled his lips. When he tried to resist it, the man's palm struck the other end. It tore through his lip, clunked against his teeth and then twisted into his tongue. Blood welled its metal taste. The cane was a nail through his face. He vibrated with terror as the man put his mouth to the other end of it. He watched the cheeks inflate. The man spat out and Carnelian choked and gagged as something like a fruit stone punched into his throat. He tried to vomit it out but the cane was in the way. It melted down into him. The cane rasping out of his mouth allowed him to rack out some coughs. He gulped, trying to bail the blood from his mouth with his tongue. His hands flailed for the lip of the urn as he tried to drag himself out of its maw. Voices were barking remotely. Rays of light as sharp as spears. His head sank up to the ears between his knees. His hands folded and tucked into the urn. His body was a deadman's. He felt the darkness coming. A night sky pressing down upon his head and then a grinding that locked him into a world crammed full with his flesh in which the only sound was breathing.